BUREAU FOR PARANORMAL RESEARCH AND DEFENSE

CREATED BY MIKE MIGNOLA

HELL ON EARTH

VOLUME 1

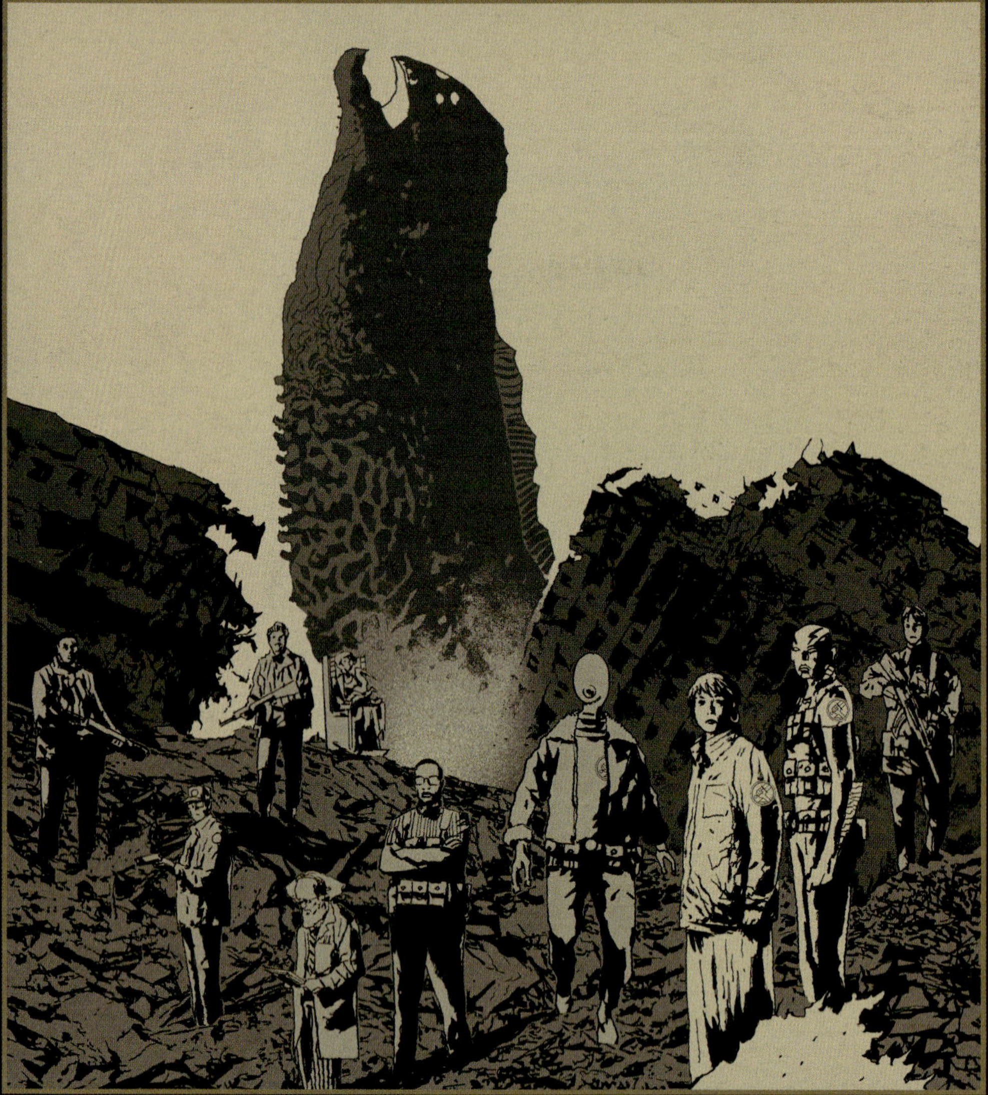

Liz Sherman has been AWOL since releasing her devastating fire at the center of the earth and hastening the world-wide crisis. Director Kate Corrigan's closest allies remain Abe Sapien, Johann Kraus, and the Egyptian mummy Panya, while traditional soldiers round out the ranks of a more militarized Bureau for Paranormal Research and Defense, taking their orders from the United Nations.

MIKE MIGNOLA'S
B.P.R.D.
HELL ON EARTH
VOLUME 1

STORY BY
MIKE MIGNOLA AND **JOHN ARCUDI**

NEW WORLD, *SEATTLE*, AND *GODS*
ART BY **GUY DAVIS**

MONSTERS AND *RUSSIA*
ART BY **TYLER CROOK**

AN UNMARKED GRAVE
ART BY **DUNCAN FEGREDO**

COLORS BY **DAVE STEWART**
LETTERS BY **CLEM ROBINS**
COVER ART BY **LAURENCE CAMPBELL** WITH **DAVE STEWART**
CHAPTER BREAK ART BY **GUY DAVIS** WITH **DAVE STEWART, RYAN SOOK, DAVE JOHNSON,** AND **DUNCAN FEGREDO**

PUBLISHER **MIKE RICHARDSON**
EDITOR **KATII O'BRIEN**
ASSISTANT EDITOR **JENNY BLENK**
COLLECTION DESIGNER **PATRICK SATTERFIELD**
DIGITAL ART TECHNICIAN **ANN GRAY**

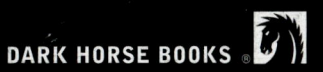

DARK HORSE BOOKS

Neil Hankerson EXECUTIVE VICE PRESIDENT • Tom Weddle CHIEF FINANCIAL OFFICER • Randy Stradley VICE PRESIDENT OF PUBLISHING • Nick McWhorter CHIEF BUSINESS DEVELOPMENT OFFICER • Dale LaFountain CHIEF INFORMATION OFFICER • Matt Parkinson VICE PRESIDENT OF MARKETING • Vanessa Todd-Holmes VICE PRESIDENT OF PRODUCTION AND SCHEDULING • Mark Bernardi VICE PRESIDENT OF BOOK TRADE AND DIGITAL SALES • Ken Lizzi GENERAL COUNSEL Dave Marshall EDITOR IN CHIEF • Davey Estrada EDITORIAL DIRECTOR • Chris Warner SENIOR BOOKS EDITOR • Cary Grazzini DIRECTOR OF SPECIALTY PROJECTS • Lia Ribacchi ART DIRECTOR Matt Dryer DIRECTOR OF DIGITAL ART AND PREPRESS • Michael Gombos SENIOR DIRECTOR OF LICENSED PUBLICATIONS • Kari Yadro DIRECTOR OF CUSTOM PROGRAMS • Kari Torson DIRECTOR OF INTERNATIONAL LICENSING • Sean Brice DIRECTOR OF TRADE SALES

Published by Dark Horse Books
A division of Dark Horse Comics LLC
10956 SE Main Street
Milwaukie, OR 97222

DarkHorse.com
Comic Shop Locator Service: comicshoplocator.com

First edition: March 2021
ISBN 978-1-50671-970-2

10 9 8 7 6 5 4 3 2 1
Printed in China

Library of Congress Cataloging-in-Publication Data

Names: Mignola, Mike, author. | Arcudi, John, author. | Davis, Guy, 1966- illustrator. | Crook, Tyler, illustrator. | Fegredo, Duncan, illustrator. | Stewart, Dave, colourist. | Robins, Clem, 1955- letterer.

Title: B.P.R.D. Hell on Earth / story by Mike Mignola and John Arcudi ; art by Guy Davis, Tyler Crook, Duncan Fegredo ; colors by Dave Stewart ; letters by Clem Robins.
Other titles: At head of title: Mike Mignola's
Description: First edition. | Milwaukie, OR : Dark Horse Books, 2020- | "This book collects B.P.R.D. Hell on Earth volumes 1-3, the B.P.R.D. Hell on Earth: Seattle ashcan, and 'B.P.R.D.: An Unmarked Grave,' from Dark Horse Presents #8, all originally published by Dark Horse Comics."
| Summary: "The plague of frogs has ended, but earth will never be the same, and the fractured B.P.R.D. struggles to battle dangerous monsters and humans alike, from a trailer-park cult to a Russian town ravaged by a zombie-like virus. Guy Davis's final B.P.R.D. stories set the stage for Tyler Crook's (Harrow County) backwoods-horror debut, as Liz Sherman hides from a world that she helped push toward Armageddon, and Abe Sapien is shot down by a girl who's seen the world to come"-- Provided by publisher.
Identifiers: LCCN 2020014107 | ISBN 9781506719702 (v. 1 ; paperback)
Classification: LCC PN6727.M53 B24 2020 | DDC 741.5/973--dc23
LC record available at https://lccn.loc.gov/2020014107

B.P.R.D.™ HELL ON EARTH™© 2011, 2012, 2017, 2021 Mike Mignola. Abe Sapien, Hellboy, Liz Sherman, and all other prominently featured characters are trademarks of Mike Mignola. Dark Horse Books® and the Dark Horse logo are registered trademarks of Dark Horse Comics LLC. All rights reserved. No portion of this publication may be reproduced or transmitted, in any form or by any means, without the express written permission of Dark Horse Comics LLC. Names, characters, places, and incidents featured in this publication either are the product of the author's imagination or are used fictitiously. Any resemblance to actual persons (living or dead), events, institutions, or locales, without satiric intent, is coincidental.

This book collects B.P.R.D. Hell on Earth Volumes 1-3, the B.P.R.D. Hell on Earth: Seattle ashcan, and "B.P.R.D.: An Unmarked Grave" from Dark Horse Presents #8, all originally published by Dark Horse Comics.

BUREAU FOR PARANORMAL • RESEARCH AND DEFENSE •

In *Bride of Frankenstein* (my all-time favorite monster movie) the great Dr. Pretorius raises a glass of gin (his only weakness) and toasts, "To a new world of gods and monsters." And in the *B.P.R.D./Hellboy* world that's where we are now.

Way back in the very first *Hellboy* story (*Seed of Destruction*, 1994) I turned four poor, unsuspecting Arctic explorers into frog monsters. Hellboy shot one as it tried to escape out a bathroom window and I dropped a house on the other three, and I figured that was that. But no. Ten years later I introduced a new batch of frog monsters in the *B.P.R.D.: Plague of Frogs* miniseries. Liz Sherman torched some of them, some were captured (and whatever happened to them?), but a bunch of them got away to cause more trouble. A lot of other strange stuff cropped up in *B.P.R.D.* over the years, but more often than not the frogs were there somewhere. They were the ongoing problem that ultimately defined that first arc of stories, so much so that we now refer to that entire arc as *Plague of Frogs*. But now Liz has torched the last of those frogs (in *King of Fear*), so all that's behind us, right? This is a whole new beginning, and we're back at square one, right? If you think that, then you haven't yet read the book you're holding: Those frogs may be gone, but they did a lot of damage. They set a lot of things in motion, and who knows where it will end? Well, John Arcudi and I know (at least we *think* we know), but we're not telling. Not yet.

I've been saying it for a few years now—one of the things that separates our little *B.P.R.D./Hellboy* world from some of the other comic-book worlds out there is that when we break stuff it often stays broken, or, *if* it's fixed, it's just never quite like it was before. Sometimes things don't break all at once—they crack, and those cracks get bigger and bigger until . . . well, you'll see. There is no magic pill for our heroes, no magic spell for them to read that will get the world and their lives back to square one.

This story, *New World*, is the first of a whole new arc of stories. It is a relatively small story—the scale of it is small compared to the giant robots, frog armies, and fireworks of the last couple of books—but, believe me, this series is called *Hell on Earth* for a reason. The cracks are showing, and I'm pretty sure I smell smoke. I think it's safe to say things are going to get worse before they get better. They are certainly going to get more complicated. So pour your drink of choice (whatever your weakness may be) and toast this new world, with gods and monsters on the way.

MIKE MIGNOLA

CONTENTS

NEW WORLD
PAGE 11

SEATTLE
PAGE 131

GODS
PAGE 141

MONSTERS
PAGE 213

RUSSIA
PAGE 261

AN UNMARKED GRAVE
PAGE 381

SKETCHBOOK
PAGE 391

NEW WORLD CHAPTER ONE

ILLUSTRATION BY **GUY DAVIS** WITH **DAVE STEWART**

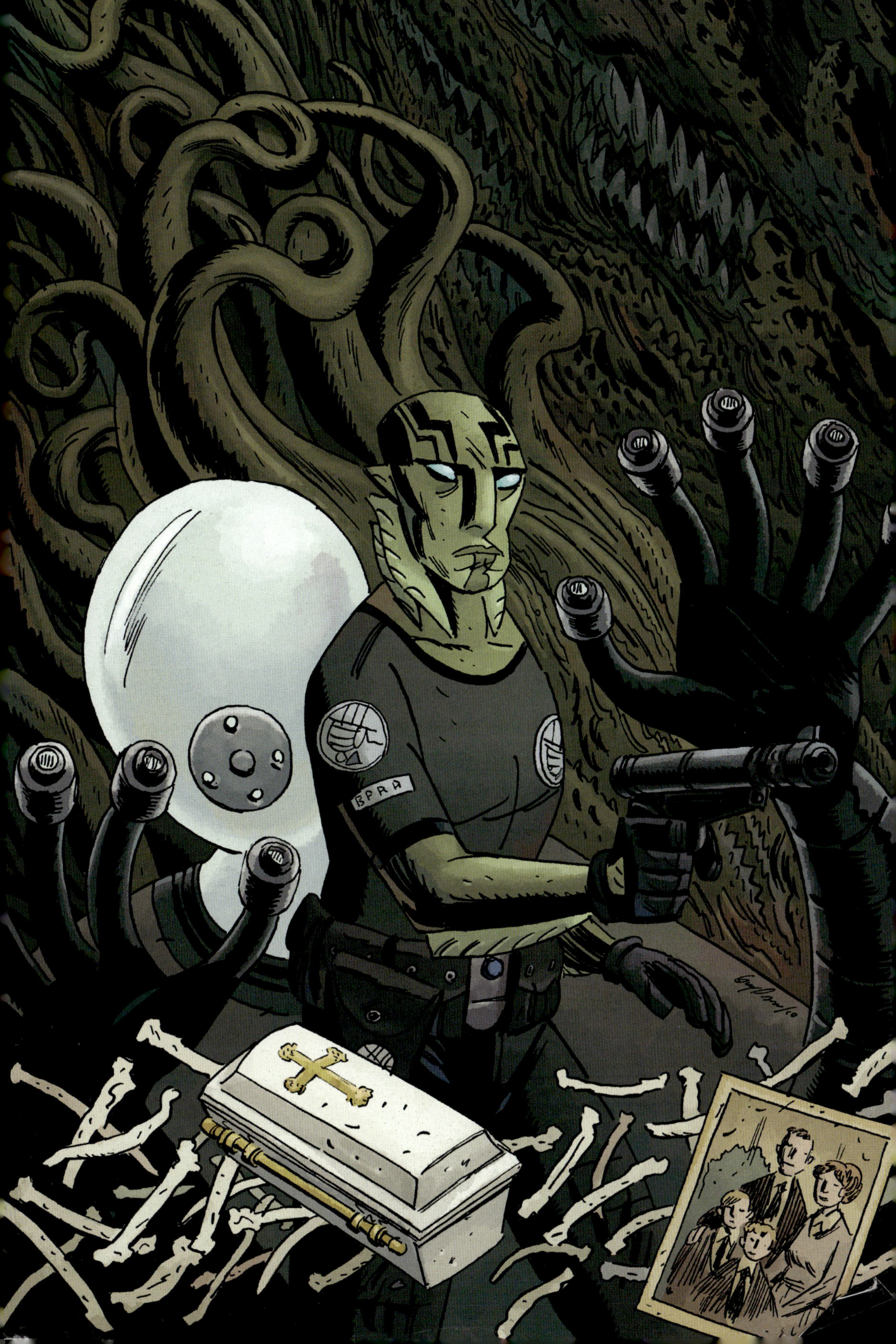
BPRA

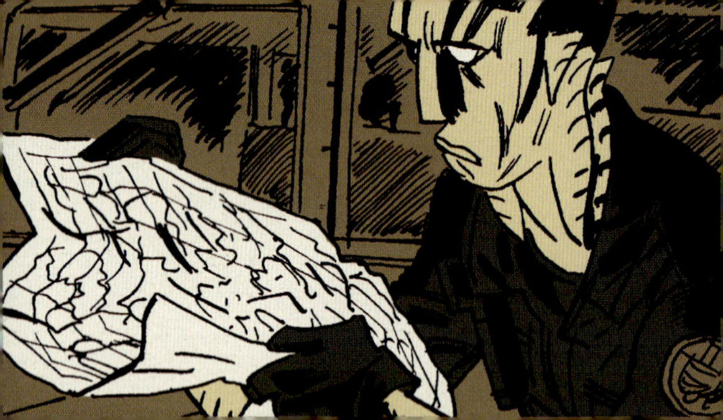

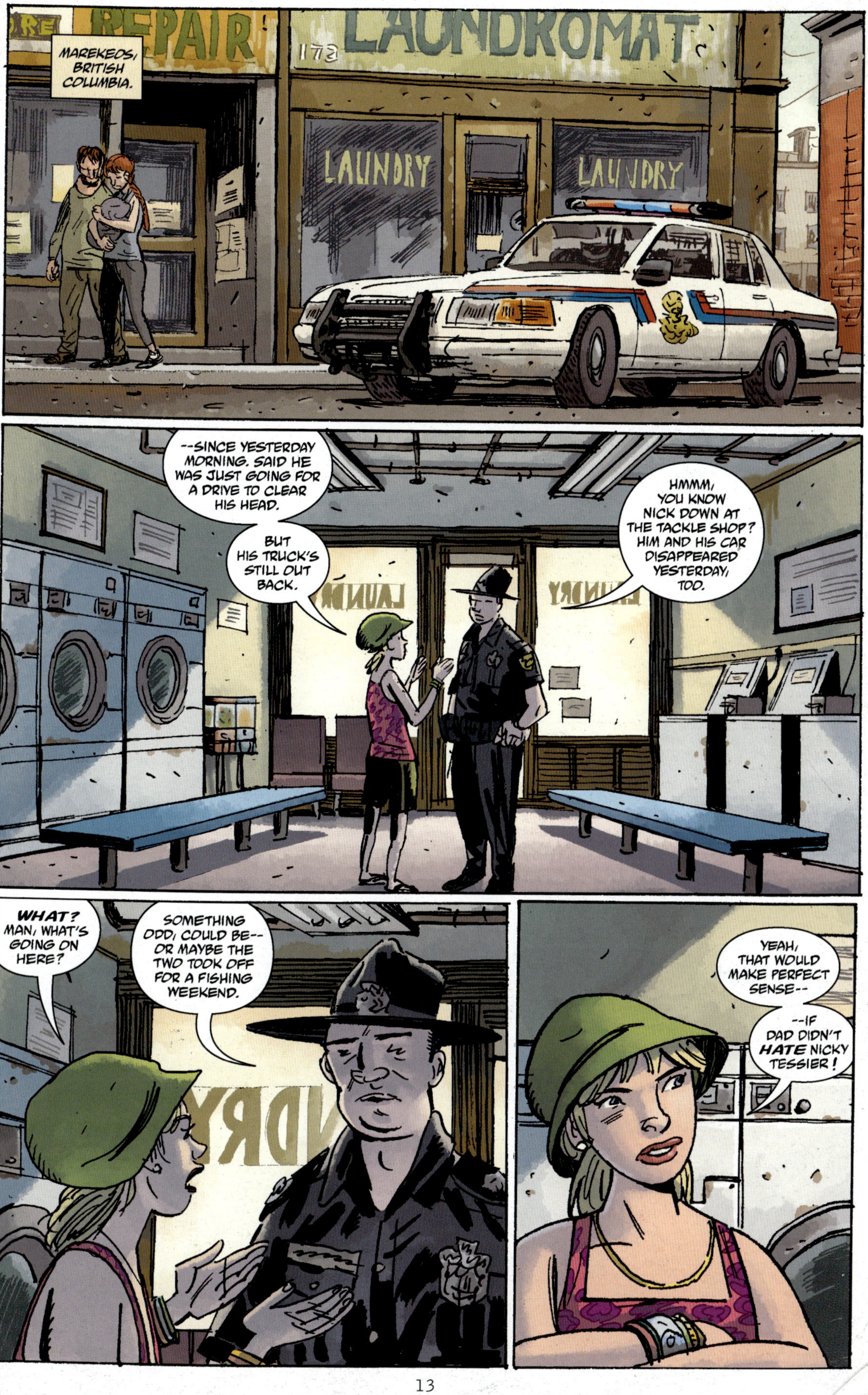
REPAIR
LAUNDROMAT
173
MAREKEOS, BRITISH COLUMBIA.
LAUNDRY
LAUNDRY
--SINCE YESTERDAY MORNING. SAID HE WAS JUST GOING FOR A DRIVE TO CLEAR HIS HEAD.
BUT HIS TRUCK'S STILL OUT BACK.
HMMM, YOU KNOW NICK DOWN AT THE TACKLE SHOP? HIM AND HIS CAR DISAPPEARED YESTERDAY, TOO.
WHAT? MAN, WHAT'S GOING ON HERE?
SOMETHING ODD, COULD BE-- OR MAYBE THE TWO TOOK OFF FOR A FISHING WEEKEND.
YEAH, THAT WOULD MAKE PERFECT SENSE--
--IF DAD DIDN'T HATE NICKY TESSIER!

ELLIE, SEVEN YEARS AGO, YOUR DAD COULD AFFORD TO HATE NICKY.
BUT WITH JOBS DRYING UP, THERE JUST AIN'T MANY FISHING PARTNERS LEFT HEREABOUTS.
HE WOULDN'T LEAVE WITHOUT SAYING SOME-THING. HE WOULD HAVE CALLED ME.
BET YOU'RE RIGHT, BUT YOU KNOW HOW CELL-PHONE RECEPTION IS OUT HERE SOMETIMES.
SO YOU'RE NOT GOING TO LOOK FOR HIM?!
COURSE I'LL LOOK FOR HIM. I JUST DON'T WANT YOU TO WORRY OVER WHAT MIGHT BE NOTHING.
YEAH, OKAY. MAYBE YOU'RE RIGHT.
SURE HOPE I AM. NOW IF YOU THINK OF ANYTHING ELSE, ANYTHING AT ALL, CALL IT IN, OKAY?

SNAP
SHERIFF, I JUST REMEMBERED THAT TODAY DADDY WAS SUPPOSED--
SHERIFF?
173 LAUNDROMAT

Victoria Clarion-Gazette

The Return of Bigfoot?

Once again the British Columbia forest is alive with the rumors of strange sightings and stranger theories. No one is using the name "Bigfoot," and in fact, none of the signature giant footprints have been found, but it's hard not to think of ol' Sasquatch when you hear what some of the eyewitnesses have to say.

"Tall, like ten feet at least. No kidding," swears Michael Jennings. "And pale white as any snow you ever laid eyes on." No other witnesses have as yet corre— Jennings' story, but his credibility is hard to dispute. Ini—taken on the air of a crusade, as provin— along with television an—

but few experts on the subject from th—and although

BRINGG

BPRD Headquarters Calling

BRINGG

"HI, KATE. WOW, YOU STILL AREN'T SLEEPING, ARE YOU?"

"NOT MUCH."

"ANYTHING NEW?"

16

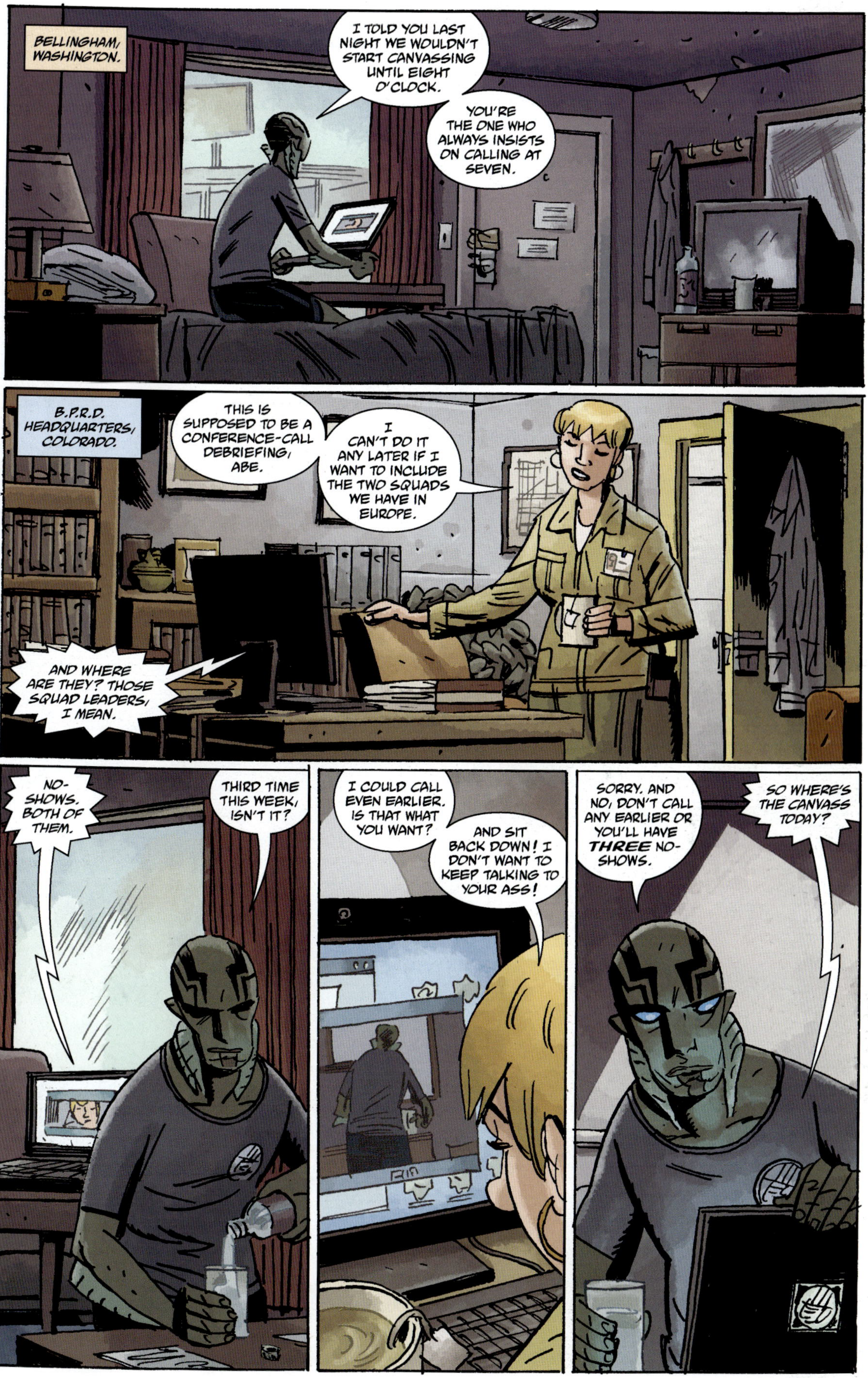
BELLINGHAM, WASHINGTON.
I TOLD YOU LAST NIGHT WE WOULDN'T START CANVASSING UNTIL EIGHT O'CLOCK.
YOU'RE THE ONE WHO ALWAYS INSISTS ON CALLING AT SEVEN.
B.P.R.D. HEADQUARTERS, COLORADO.
THIS IS SUPPOSED TO BE A CONFERENCE-CALL DEBRIEFING, ABE.
I CAN'T DO IT ANY LATER IF I WANT TO INCLUDE THE TWO SQUADS WE HAVE IN EUROPE.
AND WHERE ARE THEY? THOSE SQUAD LEADERS, I MEAN.
NO-SHOWS. BOTH OF THEM.
THIRD TIME THIS WEEK, ISN'T IT?
I COULD CALL EVEN EARLIER. IS THAT WHAT YOU WANT?
AND SIT BACK DOWN! I DON'T WANT TO KEEP TALKING TO YOUR ASS!
SORRY. AND NO, DON'T CALL ANY EARLIER OR YOU'LL HAVE THREE NO-SHOWS.
SO WHERE'S THE CANVASS TODAY?

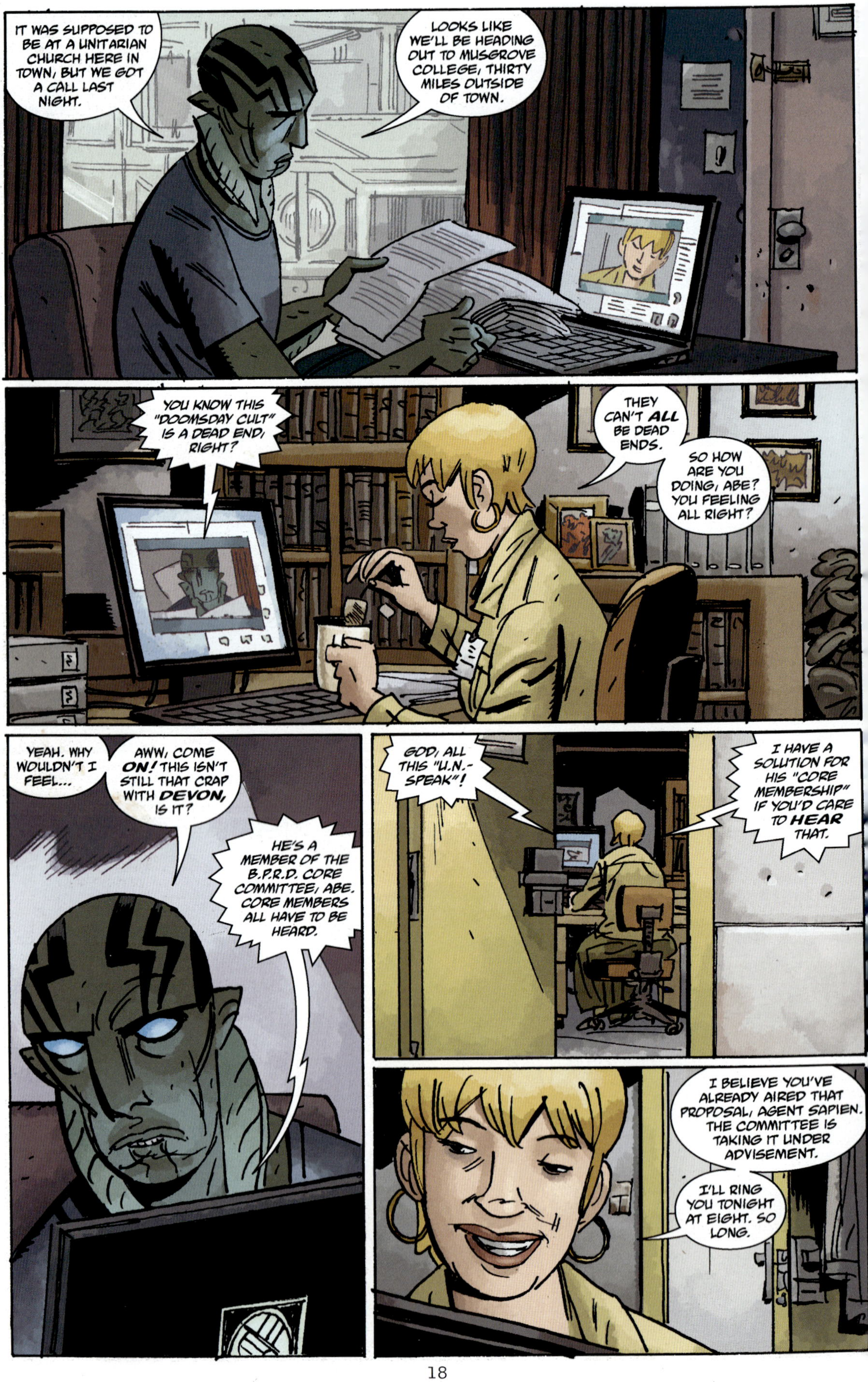
IT WAS SUPPOSED TO BE AT A UNITARIAN CHURCH HERE IN TOWN, BUT WE GOT A CALL LAST NIGHT.
LOOKS LIKE WE'LL BE HEADING OUT TO MUSGROVE COLLEGE, THIRTY MILES OUTSIDE OF TOWN.
YOU KNOW THIS "DOOMSDAY CULT" IS A DEAD END, RIGHT?
THEY CAN'T **ALL** BE DEAD ENDS.
SO HOW ARE YOU DOING, ABE? YOU FEELING ALL RIGHT?
YEAH. WHY WOULDN'T I FEEL...
AWW, COME **ON!** THIS ISN'T STILL THAT CRAP WITH **DEVON,** IS IT?
HE'S A MEMBER OF THE B.P.R.D. CORE COMMITTEE, ABE. CORE MEMBERS ALL HAVE TO BE HEARD.
GOD, ALL THIS "U.N.-SPEAK"!
I HAVE A SOLUTION FOR HIS "CORE MEMBERSHIP" IF YOU'D CARE TO **HEAR** THAT.
I BELIEVE YOU'VE ALREADY AIRED THAT PROPOSAL, AGENT SAPIEN. THE COMMITTEE IS TAKING IT UNDER ADVISEMENT.
I'LL RING YOU TONIGHT AT EIGHT. SO LONG.

YOU SHOULDN'T JOKE ABOUT IT, DR. CORRIGAN.
DAMMIT! DEVON, YOU SCARED THE HELL OUT OF ME!
HE KEEPS TRYING TO GET YOU TO FIRE ME, AND YOU LAUGH IT OFF?
DEVON, YOU'VE BEEN SUGGESTING HE MIGHT BE THE ANTICHRIST. I'D SAY HE'S HANDLING IT FAIRLY WELL.
I'M NOT SUGGESTING ANYTHING. I'M ONLY REPEATING--
--WHAT SOME PSYCHOTIC, SKULL-FACED MONSTER PREACHED ABOUT ABE BEING THE LEADER OF A NEW RACE OF FROGS.
HE WAS MANIPULATING YOU, DEVON. TRYING TO GET YOU TO TURN ON ONE ANOTHER, THAT'S ALL.
IF THAT'S ALL IT IS, WHY ARE YOU STILL KEEPING CLOSE TABS ON ABE?
JESUS CHRIST, DEVON! YOU'RE DRIVING ME CRAZY WITH THIS NONSENSE.
CLIMB OFF MY BACK, OKAY?

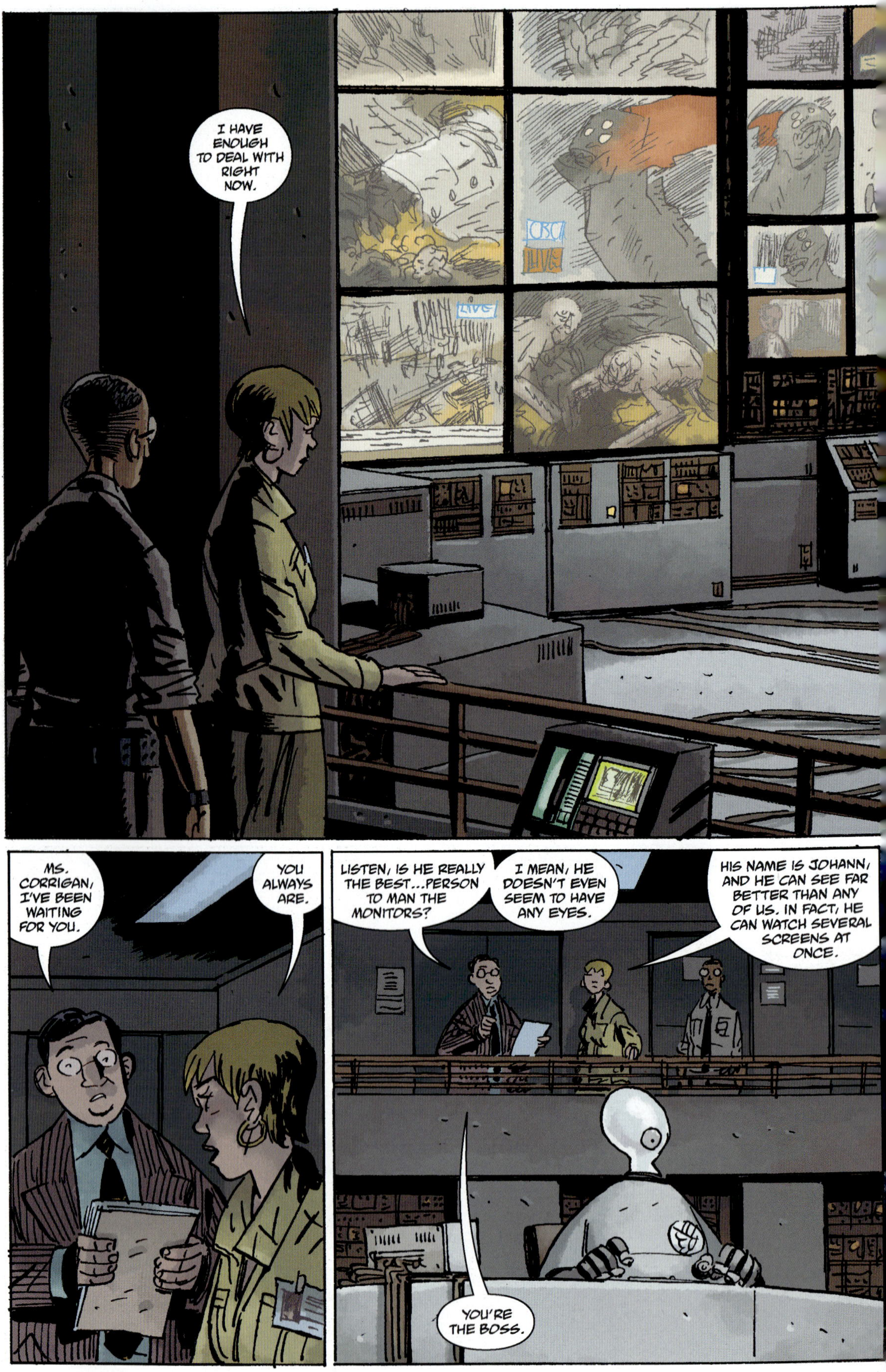

I HAVE ENOUGH TO DEAL WITH RIGHT NOW.
MS. CORRIGAN, I'VE BEEN WAITING FOR YOU.
YOU ALWAYS ARE.
LISTEN, IS HE REALLY THE BEST...PERSON TO MAN THE MONITORS?
I MEAN, HE DOESN'T EVEN SEEM TO HAVE ANY EYES.
HIS NAME IS JOHANN, AND HE CAN SEE FAR BETTER THAN ANY OF US. IN FACT, HE CAN WATCH SEVERAL SCREENS AT ONCE.
YOU'RE THE BOSS.

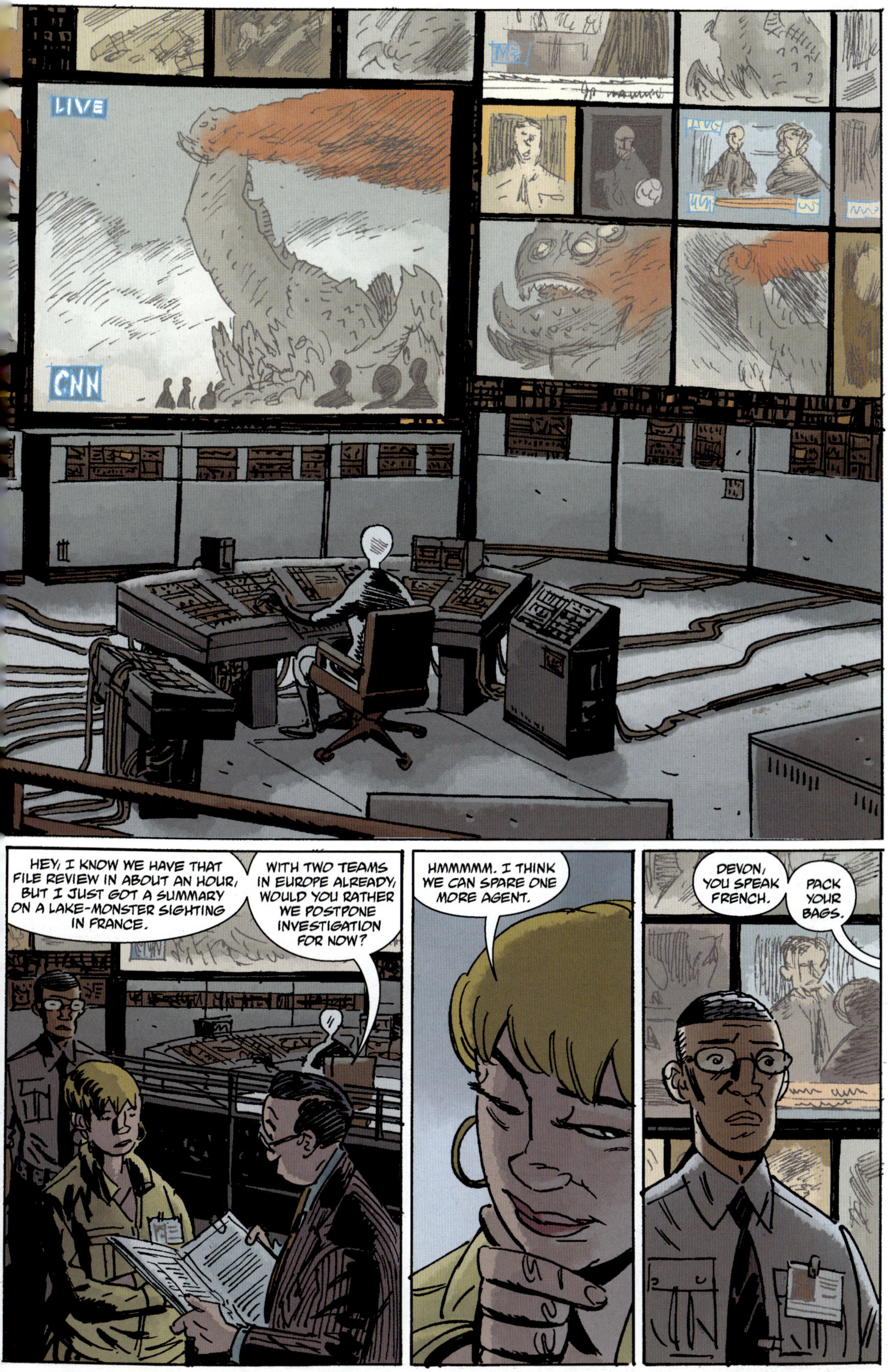
LIVE
CNN
HEY, I KNOW WE HAVE THAT FILE REVIEW IN ABOUT AN HOUR, BUT I JUST GOT A SUMMARY ON A LAKE-MONSTER SIGHTING IN FRANCE.
WITH TWO TEAMS IN EUROPE ALREADY, WOULD YOU RATHER WE POSTPONE INVESTIGATION FOR NOW?
HMMMMM. I THINK WE CAN SPARE ONE MORE AGENT.
DEVON, YOU SPEAK FRENCH.
PACK YOUR BAGS.

CNN
--NOT A MATTER O' WHAT'S FOR THE BEST. I JUST DON'T SEE WHY THE U.N. NEEDS TO COME IN HERE TELLIN' US WHAT MIGHT BE BEST.
SERVICE
AND IF THE U.N. IS BACKING UP THAT B.V.D.T., WELL, REASON ENOUGH TO BE SUSPICIOUS OF 'EM, YOU ASK ME.
IT'S A WORLDWIDE PROBLEM, THOUGH. AND THE B.P.R.D. WAS RESPONSIBLE FOR DEFEATING THAT GIANT BEAST IN NEBRASKA LAST YEAR. YOU KNOW THAT, RIGHT?
HEAR THAT? WE GOT TALKING CATFISH AND GHOSTS FIGHTING OUR BATTLES.
TRADING MONSTERS FOR MONSTERS!
LOOK, WE TOOK CARE OF THE NAZIS, DIDN'T WE? AND THE COMMIES. THE WHOLE WORLD NEEDED OUR HELP, NOT T'OTHER WAY 'ROUND.
WHAT GOES ON IN CHINA, I DON'T KNOW, BUT LET AMERICANS TAKE CARE OF AMERICA.
HUMAN AMERICANS, AT THAT!

B.P.R.D. HEADQUARTERS, COLORADO.
HI, PANYA.
KATHERINE, LOOK AT YOU! YOU WORK TOO HARD, DEAR.
YOU KNOW, JUST ONCE I WISH SOMEONE WOULD LIE AND TELL ME HOW PRETTY I LOOK.
WELL, YOUR SKIRT IS CERTAINLY LOVELY.
THAT'S A START.
PANYA, I'VE BEEN MEANING TO TELL YOU...
I'M SORRY WE STILL HAVEN'T FOUND LIZ. YOU TWO WERE CLOSE.
IT'S ALL RIGHT, KATHERINE. YOU'VE DONE--ARE STILL DOING--ALL YOU CAN. SHE'S YOUR FRIEND TOO, AFTER ALL.
JUST TAKE CARE OF YOURSELF, DEAR.
BZZZ
BZZZ
CALL
C. GIAROCCO INCOMING

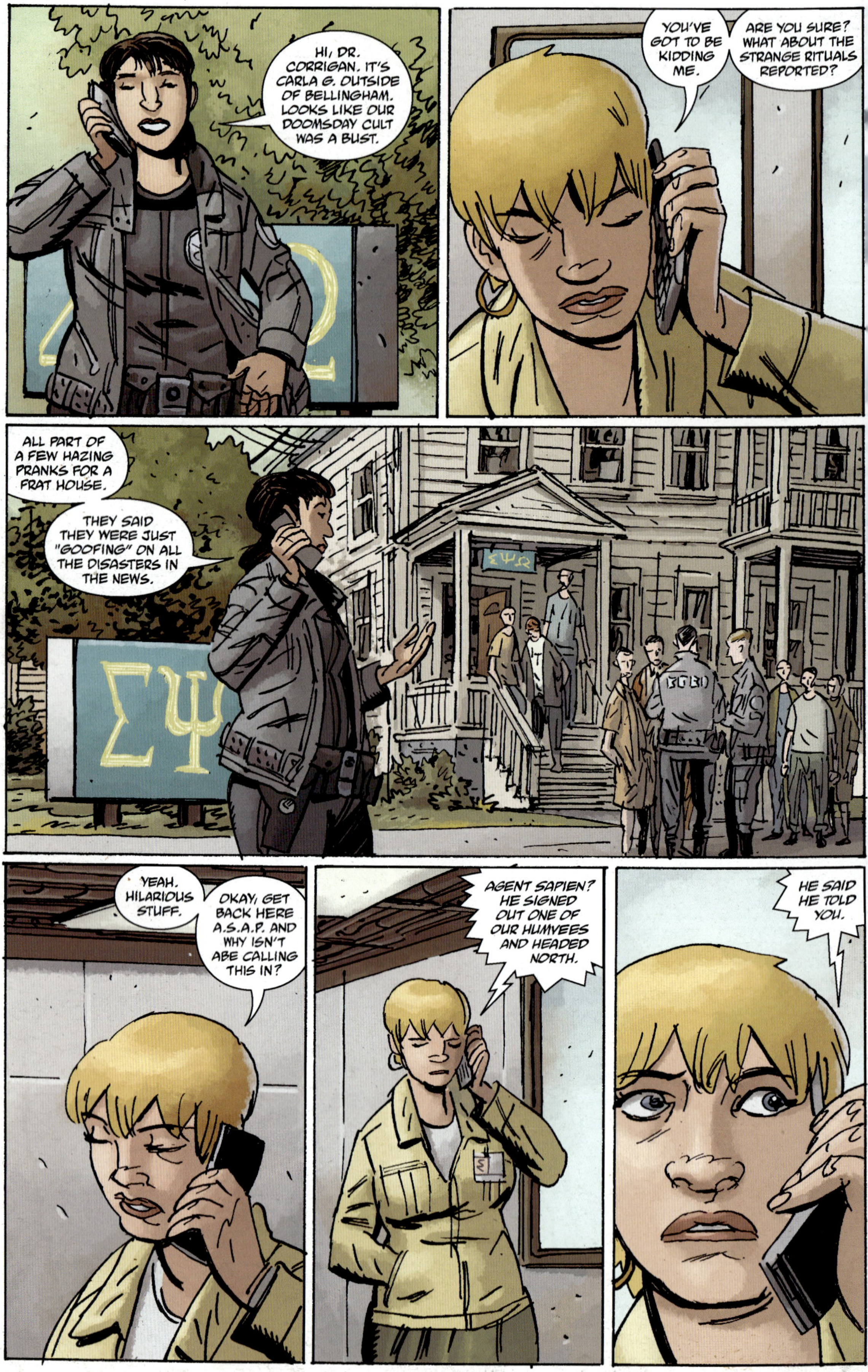
HI, DR. CORRIGAN. IT'S CARLA G. OUTSIDE OF BELLINGHAM. LOOKS LIKE OUR DOOMSDAY CULT WAS A BUST.
YOU'VE GOT TO BE KIDDING ME.
ARE YOU SURE? WHAT ABOUT THE STRANGE RITUALS REPORTED?
ALL PART OF A FEW HAZING PRANKS FOR A FRAT HOUSE.
THEY SAID THEY WERE JUST "GOOFING" ON ALL THE DISASTERS IN THE NEWS.
ΣΨΩ
ΣΨ
YEAH. HILARIOUS STUFF.
OKAY, GET BACK HERE A.S.A.P. AND WHY ISN'T ABE CALLING THIS IN?
AGENT SAPIEN? HE SIGNED OUT ONE OF OUR HUMVEES AND HEADED NORTH.
HE SAID HE TOLD YOU.

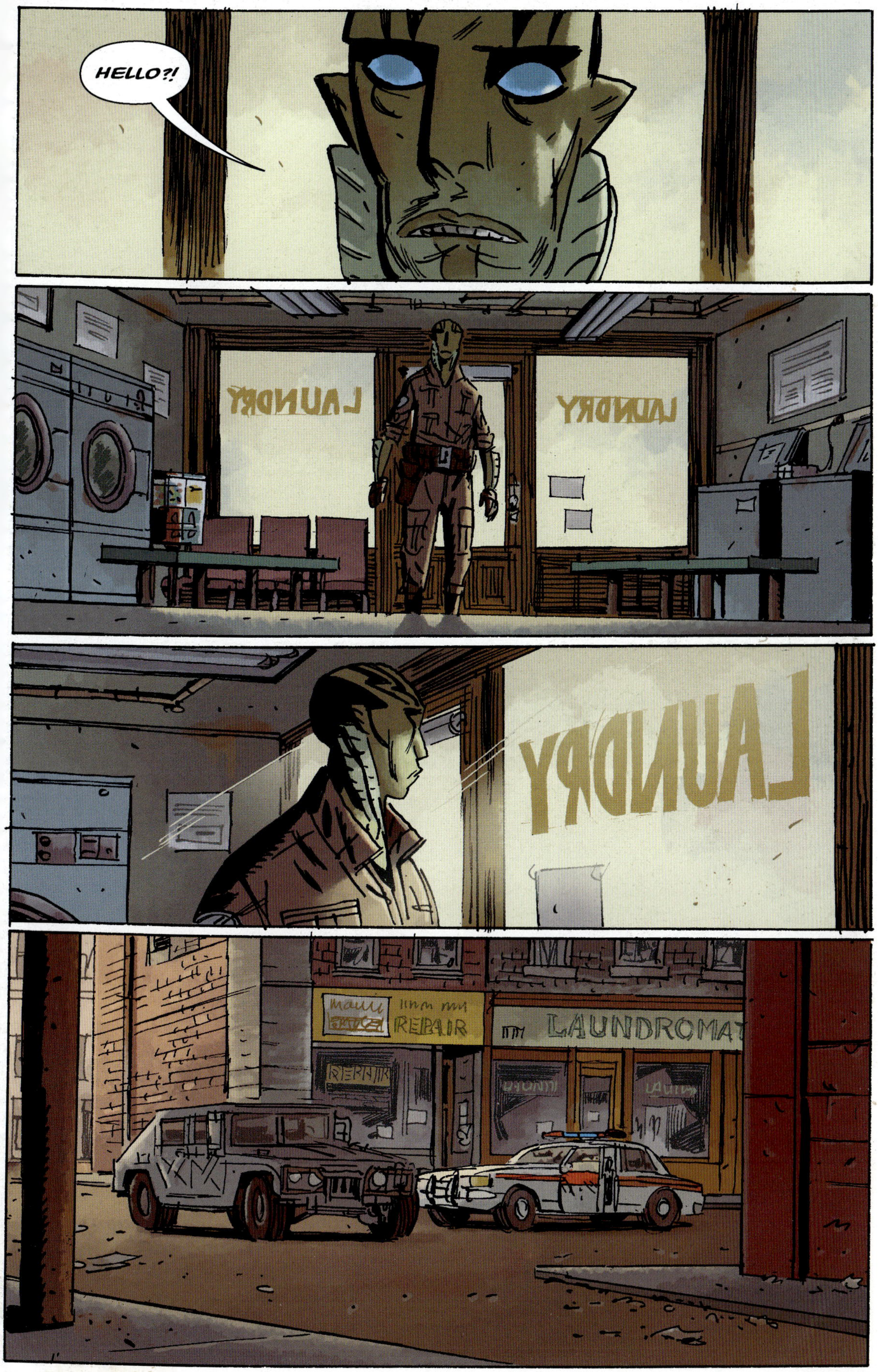
HELLO?!
LAUNDRY
LAUNDRY
LAUNDRY
REPAIR
LAUNDROMAT

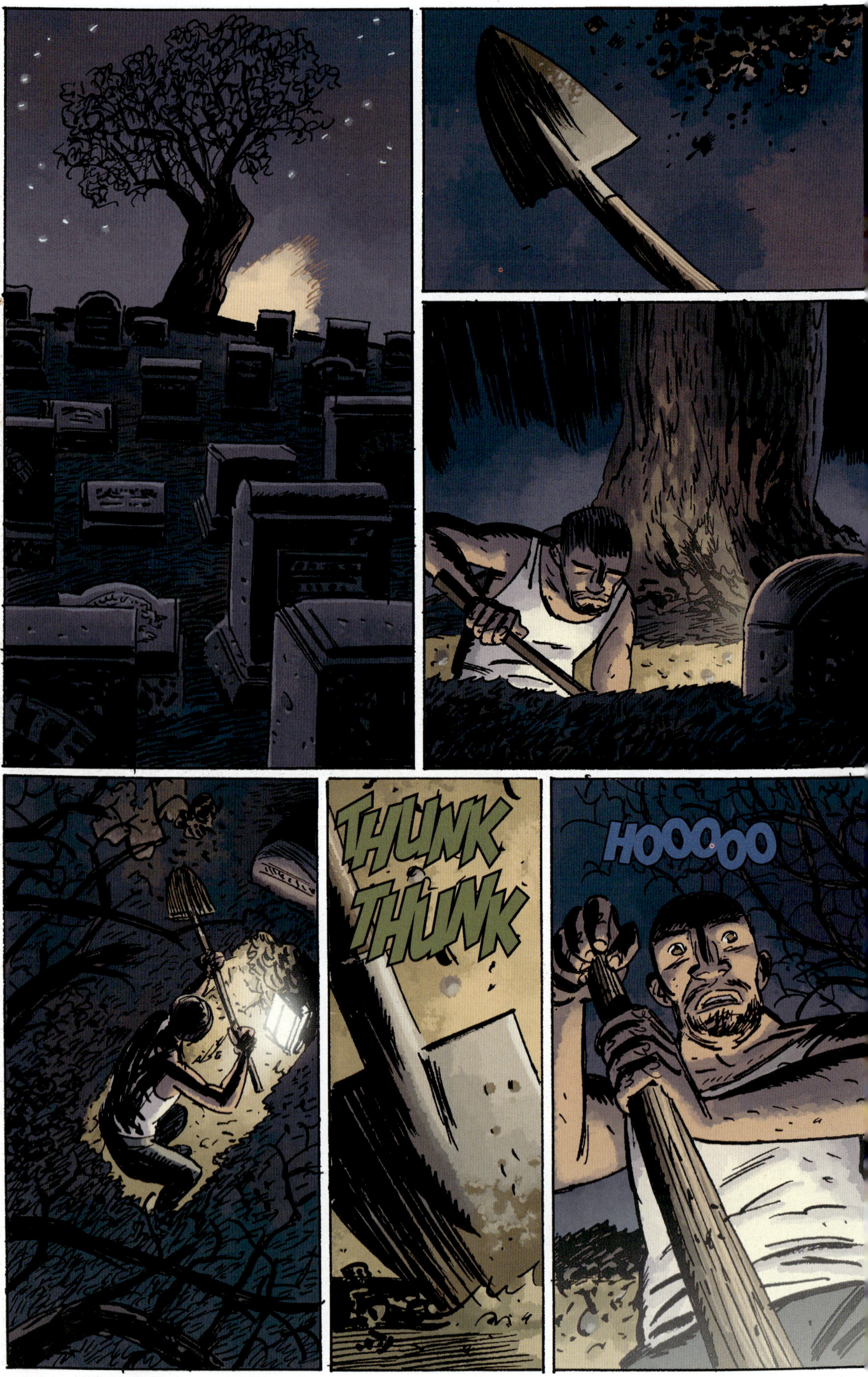
THUNK
THUNK
HOOOOO

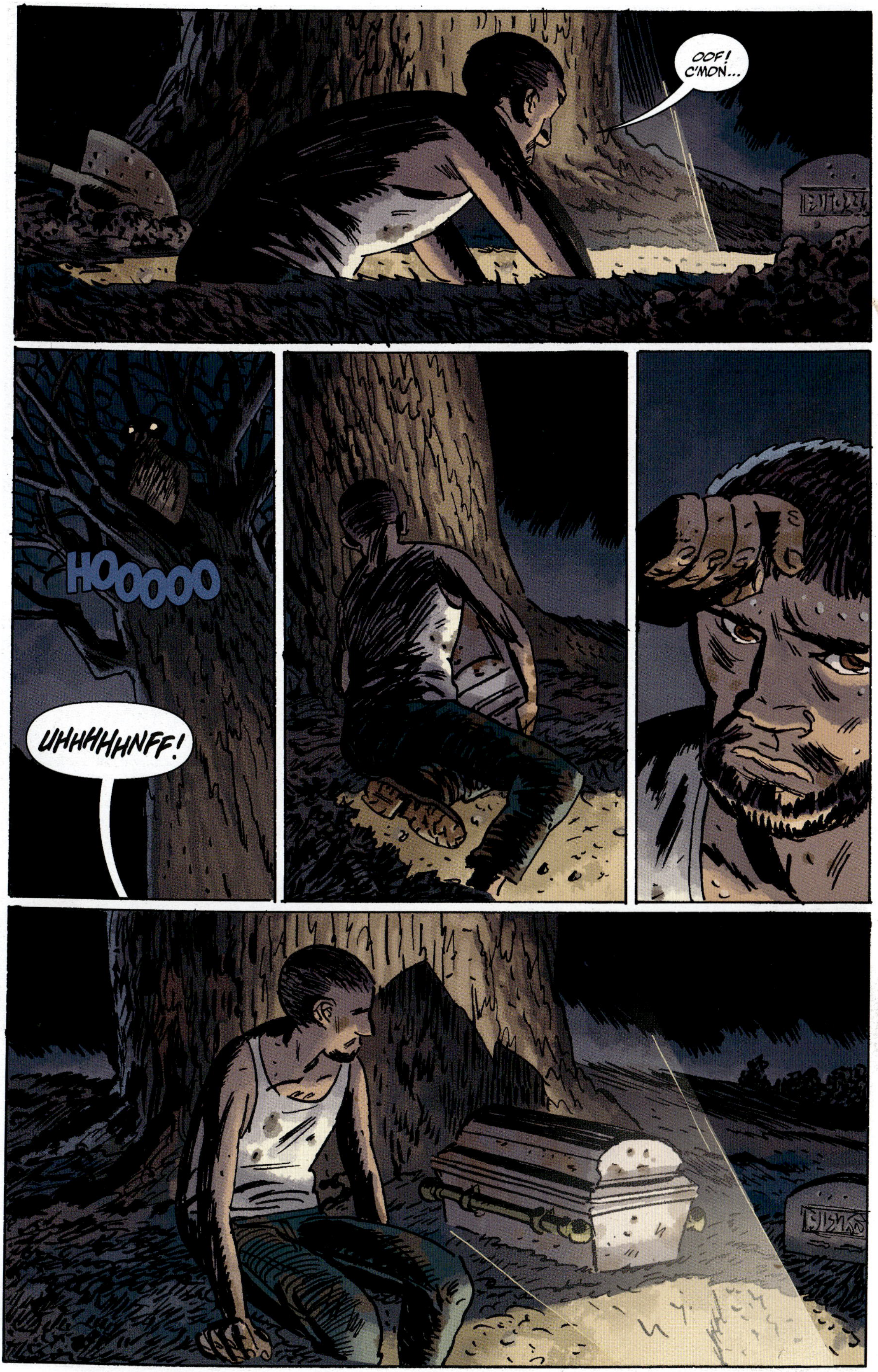
OOF! C'MON...
HOOOOO
UHHHHHNFF!

GOD DAMMIT, ABE. PICK UP!
WOW, YOU MUST HAVE TWENTY YEARS' WORTH OF FILES HERE!
SIXTY, ACTUALLY. ALL SHIPPED OVER WHEN THE CONNECTICUT HEADQUARTERS SHUT DOWN.
IT'S THE TWENTY-FIRST CENTURY, DOCTOR. THESE SHOULD BE DIGITAL.
WE HAVE A SCANNER DOWNSTAIRS. YOU CAN START ANY TIME.
THIS...THIS WHOLE EXPERIENCE IS DIFFERENT FROM WHAT I EXPECTED.
TYNON, DARYL
I THOUGHT YOUR WORK WAS ALL ABOUT MONSTERS, BUT I SEE A LOT OF NORMAL FOLKS IN HERE.
LIKE THIS FAMILY.
WHAT WAS THEIR STORY? HAUNTED BY A GHOST?
SOMETHING LIKE THAT.

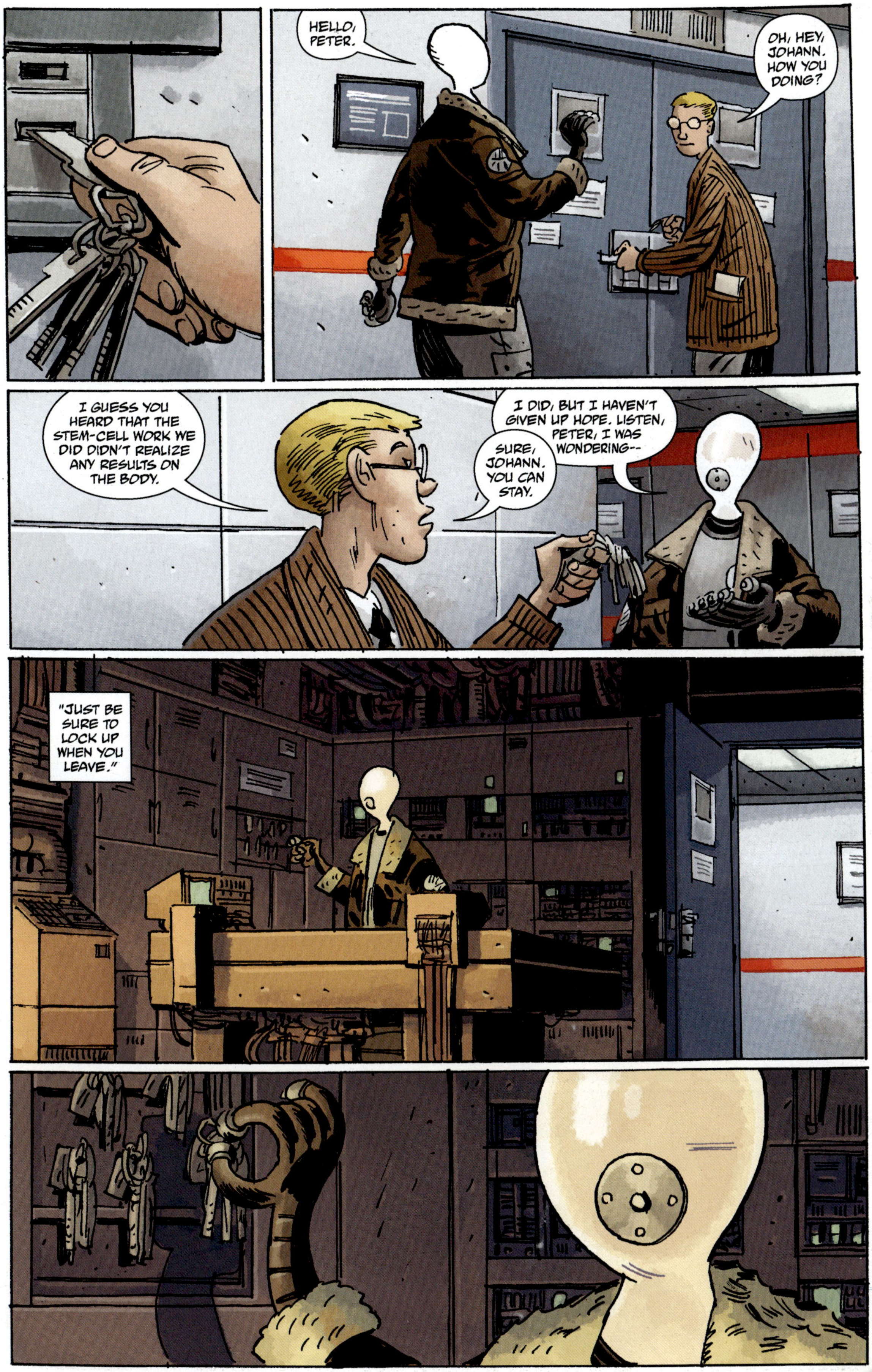
HELLO, PETER.
OH, HEY, JOHANN. HOW YOU DOING?
I GUESS YOU HEARD THAT THE STEM-CELL WORK WE DID DIDN'T REALIZE ANY RESULTS ON THE BODY.
I DID, BUT I HAVEN'T GIVEN UP HOPE. LISTEN, PETER, I WAS WONDERING--
SURE, JOHANN. YOU CAN STAY.
"JUST BE SURE TO LOCK UP WHEN YOU LEAVE."

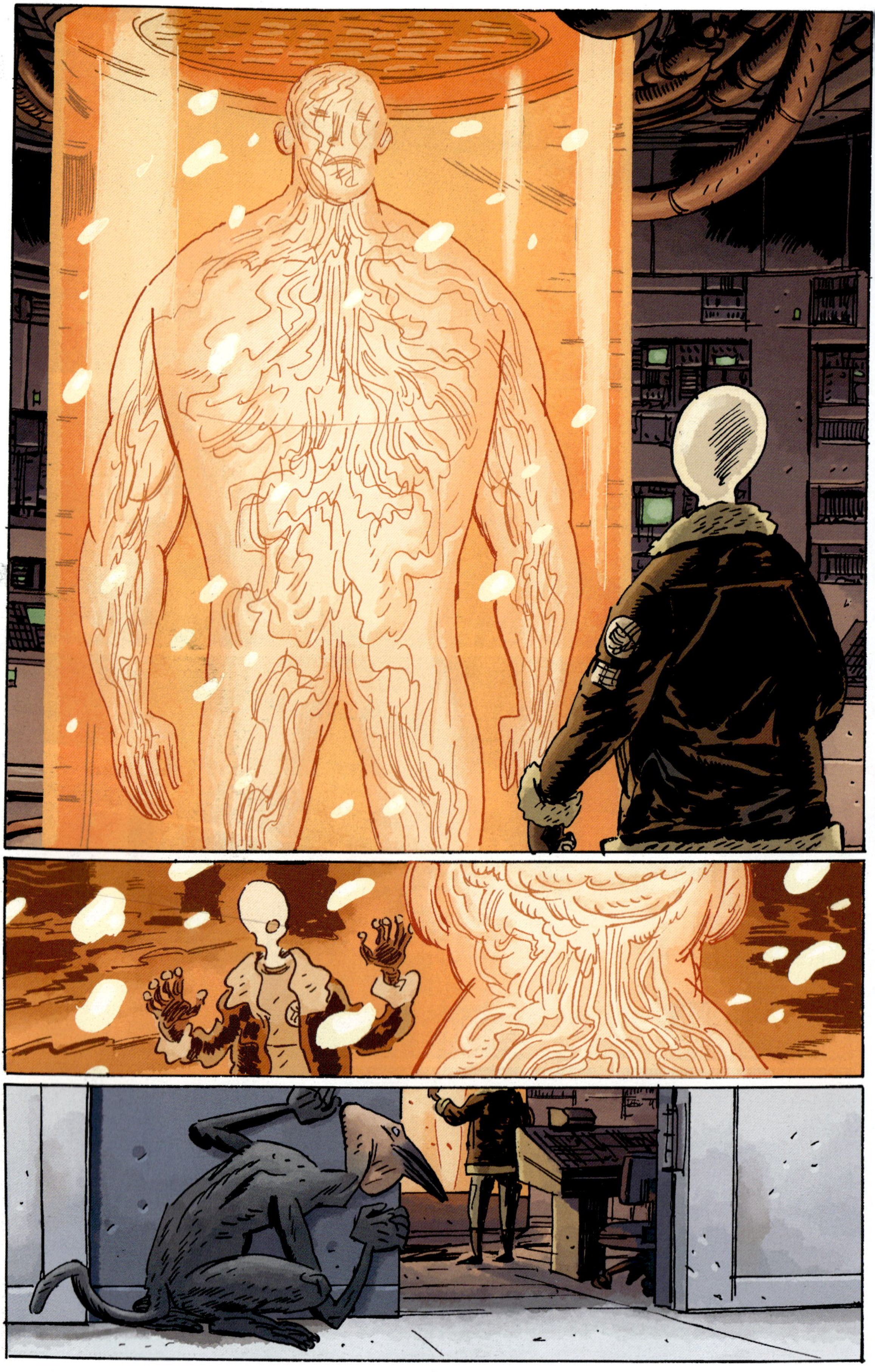

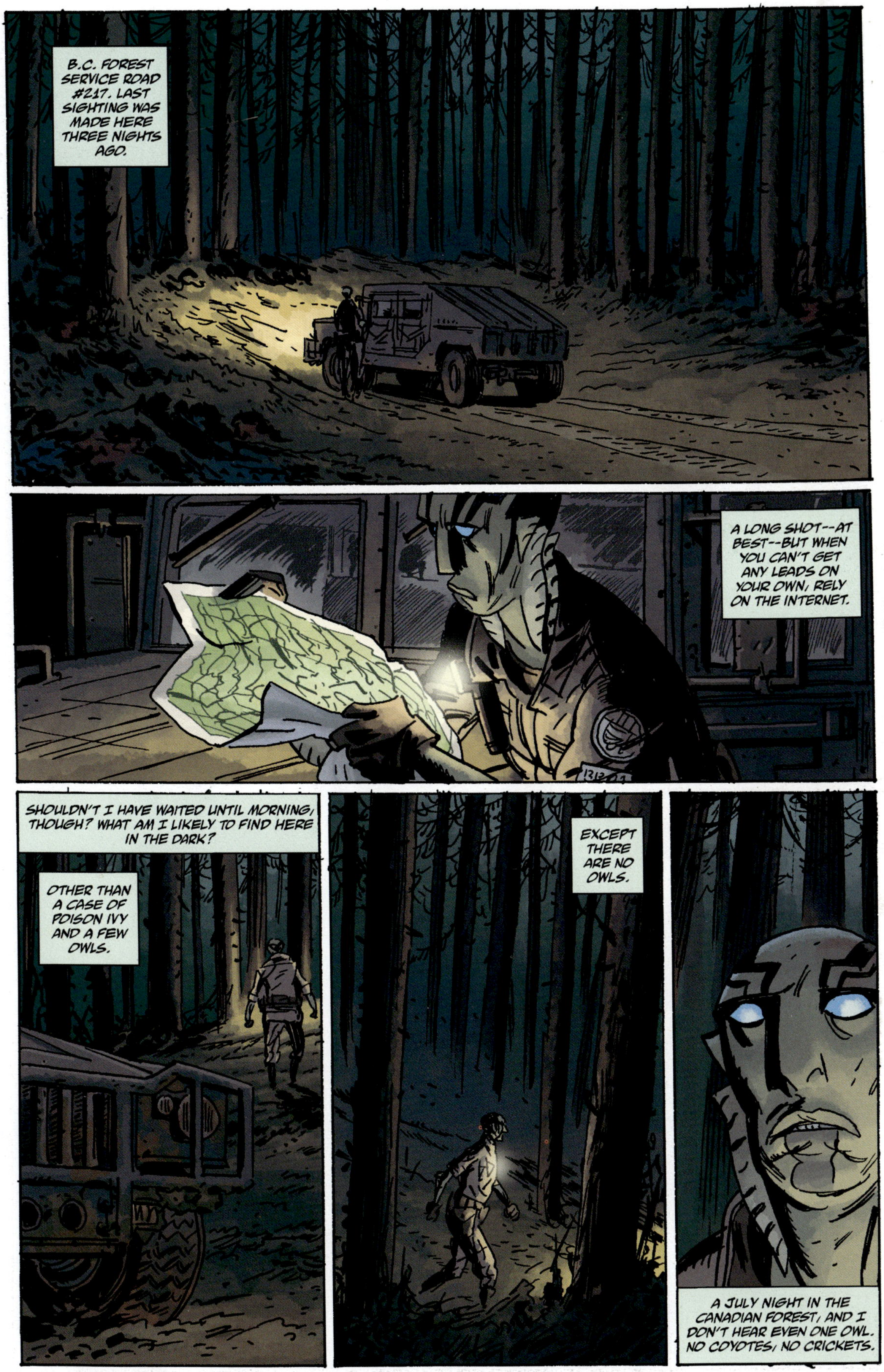
B.C. FOREST SERVICE ROAD #217. LAST SIGHTING WAS MADE HERE THREE NIGHTS AGO.
A LONG SHOT--AT BEST--BUT WHEN YOU CAN'T GET ANY LEADS ON YOUR OWN, RELY ON THE INTERNET.
SHOULDN'T I HAVE WAITED UNTIL MORNING, THOUGH? WHAT AM I LIKELY TO FIND HERE IN THE DARK?
OTHER THAN A CASE OF POISON IVY AND A FEW OWLS.
EXCEPT THERE ARE NO OWLS.
A JULY NIGHT IN THE CANADIAN FOREST, AND I DON'T HEAR EVEN ONE OWL. NO COYOTES, NO CRICKETS.

I DON'T HEAR ANYTHING.
HOW IS THAT POSSIBLE?
IT'S JUST LIKE THAT SMALL TOWN. EVERY-THING GONE.
NO. NOT EVERYTHING.
DON'T HEAR IT, CAN'T SEE IT--
--BUT I FEEL IT.

WHAT IS THE MATTER WITH ME, COMING OUT HERE ALONE AT NIGHT?
COMING OUT HERE AT ALL.
WHAT DID I THINK WAS GOING TO HAP--
KRAK

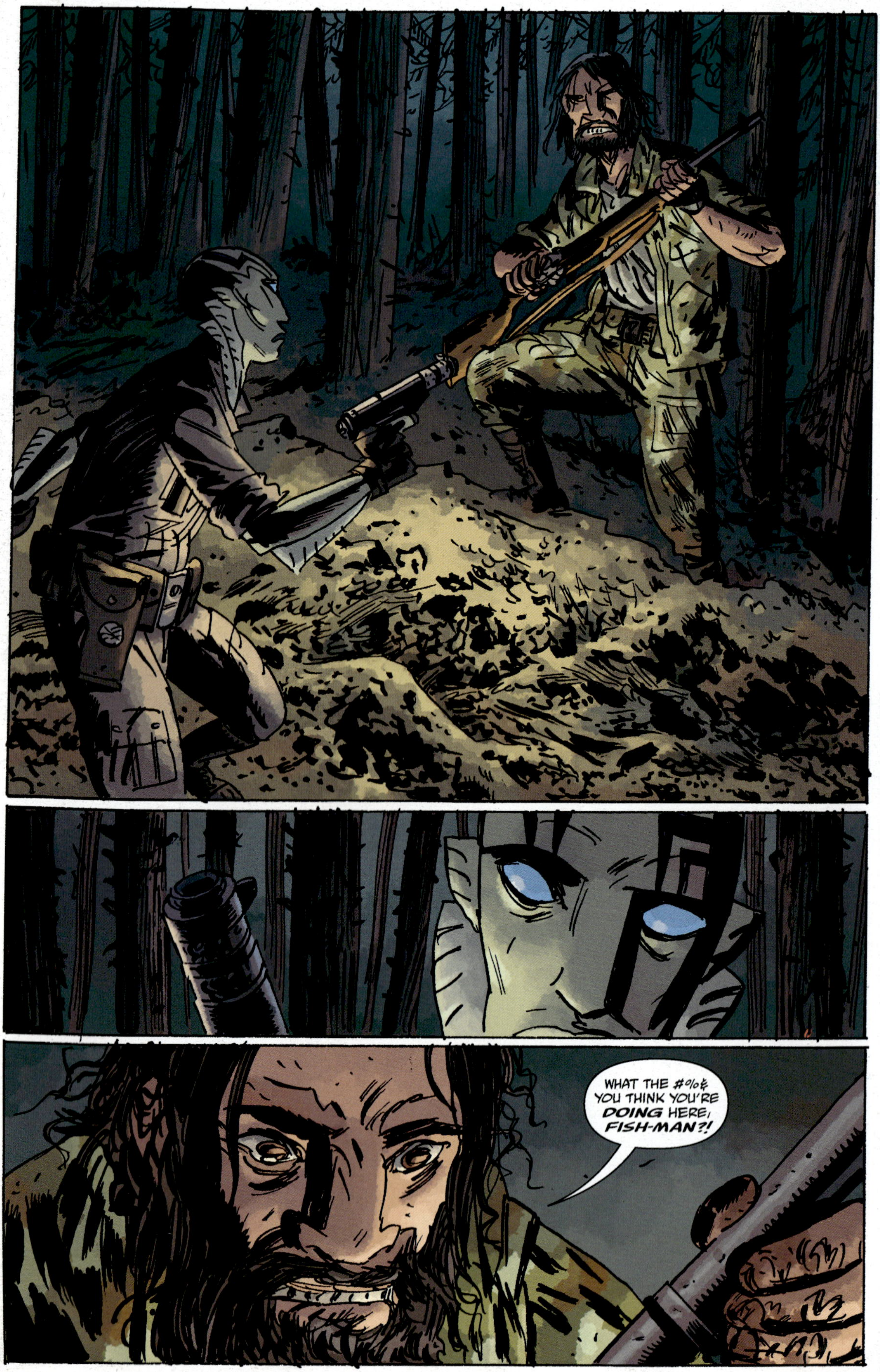
WHAT THE #%& YOU THINK YOU'RE ***DOING*** HERE, ***FISH-MAN?!***

NEW WORLD CHAPTER TWO

ILLUSTRATION BY **GUY DAVIS** WITH **DAVE STEWART**

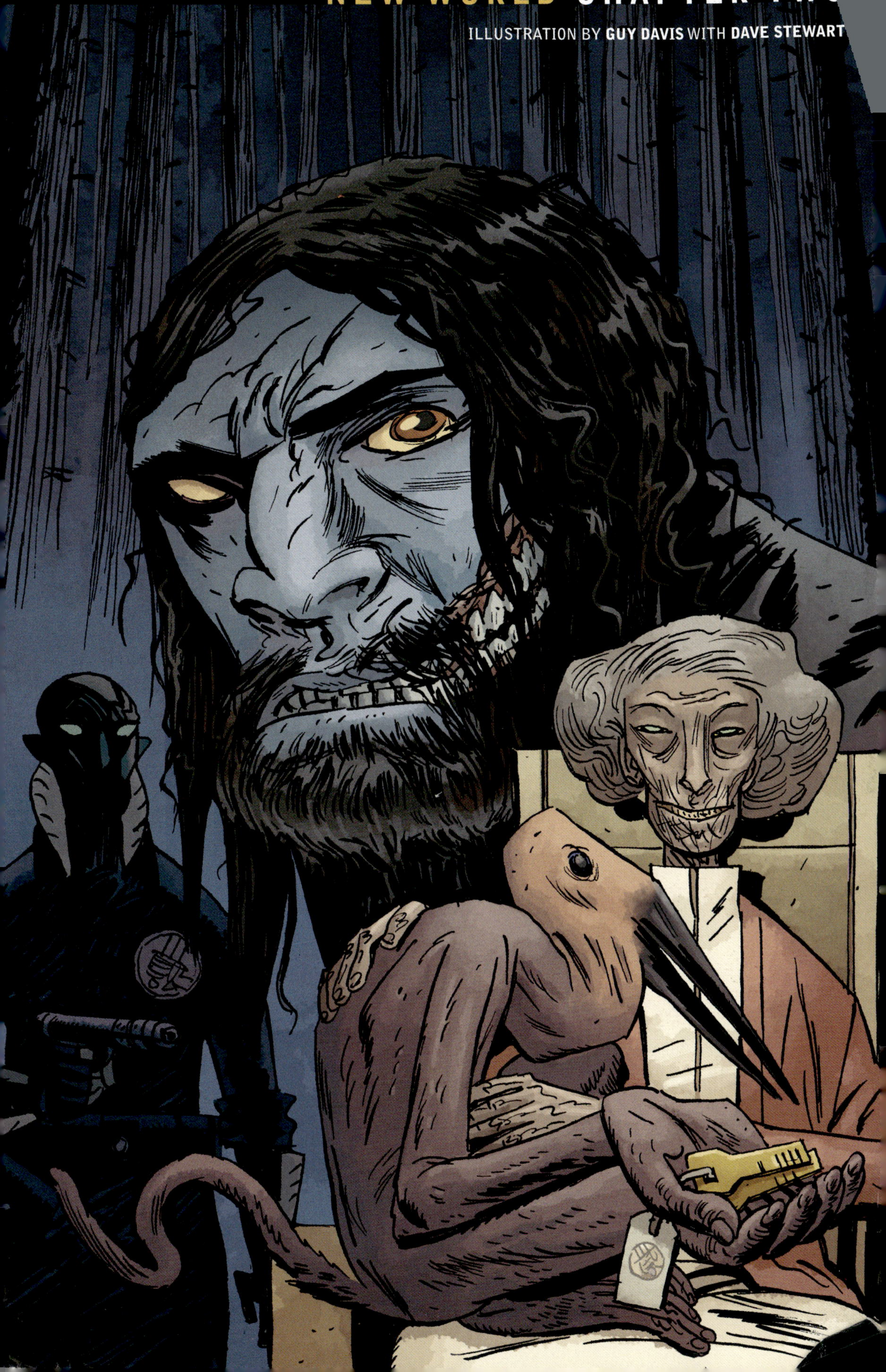

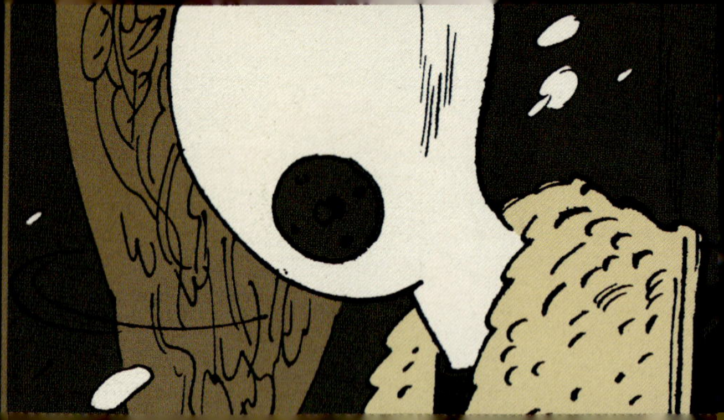

DR. CORRIGAN!
THERE YOU ARE.
I JUST WANTED TO GO OVER SOME SCHEDULING ISSUES WITH YOU IF YOU HAVE A MOMENT.
WE'RE RUNNING SHORT OF AGENTS WE CAN SPARE FOR MONITOR DUTY.
CALL JOHANN. HE CAN ALWAYS PICK UP A SHIFT.
WELL, UH, SEE, THAT'S JUST IT. I TRIED THAT, AND HE SAID HE WOULDN'T BE AVAILABLE.
WHAT?!

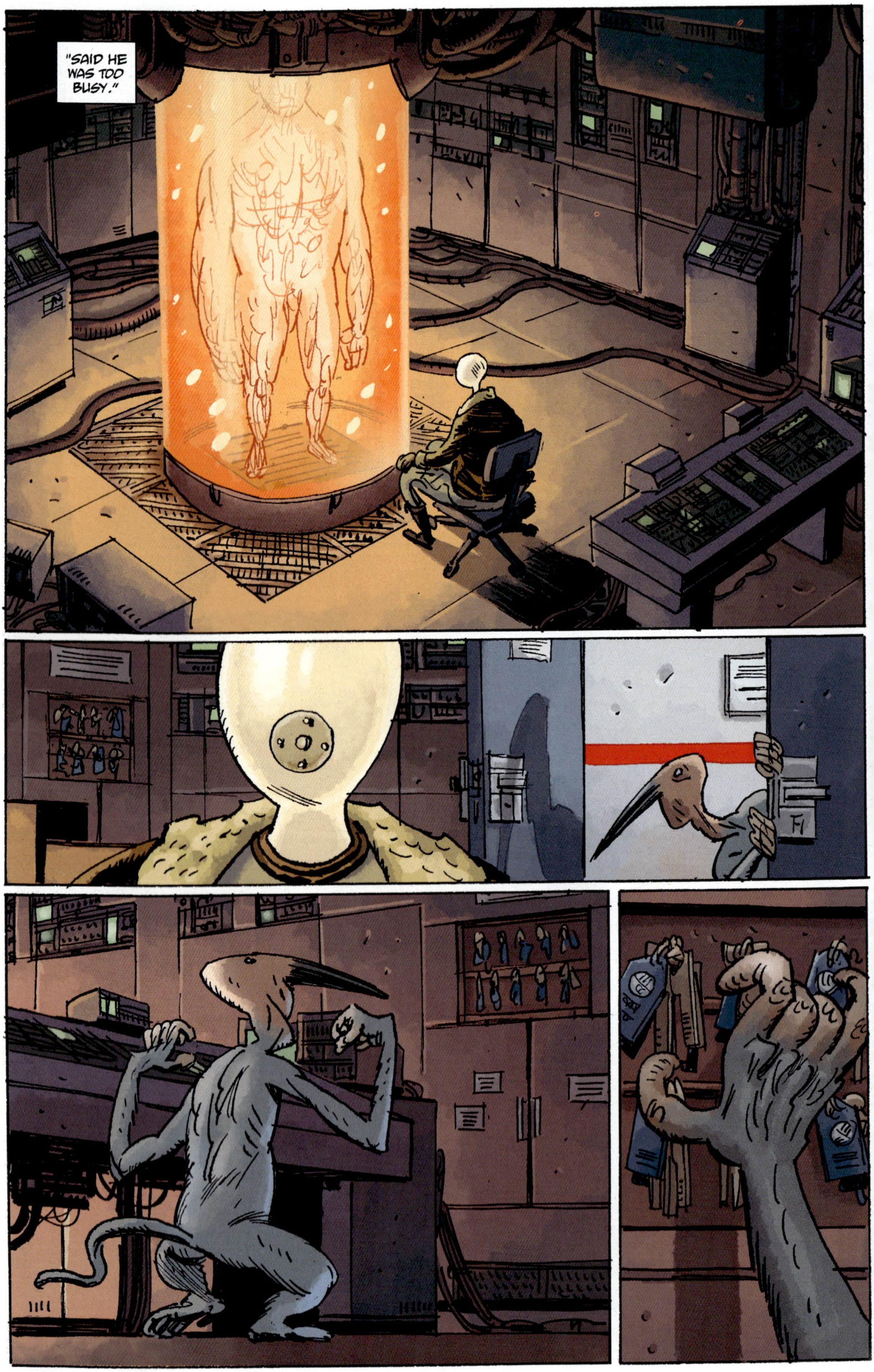
"SAID HE WAS TOO BUSY."

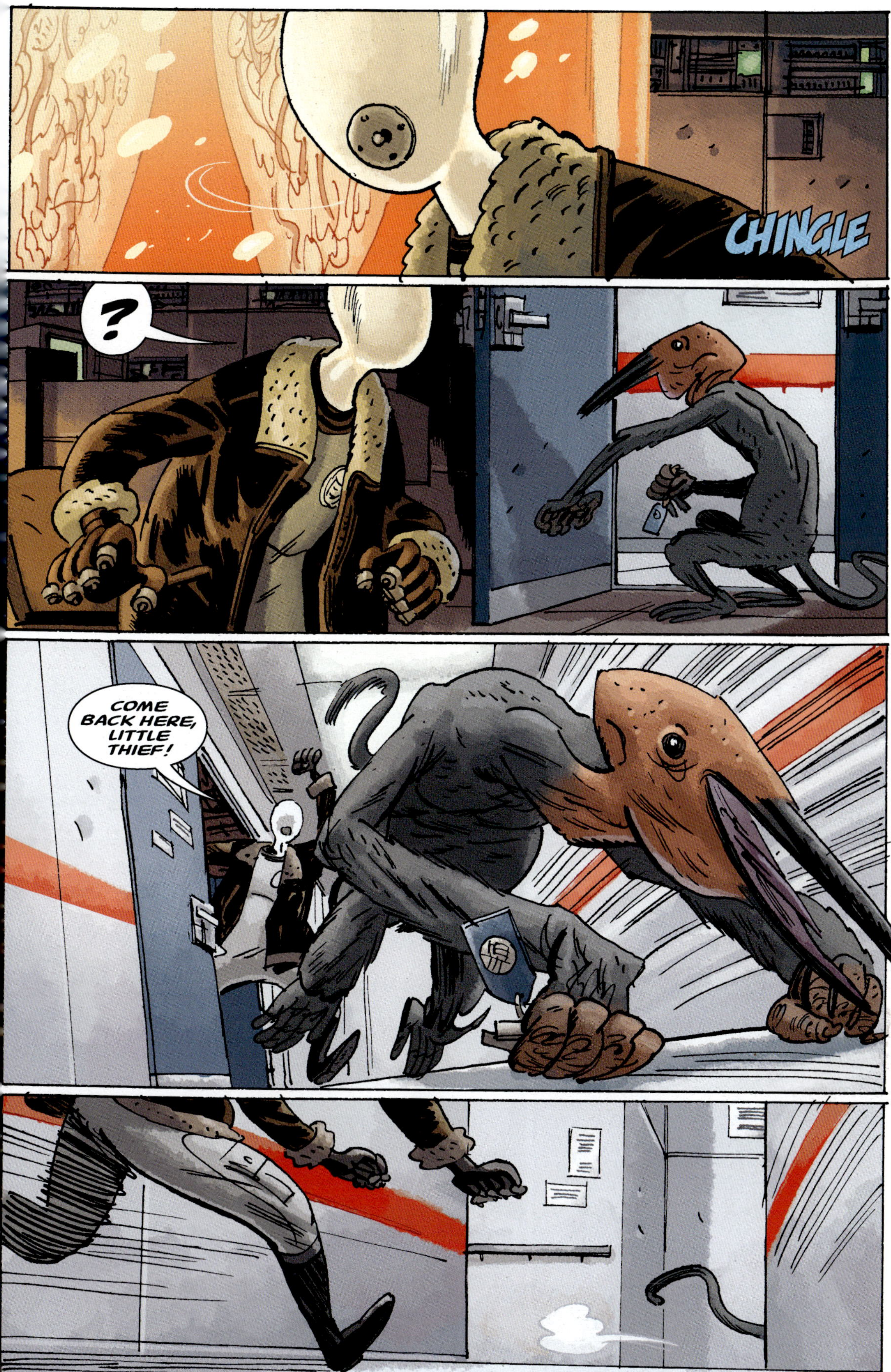
CHINGLE
?
COME BACK HERE, LITTLE THIEF!

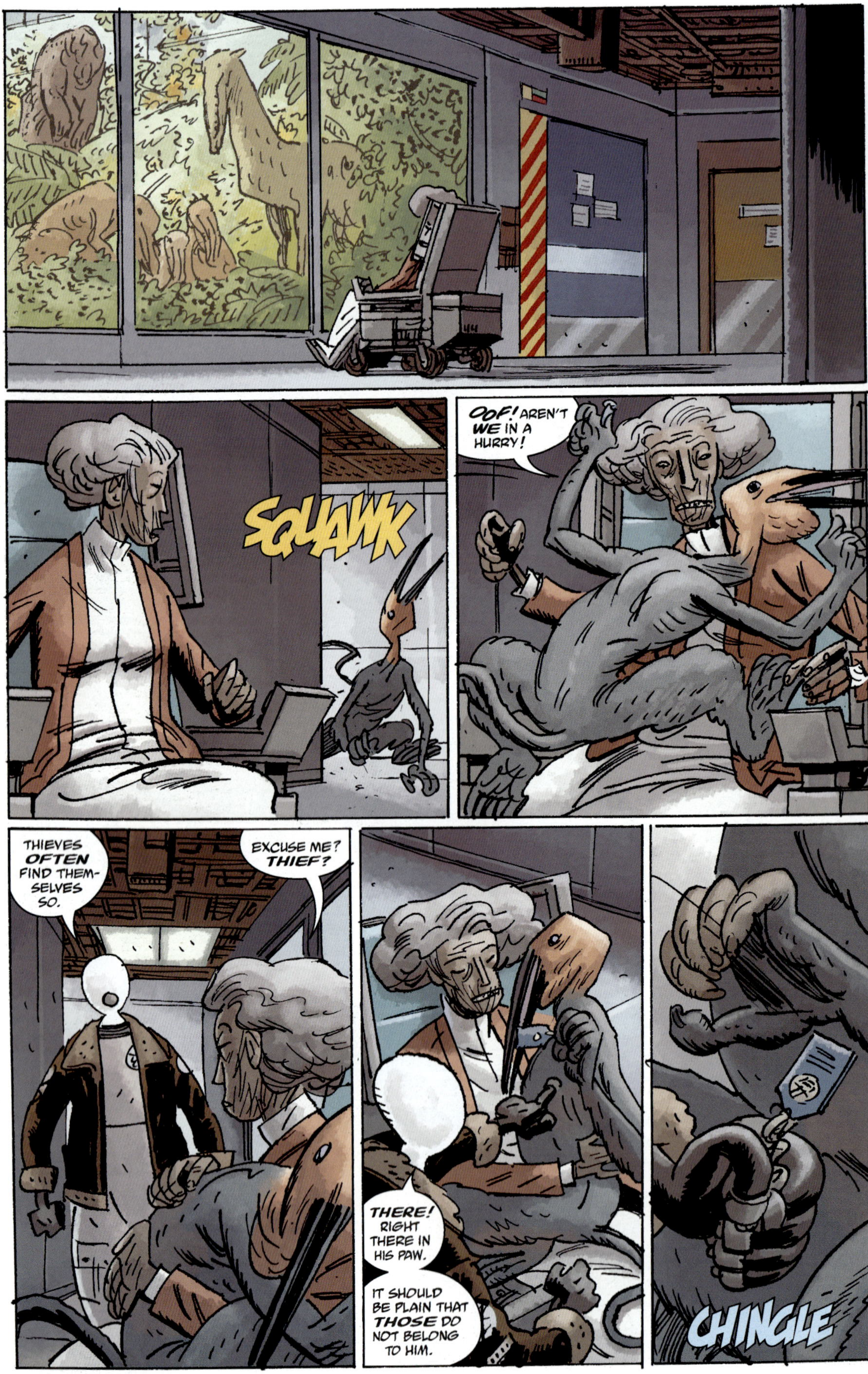
SQUAWK
OOF! AREN'T WE IN A HURRY!
THIEVES OFTEN FIND THEMSELVES SO.
EXCUSE ME? THIEF?
THERE! RIGHT THERE IN HIS PAW.
IT SHOULD BE PLAIN THAT THOSE DO NOT BELONG TO HIM.
CHINGLE

COVETOUS LITTLE GOBLIN!
OH, CALM DOWN, AGENT KRAUS! THE POOR THING DIDN'T ACT OUT OF MALICE. HE'S ONLY AN ANIMAL.
RIGHT. ANOTHER ONE OF YOUR PRECIOUS HYBRID ANIMALS.
YOU SEEM TO LOVE THEM MORE, TO HAVE MORE RESPECT FOR THEM, THAN YOU DO YOUR FELLOW...
WHAT? WHAT ARE YOU LOOKING AT?

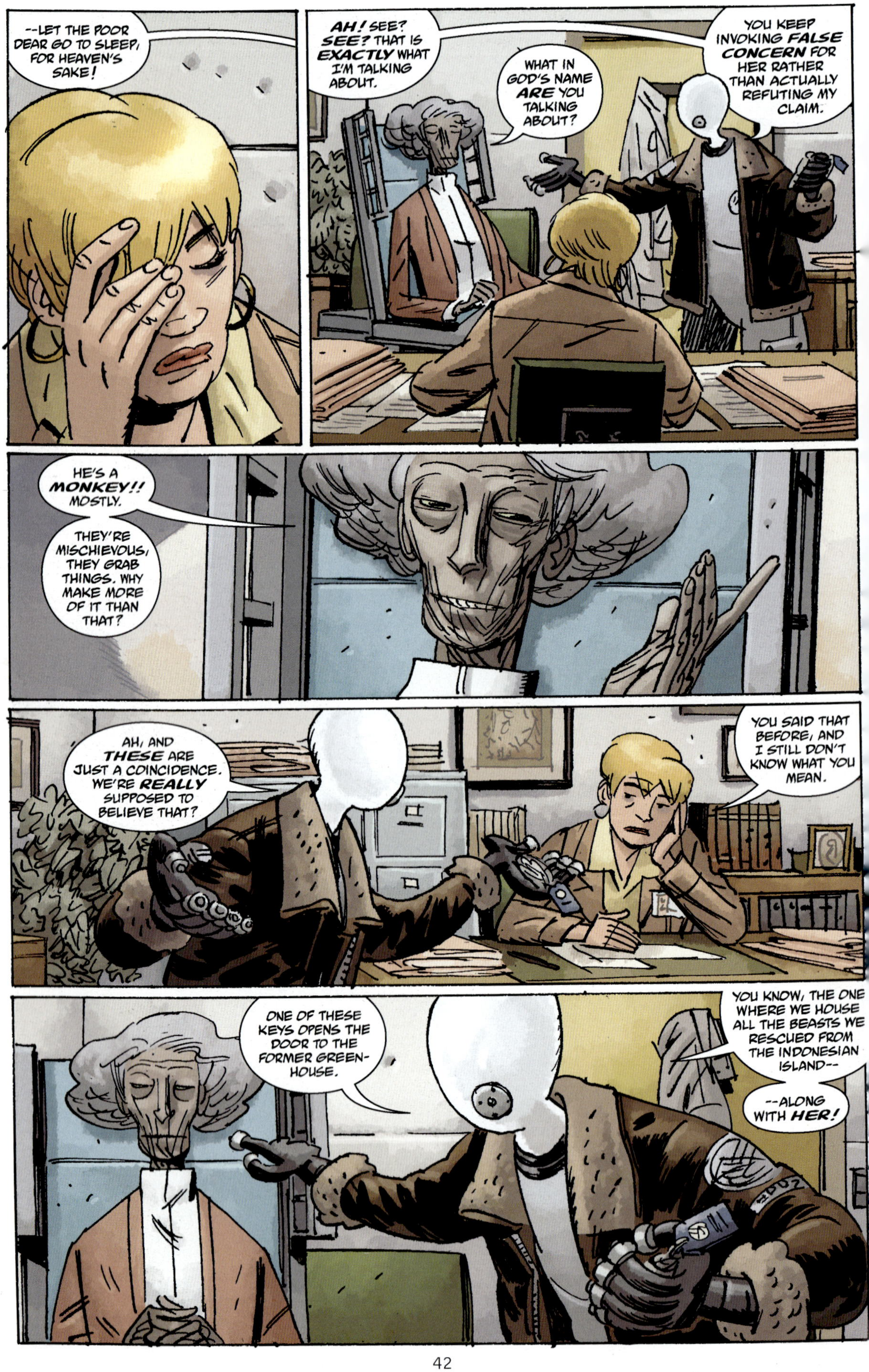

--LET THE POOR DEAR GO TO SLEEP, FOR HEAVEN'S SAKE!
AH! SEE? SEE? THAT IS EXACTLY WHAT I'M TALKING ABOUT.
WHAT IN GOD'S NAME ARE YOU TALKING ABOUT?
YOU KEEP INVOKING FALSE CONCERN FOR HER RATHER THAN ACTUALLY REFUTING MY CLAIM.
HE'S A MONKEY!! MOSTLY.
THEY'RE MISCHIEVOUS, THEY GRAB THINGS. WHY MAKE MORE OF IT THAN THAT?
AH, AND THESE ARE JUST A COINCIDENCE. WE'RE REALLY SUPPOSED TO BELIEVE THAT?
YOU SAID THAT BEFORE, AND I STILL DON'T KNOW WHAT YOU MEAN.
ONE OF THESE KEYS OPENS THE DOOR TO THE FORMER GREEN-HOUSE.
YOU KNOW, THE ONE WHERE WE HOUSE ALL THE BEASTS WE RESCUED FROM THE INDONESIAN ISLAND--
--ALONG WITH HER!

THE PELICAN-MONKEY STOLE THE KEYS ON PURPOSE?
PREPOSTEROUS!
WE KNOW WHAT YOU DO, PANYA!
YOU GET INTO THE MINDS OF ANIMALS OF LOWER INTELLIGENCE AND USE THEIR BODIES LIKE PUPPETS. THAT'S HOW YOU CONTACTED US IN THE FIRST PLACE, ISN'T IT?
AND SHE'S BEEN TRYING TO GET US TO RELEASE THOSE CREATURES SINCE SHE ARRIVED. IT ALL MAKES SENSE.
DOES IT? AFTER I RELEASED THE ANIMALS, THEN WHAT WAS I GOING TO DO?
AFTER ALL, DEAR, YOU WOULD JUST ROUND THEM UP AND PUT THEM BACK.
SEEMS A SILLY THING FOR ME TO DO.
THERE! THAT PATRONIZING TONE AGAIN!!
SHUT UP!!

YOU SEE THESE? THESE ARE FILES OF CASES I NEVER WOULD HAVE TAKEN SIX MONTHS AGO!
IN FACT, I NEVER WOULD HAVE EVEN HEARD ABOUT THEM!
BUT NOW, WITH THE U.N. MONEY KEEPING OUR DOORS OPEN, WE'VE GOT U.N. OVER-SIGHT.
FWAP
OVERSIGHT THAT MEANS I HAVE TO CHECK OUT EVERY SINGLE CREAKY BOARD THEY SAY I HAVE TO.
MY DAYS--AND MY NIGHTS!--ARE FILLED WITH THIS CRAP!!
AND YOU WAKE ME UP WITH YOUR PARANOID FANTASY?!
WHICH, BY THE WAY, YOU WOULD NEVER HAVE HAD IF YOU'D BEEN WHERE YOU WERE SUPPOSED TO BE--ON MONITOR DUTY!!
A DUTY YOU'RE GOING TO FULFILL RIGHT NOW!
BUT, KATHERINE--
AND GIVE ME THOSE GOD DAMN KEYS!!!

BRAVA, DEAR! BRAVA!
CLAP CLAP CLAP
OH, GIVE IT A REST!
I-- WELL, I--
THIS WASN'T A COINCIDENCE.
YOUR MONKEY-PELICAN PAL'S NOT ENOUGH FOR YOU ANYMORE, IS THAT IT?
IF YOU WANT SOMETHING, YOU CAN'T JUST TAKE IT! THAT'S NOT THE WAY THINGS ARE RUN AROUND HERE!
SWEETIE--
CUT THE CRAP, PANYA! YOU'VE BEEN DOING YOUR BEST TO STAY ON THE FRINGES OF OUR GROUP FOR MONTHS.
EITHER YOU'RE PART OF OUR TEAM OR YOU'RE NOT.
FIGURE IT OUT.

"NOW GET OUT AND LET ME SLEEP!"
--JOINING US NOW FROM OUR ATLANTA STUDIO. GOOD EVENING, REVEREND NEDIN, AND THANK YOU FOR JOINING US.
WHAT CHOICE DID I HAVE, ERICA?
PEOPLE ARE SCARED--AND THEY SHOULD BE! ALL THAT WE'VE DONE, ALL OF OUR SINS, COME DOWN TO THIS, DON'T THEY?

BECAUSE THIS ISN'T THE END OF IT. AS TERRIBLE AS IT IS, IT'S JUST THE BEGINNING.
THE WAY THIS NATION, THE WAY WE MOCK GOD WITH OUR DISREGARD FOR HUMAN LIFE, WE SHOULD HAVE EXPECTED IT.
WHAT HAPPENED TO ROME WHEN THEY INVADED SOVEREIGN NATIONS? WHAT HAPPENED TO GERMANY? THE ALMIGHTY DOES NOT FAVOR THE BELLICOSE. HE DOES NOT!
OKAY, PAT, YOU HEARD THE REVEREND.
I SURE DID, AND I'VE HEARD IT BEFORE. RIGHT AFTER 9/11 THIS SAME SORT OF RHETORIC WAS TROTTED OUT, THOUGH I'M A LITTLE SURPRISED THIS TIME.
AFTER ALL, THE WHOLE WORLD HAS SEEN CATASTROPHE. I'M SORRY, BUT YOU CAN'T POINT THE FINGER AT AMERICA THIS TIME.
THAT'S WHERE YOU'RE WRONG, PATRICK. AMERICA'S GOT TO TAKE A LOT OF BLAME FOR THIS.
I REALLY BELIEVE THAT THE PAGANS, AND THE FALSE CHRISTIANS, AND THE SECULARISTS WHO HAVE ALL, THROUGH THEIR ACTIONS, REJECTED THE PATH OF CHRIST--WELL, I POINT MY FINGER RIGHT IN THEIR FACE.
BUT THEN YOU'RE ALSO RIGHT, PATRICK. BECAUSE IT ISN'T ONLY AMERICA.
ALL OVER THIS ONCE-BLESSED EARTH, YOU'VE GOT PEOPLE ACTING LIKE BARBARIANS, KILLING AND OPPRESSING.

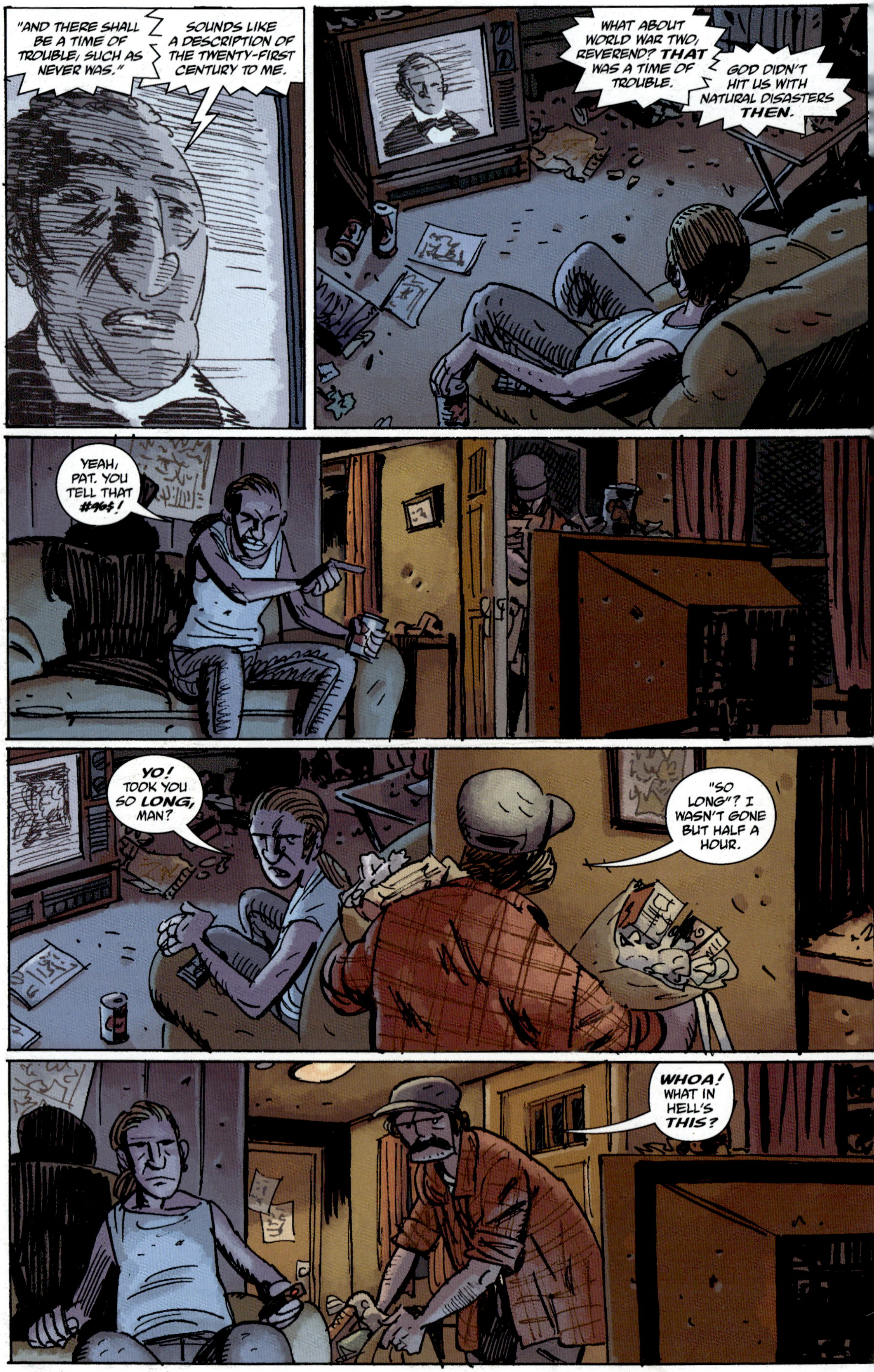
"AND THERE SHALL BE A TIME OF TROUBLE, SUCH AS NEVER WAS."
SOUNDS LIKE A DESCRIPTION OF THE TWENTY-FIRST CENTURY TO ME.
WHAT ABOUT WORLD WAR TWO, REVEREND? THAT WAS A TIME OF TROUBLE.
GOD DIDN'T HIT US WITH NATURAL DISASTERS THEN.
YEAH, PAT. YOU TELL THAT #%$!
YO! TOOK YOU SO LONG, MAN?
"SO LONG"? I WASN'T GONE BUT HALF A HOUR.
WHOA! WHAT IN HELL'S THIS?

HEY NOW!
HUSH!
YOU KNOW YOU DON'T WATCH NO T.V. WHEN SHE'S ASLEEP!
THIS AIN'T RIGHT. I PAY RENT, SAME AS YOU. I GOT A EQUAL VOTE.
NUH-UH, BOY.
HER IN THERE? SHE'D BE THE ONLY ONE GOT ANY VOTE. GET YERSELF CLEAR ON THAT.
AWW, #$%¢# THIS $¢*#, MAN!

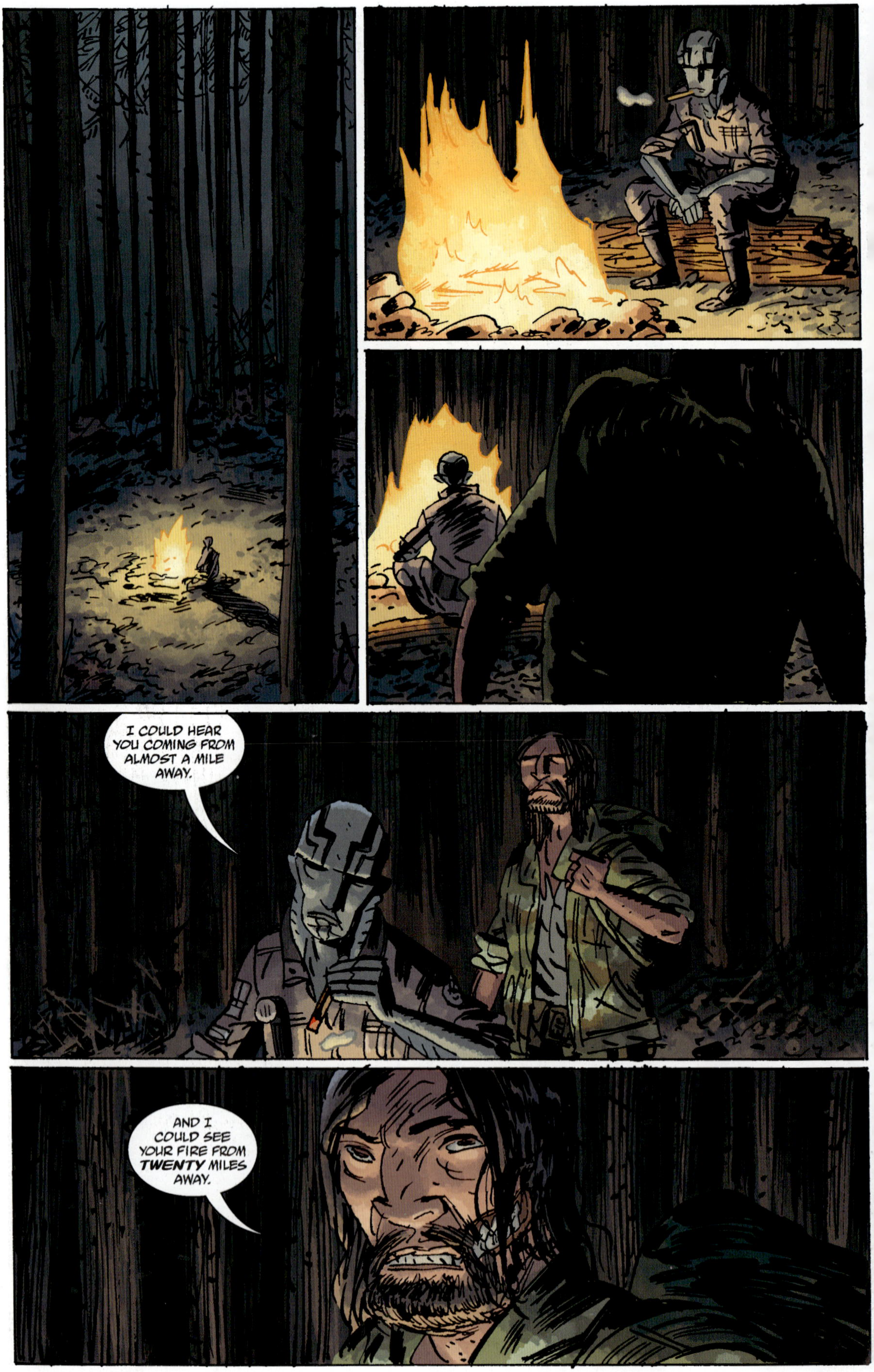
I COULD HEAR YOU COMING FROM ALMOST A MILE AWAY.
AND I COULD SEE YOUR FIRE FROM TWENTY MILES AWAY.

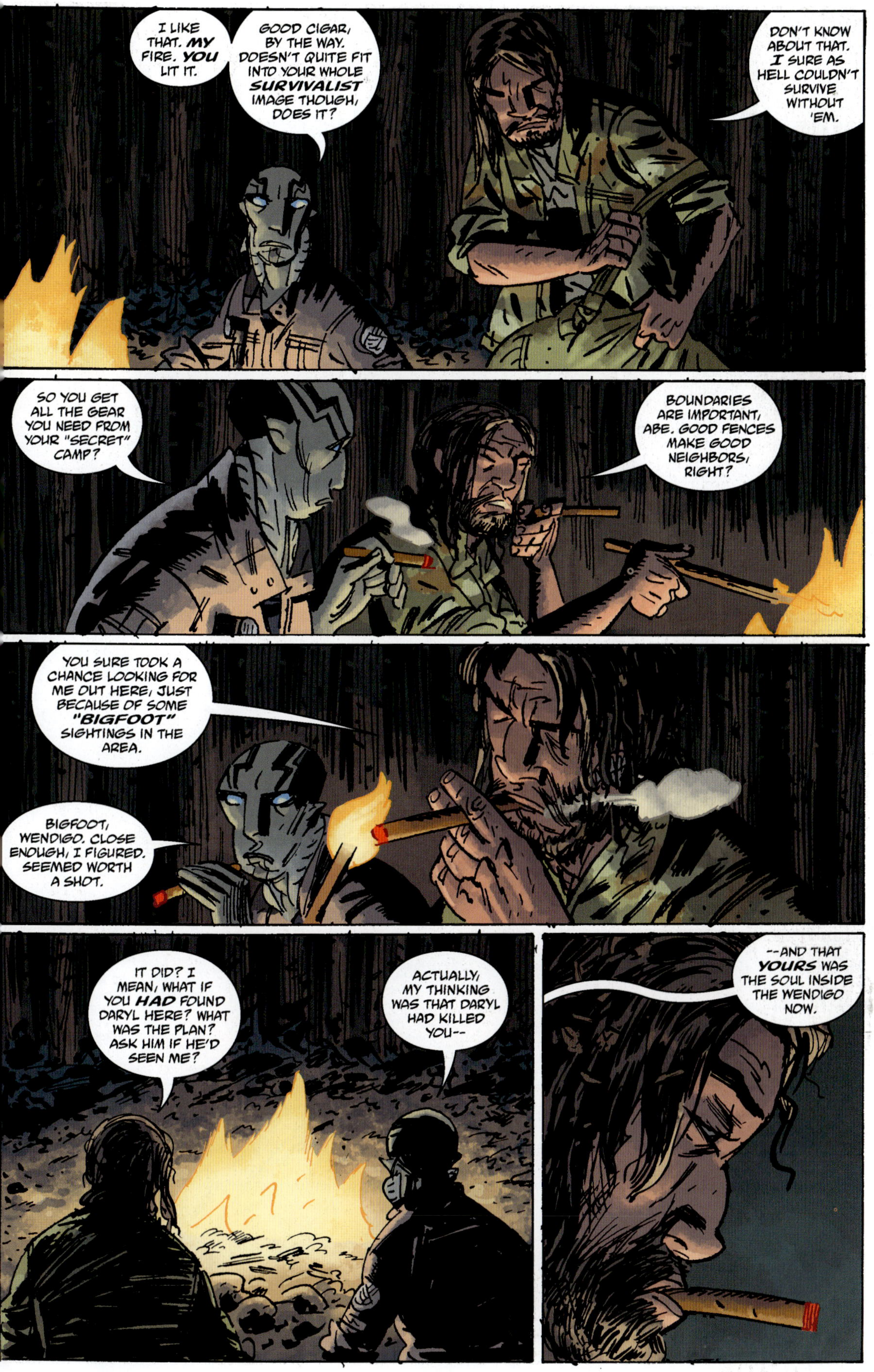
I LIKE THAT. MY FIRE. YOU LIT IT.
GOOD CIGAR, BY THE WAY. DOESN'T QUITE FIT INTO YOUR WHOLE SURVIVALIST IMAGE THOUGH, DOES IT?
DON'T KNOW ABOUT THAT. I SURE AS HELL COULDN'T SURVIVE WITHOUT 'EM.
SO YOU GET ALL THE GEAR YOU NEED FROM YOUR "SECRET" CAMP?
BOUNDARIES ARE IMPORTANT, ABE. GOOD FENCES MAKE GOOD NEIGHBORS, RIGHT?
YOU SURE TOOK A CHANCE LOOKING FOR ME OUT HERE, JUST BECAUSE OF SOME "BIGFOOT" SIGHTINGS IN THE AREA.
BIGFOOT, WENDIGO. CLOSE ENOUGH, I FIGURED. SEEMED WORTH A SHOT.
IT DID? I MEAN, WHAT IF YOU HAD FOUND DARYL HERE? WHAT WAS THE PLAN? ASK HIM IF HE'D SEEN ME?
ACTUALLY, MY THINKING WAS THAT DARYL HAD KILLED YOU--
--AND THAT YOURS WAS THE SOUL INSIDE THE WENDIGO NOW.

LOOK, ABE, I'M...
THAT WASN'T ME. THAT...
"I **NEVER** COULD HAVE DONE THAT, ANY OF IT. ***NEVER!***"

I WAS TRAPPED INSIDE THAT THING, SEEING IT ALL HAPPEN. SEEING ITS CLAWS RIP INTO MY MEN.
BUT IT *WASN'T* ME.
BEN.
I WOULDN'T HAVE COME HERE ALONE IF I THOUGHT IT WAS.
OKAY.
OKAY. THANKS.
I'VE BEEN LOOKING FOR YOU BECAUSE I THOUGHT YOU MIGHT NEED HELP.
AND I KNEW YOU WOULDN'T COME TO US LOOKING FOR IT YOURSELF.
AND I *STILL* WON'T GO BACK WITH YOU.
YOU CAN'T EXPECT ME TO FACE THOSE MEN AGAIN. OR KATE. OR LIZ.
OR JOHANN.

THIS IS WHERE I BELONG NOW.
OUT HERE, WHERE THERE'S NO ONE TO HURT.
NO. NO ONE.
I ALMOST FORGOT, BUT A FEW HOURS AGO I WAS IN THIS TOWN ABOUT TWENTY MILES SOUTH-WEST--
MAREKEOS?
YOU KNOW, DON'T YOU?
WHY ELSE WOULD I BE PRACTICING LOUSY LIGHT DISCIPLINE?
HAPPENED A FEW WEEKS BACK. NOT A SOUL IN TOWN. NO SIGN OF ANYONE AT ALL.
NO SIGN. JUST EMPTY. LIKE THIS FOREST.
BECAUSE I HAVEN'T HEARD A SINGLE ANIMAL TONIGHT SINCE I LEFT THE CAR.
BUT THERE IS SOME-THING OUT THERE.
I FELT IT BEFORE. SOMETHING THAT PULLED AT ME. IT ALMOST HURT.
DON'T START, ABE.

WHEN DID I EVER STOP? THIS IS MY JOB.
YOU DO KNOW WHAT'S GOING ON IN THE WORLD.
I KNOW. THE WHOLE THING'S GONE TO $#&%!
BUT, SEE, I'VE HEARD HOW THE BUREAU'S BEEN HANDLING THINGS. A WHOLE BATTALION WIPED OUT IN CHINA?
I WON'T LET THAT HAPPEN HERE.
YOU WON'T LET IT HAPPEN.
SO YOU NEVER STOPPED EITHER.
NO.
LISTEN, I GOT A LOT OF GHOSTS LOOKING OVER MY SHOULDER, WAITING FOR ME TO MAKE THINGS RIGHT.
AND THIS IS WHERE I CAN DO THAT. HERE. NOWHERE ELSE.
SO YEAH, THERE IS SOMETHING OUT THERE, BUT I CAN HANDLE IT. AND IF I CAN'T...
WHO CARES IF I DIE?

OKAY, WELL, I'M HERE NOW, AND I DIDN'T BRING A BATTALION, SO MAYBE YOU COULD FILL ME IN.
MAYBE. TOMORROW, THOUGH.
RIGHT NOW, LET'S GET SOME SHUT-EYE.

THE LOCALS CALL IT HELL'S KETTLE. I MEAN, IF THERE WERE ANY LOCALS LEFT.
NAMED FOR THE LAKES IN ENGLAND?
COULDN'T TELL YOU. IT'S JUST A REALLY DEEP LAKE. BOTTOMLESS, SUPPOSEDLY.
ANYWAY, THIS IS THE CENTER OF IT ALL. ALL THOSE BAD VIBES COME FROM RIGHT HERE--AND IT ONLY STARTED ABOUT A MONTH AGO.
BEEN TRYING TO FIGURE IT OUT, BUT THAT TANNIC WATER, BLACK AS TAR...THERE'S JUST NO WAY TO KNOW WHAT'S DOWN THERE.
WELL, THERE IS ONE WAY, RIGHT?
LUCKY YOU SHOWED UP, ISN'T IT?
YOU KNOW, THERE IS EQUIPMENT PEOPLE USE TO DO JUST THIS SORT OF THING. YOU REALIZE THAT.
NO $#!%? DO ME A FAVOR, THEN? BRING ME SOME ON YOUR NEXT VISIT?

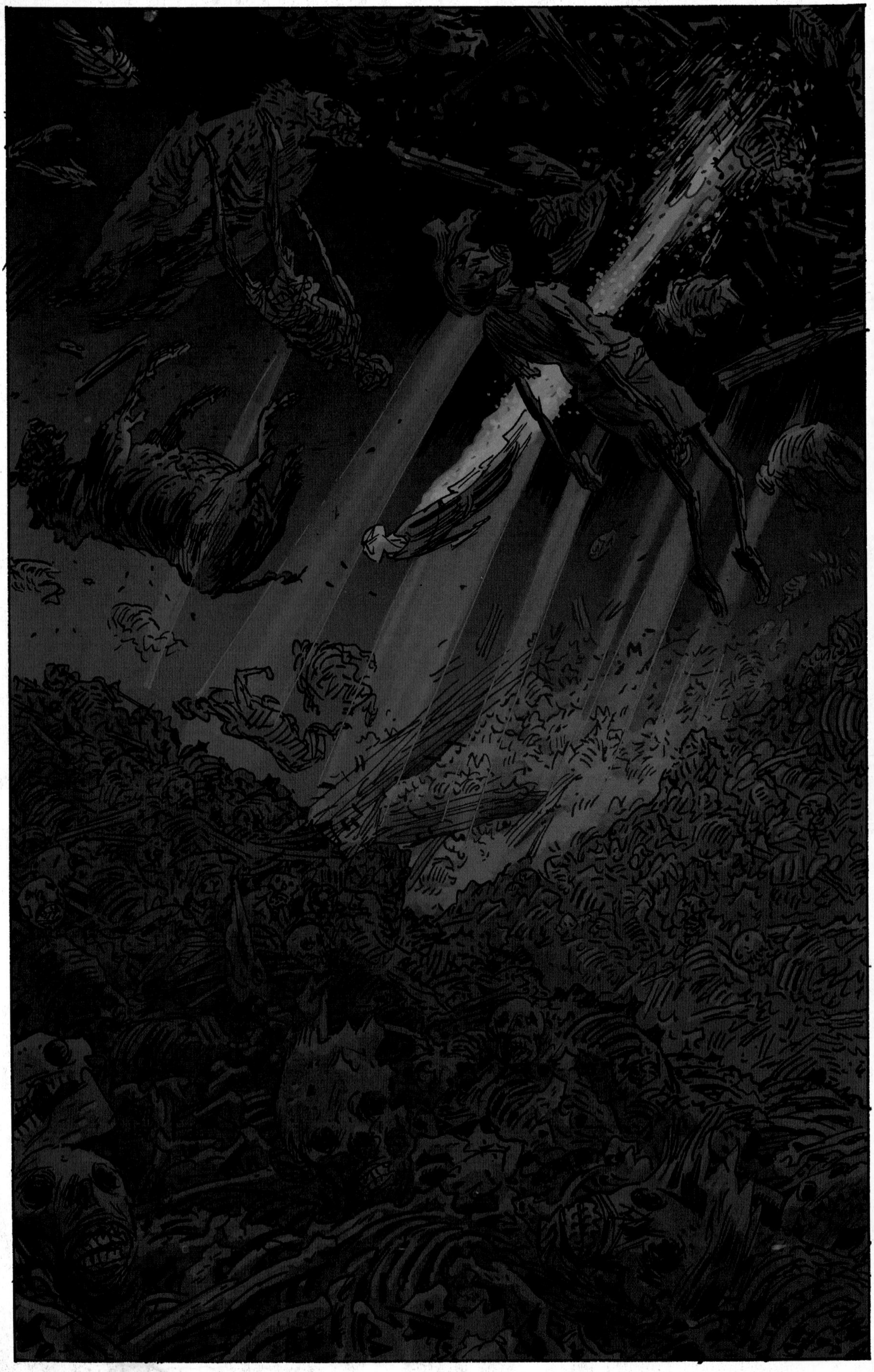

NEW WORLD CHAPTER THREE

ILLUSTRATION BY **GUY DAVIS** WITH **DAVE STEWART**

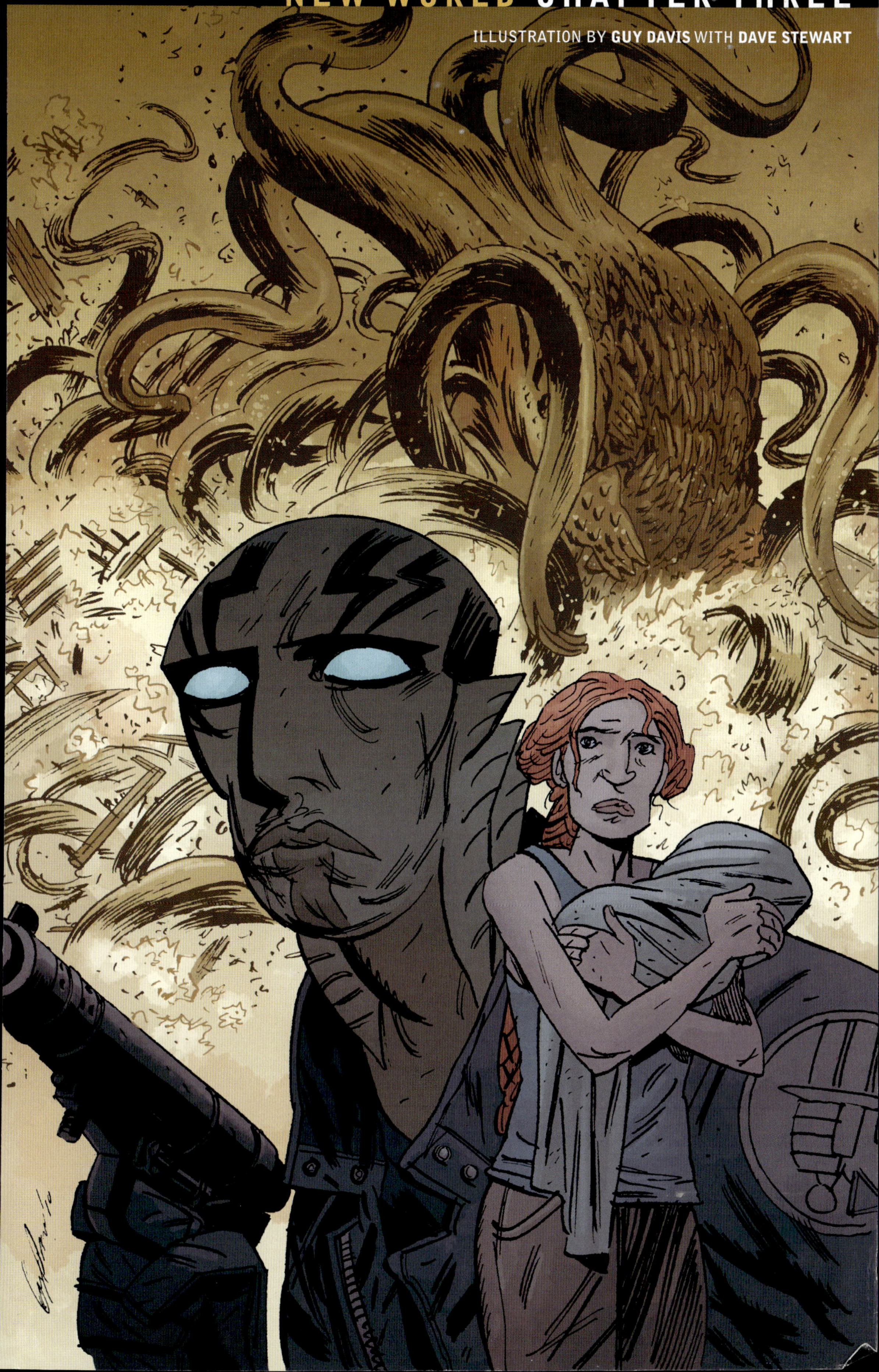

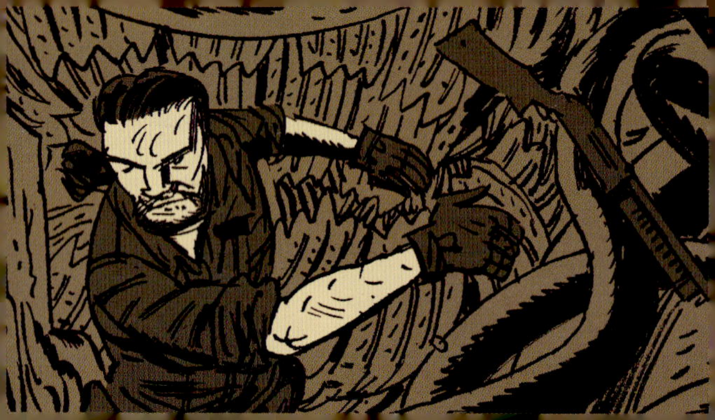

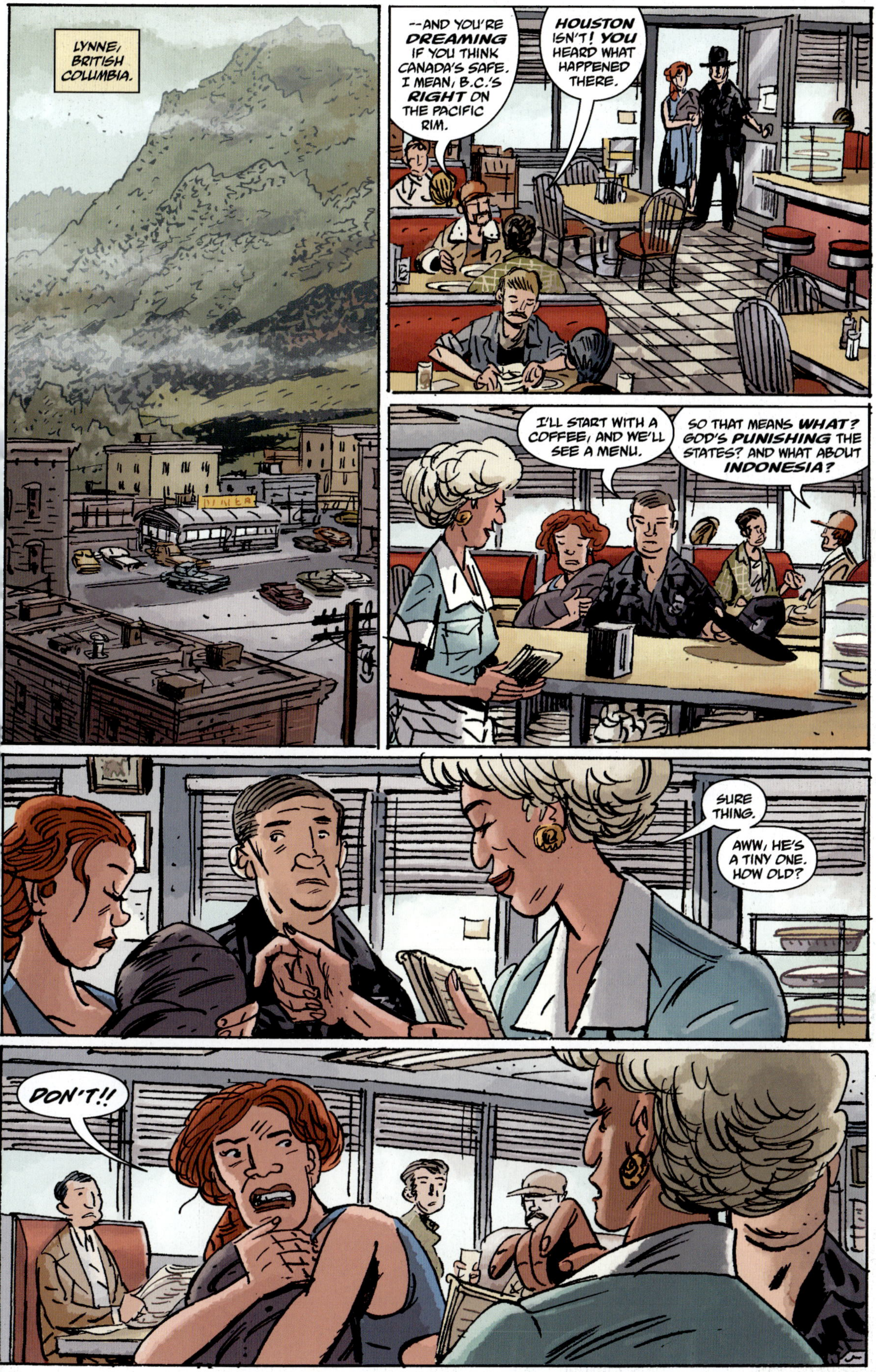
LYNNE, BRITISH COLUMBIA.
--AND YOU'RE DREAMING IF YOU THINK CANADA'S SAFE. I MEAN, B.C.'S RIGHT ON THE PACIFIC RIM.
HOUSTON ISN'T! YOU HEARD WHAT HAPPENED THERE.
I'LL START WITH A COFFEE, AND WE'LL SEE A MENU.
SO THAT MEANS WHAT? GOD'S PUNISHING THE STATES? AND WHAT ABOUT INDONESIA?
SURE THING.
AWW, HE'S A TINY ONE. HOW OLD?
DON'T!!

DAMN! WHAT'S THAT ABOUT?
COFF WHO KNOWS. NEW MOMMAS COFF COFF GET EDGY.
WHAT WOULD YOU KNOW ABOUT "NEW MOMMAS"? YOU NEVER EVEN BEEN CLOSE TO MARRIED.
COFF COFF COFF NEITHER COFF COFF NEITHER COFF YOU COFF--
JESUS CHRIST, EUGENE!
COFF
COFF
WHEEZE
HEY! HEY!! EUGENE'S CHOKING!
COFF
COFF
COFF
WHAT'S WRONG? WHAT HAPPENED?
I DON'T KNOW. MAYBE HE NEEDS THAT HEIMLICH MANEUVER!

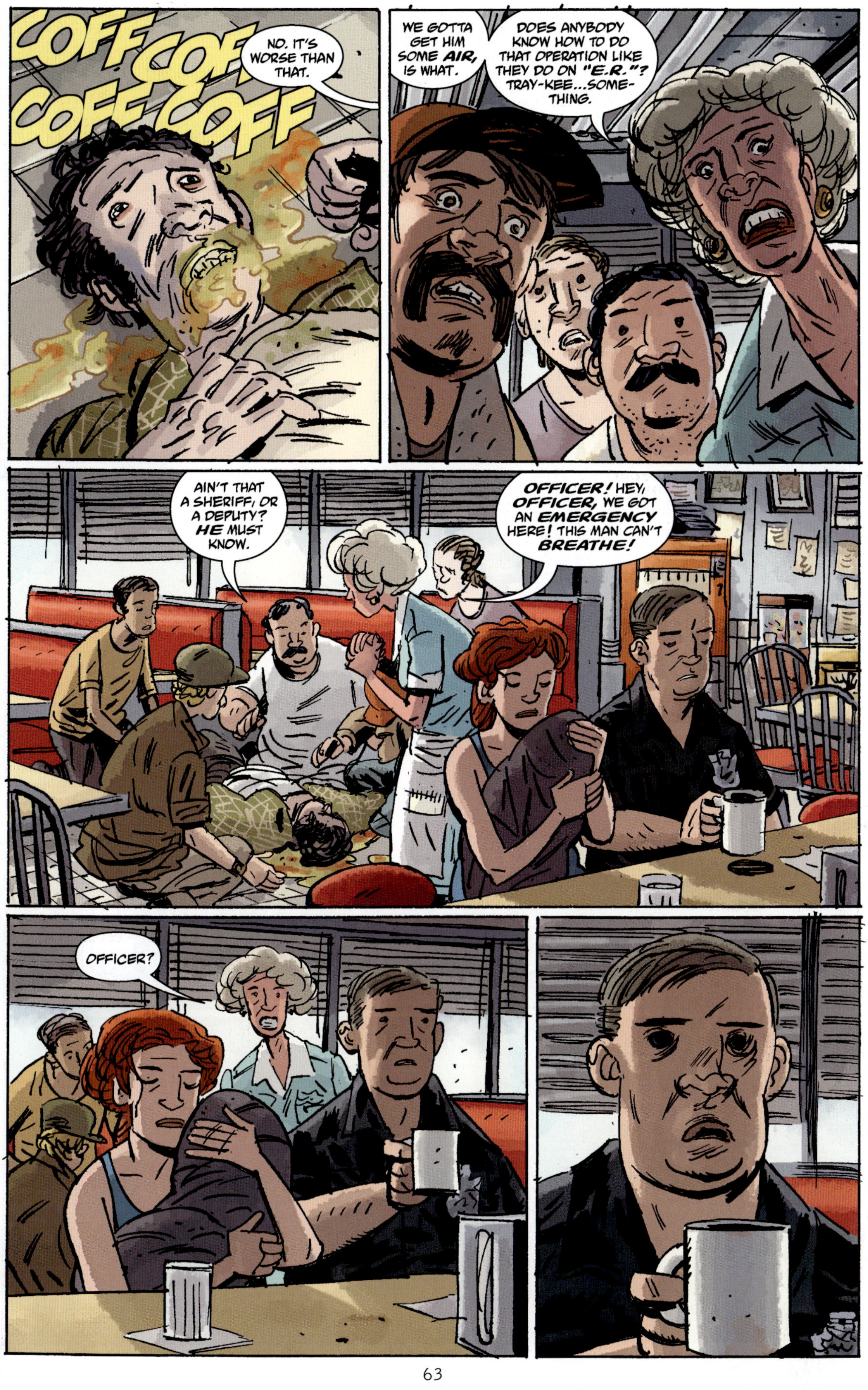
COFF COFF COFF COFF
NO. IT'S WORSE THAN THAT.
WE GOTTA GET HIM SOME AIR, IS WHAT.
DOES ANYBODY KNOW HOW TO DO THAT OPERATION LIKE THEY DO ON "E.R."? TRAY-KEE...SOME-THING.
AIN'T THAT A SHERIFF, OR A DEPUTY? HE MUST KNOW.
OFFICER! HEY, OFFICER, WE GOT AN EMERGENCY HERE! THIS MAN CAN'T BREATHE!
OFFICER?

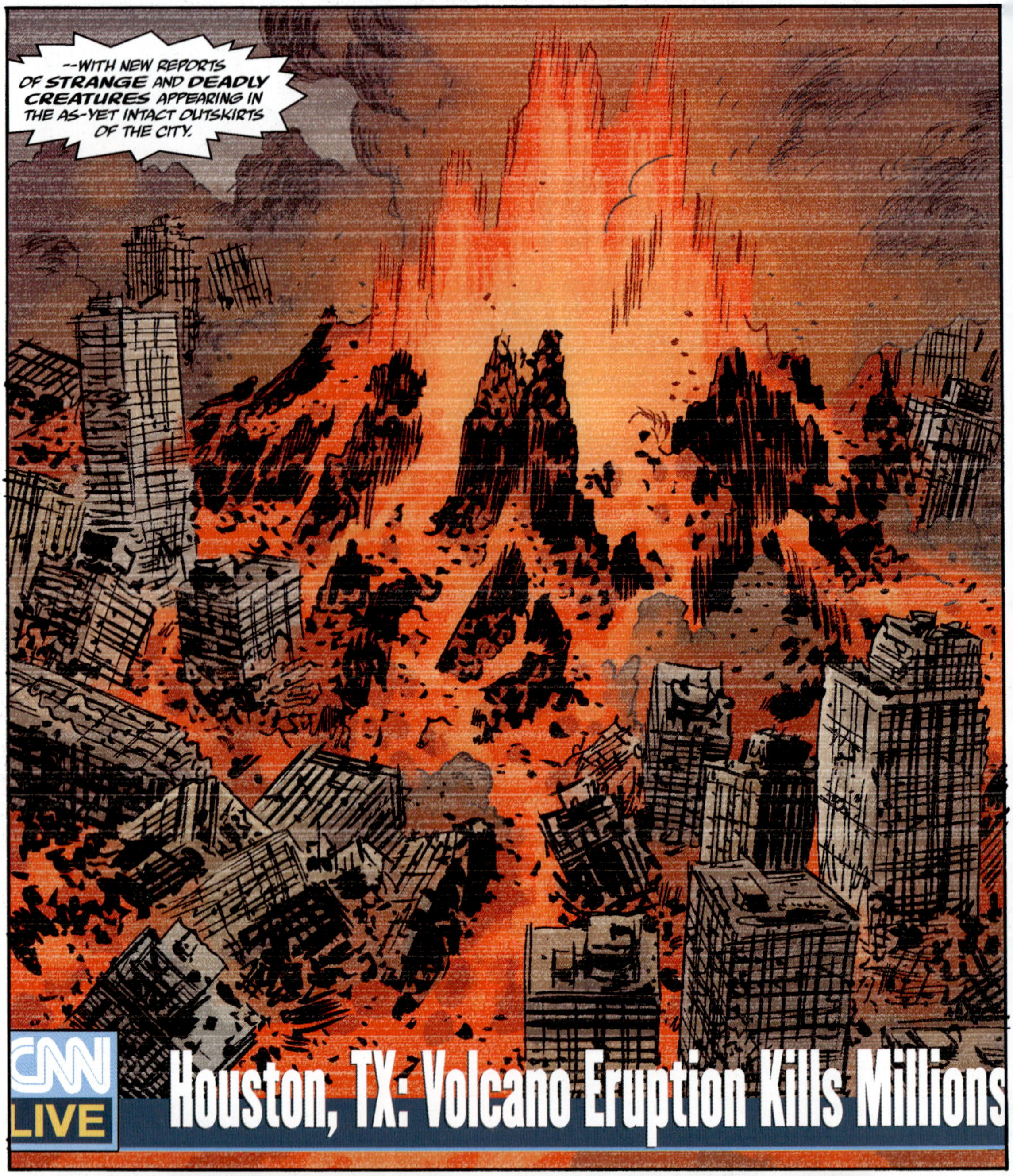
--WITH NEW REPORTS OF STRANGE AND DEADLY CREATURES APPEARING IN THE AS-YET INTACT OUTSKIRTS OF THE CITY.
CNN LIVE
Houston, TX: Volcano Eruption Kills Millions

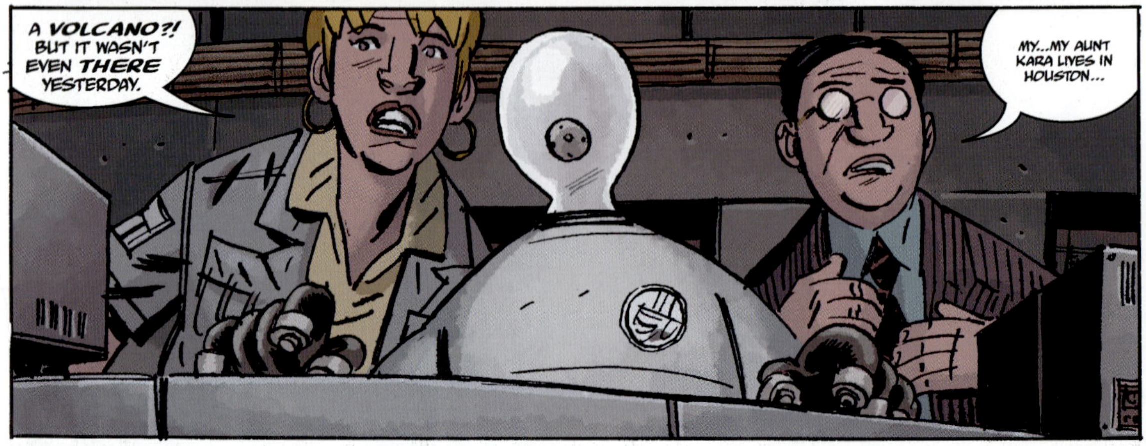
A VOLCANO?! BUT IT WASN'T EVEN THERE YESTERDAY.
MY...MY AUNT KARA LIVES IN HOUSTON...

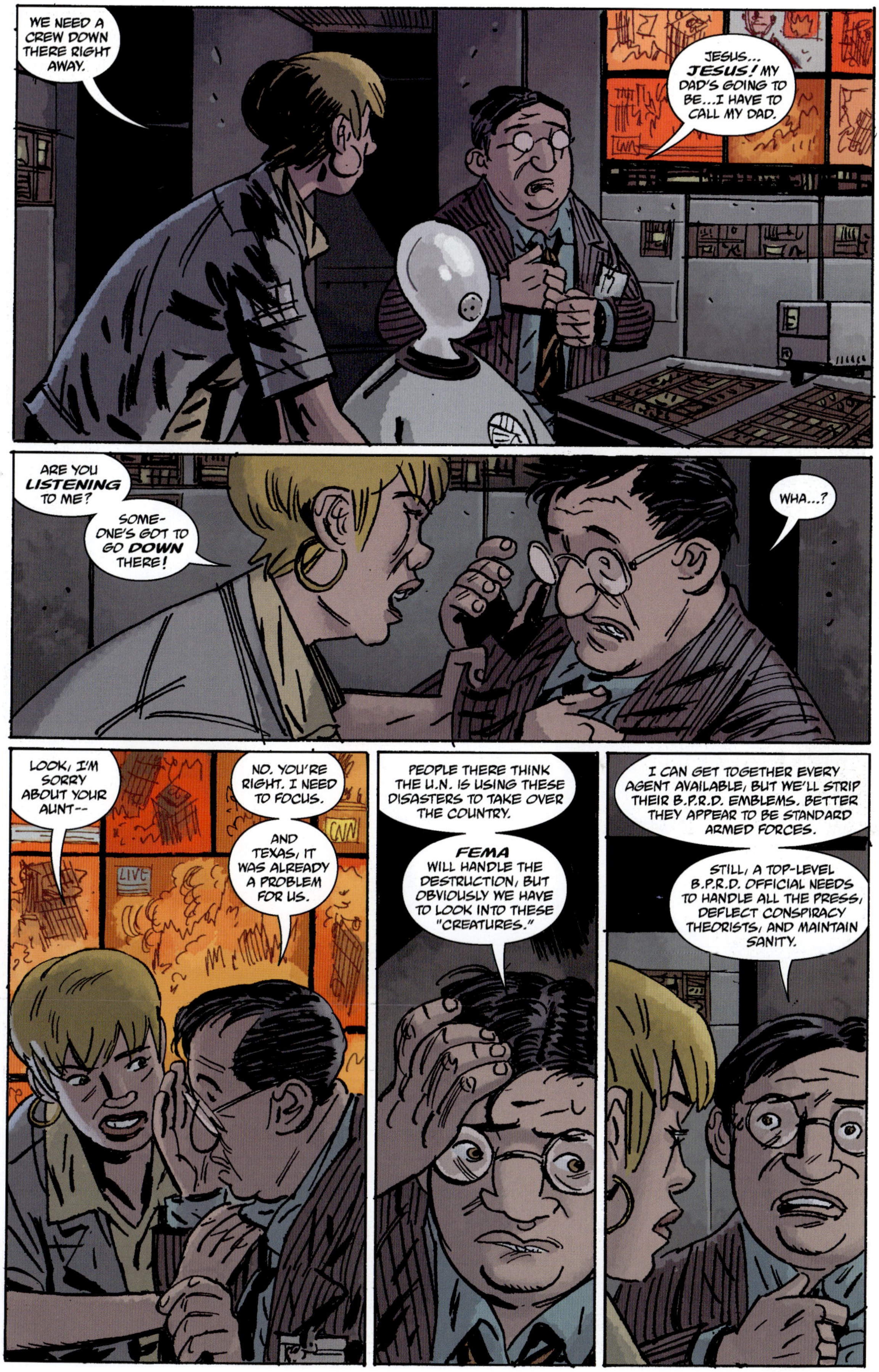
WE NEED A CREW DOWN THERE RIGHT AWAY.
JESUS... JESUS! MY DAD'S GOING TO BE...I HAVE TO CALL MY DAD.
ARE YOU LISTENING TO ME?
SOME-ONE'S GOT TO GO DOWN THERE!
WHA...?
LOOK, I'M SORRY ABOUT YOUR AUNT--
NO. YOU'RE RIGHT. I NEED TO FOCUS.
AND TEXAS, IT WAS ALREADY A PROBLEM FOR US.
CNN
LIVE
PEOPLE THERE THINK THE U.N. IS USING THESE DISASTERS TO TAKE OVER THE COUNTRY.
FEMA WILL HANDLE THE DESTRUCTION, BUT OBVIOUSLY WE HAVE TO LOOK INTO THESE "CREATURES."
I CAN GET TOGETHER EVERY AGENT AVAILABLE, BUT WE'LL STRIP THEIR B.P.R.D. EMBLEMS. BETTER THEY APPEAR TO BE STANDARD ARMED FORCES.
STILL, A TOP-LEVEL B.P.R.D. OFFICIAL NEEDS TO HANDLE ALL THE PRESS, DEFLECT CONSPIRACY THEORISTS, AND MAINTAIN SANITY.

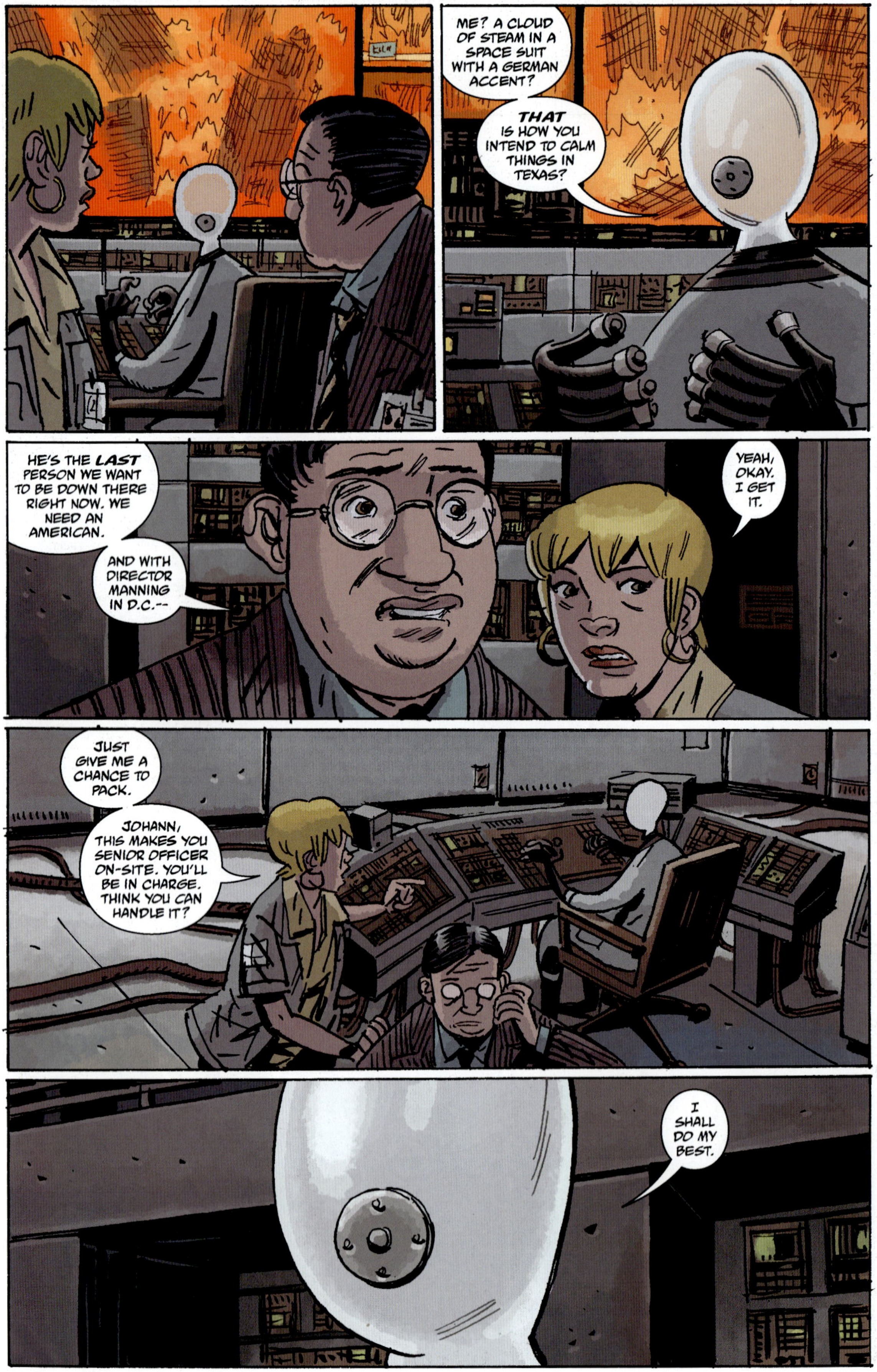
ME? A CLOUD OF STEAM IN A SPACE SUIT WITH A GERMAN ACCENT?
THAT IS HOW YOU INTEND TO CALM THINGS IN TEXAS?
HE'S THE LAST PERSON WE WANT TO BE DOWN THERE RIGHT NOW. WE NEED AN AMERICAN.
AND WITH DIRECTOR MANNING IN D.C.--
YEAH, OKAY. I GET IT.
JUST GIVE ME A CHANCE TO PACK.
JOHANN, THIS MAKES YOU SENIOR OFFICER ON-SITE. YOU'LL BE IN CHARGE. THINK YOU CAN HANDLE IT?
I SHALL DO MY BEST.

SEE? SEE, ABE?
THIS IS WHAT I WAS AFRAID OF. YOUR DAMN BUREAUCRATIC APPROACH. DIDN'T I MAKE IT CLEAR? I DON'T WANT THE R.C.M.P.--OR ANYBODY ELSE-- IN ON THIS.
WHAT HAVE YOU GOT RIGHT NOW, BEN? A "FEELING." A FEELING OF "SOMETHING" OUT THERE.
WE NEED A STARTING POINT, AND A VICTIM'S I.D. MIGHT GET US THAT.
#%&$! THAT SMELL!
YOU KNOW, IF WE HAD JOHANN HERE, WE WOULDN'T EVEN--
AHA!
LICENCE
"TESSIER, NICHOLAS. MAREKEOS, B.C."
ALL RIGHT, NOW WE NEED A PHONE. LET'S HEAD BACK TO THE CAR.
NOT JUST YET.

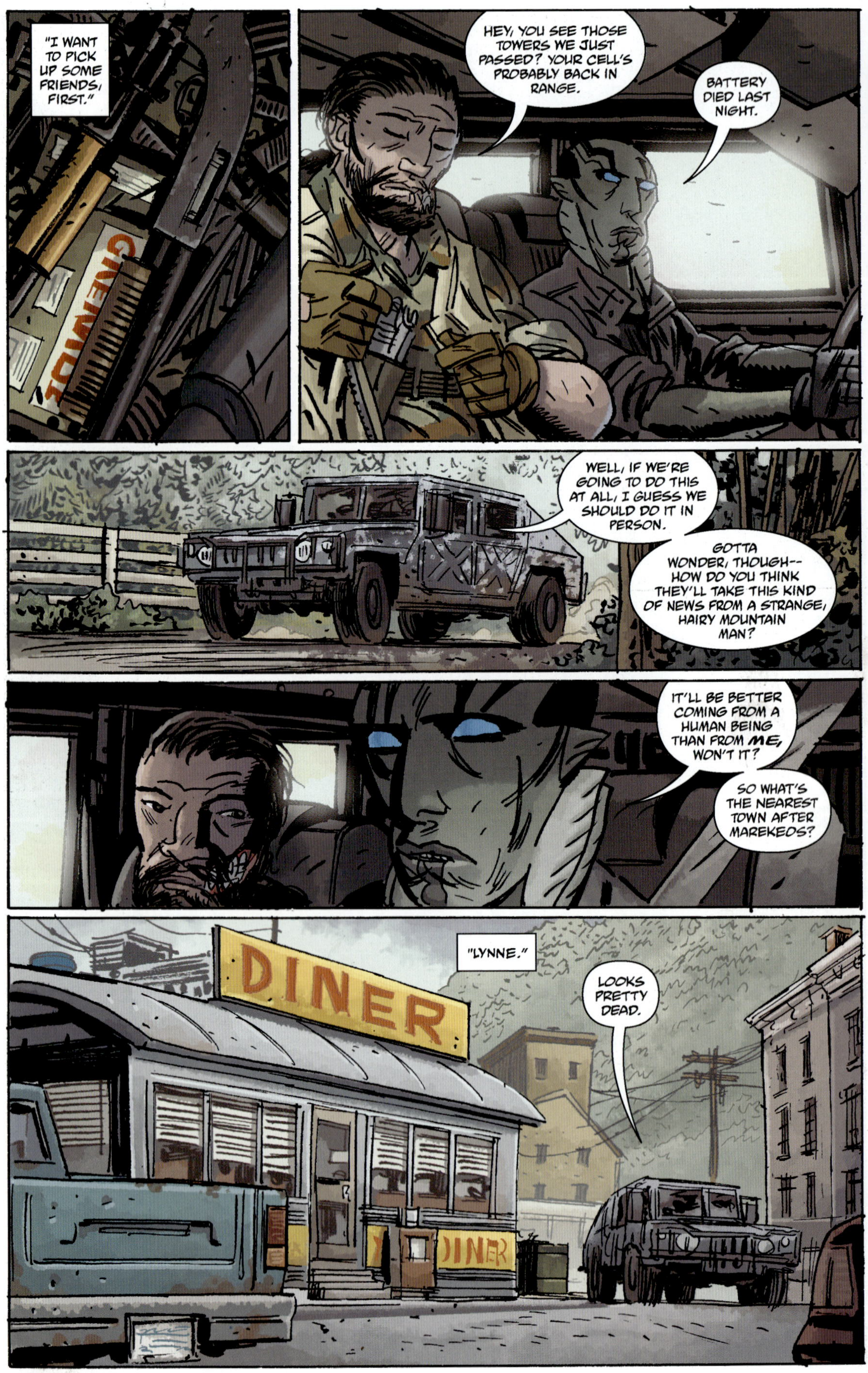
"I WANT TO PICK UP SOME FRIENDS, FIRST."
HEY, YOU SEE THOSE TOWERS WE JUST PASSED? YOUR CELL'S PROBABLY BACK IN RANGE.
BATTERY DIED LAST NIGHT.
WELL, IF WE'RE GOING TO DO THIS AT ALL, I GUESS WE SHOULD DO IT IN PERSON.
GOTTA WONDER, THOUGH-- HOW DO YOU THINK THEY'LL TAKE THIS KIND OF NEWS FROM A STRANGE, HAIRY MOUNTAIN MAN?
IT'LL BE BETTER COMING FROM A HUMAN BEING THAN FROM ME, WON'T IT?
SO WHAT'S THE NEAREST TOWN AFTER MAREKEOS?
"LYNNE."
DINER
LOOKS PRETTY DEAD.

NOPE. WE'RE GOOD. SEE?
DINER
HEY, FOLKS. CAN YOU TELL ME WHERE THE SHERIFF'S OFFICE IS?
?
OH, #&$% NO...
START THE ENGINE!!
START THE ENGINE NOW!!!

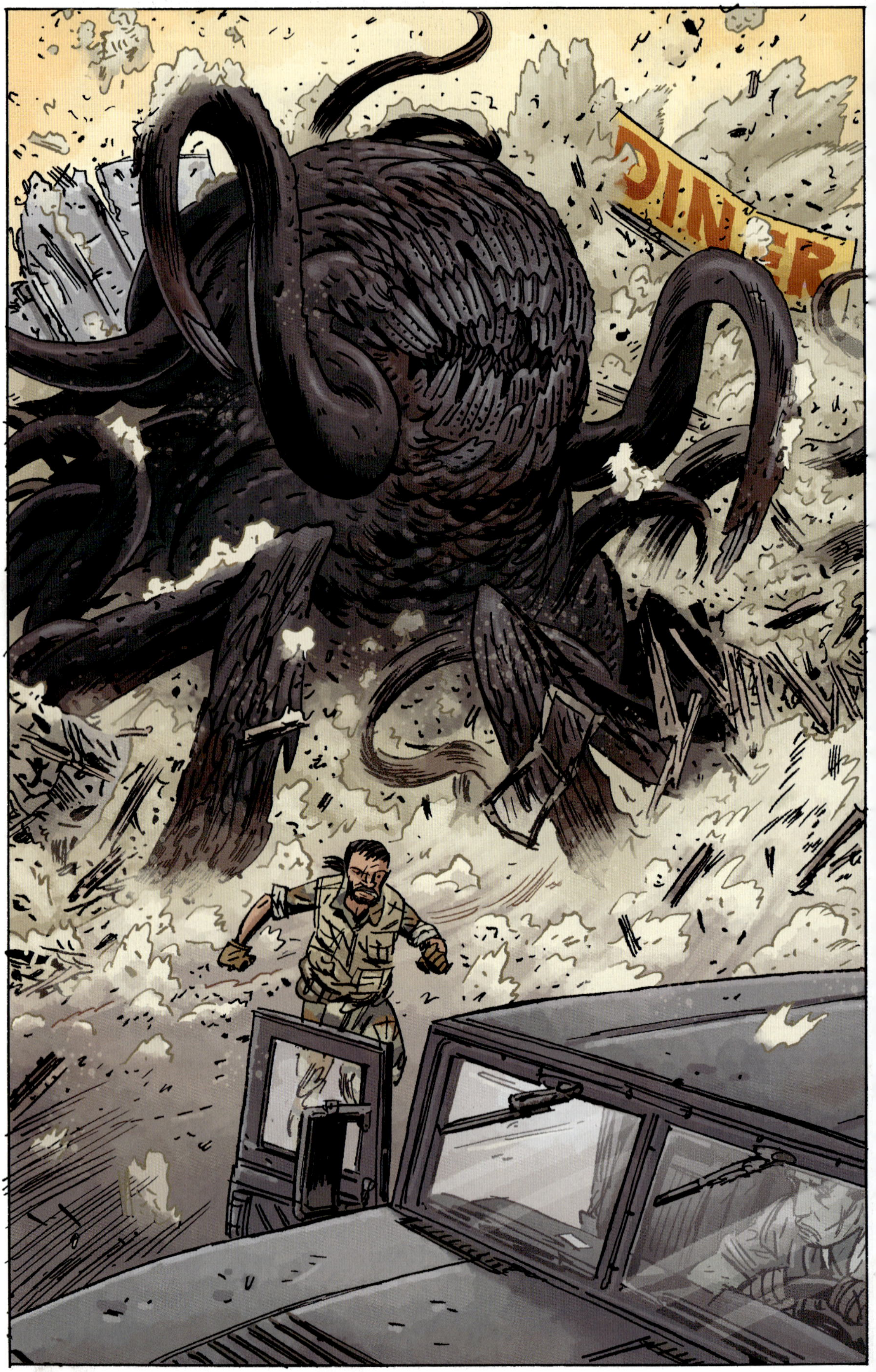
DINER

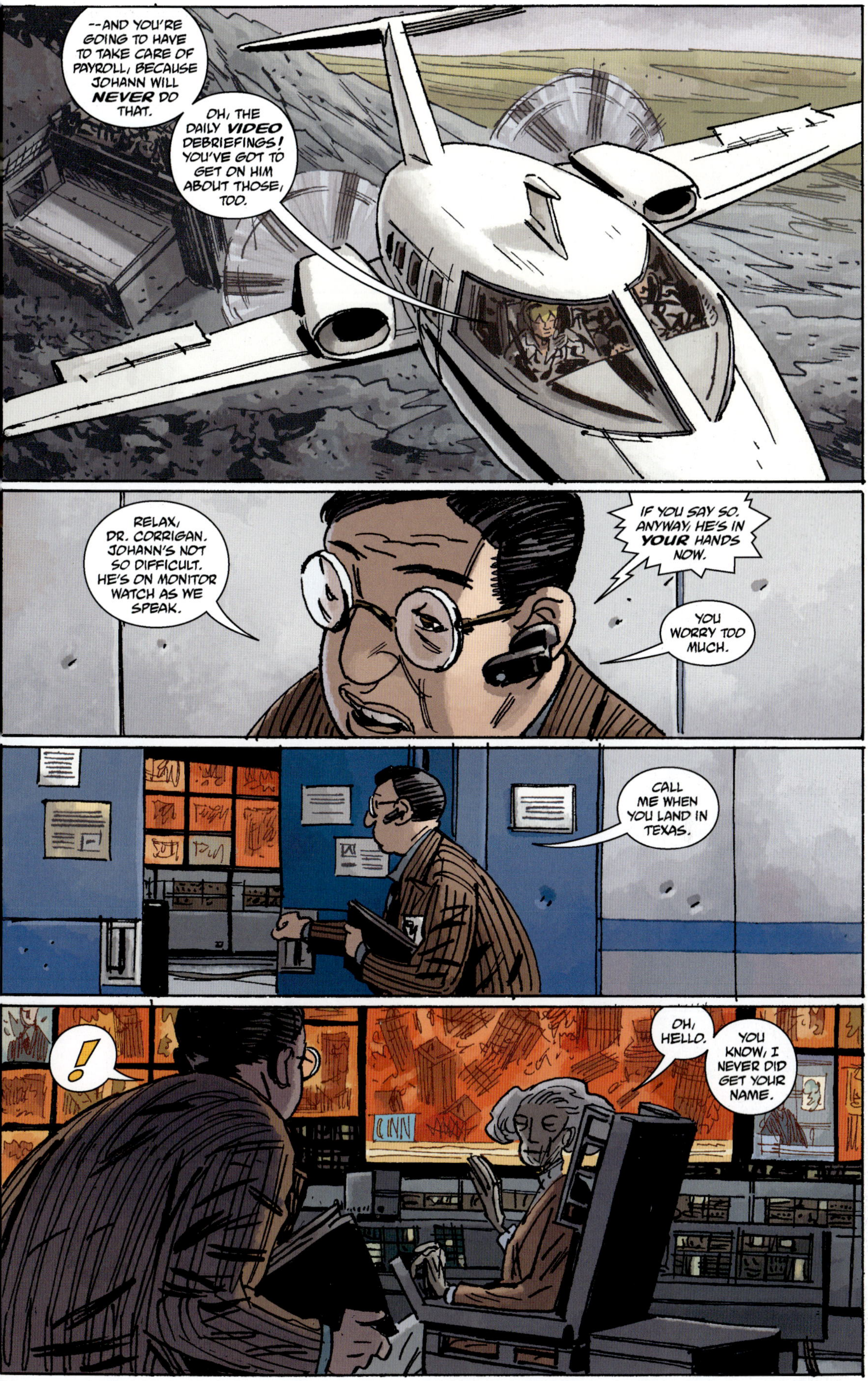
--AND YOU'RE GOING TO HAVE TO TAKE CARE OF PAYROLL, BECAUSE JOHANN WILL NEVER DO THAT.
OH, THE DAILY VIDEO DEBRIEFINGS! YOU'VE GOT TO GET ON HIM ABOUT THOSE, TOO.
RELAX, DR. CORRIGAN. JOHANN'S NOT SO DIFFICULT. HE'S ON MONITOR WATCH AS WE SPEAK.
IF YOU SAY SO. ANYWAY, HE'S IN YOUR HANDS NOW.
YOU WORRY TOO MUCH.
CALL ME WHEN YOU LAND IN TEXAS.
!
OH, HELLO.
YOU KNOW, I NEVER DID GET YOUR NAME.

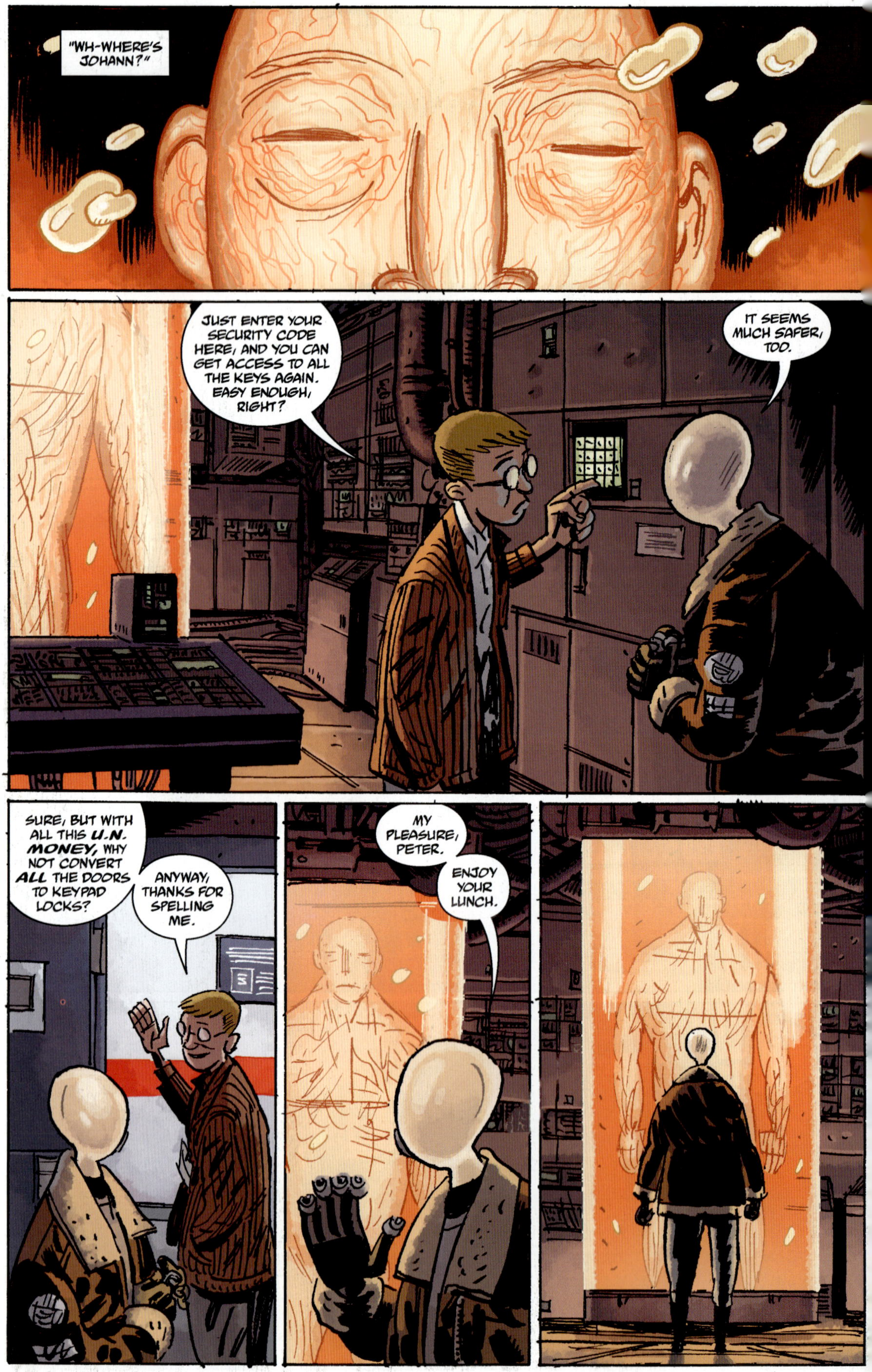
"WH-WHERE'S JOHANN?"
JUST ENTER YOUR SECURITY CODE HERE, AND YOU CAN GET ACCESS TO ALL THE KEYS AGAIN. EASY ENOUGH, RIGHT?
IT SEEMS MUCH SAFER, TOO.
SURE, BUT WITH ALL THIS U.N. MONEY, WHY NOT CONVERT ALL THE DOORS TO KEYPAD LOCKS?
ANYWAY, THANKS FOR SPELLING ME.
MY PLEASURE, PETER.
ENJOY YOUR LUNCH.

GOD DAMMIT, ABE, MOVE THIS THING!!
THAT COUPLE! WE SHOULD CHECK--
THEY'RE THE LAST ONES NEEDING HELP HERE.
SCREECH
NOW LET'S GO!!
KRONCH

BOOM
THAT'S RIGHT, $#$% FACE! I DON'T DIE EASY!!
BOOM CHUK BOOM CHUK BOOM

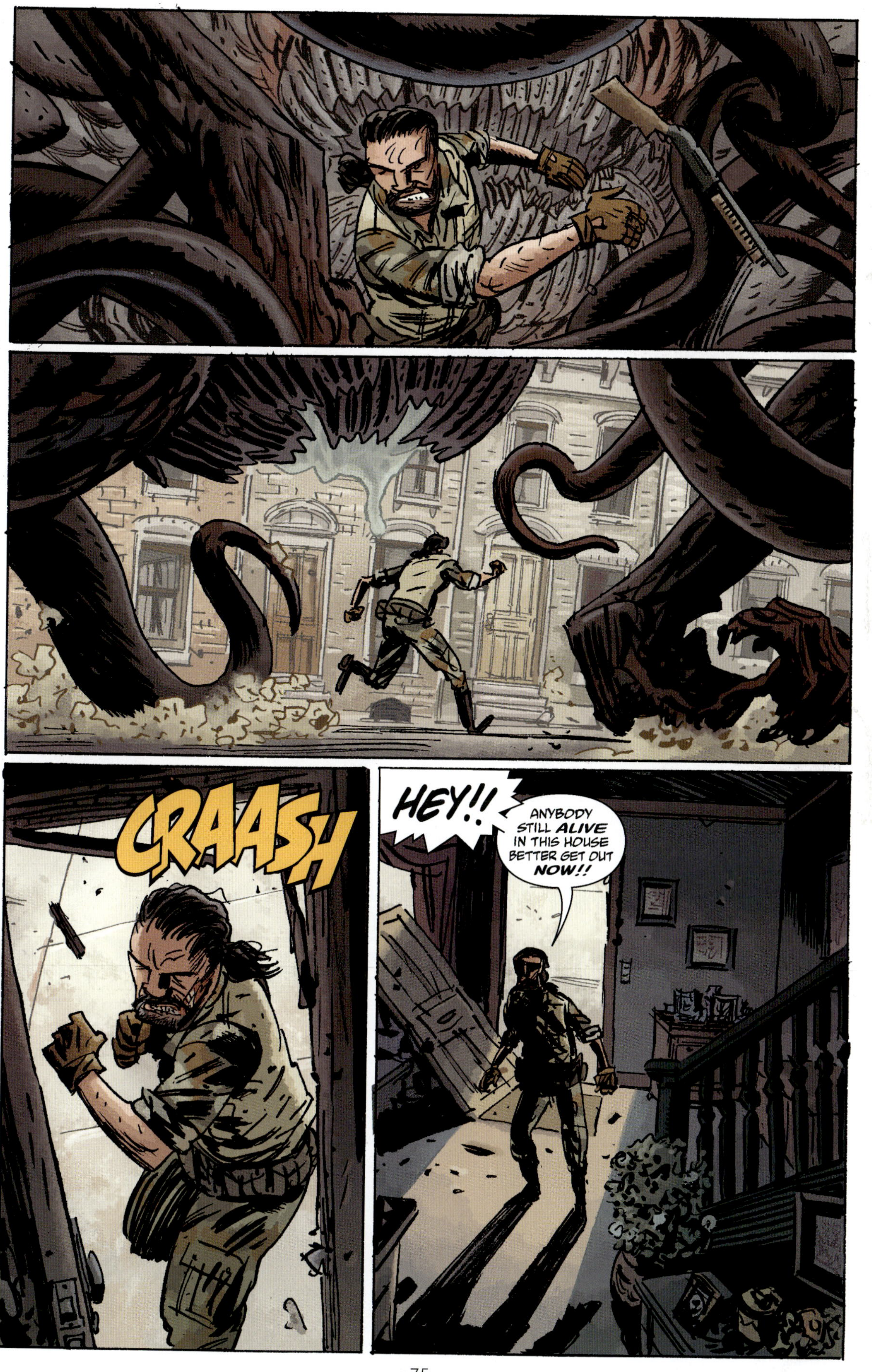
CRAASH
HEY!!
ANYBODY STILL ALIVE IN THIS HOUSE BETTER GET OUT NOW!!

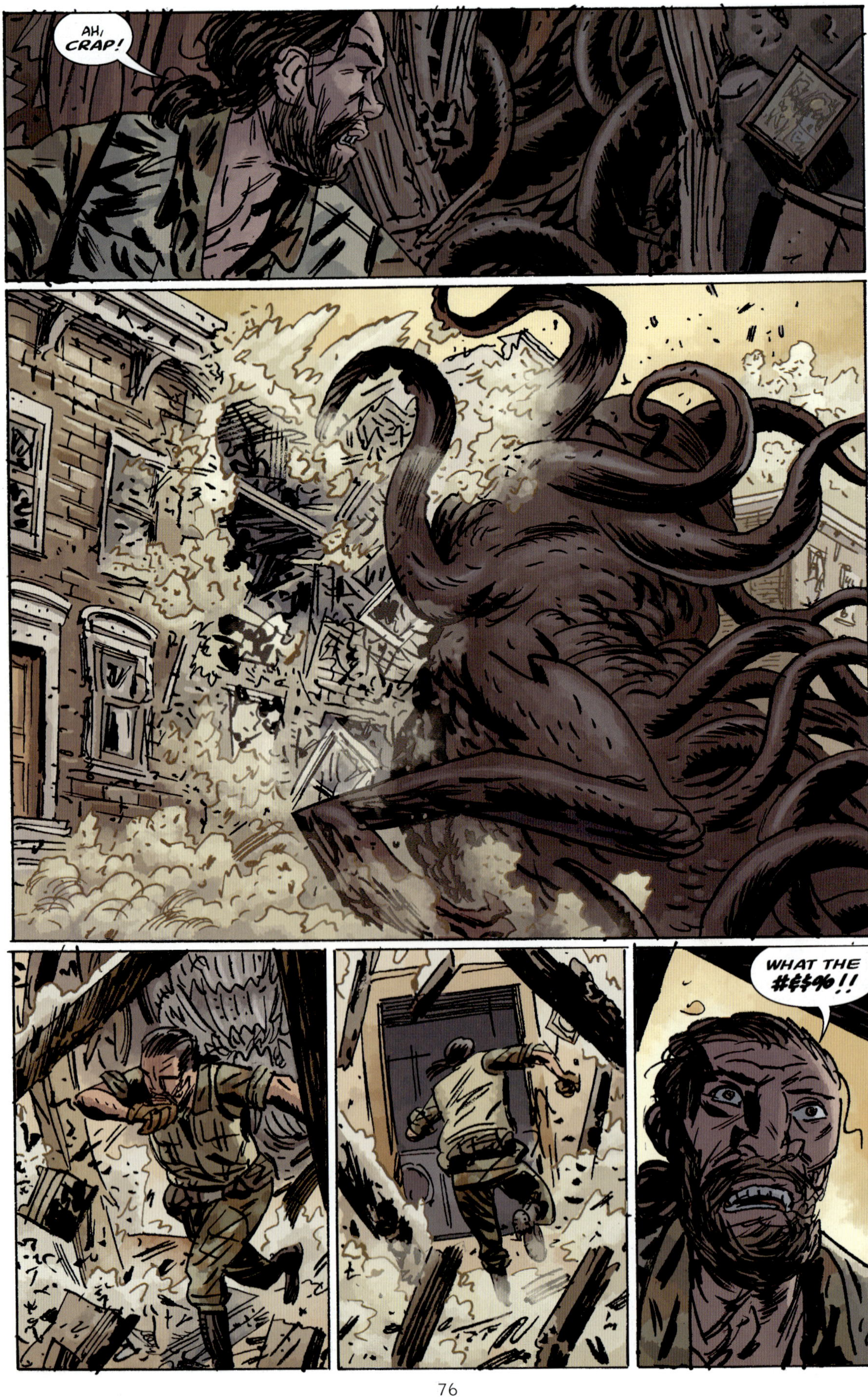
AH, CRAP!
WHAT THE #&$%!!

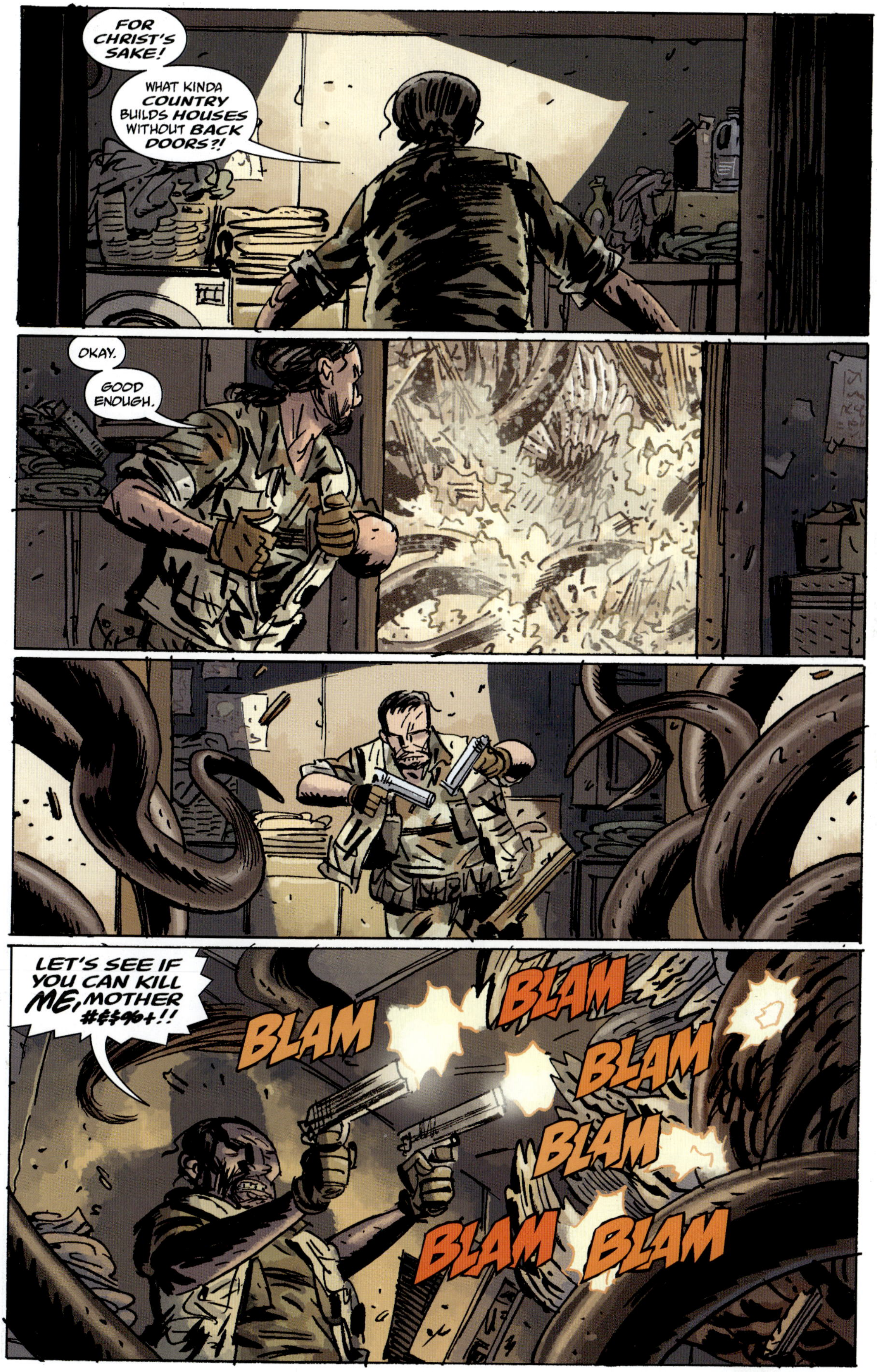

FOR CHRIST'S SAKE!
WHAT KINDA COUNTRY BUILDS HOUSES WITHOUT BACK DOORS?!
OKAY.
GOOD ENOUGH.
LET'S SEE IF YOU CAN KILL ME, MOTHER #$$%+!!
BLAM
BLAM
BLAM
BLAM
BLAM
BLAM

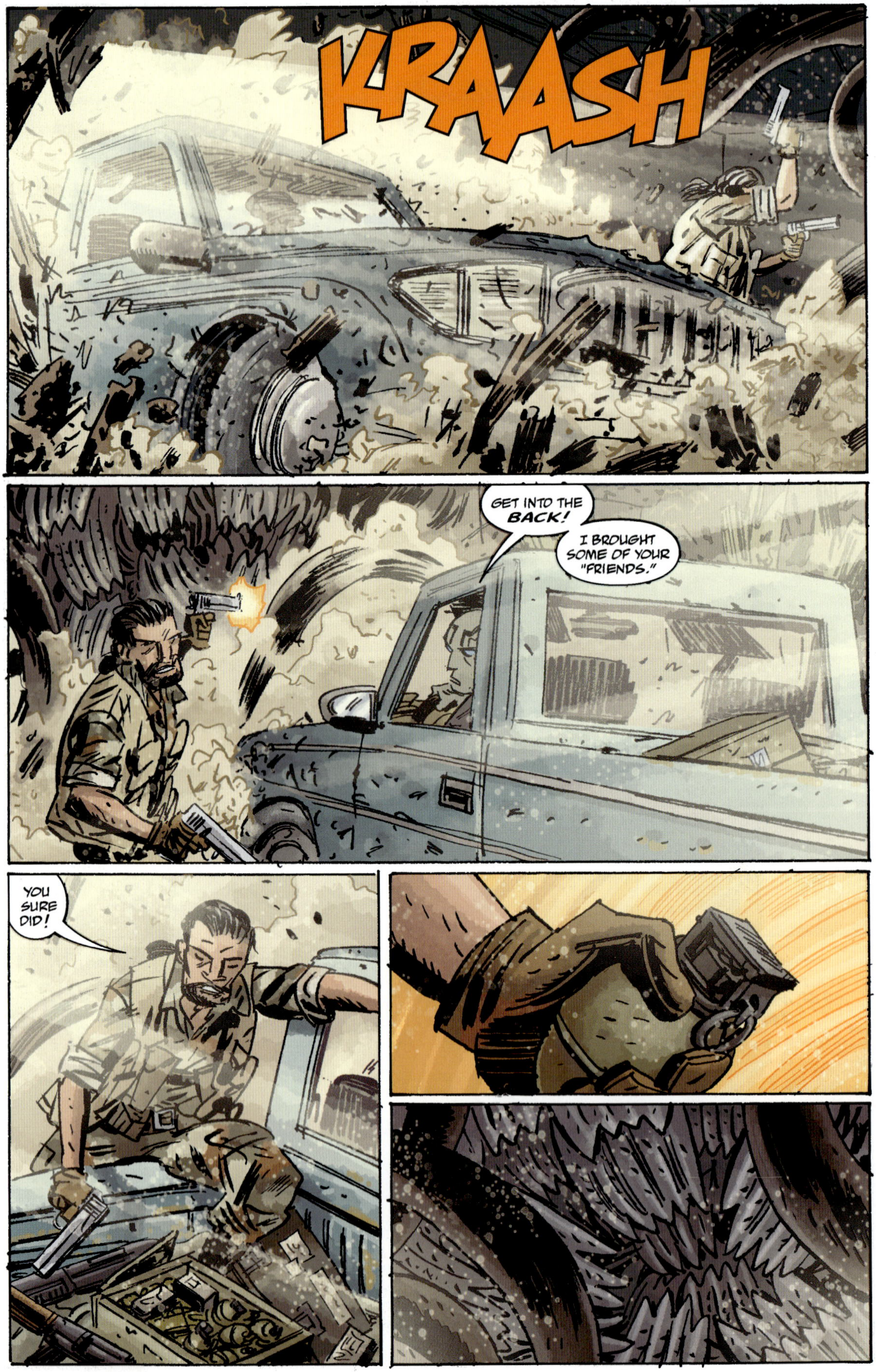
KRAASH
GET INTO THE BACK!
I BROUGHT SOME OF YOUR "FRIENDS."
YOU SURE DID!

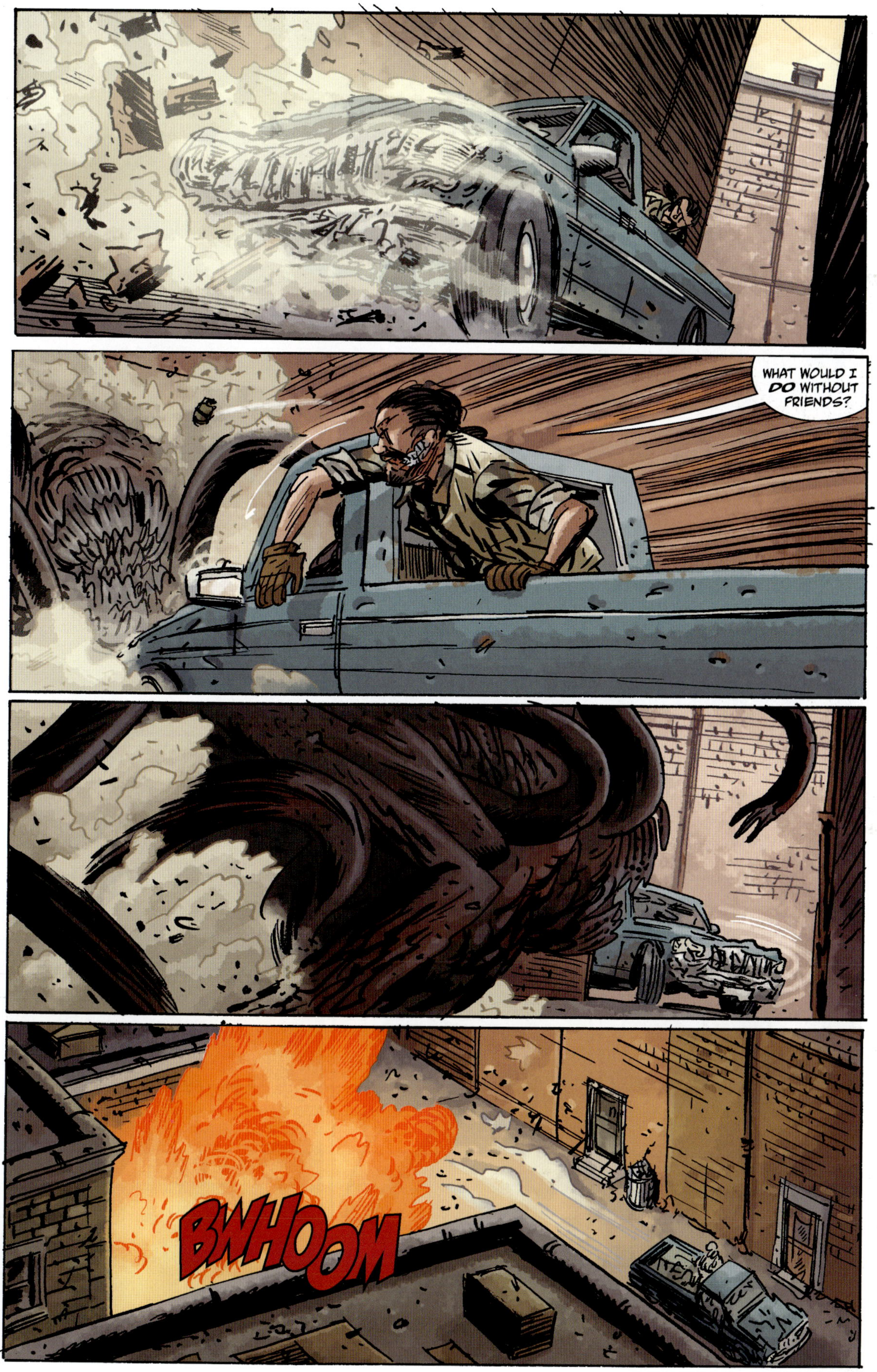
WHAT WOULD I DO WITHOUT FRIENDS?
BWHOOM

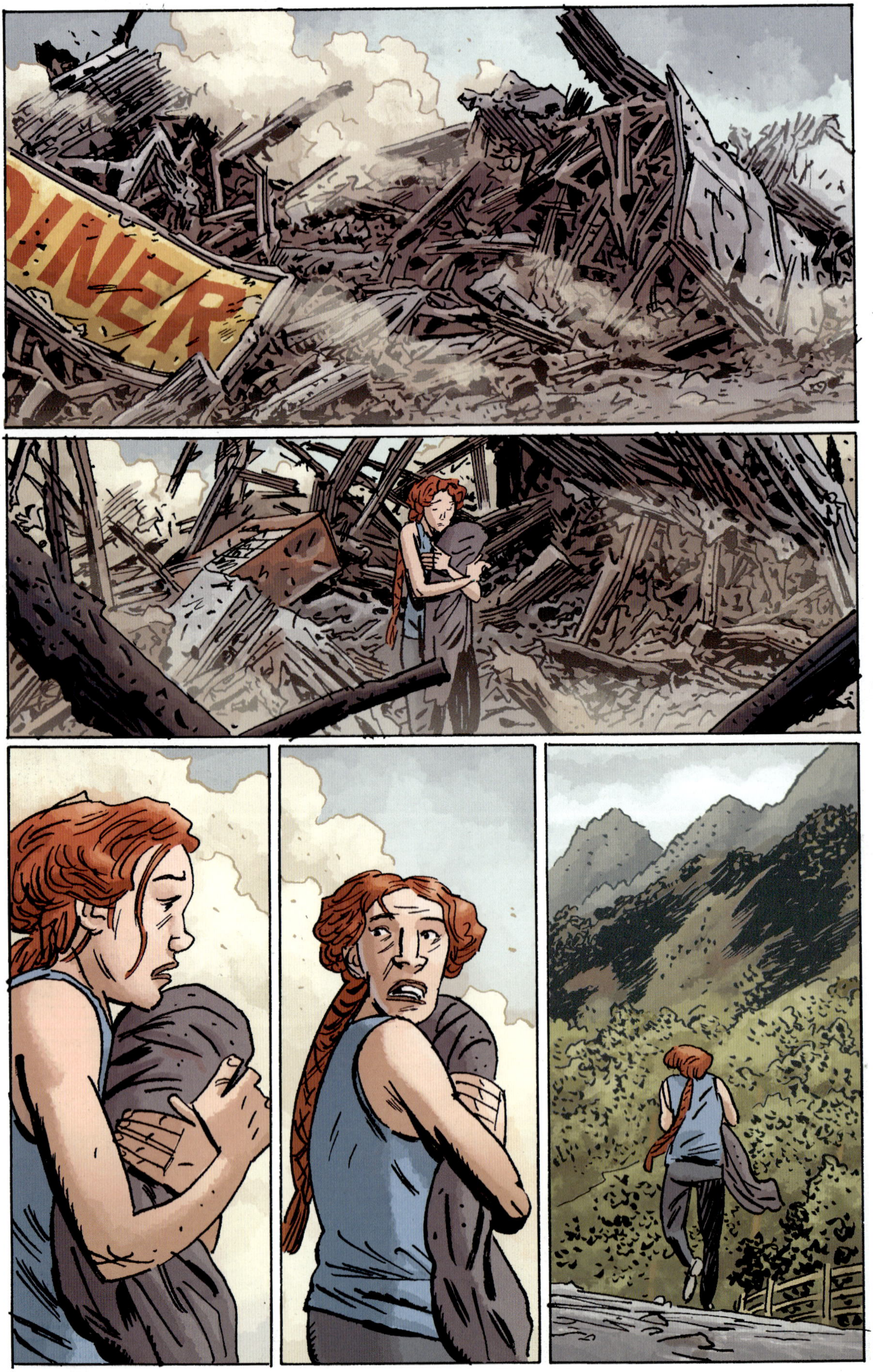

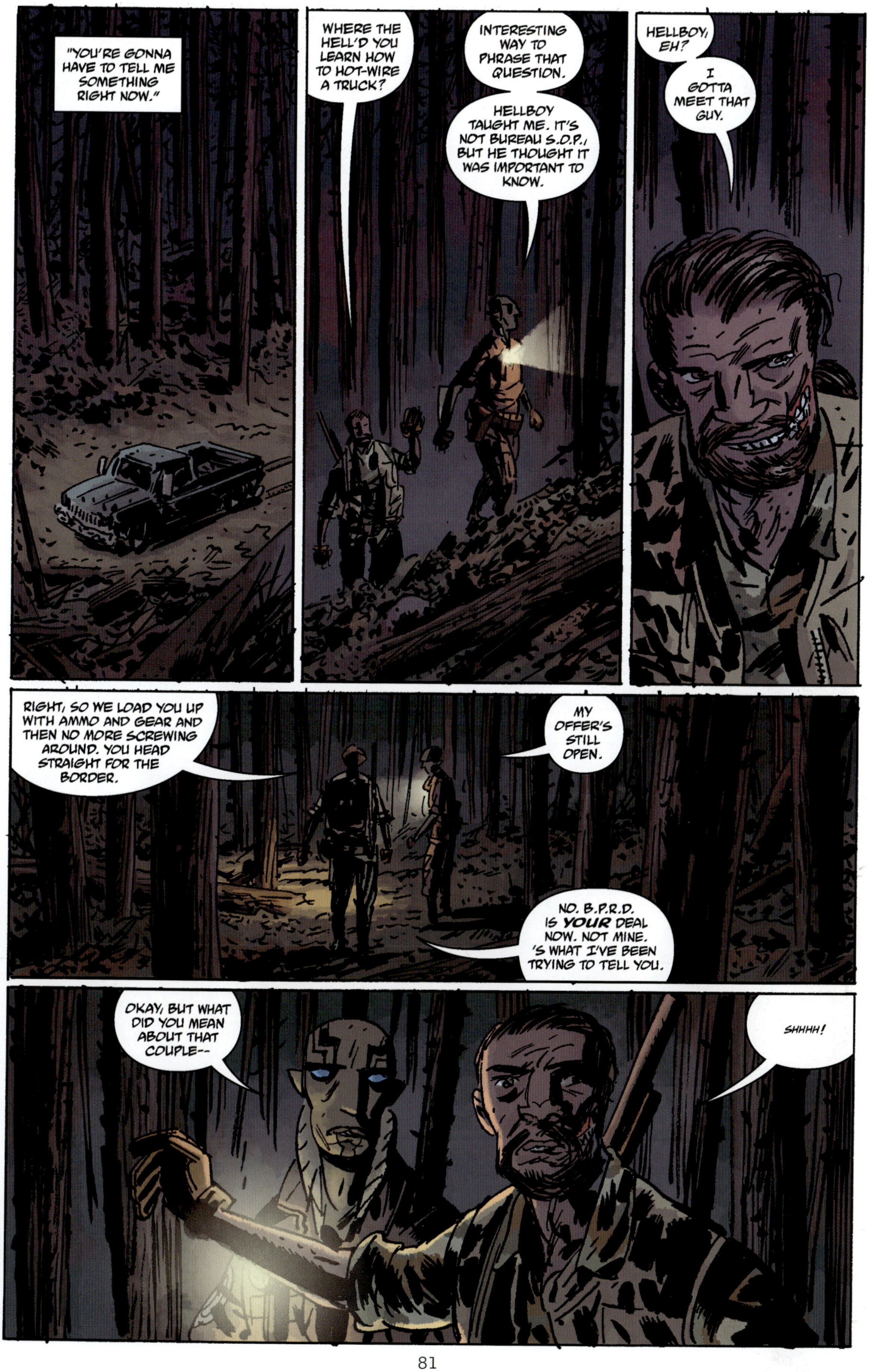
"YOU'RE GONNA HAVE TO TELL ME SOMETHING RIGHT NOW."
WHERE THE HELL'D YOU LEARN HOW TO HOT-WIRE A TRUCK?
INTERESTING WAY TO PHRASE THAT QUESTION.
HELLBOY TAUGHT ME. IT'S NOT BUREAU S.O.P., BUT HE THOUGHT IT WAS IMPORTANT TO KNOW.
HELLBOY, EH?
I GOTTA MEET THAT GUY.
RIGHT, SO WE LOAD YOU UP WITH AMMO AND GEAR AND THEN NO MORE SCREWING AROUND. YOU HEAD STRAIGHT FOR THE BORDER.
MY OFFER'S STILL OPEN.
NO. B.P.R.D. IS YOUR DEAL NOW. NOT MINE. 'S WHAT I'VE BEEN TRYING TO TELL YOU.
OKAY, BUT WHAT DID YOU MEAN ABOUT THAT COUPLE--
SHHHH!

WHAT? WHAT IS IT?
YOU DON'T SMELL THAT?
SOMEONE ELSE IS OUT HERE. A MAN.
RIGHT UP AHEAD.
PLEASE STOP WHISPERING.
AND YOU DON'T HAVE TO WORRY. I'M NOT HERE FOR YOU.
I'M HERE FOR MY **SON**.

NEW WORLD CHAPTER FOUR

ILLUSTRATION BY **GUY DAVIS** WITH **DAVE STEWART**

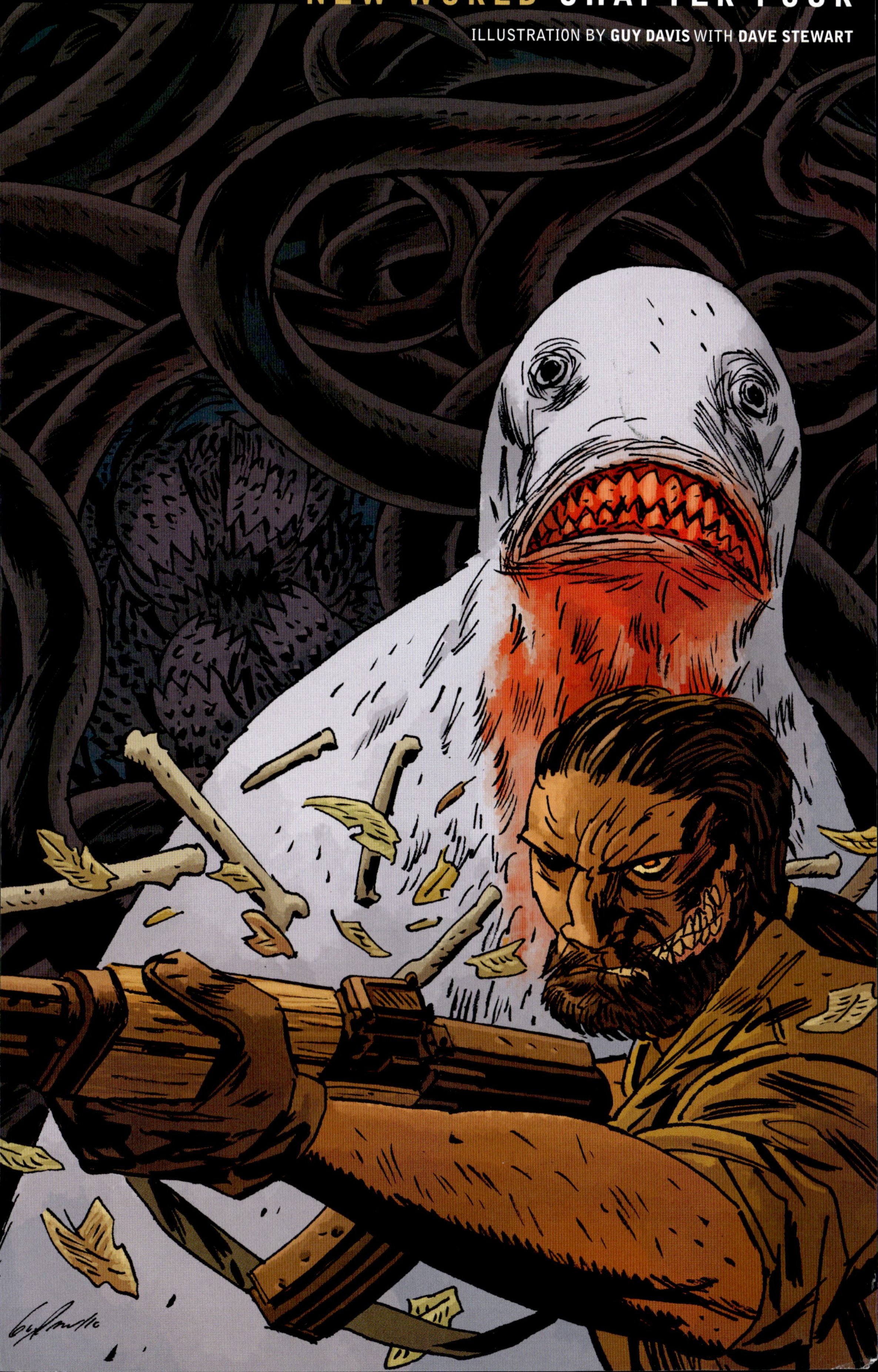

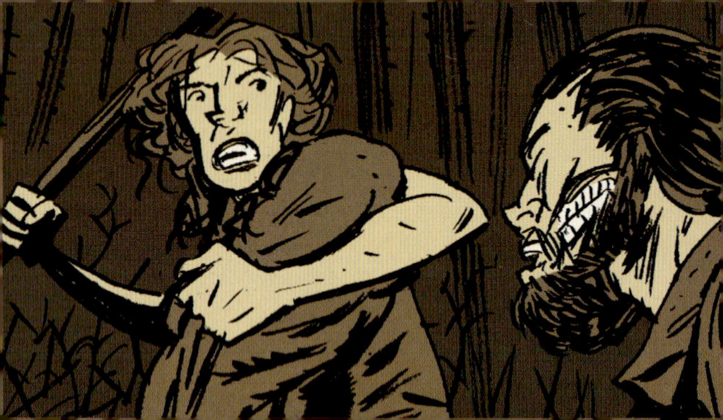

SAUER CITY, IDAHO.
THAT'S WHERE WE'RE FROM.
"WE"?
ME AND THE WIFE...
...AND MY SON.
CRACK
FSSSSSSSSSS

I REALIZE HE'S DEAD, ALL RIGHT? DON'T LOOK AT ME LIKE THAT.
HOW YOU TWO CAN BE THINKING I'M CRAZY IS... WELL, THAT'S CRAZY.
LISTEN, MR. KIHNL, YOU SAID YOU KNOW SOMETHING-- SOMETHING WE SHOULD KNOW.
I DO. WELL, I MEAN I DON'T KNOW HOW ANY OF IT HAPPENED, BUT WHAT HAPPENED-- YEAH, I KNOW THAT.
"I WAS STATIONED OVER IN FORT FUHRMAN WHEN MY ORDERS CAME THROUGH TO SHIP OUT. I'D BEEN EXPECTING IT. NESSA--SHE'S MY WIFE--WAS SEVEN MONTHS PREGNANT, THOUGH. I HATED TO LEAVE.
"BUT I DID. WENT AND STARTED MY TOUR.
"YEAH, A TWELVE-MONTH TOUR, AND I WASN'T EVEN IN-COUNTRY TWO WEEKS.

"I.E.D.
"TORE MY LEFT LEG UP BIG TIME. NOT AN OVERNIGHT STAY, YOU SEE? AND BY THEN, NESSA COULDN'T FLY ANYMORE.
"WROTE ME EVERY DAY, ALMOST. EXCEPT THE DAY JAXON WAS BORN, OF COURSE.
"SO I MISSED THAT, BUT GOT HOME AS SOON AS I COULD.
"IF YOU COULD CALL IT A HOME.
"NESSA SAID JAXON WAS SICK. WOULDN'T LET ME ANYWHERE NEAR HIM.
"SHE, ON THE OTHER HAND, NEVER LEFT HIS SIDE.
"IT WAS WEIRD, AND I STARTED THINKING MAYBE NESSA WAS THE ONE WHO WAS SICK.

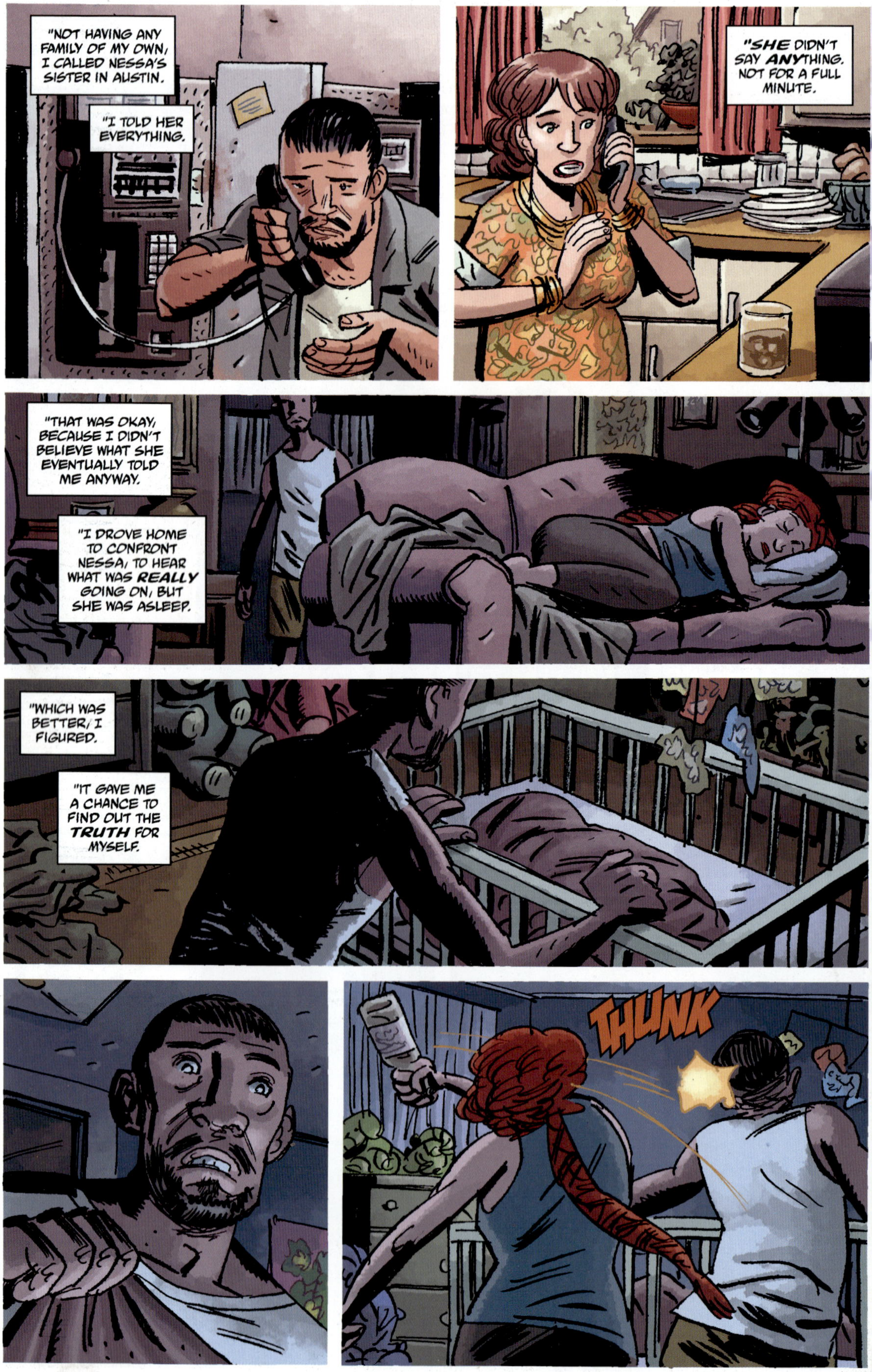
"NOT HAVING ANY FAMILY OF MY OWN, I CALLED NESSA'S SISTER IN AUSTIN.
"I TOLD HER EVERYTHING.
"SHE DIDN'T SAY ANYTHING. NOT FOR A FULL MINUTE.
"THAT WAS OKAY, BECAUSE I DIDN'T BELIEVE WHAT SHE EVENTUALLY TOLD ME ANYWAY.
"I DROVE HOME TO CONFRONT NESSA, TO HEAR WHAT WAS REALLY GOING ON, BUT SHE WAS ASLEEP.
"WHICH WAS BETTER, I FIGURED.
"IT GAVE ME A CHANCE TO FIND OUT THE TRUTH FOR MYSELF.
THUNK

"WHEN I WOKE UP, SHE WAS GONE. BUT SHE'D CALLED AN AMBULANCE.
"COPS WANTED ME TO FILE CHARGES, SO I DID THAT, JUST TO SHUT 'EM UP.
"BUT I'D ALREADY WORKED OUT ANOTHER PLAN."
JAXON KUHL
I FIGURE IF I SHOW HER--IF SHE SEES OUR BOY IN HERE--MAYBE THAT SNAPS HER OUT OF THIS.
SHE CALLED AN AMBULANCE FOR ME, RIGHT? SHE STILL CARES, SO MAYBE SHE'LL COME BACK TO ME--AWAY FROM THAT THING.
BUT WHY ARE YOU HERE? WHY OUR CAMP, AND HOW?
NESSA, SHE'S STILL USING MY CREDIT CARD. BOUGHT BREAKFAST IN A TOWN CALLED MAREKEOS NEAR HERE.
IT'S EMPTY. NESSA WAS THERE AND IN A FEW HOURS... EVERYBODY'S GONE.

LAST NIGHT, FROM THE ROAD, I SAW YOUR FIRE.
FIGURED WHOEVER WAS STICKING AROUND A GHOST TOWN LIKE THAT MIGHT KNOW SOMETHING, SO I CAME UP HERE AND...WELL, JUST WAITED.
WHEN YOU SHOWED UP, I KNEW. YOU'RE PART OF THE PARANORMAL BUREAU. I SAW YOU ON T.V.
YOU'RE HERE TO FIGHT MONSTERS. YOU'RE HERE BECAUSE OF MY NESSA. THOSE FOLKS THAT DISAPPEARED, SHE DID THAT, DIDN'T SHE?
THE WOMAN WE SAW IN LYNNE. THAT'S WHAT YOU MEANT--
SHH!
WHAT IS IT?
SOMETHING.

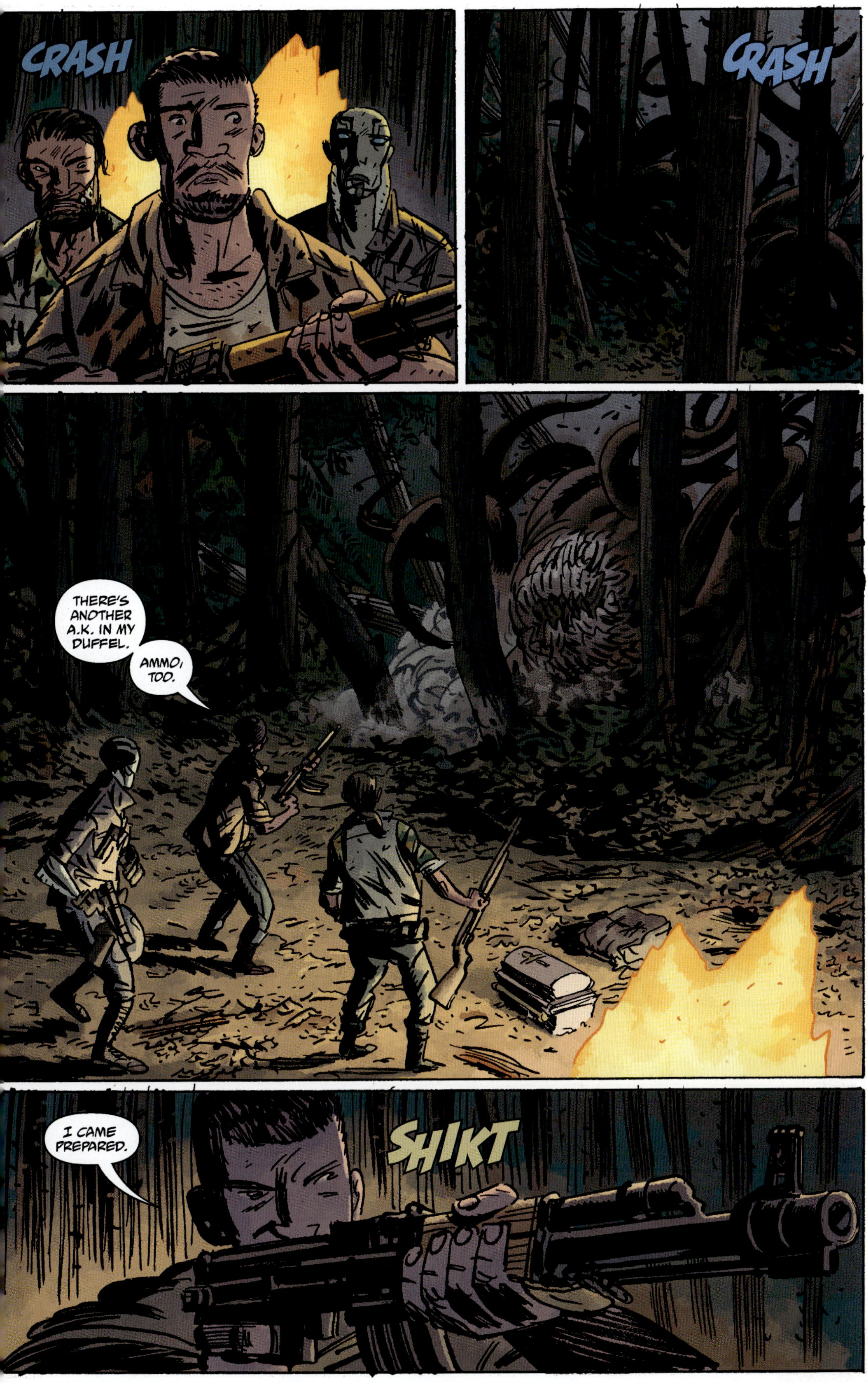
CRASH
CRASH
THERE'S ANOTHER A.K. IN MY DUFFEL.
AMMO, TOO.
I CAME PREPARED.
SHIKT

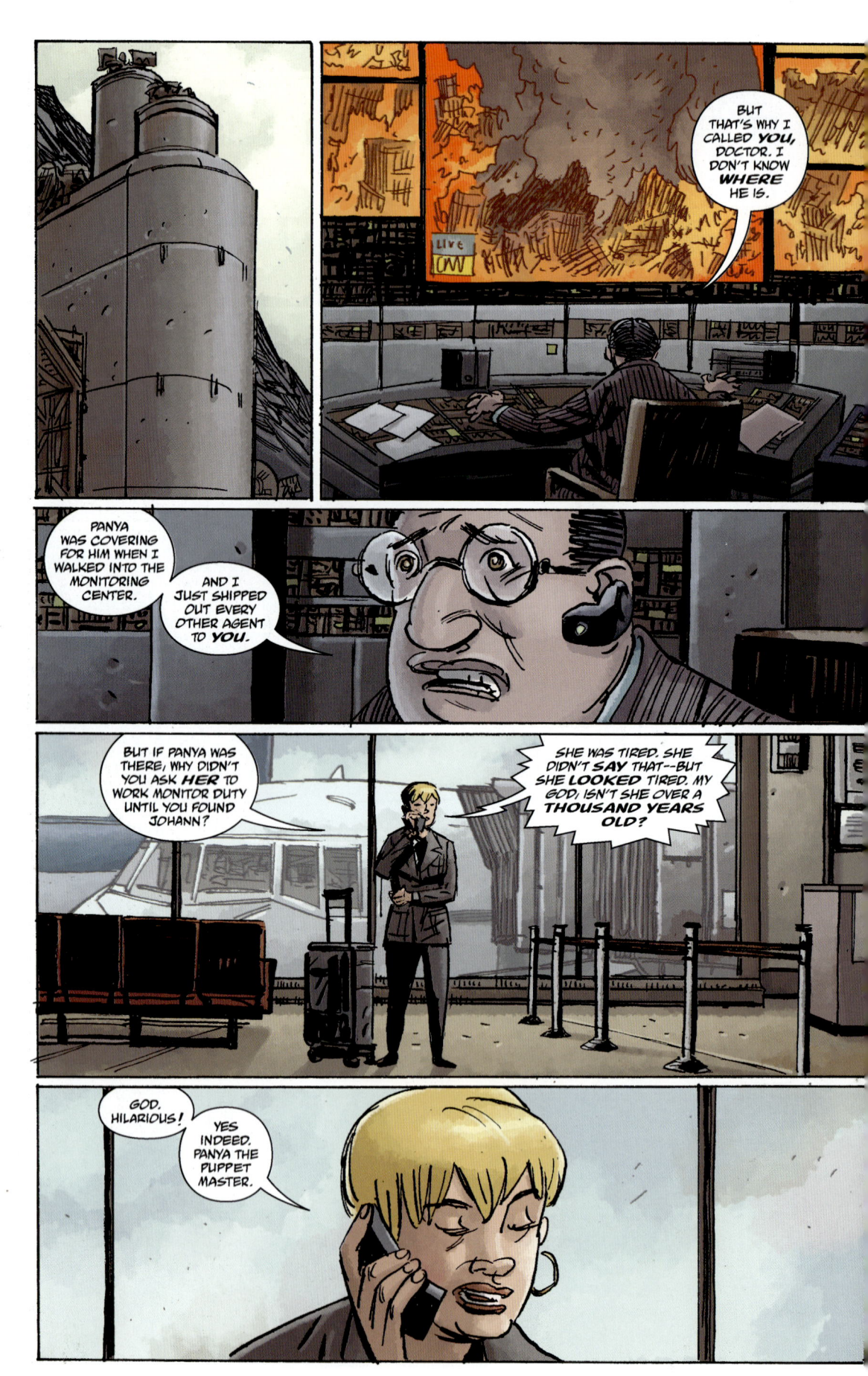

"BUT THAT'S WHY I CALLED **YOU**, DOCTOR. I DON'T KNOW **WHERE** HE IS.

"PANYA WAS COVERING FOR HIM WHEN I WALKED INTO THE MONITORING CENTER.

"AND I JUST SHIPPED OUT EVERY OTHER AGENT TO **YOU**."

"BUT IF PANYA WAS THERE, WHY DIDN'T YOU ASK **HER** TO WORK MONITOR DUTY UNTIL YOU FOUND JOHANN?"

"SHE WAS TIRED. SHE DIDN'T **SAY** THAT--BUT SHE **LOOKED** TIRED. MY GOD, ISN'T SHE OVER A **THOUSAND YEARS OLD**?"

"GOD. HILARIOUS!"

"YES INDEED. PANYA THE PUPPET MASTER."

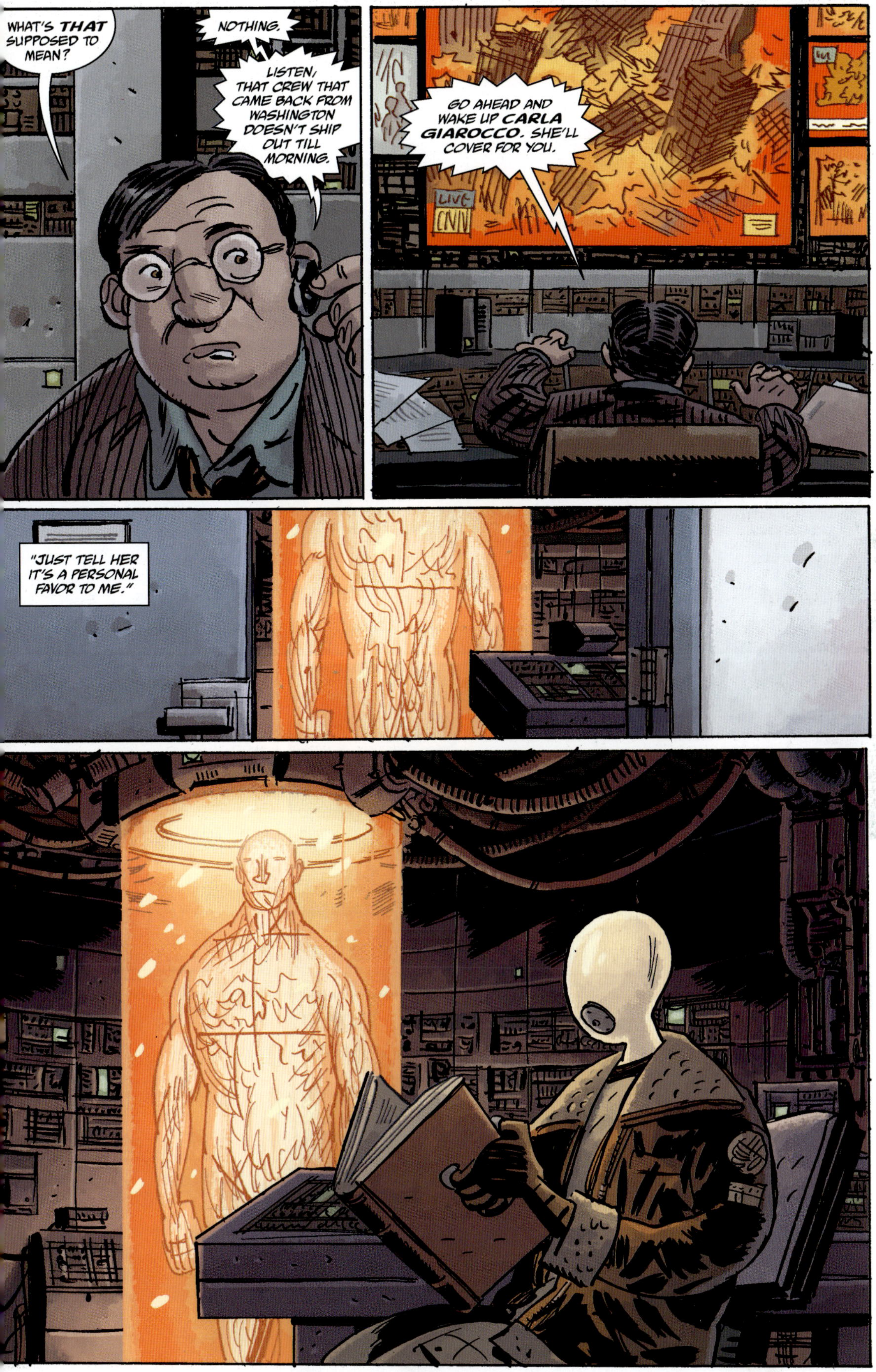
WHAT'S THAT SUPPOSED TO MEAN?
NOTHING.
LISTEN, THAT CREW THAT CAME BACK FROM WASHINGTON DOESN'T SHIP OUT TILL MORNING.
GO AHEAD AND WAKE UP CARLA GIAROCCO. SHE'LL COVER FOR YOU.
LIVE
CNN
"JUST TELL HER IT'S A PERSONAL FAVOR TO ME."

BEEP BEEP BEEP

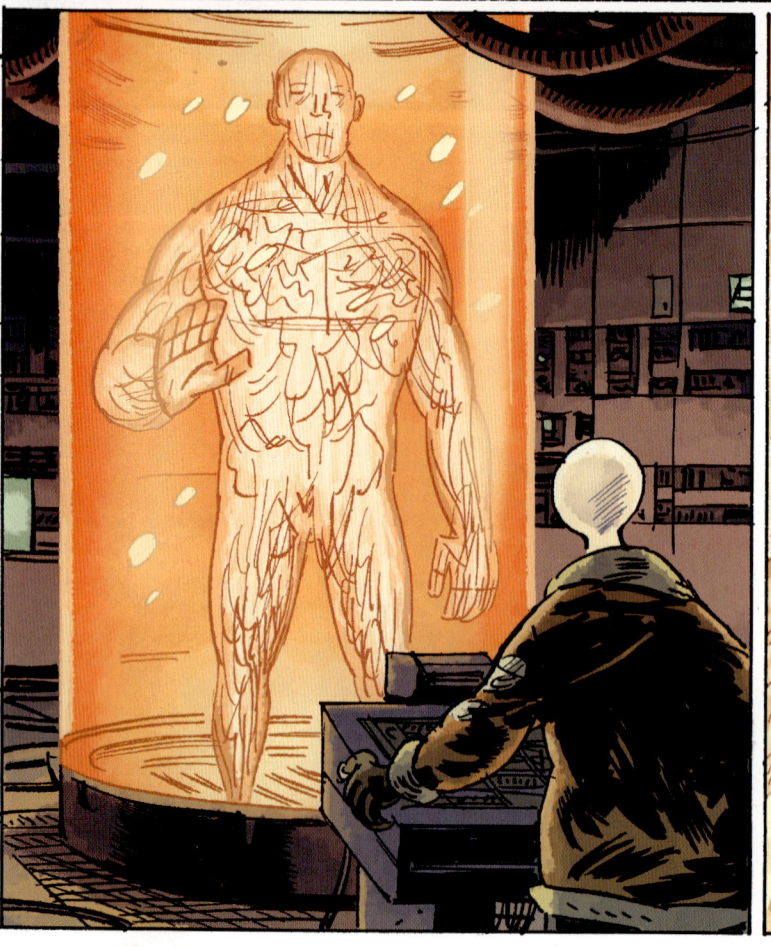

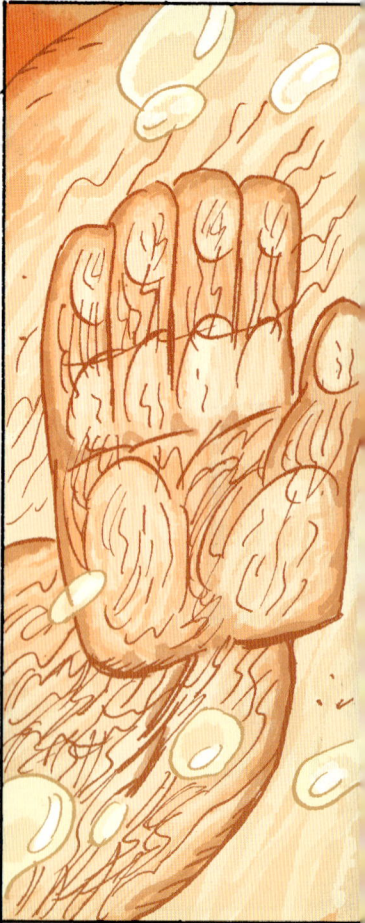

BRAIN-WAVE FUNCTION?

94

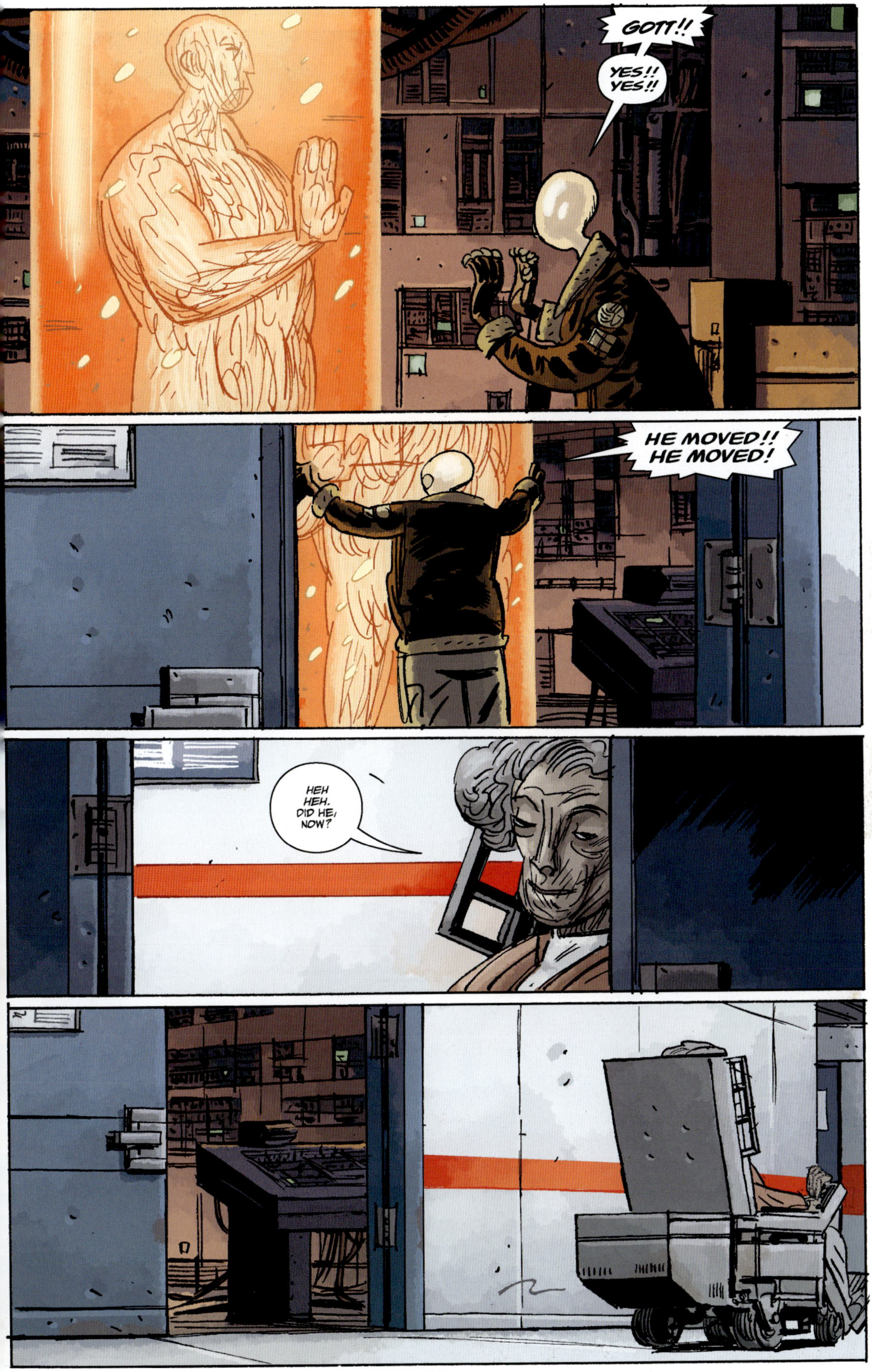
GOTT!!
YES!! YES!!
HE MOVED!! HE MOVED!
HEH HEH. DID HE, NOW?

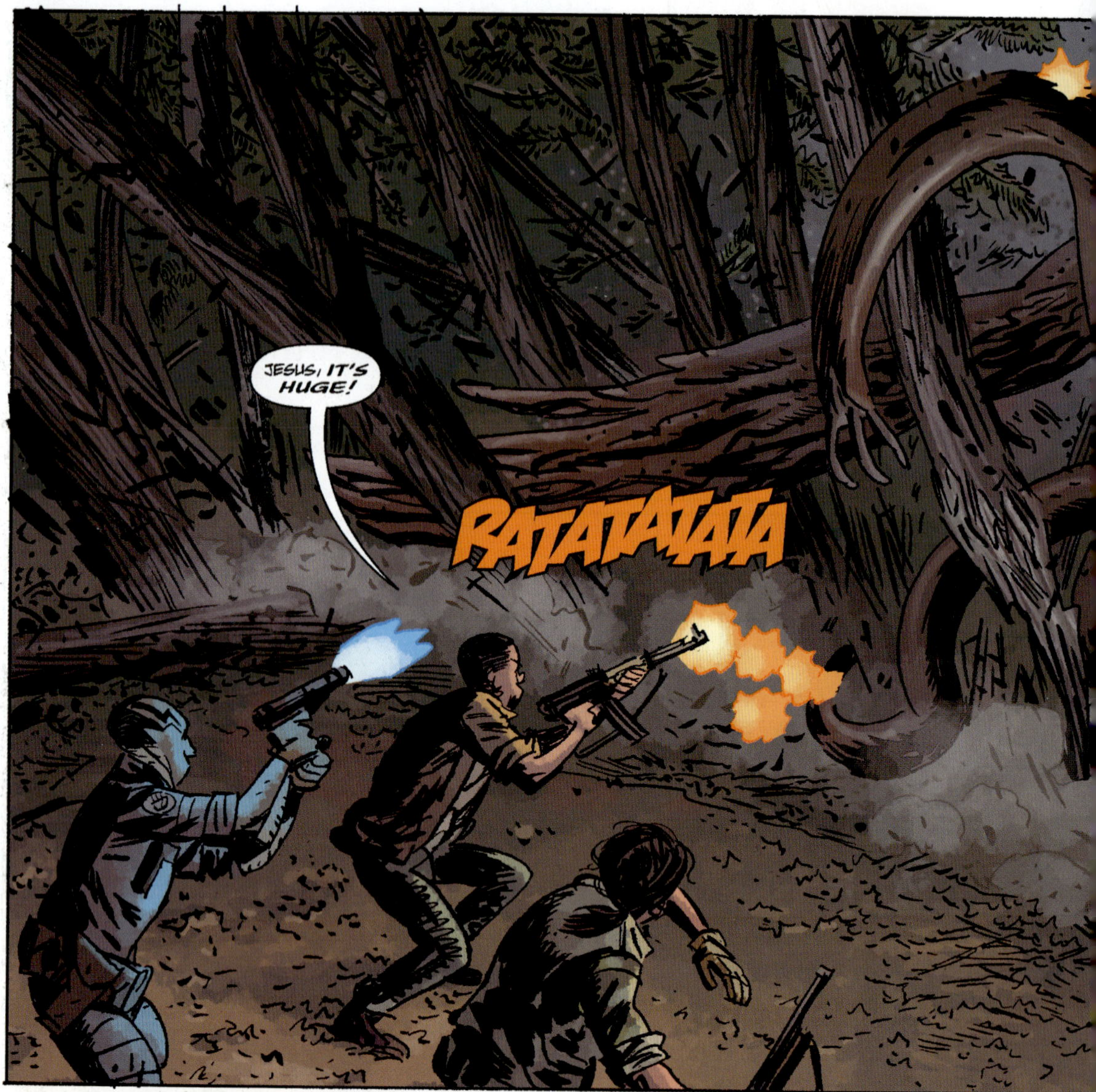
JESUS, IT'S HUGE!
RATATATATA

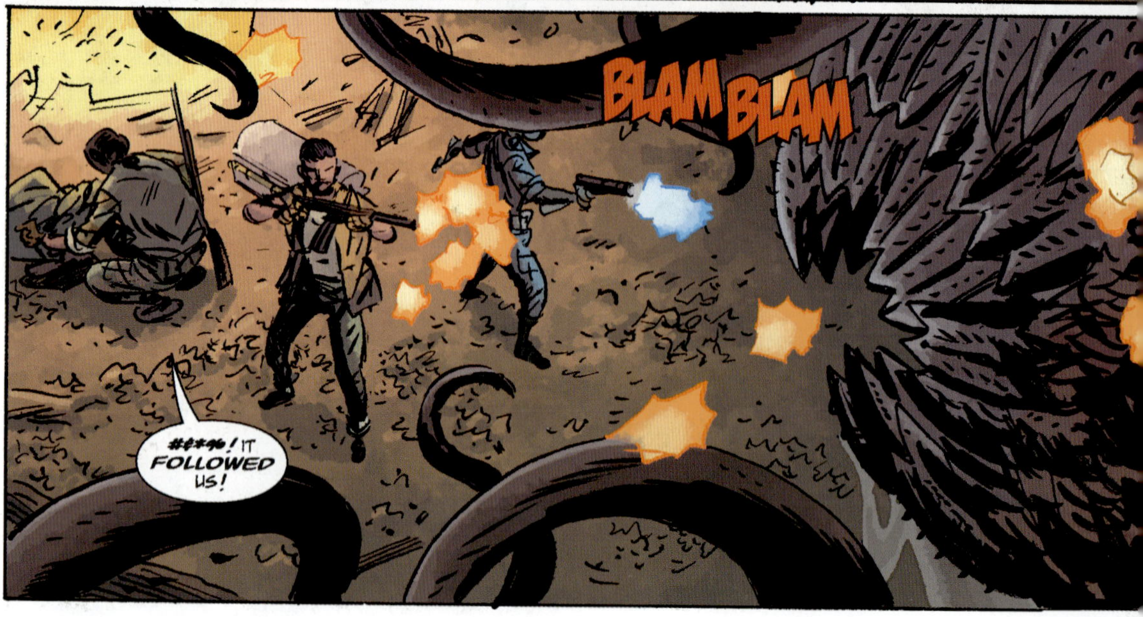
BLAM BLAM
#@*%! IT FOLLOWED US!

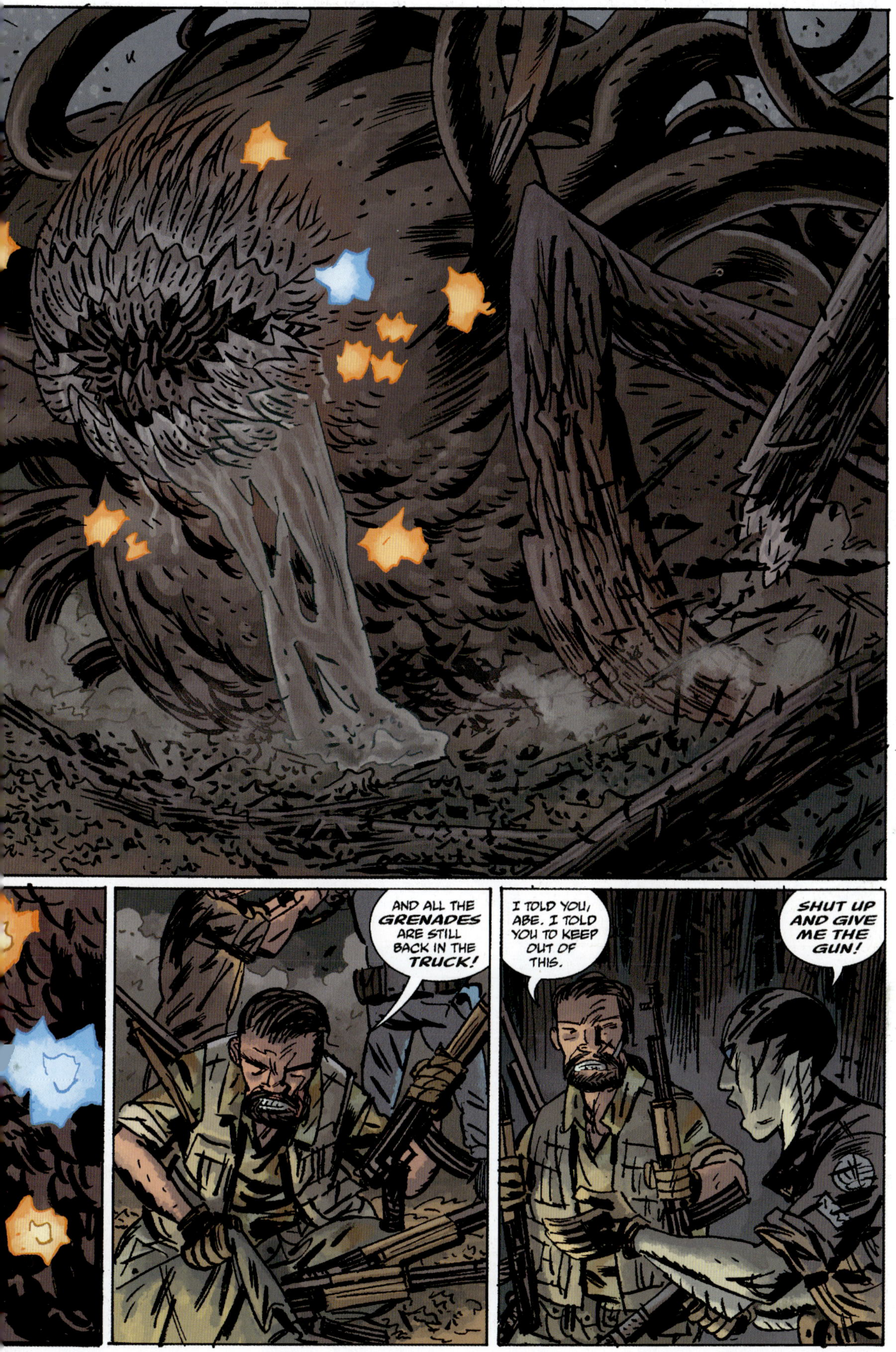
AND ALL THE GRENADES ARE STILL BACK IN THE TRUCK!
I TOLD YOU, ABE. I TOLD YOU TO KEEP OUT OF THIS.
SHUT UP AND GIVE ME THE GUN!

YOU MOTHER#$*%!! WHERE IS SHE?!
I KNOW SHE'S HERE. I KNOW YOU GOT HER.
GIVE ME BACK MY NESSA!
UHHHHH...

GIVE ME BACK MY WIFE!!
GOD, NO. NO.
AAAA--!!
CRUNCH
HELL!
BEN, I'M OUT. GIVE ME ANOTHER CLIP.
BEN...?
AIIIIIII

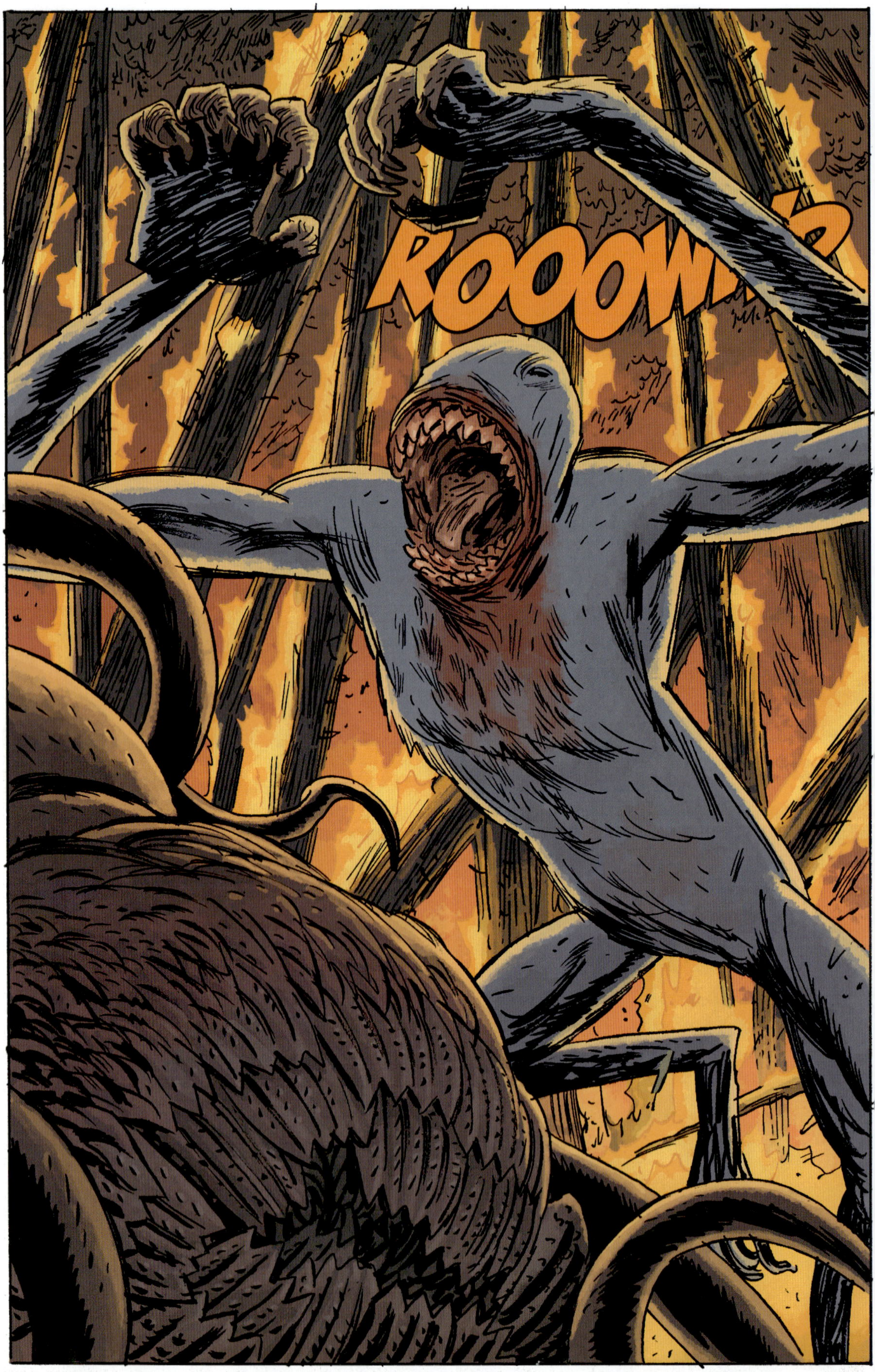
ROOOW

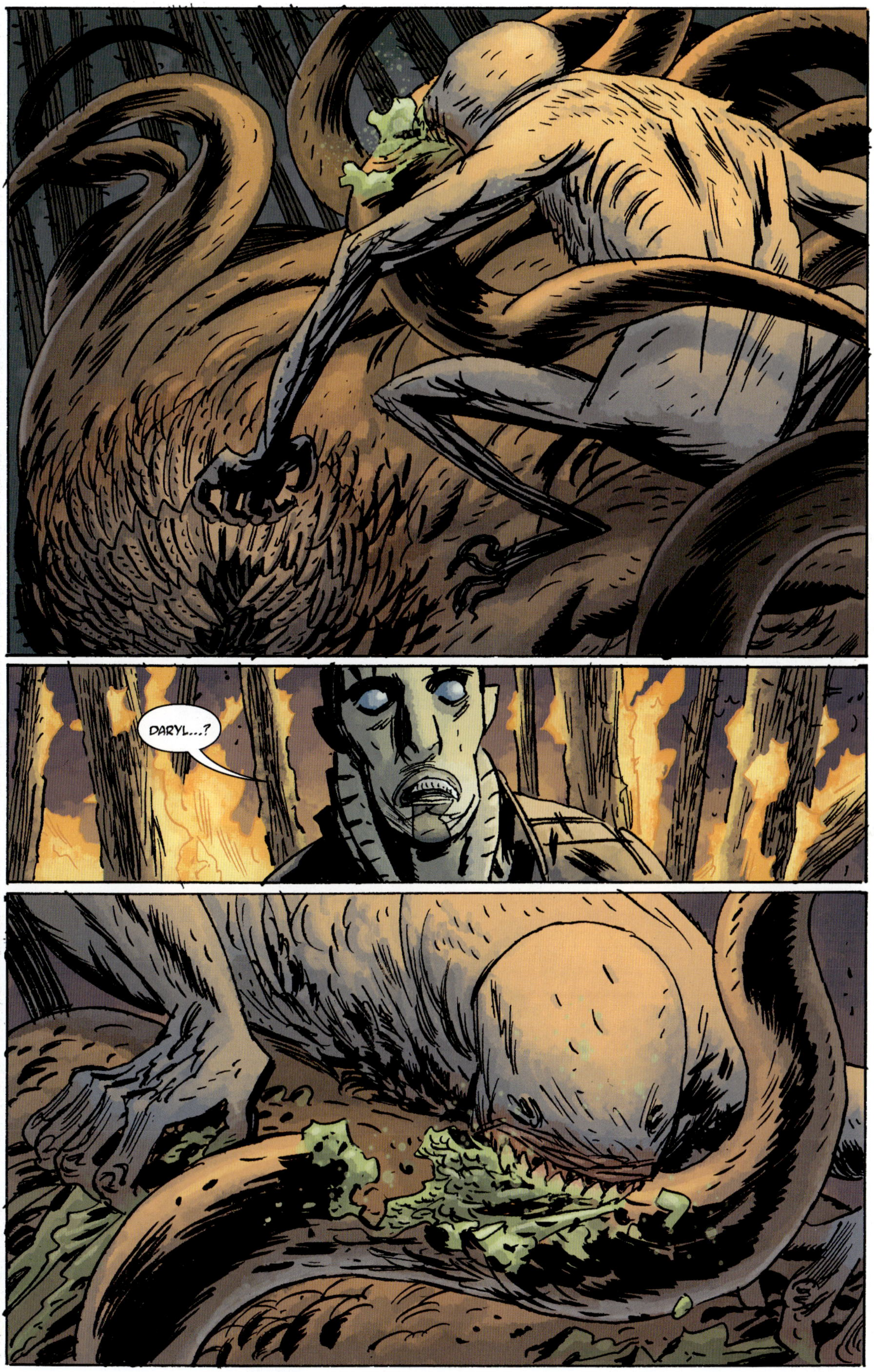
DARYL...?

I KNOW SHE'S HERE! I KNOW YOU GOT HER!
THAT'S RIGHT. SHE'S HERE.
THING DIDN'T FOLLOW US. FOLLOWED HER.
PUMP BULLETS INTO THAT MONSTER ALL NIGHT. WHERE'LL THAT GET US?
YOU, YOU BITCH. IT'S YOU.
YOU'RE HERE, AND I SWEAR--

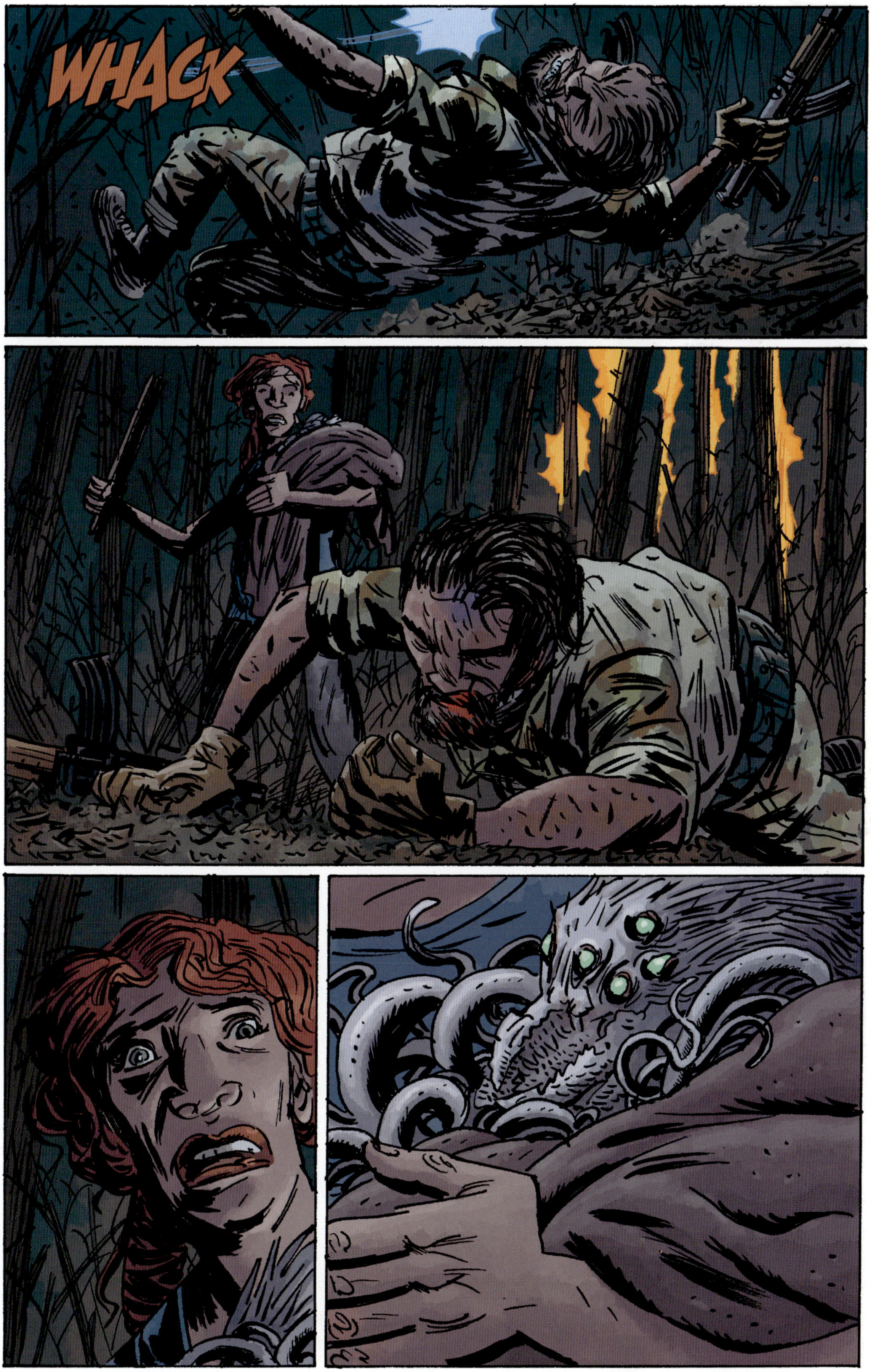
WHACK

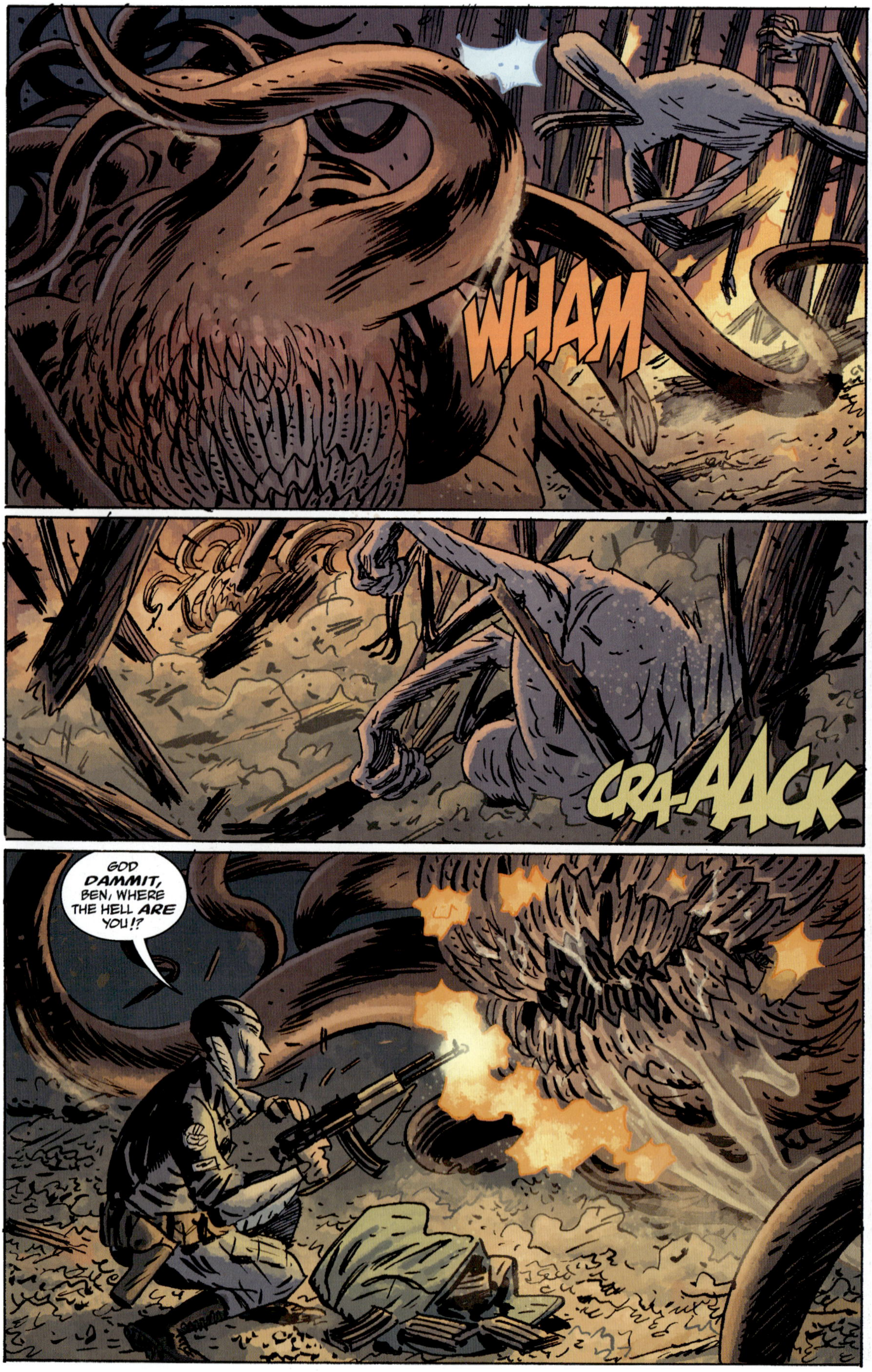
WHAM
CRA-AACK
GOD DAMMIT, BEN, WHERE THE HELL ARE YOU!?

REALLY GOT A THING FOR CRACKING GUYS OVER THE SKULL, EH?
YOU AND FREAK PUPPY THERE.
STAY AWAAAY!!
OOOF!
YOU SHOULD STICK TO CLOCKING PEOPLE WHO CARE ABOUT YOU, THOUGH.
PEOPLE LIKE YOUR HUSBAND, POOR STUPID BASTARD.

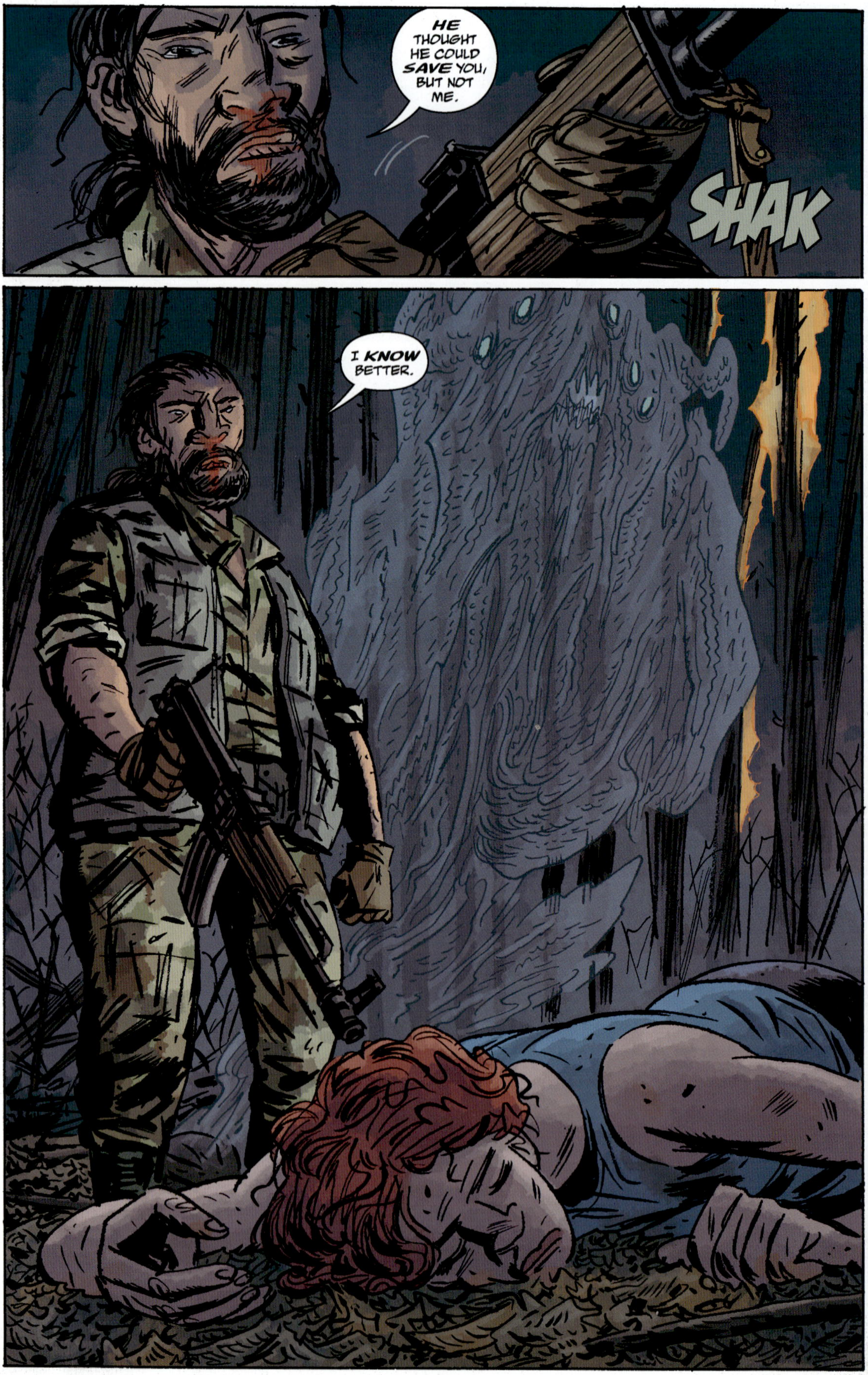
HE THOUGHT HE COULD SAVE YOU, BUT NOT ME.
SHAK
I KNOW BETTER.

NEW WORLD CHAPTER FIVE

ILLUSTRATION BY **GUY DAVIS** WITH **DAVE STEWART**

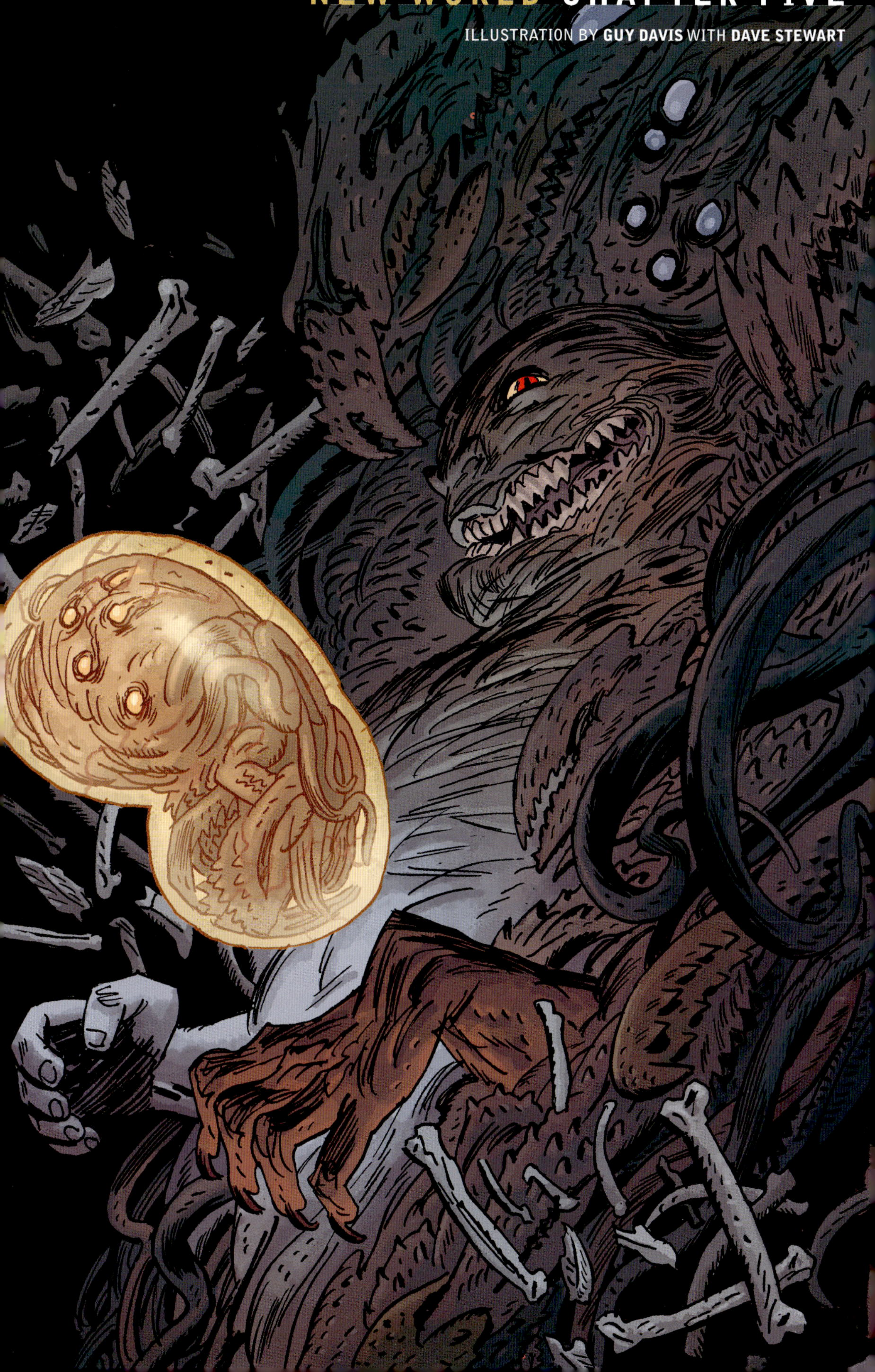

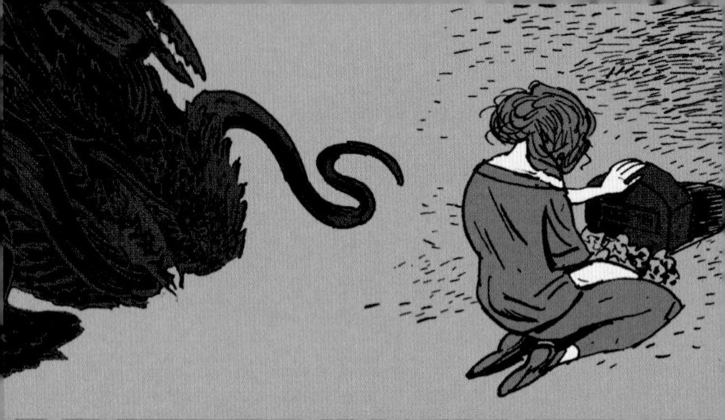

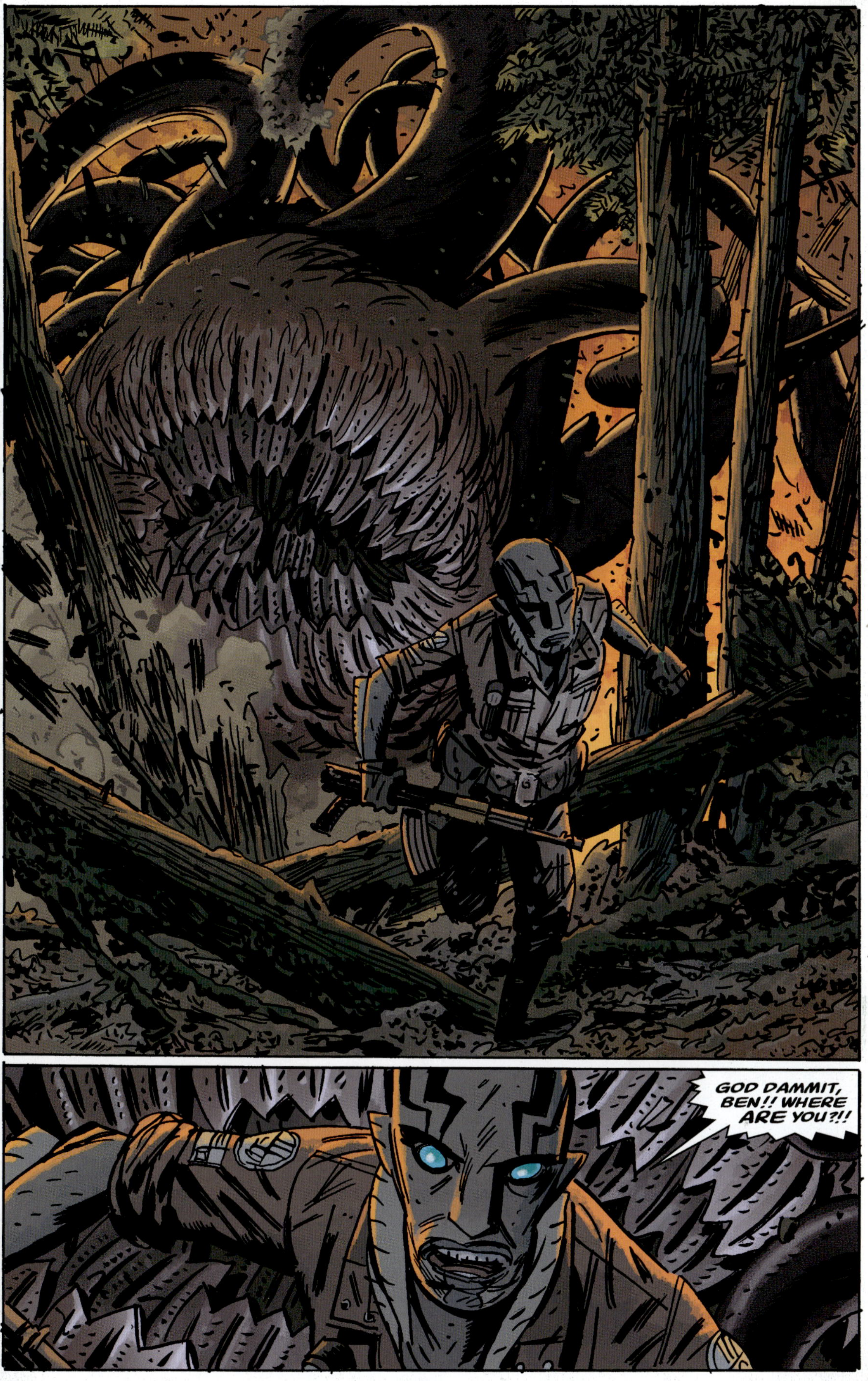
GOD DAMMIT, BEN!! WHERE ARE YOU?!!

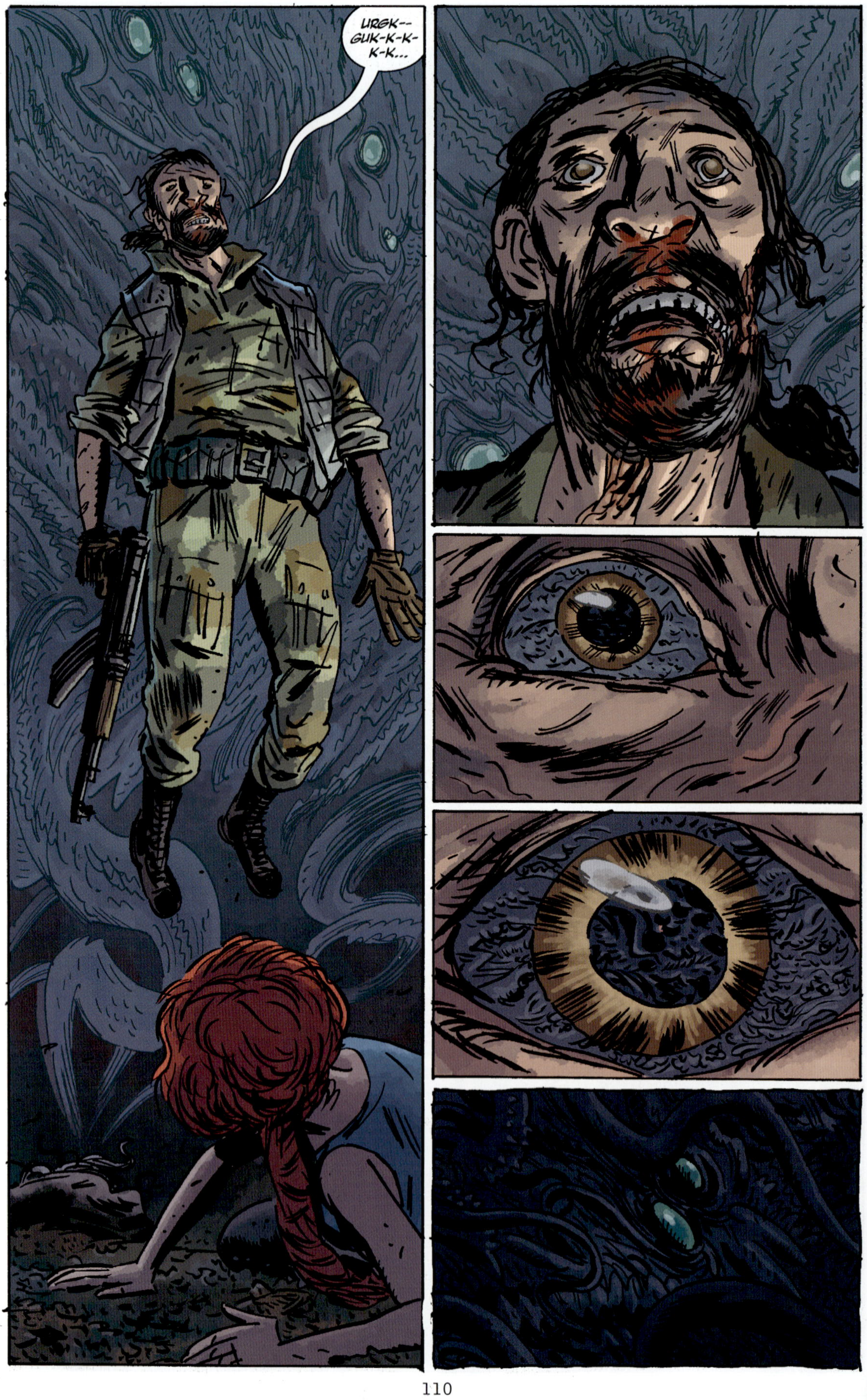
URGK--
GUK-K-K-
K-K...

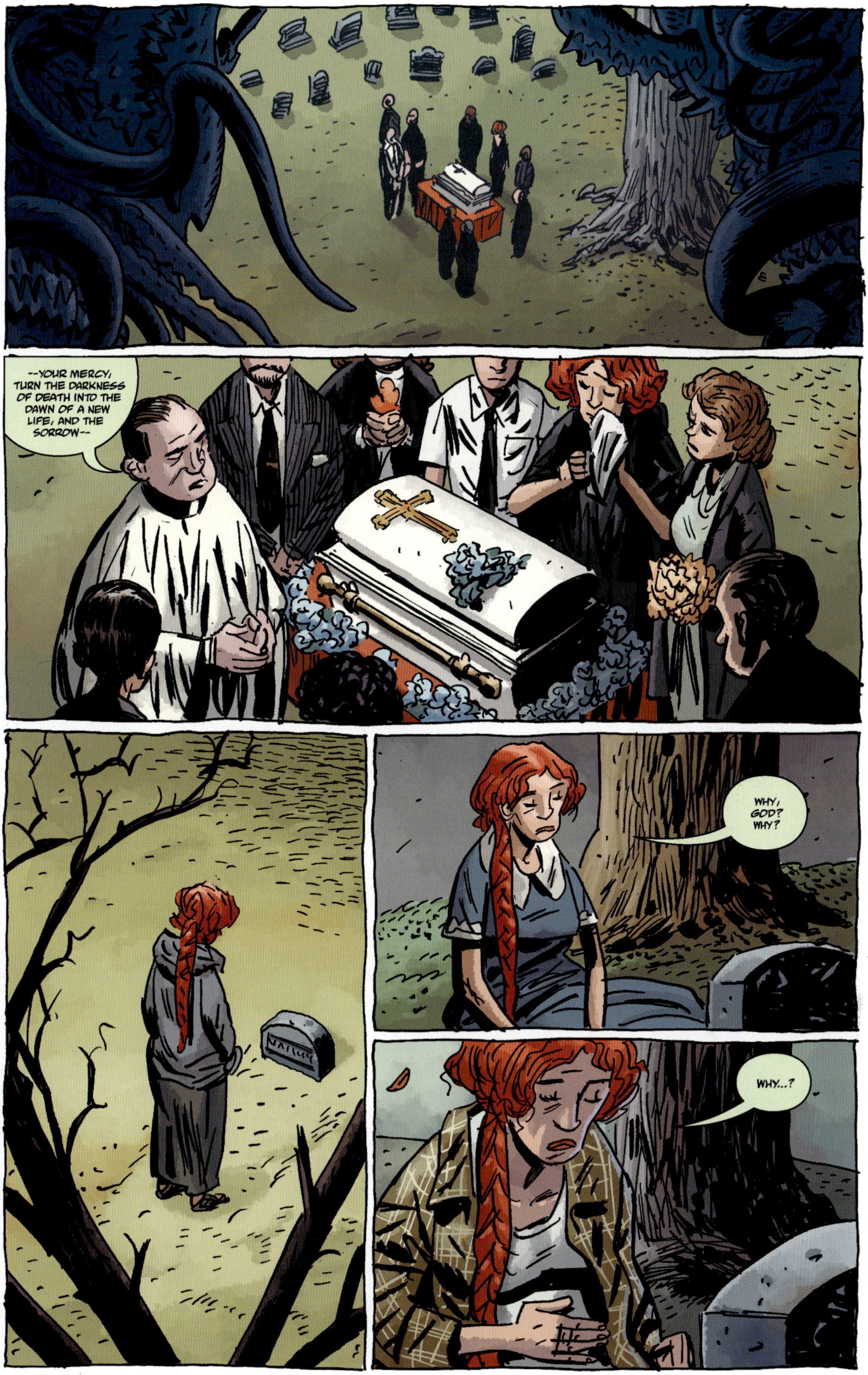
--YOUR MERCY, TURN THE DARKNESS OF DEATH INTO THE DAWN OF A NEW LIFE, AND THE SORROW--
WHY, GOD? WHY?
WHY...?

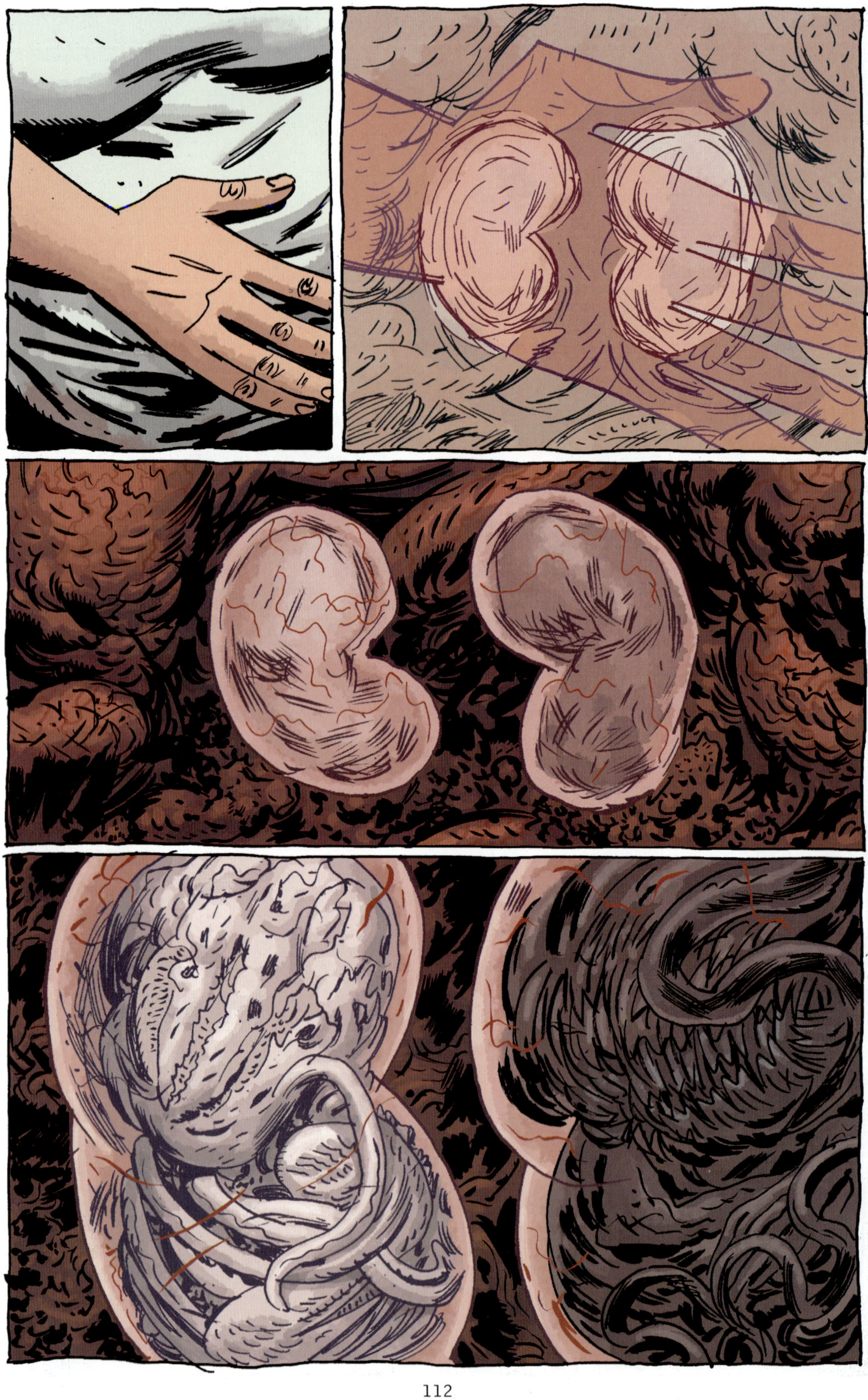

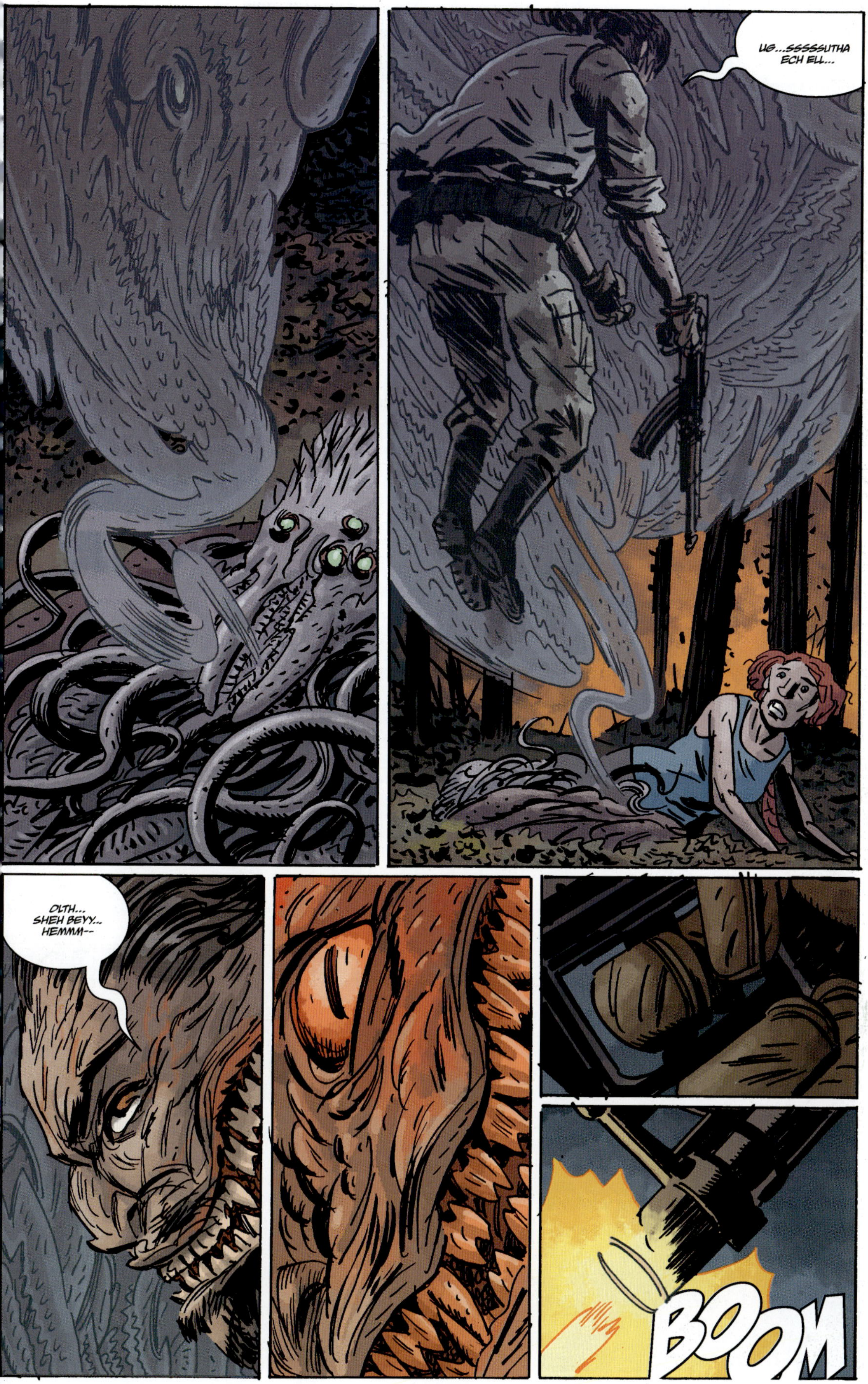
UG...SSSSSUTHA ECH ELL...
OLTH... SHEH BEYY... HEMMM--
BOOM

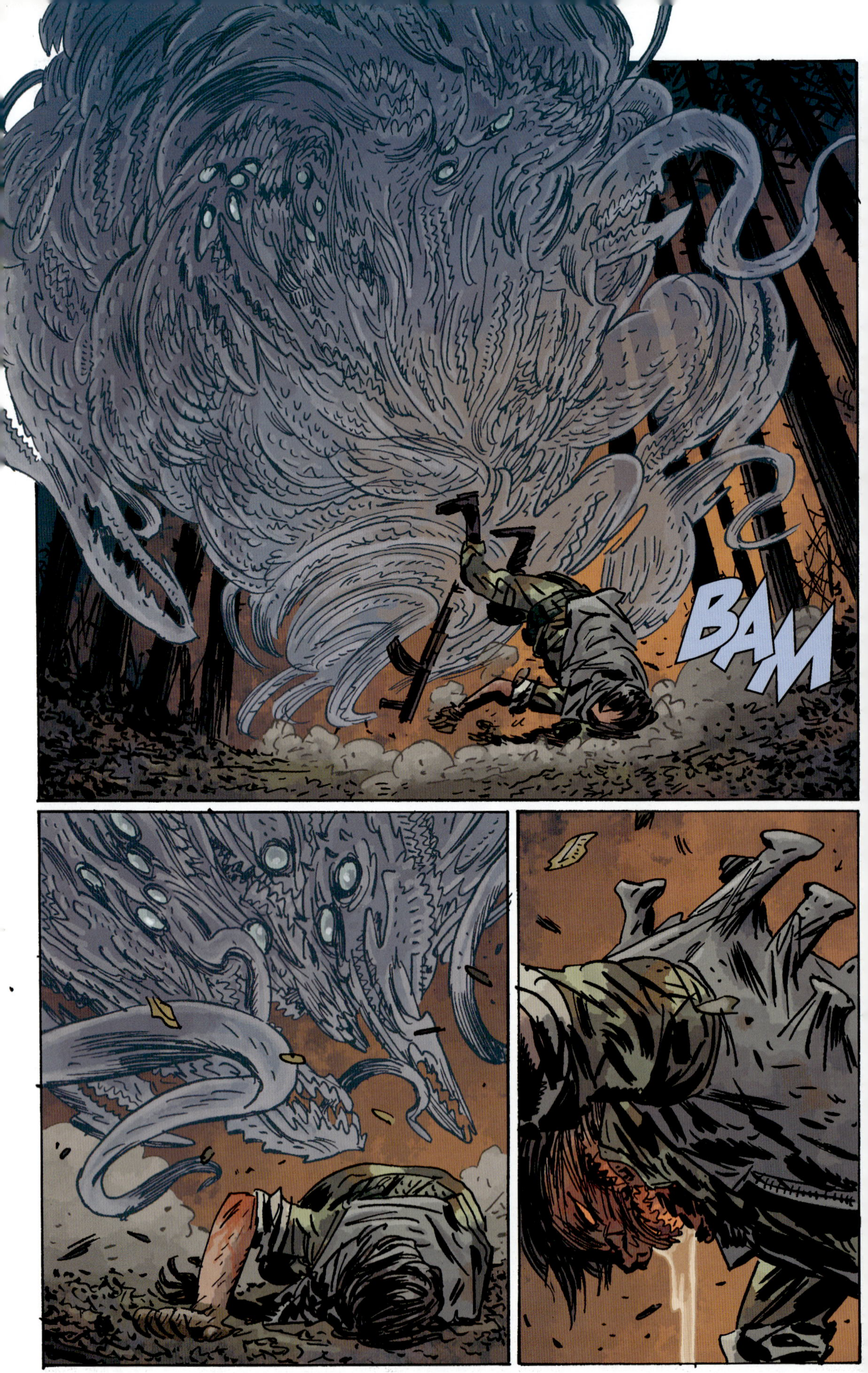
BAM

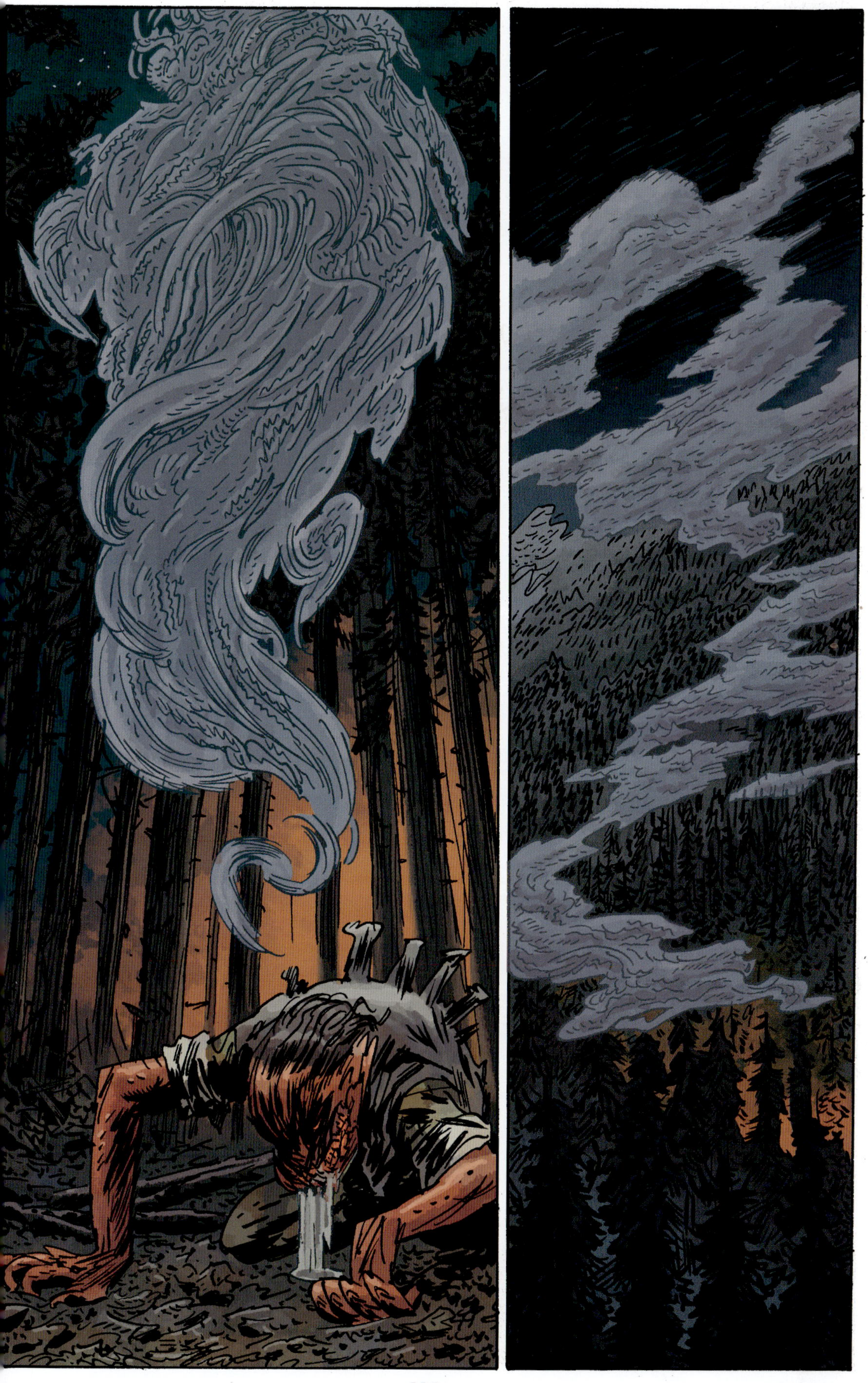

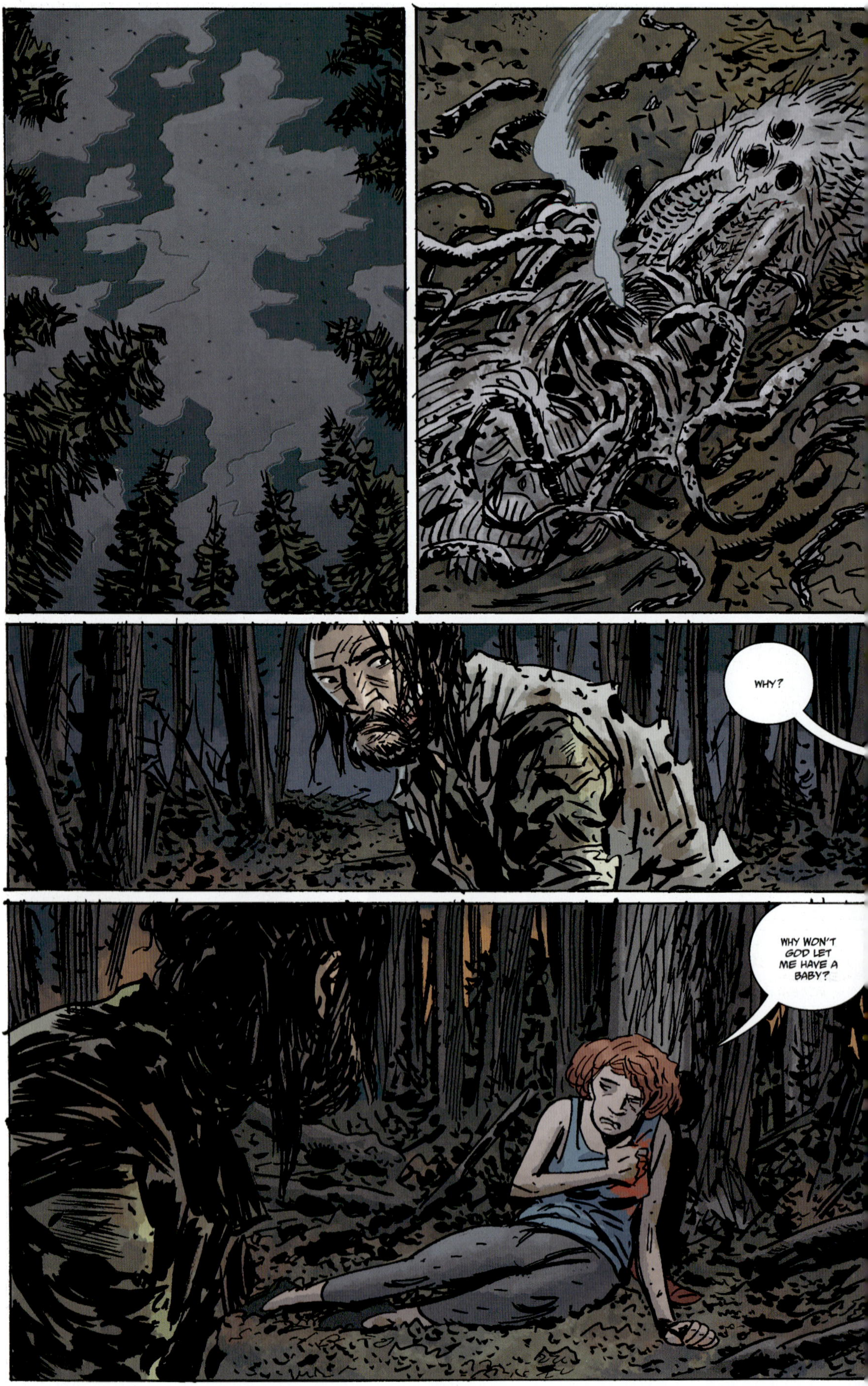
WHY?
WHY WON'T GOD LET ME HAVE A BABY?

WHAT--I DON'T...?
DEAD? IT JUST DIED?
JUST LIKE I FIGURED.
JESUS, BEN! I THOUGHT YOU WERE DEAD, OR WORSE.
AND **WHAT** DID YOU FIGURE?
COME ON.
I'LL TELL YOU ALL ABOUT IT WHILE WE'RE DIGGING.

THUNK
THUNK
BACK UP A SECOND. YOU CAN READ MINDS NOW?
NO, THAT ISN'T IT. THAT THING WAS TRYING TO GET INTO MY HEAD, I THINK, BUT I ENDED UP INSIDE OF ITS...WELL, ITS MIND, I GUESS.
OKAY, SO WHERE DID MRS. KIHNL FIND IT?
SHE DIDN'T.
IT FOUND HER.

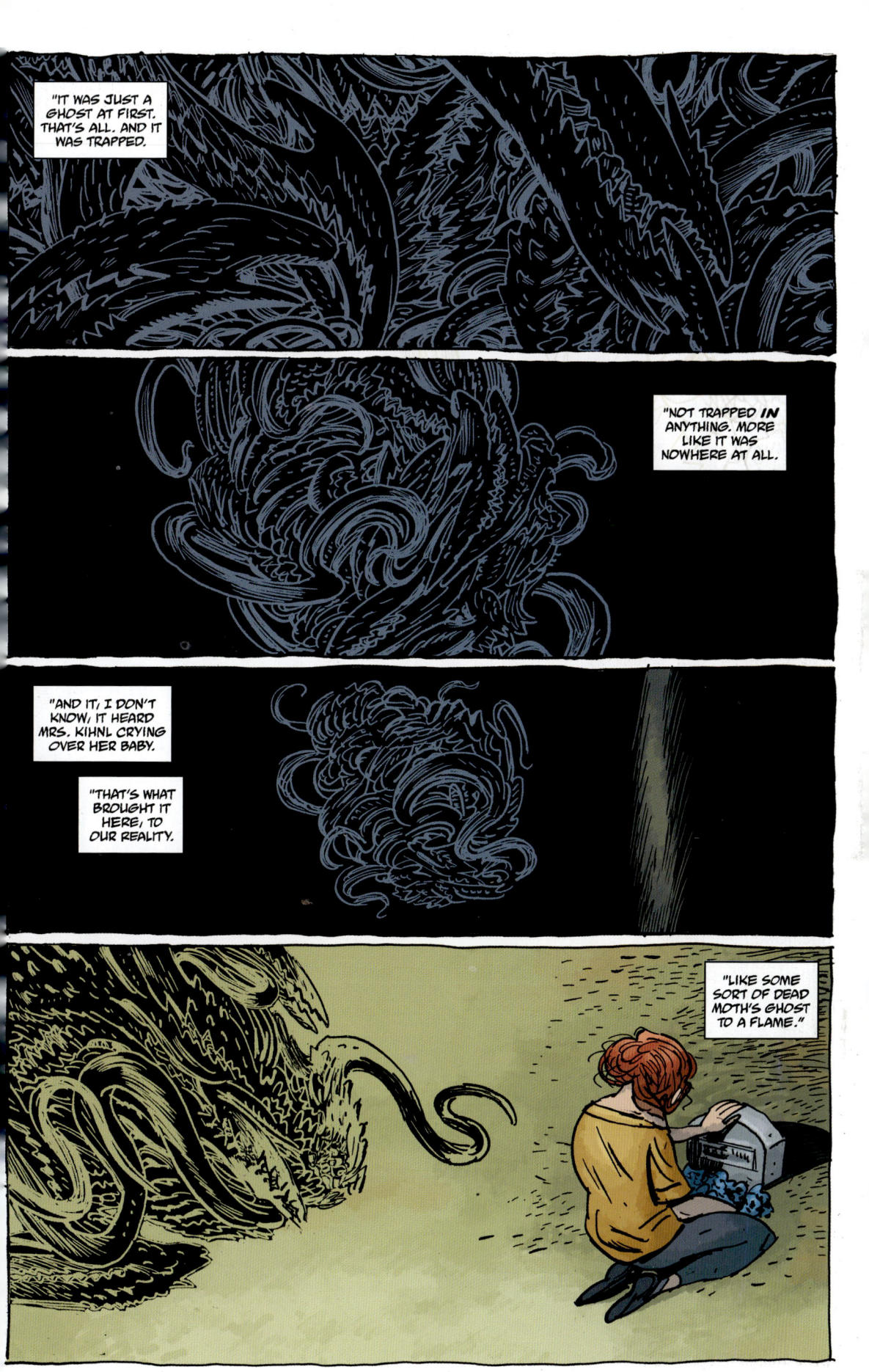

"IT WAS JUST A GHOST AT FIRST. THAT'S ALL. AND IT WAS TRAPPED.

"NOT TRAPPED *IN* ANYTHING. MORE LIKE IT WAS NOWHERE AT ALL.

"AND IT, I DON'T KNOW, IT HEARD MRS. KIHNL CRYING OVER HER BABY.

"THAT'S WHAT BROUGHT IT HERE, TO OUR REALITY.

"LIKE SOME SORT OF DEAD MOTH'S GHOST TO A FLAME."

BUT THAT'S ALL IT WAS--A SPIRIT. IT WANTED TO BECOME FLESH--AND HERE'S THE DISGUSTING PART--
"IT ENTERED HER BODY AND USED HER EGGS--FROM HER OVARIES--TO BUILD A BODY FOR ITSELF--
"--AND FOR A TWIN 'BROTHER.'
"SHE DELIVERED IT AS A LARVA. IT WAS WAITING TO GROW INTO ONE OF THOSE BIG MONSTERS--LIKE THE ONE IN NEBRASKA.
"TAKES A LOT OF TIME FOR THAT, THOUGH, SO IT WANTED PROTECTION.
"THAT'S WHAT ITS 'BROTHER' WAS ALL ABOUT, AND IT CLEANED OUT THE WOODS TO GET BIG ENOUGH FOR THE JOB.

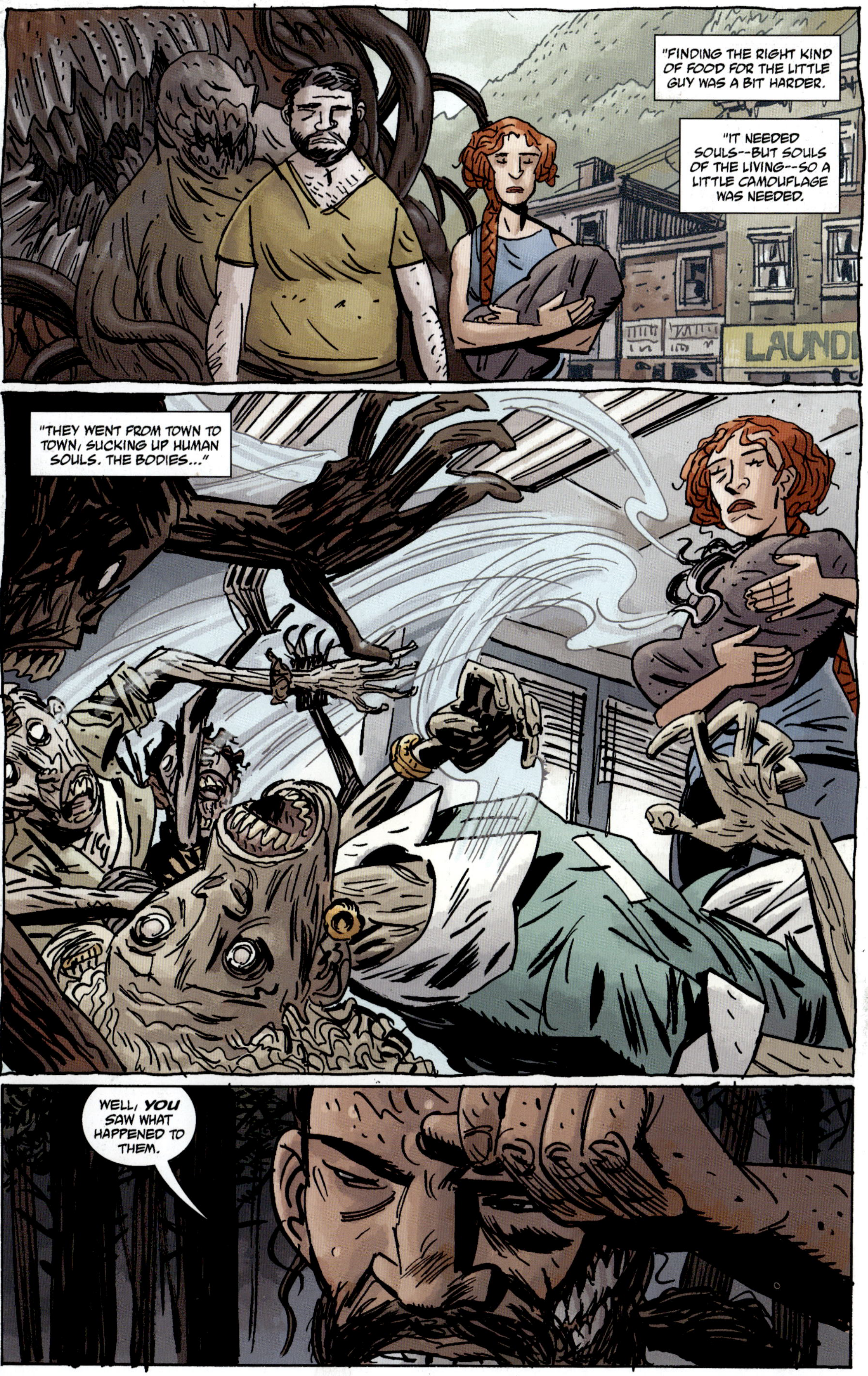
"FINDING THE RIGHT KIND OF FOOD FOR THE LITTLE GUY WAS A BIT HARDER.
"IT NEEDED SOULS--BUT SOULS OF THE LIVING--SO A LITTLE CAMOUFLAGE WAS NEEDED.
LAUND
"THEY WENT FROM TOWN TO TOWN, SUCKING UP HUMAN SOULS. THE BODIES..."
WELL, *YOU* SAW WHAT HAPPENED TO THEM.

ANYWAY, THAT'S WHAT MADE ME REALIZE MRS. KIHNL WAS THE ANCHOR FOR THIS CREATURE. SHE WAS WHAT KEPT ITS SPIRIT HERE.
A BULLET IN HER HEART WAS THE ONLY WAY OUT.
ALL THIS BECAUSE OF ONE WOMAN'S GRIEF?
THAT'S WHAT BROUGHT THIS MONSTER OUT OF ITS PRISON?
THERE'S SO MUCH PAIN IN THE WORLD, WHY HASN'T THIS HAPPENED BEFORE?
WE DON'T KNOW THAT IT HASN'T, DO WE?
BUT IF YOU THINK ABOUT IT, EVERYTHING THAT'S HAPPENING IN THIS WORLD RIGHT NOW? ALL THAT CRAZINESS?
WE'RE AT A TIPPING POINT. THINGS ARE COMING APART. THIS "GHOST," OR WHATEVER, IT MAYBE JUST SLIPPED THROUGH ONE OF THE RIPS.

JESUS...
BEN, YOU DIDN'T TELL ME DARYL WAS HERE. WITH YOU.
NO, I DIDN'T.
GRAB THE OTHER END, WILL YOU?
NO ANIMALS IN THESE WOODS NOW, BUT--
--BUT SINCE WE KILLED THE THING THAT SCARED THEM OFF, THEY'LL BE BACK SOON.
DON'T WORRY. WHEN I BRING BACK THE BUREAU'S INVESTIGATION TEAM, WE'LL GET THE KIHNLS HOME.
I CAN WAIT A DAY OR SO BEFORE I CALL THIS IN. GIVE YOU A LITTLE LEAD TIME TO CLEAR OUT?
"LEAD TIME"?
ABE, BEFORE YOU EVER GET TO A TOWN WITH A WORKING PHONE, WE'LL BE A MILLION MILES FROM THIS SPOT.

THAT CROSS SHOULD MAKE IT EASY FOR YOUR BOYS TO FIND.
JUST HOPE KIHNL ISN'T A JEWISH NAME.
BEN, THAT "TIPPING POINT" STUFF. IF IT'S TRUE, YOU HAVE TO COME BACK. WE'LL NEED ALL THE HELP WE CAN GET.
FIGHTING THE WRONG WAR? CAN'T HELP YOU WITH THAT.
I TRIED TO MILITARIZE THINGS IN THE BUREAU--TRIED TO MOBILIZE FORCES. MAYBE THEN IT WAS RIGHT, BUT IT'S ALL WRONG NOW.
THAT GIANT THING IN CALIFORNIA? THAT'S NOT YOUR PROBLEM.
NOT WHEN THE REAL INVASION IS GOING ON IN PEOPLE'S MINDS--AND THEIR WOMBS, FOR CHRIST'S SAKE!
THAT, ABE, IS HOW THE WORLD'S GONNA BE DESTROYED RIGHT OUT FROM UNDER YOU WHILE YOU'RE HOLED-UP THERE IN THE ROCKY MOUNTAINS.
BUT YOU CAN SAVE IT FROM RIGHT HERE?
HEY, I THINK WE DID A HELL OF A JOB, DON'T YOU?
LOOK, WHATEVER. THE UPSHOT IS, I CAN'T HELP YOU.

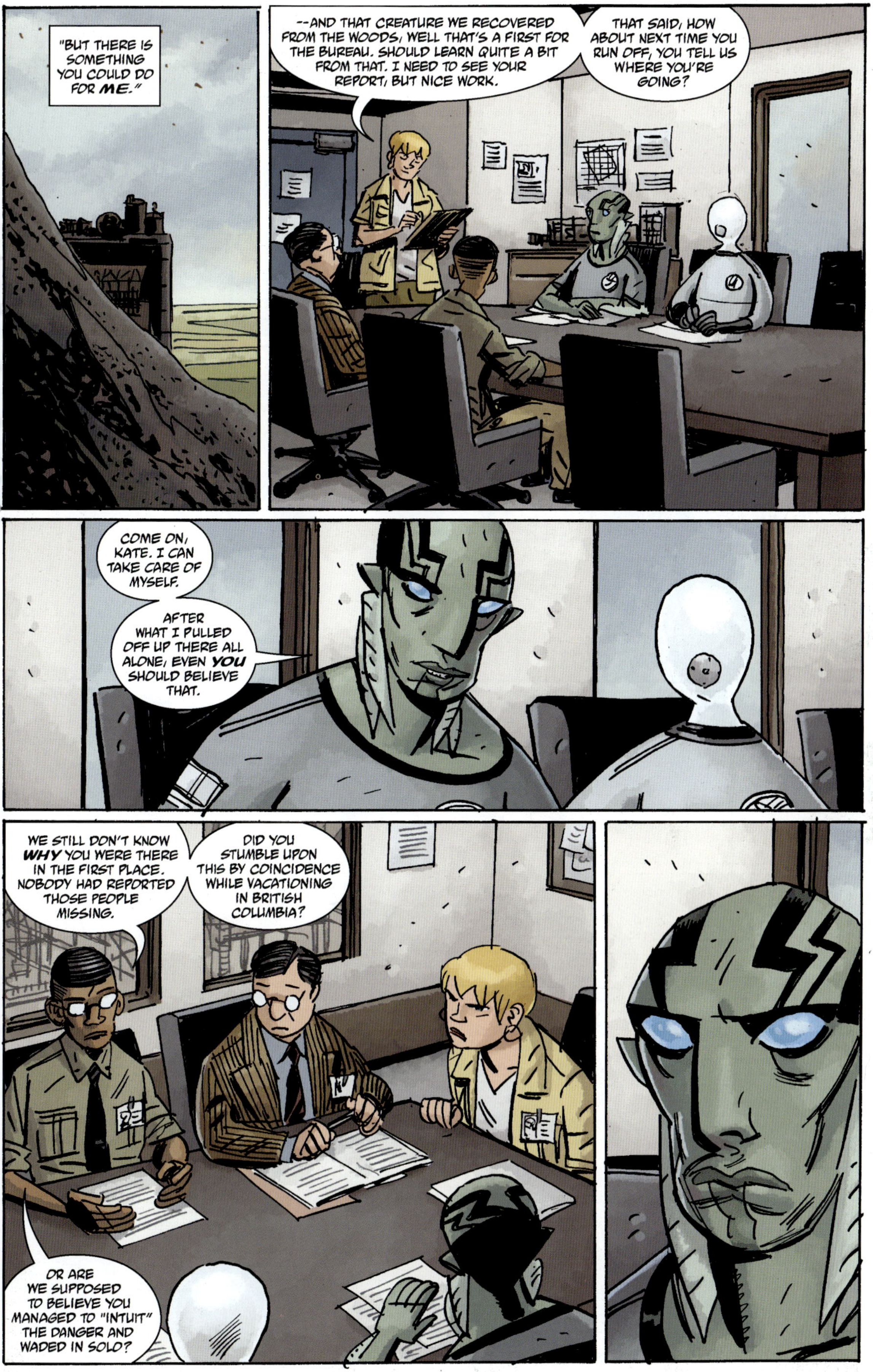
"BUT THERE IS SOMETHING YOU COULD DO FOR *ME*."
--AND THAT CREATURE WE RECOVERED FROM THE WOODS, WELL THAT'S A FIRST FOR THE BUREAU. SHOULD LEARN QUITE A BIT FROM THAT. I NEED TO SEE YOUR REPORT, BUT NICE WORK.
THAT SAID, HOW ABOUT NEXT TIME YOU RUN OFF, YOU TELL US WHERE YOU'RE GOING?
COME ON, KATE. I CAN TAKE CARE OF MYSELF.
AFTER WHAT I PULLED OFF UP THERE ALL ALONE, EVEN *YOU* SHOULD BELIEVE THAT.
WE STILL DON'T KNOW *WHY* YOU WERE THERE IN THE FIRST PLACE. NOBODY HAD REPORTED THOSE PEOPLE MISSING.
DID YOU STUMBLE UPON THIS BY COINCIDENCE WHILE VACATIONING IN BRITISH COLUMBIA?
OR ARE WE SUPPOSED TO BELIEVE YOU MANAGED TO "INTUIT" THE DANGER AND WADED IN SOLO?

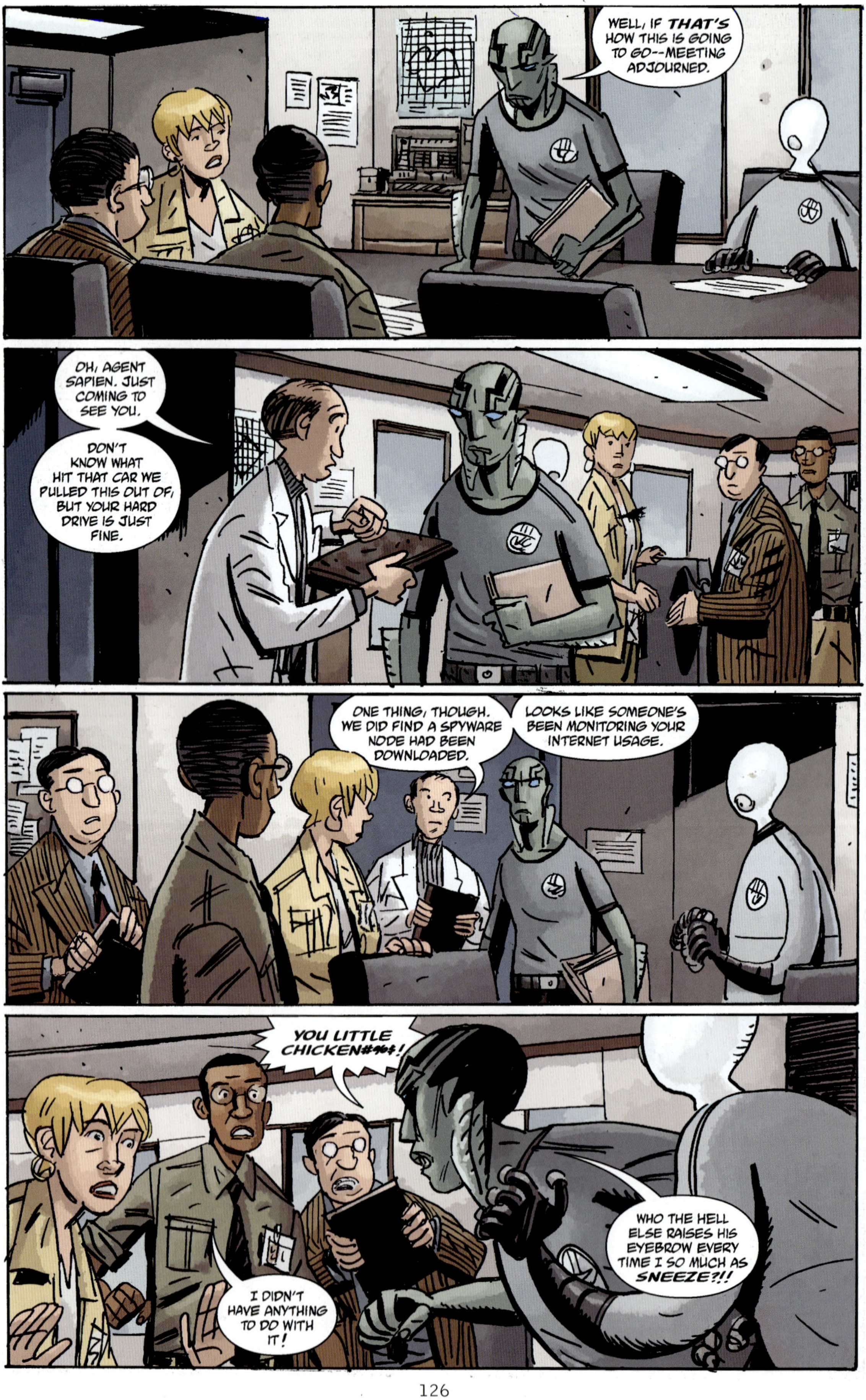
WELL, IF THAT'S HOW THIS IS GOING TO GO--MEETING ADJOURNED.
OH, AGENT SAPIEN. JUST COMING TO SEE YOU.
DON'T KNOW WHAT HIT THAT CAR WE PULLED THIS OUT OF, BUT YOUR HARD DRIVE IS JUST FINE.
ONE THING, THOUGH. WE DID FIND A SPYWARE NODE HAD BEEN DOWNLOADED.
LOOKS LIKE SOMEONE'S BEEN MONITORING YOUR INTERNET USAGE.
YOU LITTLE CHICKEN#%$!
WHO THE HELL ELSE RAISES HIS EYEBROW EVERY TIME I SO MUCH AS SNEEZE?!!
I DIDN'T HAVE ANYTHING TO DO WITH IT!

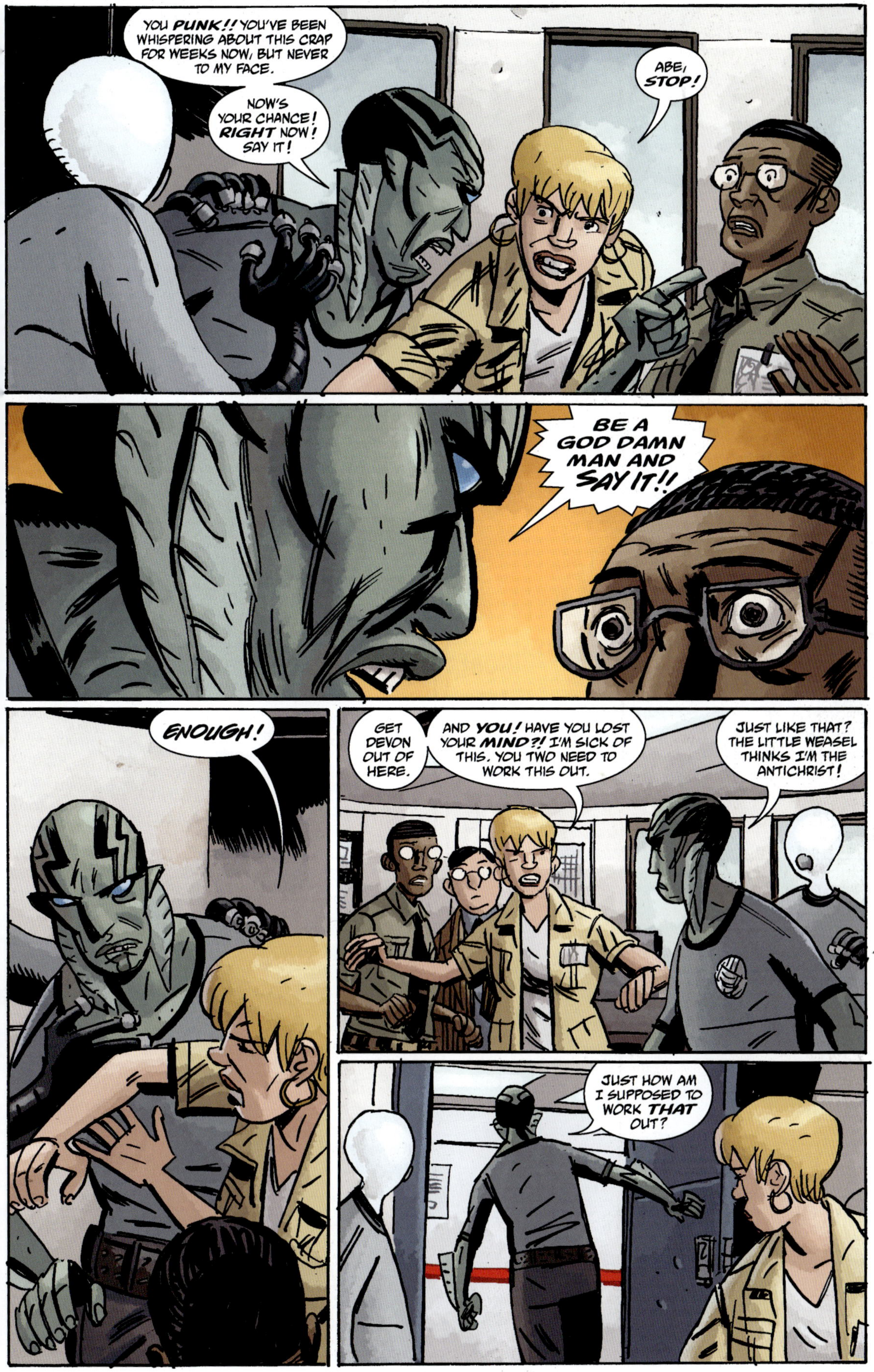
YOU PUNK!! YOU'VE BEEN WHISPERING ABOUT THIS CRAP FOR WEEKS NOW, BUT NEVER TO MY FACE.
NOW'S YOUR CHANCE! RIGHT NOW! SAY IT!
ABE, STOP!
BE A GOD DAMN MAN AND SAY IT!!
ENOUGH!
GET DEVON OUT OF HERE.
AND YOU! HAVE YOU LOST YOUR MIND?! I'M SICK OF THIS. YOU TWO NEED TO WORK THIS OUT.
JUST LIKE THAT? THE LITTLE WEASEL THINKS I'M THE ANTICHRIST!
JUST HOW AM I SUPPOSED TO WORK THAT OUT?

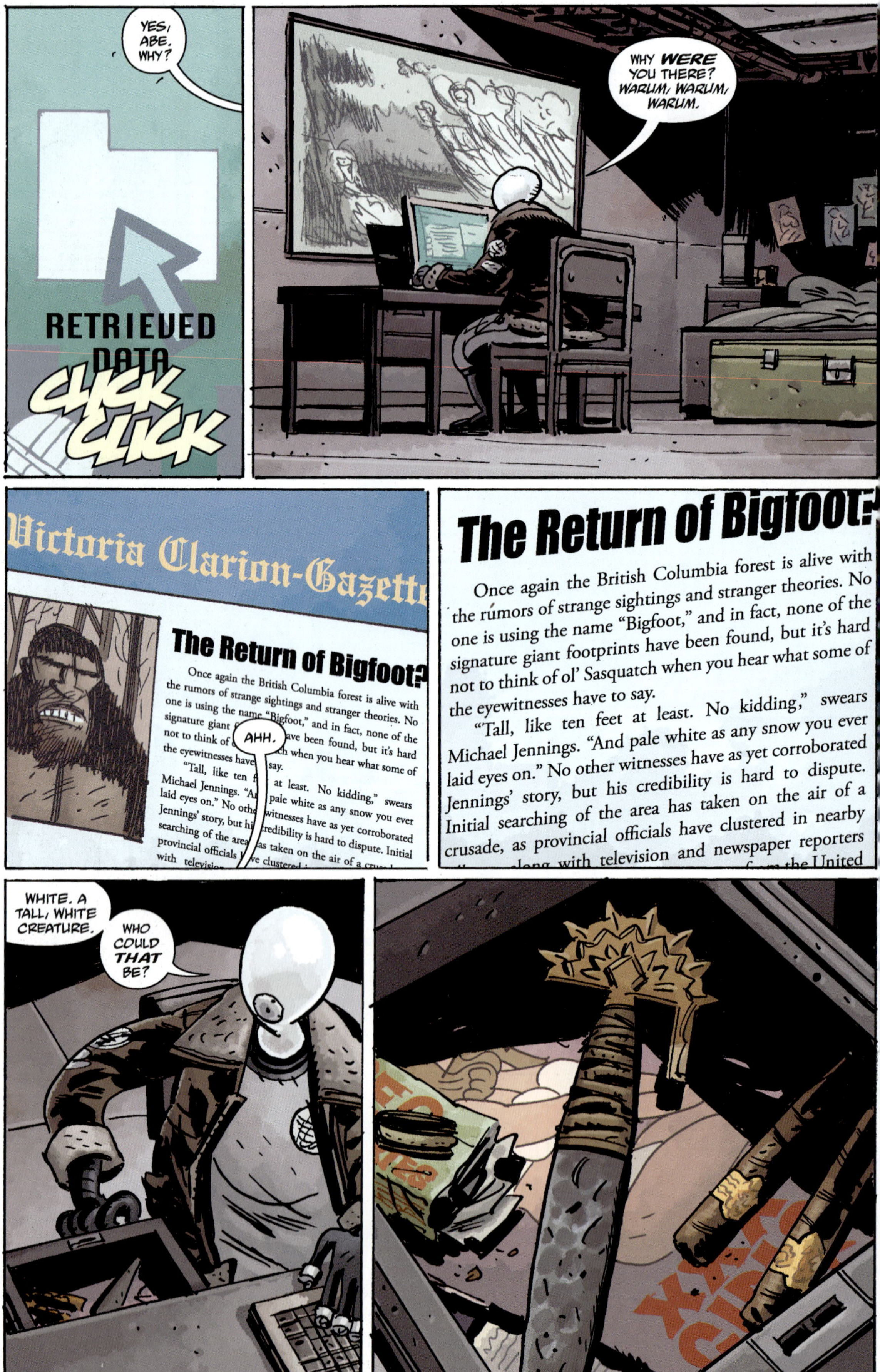
YES, ABE. WHY?
RETRIEVED DATA
CLICK CLICK
WHY WERE YOU THERE? WARUM, WARUM, WARUM.
Victoria Clarion-Gazette
The Return of Bigfoot?
AHH.
The Return of Bigfoot?
Once again the British Columbia forest is alive with the rumors of strange sightings and stranger theories. No one is using the name "Bigfoot," and in fact, none of the signature giant footprints have been found, but it's hard not to think of ol' Sasquatch when you hear what some of the eyewitnesses have to say.
"Tall, like ten feet at least. No kidding," swears Michael Jennings. "And pale white as any snow you ever laid eyes on." No other witnesses have as yet corroborated Jennings' story, but his credibility is hard to dispute. Initial searching of the area has taken on the air of a crusade, as provincial officials have clustered in nearby with television and newspaper reporters
WHITE. A TALL, WHITE CREATURE.
WHO COULD THAT BE?

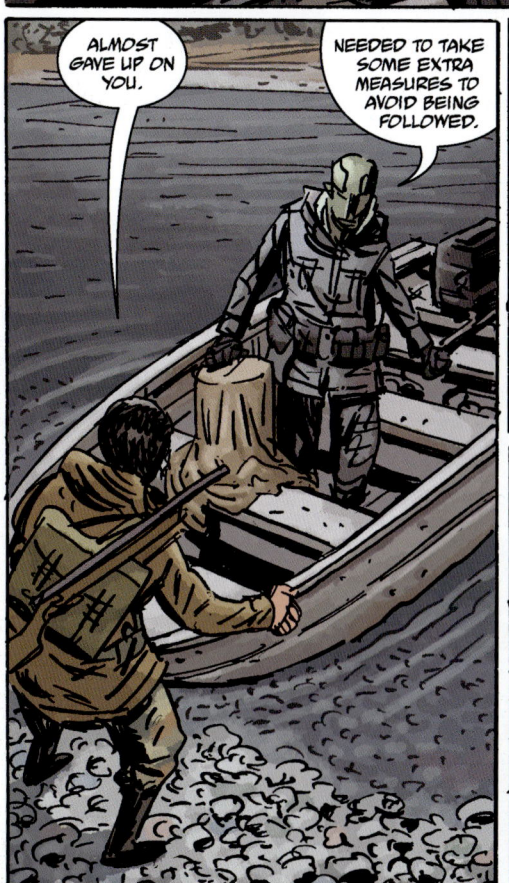

Panel 2:
— OVER HERE!

Panel 3:
— ALMOST GAVE UP ON YOU.
— NEEDED TO TAKE SOME EXTRA MEASURES TO AVOID BEING FOLLOWED.

Panel 4:
— FOLLOWED? YOU DIDN'T--
— NO, I DIDN'T TELL THEM ABOUT YOU. IT'S JUST THAT...YOU KNOW WHAT, IT'S A LONG STORY.

Panel 5:
— SO'D YOU FIND IT?
— I'M HERE, RIGHT?

LAMINATED. NICE TOUCH.
AND A SURPRISE. COHIBAS!
WORKING FOR THE U.N. HAS ITS PERKS.
WE'LL HAVE TO SMOKE A FEW OF THESE ON YOUR NEXT VISIT.
SURE. IF THE WORLD'S STILL HERE.
KEEP YOUR HEAD DOWN, BROTHER.
THE END

SEATTLE

ILLUSTRATION BY **GUY DAVIS** WITH **DAVE STEWART**

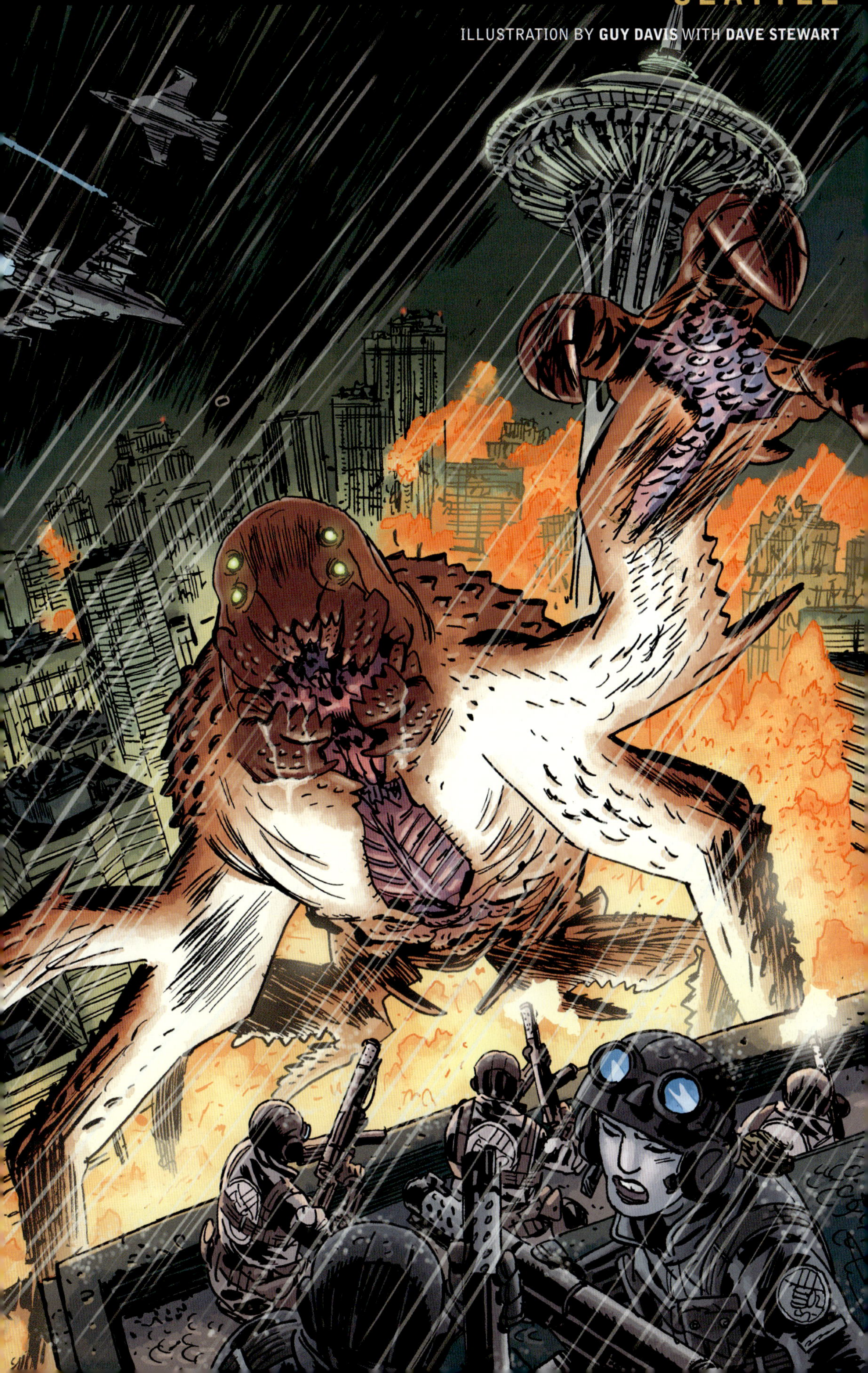

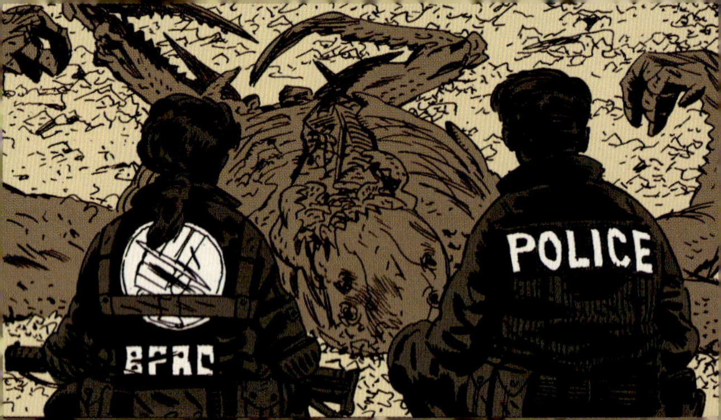

POLICE

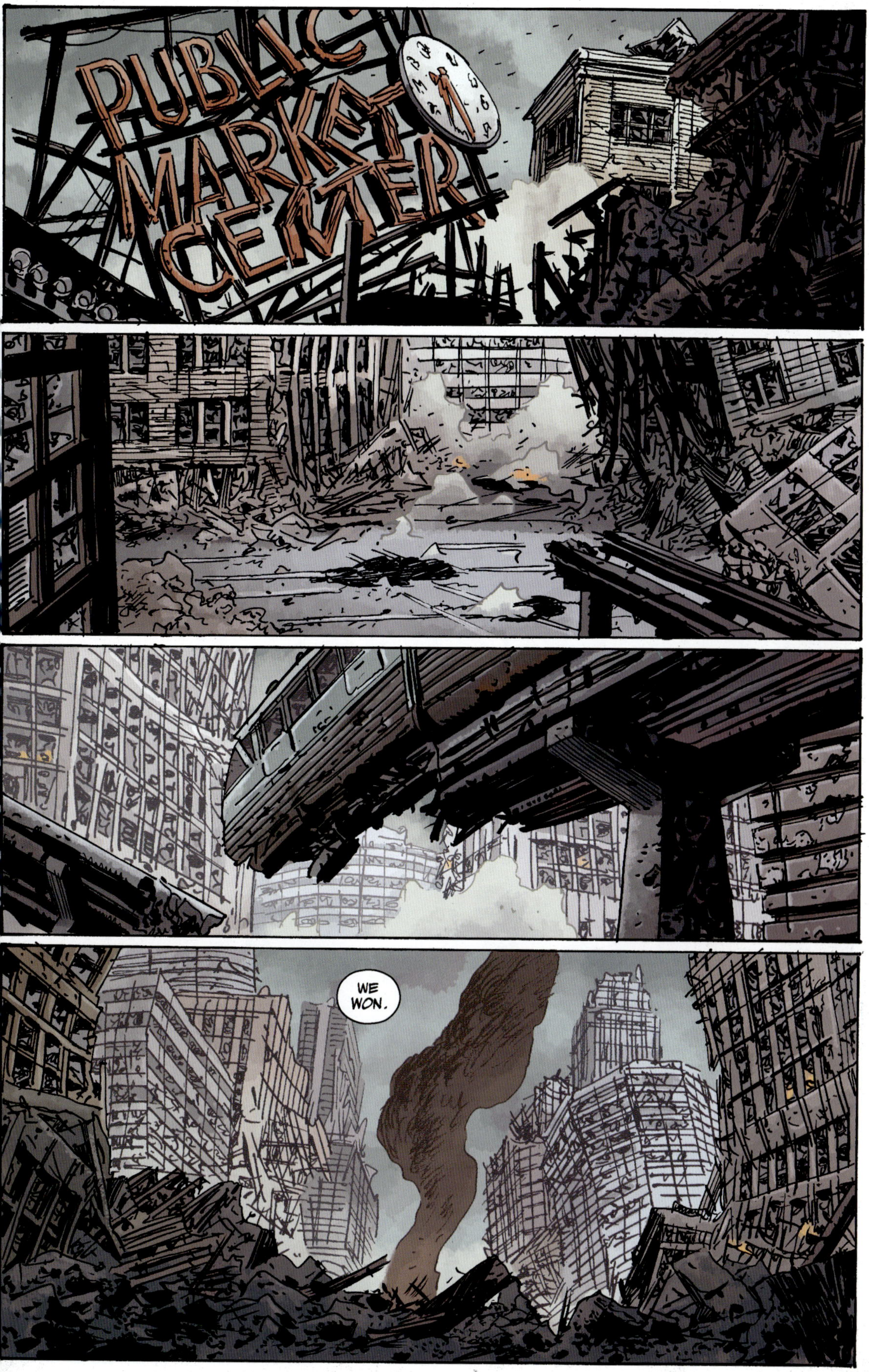
PUBLIC
MARKET
CENTER
WE WON.

YES, THAT'S WHAT I SAID. EVERYTHING'S FINE.

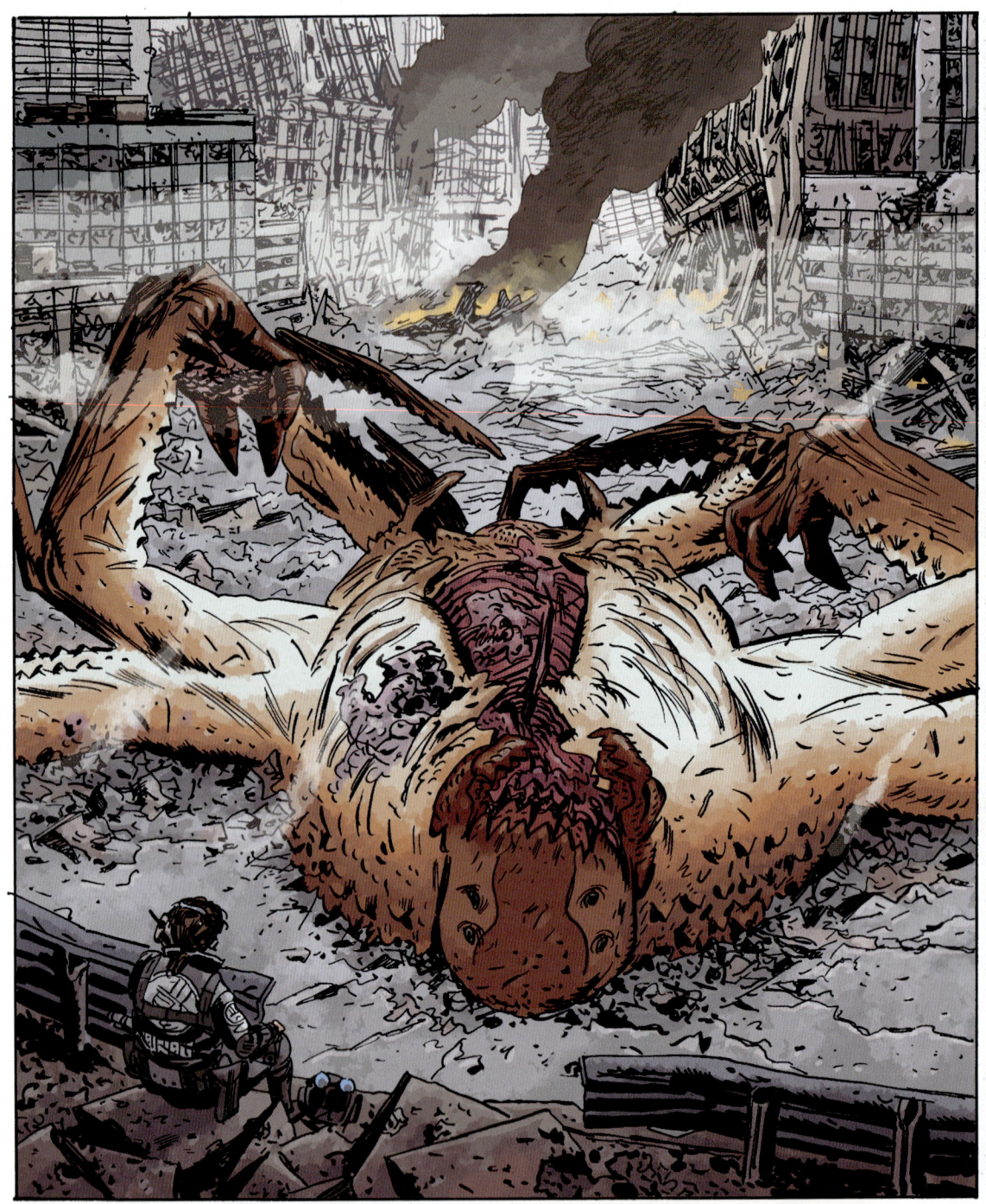

ARE YOU SURE, CARLA?

BECAUSE THAT'S NOT WHAT WE'RE SEEING HERE ON C.N.N.
LIVE
SEATT
YEAH, THEY TELL ME THE FEEDS WENT OUT ABOUT HALF AN HOUR AGO.
CELLS AREN'T WORKING EITHER. THAT'S WHY I HAD TO USE THE SATELLITE PHONE, BUT TRUST ME--

--IT'S ALL OVER. I'M JUST WAITING FOR THE CLEANUP CREW.
BETTER GO. I SHOULD SAVE THE BATTERY ON THIS THING.
POLICE
HEY.
THE WICKED WITCH IS DEAD, HUH?
POL
FINALLY.
I THOUGHT I WAS THE ONLY ONE AROUND HERE. WHEN THE MISSILES STARTED FLYING, EVERYBODY CLEARED OUT.
BUM KNEE, OR I'D BE GONE TOO.
HEY, WHAT ABOUT--?
EJECTED, BUT WITH THIS WIND... WELL, LAST I SAW OF HIM HE WAS FLOATING TOWARD BELLTOWN.

LISTEN TO YOU. "BELLTOWN." YOU FROM HERE?
UPSTATE NEW YORK.
BUT MY GRANDMA LIVED IN WALLINGFORD.
EVERY SUMMER WE'D COME OUT FOR TWO WEEKS, ME AND MY BROTHERS. IT WAS AMAZING.
THE FIRST SUMMER WE WENT CANOEING IN LAKE WASHINGTON. I'D NEVER EVEN SEEN A CANOE BEFORE. IT WAS LIKE PARADISE NEXT TO ROCHESTER.
SUMMERTIME HERE? YEAH, PARADISE IS A GOOD WORD FOR IT.
POLICE
BPRD
MAYBE NOT THIS SUMMER.

I HEARD WHAT YOU SAID. ON THE PHONE.
YOU'RE WRONG. WE DIDN'T WIN.
BPRD
I DON'T THINK HE'S GETTING UP AGAIN.
OKAY, YEAH, TODAY WE WON.
BUT WE'RE NOT REALLY "WINNING," ARE WE?
POLIC
I MEAN, HALF INDONESIA'S GONE, HOUSTON'S GONE, A GIANT LOBSTER'S SQUATTIN' IN CALIFORNIA--
--AND NOW... SEATTLE.
HOW'S ROCHESTER HOLDING UP?
I DON'T KNOW WHY THIS IS HAPPENING, BUT I KNOW IT WON'T STOP. AND IF I HAD A BRAIN, WHY, I'D MOVE WAAAAAY UP TO THE MOUNTAINS AND HIDE.
WHY DON'T YOU?
THIS IS HOME.

I DON'T HEAR YOU SAYING I'M WRONG. HELL, YOU'D HAVE TO KNOW BETTER THAN I WOULD. YOU'RE IN THE BUREAU. YOU'VE GOT MORE INFORMATION THAN I DO.
DO **YOU** THINK WE CAN "WIN"?
I DON'T KNOW...
MAYBE WE CAN'T. BUT MAYBE WE'RE NOT EVEN SUPPOSED TO.
WHAT?
POLICE
YOU'RE A COP. HAS ANYBODY ON THE FORCE EVER THOUGHT **YOU** GUYS WERE REALLY GOING TO "WIN" SOMEDAY?
DOESN'T STOP YOU FROM DOING YOUR JOB, DOES IT?
AHHH, HERE THEY COME.
POLICE

SO YOU'RE SAYING THAT THIS IS HOW IT'S GOING TO BE FROM NOW ON? YOU AND THE U.N. JUST TRYING TO STAY ONE STEP AHEAD OF MONSTERS AND VOLCANOES?
MAYBE.
KEE-RIST! WELL, THAT JUST MAKES YOU WANNA GO OUT AND GET DRUNK, DOESN'T IT?
DOESN'T IT?
NOPE.
MAKES ME WANT TO HEAD HOME AND HUG MY THREE-YEAR-OLD SON.
POLICE
THE END

GODS CHAPTER ONE

ILLUSTRATION BY **RYAN SOOK**

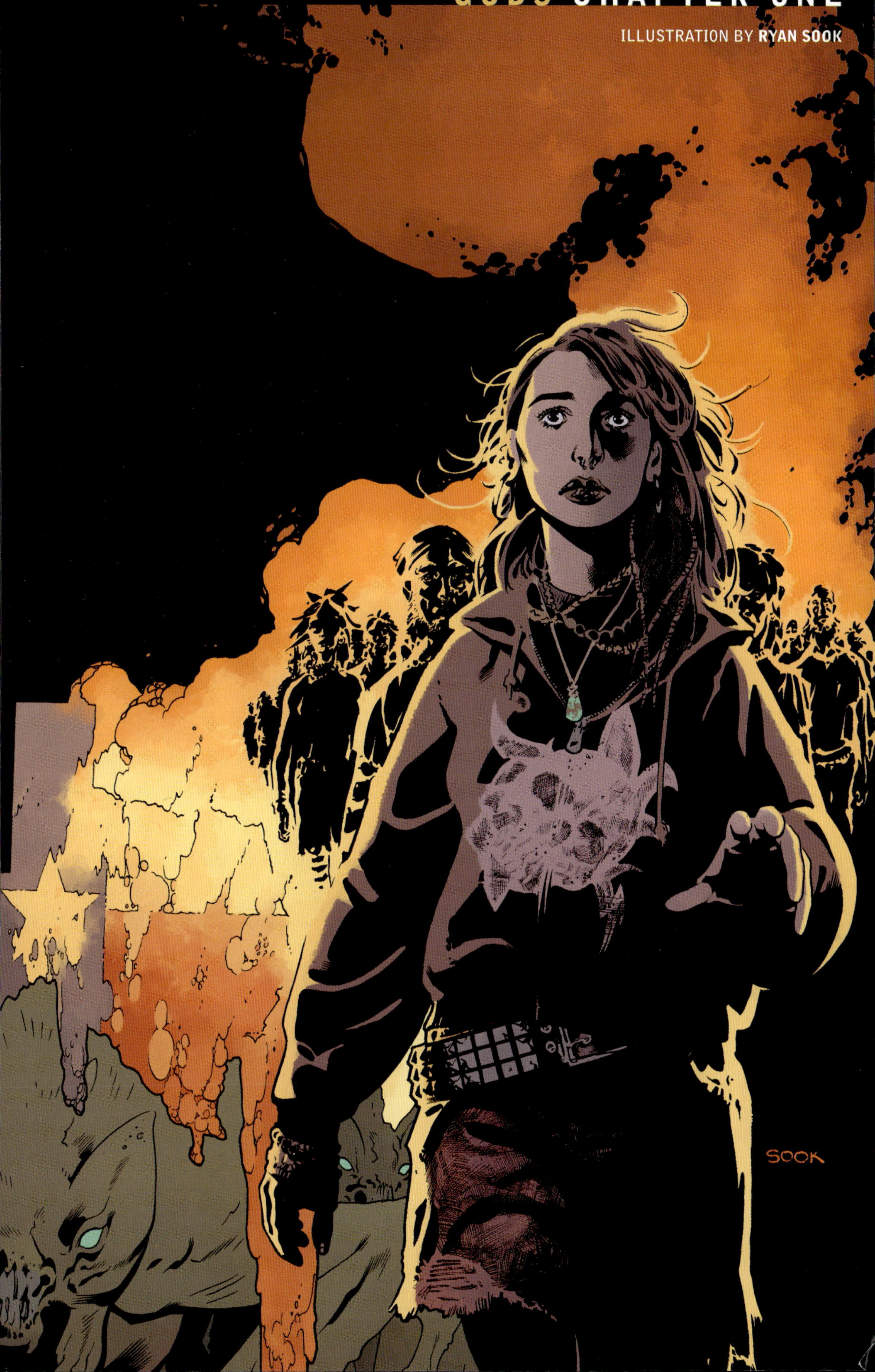
SOOK

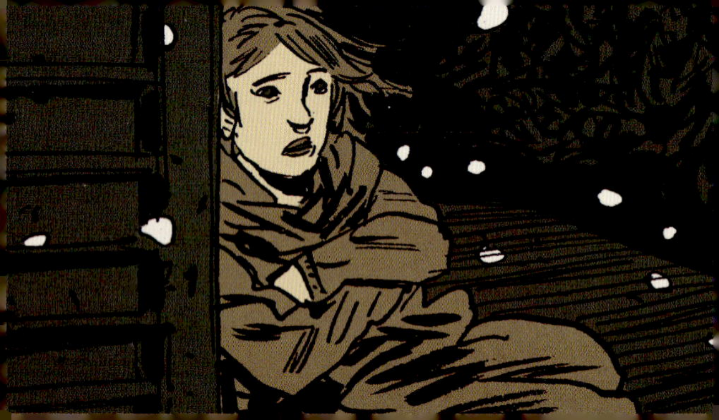

RRRAAAR
YEAH, I KNOW FOLKS IS TRYIN' T' GET OUTTA TEXAS, BUT THAT AIN'T **OUR** PROBLEM.
I **DON'T** GOT A PROBLEM WITH IT, BUT SO FAR THIS WEEK WE AIN'T FOUND ONE RIDER.
NOT ONE. SO WHAT'S THE POINT?
KEEP HOPE ALIVE, CHAZ. KEEP IT ALIVE.

COFF
COFF
AH, SEE? RIGHT THERE.
BOUND TO BE ONE SOONER OR LATER.
COME ON. OUT!
WAIT NOW. TAKE IT EASY. MY FRIEND'S SICK.
OKAY. WE LET HIM IN, THEN.
GRRRR
RAWF!
I DIDN'T SAY I WOULDN'T COME OUT.
I JUST WAS SAYING--

SHUT UP!
THWAK
GOD DAMN BEANER! NO FREE RIDE OUTTA HELL FOR YOU! NOT ON MY SHIFT!
WHUMP
ENOUGHA THAT.

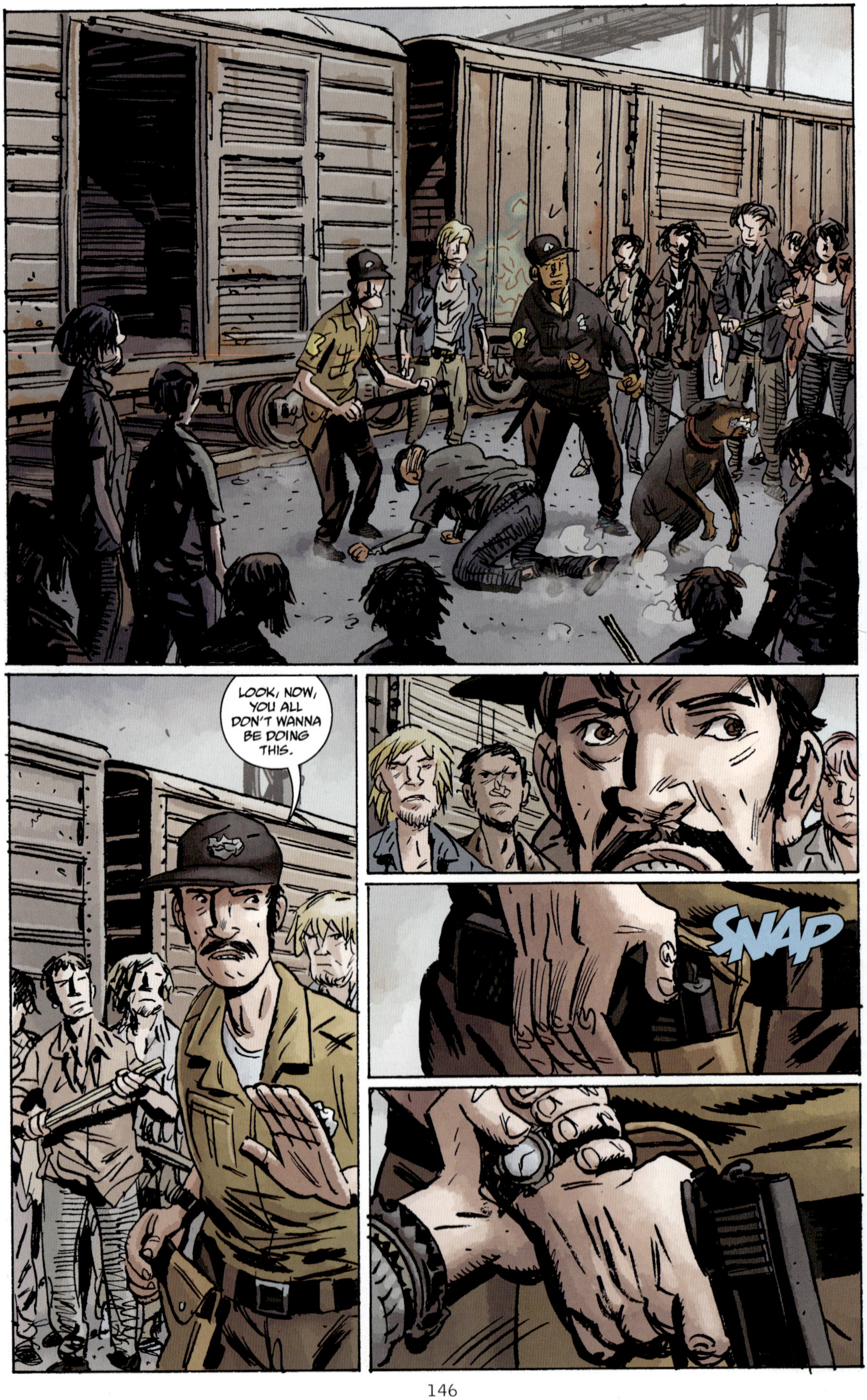
LOOK, NOW, YOU ALL DON'T WANNA BE DOING THIS.
SNAP

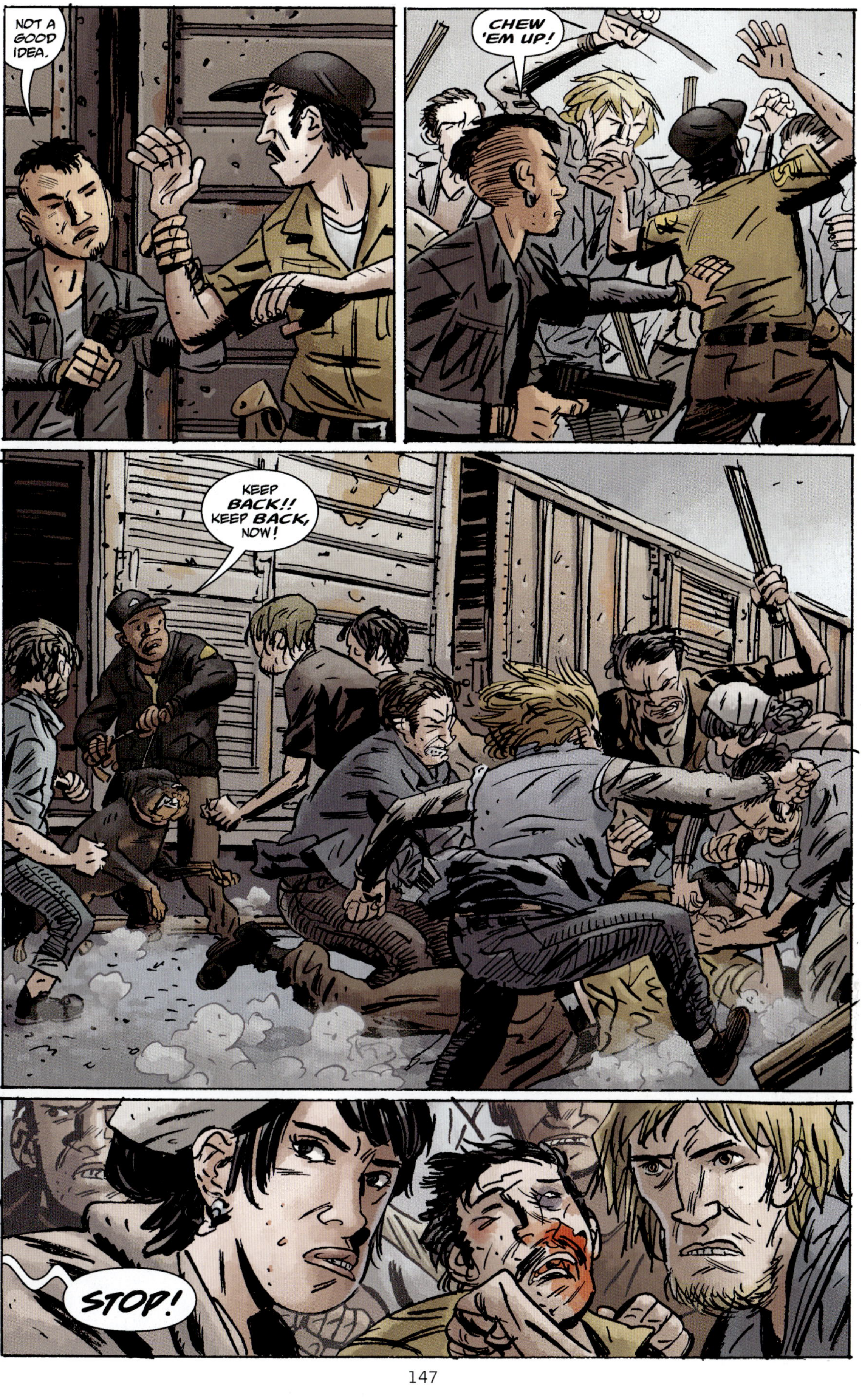
NOT A GOOD IDEA.
CHEW 'EM UP!
KEEP BACK!! KEEP BACK, NOW!
STOP!

LET 'EM GO.
COFF COFF COFF
WHY YOU LOOKING AT ME, MAN?
YOU HEARD HER.

MAN, YOU GUYS WERE GONE FOREVER! HOW 'BOUT THOSE MEDS?
JUST COUGH SYRUP. LIKE I TOLD YOU, ONLY DRUGSTORE IN THIS TOWN, 'SCRIPS ARE UNDER LOCK AND KEY.
SHOULDN'TA LET THEM GO.
BE BACK WITH REAL COPS IN NO TIME. SHOTGUNS AND EVERYTHING. YOU KNOW THAT, RIGHT?
THAT'S WHAT FENIX WANTED.
WHAT'S THAT ABOUT, ANYWAY? SIXTEEN-YEAR-OLD GIRL TELLING EVERYBODY WHAT TO DO?
YOU DON'T LIKE IT?
NO, NO. DON'T GET ME WRONG.
I MEAN, I'M GLAD I MET UP WITH YOU GUYS AND ALL. FEEL A LOT SAFER, BELIEVE ME.
"I'M JUST THINKIN'...WHAT'S THE DEAL?"

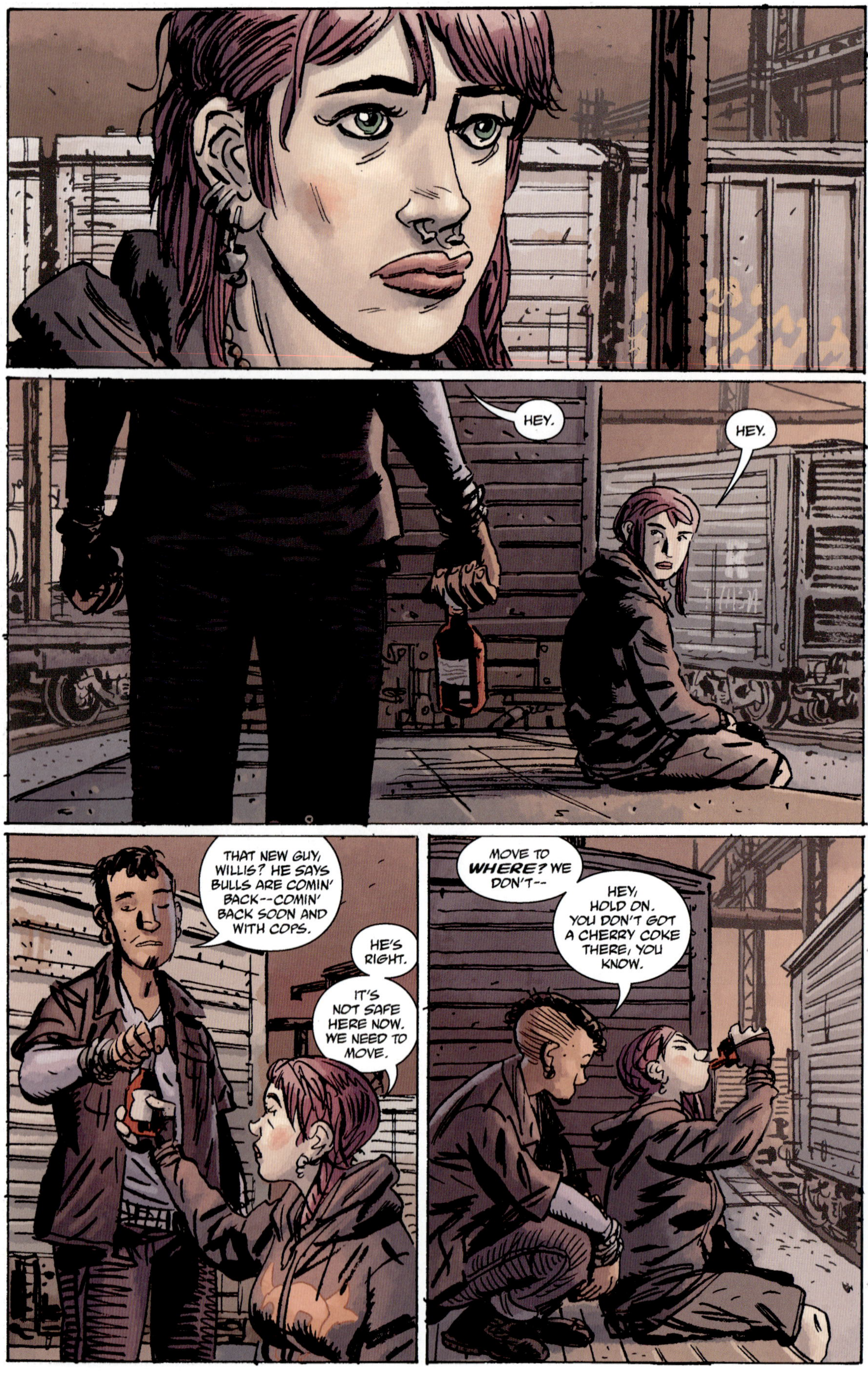
HEY.
HEY.
THAT NEW GUY, WILLIS? HE SAYS BULLS ARE COMIN' BACK--COMIN' BACK SOON AND WITH COPS.
HE'S RIGHT.
IT'S NOT SAFE HERE NOW. WE NEED TO MOVE.
MOVE TO *WHERE?* WE DON'T--
HEY, HOLD ON. YOU DON'T GOT A CHERRY COKE THERE, YOU KNOW.

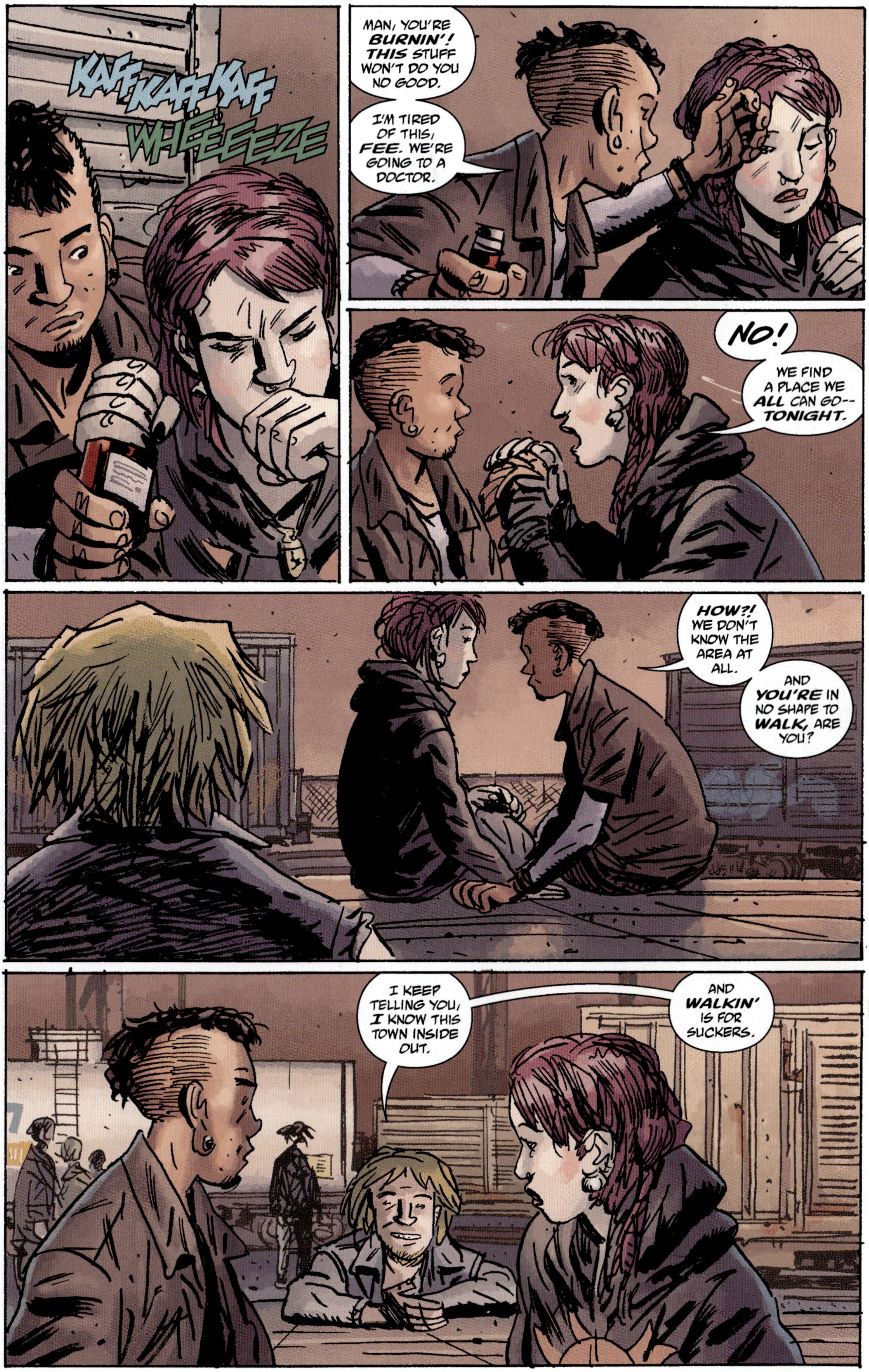
KAFF KAFF KAFF
WHEEEEEZE
MAN, YOU'RE **BURNIN'! THIS** STUFF WON'T DO YOU NO GOOD.
I'M TIRED OF THIS, **FEE**. WE'RE GOING TO A DOCTOR.
NO!
WE FIND A PLACE WE **ALL** CAN GO-- **TONIGHT.**
HOW?! WE DON'T KNOW THE AREA AT ALL.
AND **YOU'RE** IN NO SHAPE TO **WALK,** ARE YOU?
I KEEP TELLING YOU, **I** KNOW THIS TOWN INSIDE OUT.
AND **WALKIN'** IS FOR SUCKERS.

THAT WAS PRETTY SLICK. NEVER SAW ANY-BODY HOT-WIRE A CAR BEFORE.
AH, THE OLDER MAKES ARE A CINCH.
AND ALL THAT'S BEEN GOING ON LATELY, THIS TOWN'S HALF-ABANDONED. LIKE A BIG PARKING LOT, REALLY.
BE WHERE WE NEED TO BE TEN, FIFTEEN MINUTES.
PLENTY OF TIME TO FILL ME IN ON JOAN OF ARC.
HEY, KEEP IT DOWN, WILL YA?
DEAD TO THE WORLD.
SO...? I'VE EARNED IT, HAVEN'T I?
YEAH, I GUESS.
"OKAY, WE WERE IN HOUSTON TWO WEEKS AGO. ME, FENIX, DINGO, SOME OTHERS.

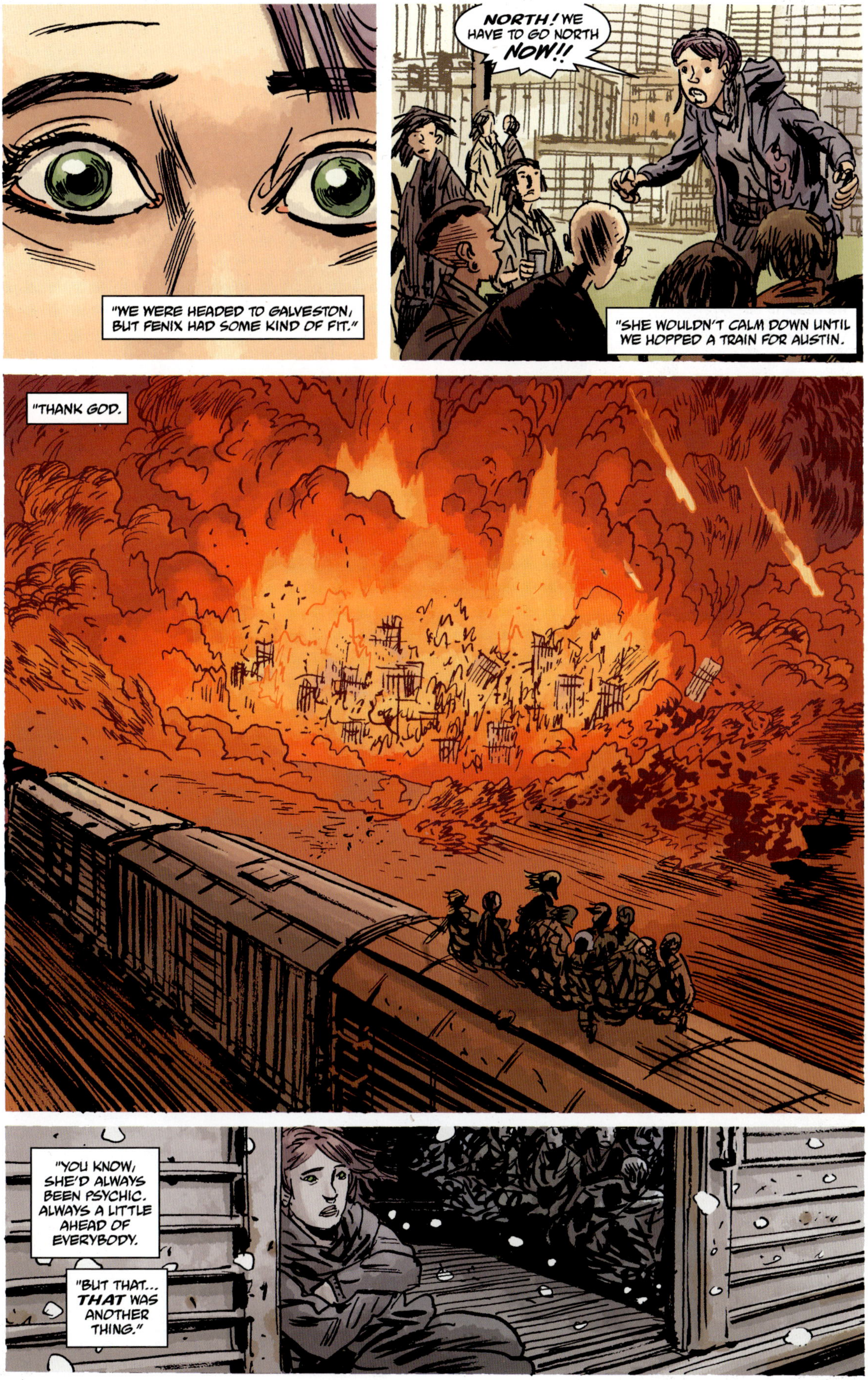
"WE WERE HEADED TO GALVESTON, BUT FENIX HAD SOME KIND OF FIT."
NORTH! WE HAVE TO GO NORTH NOW!!
"SHE WOULDN'T CALM DOWN UNTIL WE HOPPED A TRAIN FOR AUSTIN.
"THANK GOD.
"YOU KNOW, SHE'D ALWAYS BEEN PSYCHIC. ALWAYS A LITTLE AHEAD OF EVERYBODY.
"BUT THAT... THAT WAS ANOTHER THING."

DAMN! LUCKY BREAK FOR YOU GUYS.
YOU KNOW, I HEARD ANIMALS CAN SENSE STUFF LIKE THAT, TOO. EARTHQUAKES AND STUFF.
WEEK LATER--
"--WE ALL THOUGHT WE WERE SAFE WHEN WE GOT TO SAN ANGELO, BUT FENIX KEPT US MOVING.
"SOMEHOW SHE KNEW ALL ABOUT WHAT WAS COMING OUR WAY."
WHEW! YEAH, I HEARD ABOUT THOSE MOTHERS.
EVER SINCE THE VOLCANO BLEW IN HOUSTON, THEY BEEN SHOWING UP.

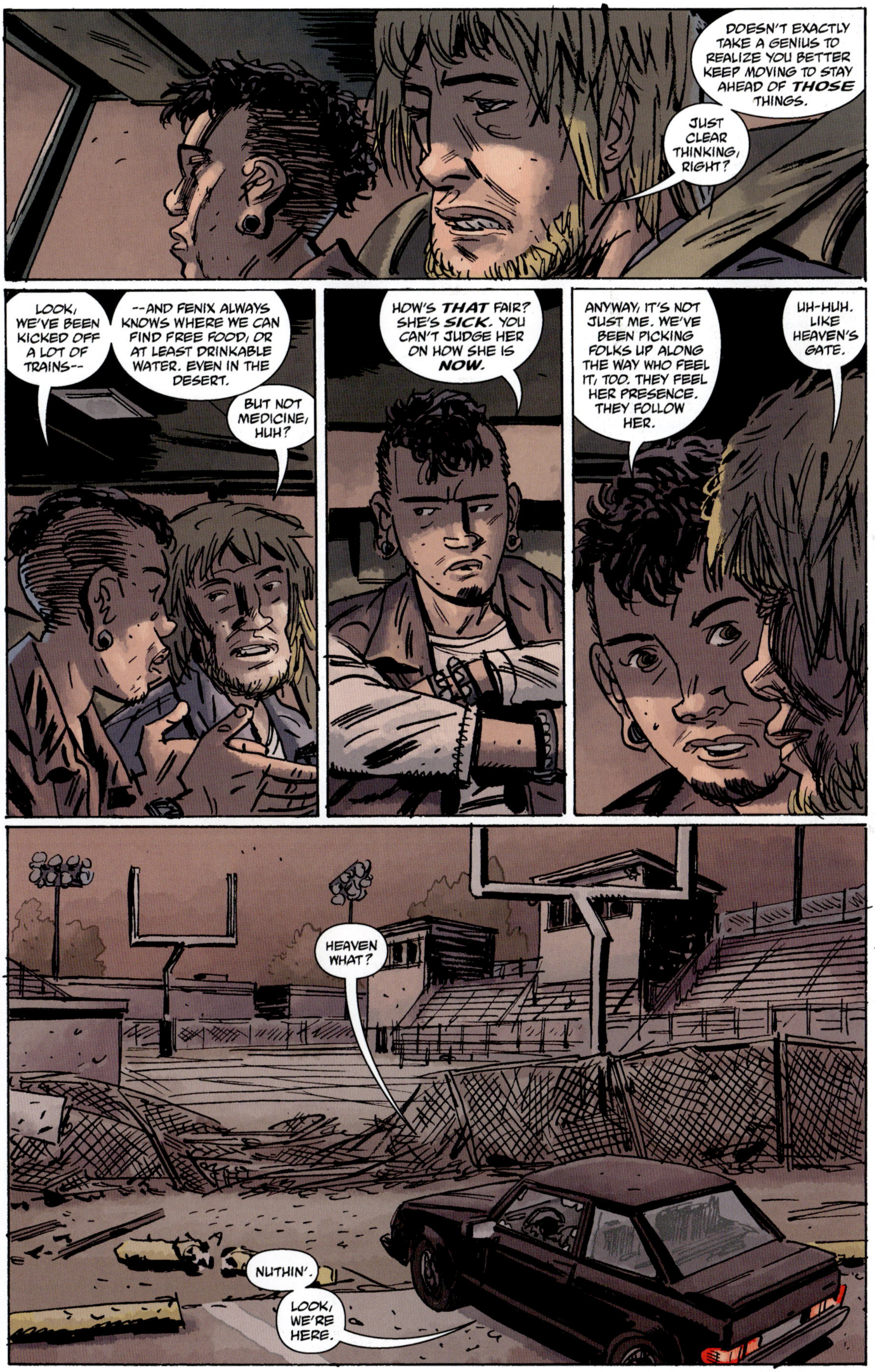
DOESN'T EXACTLY TAKE A GENIUS TO REALIZE YOU BETTER KEEP MOVING TO STAY AHEAD OF THOSE THINGS.
JUST CLEAR THINKING, RIGHT?
LOOK, WE'VE BEEN KICKED OFF A LOT OF TRAINS--
--AND FENIX ALWAYS KNOWS WHERE WE CAN FIND FREE FOOD, OR AT LEAST DRINKABLE WATER. EVEN IN THE DESERT.
BUT NOT MEDICINE, HUH?
HOW'S THAT FAIR? SHE'S SICK. YOU CAN'T JUDGE HER ON HOW SHE IS NOW.
ANYWAY, IT'S NOT JUST ME. WE'VE BEEN PICKING FOLKS UP ALONG THE WAY WHO FEEL IT, TOO. THEY FEEL HER PRESENCE. THEY FOLLOW HER.
UH-HUH. LIKE HEAVEN'S GATE.
HEAVEN WHAT?
NUTHIN'.
LOOK, WE'RE HERE.

EMPTY FOR YEARS. KIDS ALL GO TO HIGH SCHOOL NEXT TOWN OVER NOW.
ROOM FOR EVERY-BODY, HIGH WALLS GIVE US COVER FROM THE STREET...
...AND YOU TWO CAN STAY IN THE LOCKER ROOMS.
LITTLE PRIVACY BE NICE, RIGHT?
NO.
WHAT?
AH, YOU GOTTA BE KIDDING ME. GIMME **ONE** GOOD REASON.
YOU DON'T NEED A REASON. WE'RE JUST NOT STAYING HERE.
YOU MEAN **YOU** AREN'T.

WOW! SO WHAT HAPPENED THEN?
COMMUNITY POOL
WELL, THEN HE TOLD US ABOUT THIS PLACE, LET US HAVE THE CAR, AND GAVE US DIRECTIONS.
12
HE'S GOOD PEOPLE, DINGO. HE'S JUST NOT BUYING FENIX'S SECOND SIGHT.
WELL, GIRL IS SICK.
OH, NOW YOU TOO.

JORGE, SHE'S SICK! FEVER SHE'S GOT, PEOPLE SAY ALL KINDS STUFF. WE NEED TO BE GETTING HER TO A DOC.
YOU THINK I DON'T KNOW THAT? YOU THINK I DIDN'T SAY THAT TO HER? SHE DON'T WANNA GO.
12
AND THAT NEW FRIEND WON'T LET US TAKE HER.
OKAY, GREAT FOR HER. BUT WHAT ABOUT ALLS US?
WE OUT HERE IN THE OPEN. COPS, ANYBODY, CAN COME RIGHT DOWN ON OUR ASSES.
NAH, YOU DON'T GOT TO WORRY ABOUT THAT.

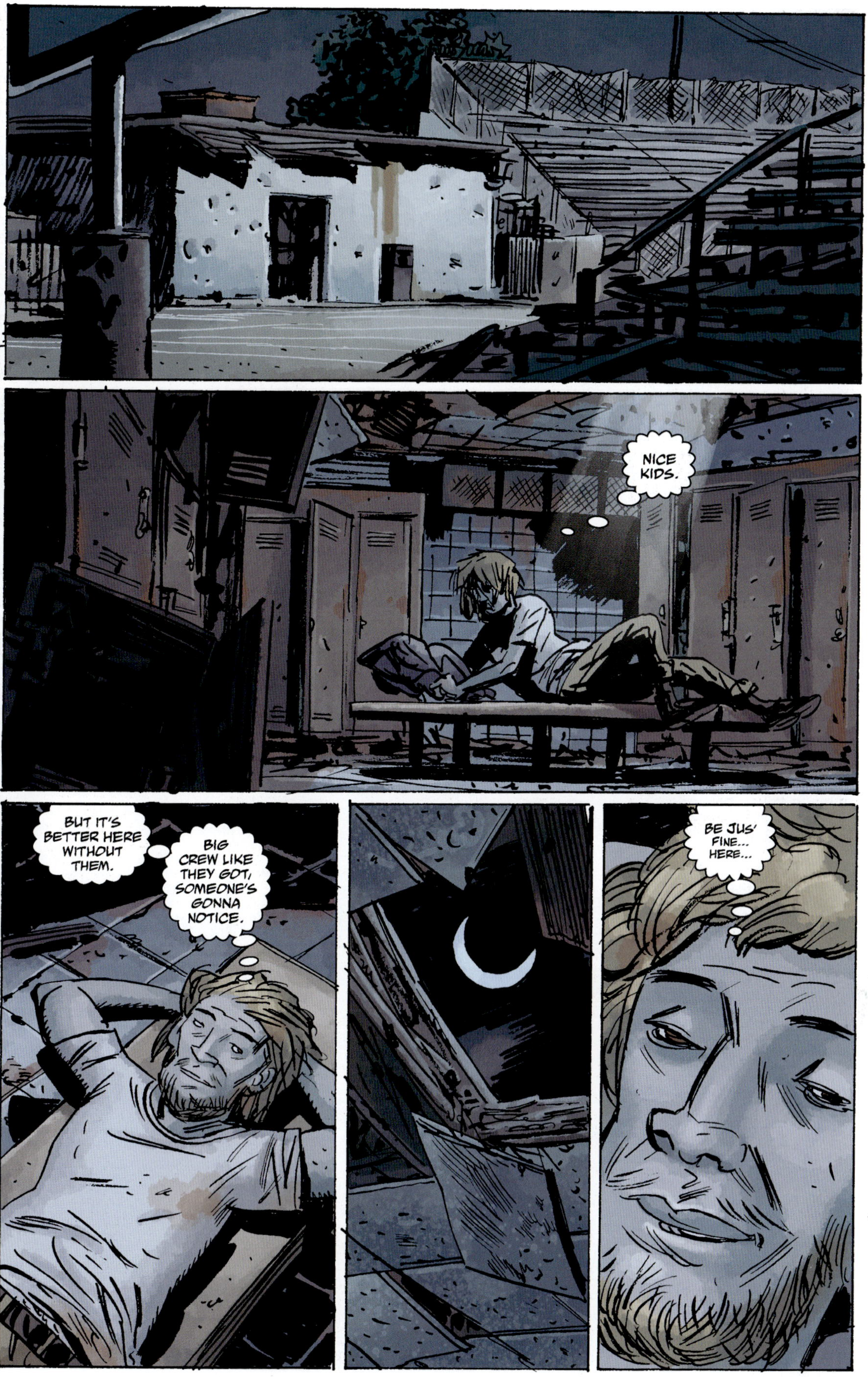
NICE KIDS.
BUT IT'S BETTER HERE WITHOUT THEM.
BIG CREW LIKE THEY GOT, SOMEONE'S GONNA NOTICE.
BE JUS' FINE... HERE...

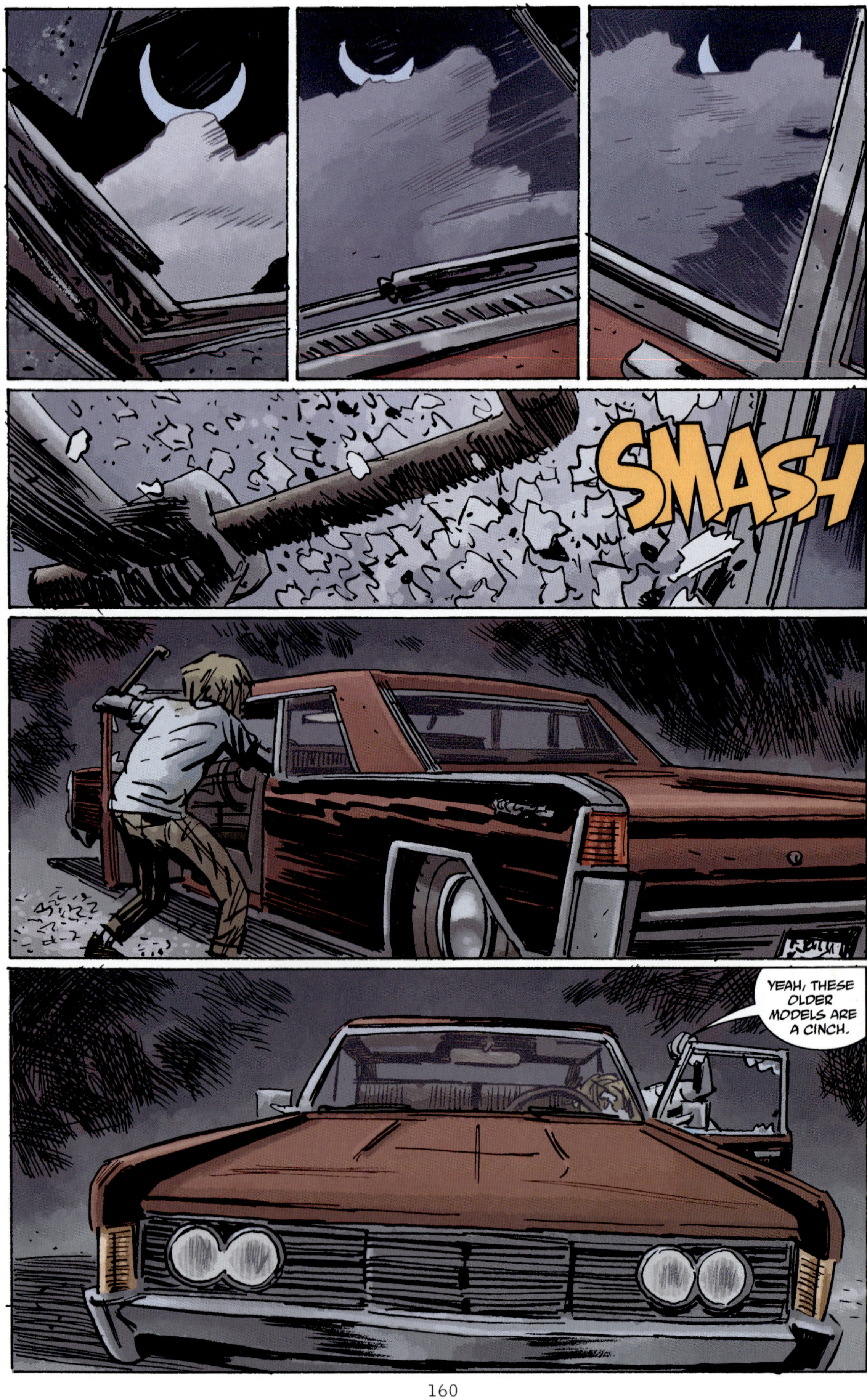
SMASH
YEAH, THESE OLDER MODELS ARE A CINCH.

YEEEHAAA!
REAL COPS NOW, HUH? SHOTGUNS AND EVERY-THING!
WELL, #$%& YOU!!!
HA HA HA HA! I KEEP TELLIN' YOU, I KNOW THIS TOWN!
!

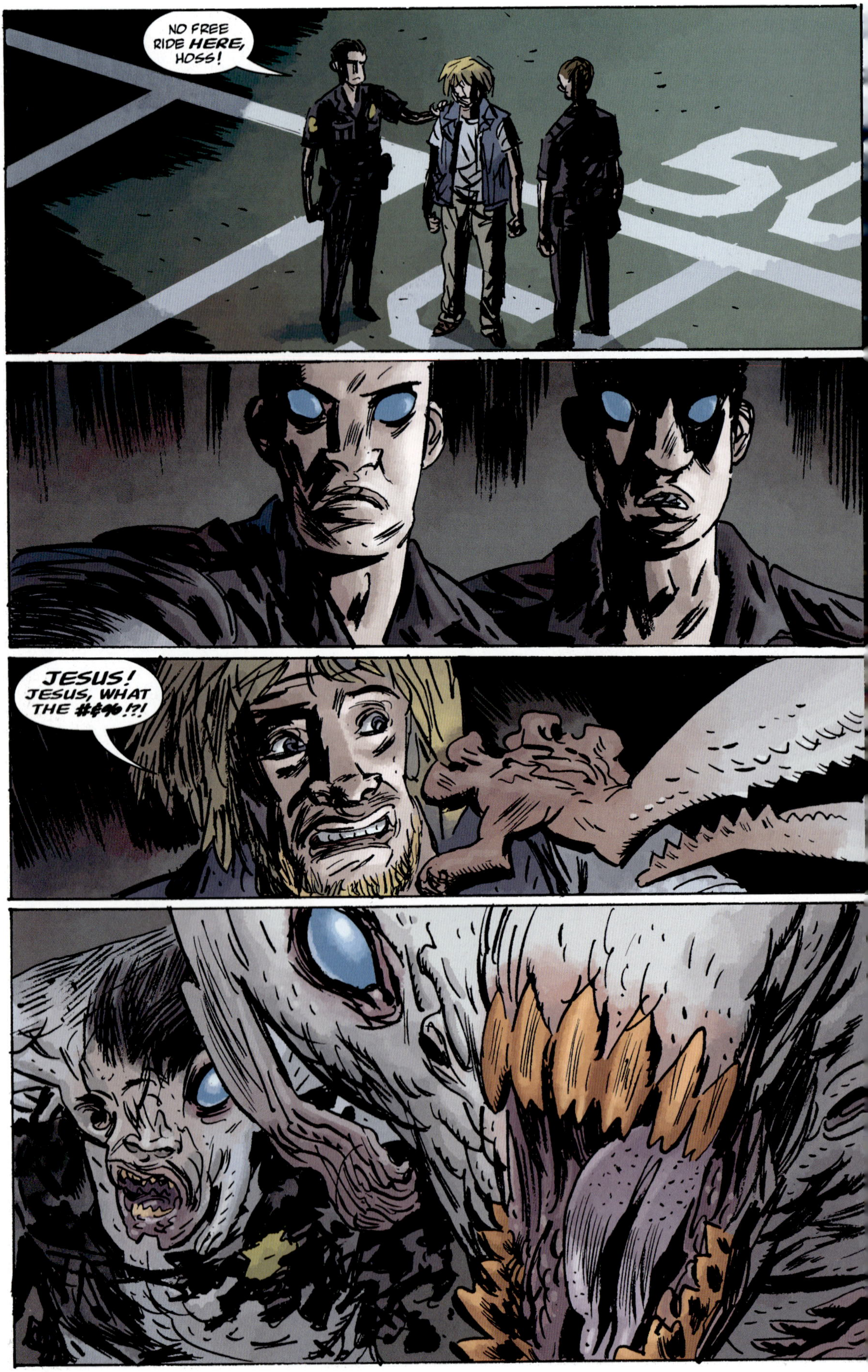
NO FREE RIDE HERE, HOSS!
JESUS! JESUS, WHAT THE #$%!?!

GAAAH!
AW, CRAP! OH, NO. WHAT'S THAT?
CLICK
DAMN! DAMNDAMN DAMNDAMN DAMN!
AND THEY HEARD ME. WHEN I WOKE UP, THEY HEARD THAT.
THEY KNOW I'M HERE.
IF THEY GOT GUNS, OKAY, THAT'S THAT.
BUT IF THEY DON'T, THEN MAYBE...

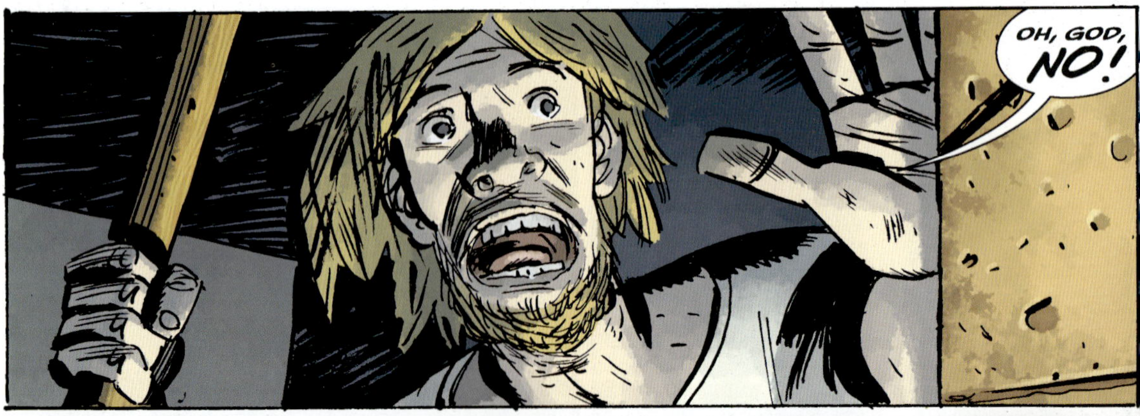
OH, GOD, NO!

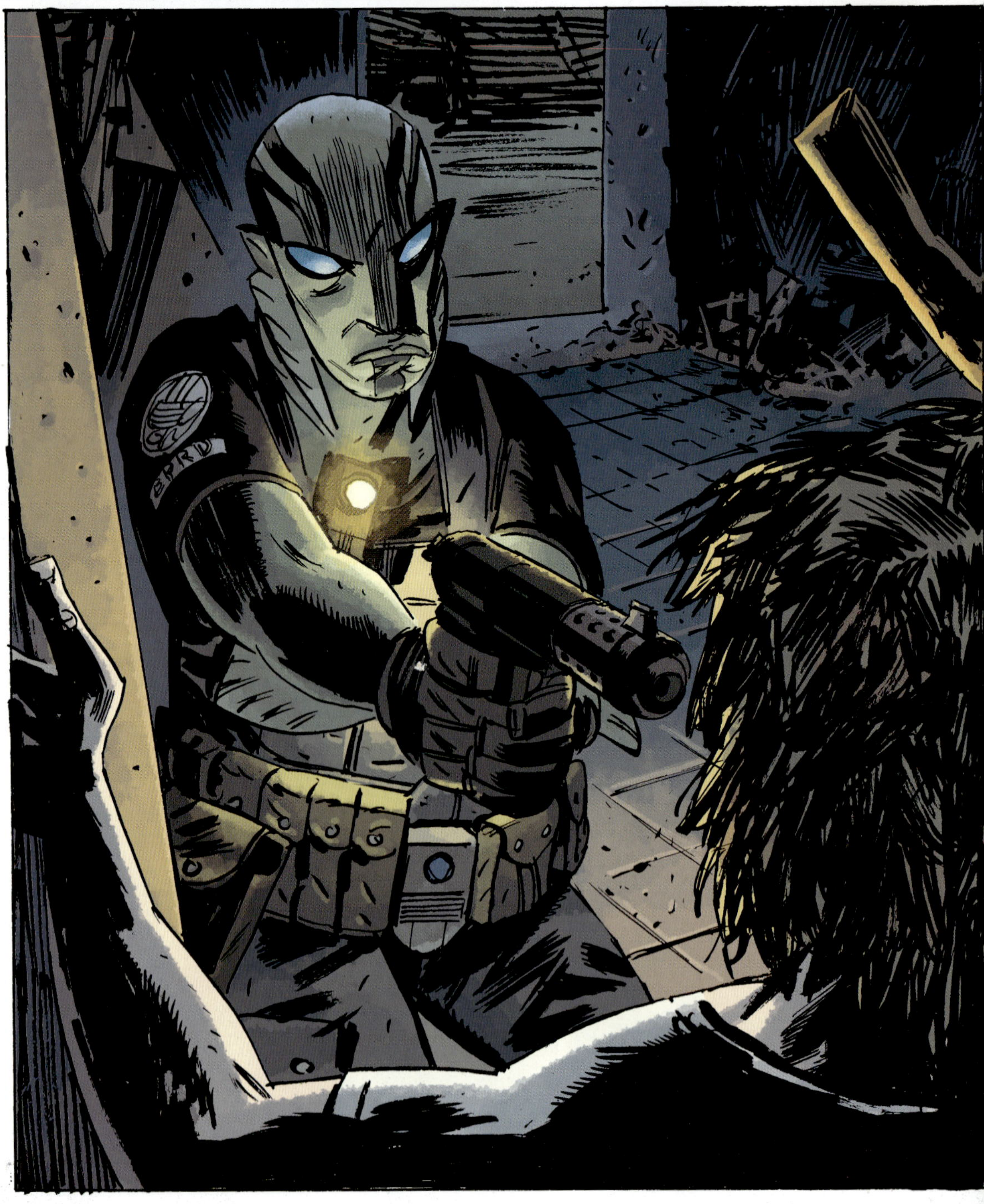

GODS CHAPTER TWO

ILLUSTRATION BY **RYAN SOOK**

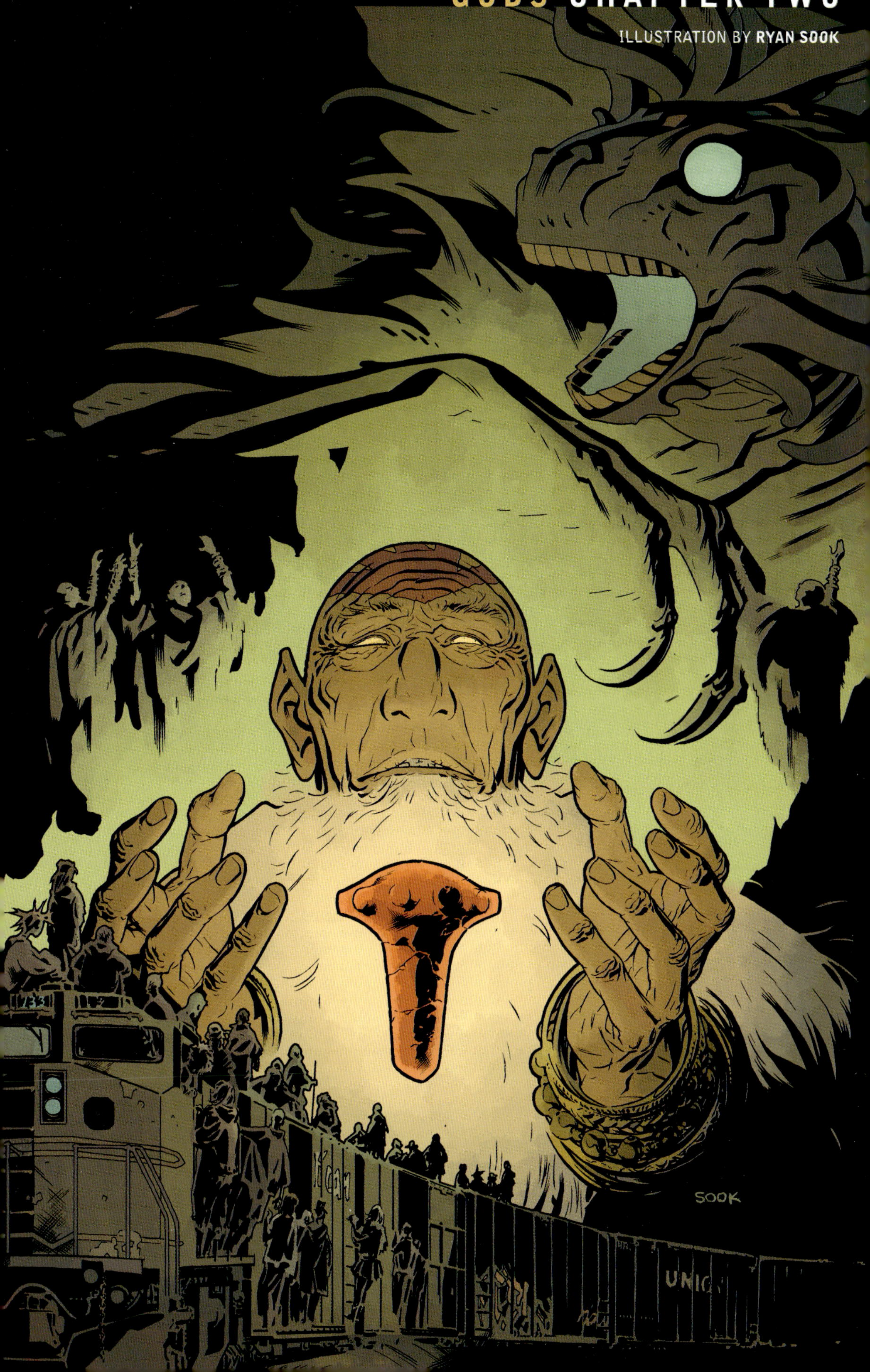
SOOK

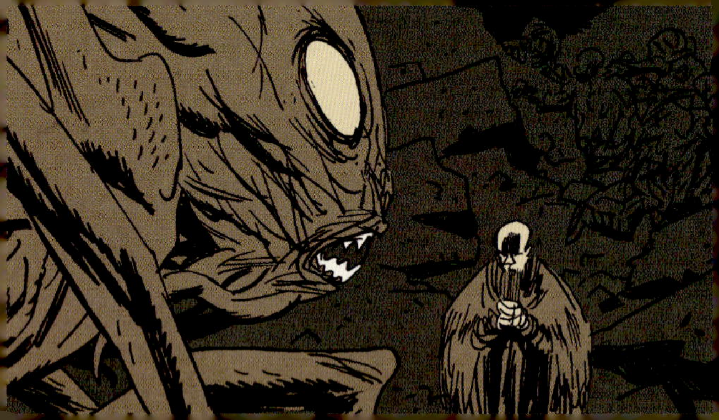

ABE, PLEASE.
WE CAN'T PUT THIS TALK OFF ANY LONGER.
I CAN TALK STANDING UP.
AND YOU CAN BE JUST AS MUCH OF AN #%&%@ SITTING DOWN.
NOW SIT!

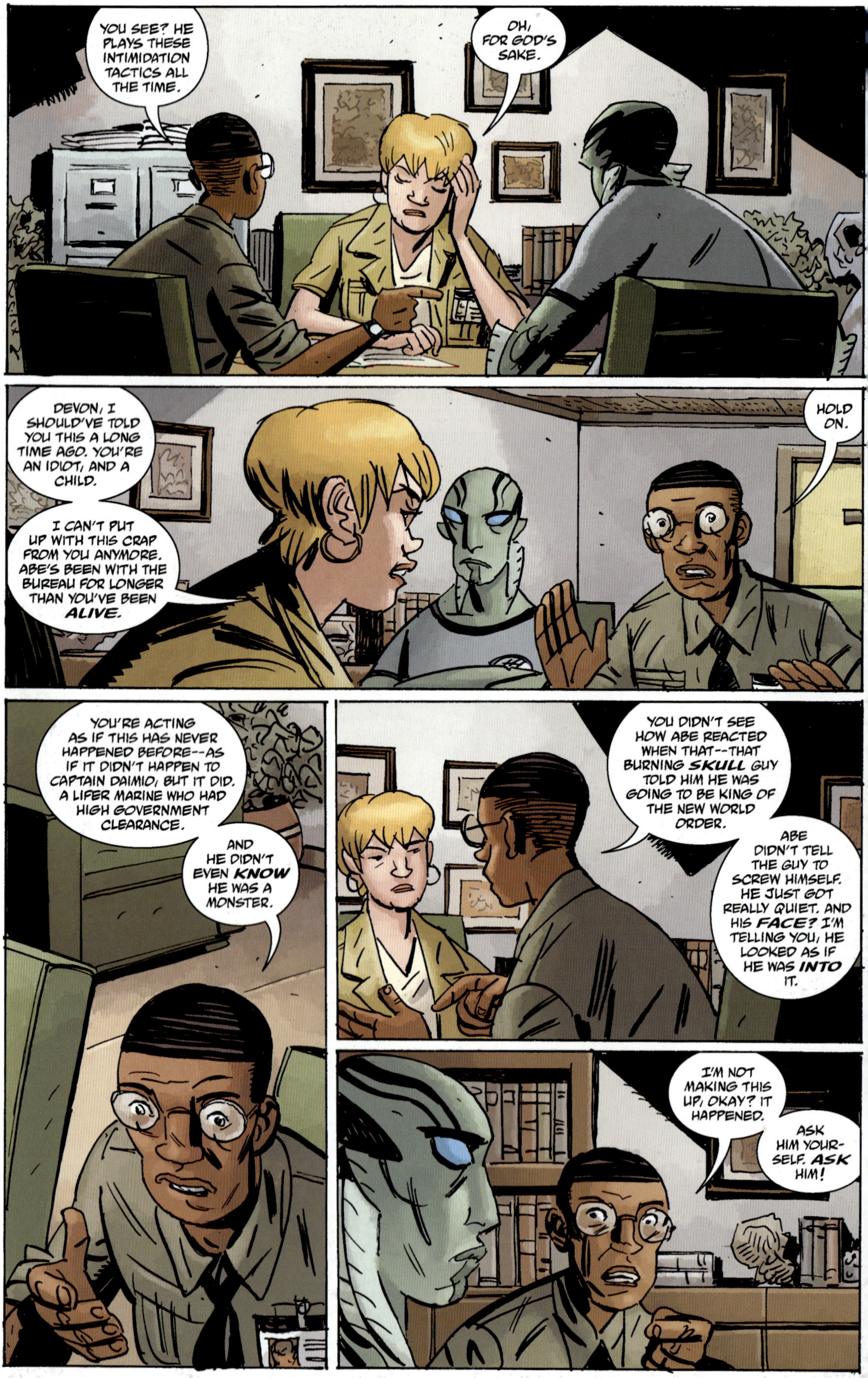
YOU SEE? HE PLAYS THESE INTIMIDATION TACTICS ALL THE TIME.
OH, FOR GOD'S SAKE.
DEVON, I SHOULD'VE TOLD YOU THIS A LONG TIME AGO. YOU'RE AN IDIOT, AND A CHILD.
I CAN'T PUT UP WITH THIS CRAP FROM YOU ANYMORE. ABE'S BEEN WITH THE BUREAU FOR LONGER THAN YOU'VE BEEN ALIVE.
HOLD ON.
YOU'RE ACTING AS IF THIS HAS NEVER HAPPENED BEFORE--AS IF IT DIDN'T HAPPEN TO CAPTAIN DAIMIO, BUT IT DID. A LIFER MARINE WHO HAD HIGH GOVERNMENT CLEARANCE.
AND HE DIDN'T EVEN KNOW HE WAS A MONSTER.
YOU DIDN'T SEE HOW ABE REACTED WHEN THAT--THAT BURNING SKULL GUY TOLD HIM HE WAS GOING TO BE KING OF THE NEW WORLD ORDER.
ABE DIDN'T TELL THE GUY TO SCREW HIMSELF. HE JUST GOT REALLY QUIET. AND HIS FACE? I'M TELLING YOU, HE LOOKED AS IF HE WAS INTO IT.
I'M NOT MAKING THIS UP, OKAY? IT HAPPENED.
ASK HIM YOURSELF. ASK HIM!

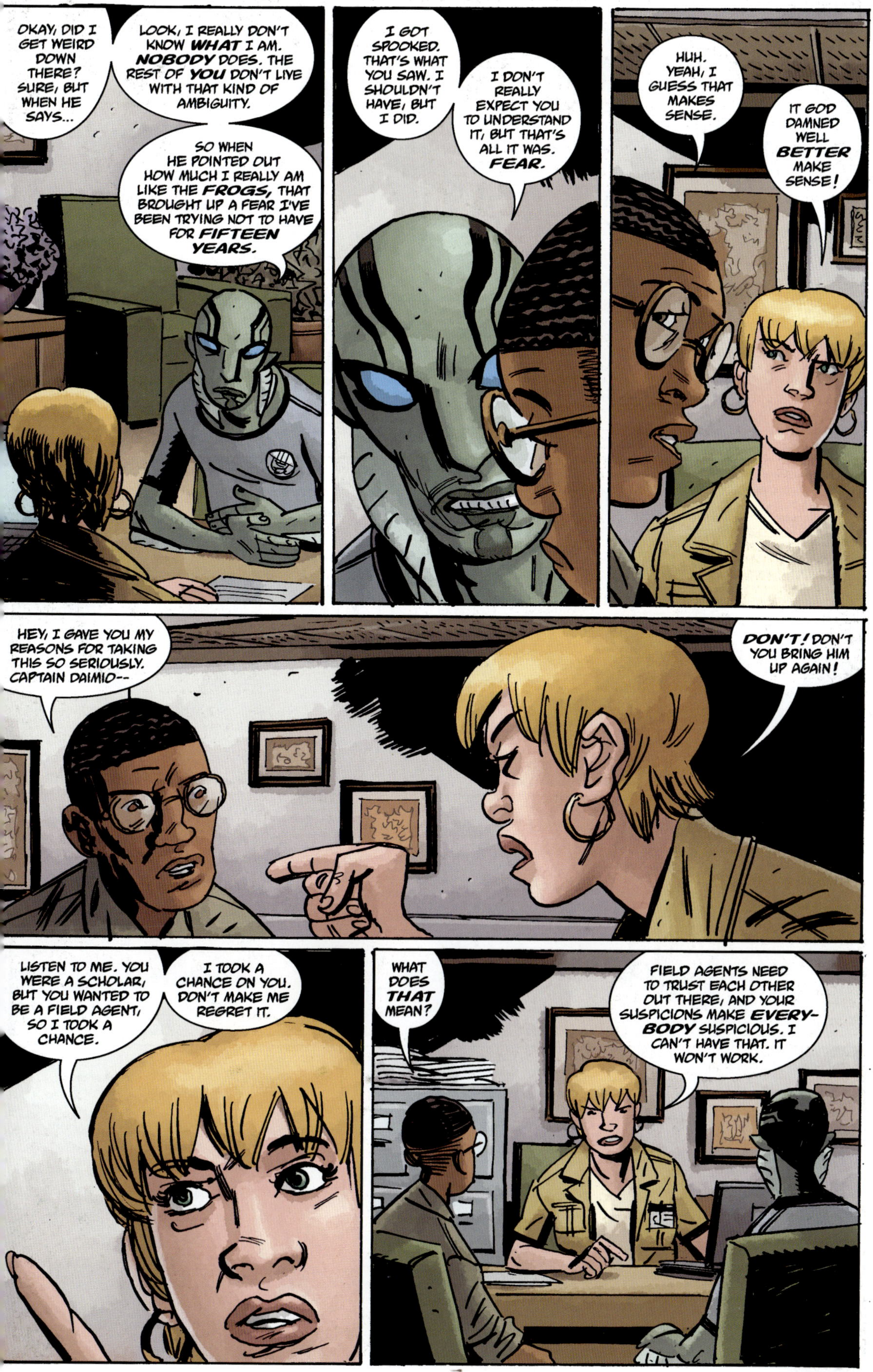
OKAY, DID I GET WEIRD DOWN THERE? SURE, BUT WHEN HE SAYS...
LOOK, I REALLY DON'T KNOW WHAT I AM. NOBODY DOES. THE REST OF YOU DON'T LIVE WITH THAT KIND OF AMBIGUITY.
SO WHEN HE POINTED OUT HOW MUCH I REALLY AM LIKE THE FROGS, THAT BROUGHT UP A FEAR I'VE BEEN TRYING NOT TO HAVE FOR FIFTEEN YEARS.
I GOT SPOOKED. THAT'S WHAT YOU SAW. I SHOULDN'T HAVE, BUT I DID.
I DON'T REALLY EXPECT YOU TO UNDERSTAND IT, BUT THAT'S ALL IT WAS. FEAR.
HUH. YEAH, I GUESS THAT MAKES SENSE.
IT GOD DAMNED WELL BETTER MAKE SENSE!
HEY, I GAVE YOU MY REASONS FOR TAKING THIS SO SERIOUSLY. CAPTAIN DAIMIO--
DON'T! DON'T YOU BRING HIM UP AGAIN!
LISTEN TO ME. YOU WERE A SCHOLAR, BUT YOU WANTED TO BE A FIELD AGENT, SO I TOOK A CHANCE.
I TOOK A CHANCE ON YOU. DON'T MAKE ME REGRET IT.
WHAT DOES THAT MEAN?
FIELD AGENTS NEED TO TRUST EACH OTHER OUT THERE, AND YOUR SUSPICIONS MAKE EVERYBODY SUSPICIOUS. I CAN'T HAVE THAT. IT WON'T WORK.

AND YOU SHOULD ALSO KNOW THAT ABE'S BEEN STRAIGHT WITH ME ABOUT ALL THIS. HE NEVER MADE ANY COUNTER ACCUSATIONS AGAINST YOU.
NO. JUST ASKED YOU TO FIRE ME ONCE A WEEK.
WELL, IF I FIND MYSELF HAVING TO CHOOSE--
ALL RIGHT! ALL RIGHT, I GET IT. I TOOK IT TOO FAR. I WAS SCARED MYSELF, OKAY?
ABE, I HOPE YOU UNDERSTAND THIS WAS NEVER PERSONAL.
BECAUSE KATE'S RIGHT. YOU HAVE BEEN STRAIGHT. WITH HER, AND WITH ME.
ISN'T THERE A DEBRIEFING WE NEED TO GET TO?

THIS IS A CHANGING WORLD.
AND MAN IS AN ADAPTABLE ANIMAL.
THE SOUTHWEST PART OF THIS COUNTRY IS RAPIDLY LOSING ITS STATIONARY POPULATIONS, ESPECIALLY FROM URBAN CENTERS.
WHICH MAKES *SENSE*, GIVEN THAT A CITY CAN DISAPPEAR OVERNIGHT AS *HOUSTON* DID.
INVERSELY, THERE'S AN INCREASINGLY LARGE *NOMADIC* POPULATION.
WE'RE SEEING, IN FACT, A RISE OF A KIND OF "BEDOUIN" CLASS, AS TIGHTLY KNIT AND AS WARY OF STRANGERS AS THAT ANALOGY SUGGESTS.
WHAT THE HELL *IS* THIS? A SOCIOLOGY CLASS?

NO, AGENT SAPIEN. IT'S NOT.
IT MIGHT BE, BUT FOR ONE THING.
HER.
SHE'S BECOMING SORT OF A LEGEND AMONG THESE "BEDOUINS," A LARGE NUMBER OF WHOM SHE IS REPORTED TO HAVE SAVED FROM THE HOUSTON DISASTER THROUGH AN UNCANNY SECOND SIGHT.
CUTE, FOR A LEGEND.
DO WE KNOW HER NAME?
FENIX SAW THIS COMING
INDEED WE DO.
THESE ARE ALL OVER TEXAS.

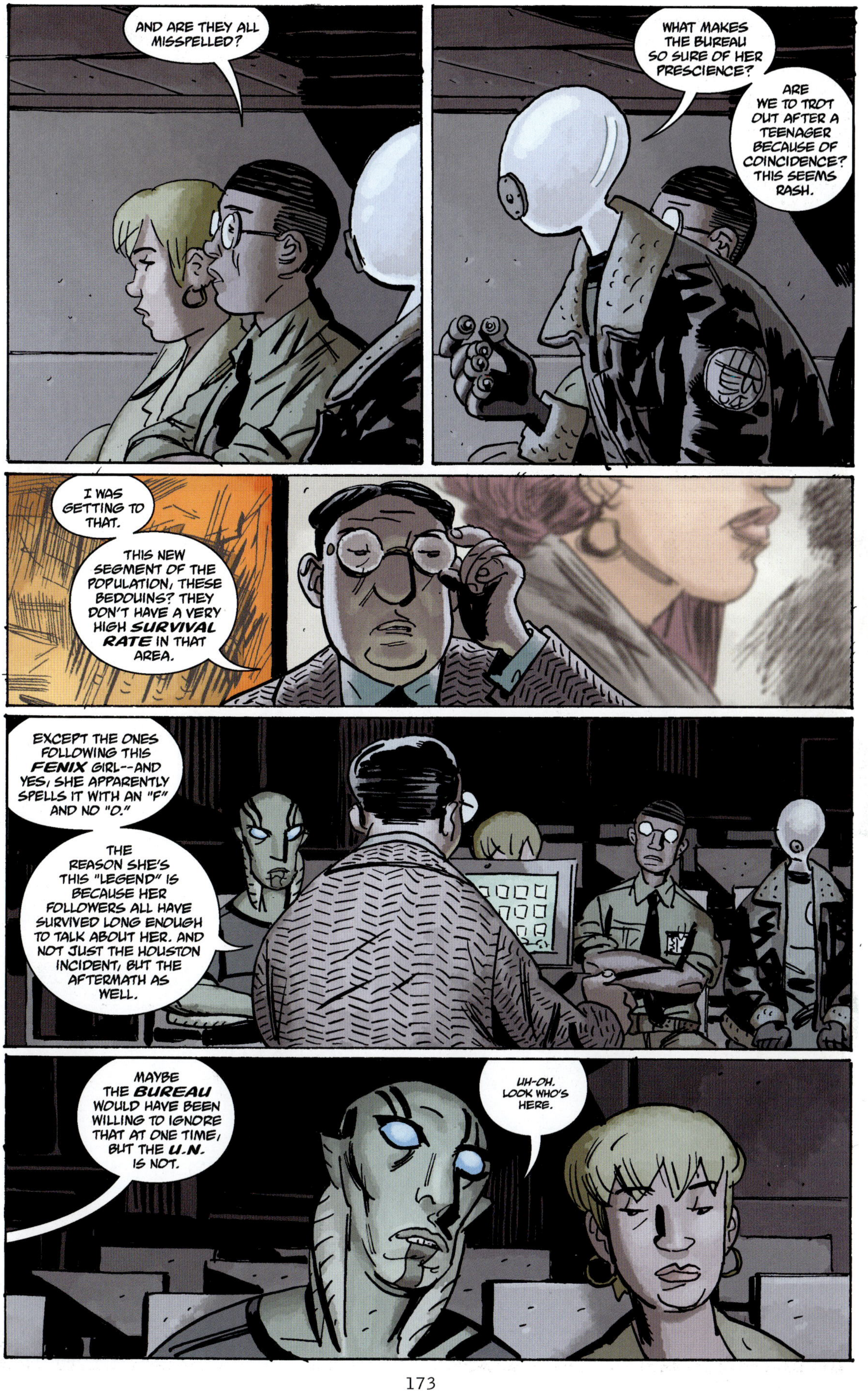
AND ARE THEY ALL MISSPELLED?
WHAT MAKES THE BUREAU SO SURE OF HER PRESCIENCE?
ARE WE TO TROT OUT AFTER A TEENAGER BECAUSE OF COINCIDENCE? THIS SEEMS RASH.
I WAS GETTING TO THAT.
THIS NEW SEGMENT OF THE POPULATION, THESE BEDOUINS? THEY DON'T HAVE A VERY HIGH SURVIVAL RATE IN THAT AREA.
EXCEPT THE ONES FOLLOWING THIS FENIX GIRL--AND YES, SHE APPARENTLY SPELLS IT WITH AN "F" AND NO "O."
THE REASON SHE'S THIS "LEGEND" IS BECAUSE HER FOLLOWERS ALL HAVE SURVIVED LONG ENOUGH TO TALK ABOUT HER. AND NOT JUST THE HOUSTON INCIDENT, BUT THE AFTERMATH AS WELL.
MAYBE THE BUREAU WOULD HAVE BEEN WILLING TO IGNORE THAT AT ONE TIME, BUT THE U.N. IS NOT.
UH-OH. LOOK WHO'S HERE.

OH BOY.
AH, PROFESSOR O'DONNELL.
WHAT CAN WE HELP YOU WITH?
PROFESSOR?
YOU DON'T KNOW WHAT'S GOING ON IN TEXAS.
UMM, ACTUALLY, I DO. THAT'S JUST WHAT I'VE BEEN--
IT ALL HAPPENED BEFORE.
AND NOW IT'S HAPPENING AGAIN.

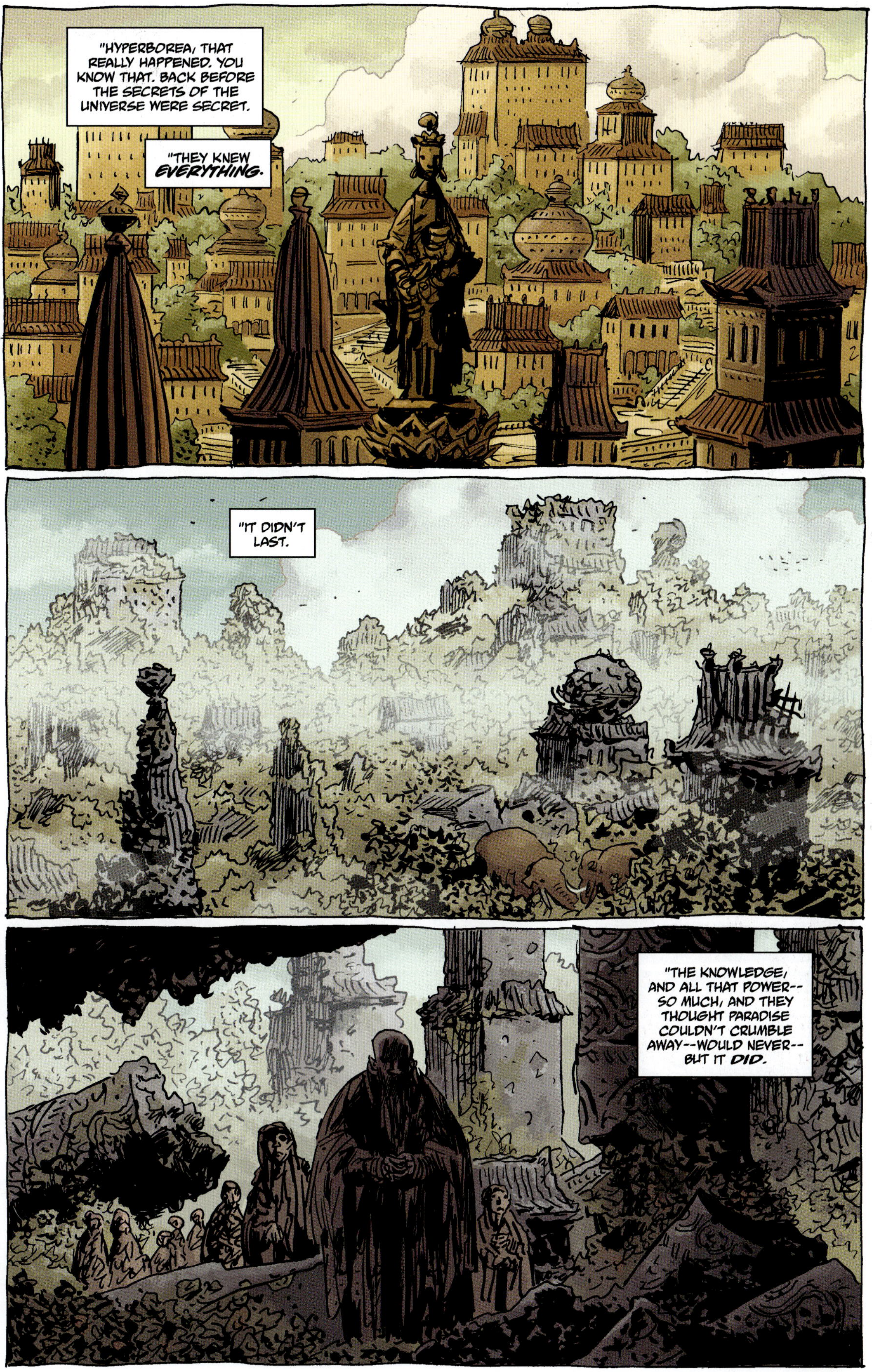
"HYPERBOREA, THAT REALLY HAPPENED. YOU KNOW THAT. BACK BEFORE THE SECRETS OF THE UNIVERSE WERE SECRET.
"THEY KNEW *EVERYTHING*.
"IT DIDN'T LAST.
"THE KNOWLEDGE, AND ALL THAT POWER-- SO MUCH, AND THEY THOUGHT PARADISE COULDN'T CRUMBLE AWAY--WOULD NEVER-- BUT IT *DID*.

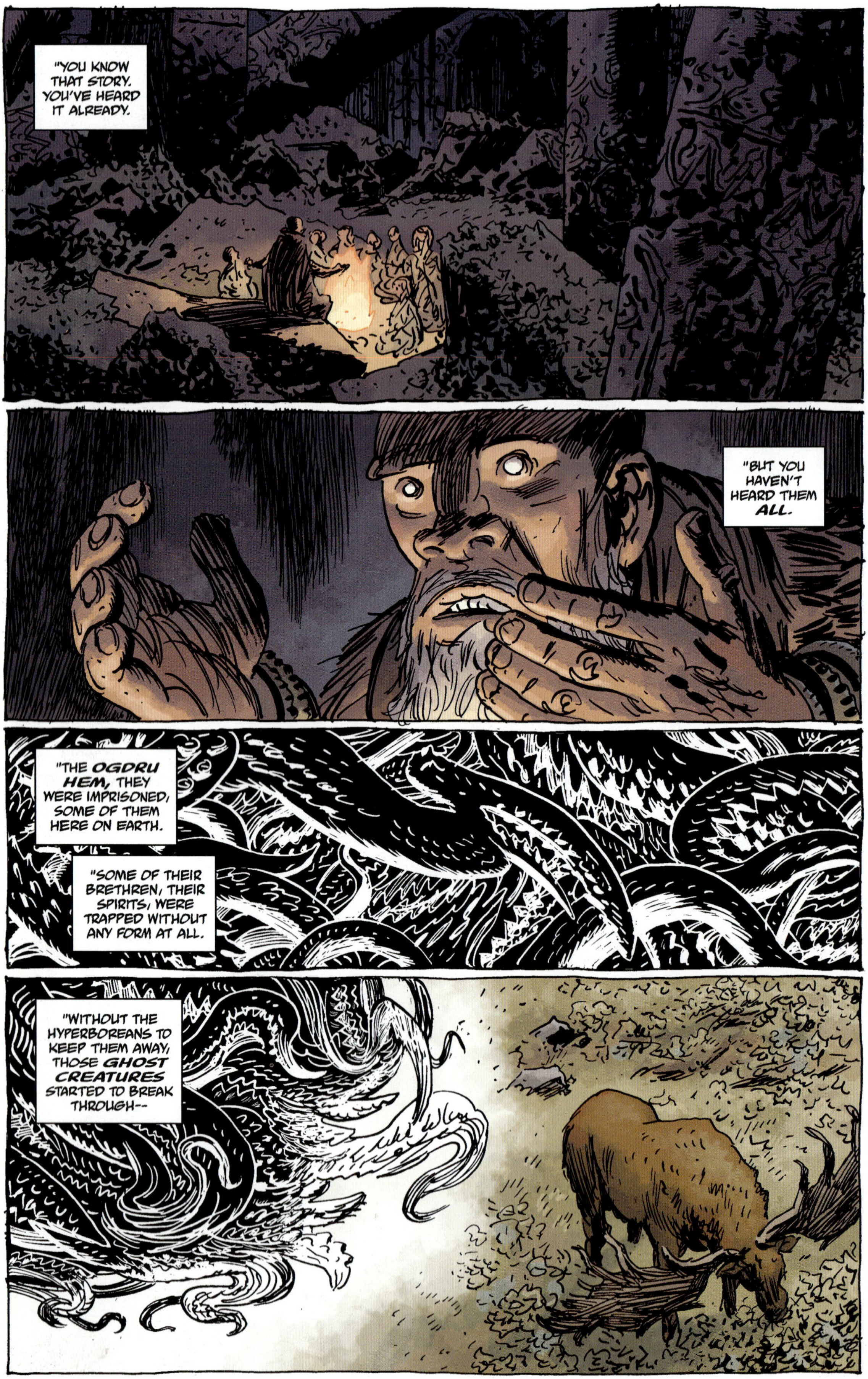
"YOU KNOW THAT STORY. YOU'VE HEARD IT ALREADY.
"BUT YOU HAVEN'T HEARD THEM ALL.
"THE OGDRU HEM, THEY WERE IMPRISONED, SOME OF THEM HERE ON EARTH.
"SOME OF THEIR BRETHREN, THEIR SPIRITS, WERE TRAPPED WITHOUT ANY FORM AT ALL.
"WITHOUT THE HYPERBOREANS TO KEEP THEM AWAY, THOSE GHOST CREATURES STARTED TO BREAK THROUGH--

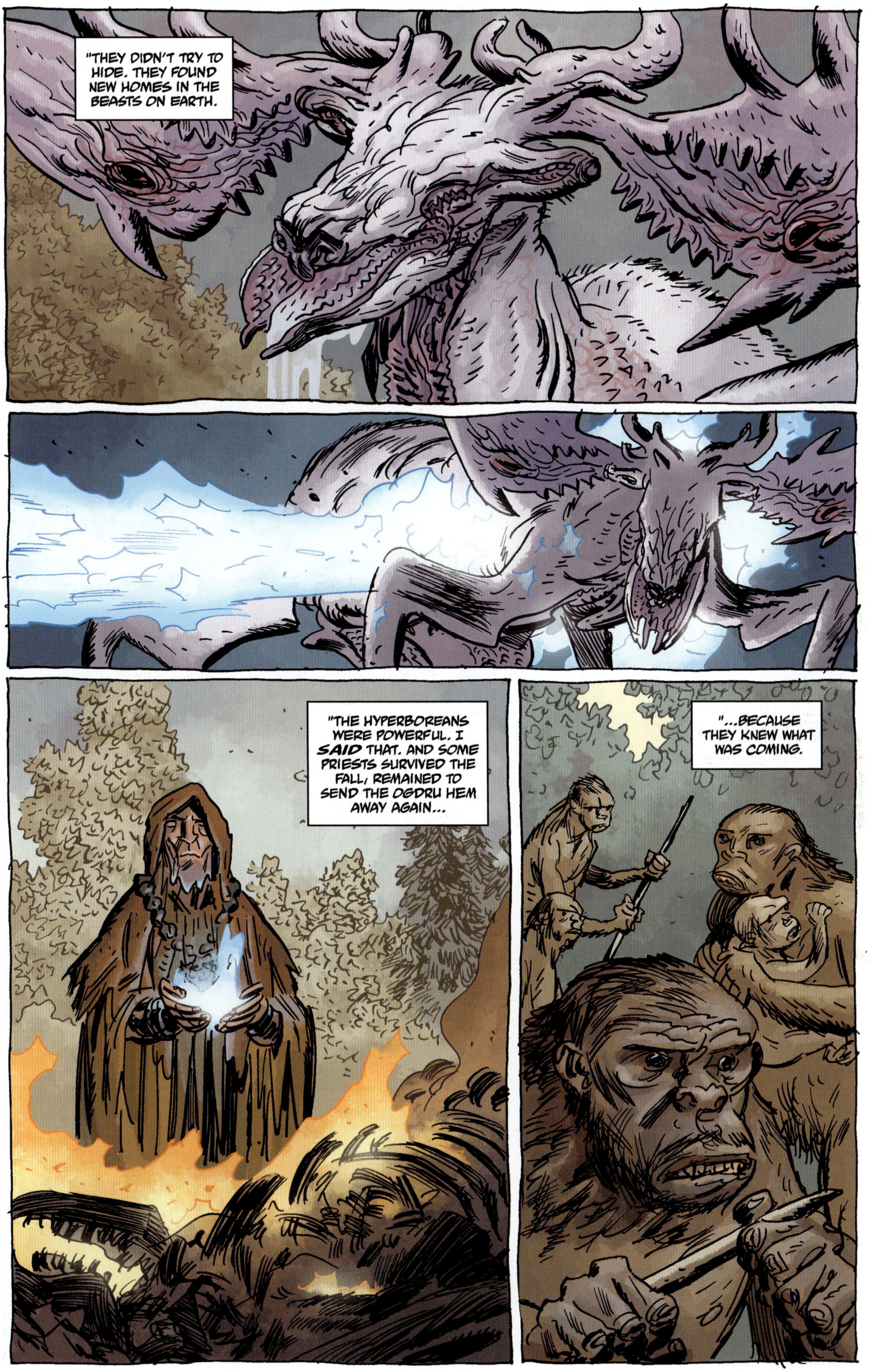
"THEY DIDN'T TRY TO HIDE. THEY FOUND NEW HOMES IN THE BEASTS ON EARTH.
"THE HYPERBOREANS WERE POWERFUL. I SAID THAT. AND SOME PRIESTS SURVIVED THE FALL, REMAINED TO SEND THE OGDRU HEM AWAY AGAIN...
"...BECAUSE THEY KNEW WHAT WAS COMING.

"NEW HOMES FOR THE PHANTOMS TO HIDE IN, BETTER HOMES FOR THE RESURRECTIONS OF THE PROGENY OF THE OGDRU JAHAD. THAT'S WHAT THIS NEXT RACE OF MAN COULD BE.
"A YOUNG RACE STILL WEAK, LIKE CHILDREN.
"AND LIKE CHILDREN, CURIOUS, AND CLEVER, AND MALLEABLE.
"WHO WOULD SHAPE THEM? A NEW WORLD, A WORLD WITHOUT THE WATCHERS, WITHOUT KINGS--SO WHO WOULD RAISE THESE CHILDREN TO TAKE CONTROL?
"AND CONTROL OF WHAT?

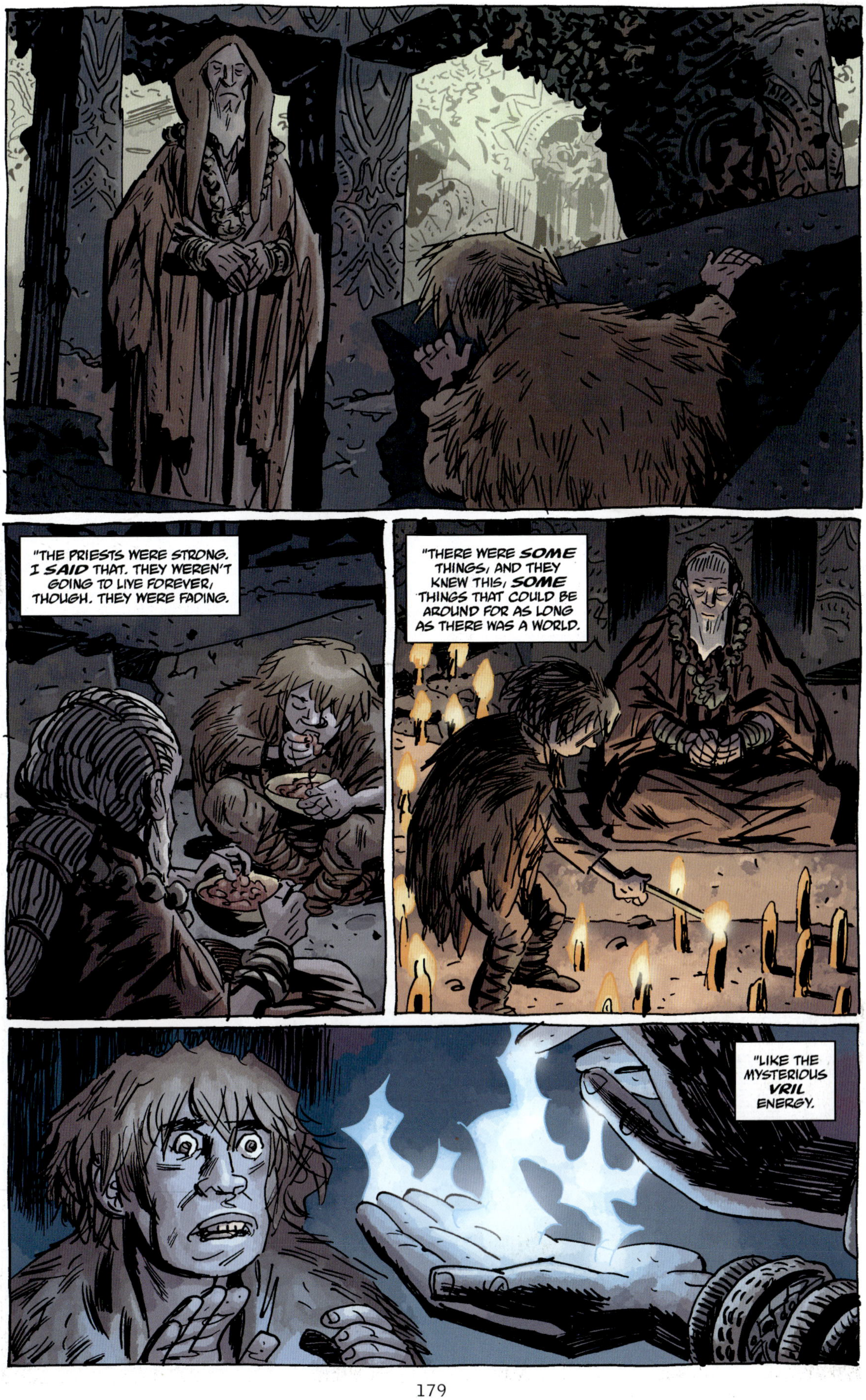
"THE PRIESTS WERE STRONG. I SAID THAT. THEY WEREN'T GOING TO LIVE FOREVER, THOUGH. THEY WERE FADING.
"THERE WERE SOME THINGS, AND THEY KNEW THIS, SOME THINGS THAT COULD BE AROUND FOR AS LONG AS THERE WAS A WORLD.
"LIKE THE MYSTERIOUS VRIL ENERGY.

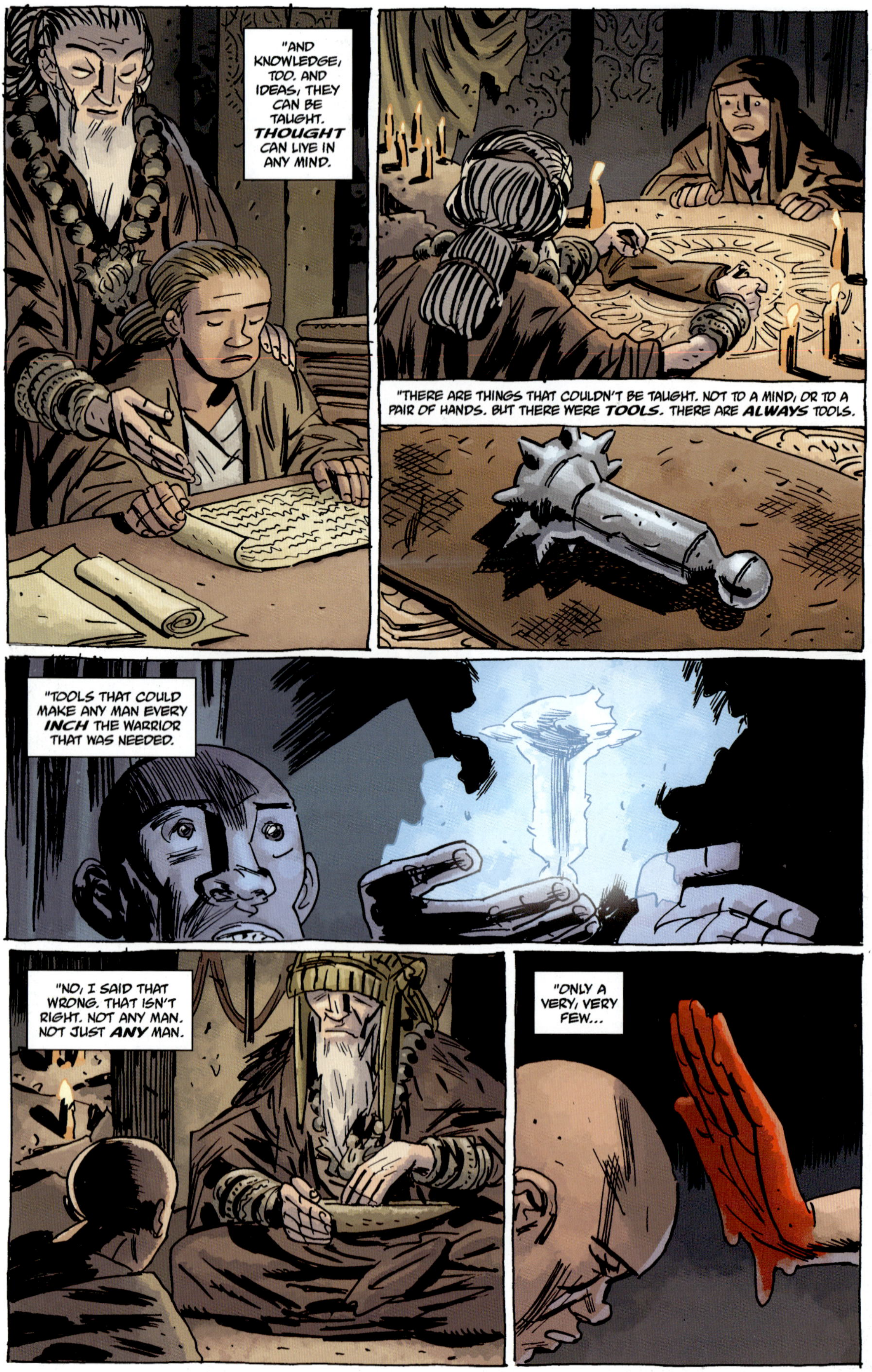
"AND KNOWLEDGE, TOO. AND IDEAS, THEY CAN BE TAUGHT. THOUGHT CAN LIVE IN ANY MIND.
"THERE ARE THINGS THAT COULDN'T BE TAUGHT. NOT TO A MIND, OR TO A PAIR OF HANDS. BUT THERE WERE TOOLS. THERE ARE ALWAYS TOOLS.
"TOOLS THAT COULD MAKE ANY MAN EVERY INCH THE WARRIOR THAT WAS NEEDED.
"NO, I SAID THAT WRONG. THAT ISN'T RIGHT. NOT ANY MAN. NOT JUST ANY MAN.
"ONLY A VERY, VERY FEW...

"AND THAT'S THE STORY YOU DIDN'T KNOW.
"PART OF IT. PART OF THE STORY.
"THE NEW PRIESTS, THE SHAMANS, THEY LIVED THEIR NOMADIC MISSION, NOT DOING WHAT YOU SAY. NOT AVOIDING EVIL.
"BECAUSE WHEN ENOUGH OF THE OGDRU HEM RETURNED, THEY WOULD CALL BACK THE OGDRU JAHAD.
"THE SHAMANS COULDN'T RUN FROM THAT."
NO!
STEP AWAY.

STEP AWAY? BUT THIS MAN IS A VICTIM OF THE OGDRU CULT.
HO, HO! YOUR PRIEST IS WISE. HE SEES!
HE IS THE ONE WHO HAS THE EYES TO SEE!
SO THEN I MUST SUCK THEM FROM HIS HEAD!!

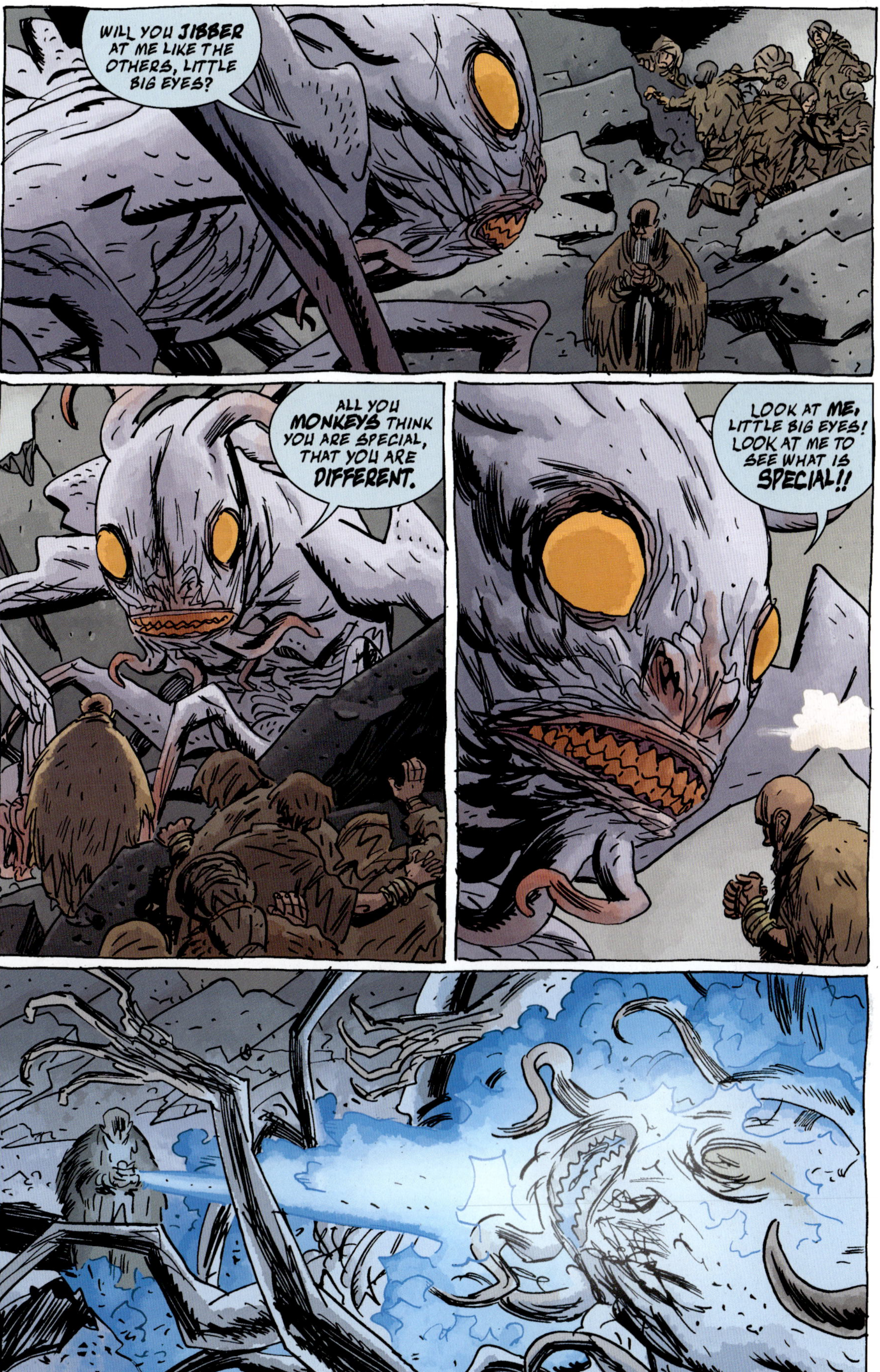
WILL YOU JIBBER AT ME LIKE THE OTHERS, LITTLE BIG EYES?
ALL YOU MONKEYS THINK YOU ARE SPECIAL, THAT YOU ARE DIFFERENT.
LOOK AT ME, LITTLE BIG EYES! LOOK AT ME TO SEE WHAT IS SPECIAL!!

YOUR NAME, LITTLE RAT!! TELL ME SO THAT I CAN FIND YOUR SOUL IN YOUR PUNY HELL AND EAT IT.
TELL ME!!!
SHONCHIN.

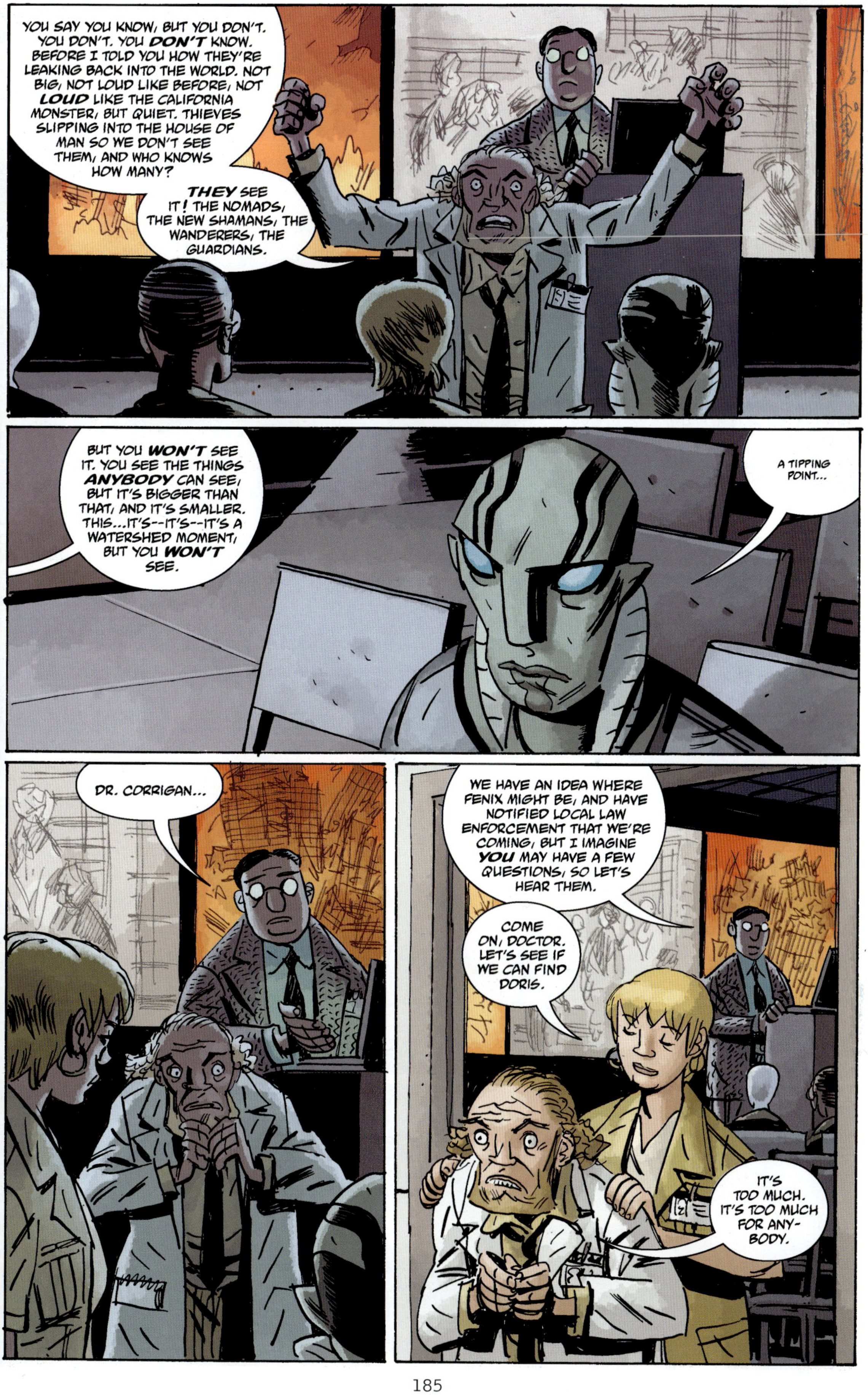
YOU SAY YOU KNOW, BUT YOU DON'T. YOU DON'T. YOU DON'T KNOW. BEFORE I TOLD YOU HOW THEY'RE LEAKING BACK INTO THE WORLD. NOT BIG, NOT LOUD LIKE BEFORE, NOT LOUD LIKE THE CALIFORNIA MONSTER, BUT QUIET. THIEVES SLIPPING INTO THE HOUSE OF MAN SO WE DON'T SEE THEM, AND WHO KNOWS HOW MANY?
THEY SEE IT! THE NOMADS, THE NEW SHAMANS, THE WANDERERS, THE GUARDIANS.
BUT YOU WON'T SEE IT. YOU SEE THE THINGS ANYBODY CAN SEE, BUT IT'S BIGGER THAN THAT, AND IT'S SMALLER. THIS...IT'S--IT'S--IT'S A WATERSHED MOMENT, BUT YOU WON'T SEE.
A TIPPING POINT...
DR. CORRIGAN...
WE HAVE AN IDEA WHERE FENIX MIGHT BE, AND HAVE NOTIFIED LOCAL LAW ENFORCEMENT THAT WE'RE COMING, BUT I IMAGINE YOU MAY HAVE A FEW QUESTIONS, SO LET'S HEAR THEM.
COME ON, DOCTOR. LET'S SEE IF WE CAN FIND DORIS.
IT'S TOO MUCH. IT'S TOO MUCH FOR ANY-BODY.

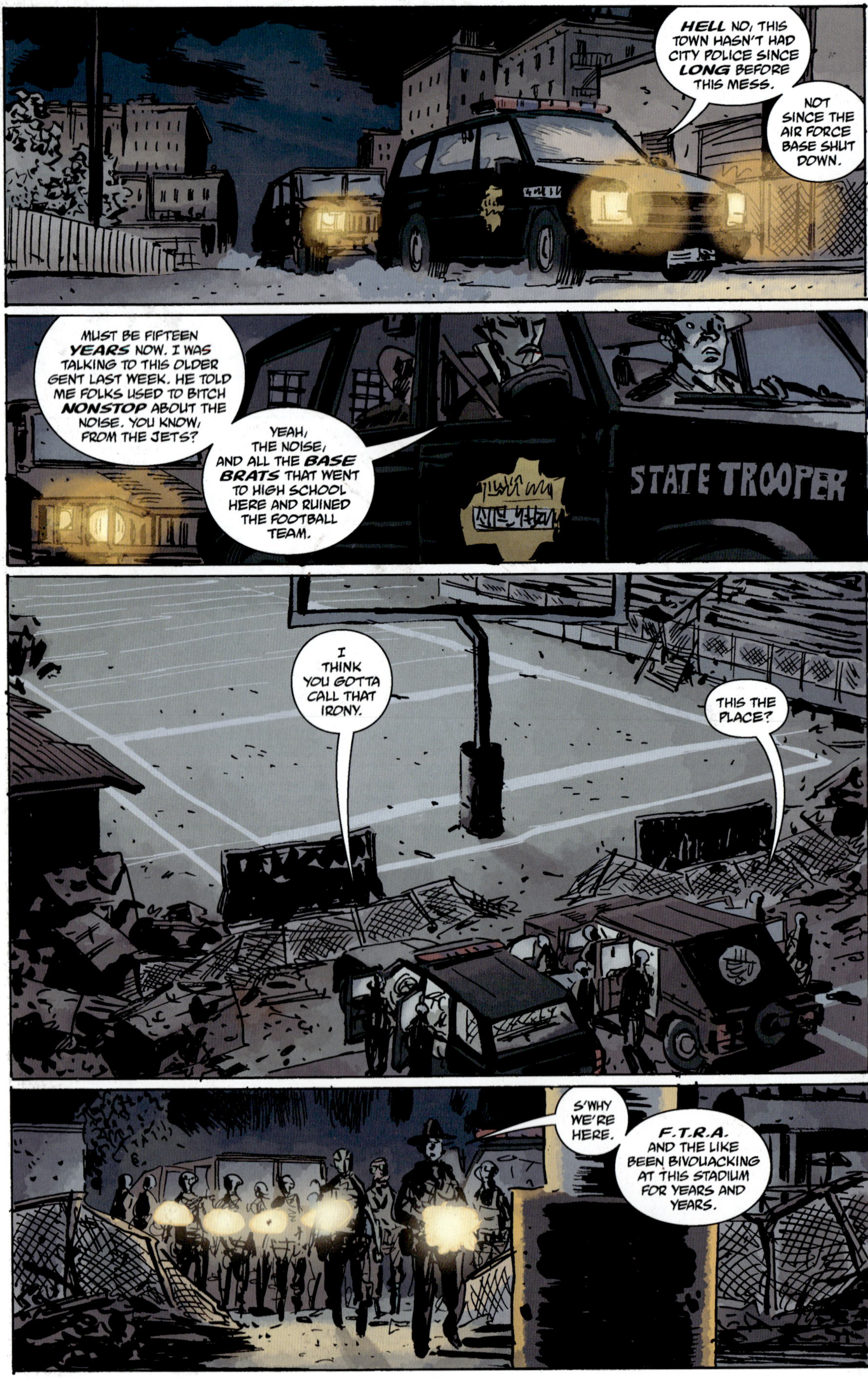
HELL NO, THIS TOWN HASN'T HAD CITY POLICE SINCE LONG BEFORE THIS MESS.
NOT SINCE THE AIR FORCE BASE SHUT DOWN.
MUST BE FIFTEEN YEARS NOW. I WAS TALKING TO THIS OLDER GENT LAST WEEK. HE TOLD ME FOLKS USED TO BITCH NONSTOP ABOUT THE NOISE. YOU KNOW, FROM THE JETS?
YEAH, THE NOISE, AND ALL THE BASE BRATS THAT WENT TO HIGH SCHOOL HERE AND RUINED THE FOOTBALL TEAM.
STATE TROOPER
I THINK YOU GOTTA CALL THAT IRONY.
THIS THE PLACE?
S'WHY WE'RE HERE.
F.T.R.A. AND THE LIKE BEEN BIVOUACKING AT THIS STADIUM FOR YEARS AND YEARS.

HMM.
NOT AS POPULAR AS IT USED TO BE, I GUESS.
WELL, YOU NEVER CAN TELL. I'LL TRY THEM "NOSEBLEED" SEATS.
I DON'T REALLY SEE THE POINT.
WELL, WE **ARE** ONLY LOOKING FOR ONE GIRL.
NO, WE'RE LOOKING FOR A GIRL WITH A WHOLE ARMY OF FOLLOWERS. IF IT TURNS OUT SHE'S HERE ALL ALONE, THEN SHE'S **NOT** WHO WE THINK SHE IS.
GAAAH!
HOLD ON. THE TROOPER KNOWS THIS WRECK BETTER THAN WE DO. LET'S GET HIM.
OKAY, YOU GET HIM.
MEAN-WHILE, I'LL DO MY JOB.

WAS THAT ONE OF YOUR MEN YELLING?
NO. THERE'S SOMEBODY IN THE LOCKER ROOM. AGENT SAPIEN WENT IN TO--
OH, GOD NO!
BLAM

GODS CHAPTER THREE

ILLUSTRATION BY **RYAN SOOK**

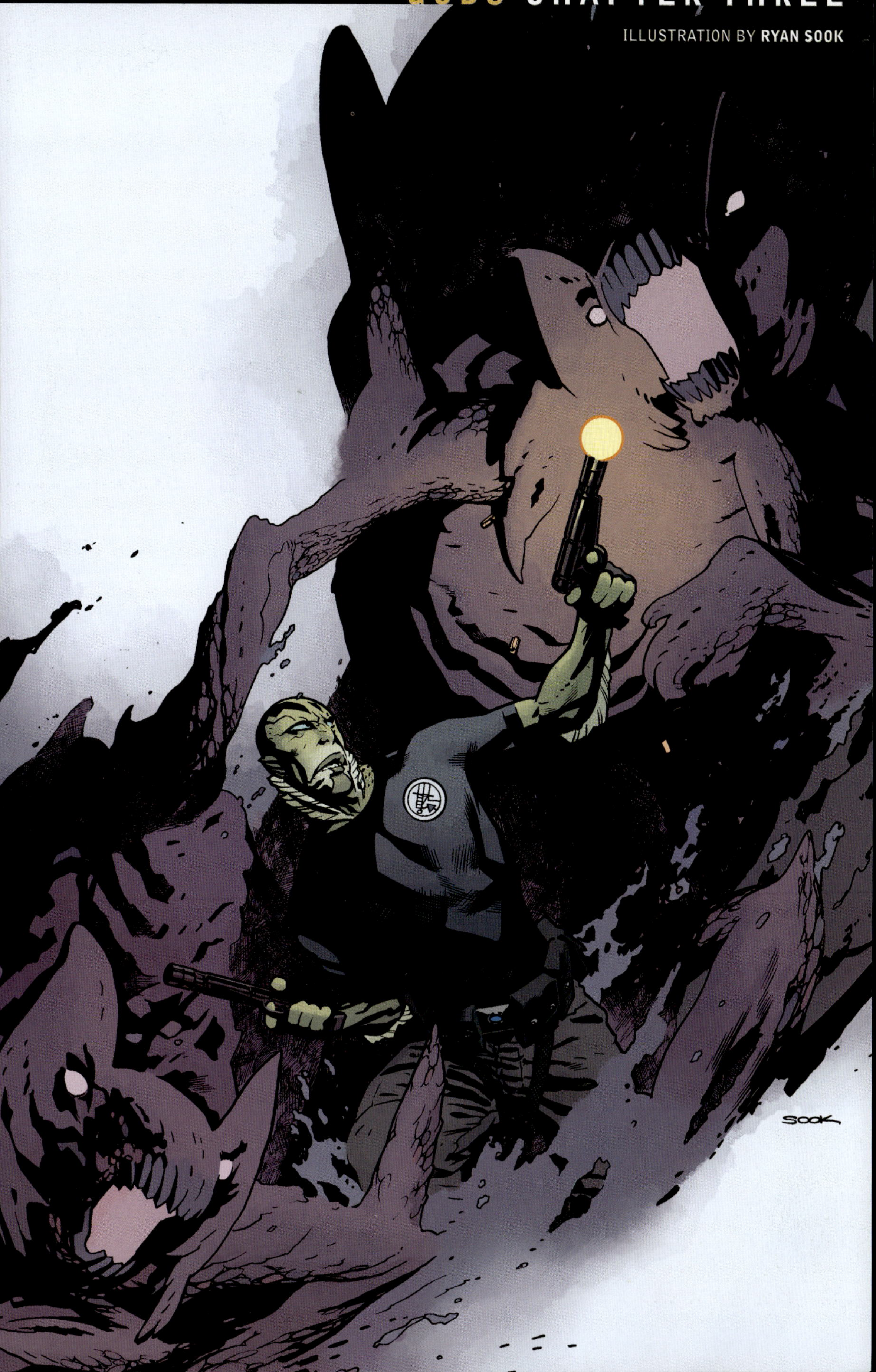
SOOK

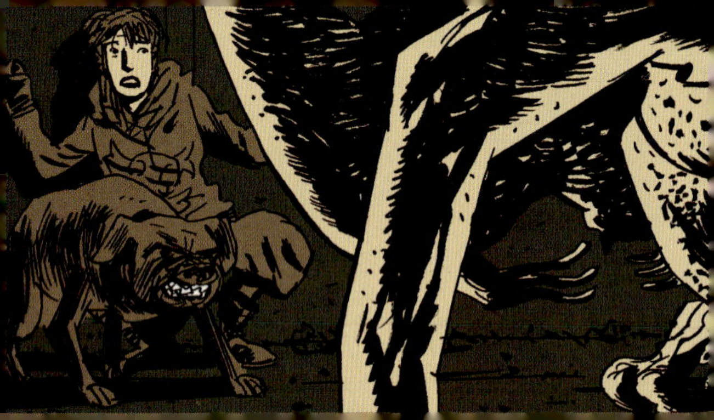

BLAM BLAM BLAM
ABE! ABE, WHAT'S GOING ON IN THERE?!
EEEEEEEE!
OOF!
BLAMBLAMBLAM
AGENT SAPIEN, WHAT IN HELL ARE YOU SHOOTING--

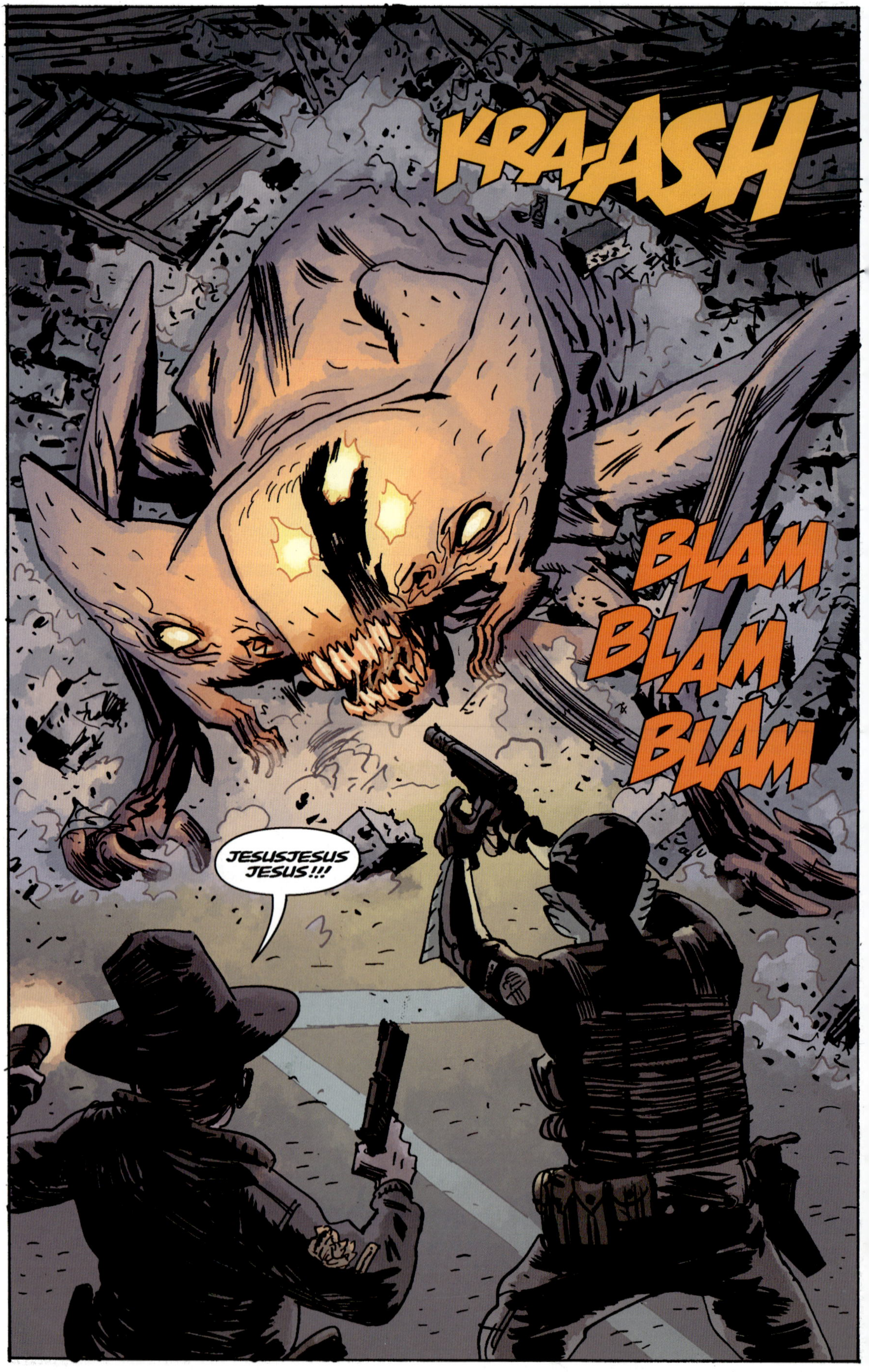
KRA-ASH
BLAM
BLAM
BLAM
JESUSJESUS JESUS!!!

BLAM BLAM
WHAT THE HELL IS THAT THING?!
GOD DAMMIT, SOMEBODY TELL ME WHAT THAT #%$#$ THING IS!
BLAM BLAM
BLAM BOOM-CHUK-BOOM
BLAM BLAM
ROOARR

#&%* DOESN'T WANNA DIE!

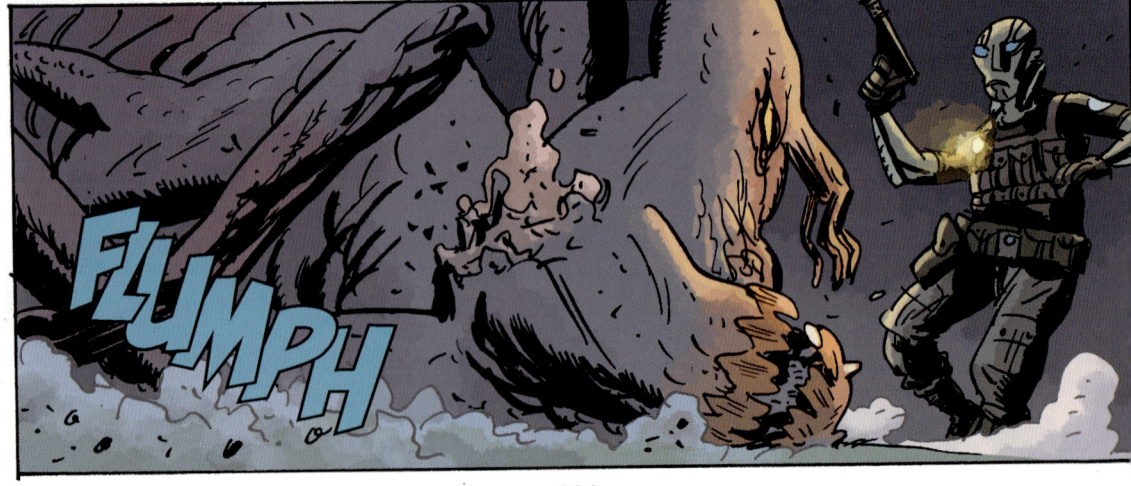

BLAM

FLUMPH

YOU CAN GET UP NOW, AGENT DEVON.
TROUBLE'S ALL OVER.
?
NO, THAT WASN'T-- I HAD TO STAY DOWN OR I WOULD'VE BEEN HIT.
HEH-HEH. TAKE IT EASY, SON. WE ALL JUST NEEDED A LAUGH.
WE HEARD ABOUT THESE THINGS. LOT TOUGHER THAN I EXPECTED, THOUGH.
CAME RIGHT UP THROUGH THE FLOOR, AND I'M TALKING ABOUT IN SECONDS.
THIS TUNNEL COULD LEAD TO A NEST. WE NEED TO SEND OUR TEAM IN THERE.

CALL IT IN.
THIS TEAM'S ALREADY GOT ITS MISSION.
ABE, THAT WAS UNCALLED FOR.
TRUST ME, DEVON--YOU'RE ONLY MAKING IT WORSE.
LOOK WHO I FINALLY CAUGHT UP WITH.
GUY CAN MOVE!
I STILL CAN'T BELIEVE IT. I CAN'T BELIEVE THE KID WAS RIGHT.
WHO WAS RIGHT?

12
12
HEY, JORGE. MORNING JOLT ON ITS WAY.
JORGE, MAN.
JORGE!
YO, JORGE!
WHASSAT?!
GET BACK, MOTHER-%$#&!
OH, $#&%!

DAMMIT, DINGO! WHAT THE HELL'S A MATTER WITH YOU?
OH, YEAH! GO ON! YELL AT THE GUY WHAT JUST SWIPED A BULLSEYE FOR YOU, AND WHOSE HEAD Y'ALMOST SHOT IN HALF!
GREAT, YOU WOKE THE #&@%IN' DOG UP!
I WOKE 'IM UP?
RRRROWF ROWF
WAIT A SEC. HE AIN'T EVEN LOOKIN' AT US.
ROWF ROWF ROWF
GRRR
KRUNCH
AROOO

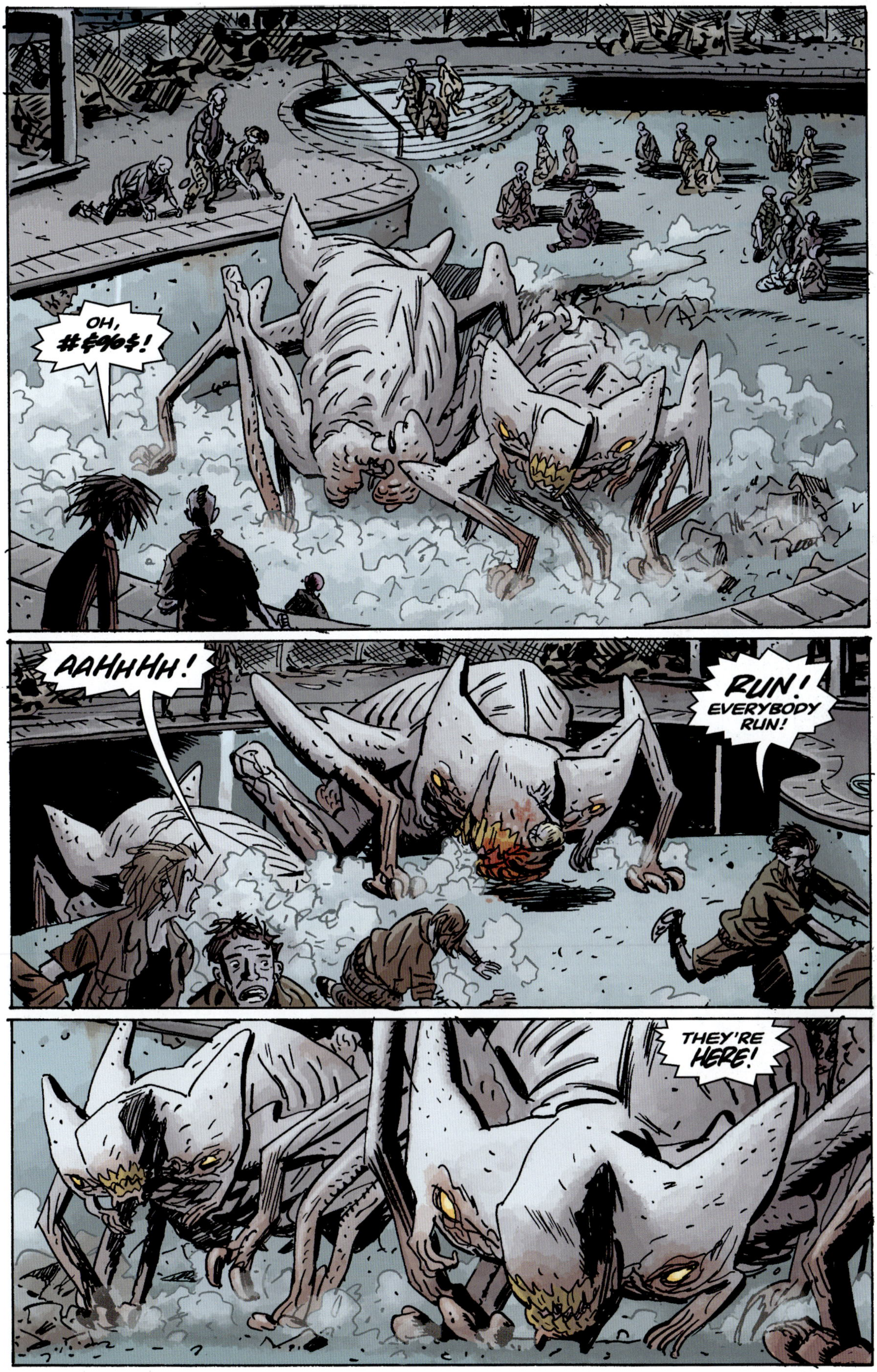
OH, #$%$!
AAHHHH!
RUN! EVERYBODY RUN!
THEY'RE HERE!

SNARRRRRRRL
FENIX...
DUDE, WHATTAYA DOIN'? SHOOT THE ₰*%$#!!
!
BLAM BLAM BLAM
I'M COMIN', BABY!

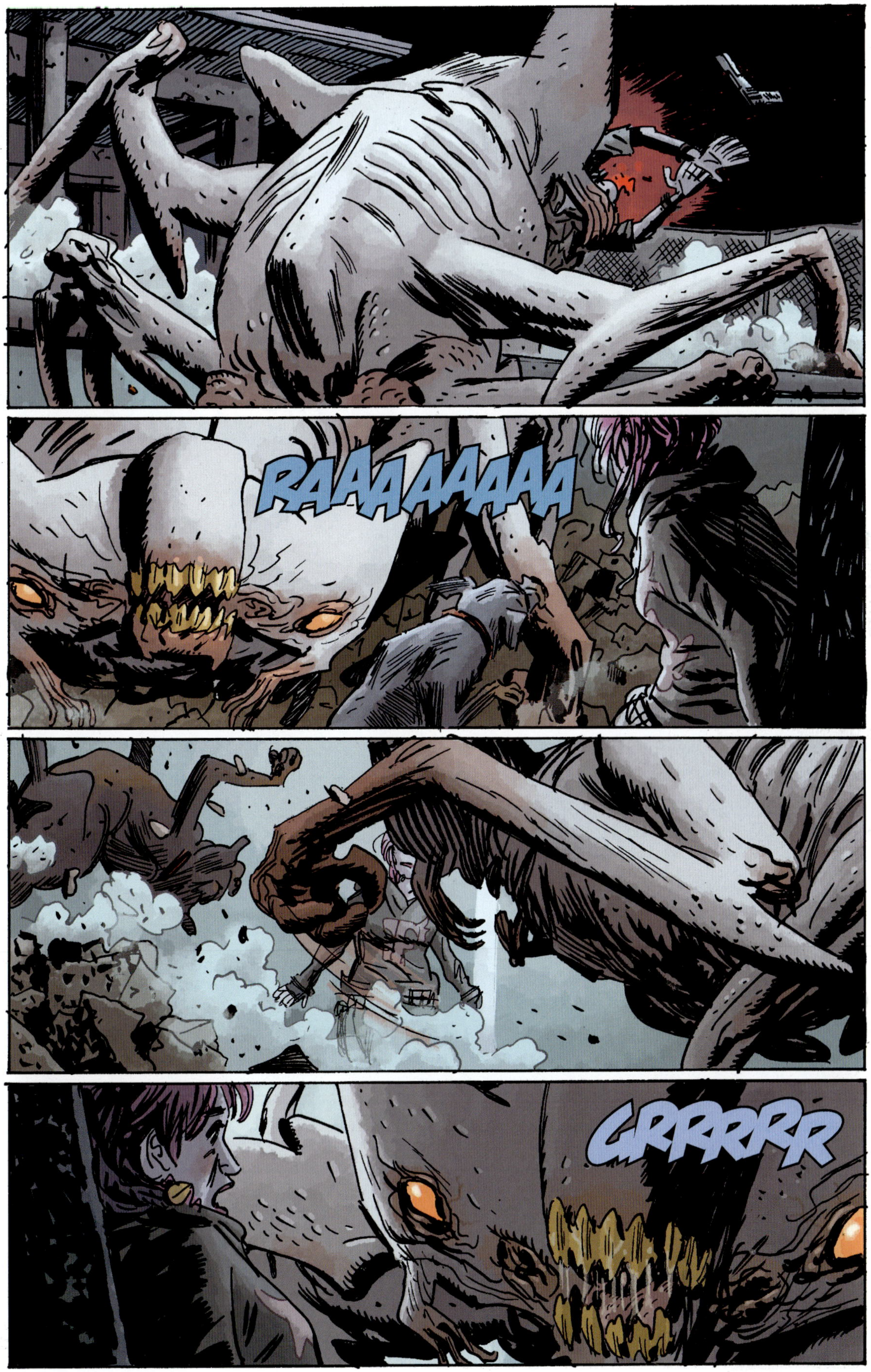
RAAAAAAAA
GRRRRR

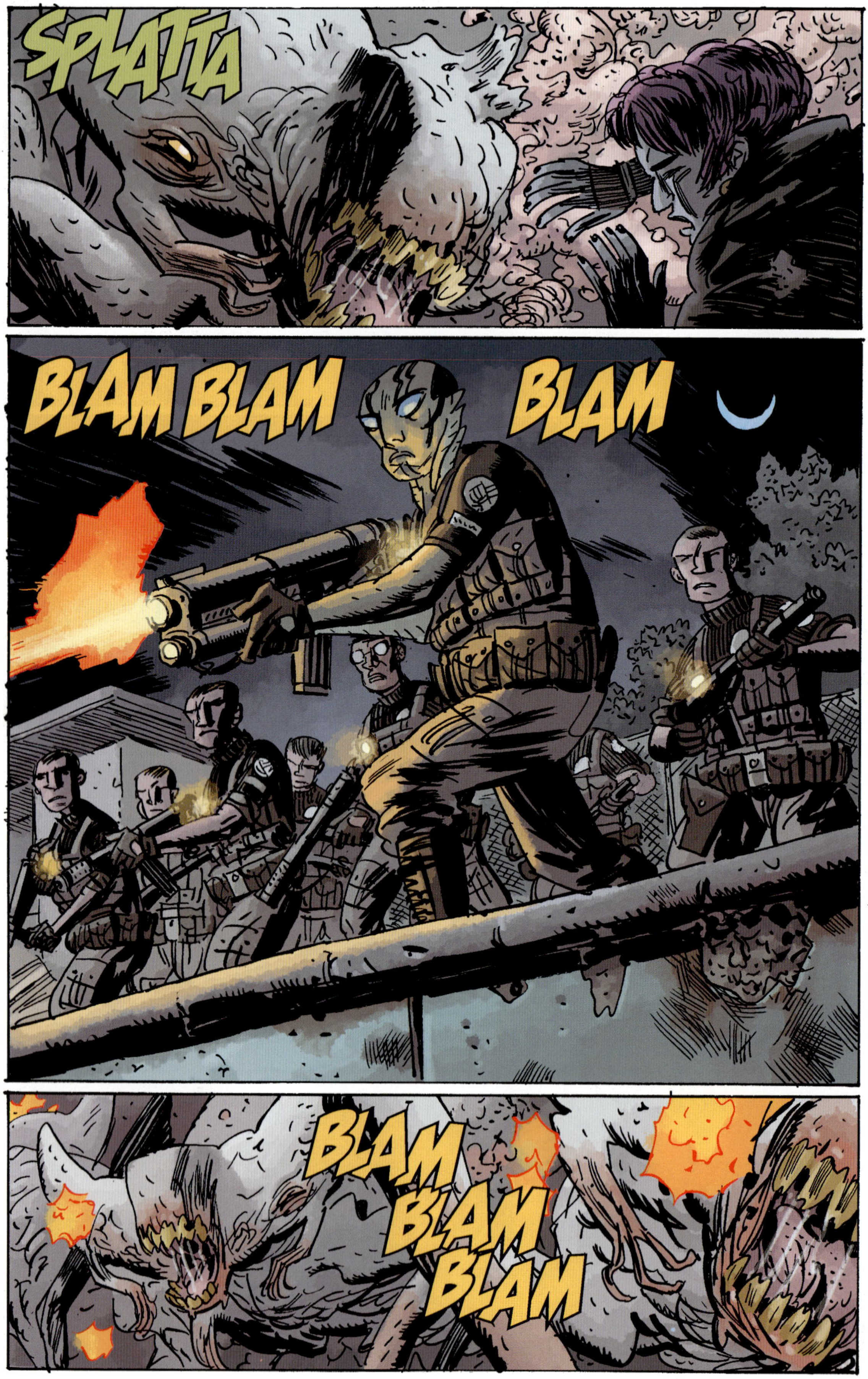
SPLATTA
BLAM BLAM
BLAM
BLAM
BLAM
BLAM

BLAM BLAM BLAM
BLAM
BOOM
BOOM
BLAM BLAM
WE GOT THIS WRAPPED UP.
GO ROUND UP THOSE "BEDOUINS"! WE NEED TO TALK TO THEM--**ALL** OF THEM!

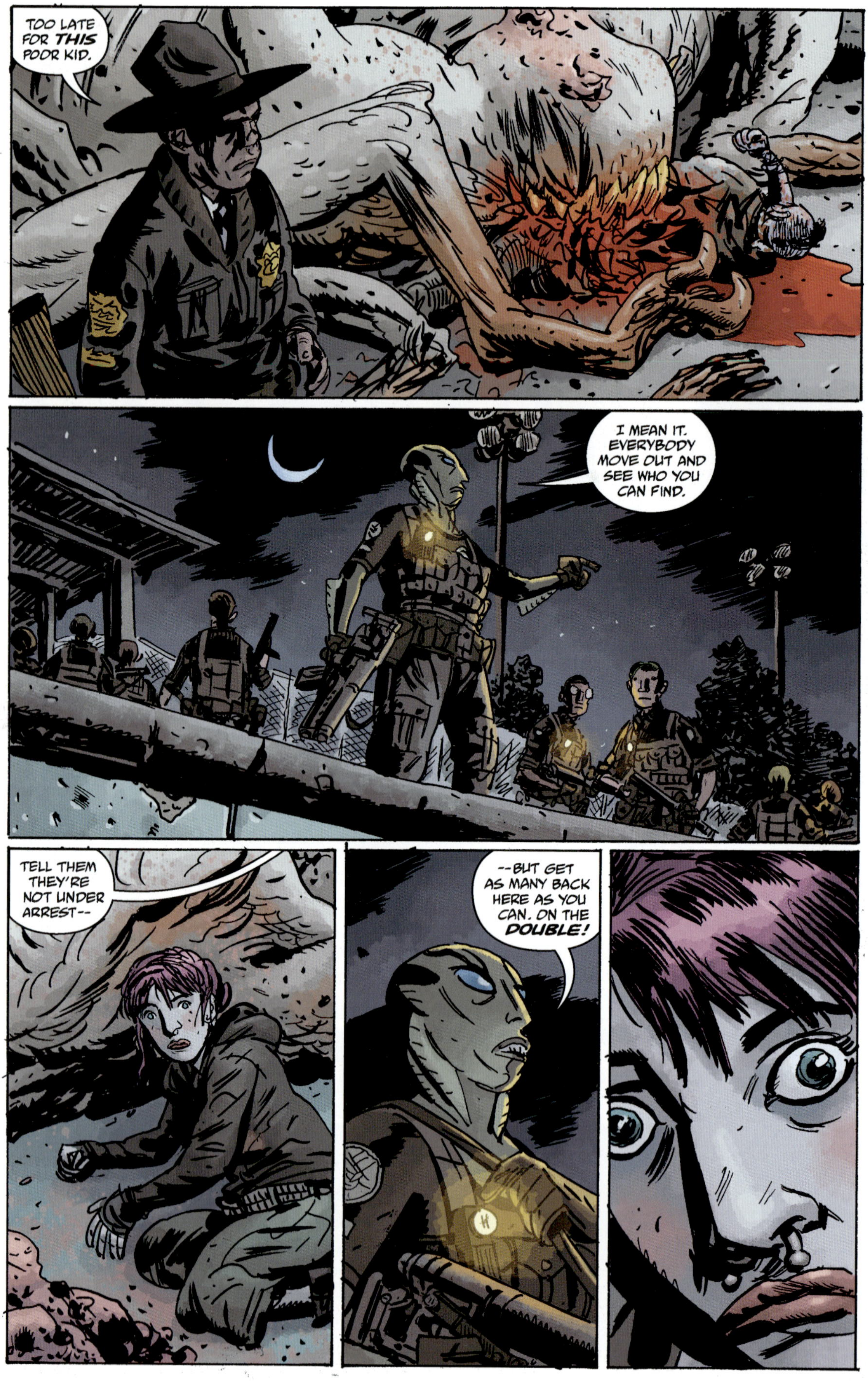
TOO LATE FOR THIS POOR KID.
I MEAN IT. EVERYBODY MOVE OUT AND SEE WHO YOU CAN FIND.
TELL THEM THEY'RE NOT UNDER ARREST--
--BUT GET AS MANY BACK HERE AS YOU CAN. ON THE DOUBLE!

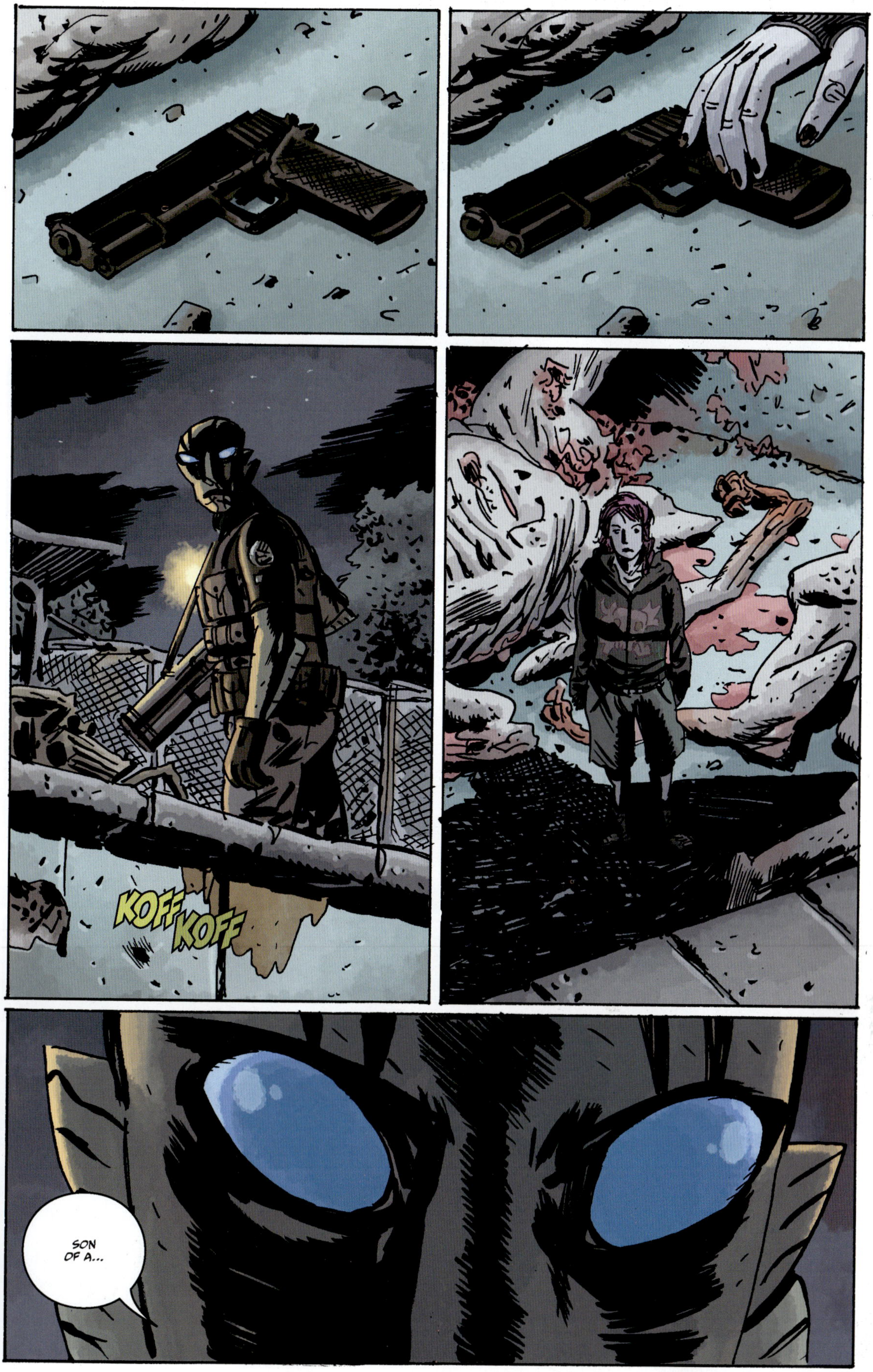
KOFF
KOFF
SON OF A...

HEY, I FOUND--
NO, WAIT!
OKAY, I WON'T CALL ANYBODY. JUST YOU AND ME, ALL RIGHT?
I'M NOT GOING TO HURT YOU. I MEAN, HECK, WE JUST SAVED YOUR LIVES, DIDN'T WE?
LOOK. NO WEAPONS, OKAY? THAT BETTER?
I KNOW I'M KIND OF SCARY LOOKING, BUT JUST HEAR ME OUT.
MY NAME'S ABE SAPIEN--

I KNOW WHO YOU ARE.
BLAM
BLAM
BLAM
BLAM
BPRD
BLAM
BLAM
BLAM
BLAM

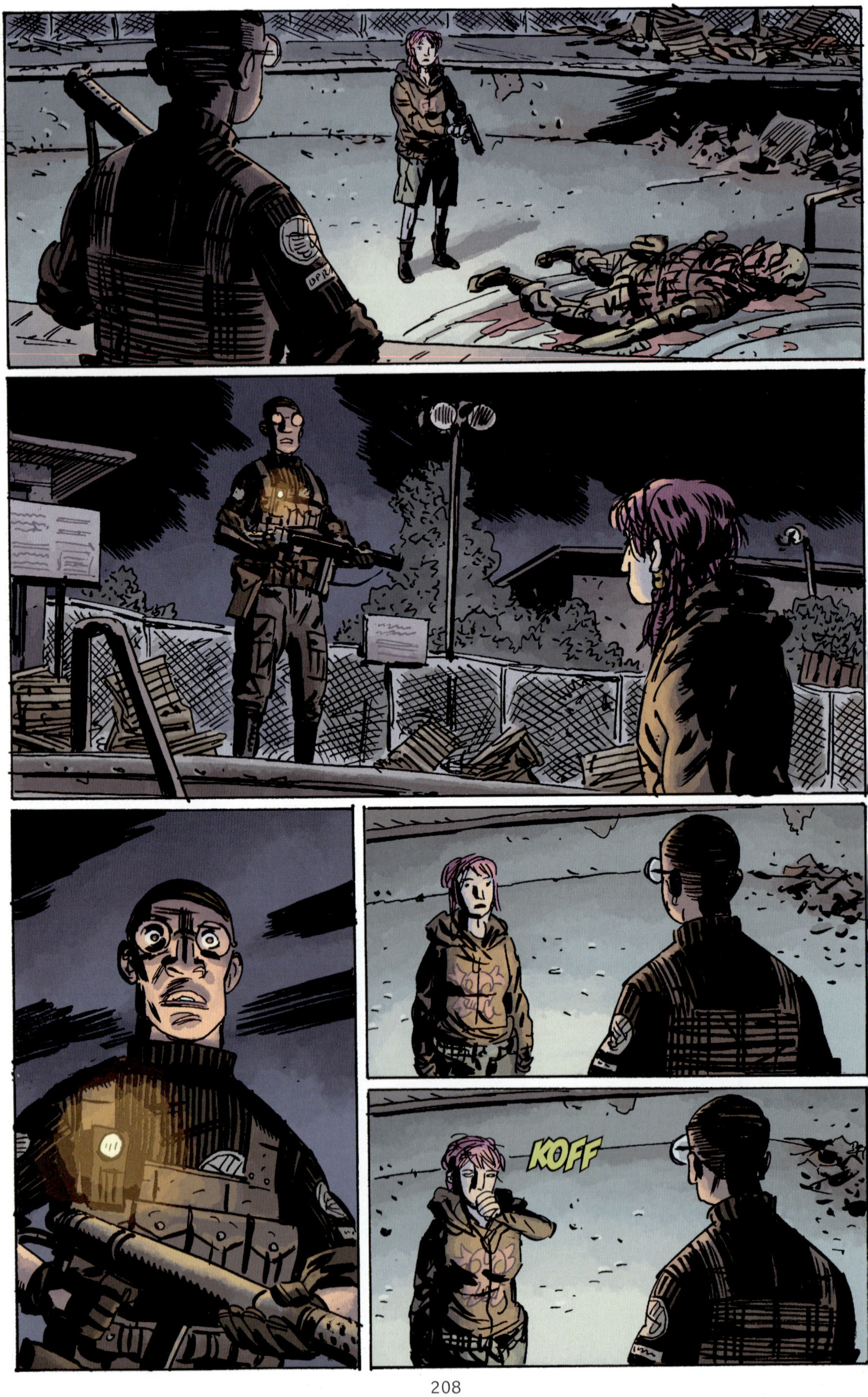
KOFF

--HAPPY THEY CAME ALONG. WE WOULD'VE BEEN SHUT DOWN IF THEY HADN'T, BUT CAN'T I BITCH A LITTLE ABOUT THEM?
LANGUAGE, MY DEAR. LANGUAGE!
WHA--? UHH, GOOD MORNING, PANYA.

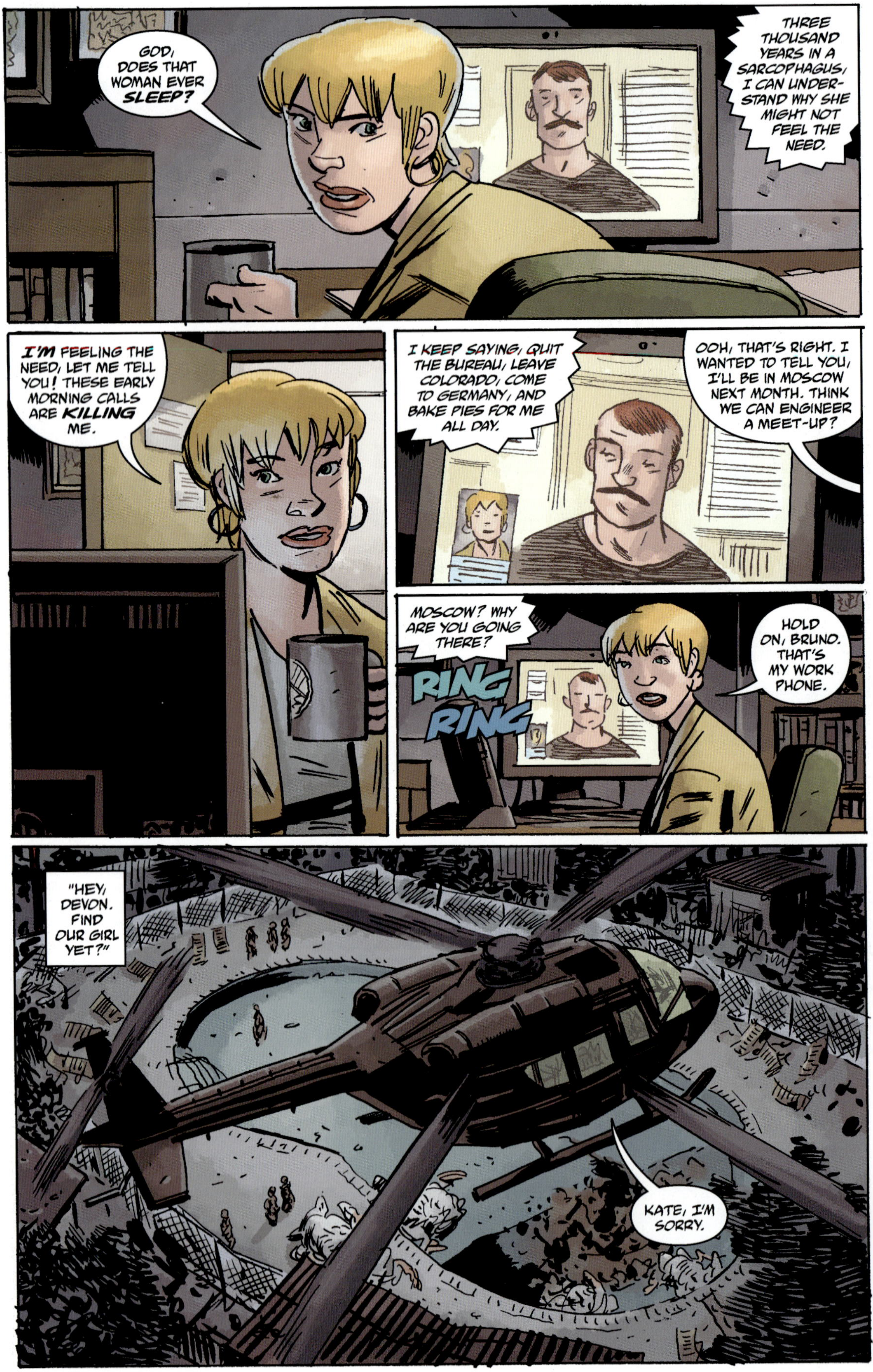
GOD, DOES THAT WOMAN EVER SLEEP?
THREE THOUSAND YEARS IN A SARCOPHAGUS, I CAN UNDER-STAND WHY SHE MIGHT NOT FEEL THE NEED.
I'M FEELING THE NEED, LET ME TELL YOU! THESE EARLY MORNING CALLS ARE KILLING ME.
I KEEP SAYING, QUIT THE BUREAU, LEAVE COLORADO, COME TO GERMANY, AND BAKE PIES FOR ME ALL DAY.
OOH, THAT'S RIGHT. I WANTED TO TELL YOU, I'LL BE IN MOSCOW NEXT MONTH. THINK WE CAN ENGINEER A MEET-UP?
MOSCOW? WHY ARE YOU GOING THERE?
RING
RING
HOLD ON, BRUNO. THAT'S MY WORK PHONE.
"HEY, DEVON. FIND OUR GIRL YET?"
KATE, I'M SORRY.

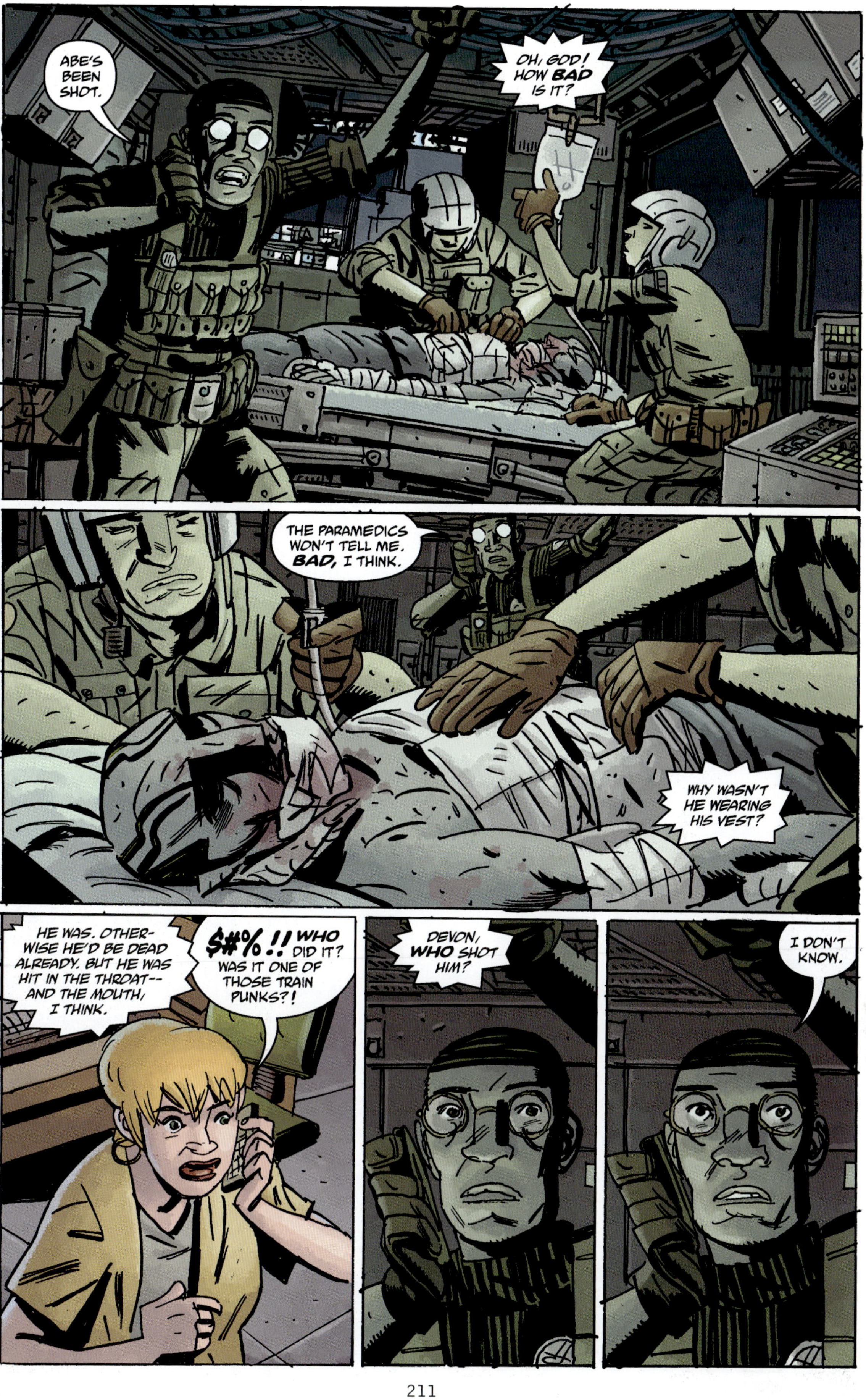
ABE'S BEEN SHOT.
OH, GOD! HOW BAD IS IT?
THE PARAMEDICS WON'T TELL ME. BAD, I THINK.
WHY WASN'T HE WEARING HIS VEST?
HE WAS. OTHERWISE HE'D BE DEAD ALREADY. BUT HE WAS HIT IN THE THROAT-- AND THE MOUTH, I THINK.
$#%!! WHO DID IT? WAS IT ONE OF THOSE TRAIN PUNKS?!
DEVON, WHO SHOT HIM?
I DON'T KNOW.

THIS EVERY-BODY?
EVERYBODY ALIVE. 'CEPT DINGO. THEY GOT HIM.
I HEARD ABOUT JORGE. I'M REAL SORRY. I SHOULDN'TA SENT YOU GUYS THERE.
IT'S NOT YOUR FAULT, WILLIS.
CAN'T STAY HERE NO MORE. WHERE YOU WANNA GO TO?
COLORADO.
THE END

MONSTERS CHAPTER ONE

ILLUSTRATION BY **RYAN SOOK**

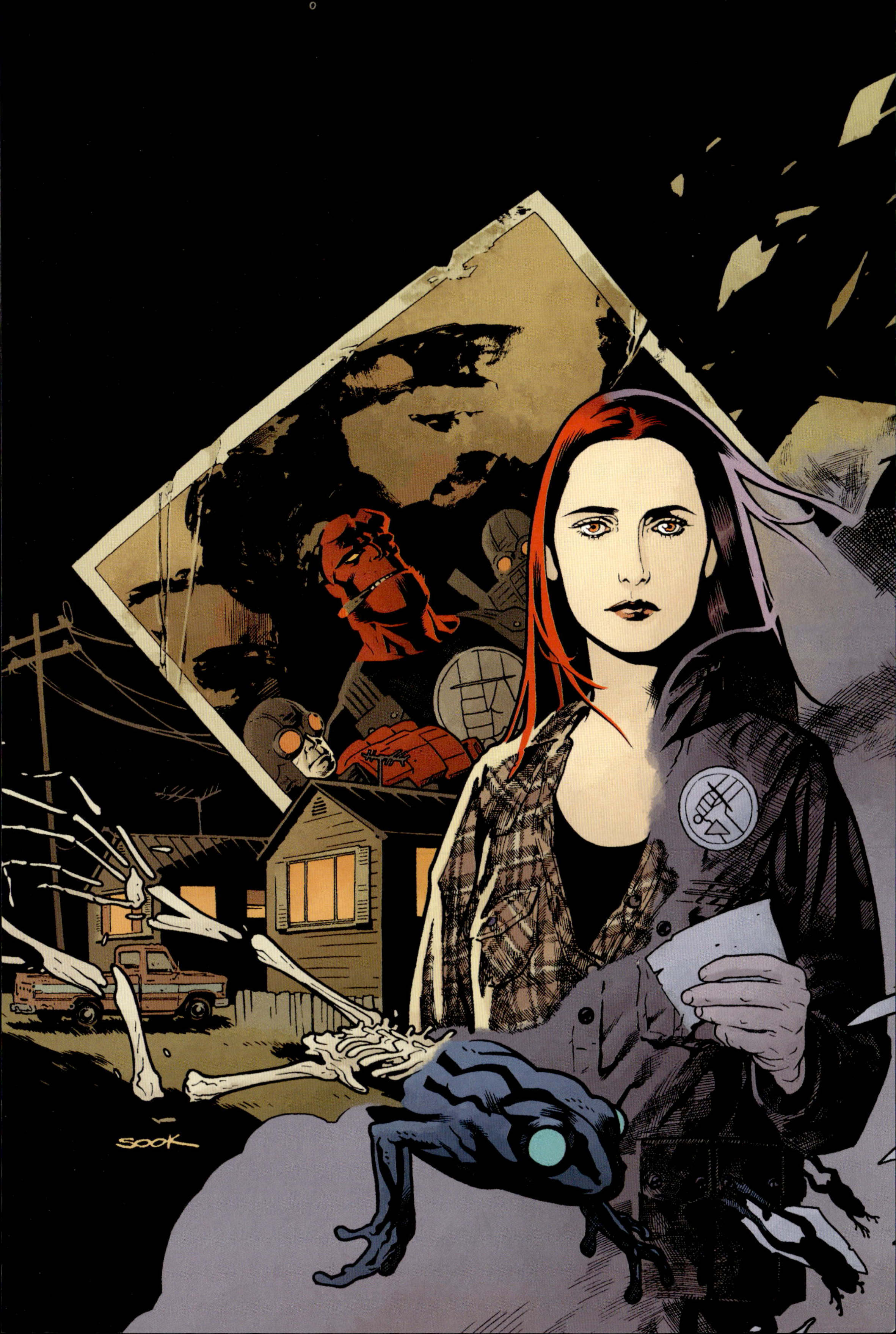
SOOK

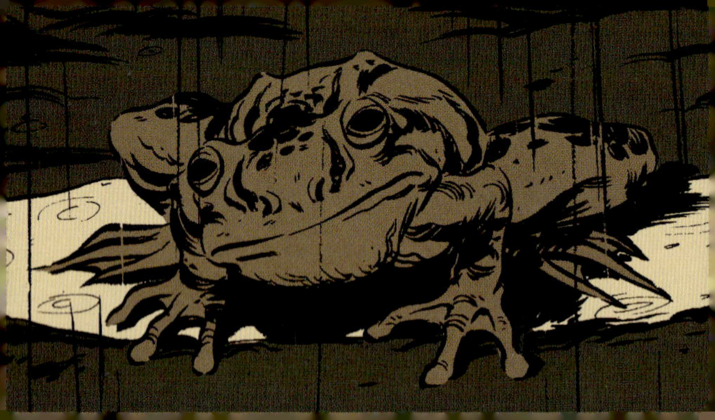

UGAR HILL PARK
AH, MAN, I HAD ENUFFA HIGH-LOW SPLIT. LET'S JUST GO BACK TO STRAIGHT.
WHY? HANDS YOU BEEN GETTIN', YOU LOSE EITHER WAY.
HAHAHA
HAHA
BUUULCH!
HEY, YOU JERK-OFFS WAN' YERSELF A **REAL** LAUGH? LAST BOTTLE RIGHT HERE.
HEY THERE, CHICA. JUS' IN TIME.
ALMOS' OUTTA BEER.

IF YOU DON'T GET YOUR FAT ASS OUT OF THIS HOUSE RIGHT NOW, YOU'RE GOING TO BE **COMPLETELY** OUT OF TEETH.
GIRLIE, YOU GOT ANY IDEA WHO IT IS--
SLAM

JESUS, LADY! HIS JAW'S ALL BUSTED.
GREAT TIME TO TAKE HIM TO A HOSPITAL.
THIS AIN'T OVER, BITCH!
YEAH IT IS.
'LIZBETH?
I'M GOING TO BED.
SLAM
I'LL GET THE MOP.

DAMN, BOY'S PUT ON WEIGHT.
I SEE JUBAL CLOCK OUT COUPLA HIGHWAY PATROLMEN ONCE, BUT DIDN'T TAKE HER BUT A SECOND TO LAY HIM OUT.
THAT'D BE 'CAUSE THAT GIRL OF JEB'S AND TODD'S USED TO BE SOME KIND OF SECRET AGENT. GOT HERSELF IN SOME TROUBLE, NOW SHE'S ON THE RUN.
SUMPIN' LIKE THAT, ANYWAY.
WHERE'D YOU HEAR THAT BULL$#@%?
'S WHAT JEB TOL' ME. SHE TOL' HIM, HE TOL' ME. MAKES SENSE, SEEIN'S HOW SHE KUNG FU'D THE CRAP OUTTA THIS BEAR.
JUS' HOPE JUBAL'S OLD LADY'S HOME. SHE GOT THE CAR KEYS.
"SECRET AGENT." MAN, THAT PONYTAIL MOTHER#$%& IS FULLA CRAP, YOU AST ME.
TODD'S THE ONE WITH A PONYTAIL, YOU MORON!
CHRIST, HOW YOU PLAY POKER AT A MAN'S HOME FOR NEAR ON A YEAR AND NOT KNOW HIS NAME?

HE'S COMING BACK. HE'S COMING BACK.
LET IT GO.
I DID. I LET GO OF ALL OF IT.
I KILLED THEM. EVERY SINGLE ONE OF THEM. I FEEL IT. THEY'RE GONE.
I'M DONE.
NO.
NO, I DON'T WANT TO.

HE'S COMING BACK. YOU DON'T NEED ME.
I'M DONE! I'M DONE!
DADDY...?
WHAT IS IT, DADDY?
PLINK PLINK PLINK
PLINK PLINK

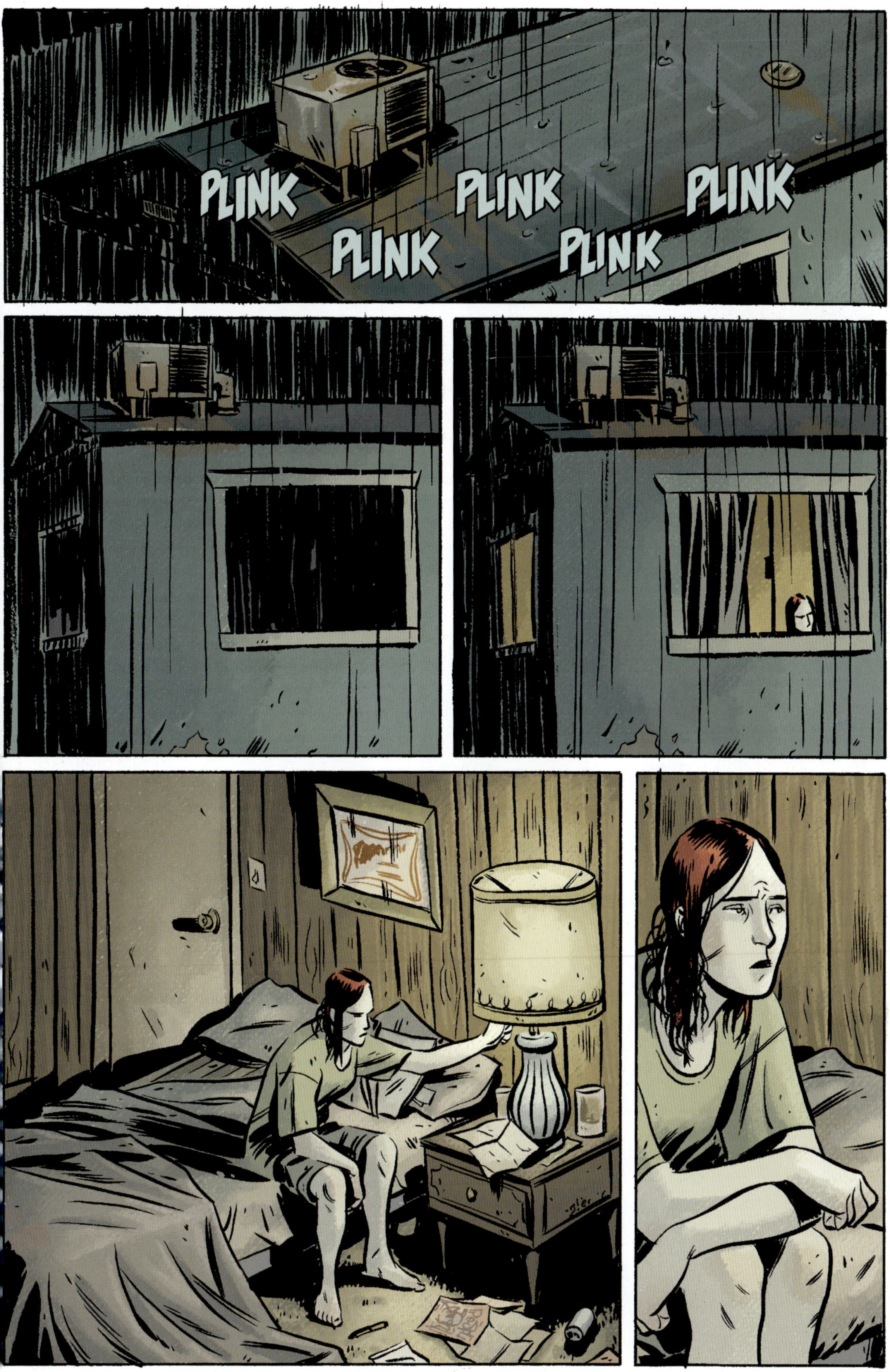
PLINK
PLINK
PLINK
PLINK
PLINK

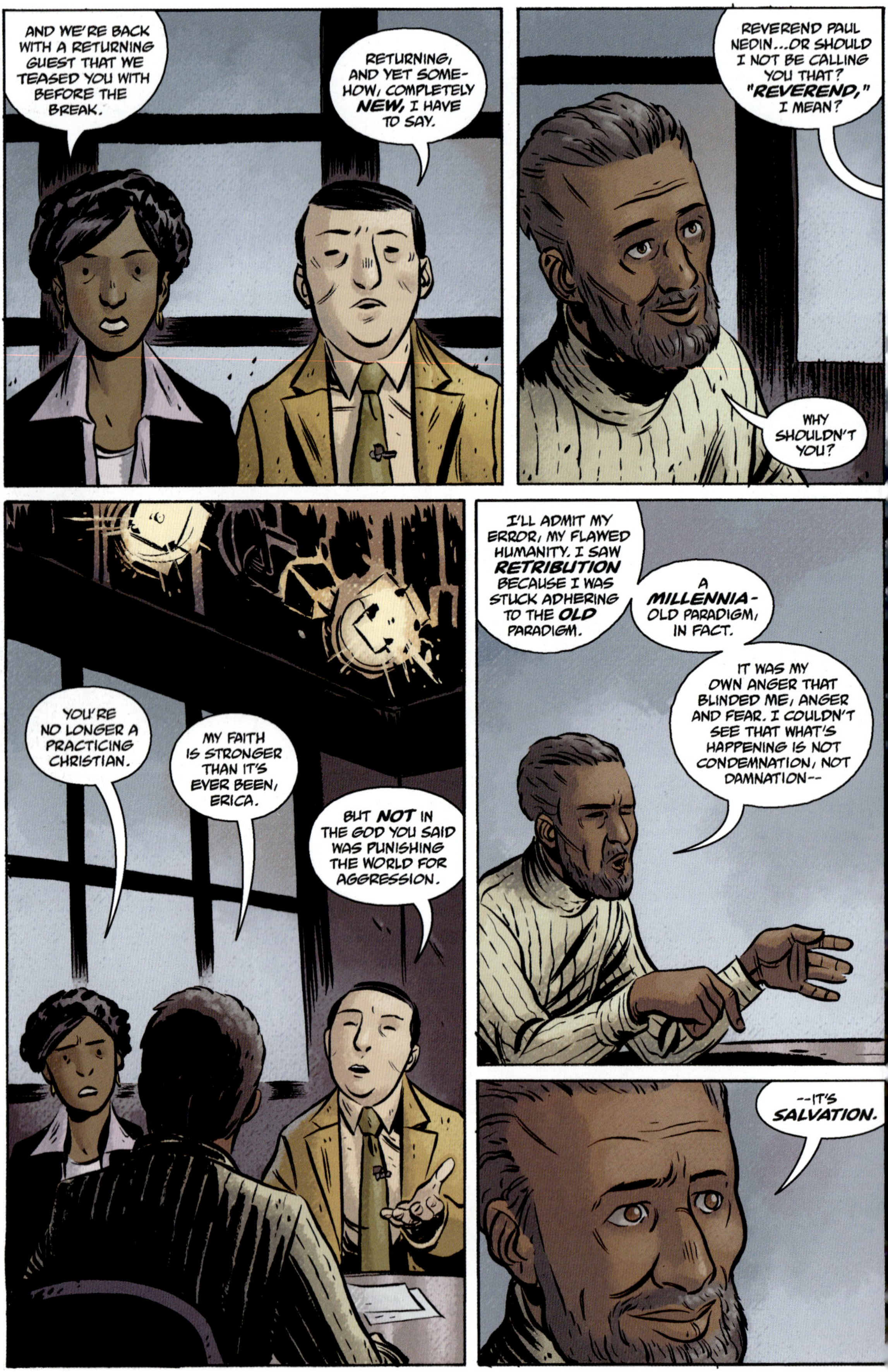
AND WE'RE BACK WITH A RETURNING GUEST THAT WE TEASED YOU WITH BEFORE THE BREAK.
RETURNING, AND YET SOME-HOW, COMPLETELY NEW, I HAVE TO SAY.
REVEREND PAUL NEDIN...OR SHOULD I NOT BE CALLING YOU THAT? "REVEREND," I MEAN?
WHY SHOULDN'T YOU?
YOU'RE NO LONGER A PRACTICING CHRISTIAN.
MY FAITH IS STRONGER THAN IT'S EVER BEEN, ERICA.
BUT NOT IN THE GOD YOU SAID WAS PUNISHING THE WORLD FOR AGGRESSION.
I'LL ADMIT MY ERROR, MY FLAWED HUMANITY. I SAW RETRIBUTION BECAUSE I WAS STUCK ADHERING TO THE OLD PARADIGM.
A MILLENNIA-OLD PARADIGM, IN FACT.
IT WAS MY OWN ANGER THAT BLINDED ME, ANGER AND FEAR. I COULDN'T SEE THAT WHAT'S HAPPENING IS NOT CONDEMNATION, NOT DAMNATION--
--IT'S SALVATION.

SO NOW YOU THINK THE EARTHQUAKES, THE VOLCANOES AND MONSTERS, THESE ARE GOOD THINGS?
NOT FOR EVERYBODY, NO.
"NOT FOR EVERY-BODY"? THEN THIS "THINNING" OF THE POPULATION, IT'S SOME KIND OF RAPTURE?
LISTEN TO YOURSELF, ERICA. THE RAPTURE IS A BUNCH OF NONSENSE.
SO THE RAPTURE'S NONSENSE, NOW? BUT ANIMAL SACRIFICES, THOSE MAKE PERFECT SENSE.
WE HAD A PIG ROAST, PATRICK. WE INAUGURATED OUR NEW CHURCH WITH A BARBECUE.
DON'T BELIEVE EVERYTHING PEOPLE SAY ON TELEVISION.
SO YOUR CHURCH DOES NOT PRACTICE ANIMAL SACRIFICE?
OF COURSE NOT.
CAN--CAN WE GET THAT GRAPHIC?
OKAY, OKAY, WE SEEM TO BE TALKING ACROSS EACH OTHER, AND I JUST WANT TO GET THIS STRAIGHT. ARE YOU SAYING THAT GOD SENT THIS THING TO "HELP" US?
OR HAVE YOU TURNED YOUR BACK ON GOD ALTOGETHER?

PATRICK, THAT IS GOD.
THIS BROTHER'S OFF HIS NUT!
KEEP IT DOWN. SHE'S SLEEPING.
DUDE, WE AGREED I CAN WATCH T.V. AT NIGHT--
RIGHT. LONG'S YOU KEEP IT DOWN, SURE, BUT YOU START ARGUIN' WITH THE THING, THAT'S WHEN IT GETS LOUD IN HERE.
NUMBER ONE, I WUN'T ARGUIN'. JUST STATIN' A FAC'!
DRIVE
AN' NUMBER TWO, I'M SICKA THIS $#%*#! CAN'T RELAX IN MY OWN HOME, AND THAT AIN'T RIGHT!
FINE. MOVE ON OUT. I LIKE THAT IDEA.
YEAH, RIGHT! LIKE YOU COULD HANDLE HER BY YERSELF.

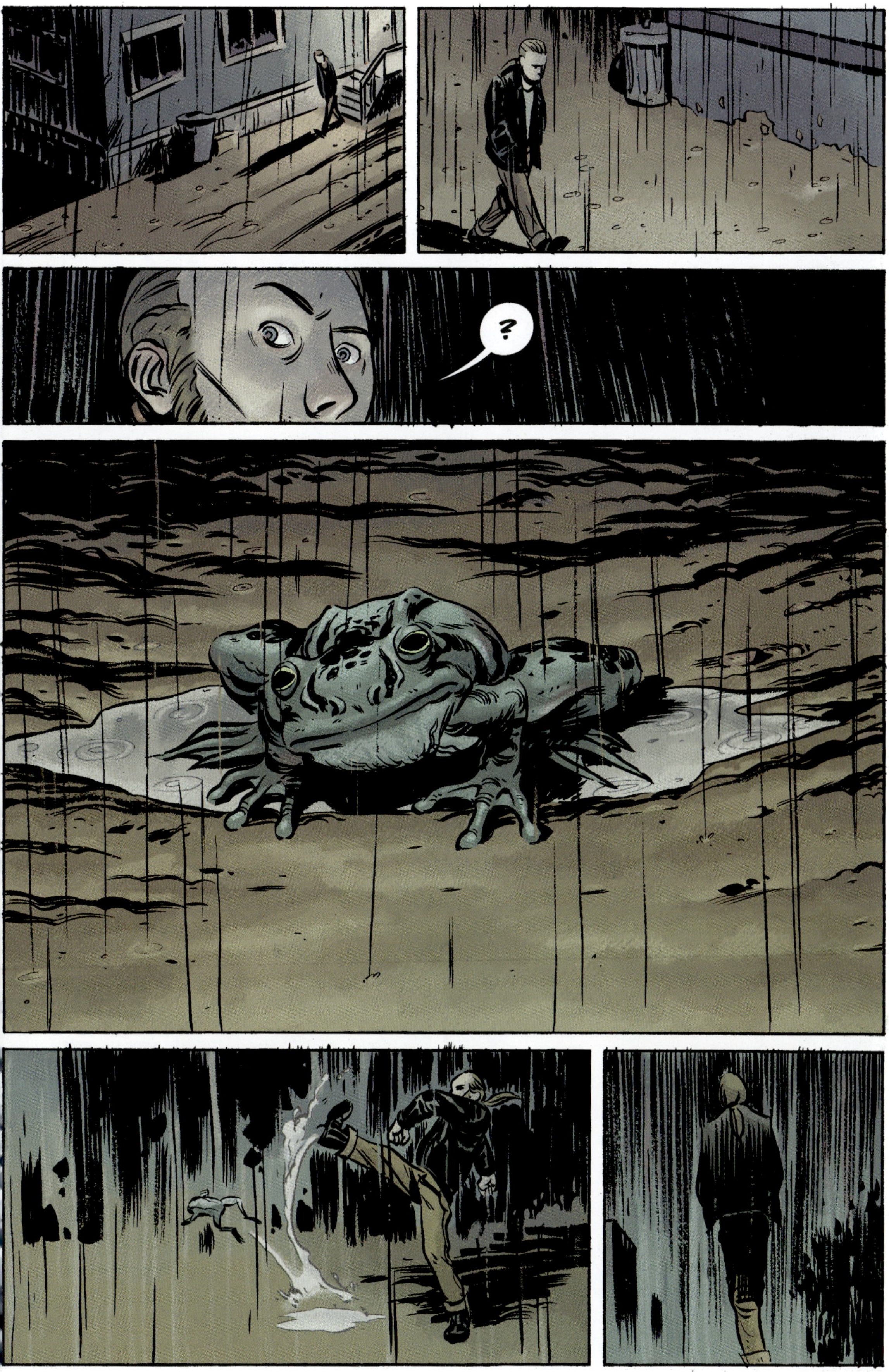
?

MAN, IT REALLY IS TOO NICE A EVENIN' FOR POKER, YOU KNOW?
YOU KEEP SAYIN' THAT-- LIKE YOU WANNA CATCH FIRE-FLIES OR SUMPIN'.
'SIDES, WE **GOTTA** GO.
JUBAL'S BEEN HOLED UP IN HIS HOUSE ALL WEEK, JAW ALL WIRED, HAVIN' TO DRINK HIS MEALS THROUGH A STRAW.
I KNOW HE LOVES HIS OL' LADY, BUT YOU TAKE HER COOKIN' AWAY FROM HER... WELL, I'M BETTIN' THEY DRIVIN' EACH OTHER CRAZY.
I TRIED TO GET HIM TO GO FISHIN' WITH US. BROKE JAW DON'T MEAN YOU CAN'T BE OUTSIDE. WOULDN'T COME.
BE A WHILE, I EXPEC'. OL' JUBAL GETTIN' TOOK DOWN BY A GAL--PROB'LY STINGS, YOU KNOW?
HOW WE SURE THERE'S EVEN ENOUGH FOLKS OVER AT JUBAL'S FOR A DECENT GAME? I MEAN, DOES HE **GOT** ANY OTHER FRIENDS?
STU, WHUT THE HELL'S A MATTER WITH YOU? WHO GIVES A DAMN ABOUT THE POKER GAME?!
JUBAL, HE'S BEEN HUMILIATED. YOU KNOW THAT WORD?
WHATEVER FRIENDS HE **DOES** GOT-- BEIN' US--WELL, HE NEEDS 'EM RIGHT NOW.

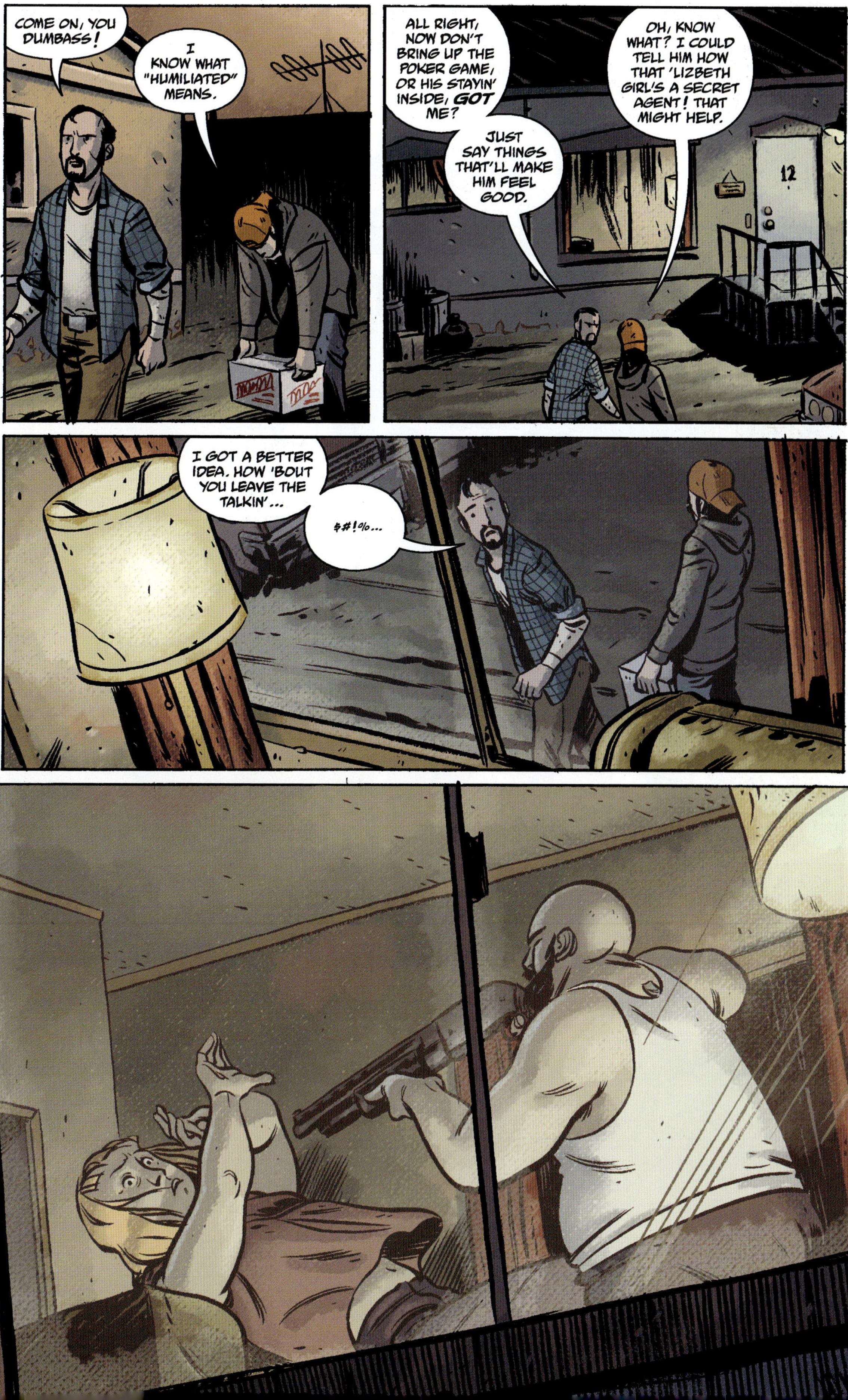
COME ON, YOU DUMBASS!
I KNOW WHAT "HUMILIATED" MEANS.
ALL RIGHT, NOW DON'T BRING UP THE POKER GAME, OR HIS STAYIN' INSIDE, GOT ME?
JUST SAY THINGS THAT'LL MAKE HIM FEEL GOOD.
OH, KNOW WHAT? I COULD TELL HIM HOW THAT 'LIZBETH GIRL'S A SECRET AGENT! THAT MIGHT HELP.
12
I GOT A BETTER IDEA. HOW 'BOUT YOU LEAVE THE TALKIN'...
$#!%...

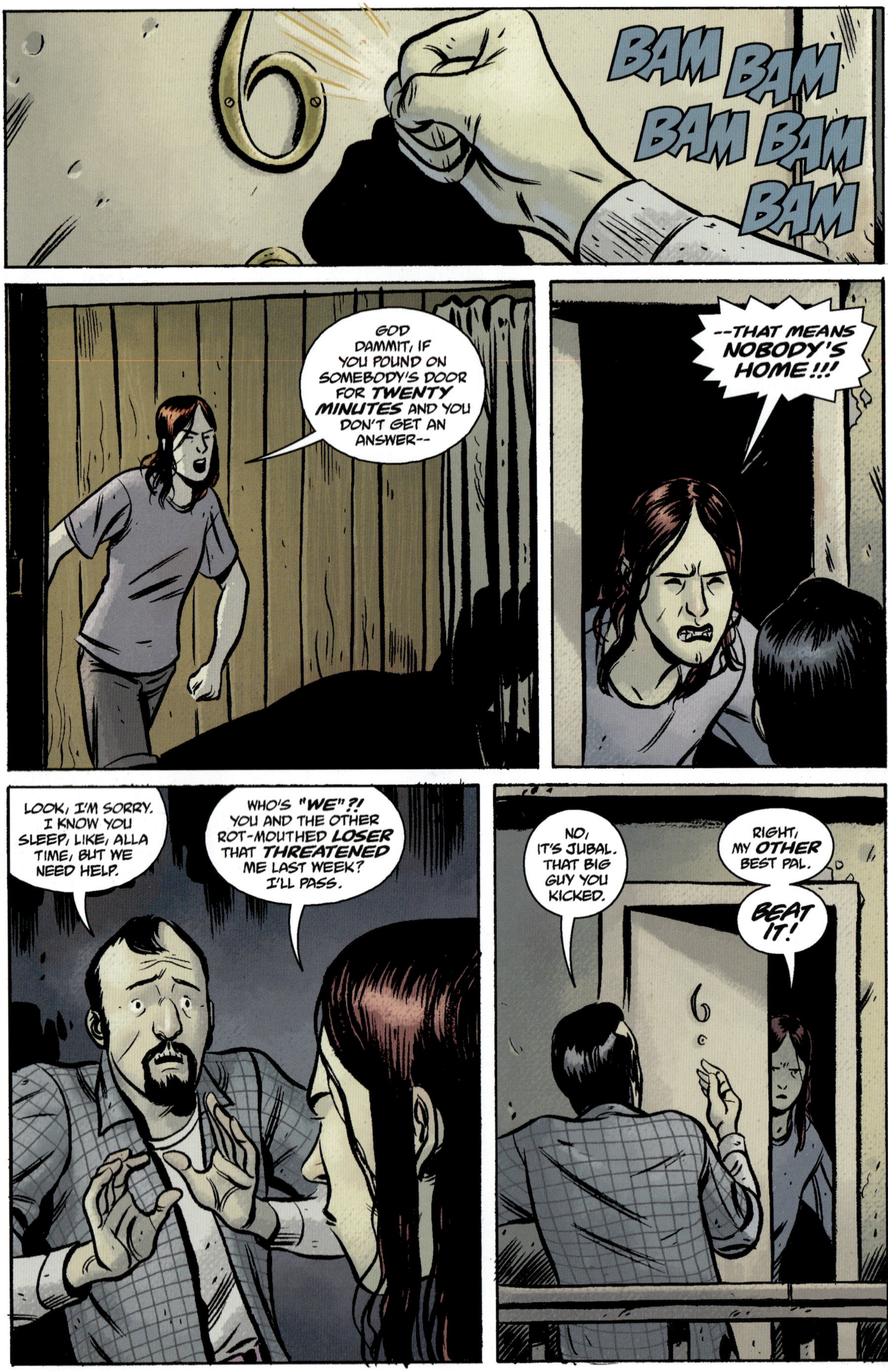
BAM BAM BAM BAM BAM
GOD DAMMIT, IF YOU POUND ON SOMEBODY'S DOOR FOR TWENTY MINUTES AND YOU DON'T GET AN ANSWER--
--THAT MEANS NOBODY'S HOME!!!
LOOK, I'M SORRY. I KNOW YOU SLEEP, LIKE, ALLA TIME, BUT WE NEED HELP.
WHO'S "WE"?! YOU AND THE OTHER ROT-MOUTHED LOSER THAT THREATENED ME LAST WEEK? I'LL PASS.
NO, IT'S JUBAL. THAT BIG GUY YOU KICKED.
RIGHT, MY OTHER BEST PAL.
BEAT IT!

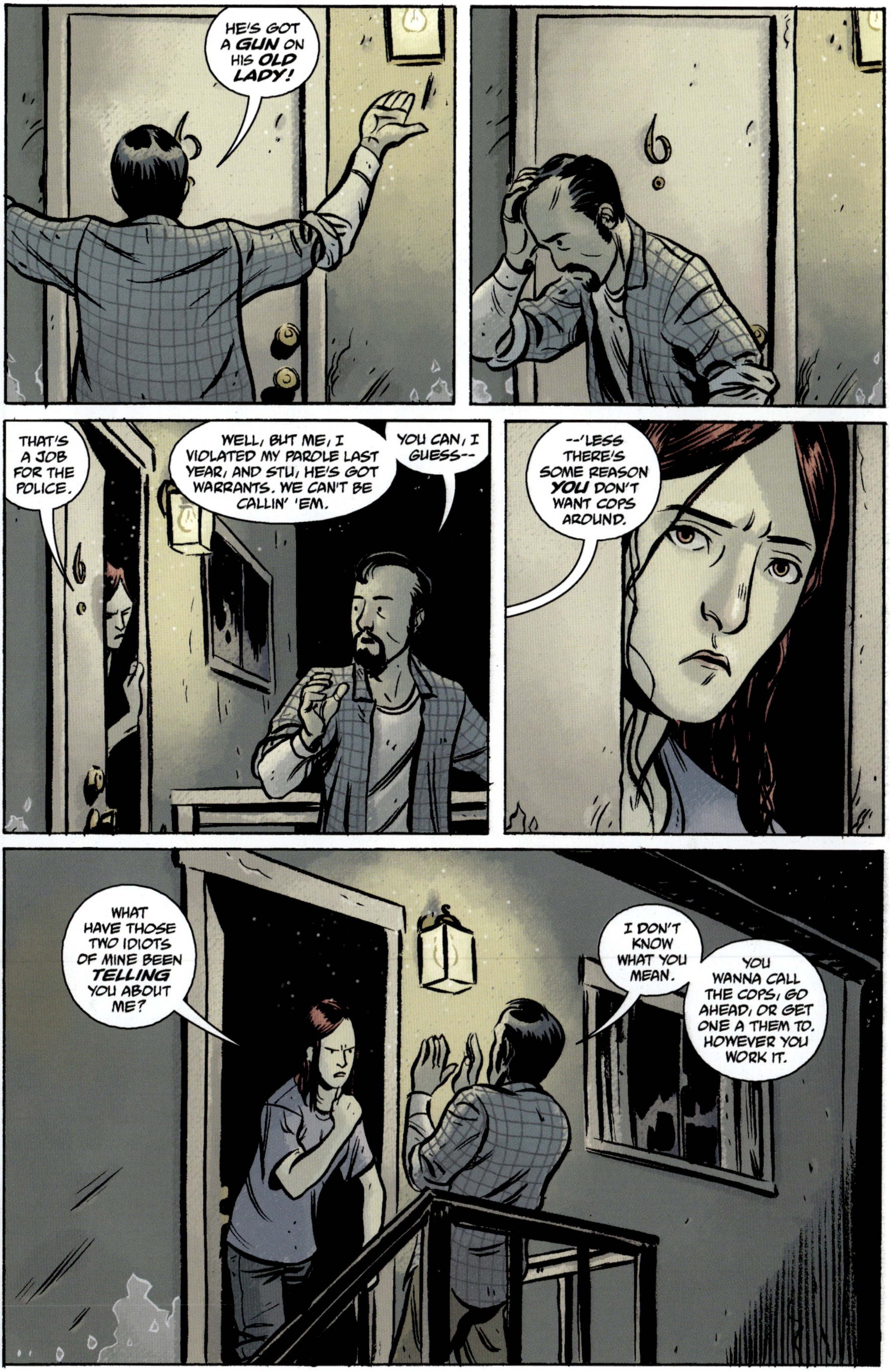
HE'S GOT A GUN ON HIS OLD LADY!
THAT'S A JOB FOR THE POLICE.
WELL, BUT ME, I VIOLATED MY PAROLE LAST YEAR, AND STU, HE'S GOT WARRANTS. WE CAN'T BE CALLIN' 'EM.
YOU CAN, I GUESS--
--'LESS THERE'S SOME REASON YOU DON'T WANT COPS AROUND.
WHAT HAVE THOSE TWO IDIOTS OF MINE BEEN TELLING YOU ABOUT ME?
I DON'T KNOW WHAT YOU MEAN.
YOU WANNA CALL THE COPS, GO AHEAD, OR GET ONE A THEM TO. HOWEVER YOU WORK IT.

THEY'RE NOT HERE, AND ANYWAY, YOU DIDN'T COME HERE FOR ME TO CALL THE COPS, DID YOU?
JUBAL'S A BASTARD, BUT HE AIN'T NEVER DONE NOTHING LIKE THIS. I THINK HE'S JUST KINDA LOST HIS HEAD, IS ALL.
AND YOU HANDLED HIM PRETTY EASY, SO...
SO YOUR IDEA IS, I KNOCK HIM OUT AGAIN, KEEP HIM OUT OF JAIL?
JUST WHY DO YOU THINK I'D DO THAT?
DIDN'T SAY I DID THINK IT.
REEBIT
HUH. YOU MAY NOT BE AS STUPID AS YOU LOOK.
REEBIT
REEBIT
REEBIT
REEBIT

DAMN, ELI, TOOK YOU LONG ENOUGH.
JUBAL FORCED HIS WIFE BACK INTO THE BEDROOM. BEEN PRETTY QUIET SINCE.
I HEARD THEM TALKING, HEARD A LADY'S VOICE, SO I KNOW SHE'S STILL--
THAT'S FOR CALLING ME A BITCH!
OOF!
#*$%
YOU!! THIS IS ALL YOUR FAULT, Y'KNOW THAT? IN HIS RIGHT MIND, JUBAL'D NEVER HURT HIS WOMAN.
BUT HE'S A PROUD MAN, AND YOU--YOU HUMILIATED HIM.
AND LET'S HOPE I CAN DO IT AGAIN.

ALL RIGHT, FAT MAN! I'M HERE AND I'M COMING IN.
APPARENTLY YOU'RE NOT MAD AT YOUR WIFE. YOU'RE MAD AT ME.
SO COME ON OUT. COME OUT AND SHOOT MY ASS-- IF YOU THINK YOU CAN.
12
WHIMPER

SHHH, DON'T BE AFRAID. I'LL GET YOU OUT OF HERE. YOU'RE GOING TO BE OKAY.
N-N-NO. IN IN IN IN THERE--
--IN THERE IN THERE IN THERE IN THERE--
--IN THERE IN THERE IN THERE IN THERE...
12

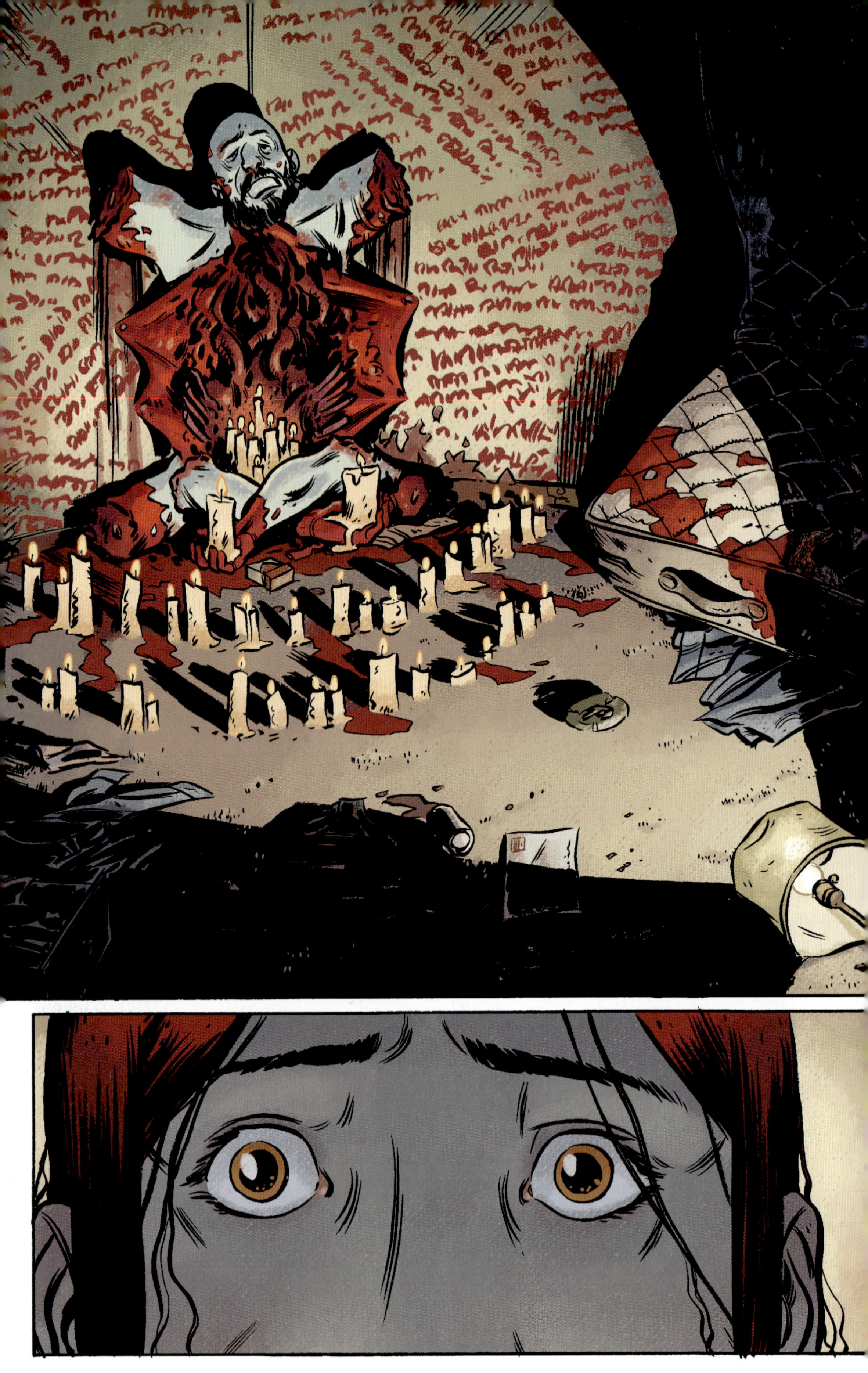

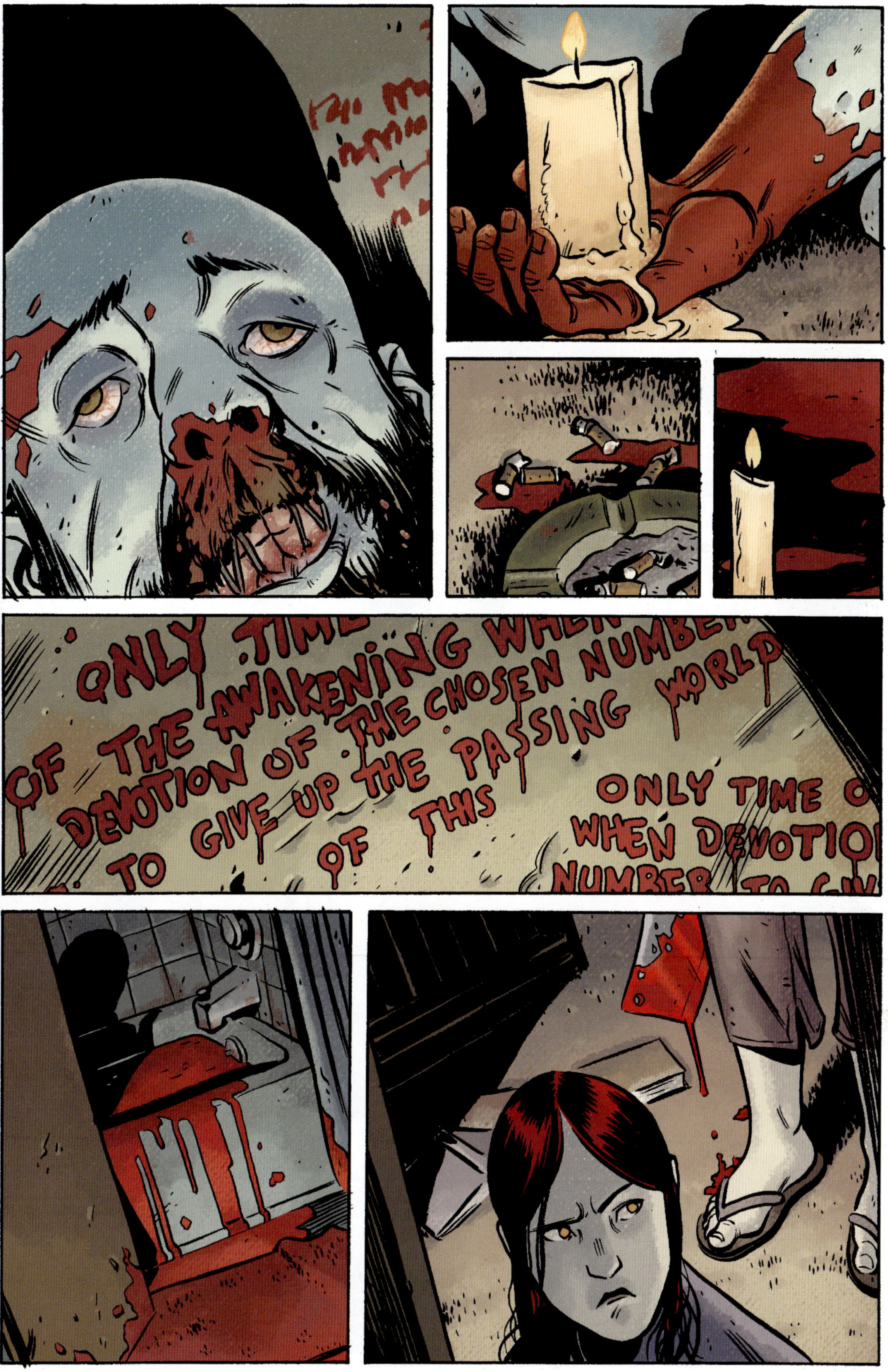
ONLY TIM
OF THE AWAKENING WHE
DEVOTION OF THE CHOSEN NUMBE
TO GIVE UP THE PASSING WORLD
OF THIS
ONLY TIME O
WHEN DEVOTIO
NUMBER

AIN'T YOU GONNA SCREAM?
I DON'T SCARE EASY.
GUESS NOT. YOU'LL DIE EASY ENOUGH, THOUGH.
TRUST ME, TRAILER MONKEY, YOU'RE GOING TO NEED A LOT MORE THAN A MEAT CLEAVER TO END ME.
THAT'S JUST IT, LIZ, HONEY.
SHE'S GOT A LOT MORE.

MONSTERS CHAPTER TWO

ILLUSTRATION BY **RYAN SOOK**

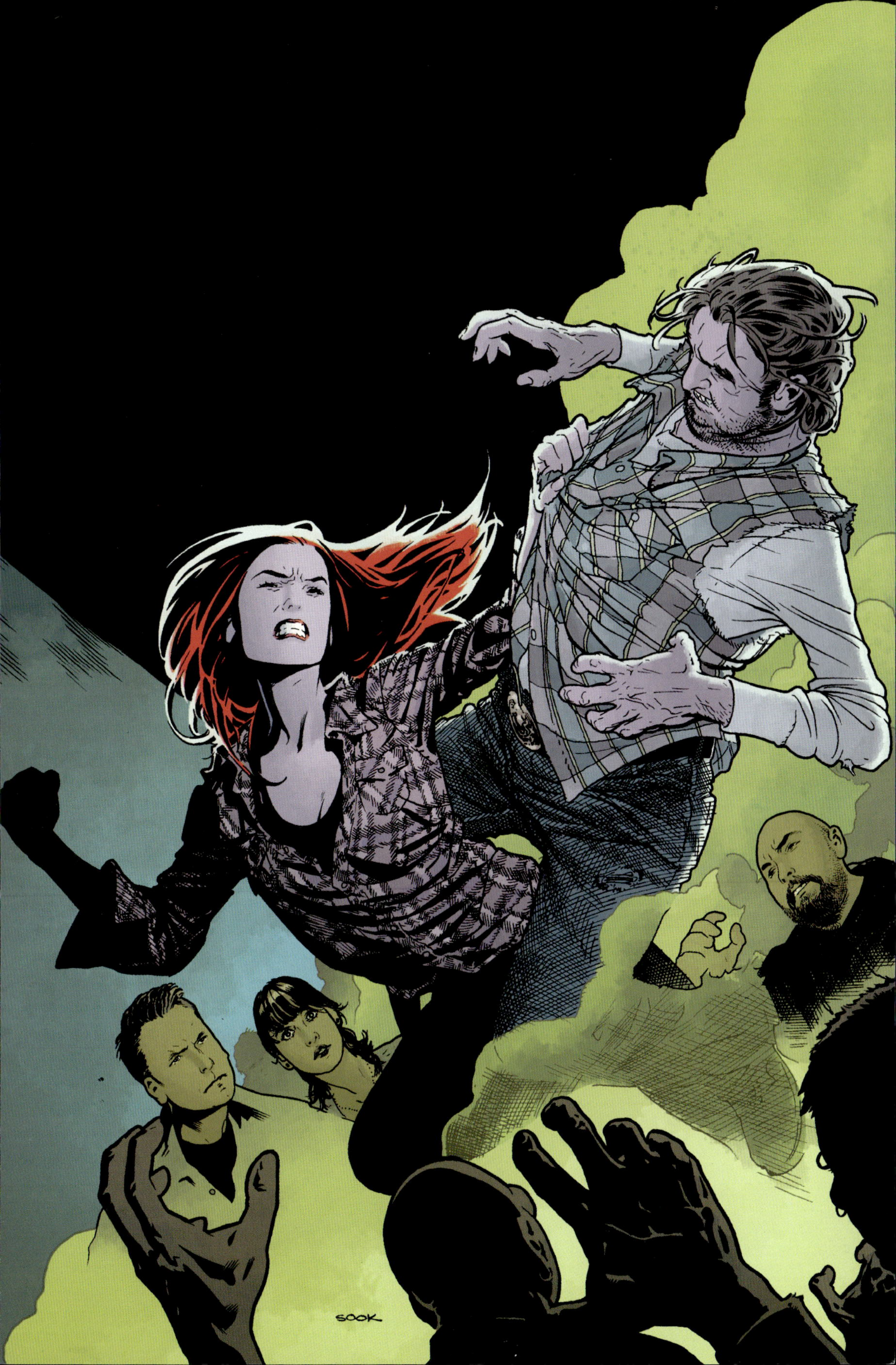
SOOK

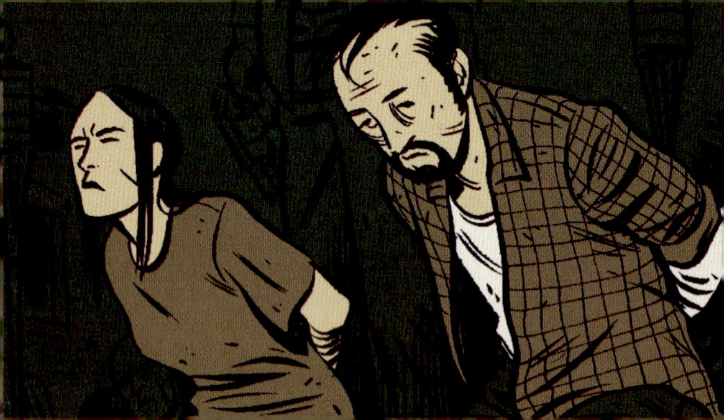

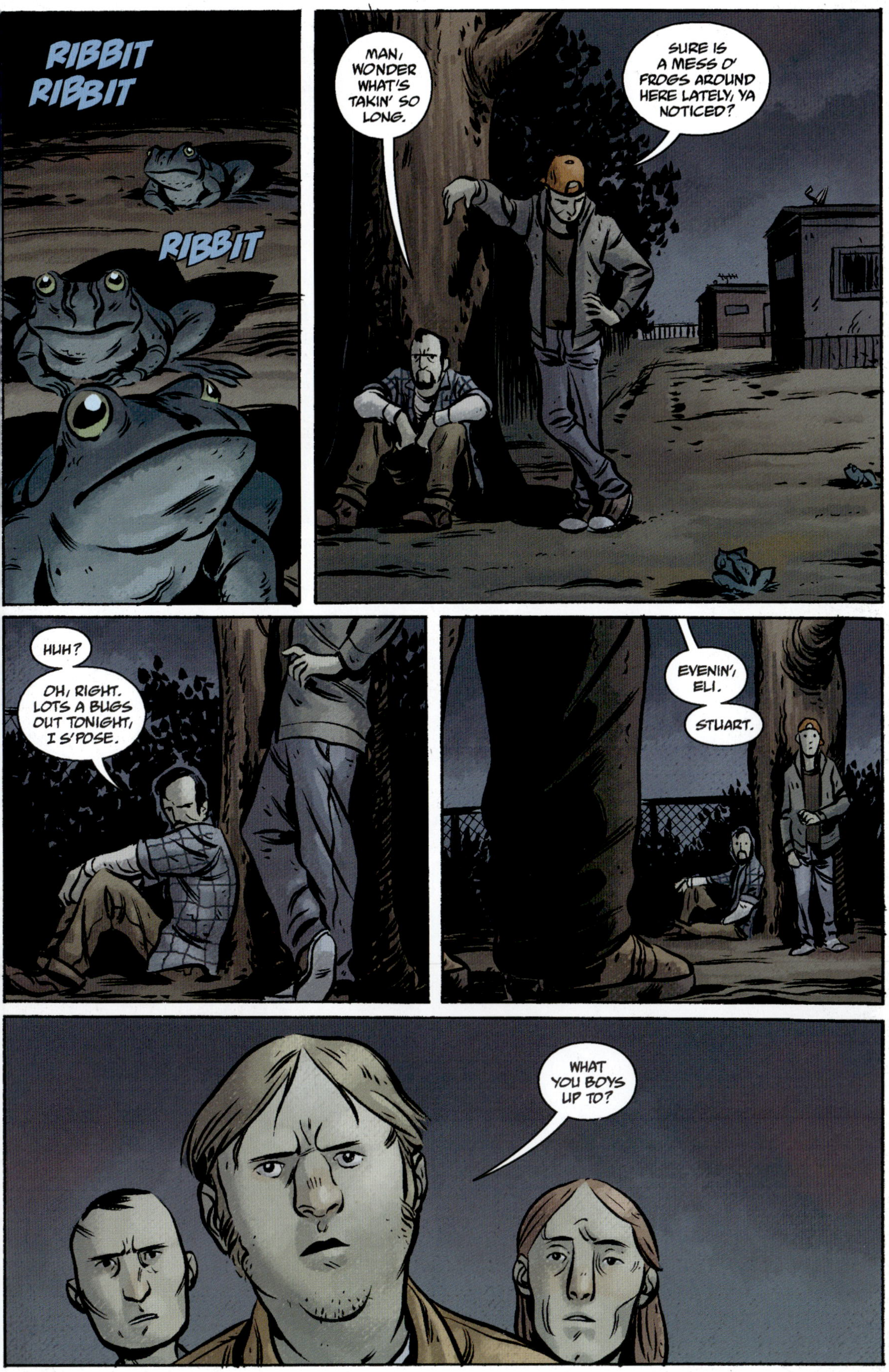

RIBBIT RIBBIT
RIBBIT
MAN, WONDER WHAT'S TAKIN' SO LONG.
SURE IS A MESS O' FROGS AROUND HERE LATELY, YA NOTICED?
HUH?
OH, RIGHT. LOTS A BUGS OUT TONIGHT, I S'POSE.
EVENIN', ELI.
STUART.
WHAT YOU BOYS UP TO?

I SWEAR, TODD, YOU'RE EVEN STUPIDER THAN I THOUGHT.
SHUT YER MOUTH, GIRL!
OR WHAT? YOU CAN'T SHOOT ME, JACKASS!
YOU'LL BLOW HOLES IN YOUR NEW GIRLFRIEND'S FACE, MAKE HER EVEN UGLIER.
AIN'T MUCH OF NOTHIN' STOPPIN' ME!
DON'T I KNOW IT.
YOU WANT HER, TODD?

SHE'S ALL YOURS!
DAMMIT, WOMAN, YOU IN MY WAY!
GOOD NIGHT, STUPID!
I CAN'T DO THIS ANYMORE. IT'S SUPPOSED TO BE ALL OVER.
I'M SUPPOSED TO BE--
12

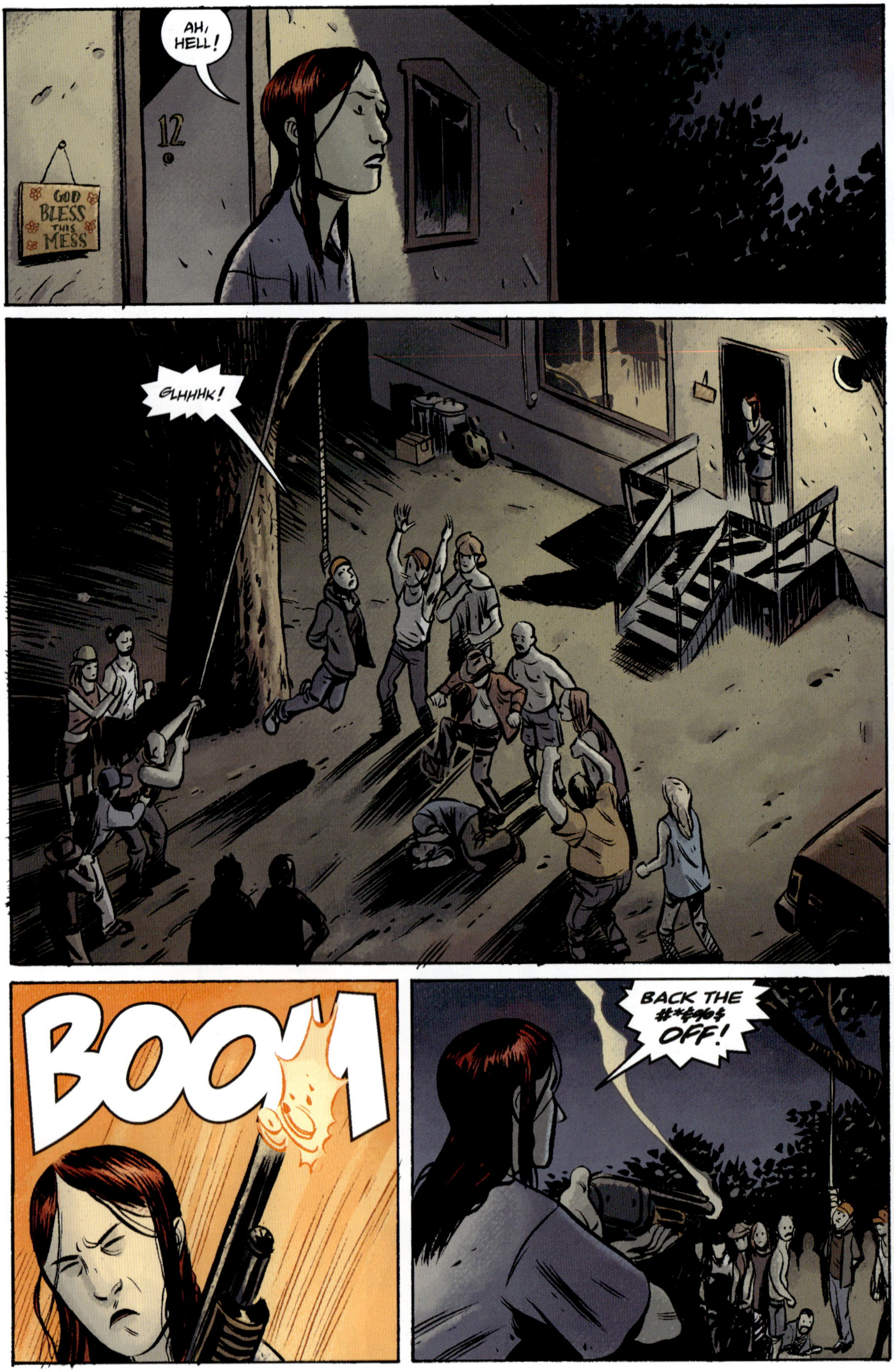
AH, HELL!
12
GOD BLESS THIS MESS
GLHHHK!
BOOM
BACK THE #*$%$ OFF!

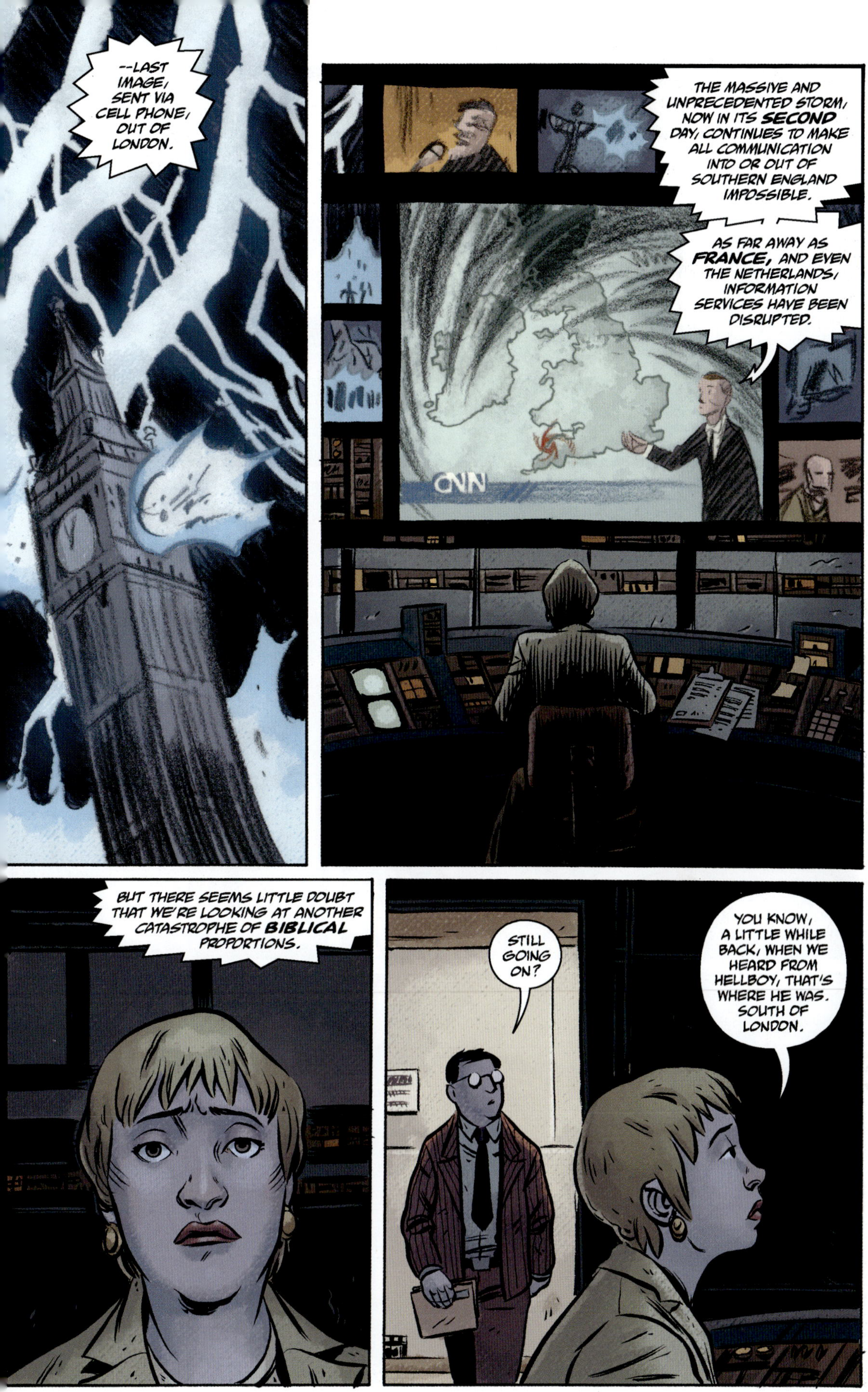
--LAST IMAGE, SENT VIA CELL PHONE, OUT OF LONDON.
THE MASSIVE AND UNPRECEDENTED STORM, NOW IN ITS SECOND DAY, CONTINUES TO MAKE ALL COMMUNICATION INTO OR OUT OF SOUTHERN ENGLAND IMPOSSIBLE.
AS FAR AWAY AS FRANCE, AND EVEN THE NETHERLANDS, INFORMATION SERVICES HAVE BEEN DISRUPTED.
CNN
BUT THERE SEEMS LITTLE DOUBT THAT WE'RE LOOKING AT ANOTHER CATASTROPHE OF BIBLICAL PROPORTIONS.
STILL GOING ON?
YOU KNOW, A LITTLE WHILE BACK, WHEN WE HEARD FROM HELLBOY, THAT'S WHERE HE WAS. SOUTH OF LONDON.

AND YOU THINK HE'S THE CAUSE?
WHAT?!!
I'M SORRY!
IT'S JUST THAT I'VE GOTTEN SO MUCH CONFLICTING INFORMATION--
YEAH, OKAY. FORGET IT. YOU NEED SOMETHING?
I...I HATE TO HAVE TO BRING THIS UP NOW, BUT YOUR MEETING IN MOSCOW--
OH, GOD. CAN'T WE POSTPONE THAT?
AT LEAST UNTIL AFTER ABE'S RECOVERED.
UM, YES, WELL, AS TO AGENT SAPIEN...
"...THAT'S ACTUALLY WHO I CAME TO TALK TO YOU ABOUT."

NOPE.
NOT GOING ANY-WHERE, ARE YOU?
STU, YOU GONNA BE OKAY?
SH *CAFF* SAVED OUR LIVES *HACKHACK HACK*
YEAH, WELL, AS ALLIES I'M GUESSING YOU TWO AREN'T WORTH A LOT, BUT I NEED ALL THE HELP I CAN GET.
YOU NEED HELP? WHAT WITH?
FOR ONE THING, MY CELL'S BACK AT THE HOUSE, SO HOW'S ABOUT YOU CALL THE COPS?
THEY TOOK OUR PHONES. FIRST THING THEY DID AFTER WE SAID WE WAS HERE TO HELP JUBAL.
WHERE IS JUBAL, ANYHOW?
CHECK THE BEDROOM. SEE WHAT YOUR NEIGHBORS HAVE BEEN UP TO.

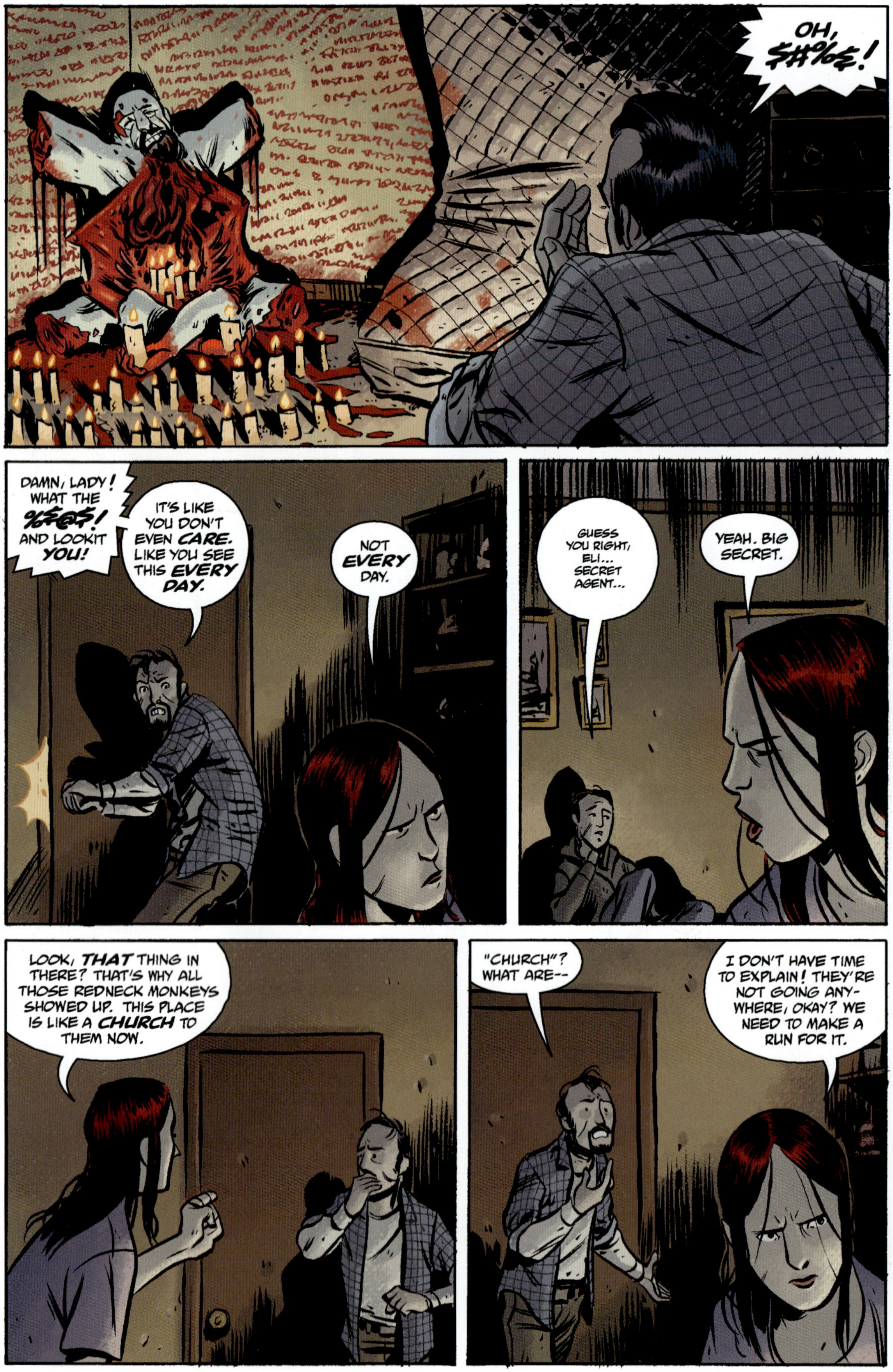

OH, $#%£!
DAMN, LADY! WHAT THE %£@$! AND LOOKIT YOU!
IT'S LIKE YOU DON'T EVEN CARE. LIKE YOU SEE THIS EVERY DAY.
NOT EVERY DAY.
GUESS YOU RIGHT, ELI... SECRET AGENT...
YEAH. BIG SECRET.
LOOK, THAT THING IN THERE? THAT'S WHY ALL THOSE REDNECK MONKEYS SHOWED UP. THIS PLACE IS LIKE A CHURCH TO THEM NOW.
"CHURCH"? WHAT ARE--
I DON'T HAVE TIME TO EXPLAIN! THEY'RE NOT GOING ANYWHERE, OKAY? WE NEED TO MAKE A RUN FOR IT.

YOU GOT A GUN, THEY DON'T. LET THEM RUN.
IT'S A TRAILER PARK, ELI. HOW FAR DO THEY HAVE TO LOOK FOR A GUN?
BESIDES, I HAVE ONE ROUND LEFT. THAT'S IT.
RUNNIN' AIN'T NO KINDA PLAN. LOOK AT STU. HE AIN'T IN NO SHAPE TO WALK, EVEN.
NO. GUESS NOT. OKAY, BUT I HAVE TO WARN YOU. PLAN B IS EVEN WORSE.
I GOT YOUR TEXT. THEY ALL STILL INSIDE?
YUP. WE CUT THE PHONE LINE, AND RHETT'S OUT BACK KEEPIN' WATCH. COURSE, SHE MIGHT HAVE A CELL.
FORGET THAT. NOW YOU GIVE RHETT A CALL. I WANNA--
KEESH
THEY MAKIN' A BREAK!
BOOM

GOD DAMN, I DON'T GET IT. IT'S ALMOST LIKE THEY AIN'T EVEN HUMAN NO MORE.
KILL 'EM!
NOT "ALMOST," ELI.
"IT'S EXACTLY LIKE THAT."
WE AIN'T GONNA MAKE IT!
JUST ANOTHER HUNDRED YARDS TO THE HIGHWAY. THAT'S ALL.
WHERE YOU GOIN'?!
DAMMIT!

YOU'RE RIGHT, LADY. THIS PLAN SUCKED!
SHUT UP, ELI!
AND STAY OUTTA MY WAY!
TWAK
SHUNK
WAK

WAK
COME ON, CRACKER BOYS! I'M NOT FINISHED YET!
ALL RIGHT, I GUESS THAT'S JUST ABOUT ENOUGH O' THAT!
HEAR THAT, YOU HILLBILLY PSYCHOS?!
NOW WE'RE FINISHED!
'LIZBETH, HONEY?
I'M TALKIN' TO YOU.

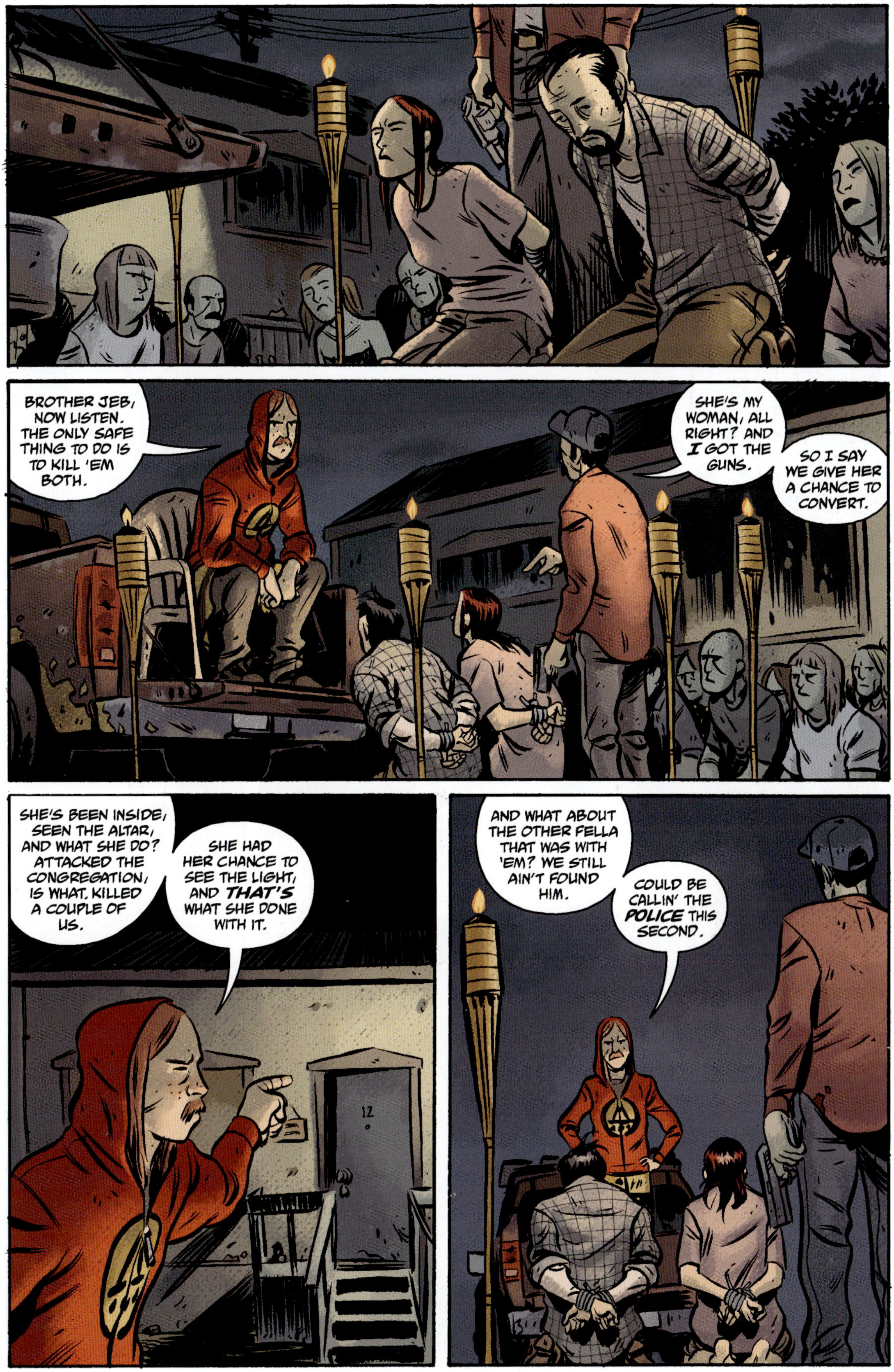
BROTHER JEB, NOW LISTEN. THE ONLY SAFE THING TO DO IS TO KILL 'EM BOTH.
SHE'S MY WOMAN, ALL RIGHT? AND I GOT THE GUNS.
SO I SAY WE GIVE HER A CHANCE TO CONVERT.
SHE'S BEEN INSIDE, SEEN THE ALTAR, AND WHAT SHE DO? ATTACKED THE CONGREGATION, IS WHAT. KILLED A COUPLE OF US.
SHE HAD HER CHANCE TO SEE THE LIGHT, AND THAT'S WHAT SHE DONE WITH IT.
12
AND WHAT ABOUT THE OTHER FELLA THAT WAS WITH 'EM? WE STILL AIN'T FOUND HIM.
COULD BE CALLIN' THE POLICE THIS SECOND.

WE'RE WASTING TIME!
KILL EVERY FROG ON THE PLANET, STILL ISN'T ENOUGH.
?
WE GOT HIS PHONE, AND FROM WHAT WE'VE BEEN ABLE
"FOCUS--"
--BUT NOT WITH EFFORT.
LET THAT FALL AWAY, LET THE PEACE FLOW THROUGH YOU. THAT IS WHEN YOU SUCCEED. ALL THINGS ARE POSSIBLE--
"--WHEN YOU STOP STRUGGLING."

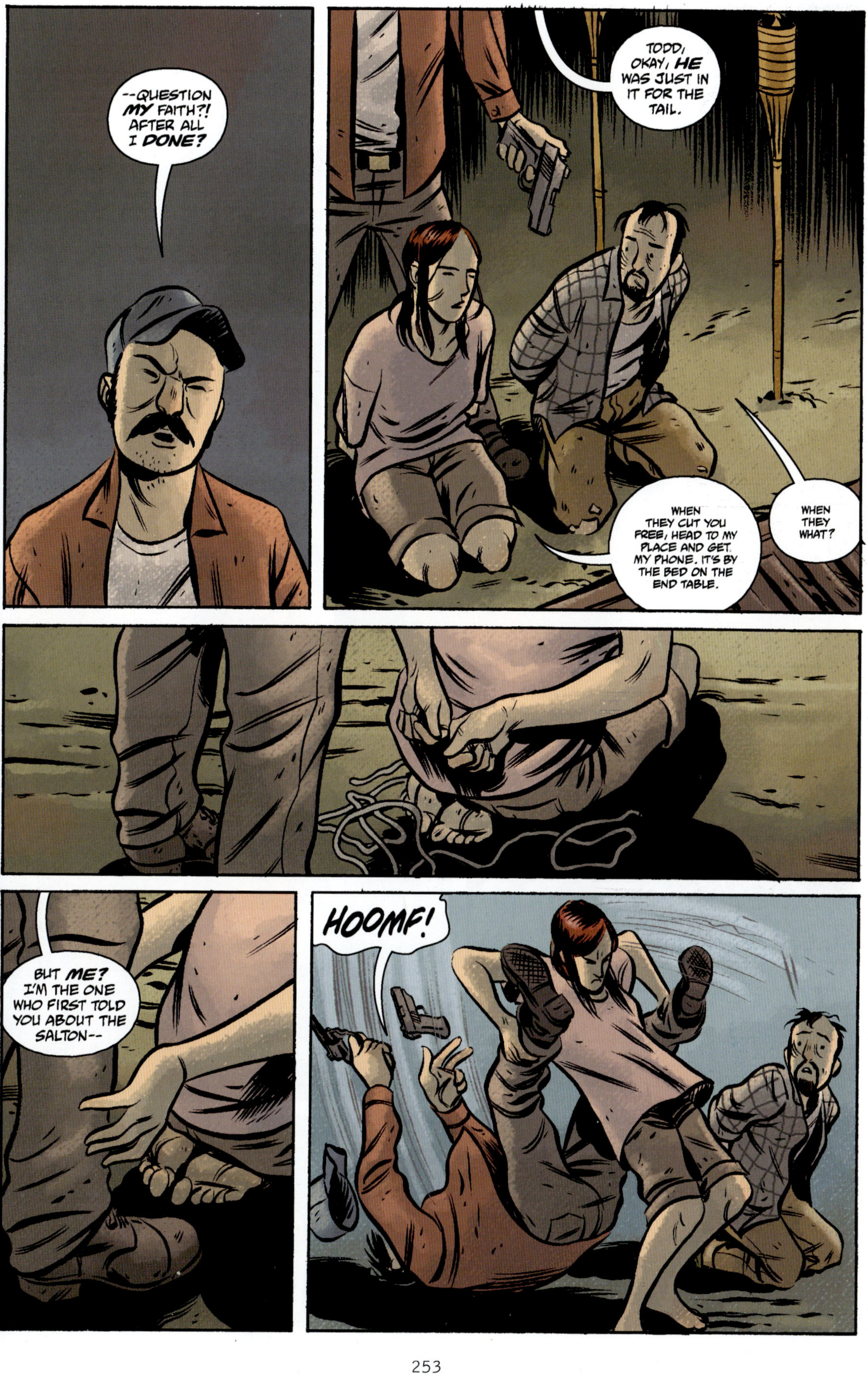
--QUESTION MY FAITH?! AFTER ALL I DONE?
TODD, OKAY, HE WAS JUST IN IT FOR THE TAIL.
WHEN THEY WHAT?
WHEN THEY CUT YOU FREE, HEAD TO MY PLACE AND GET MY PHONE. IT'S BY THE BED ON THE END TABLE.
BUT ME? I'M THE ONE WHO FIRST TOLD YOU ABOUT THE SALTON--
HOOMF!

THANKS, JEB!
AHHHH, THIS IS MORE LIKE IT!
ALL RIGHT, LISTEN UP, FAITHFUL ONES. I'VE GOT A FEW DEMANDS.
FIRST, CUT ELI FREE.
AND I SWEAR, IF ANY OF YOU SLACK-JAW CLOWNS TRIES TO FOLLOW HIM--
--IF YOU SO MUCH AS SNEEZE--
--THEN I GUESS REVEREND SCUMHOLE HERE WILL BE DOING SOME SERIOUS DYING.

BEE WOO BEE WOO
HUH! LOOKS LIKE SOMEBODY ALREADY RATTED YOU OUT.
GUESS ONE OF YOUR "FLOCK" HAS STRAYED.
DROP YOUR WEAPONS!!
WHA...?

UHHHHH...
THANK GOD YOU GOT HERE, OFFICERS!
SHE--SHE'S OUT OF HER MIND!
GOD DAMMIT LADY, I WON'T SAY IT AGAIN. DROP THE GUNS NOW!!!
FINE.

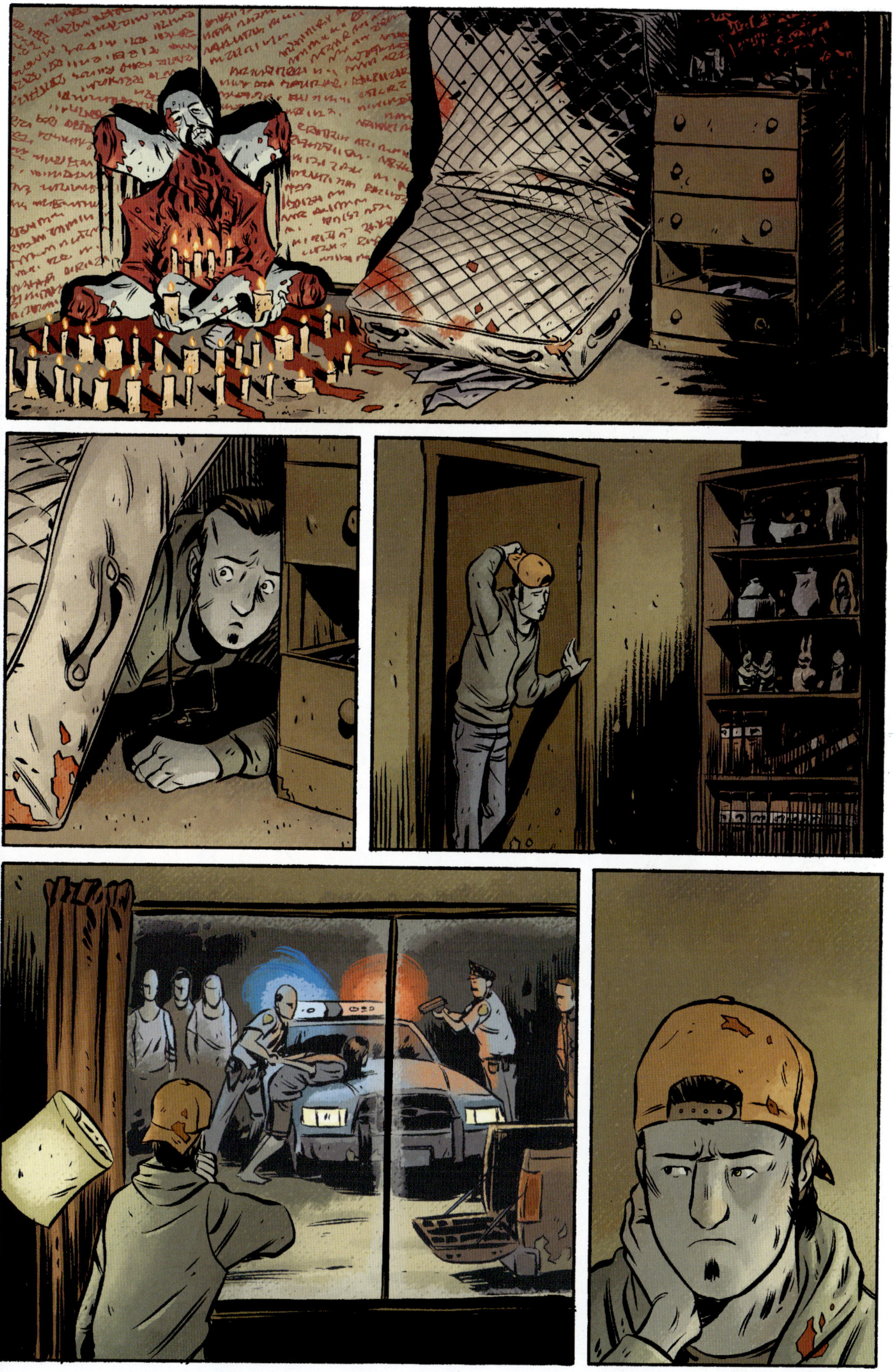

LISTEN, I'M NOT THE ONE YOU WANT--
SHUT UP!!
WE GET A CALL OF SHOTS FIRED, AND YOU'RE THE ONLY ONE WITH A GUN.
WHO ELSE WOULD WE WANT?!
KEERASH

JESUS H. GOD!!
WHAT THE FRIG IS GOING ON HERE?!
STOP!!
GET BACK HERE OR SO HELP ME--
WAIT! OH, YOU GOTTA BE KIDDING!
WHERE THE HELL'D SHE GO?!

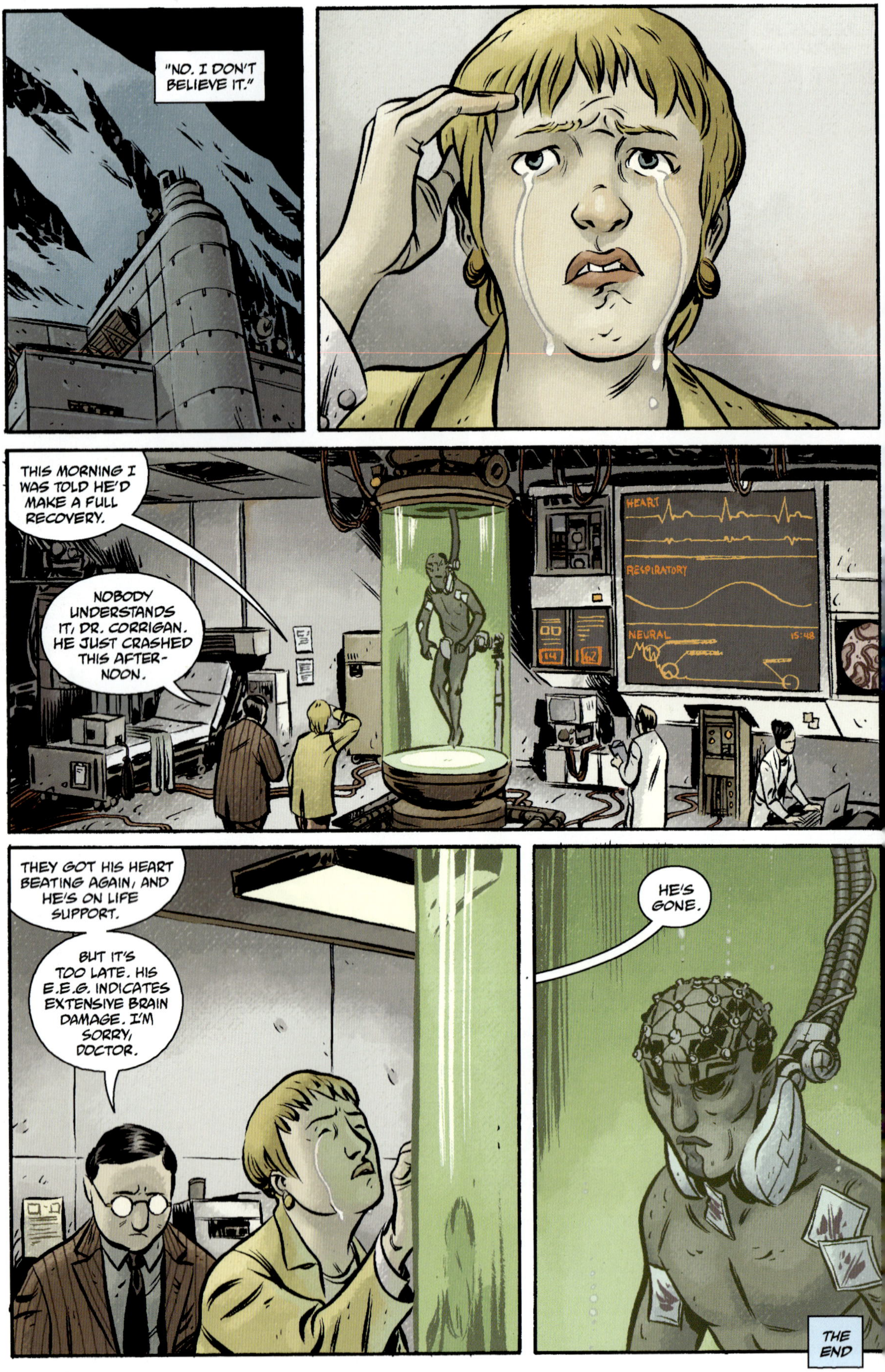
"NO. I DON'T BELIEVE IT."
THIS MORNING I WAS TOLD HE'D MAKE A FULL RECOVERY.
NOBODY UNDERSTANDS IT, DR. CORRIGAN. HE JUST CRASHED THIS AFTER-NOON.
HEART
RESPIRATORY
NEURAL
15:48
THEY GOT HIS HEART BEATING AGAIN, AND HE'S ON LIFE SUPPORT.
BUT IT'S TOO LATE. HIS E.E.G. INDICATES EXTENSIVE BRAIN DAMAGE. I'M SORRY, DOCTOR.
HE'S GONE.
THE END

RUSSIA CHAPTER ONE

ILLUSTRATION BY **DAVE JOHNSON**

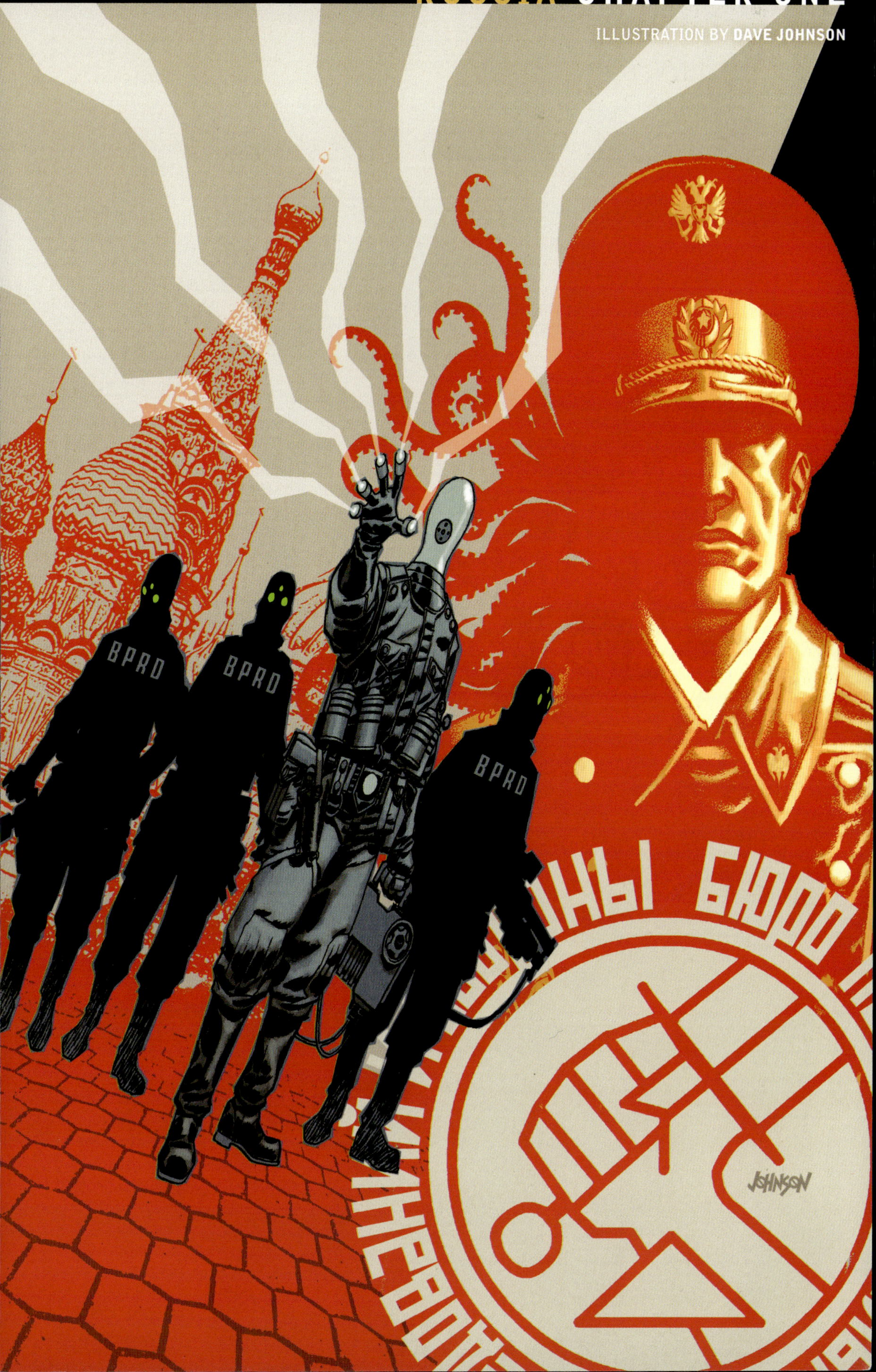
BPRD
BPRD
BPRD
JOHNSON

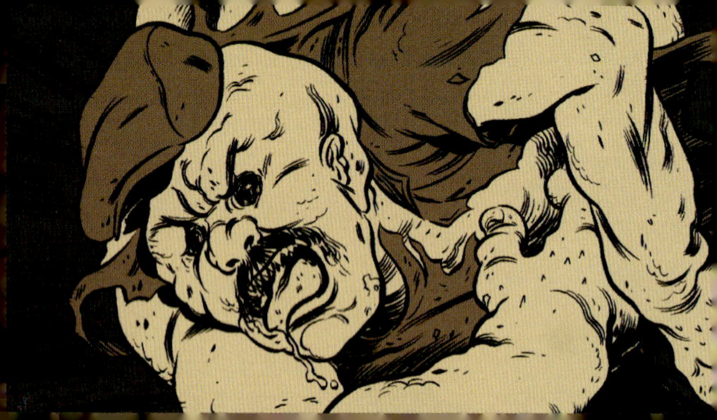

RAMPAYEDIK.

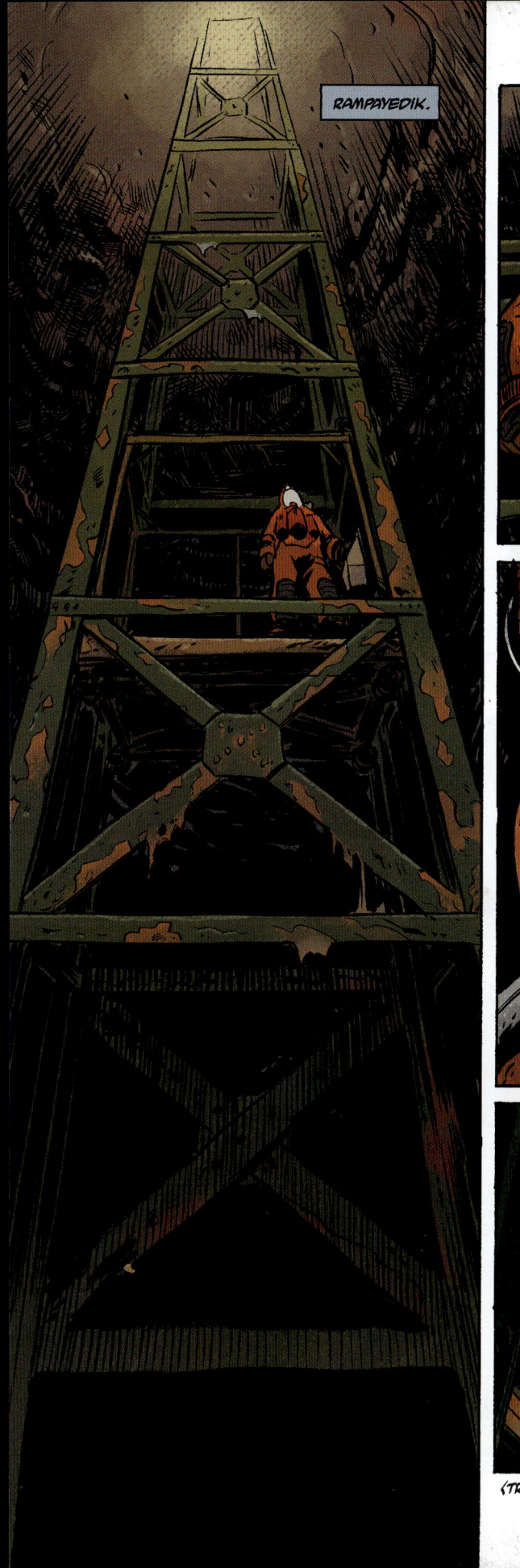

⟨JUST ABOUT THERE. YOU ARE STILL RECEIVING IMAGES, YES?⟩

⟨YES, COMMANDER. I STILL WISH YOU WOULD RECONSIDER--⟩

⟨DIMAH, ARE YOU STILL ON ABOUT THAT?⟩

⟨LET IT GO. YOU HAVE TO TRUST THAT I KNOW WHAT I'M DOING.⟩

⟨OF COURSE I TRUST YOU, COMMANDER--⟩

⟨TRANSLATED FROM THE RUSSIAN⟩

⟨--BUT HOW AM I TO TRUST THE DEVIL?⟩
⟨SO DRAMATIC, DIMAH. RELAX.⟩
⟨AHH, YOU SEE THIS?⟩
⟨YOU SEE HOW THE LIGHTS ARE STILL FUNCTIONING? I TOLD YOU IT WASN'T JUST THE ELEVATOR.⟩
⟨OF COURSE, WHO KNOWS HOW FAR THE GRID EXTENDS...⟩
СЕЙФ
ПОЖАР

⟨ALL RIGHT, I'VE SWITCHED TO THE HELMET LIGHT. IS IT ENOUGH FOR YOU TO SEE WHAT I'M SEEING?⟩
⟨NOT SO CLEARLY AS TESTS INDICATED WE WOULD, BUT YES.⟩
GLUNK
⟨AH! THAT'S A HELMET, ISN'T IT?⟩
⟨COMMANDER, IS THERE ANY OTHER SIGN OF OUR MEN?⟩
⟨COMMANDER...?⟩

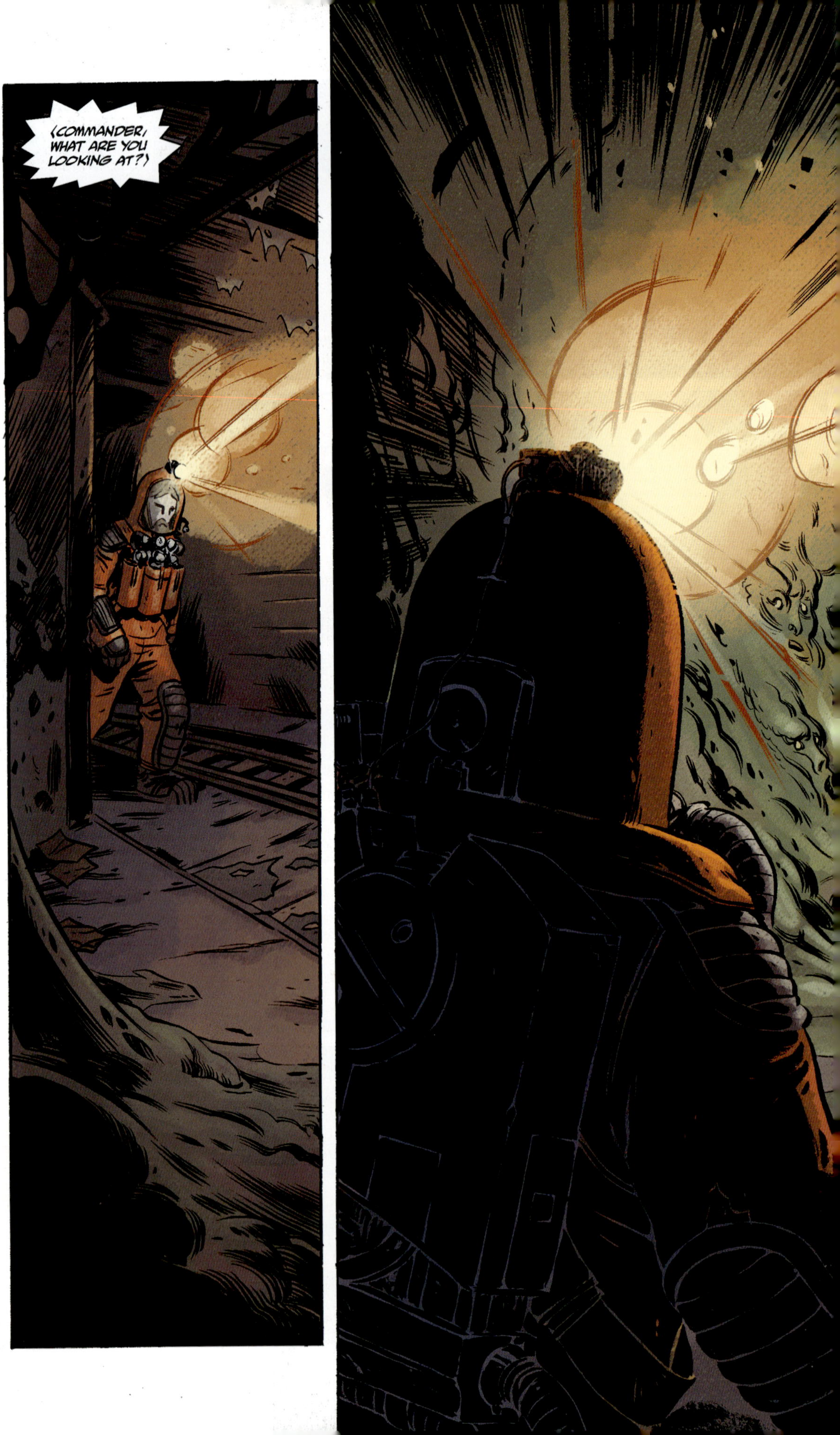
(COMMANDER, WHAT ARE YOU LOOKING AT?)

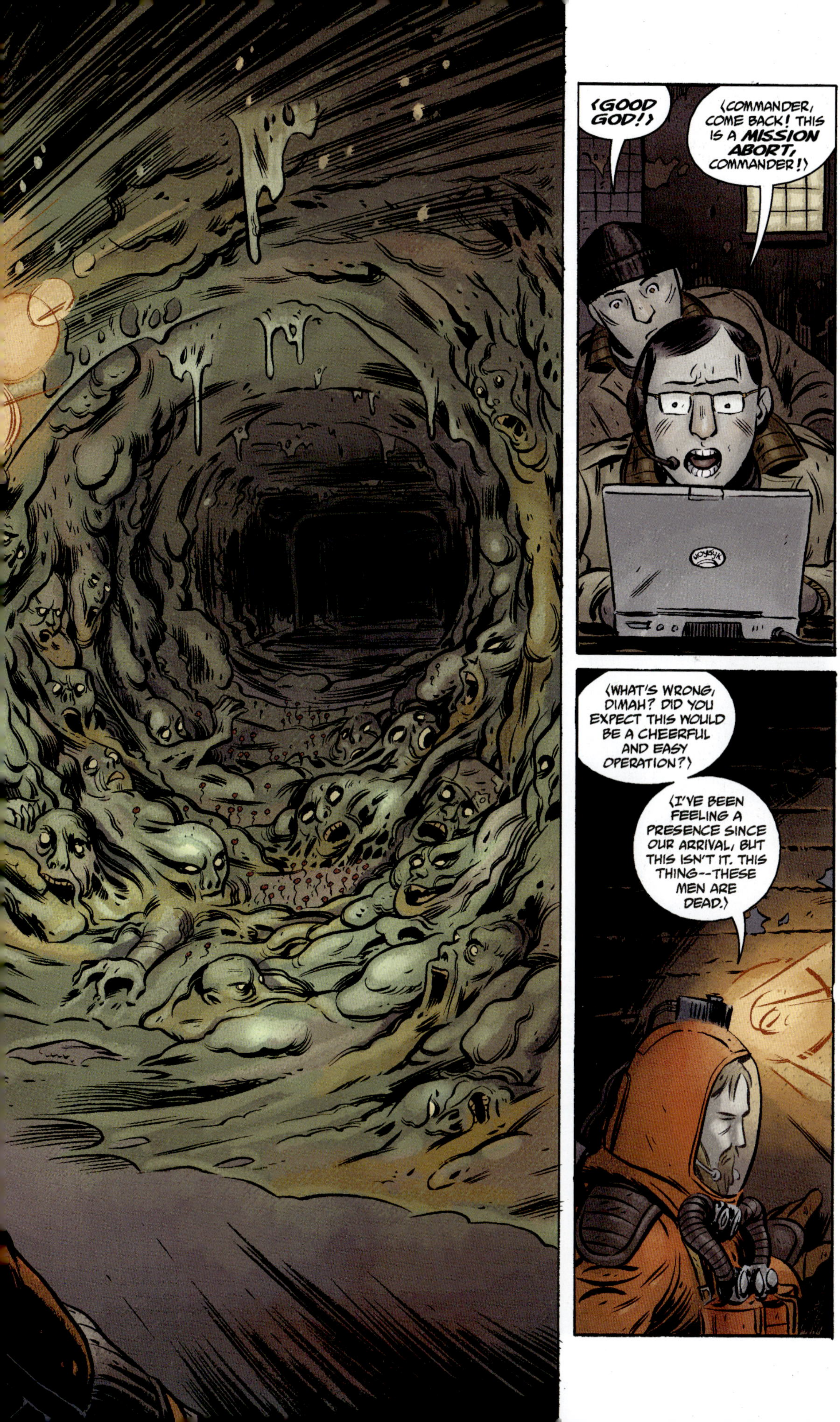
⟨GOOD GOD!⟩
⟨COMMANDER, COME BACK! THIS IS A MISSION ABORT, COMMANDER!⟩
⟨WHAT'S WRONG, DIMAH? DID YOU EXPECT THIS WOULD BE A CHEERFUL AND EASY OPERATION?⟩
⟨I'VE BEEN FEELING A PRESENCE SINCE OUR ARRIVAL, BUT THIS ISN'T IT. THIS THING--THESE MEN ARE DEAD.⟩

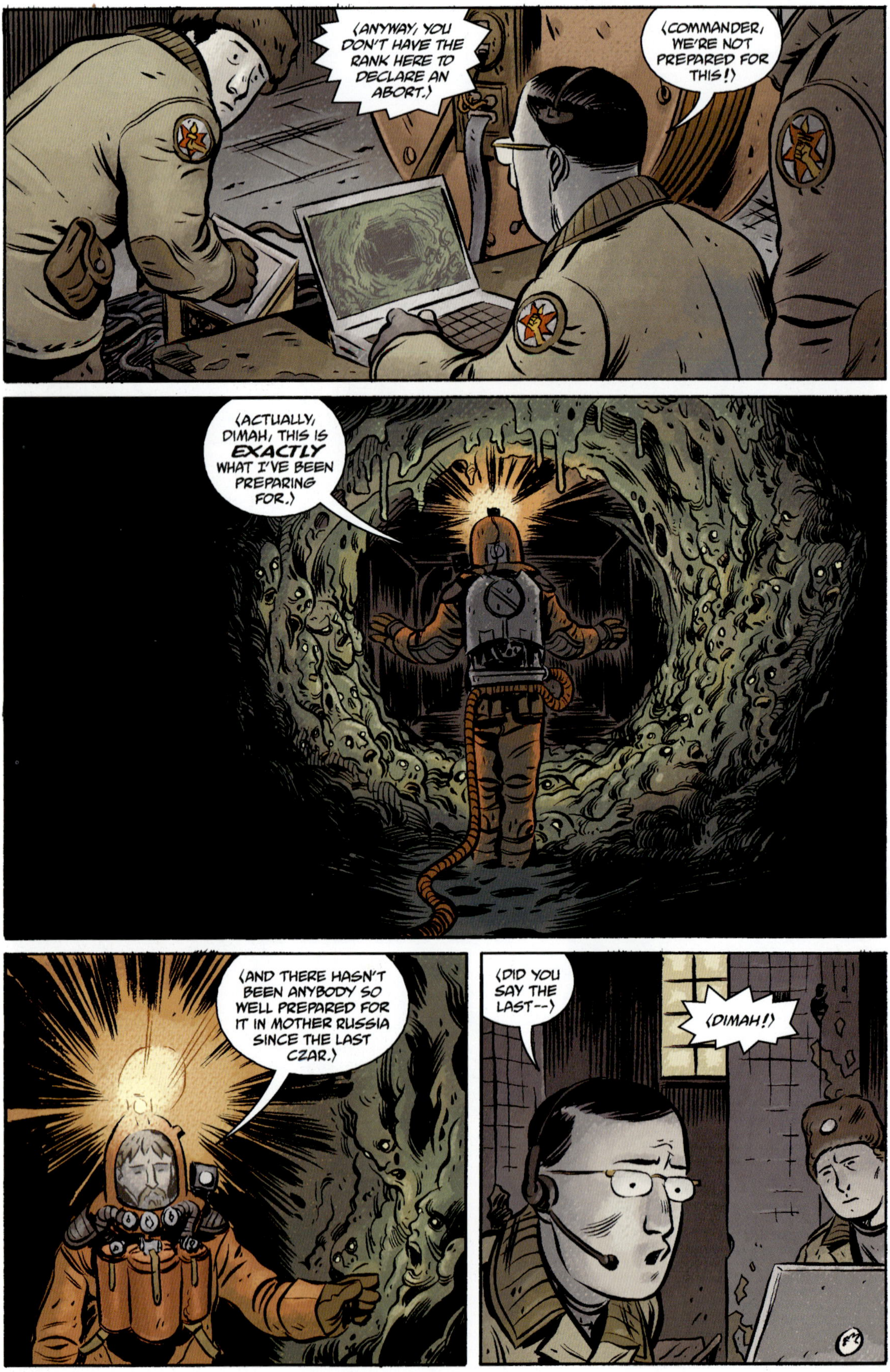
‹ANYWAY, YOU DON'T HAVE THE RANK HERE TO DECLARE AN ABORT.›
‹COMMANDER, WE'RE NOT PREPARED FOR THIS!›
‹ACTUALLY, DIMAH, THIS IS EXACTLY WHAT I'VE BEEN PREPARING FOR.›
‹AND THERE HASN'T BEEN ANYBODY SO WELL PREPARED FOR IT IN MOTHER RUSSIA SINCE THE LAST CZAR.›
‹DID YOU SAY THE LAST--›
‹DIMAH!›

‹DO YOU FEEL IT, DIMAH?›
‹DO YOU FEEL IT?›
‹COMMANDER, WE'RE LOSING YOU.›
‹ABORT! ABORT NOW!›
‹COMMANDER!›
BOOM

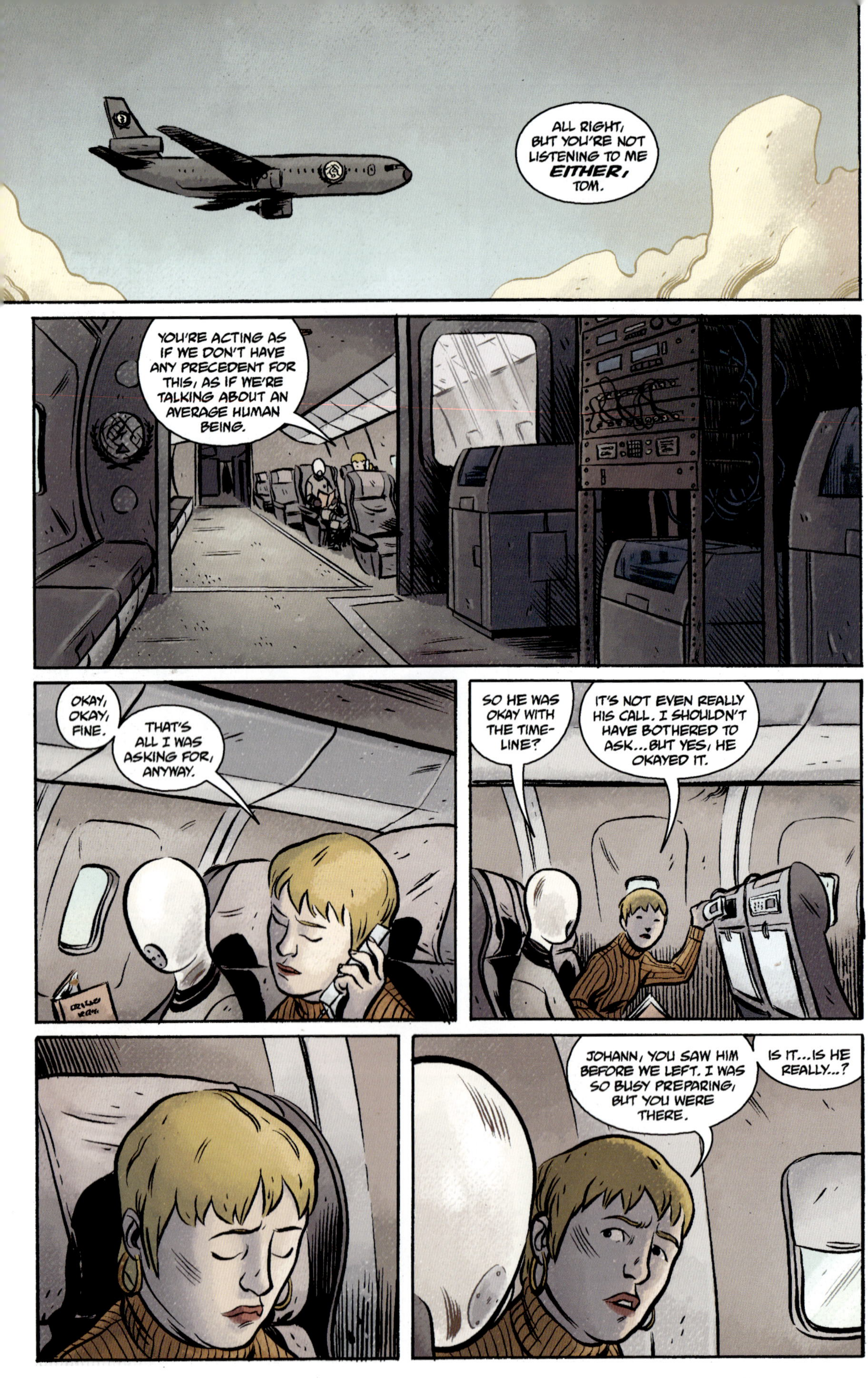
ALL RIGHT, BUT YOU'RE NOT LISTENING TO ME *EITHER,* TOM.
YOU'RE ACTING AS IF WE DON'T HAVE ANY PRECEDENT FOR THIS, AS IF WE'RE TALKING ABOUT AN AVERAGE HUMAN BEING.
OKAY, OKAY, FINE.
THAT'S ALL I WAS ASKING FOR, ANYWAY.
SO HE WAS OKAY WITH THE TIME-LINE?
IT'S NOT EVEN REALLY HIS CALL. I SHOULDN'T HAVE BOTHERED TO ASK...BUT YES, HE OKAYED IT.
JOHANN, YOU SAW HIM BEFORE WE LEFT. I WAS SO BUSY PREPARING, BUT YOU WERE THERE.
IS IT...IS HE REALLY...?

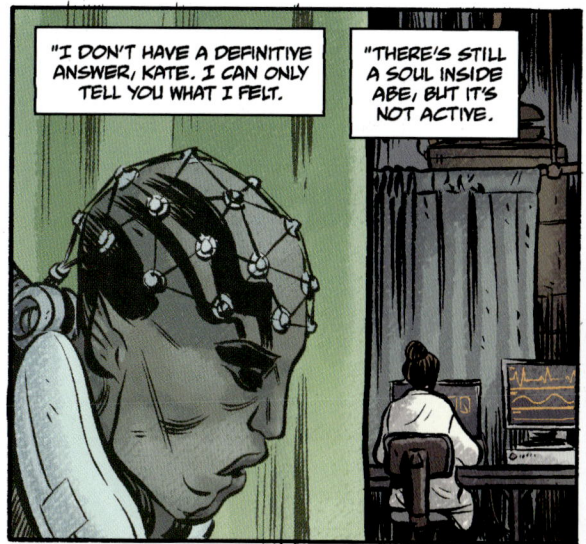

"I DON'T HAVE A DEFINITIVE ANSWER, KATE. I CAN ONLY TELL YOU WHAT I FELT.

"THERE'S STILL A SOUL INSIDE ABE, BUT IT'S NOT ACTIVE.

"IT'S NOT TRYING TO COMMUNICATE. IT FELT DESPERATE TO ME.

"IT FELT TRAPPED, AND WHEN I GET THAT FEELING, USUALLY IT MEANS..."

KATE, I THINK WE NEED TO LET HIM GO.

ON YOUR TIMELINE, OF COURSE, BUT I THINK IT'S THE ONLY WAY.

OKAY.

OKAY.

WHEN WE GET BACK.

I HAVE NOT WANTED TO SAY ANYTHING BEFORE--KNOWING YOU ARE UPSET-- BUT WHY DID YOU BRING ME?

DEVON, AFTER ALL, HAS *SOME* RUSSIAN. I DO NOT.

"NO. WE FAILED IN OUR MISSION TO FIND FENIX. I HAD TO PUT HIM BACK ON THAT.
"IF WE CAN LEARN SOMETHING ABOUT WHO SHOT ABE IN THE BARGAIN, ALL THE BETTER."
WE NEEDED A TOP AGENT ON IT, AND YOU DON'T EXACTLY TRAVEL WELL UNDERCOVER, DO YOU?
NO, I SUPPOSE NOT.
MOSCOW.

WHAT IS THIS?
THEY SEND GOONS TO MEET US? WHERE THE HELL IS THE S.S.S. CHIEF, OR A DEPUTY? OR AT LEAST AN AMBASSADOR, FOR CHRIST'S SAKE?!
HAVE YOU NOTICED WHAT THEY'RE CARRYING?
HALLO. I AM MATVEI.
DIRECTOR NICHAYKO SENDS REGRETS, BUT DON'T TO WORRY.
"WE GET YOU TO HIM FAST."

ERRRRGHH...
⟨LOOK AT YOU! I SAID TO STAY HOME, BUT NO!⟩
⟨I PROMISE YOU, OLEG, IF YOU GET ME SICK BEFORE MOTHER COMES, I WILL TORTURE YOU.⟩
WAIT! SOME-THING IS WRONG!
JOHANN?
WE NEED TO STOP! SOME-THING IS VERY **WRONG!!**
⟨OLEG, YOU ARE **EMBARRASSING** ME!⟩

MATVEL, YOU NEED TO **PULL OVER!** DO YOU UNDERSTAND?!
DA, DA, HERR KRAUS. EVERYTHING IS FINE.
FLUMP

GRGGLLLLEEEEEE!!!!!!
WHOMP
I TOLD YOU!! I TOLD YOU!!
DON'T TO WORRY. ESCALADE IS FIREPROOF.
"FIREPROOF"? WHAT ARE YOU TALKING ABOUT?

WHOOOOSHH

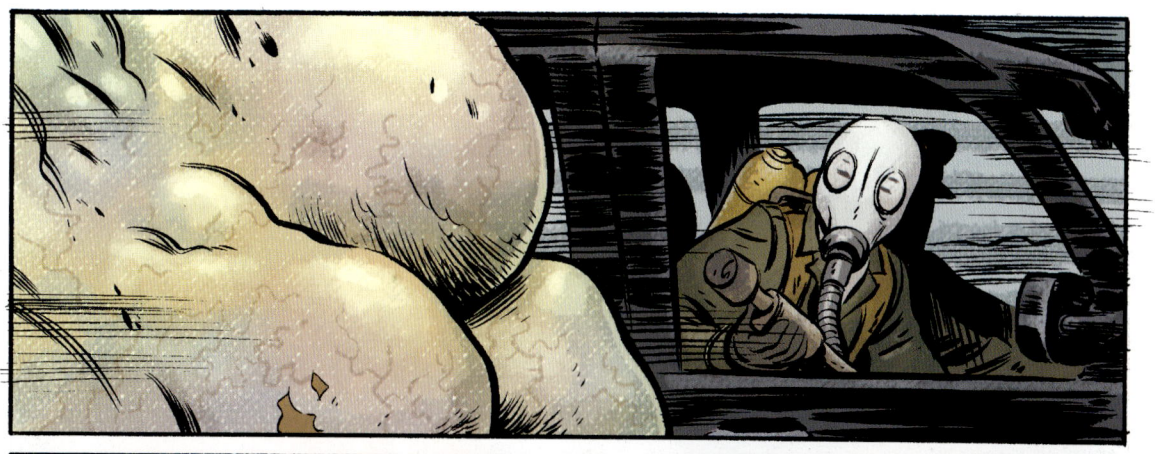

KRUNCH

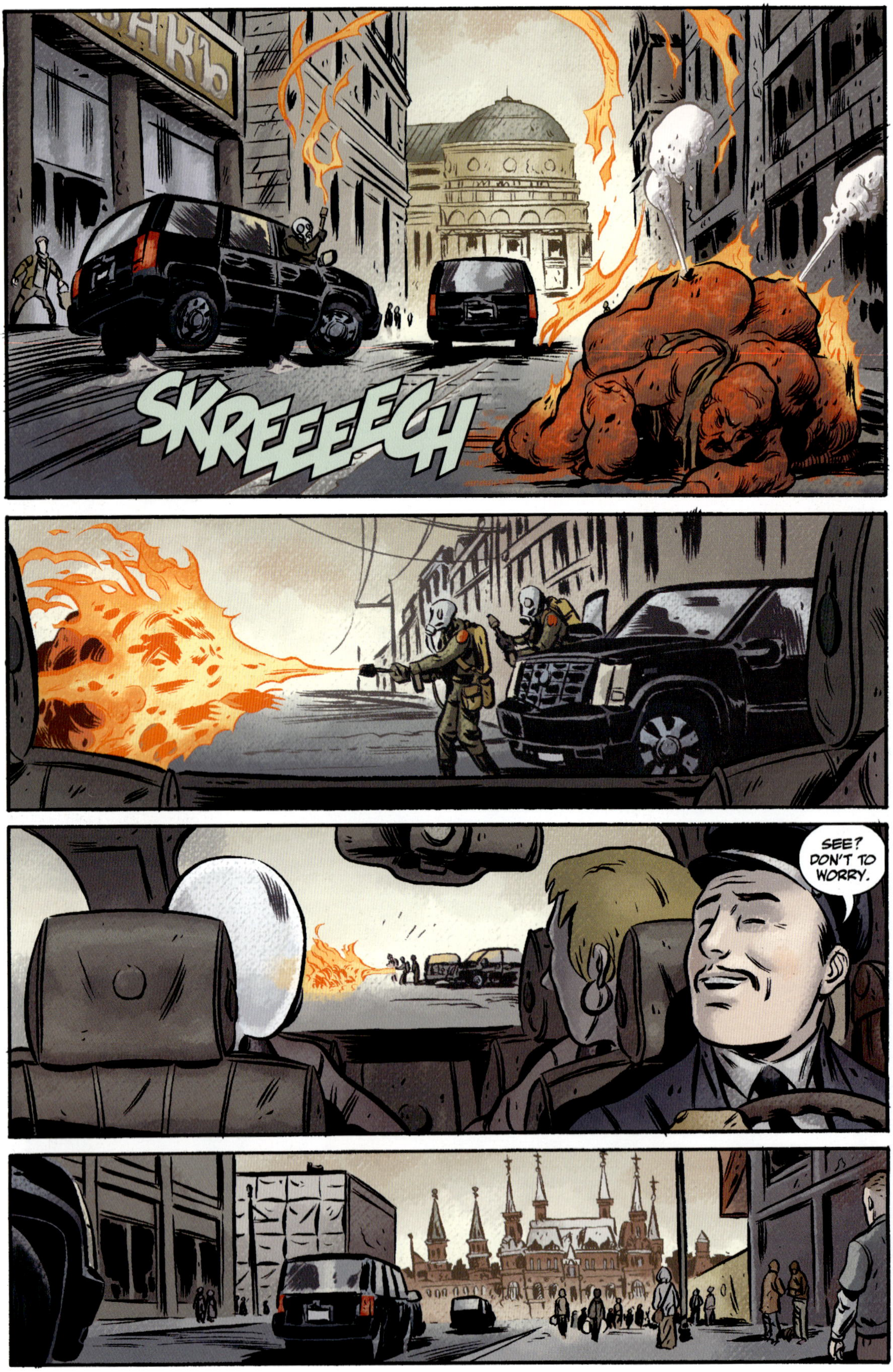

SKREEEECH
SEE? DON'T TO WORRY.

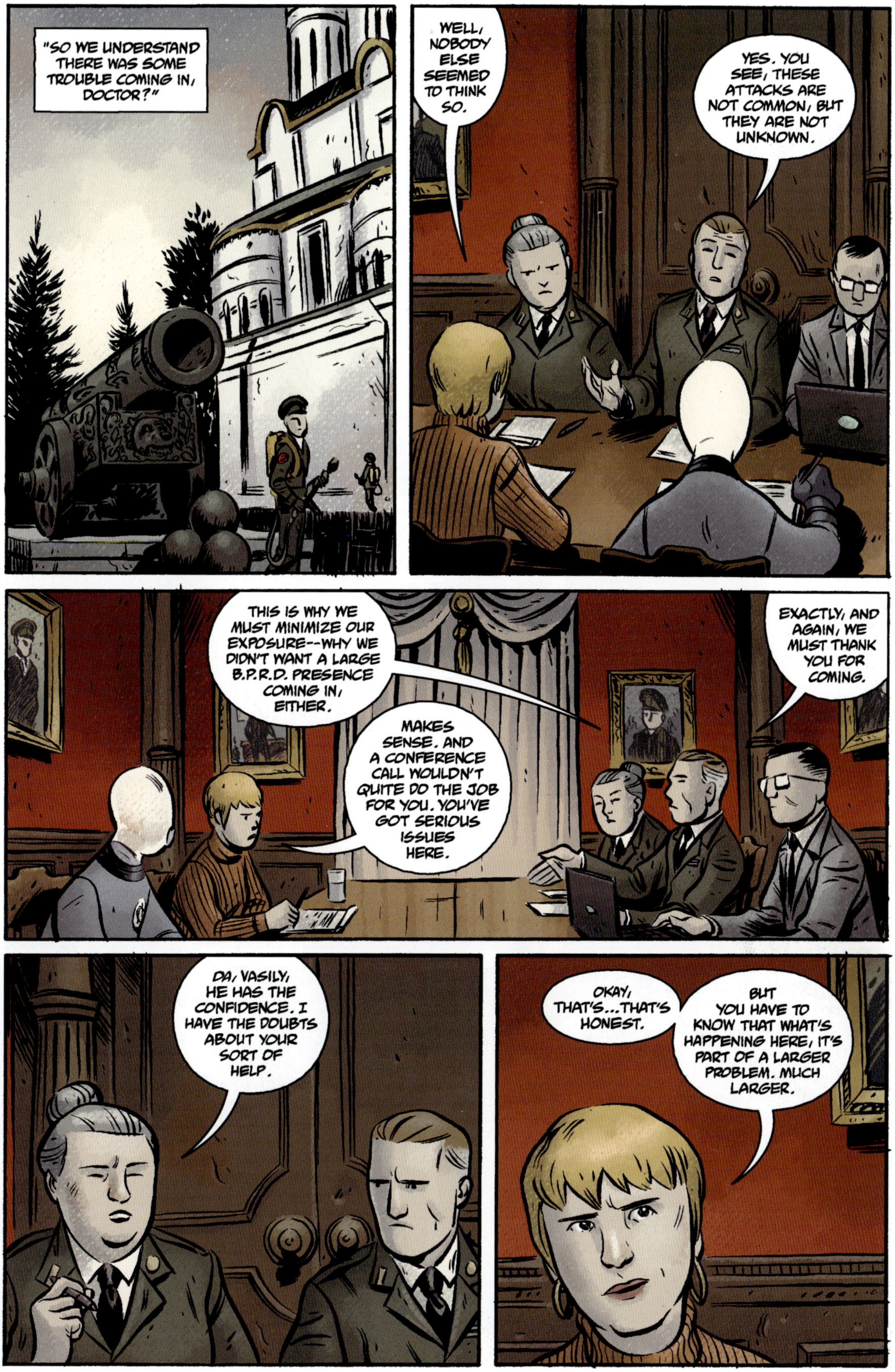
"SO WE UNDERSTAND THERE WAS SOME TROUBLE COMING IN, DOCTOR?"
WELL, NOBODY ELSE SEEMED TO THINK SO.
YES. YOU SEE, THESE ATTACKS ARE NOT COMMON, BUT THEY ARE NOT UNKNOWN.
THIS IS WHY WE MUST MINIMIZE OUR EXPOSURE--WHY WE DIDN'T WANT A LARGE B.P.R.D. PRESENCE COMING IN, EITHER.
MAKES SENSE. AND A CONFERENCE CALL WOULDN'T QUITE DO THE JOB FOR YOU. YOU'VE GOT SERIOUS ISSUES HERE.
EXACTLY, AND AGAIN, WE MUST THANK YOU FOR COMING.
DA, VASILY, HE HAS THE CONFIDENCE. I HAVE THE DOUBTS ABOUT YOUR SORT OF HELP.
OKAY, THAT'S...THAT'S HONEST.
BUT YOU HAVE TO KNOW THAT WHAT'S HAPPENING HERE, IT'S PART OF A LARGER PROBLEM. MUCH LARGER.

AND THE B.P.R.D., ESPECIALLY OUR ELITE AGENTS, HAVE AN EXCELLENT RECORD OF SUCCESS IN THIS ARENA.
BENJAMIN DAIMIO KILL DOZENS B.P.R.D. MEN. IS THIS KIND SUCCESS YOU MEAN?
WHERE THE HELL ARE YOU GETTING THIS INFORMATION?
WHERE DO WE GET IT? YOU ARE SERIOUS?
HERE. ALL IS HERE ON WIKILEAKS.
WENT UP WEEKS AGO WITH OTHER AMERICAN CLASSIFY FILES.
YOU NOT KNOW?
NO! TOO BUSY TRYING TO SAVE THE...
GOD DAMMIT, IT'S ALL HERE. EVERYTHING BEFORE OUR U.N. AFFILIATION.

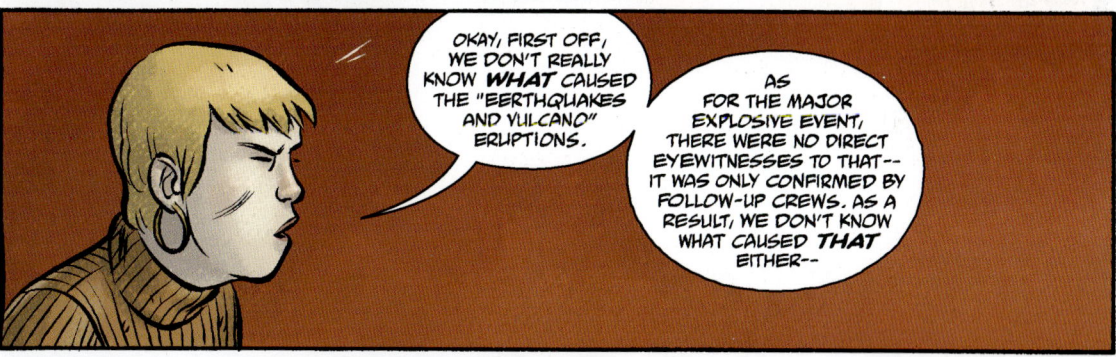

DA. LIKE MASSIVE EXPLOSION THAT DESTROYED GIANT CRABS AND CRAZY MAN WITH BLACK SKULL--AND ALSO SET OFF EARTHQUAKES AND VOLCANO ERUPTIONS.

WHAT WE ARE **NOT** SEEING IS WHERE YOUR AGENT SHERMAN--THE POWERFUL FIRE STARTER--WHERE THEN SHE WAS DURING EXPLOSION.

OR WHERE NOW SHE IS.

OKAY, FIRST OFF, WE DON'T REALLY KNOW **WHAT** CAUSED THE "EERTHQUAKES AND VULCANO" ERUPTIONS.

AS FOR THE MAJOR EXPLOSIVE EVENT, THERE WERE NO DIRECT EYEWITNESSES TO THAT-- IT WAS ONLY CONFIRMED BY FOLLOW-UP CREWS. AS A RESULT, WE DON'T KNOW WHAT CAUSED **THAT** EITHER--

"--BUT DO YOU KNOW WHAT THAT EVENT AVERTED?

"THAT SO-CALLED CRAZY MAN WAS USING THOSE GIANT CRABS AS INCUBATORS FOR MUCH LARGER CREATURES.

281

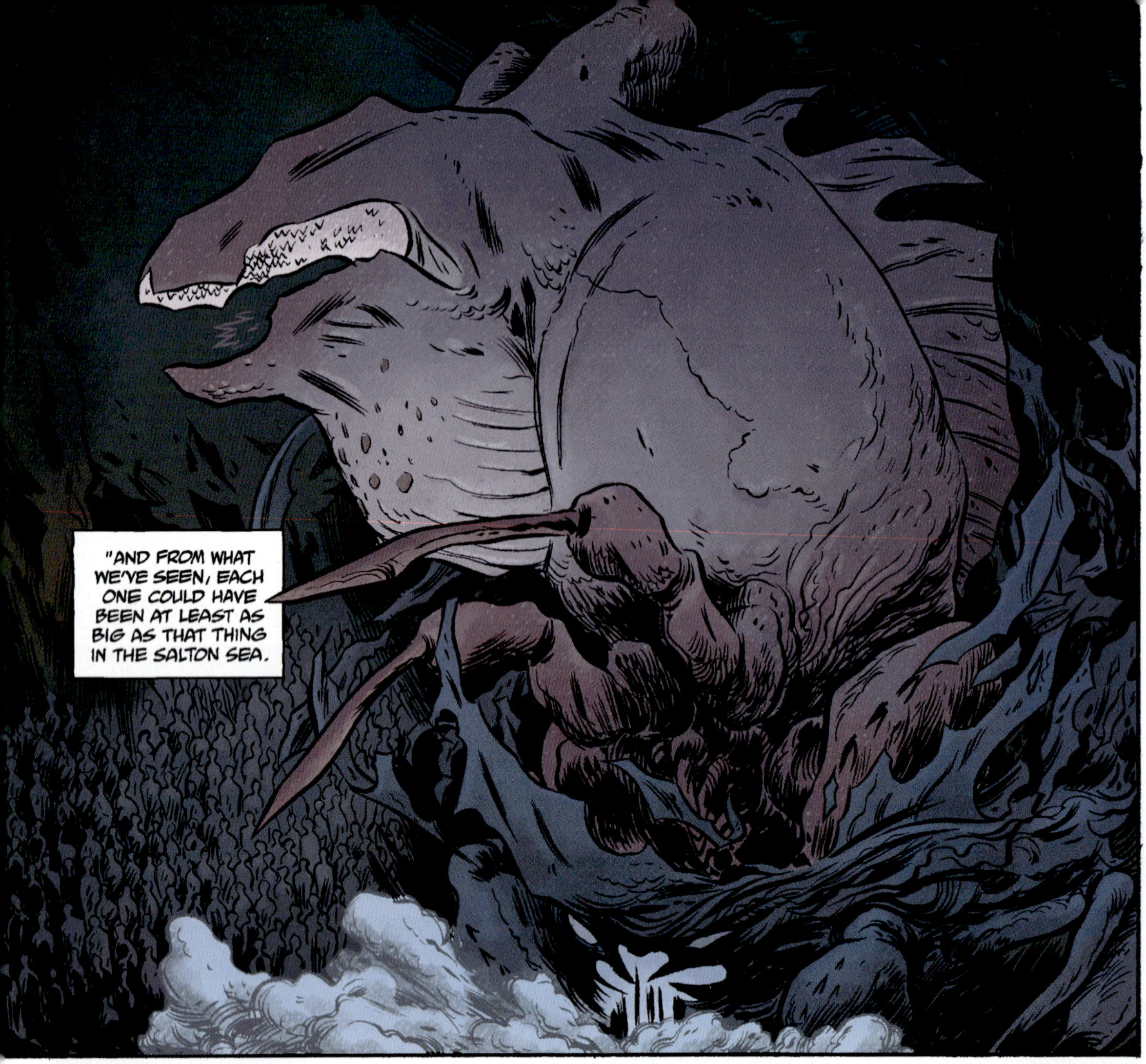
"AND FROM WHAT WE'VE SEEN, EACH ONE COULD HAVE BEEN AT LEAST AS BIG AS THAT THING IN THE SALTON SEA.

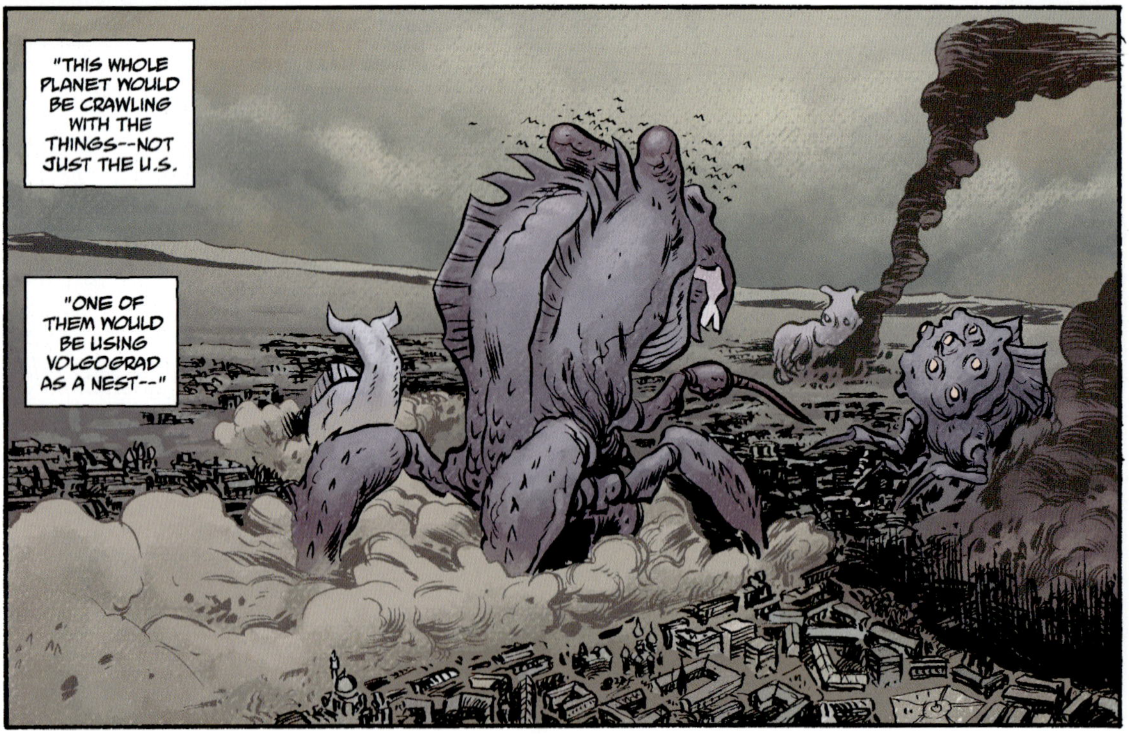
"THIS WHOLE PLANET WOULD BE CRAWLING WITH THE THINGS--NOT JUST THE U.S.
"ONE OF THEM WOULD BE USING VOLGOGRAD AS A NEST--"

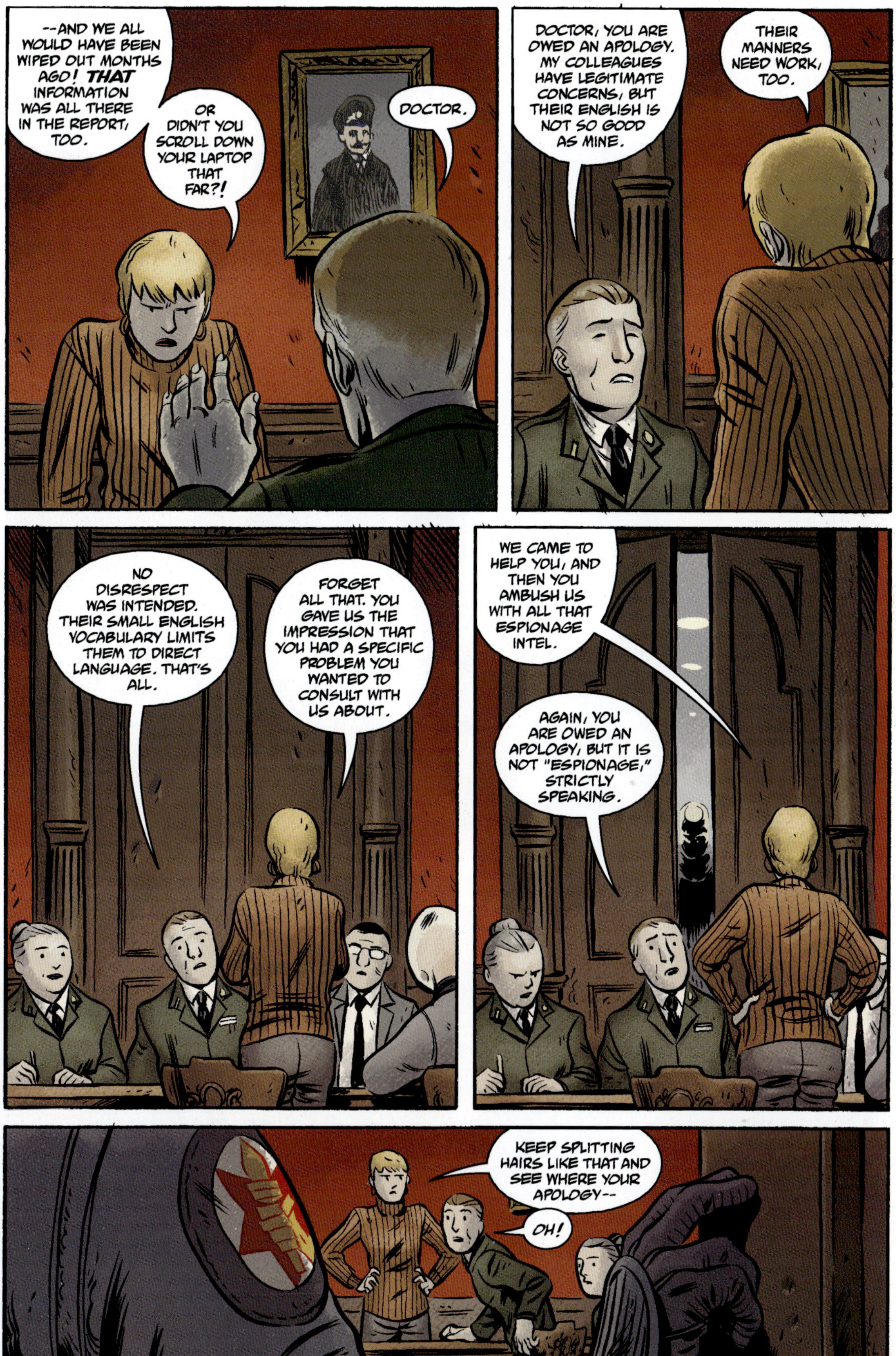
--AND WE ALL WOULD HAVE BEEN WIPED OUT MONTHS AGO! THAT INFORMATION WAS ALL THERE IN THE REPORT, TOO.
OR DIDN'T YOU SCROLL DOWN YOUR LAPTOP THAT FAR?!
DOCTOR.
DOCTOR, YOU ARE OWED AN APOLOGY. MY COLLEAGUES HAVE LEGITIMATE CONCERNS, BUT THEIR ENGLISH IS NOT SO GOOD AS MINE.
THEIR MANNERS NEED WORK, TOO.
NO DISRESPECT WAS INTENDED. THEIR SMALL ENGLISH VOCABULARY LIMITS THEM TO DIRECT LANGUAGE. THAT'S ALL.
FORGET ALL THAT. YOU GAVE US THE IMPRESSION THAT YOU HAD A SPECIFIC PROBLEM YOU WANTED TO CONSULT WITH US ABOUT.
WE CAME TO HELP YOU, AND THEN YOU AMBUSH US WITH ALL THAT ESPIONAGE INTEL.
AGAIN, YOU ARE OWED AN APOLOGY, BUT IT IS NOT "ESPIONAGE," STRICTLY SPEAKING.
KEEP SPLITTING HAIRS LIKE THAT AND SEE WHERE YOUR APOLOGY--
OH!

SO, SO SORRY TO BE LATE.
DR. CORRIGAN, AGENT KRAUS, THIS IS DIRECTOR NICHAYKO.

NO, NO, NO, NO.
PLEASE, CALL ME IOSIF!

RUSSIA CHAPTER TWO

ILLUSTRATION BY **DAVE JOHNSON**

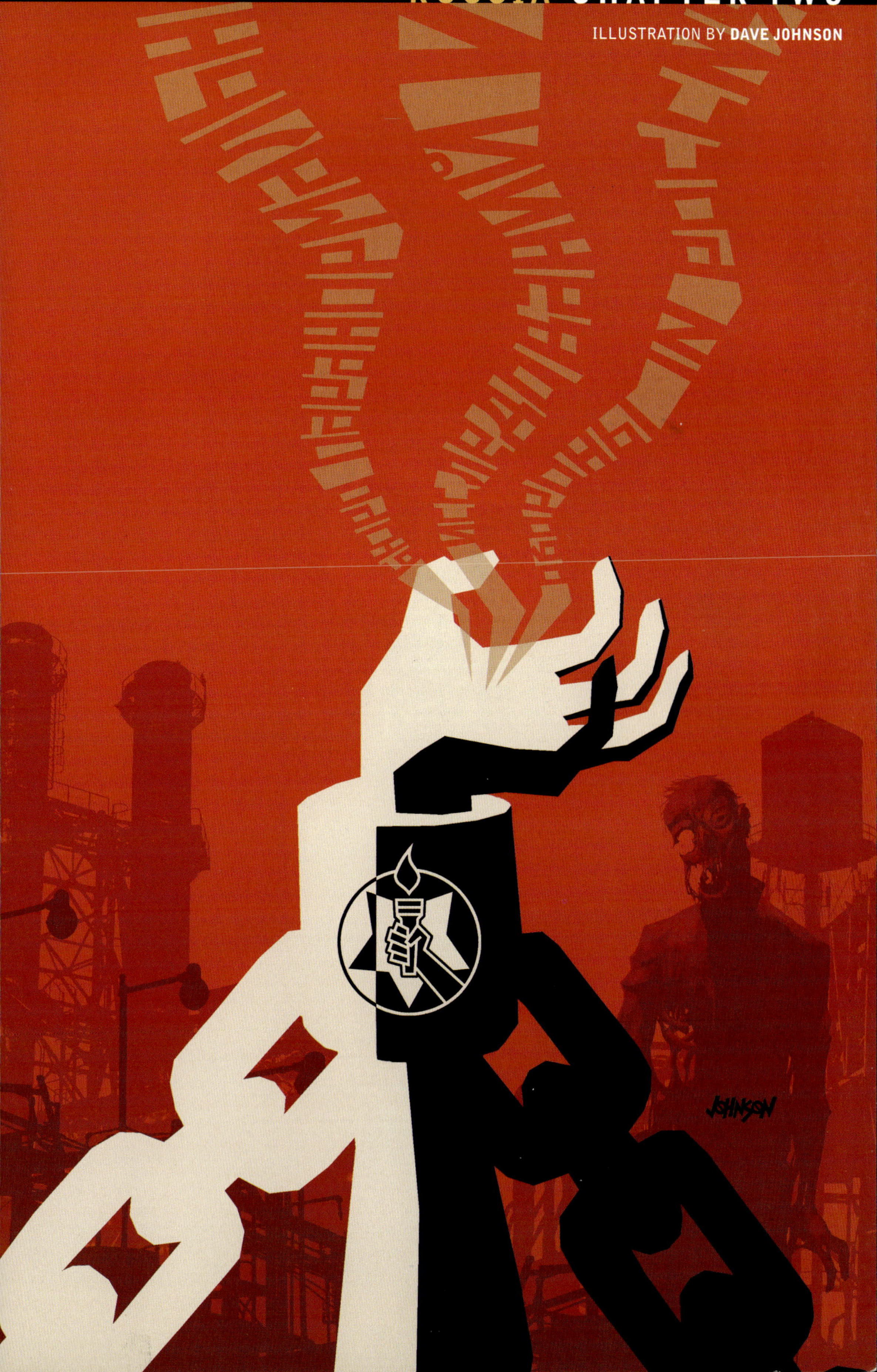

JOHNSON

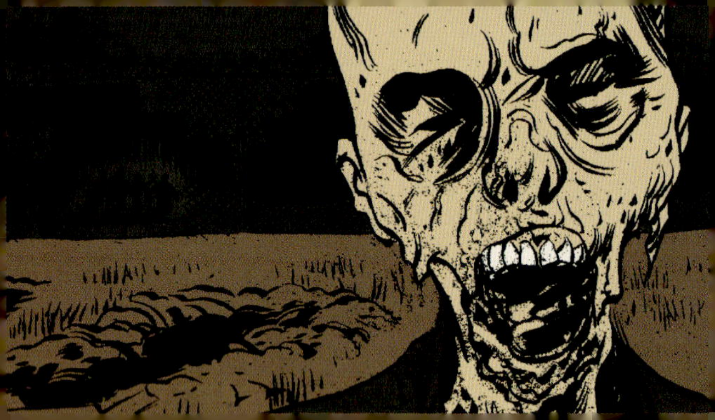

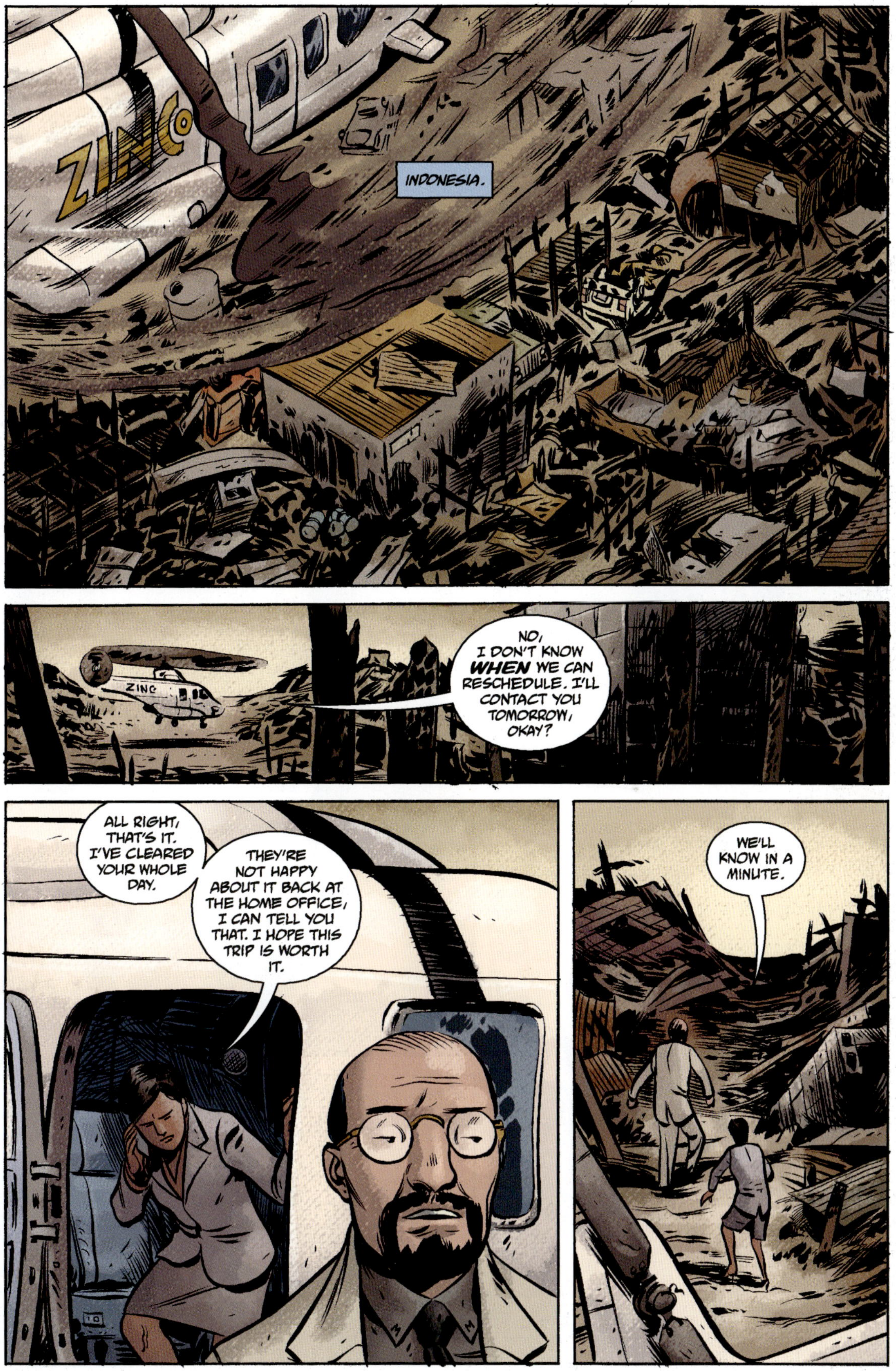
ZINCO
INDONESIA.
ZINC
NO, I DON'T KNOW WHEN WE CAN RESCHEDULE. I'LL CONTACT YOU TOMORROW, OKAY?
ALL RIGHT, THAT'S IT. I'VE CLEARED YOUR WHOLE DAY.
THEY'RE NOT HAPPY ABOUT IT BACK AT THE HOME OFFICE, I CAN TELL YOU THAT. I HOPE THIS TRIP IS WORTH IT.
WE'LL KNOW IN A MINUTE.

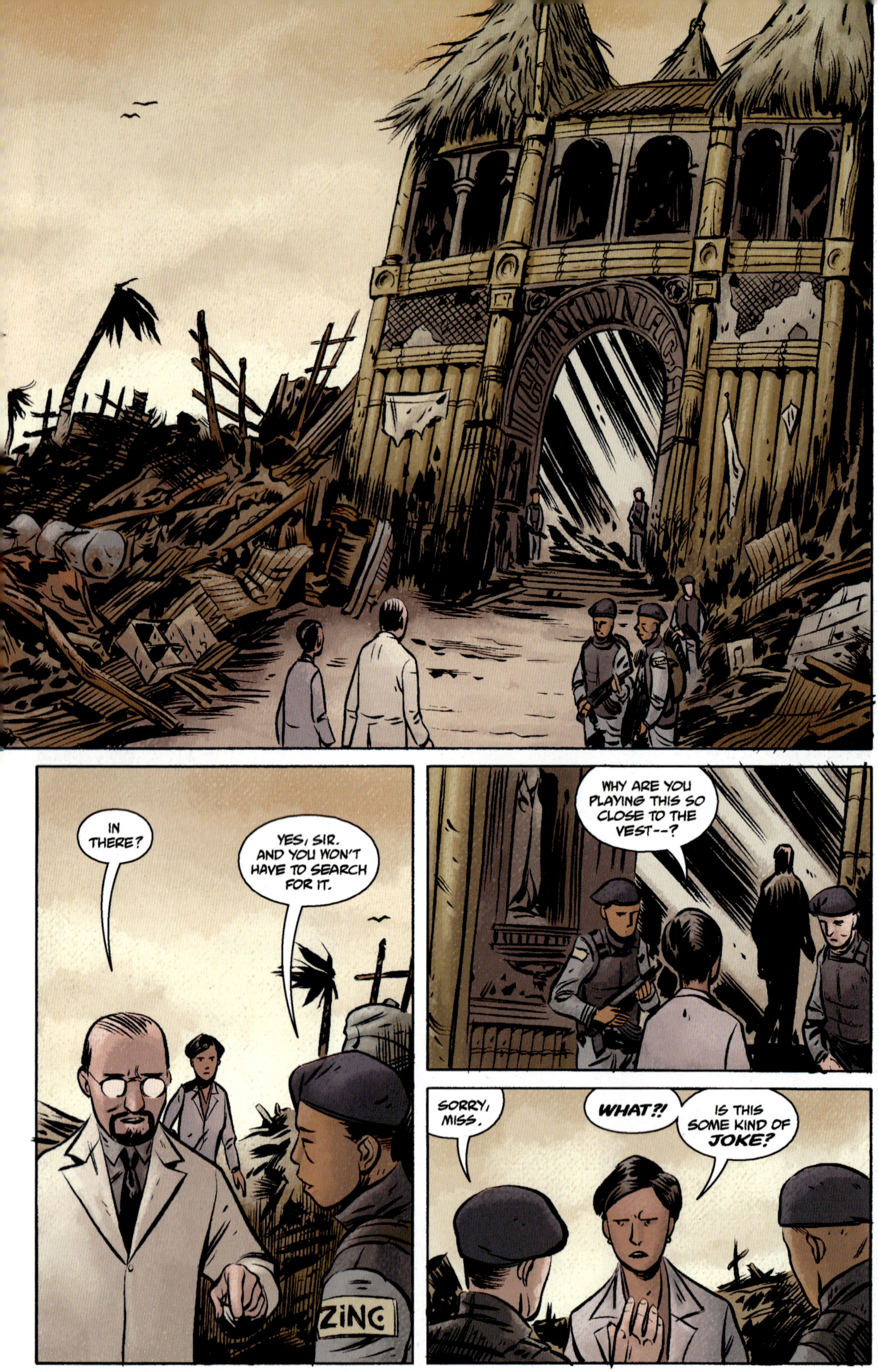
IN THERE?
YES, SIR. AND YOU WON'T HAVE TO SEARCH FOR IT.
ZINC
WHY ARE YOU PLAYING THIS SO CLOSE TO THE VEST--?
SORRY, MISS.
WHAT?!
IS THIS SOME KIND OF JOKE?

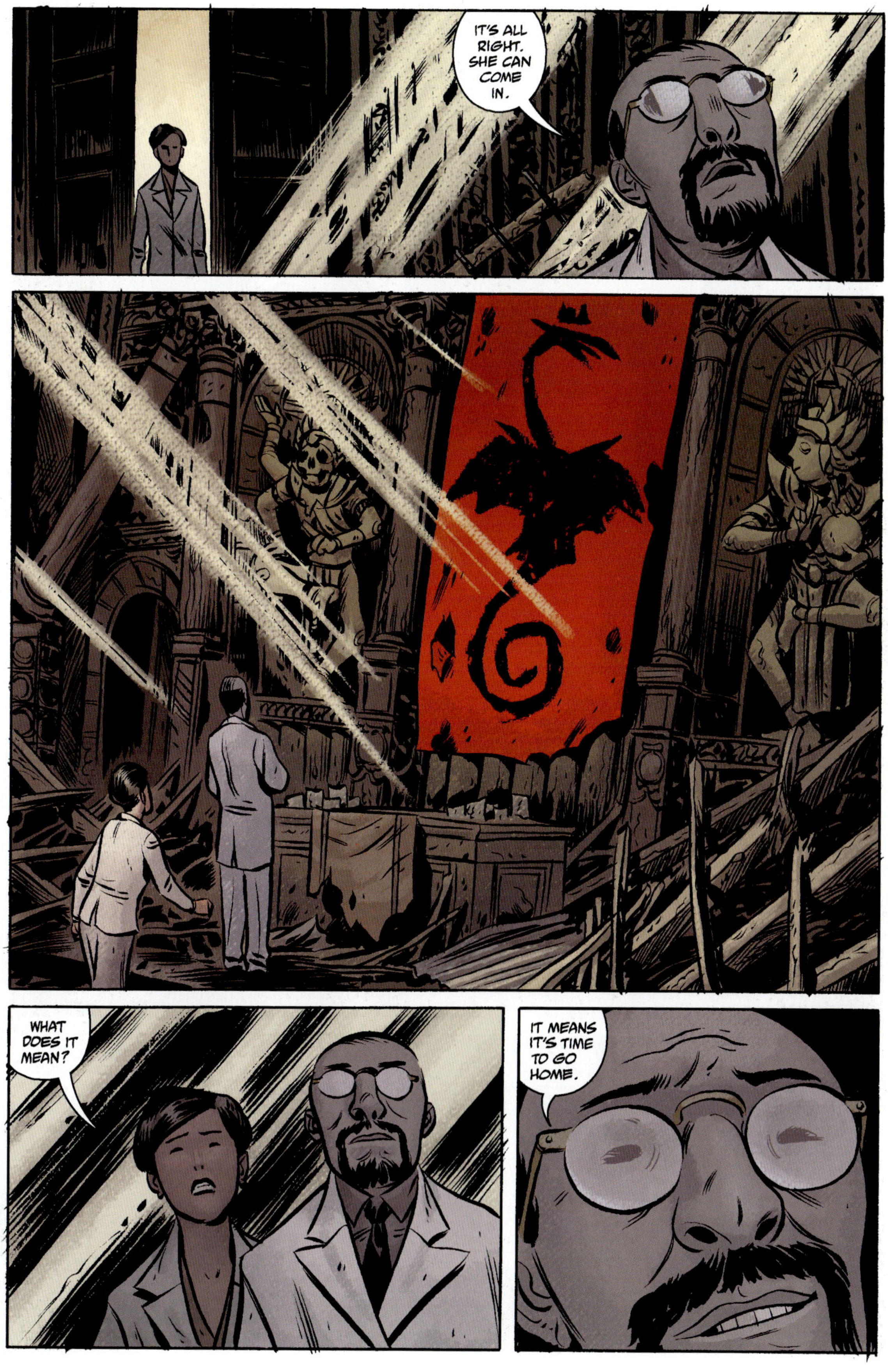
IT'S ALL RIGHT. SHE CAN COME IN.
WHAT DOES IT MEAN?
IT MEANS IT'S TIME TO GO HOME.

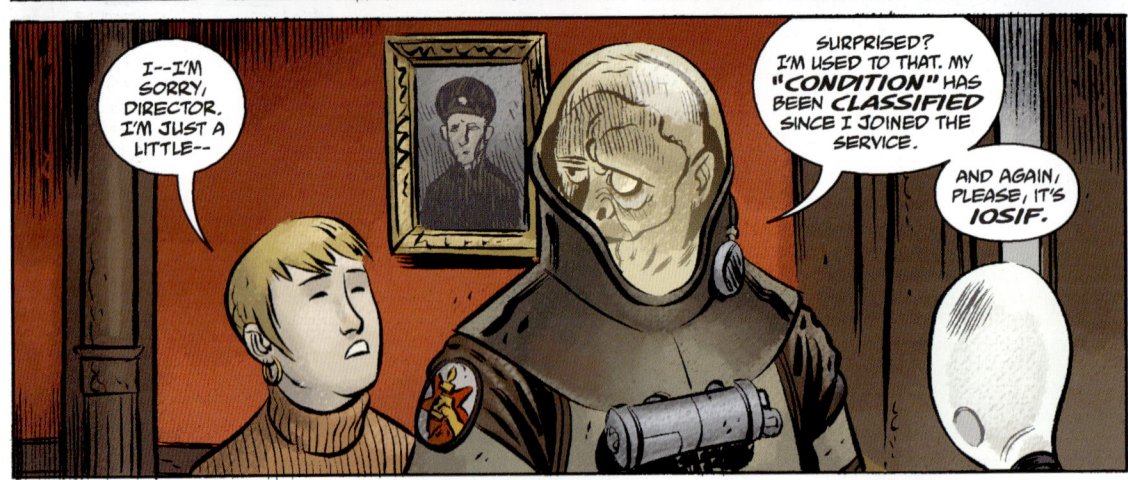

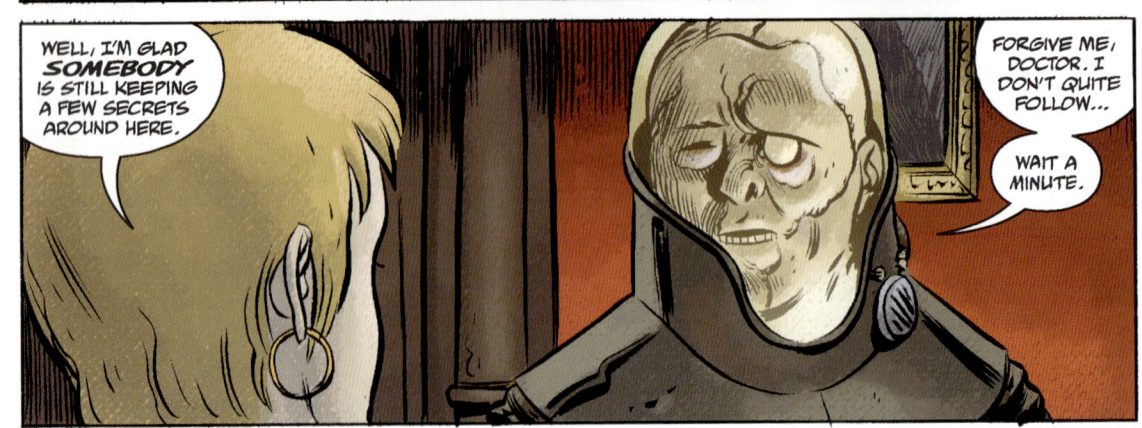

DR. CORRIGAN, SO HAPPY TO FINALLY MEET YOU. I'VE READ ALL OF YOUR BOOKS, EVERY SINGLE ARTICLE, EVERY LECTURE.

THE BUREAU IS VERY LUCKY TO HAVE YOU, BUT I REALLY DO WISH YOU STILL HAD TIME TO WRITE.

AND HERR KRAUS.

CAN YOU IMAGINE HOW LONG I'VE WANTED TO MEET *YOU*?

I--I'M SORRY, DIRECTOR. I'M JUST A LITTLE--

SURPRISED? I'M USED TO THAT. MY *"CONDITION"* HAS BEEN *CLASSIFIED* SINCE I JOINED THE SERVICE.

AND AGAIN, PLEASE, IT'S *IOSIF*.

WELL, I'M GLAD *SOMEBODY* IS STILL KEEPING A FEW SECRETS AROUND HERE.

FORGIVE ME, DOCTOR. I DON'T QUITE FOLLOW...

WAIT A MINUTE.

290

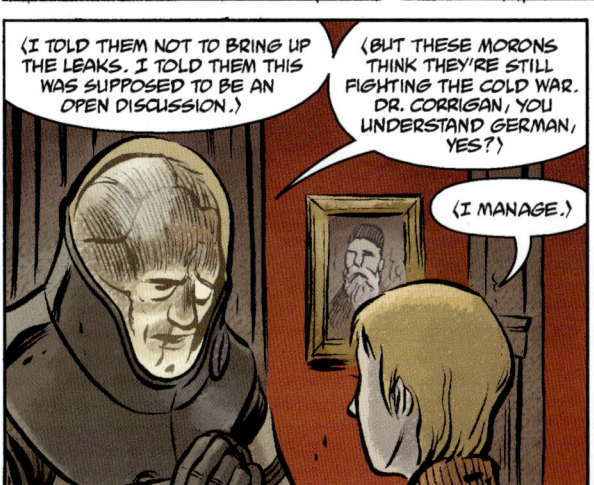

⟨I TOLD THEM NOT TO BRING UP THE LEAKS. I TOLD THEM THIS WAS SUPPOSED TO BE AN OPEN DISCUSSION.⟩

⟨BUT THESE MORONS THINK THEY'RE STILL FIGHTING THE COLD WAR. DR. CORRIGAN, YOU UNDERSTAND GERMAN, YES?⟩

⟨I MANAGE.⟩

VASILY, YOU THREE ARE NOW GOING TO TELL THE ESTEEMED DOCTOR WHY WE ASKED HER HERE. ANSWER *ALL* HER QUESTIONS. ASK A FEW OF YOUR OWN.

YES, DIRECTOR.

AND DOCTOR, I'M AFRAID YOU'LL THINK ME RUDE, BUT COULD I SPEAK TO HERR KRAUS PRIVATELY FOR A FEW MOMENTS?

YOU CAN UNDERSTAND THAT WE TWO HAVE A *LOT* TO DISCUSS, AND THERE MAY NOT BE AN OPPORTUNITY LATER.

YES! AN EXCELLENT IDEA.

⟨TRANSLATED FROM THE GERMAN⟩

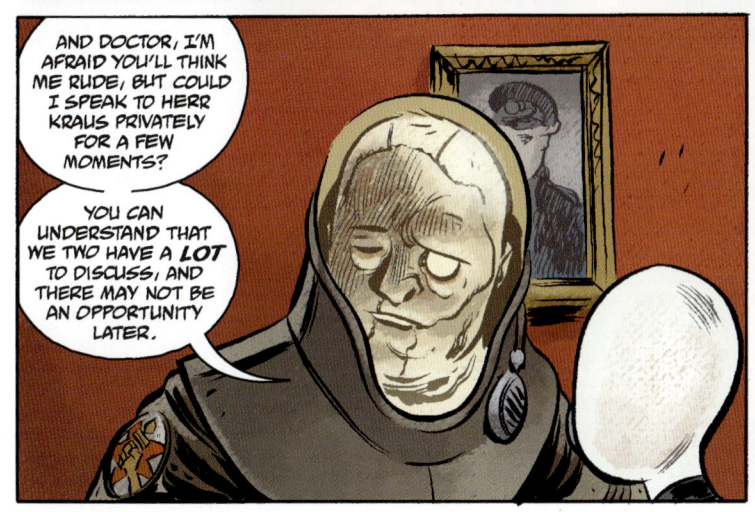

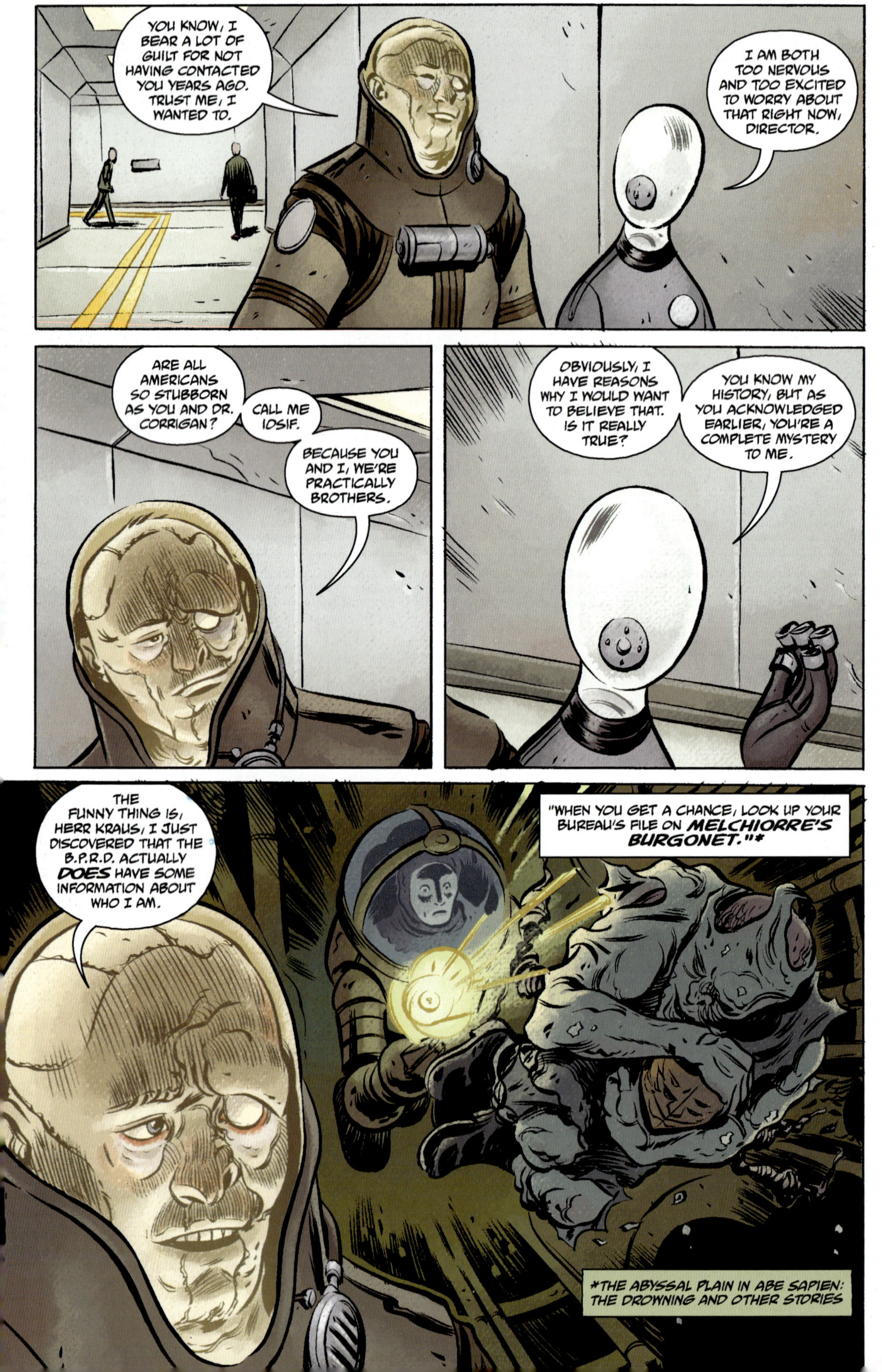
YOU KNOW, I BEAR A LOT OF GUILT FOR NOT HAVING CONTACTED YOU YEARS AGO. TRUST ME, I WANTED TO.
I AM BOTH TOO NERVOUS AND TOO EXCITED TO WORRY ABOUT THAT RIGHT NOW, DIRECTOR.
ARE ALL AMERICANS SO STUBBORN AS YOU AND DR. CORRIGAN?
CALL ME IOSIF.
BECAUSE YOU AND I, WE'RE PRACTICALLY BROTHERS.
OBVIOUSLY, I HAVE REASONS WHY I WOULD WANT TO BELIEVE THAT. IS IT REALLY TRUE?
YOU KNOW MY HISTORY, BUT AS YOU ACKNOWLEDGED EARLIER, YOU'RE A COMPLETE MYSTERY TO ME.
THE FUNNY THING IS, HERR KRAUS, I JUST DISCOVERED THAT THE B.P.R.D. ACTUALLY DOES HAVE SOME INFORMATION ABOUT WHO I AM.
"WHEN YOU GET A CHANCE, LOOK UP YOUR BUREAU'S FILE ON MELCHIORRE'S BURGONET."*
*THE ABYSSAL PLAIN IN ABE SAPIEN: THE DROWNING AND OTHER STORIES

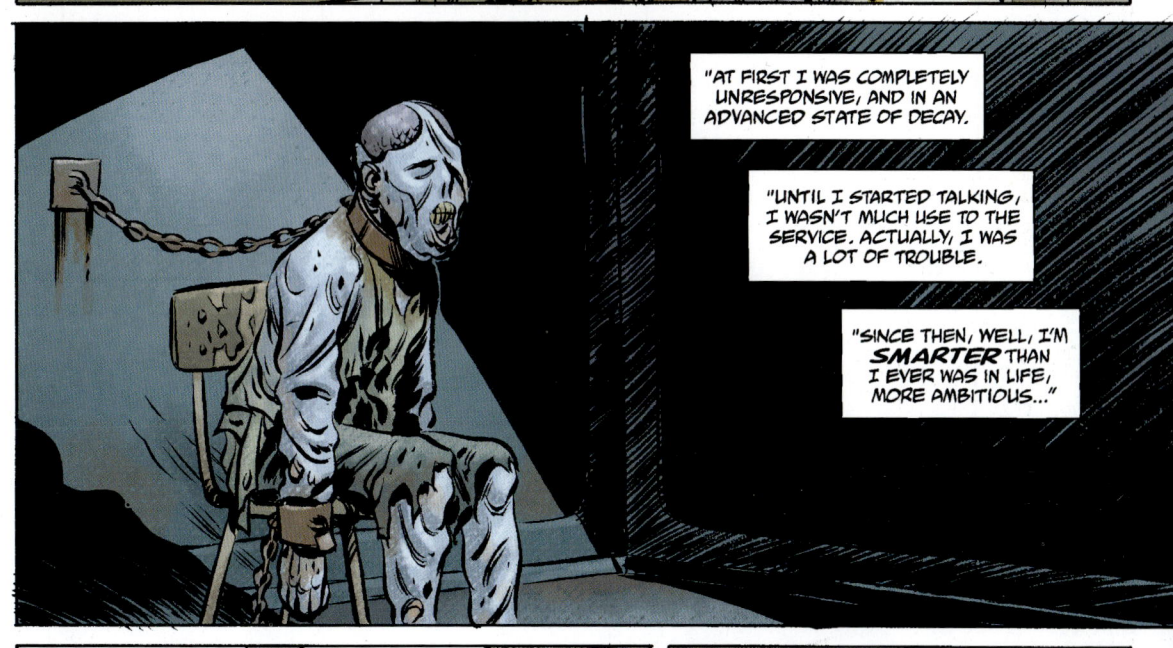

ALL YOU REALLY NEED TO KNOW IS THAT I WAS A SOLDIER IN THE SECOND WORLD WAR, *DIED*, AND WAS RESURRECTED ALMOST FORTY YEARS LATER.

NOBODY QUITE KNOWS HOW.

"AT FIRST I WAS COMPLETELY UNRESPONSIVE, AND IN AN ADVANCED STATE OF DECAY.

"UNTIL I STARTED TALKING, I WASN'T MUCH USE TO THE SERVICE. ACTUALLY, I WAS A LOT OF TROUBLE.

"SINCE THEN, WELL, I'M *SMARTER* THAN I EVER WAS IN LIFE, MORE AMBITIOUS..."

...AND I HAVE AN INTIMACY WITH DEATH AND THE SUPERNATURAL *NO ONE* ELSE IN THE SERVICE CAN CLAIM. NOT EVEN OUR PSYCHICS.

WITH THAT SORT OF INSIGHT, SUCCESS IN THE S.S.S. WAS A GIVEN. HOW COULD THEY *NOT* APPOINT ME DIRECTOR?

YOU KNOW WHAT I'M TALKING ABOUT. IT'S THE SAME KIND OF INSIGHT THAT YOU BRING TO THE BUREAU.

HERR KRAUS?

HERR KRAUS, OVER HERE.

I WANT TO SHOW YOU SOMETHING.

BEEP DEEP

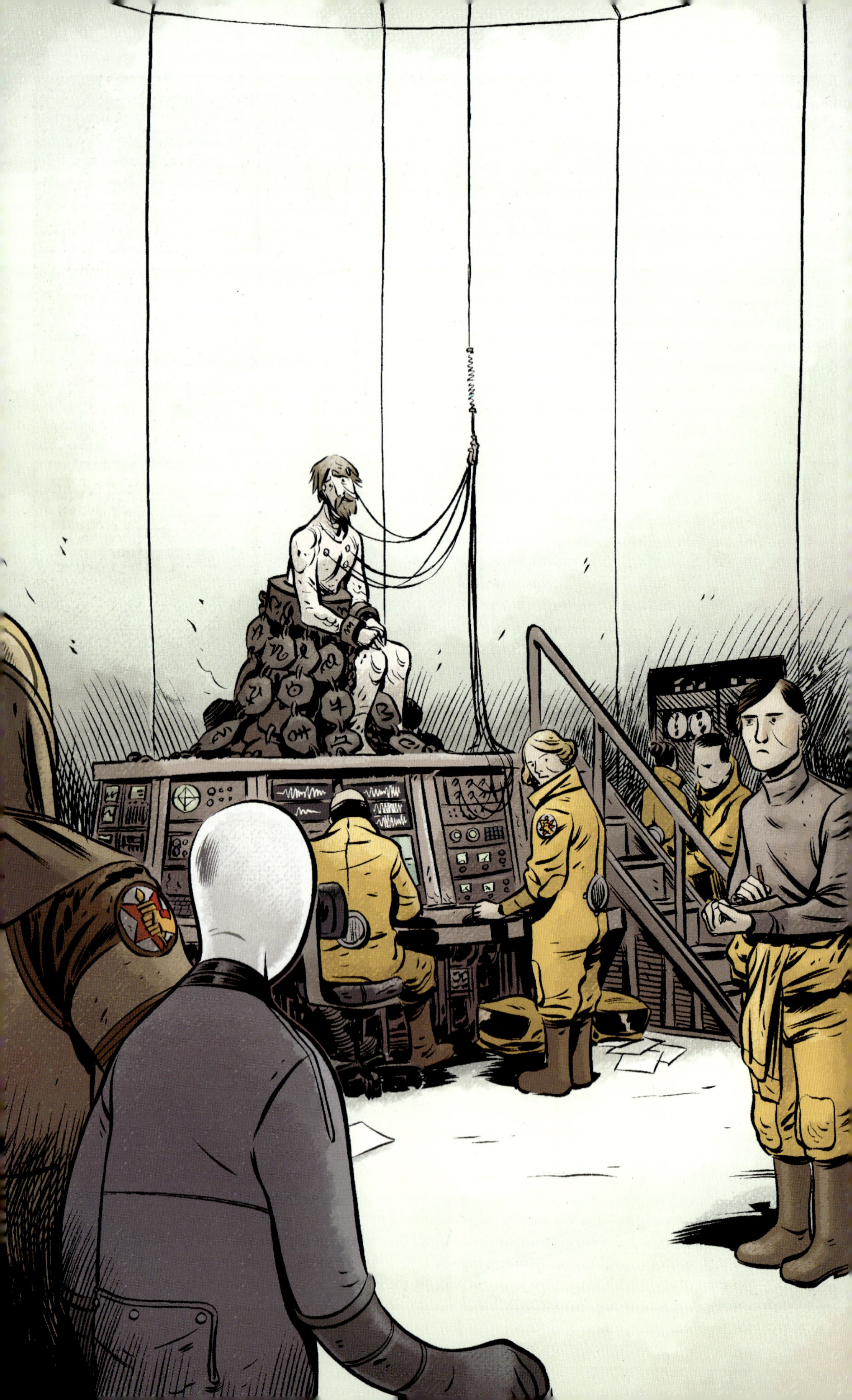

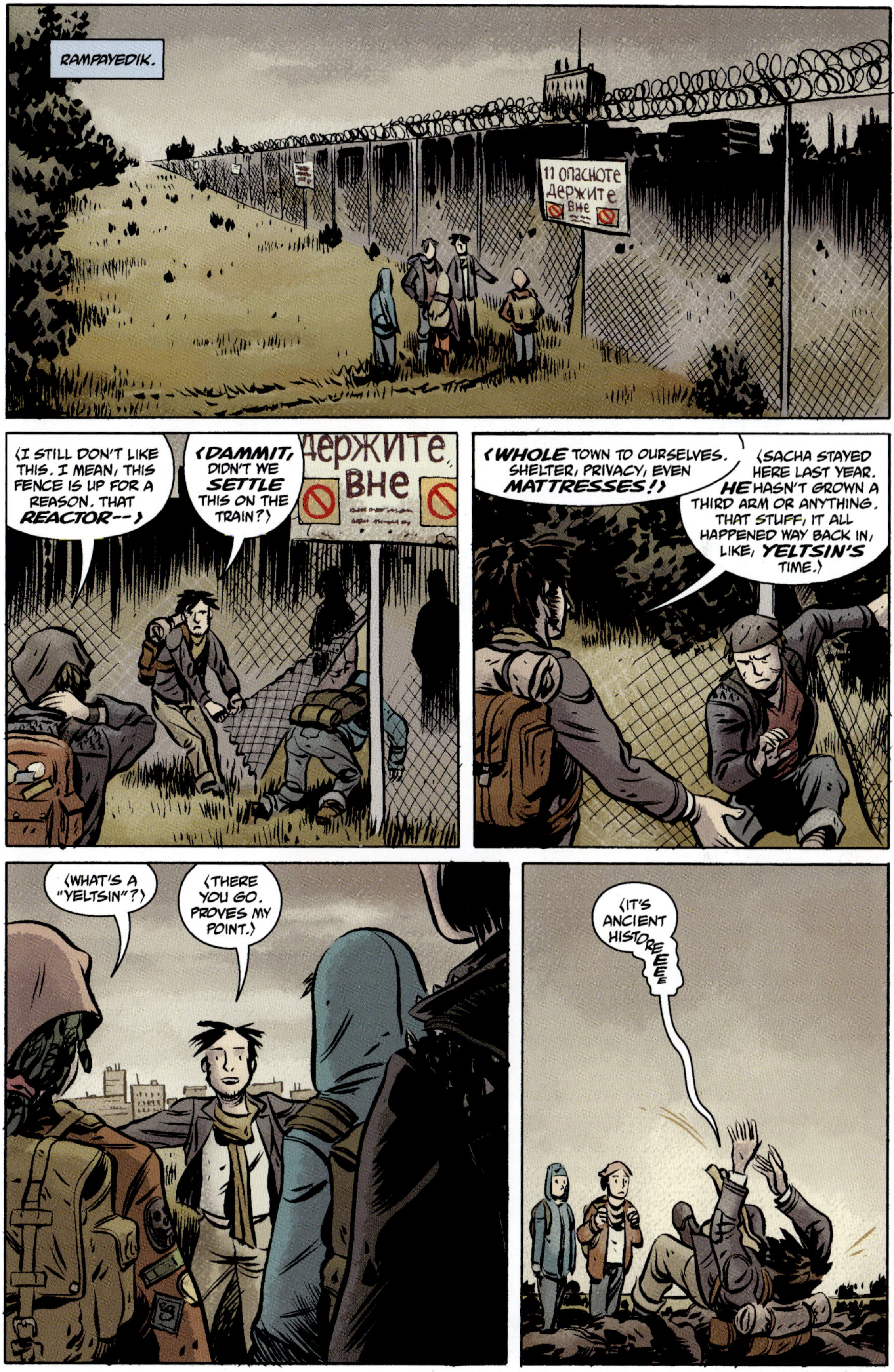
RAMPAYEDIK.
11 опасноте
держите
вне
‹I STILL DON'T LIKE THIS. I MEAN, THIS FENCE IS UP FOR A REASON. THAT REACTOR--›
‹DAMMIT, DIDN'T WE SETTLE THIS ON THE TRAIN?›
держите
вне
‹WHOLE TOWN TO OURSELVES. SHELTER, PRIVACY, EVEN MATTRESSES!›
‹SACHA STAYED HERE LAST YEAR. HE HASN'T GROWN A THIRD ARM OR ANYTHING. THAT STUFF, IT ALL HAPPENED WAY BACK IN, LIKE, YELTSIN'S TIME.›
‹WHAT'S A "YELTSIN"?›
‹THERE YOU GO. PROVES MY POINT.›
‹IT'S ANCIENT HISTOREEEEE

‹FROM THE RUSSIAN›

‹WHAT THE #€$%6 IS THIS?!›
‹HEY, BALYI, NINA, COME ON. GIVE ME A HAND.›
‹WHAT'S THE MATTER WITH YOU TWO? YOU WERE JUST GOING TO--›
‹--LEAVE ME DOWN...›
‹HOLY $#!€›
‹HEY, LOOK!›

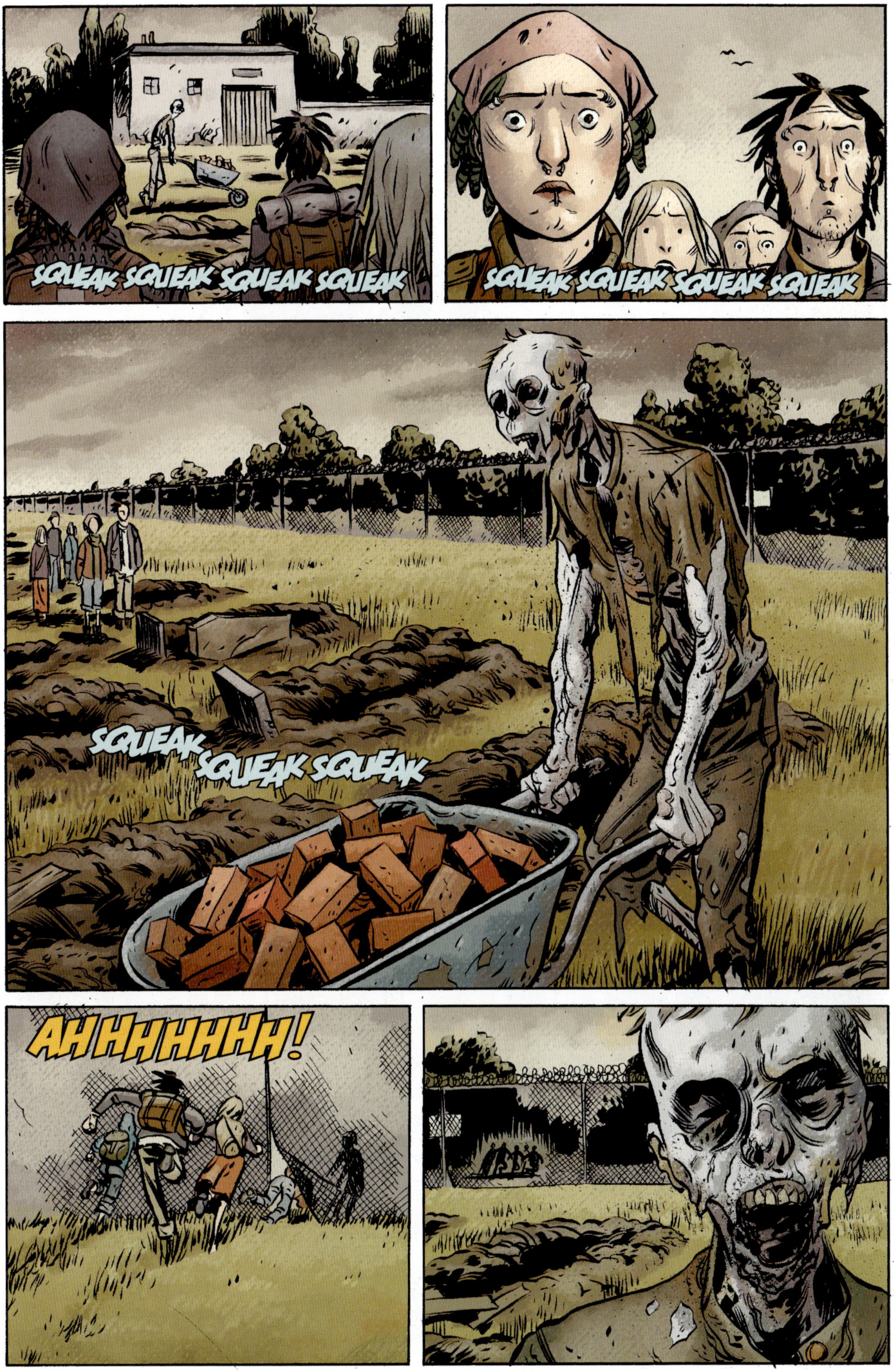
SQUEAK SQUEAK SQUEAK SQUEAK
SQUEAK SQUEAK SQUEAK SQUEAK
SQUEAK SQUEAK SQUEAK
AHHHHHHH!

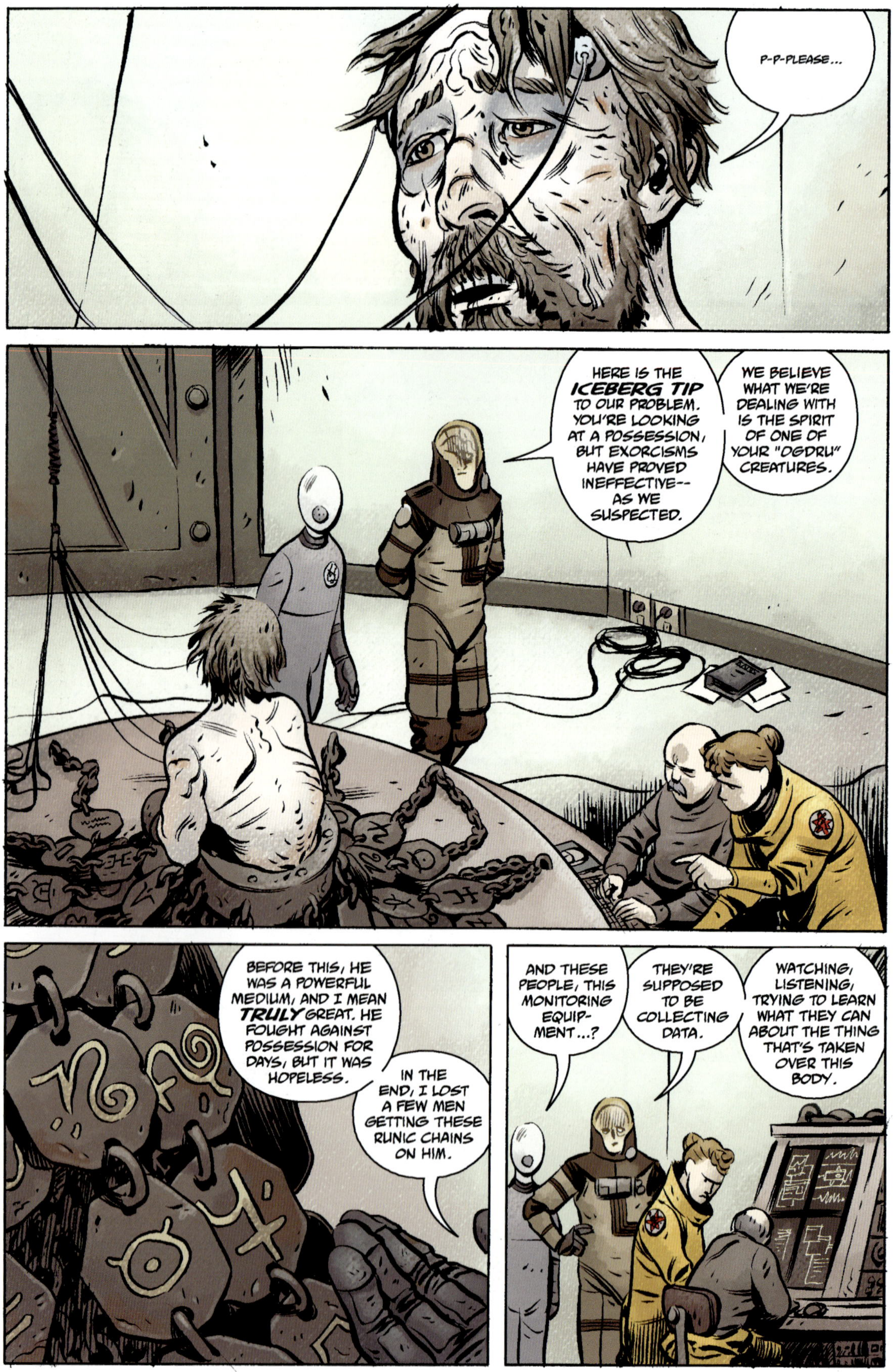
P-P-PLEASE...
HERE IS THE ICEBERG TIP TO OUR PROBLEM. YOU'RE LOOKING AT A POSSESSION, BUT EXORCISMS HAVE PROVED INEFFECTIVE-- AS WE SUSPECTED.
WE BELIEVE WHAT WE'RE DEALING WITH IS THE SPIRIT OF ONE OF YOUR "OGDRU" CREATURES.
BEFORE THIS, HE WAS A POWERFUL MEDIUM, AND I MEAN TRULY GREAT. HE FOUGHT AGAINST POSSESSION FOR DAYS, BUT IT WAS HOPELESS.
IN THE END, I LOST A FEW MEN GETTING THESE RUNIC CHAINS ON HIM.
AND THESE PEOPLE, THIS MONITORING EQUIP- MENT...?
THEY'RE SUPPOSED TO BE COLLECTING DATA.
WATCHING, LISTENING, TRYING TO LEARN WHAT THEY CAN ABOUT THE THING THAT'S TAKEN OVER THIS BODY.

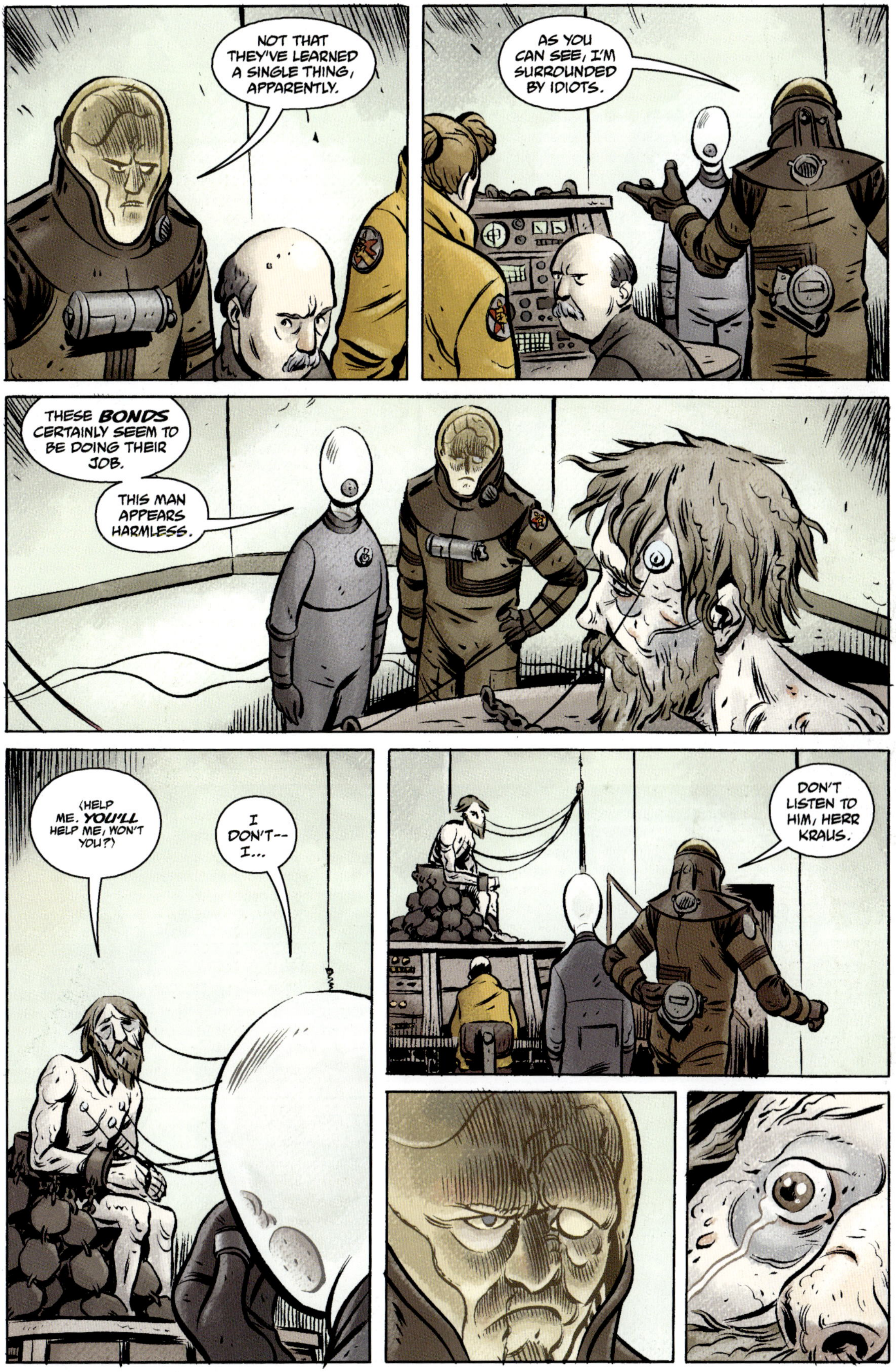
NOT THAT THEY'VE LEARNED A SINGLE THING, APPARENTLY.
AS YOU CAN SEE, I'M SURROUNDED BY IDIOTS.
THESE **BONDS** CERTAINLY SEEM TO BE DOING THEIR JOB.
THIS MAN APPEARS HARMLESS.
‹HELP ME. ***YOU'LL*** HELP ME, WON'T YOU?›
I DON'T-- I...
DON'T LISTEN TO HIM, HERR KRAUS.

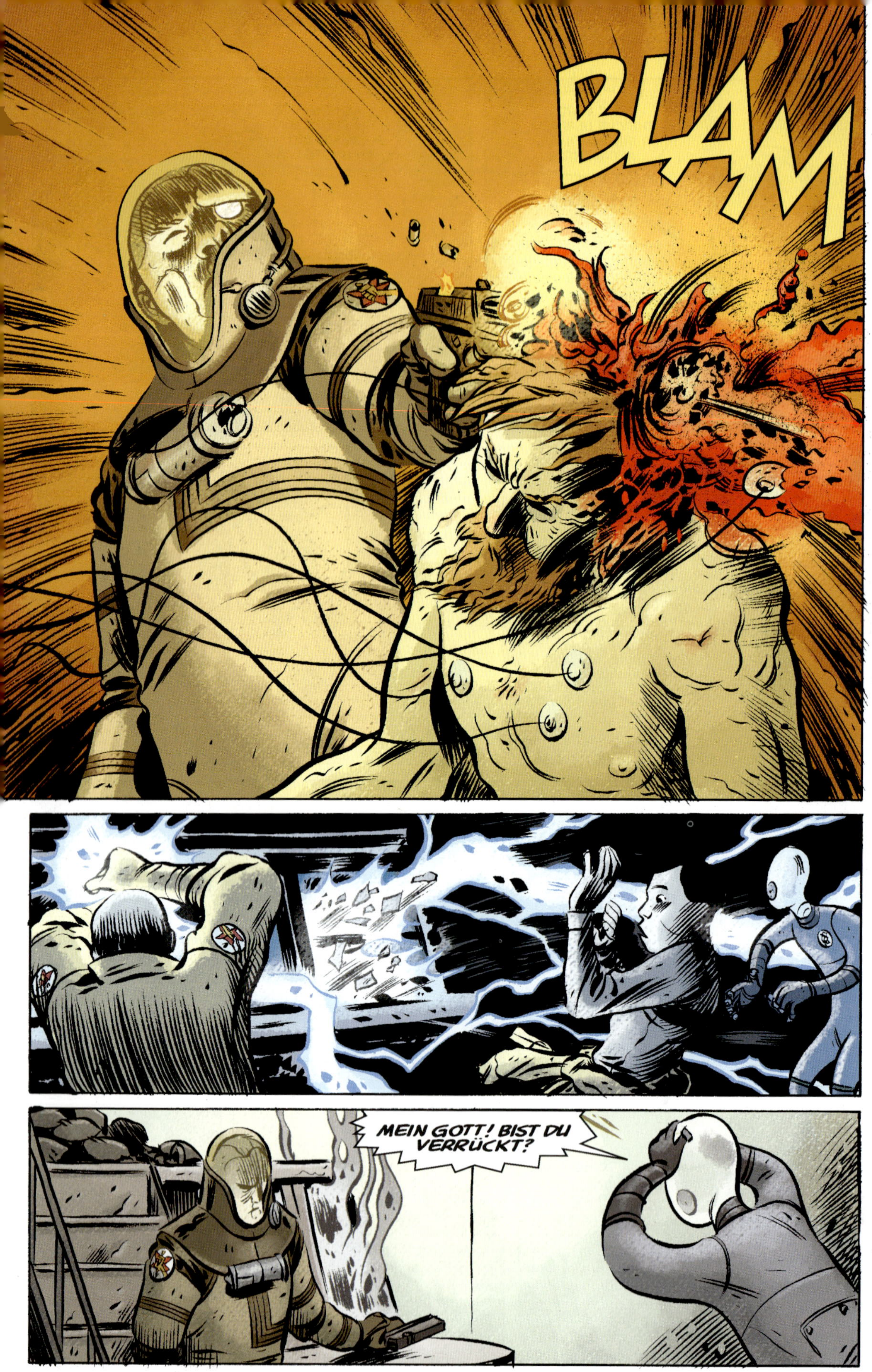
BLAM
MEIN GOTT! BIST DU VERRÜCKT?

NO, I'M NOT INSANE. HE WAS A MONSTER.
‹LOOK WHAT YOU'VE DONE! MILLIONS OF RUBLES OF EQUIPMENT RUINED--AND A RICOCHET COULD HAVE KILLED SOMEBODY!›
‹ENOUGH!›
‹OUT! EVERY-ONE!›
HERR KRAUS, YOUR BUREAU AND MY SERVICE, WE KILL HORRORS LIKE THIS ALL THE TIME.
BUT HE SEEMED--
HUMAN? HE WAS, ONCE. NOT ANYMORE.
HIS SOUL DIED MONTHS AGO. I DID THE ONLY THING I COULD FOR HIM.
HE WAS BEYOND OUR HELP--BUT NOT BEYOND REACH.
NOT ANYMORE.

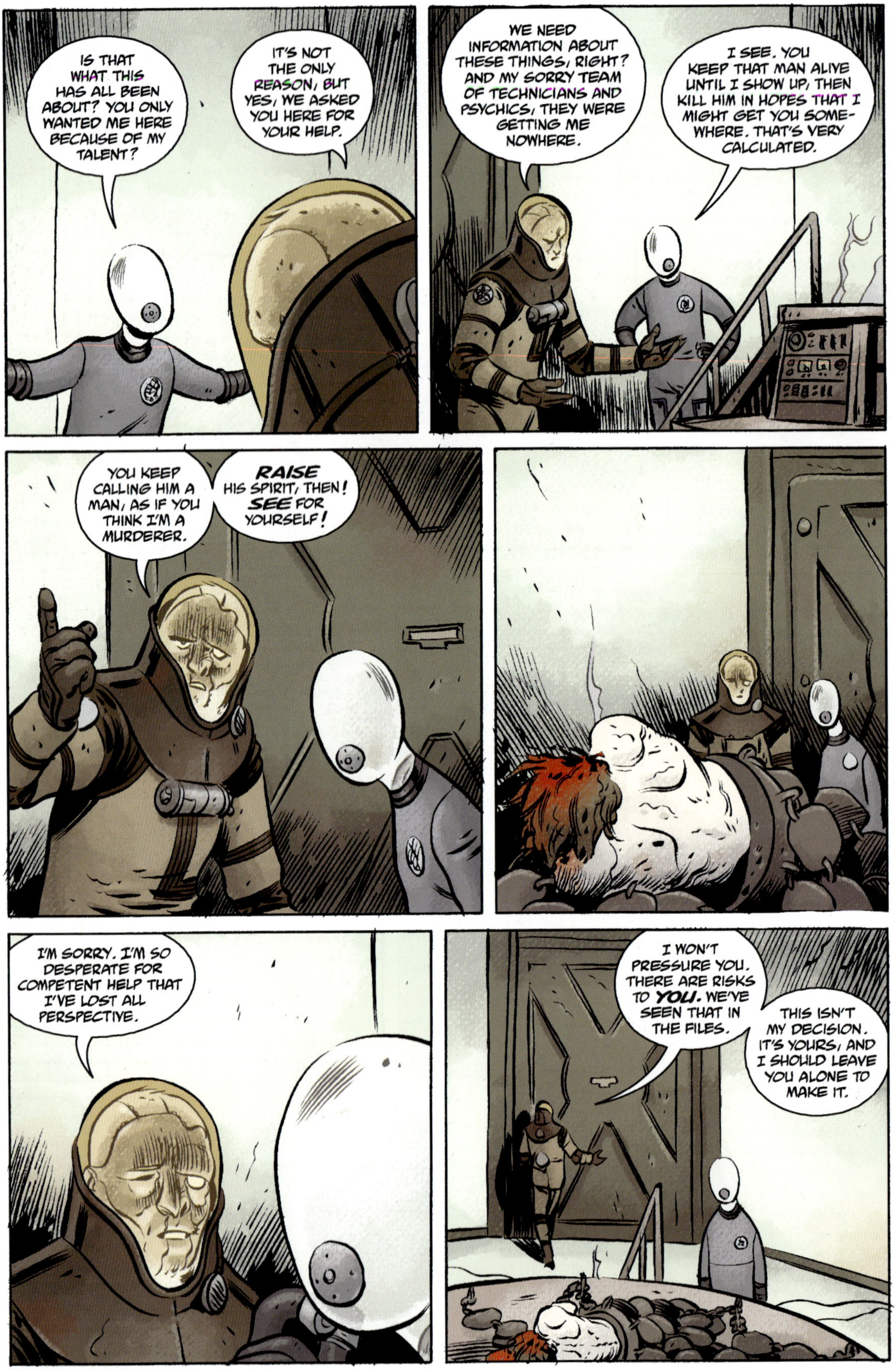
IS THAT WHAT THIS HAS ALL BEEN ABOUT? YOU ONLY WANTED ME HERE BECAUSE OF MY TALENT?
IT'S NOT THE ONLY REASON, BUT YES, WE ASKED YOU HERE FOR YOUR HELP.
WE NEED INFORMATION ABOUT THESE THINGS, RIGHT? AND MY SORRY TEAM OF TECHNICIANS AND PSYCHICS, THEY WERE GETTING ME NOWHERE.
I SEE. YOU KEEP THAT MAN ALIVE UNTIL I SHOW UP, THEN KILL HIM IN HOPES THAT I MIGHT GET YOU SOME-WHERE. THAT'S VERY CALCULATED.
YOU KEEP CALLING HIM A MAN, AS IF YOU THINK I'M A MURDERER.
RAISE HIS SPIRIT, THEN! SEE FOR YOURSELF!
I'M SORRY. I'M SO DESPERATE FOR COMPETENT HELP THAT I'VE LOST ALL PERSPECTIVE.
I WON'T PRESSURE YOU. THERE ARE RISKS TO YOU. WE'VE SEEN THAT IN THE FILES.
THIS ISN'T MY DECISION. IT'S YOURS, AND I SHOULD LEAVE YOU ALONE TO MAKE IT.

⟨IS THERE COLLUSION AFOOT?⟩
⟨PLEASE, SHARE THE MINUTES OF THIS MEETING WITH ME.⟩
⟨JUST PLANNING THE CARPOOL, SIR.⟩
⟨GOOD DAY, DIRECTOR.⟩
⟨SEE YOU TOMORROW.⟩
⟨HAVE A PLEASANT EVENING.⟩

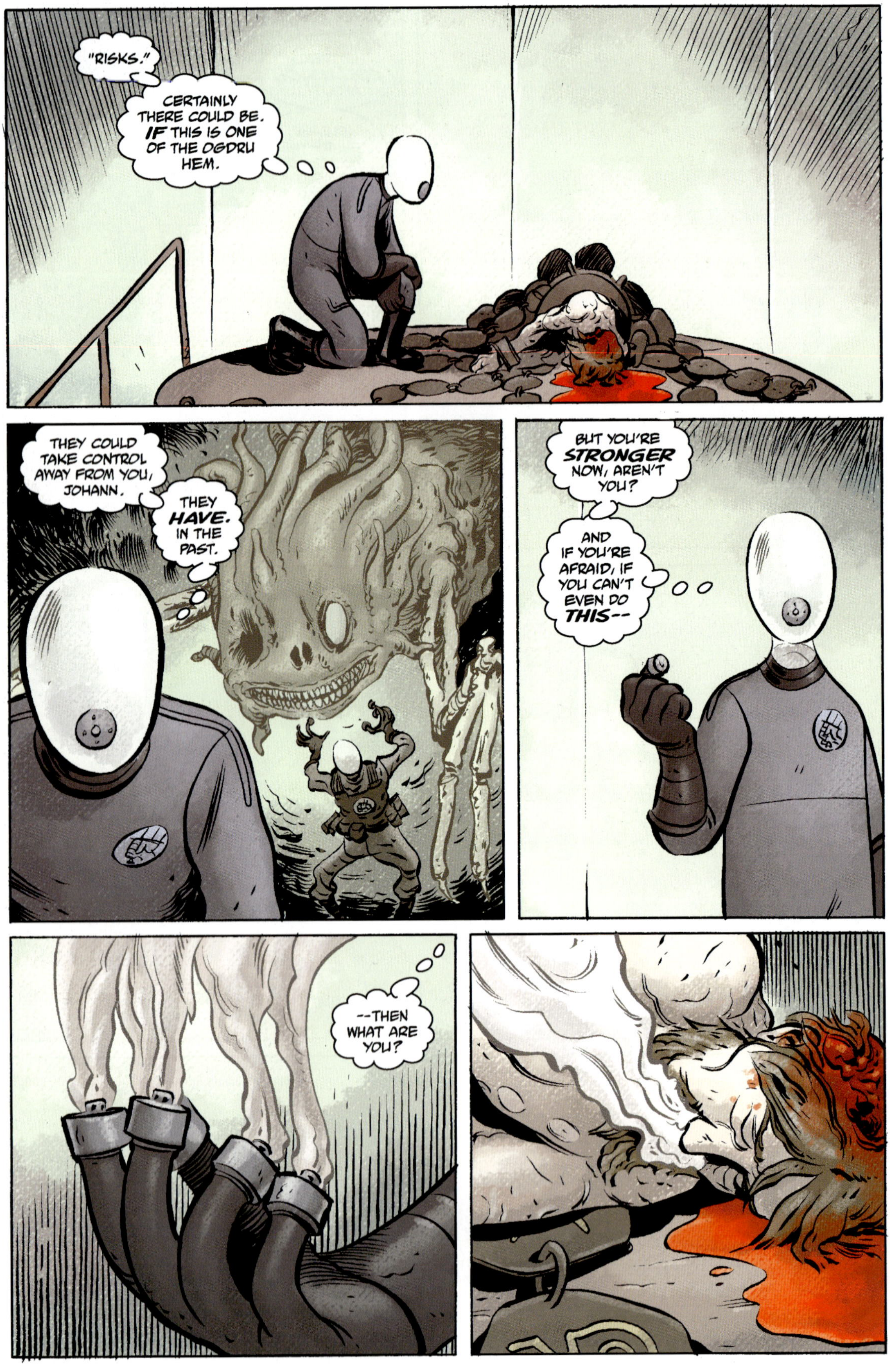
"RISKS."
CERTAINLY THERE COULD BE. IF THIS IS ONE OF THE OGDRU HEM.
THEY COULD TAKE CONTROL AWAY FROM YOU, JOHANN.
THEY HAVE. IN THE PAST.
BUT YOU'RE STRONGER NOW, AREN'T YOU?
AND IF YOU'RE AFRAID, IF YOU CAN'T EVEN DO THIS--
--THEN WHAT ARE YOU?

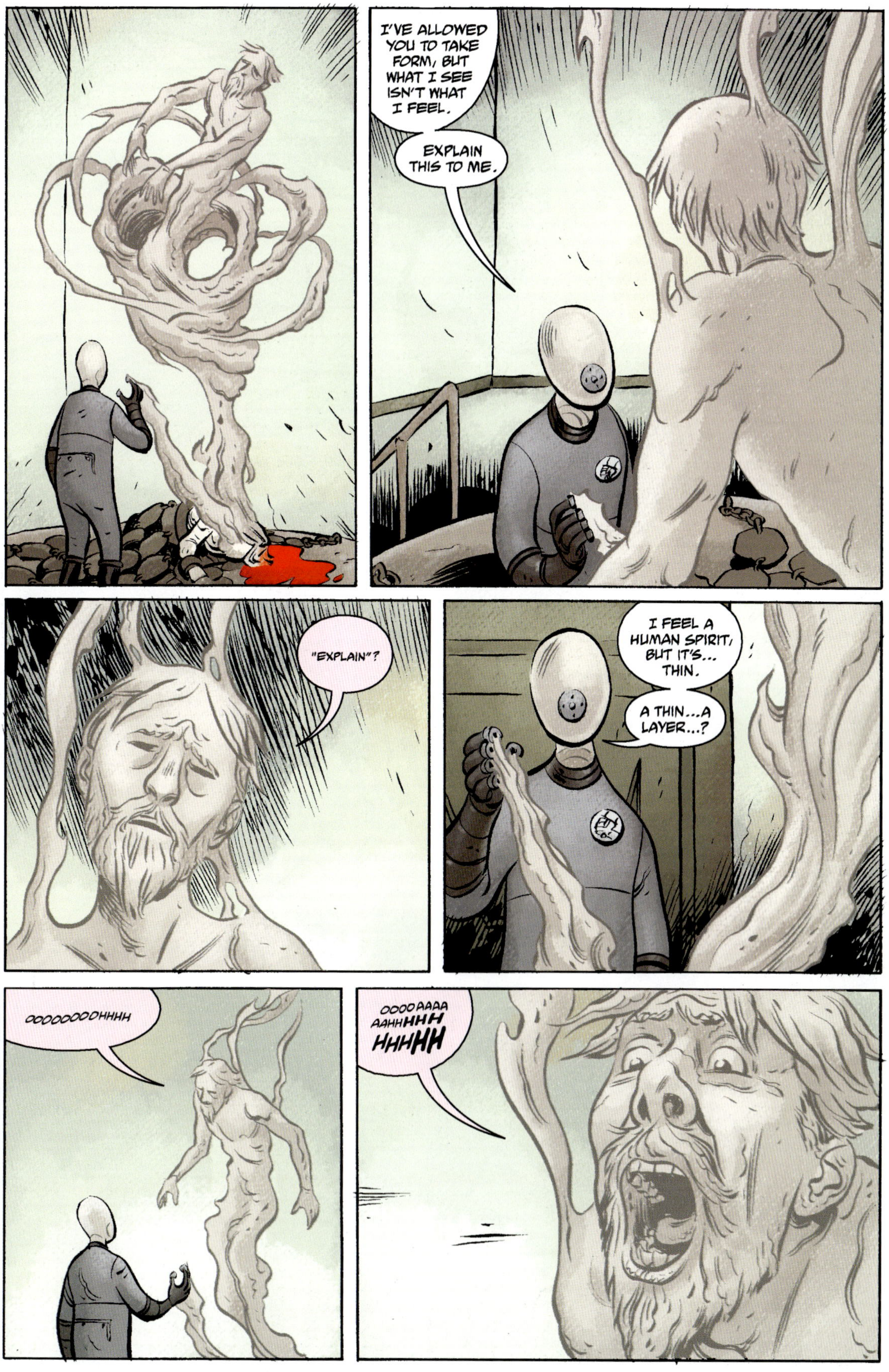
I'VE ALLOWED YOU TO TAKE FORM, BUT WHAT I SEE ISN'T WHAT I FEEL.
EXPLAIN THIS TO ME.
"EXPLAIN"?
I FEEL A HUMAN SPIRIT, BUT IT'S... THIN.
A THIN...A LAYER...?
OOOOOOOOHHHH
OOOOAAAA AAHHHHH HHHHH

HHHHHHH

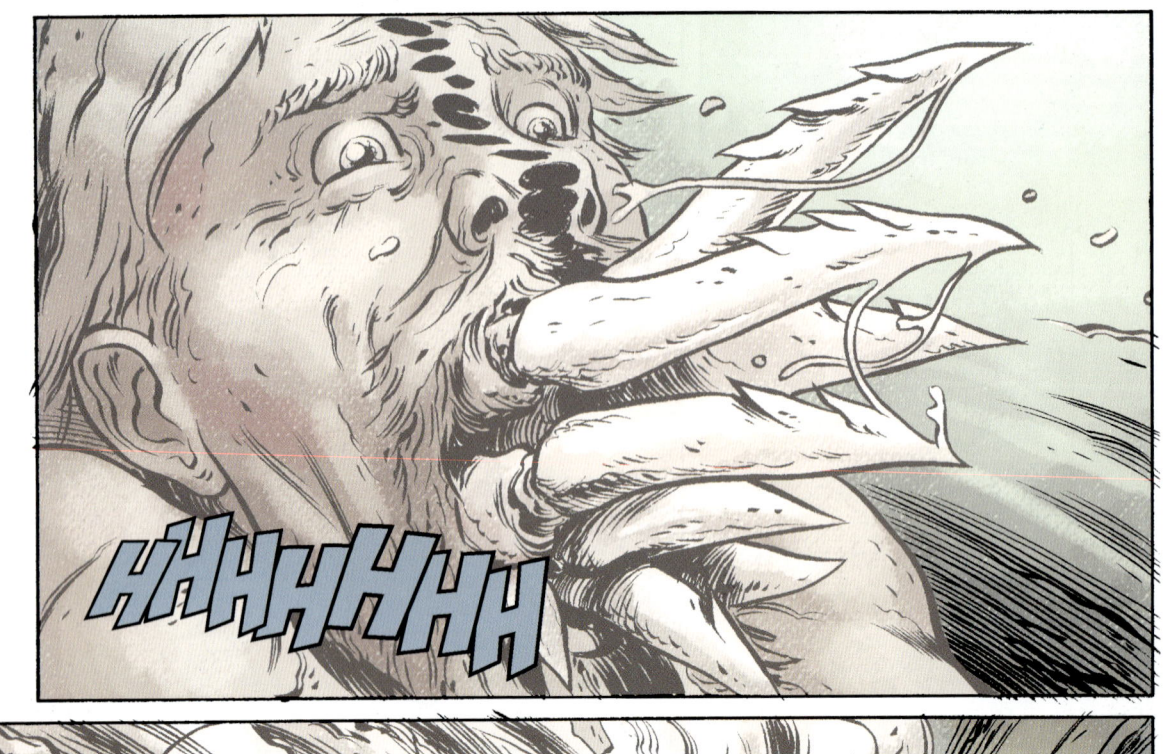

SSHRIPP

UHNGUL ETHEQ AGHRAAHN

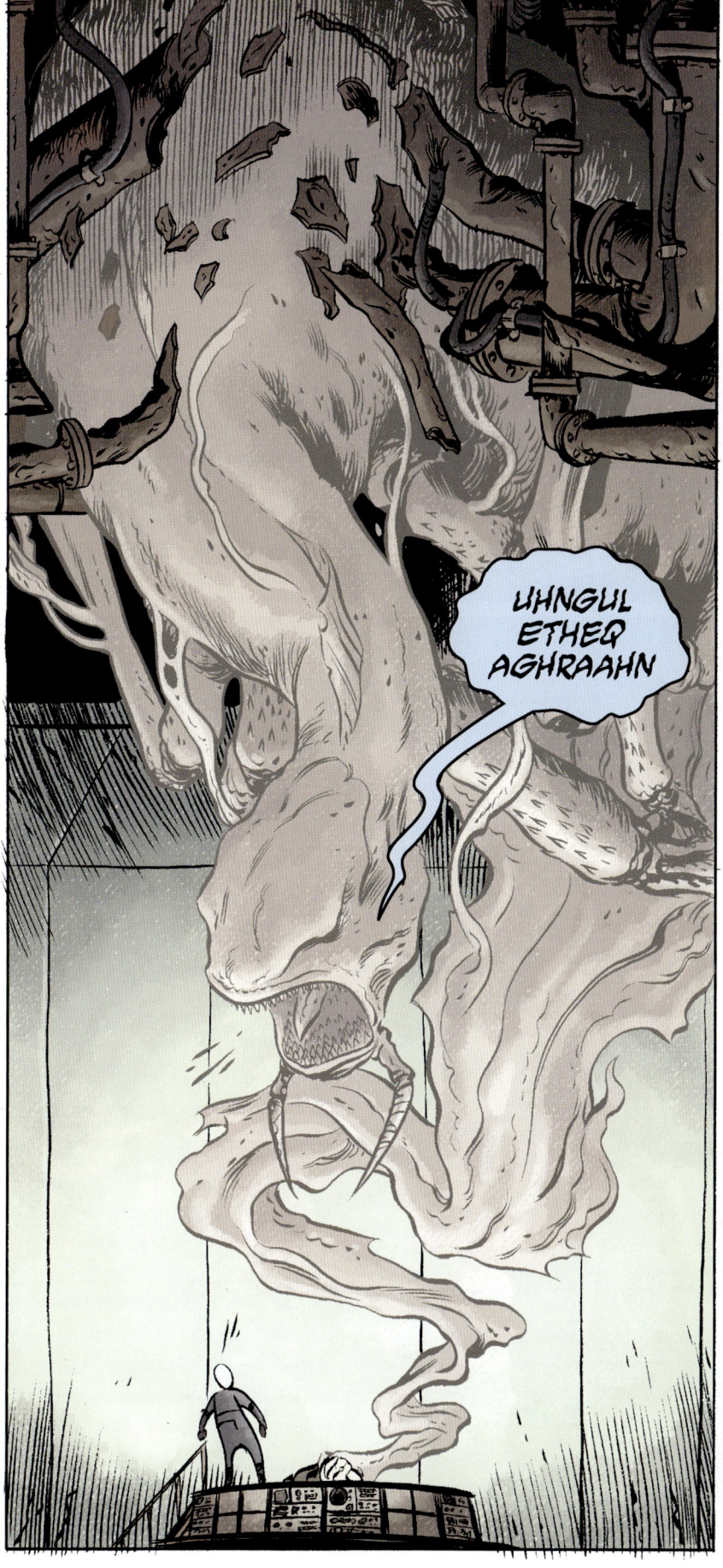

NOT THIS... THIS...TH-TH-THISSSSSS--

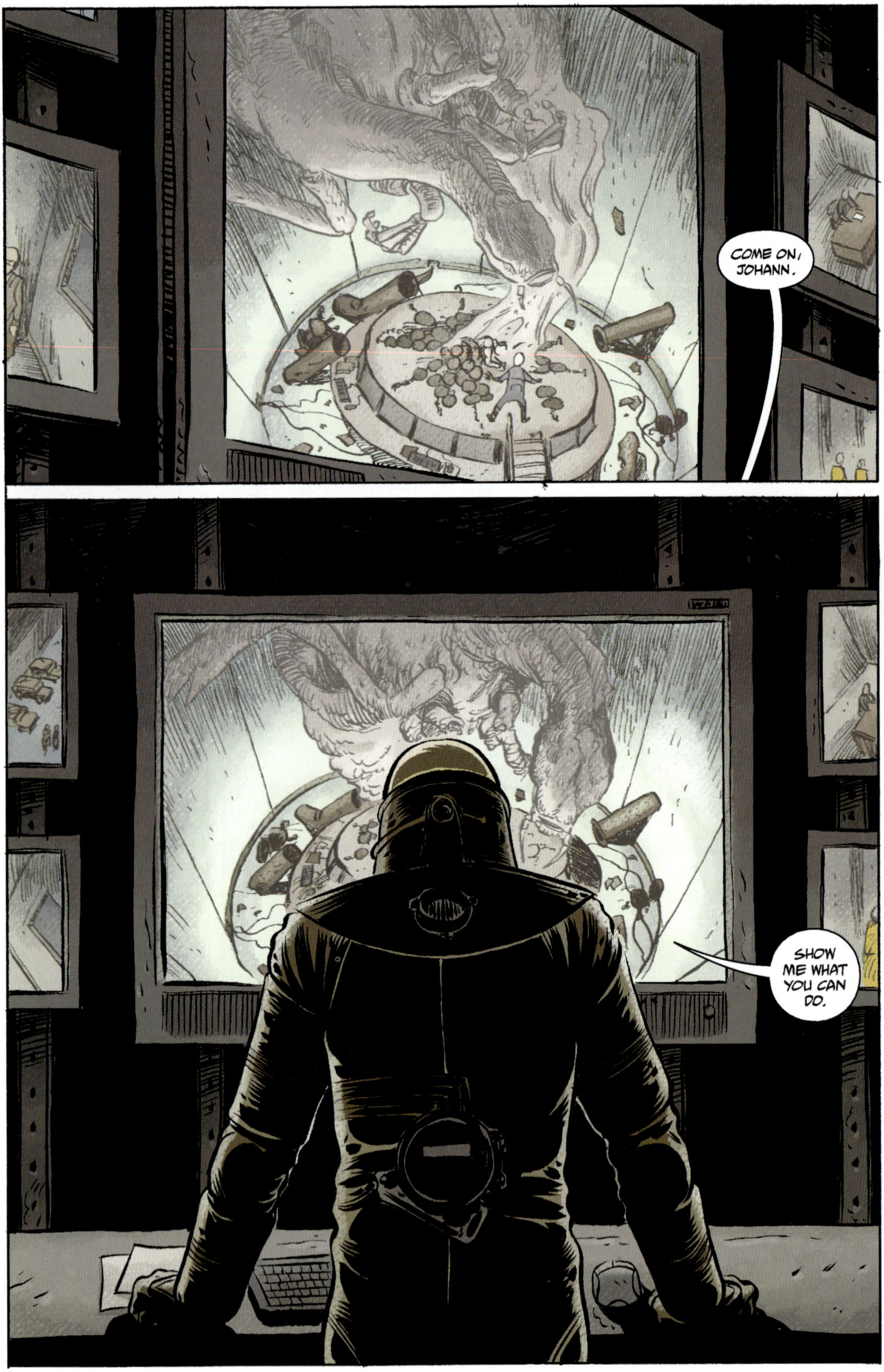
COME ON, JOHANN.
SHOW ME WHAT YOU CAN DO.

RUSSIA CHAPTER THREE

ILLUSTRATION BY **DAVE JOHNSON**

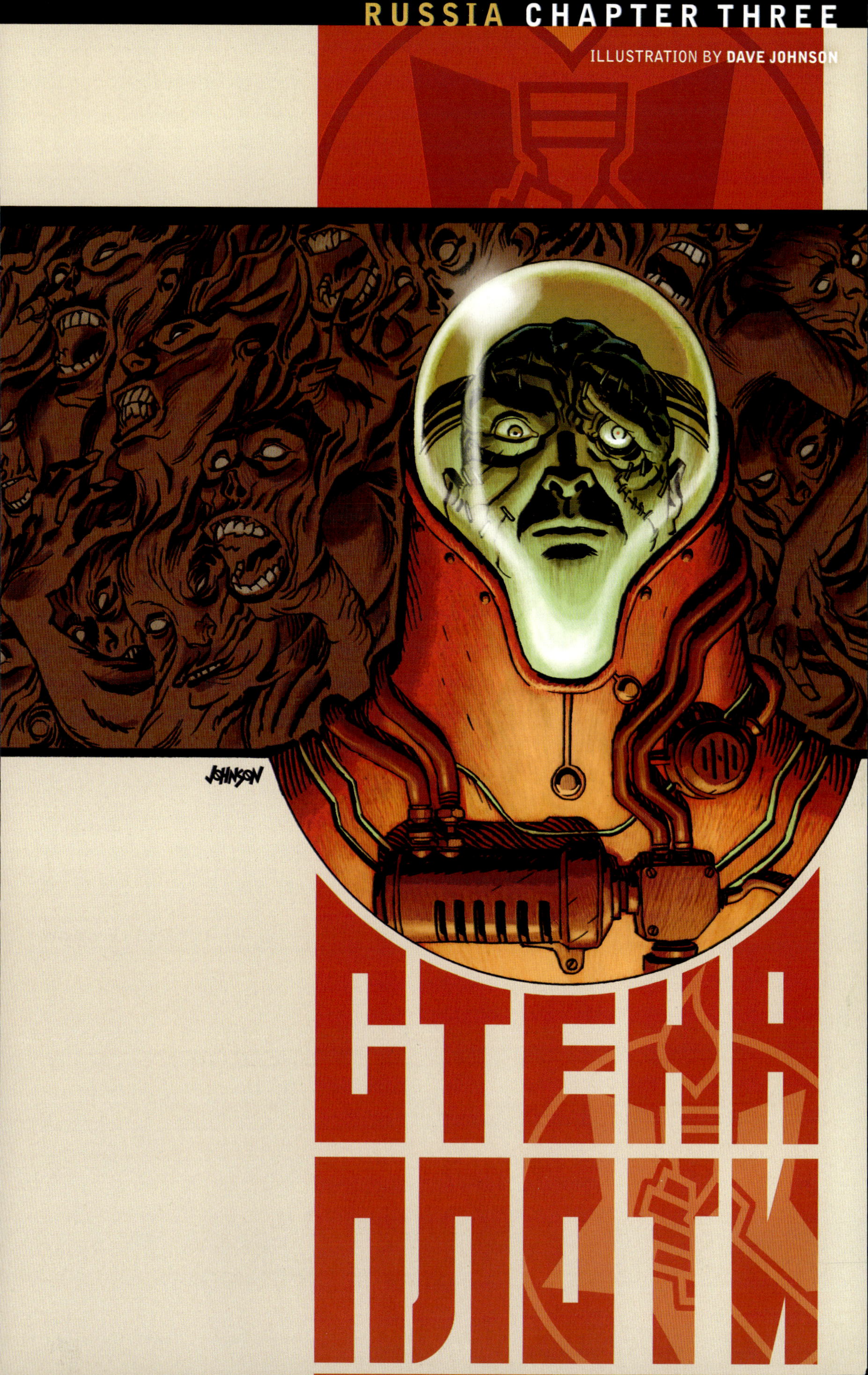
JOHNSON

СТЕНА ПЛОТИ

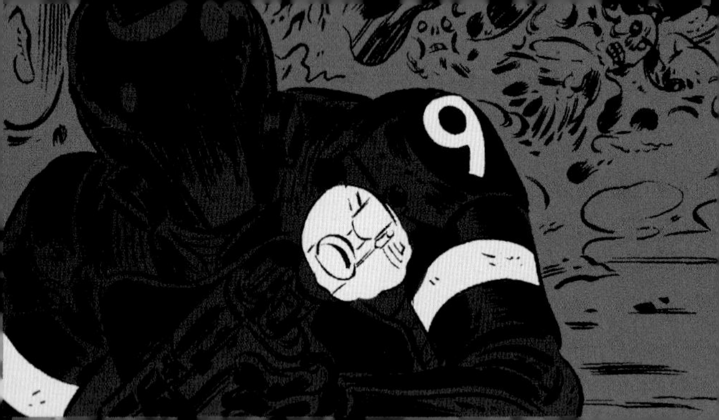

SOOOO, AREN'T YOU SUPPOSED TO BE ANSWERING SOME QUESTIONS FOR ME?
YOU HAVE NOT ASK--
YOU WANT TO KNOW WHY YOU'RE HERE, RIGHT?
I'LL TELL YOU, DOCTOR.
ALL OF IT.

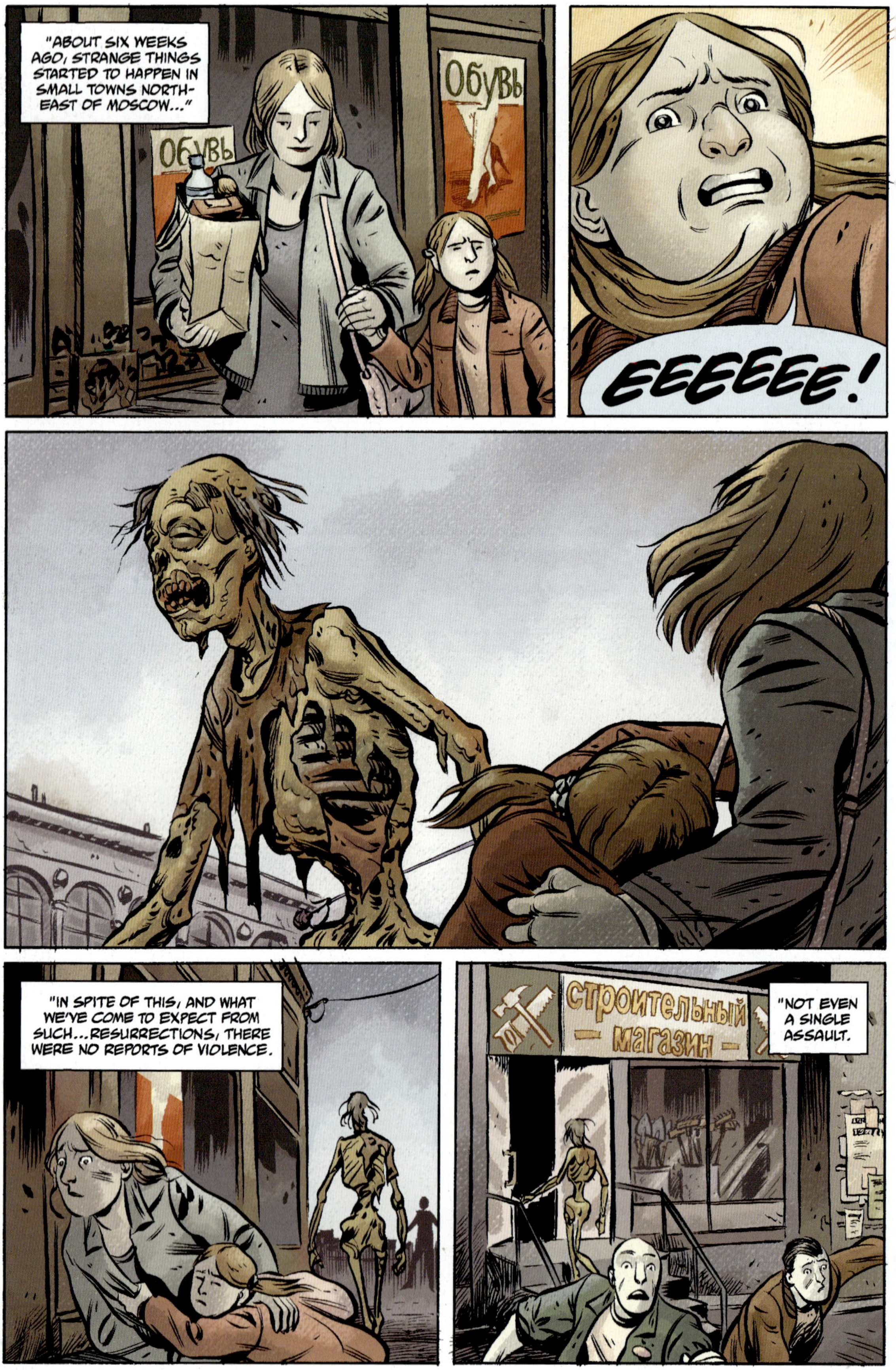
"ABOUT SIX WEEKS AGO, STRANGE THINGS STARTED TO HAPPEN IN SMALL TOWNS NORTH-EAST OF MOSCOW..."
Обувь
Обувь
EEEEEE!
"IN SPITE OF THIS, AND WHAT WE'VE COME TO EXPECT FROM SUCH...RESURRECTIONS, THERE WERE NO REPORTS OF VIOLENCE.
строительный
- магазин -
"NOT EVEN A SINGLE ASSAULT.

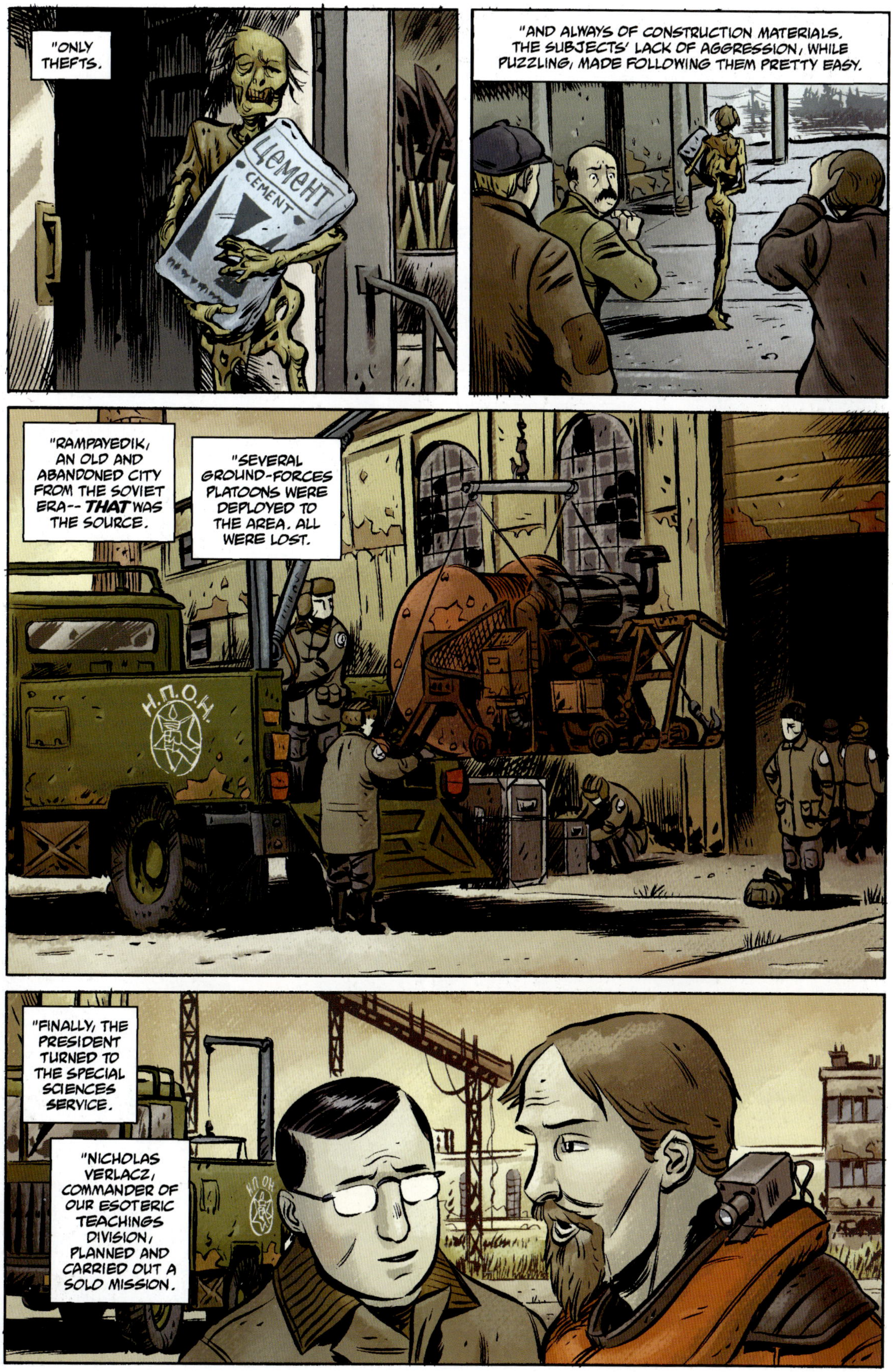
"ONLY THEFTS.
ЦЕМЕНТ
CEMENT
"AND ALWAYS OF CONSTRUCTION MATERIALS. THE SUBJECTS' LACK OF AGGRESSION, WHILE PUZZLING, MADE FOLLOWING THEM PRETTY EASY.
"RAMPAYEDIK, AN OLD AND ABANDONED CITY FROM THE SOVIET ERA-- THAT WAS THE SOURCE.
"SEVERAL GROUND-FORCES PLATOONS WERE DEPLOYED TO THE AREA. ALL WERE LOST.
Н.П.О.Н.
"FINALLY, THE PRESIDENT TURNED TO THE SPECIAL SCIENCES SERVICE.
"NICHOLAS VERLACZ, COMMANDER OF OUR ESOTERIC TEACHINGS DIVISION, PLANNED AND CARRIED OUT A SOLO MISSION.

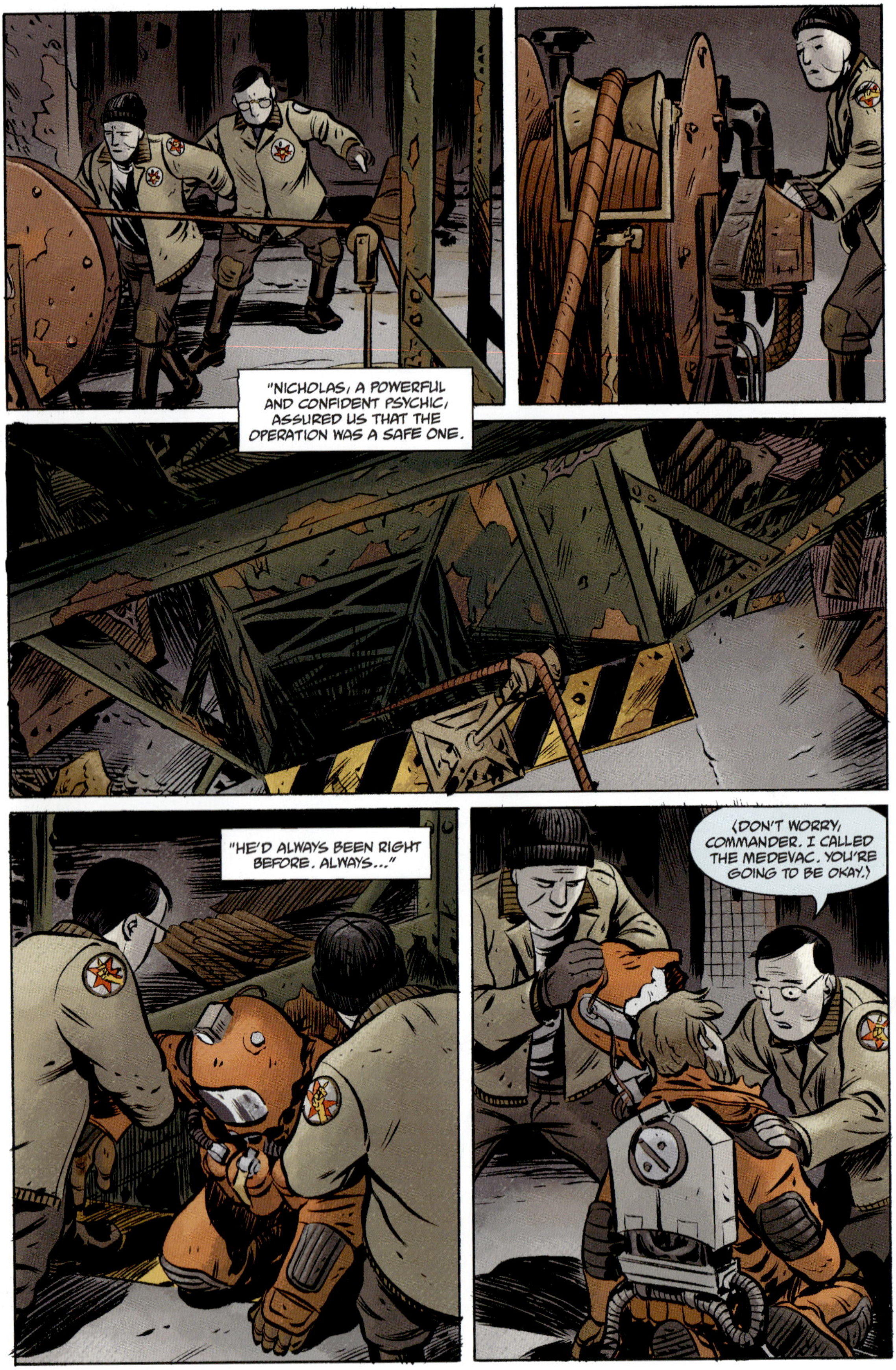
"NICHOLAS, A POWERFUL AND CONFIDENT PSYCHIC, ASSURED US THAT THE OPERATION WAS A SAFE ONE.
"HE'D ALWAYS BEEN RIGHT BEFORE. ALWAYS..."
‹DON'T WORRY, COMMANDER. I CALLED THE MEDEVAC. YOU'RE GOING TO BE OKAY.›

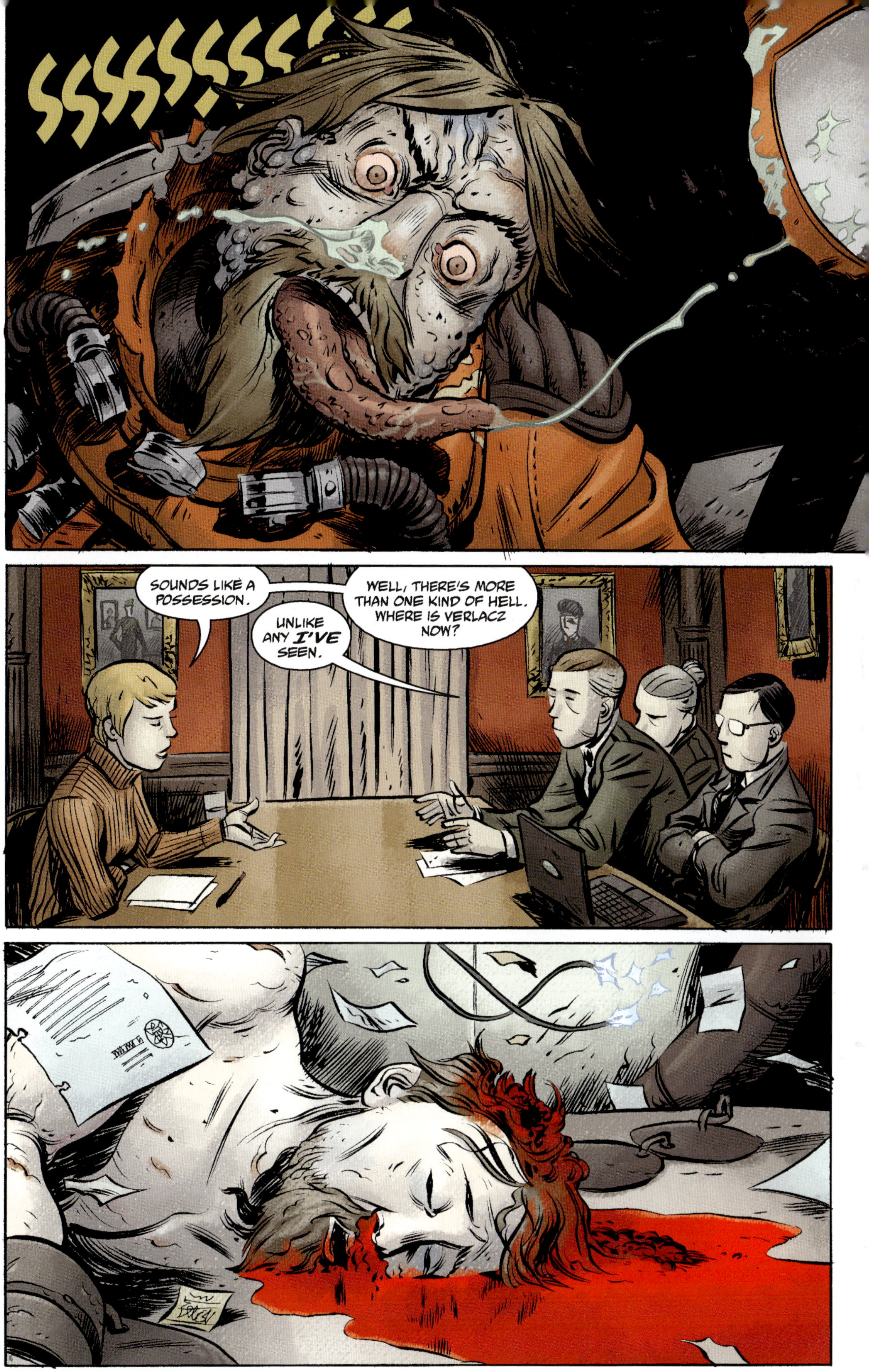
SSSSSSSSSS
SOUNDS LIKE A POSSESSION.
UNLIKE ANY I'VE SEEN.
WELL, THERE'S MORE THAN ONE KIND OF HELL. WHERE IS VERLACZ NOW?

MEHK OSLU'L ITHRABE' YIENNN

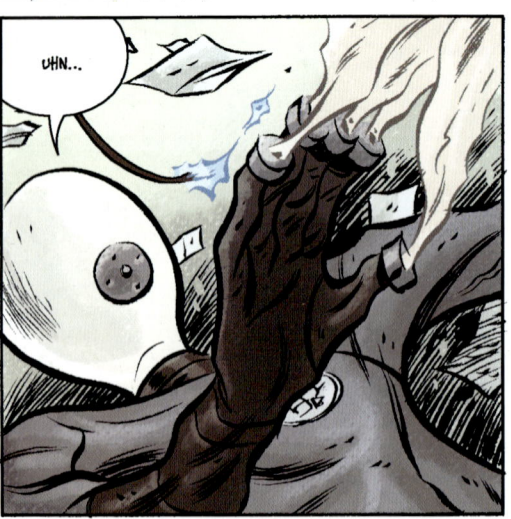

UHN...

ERF!

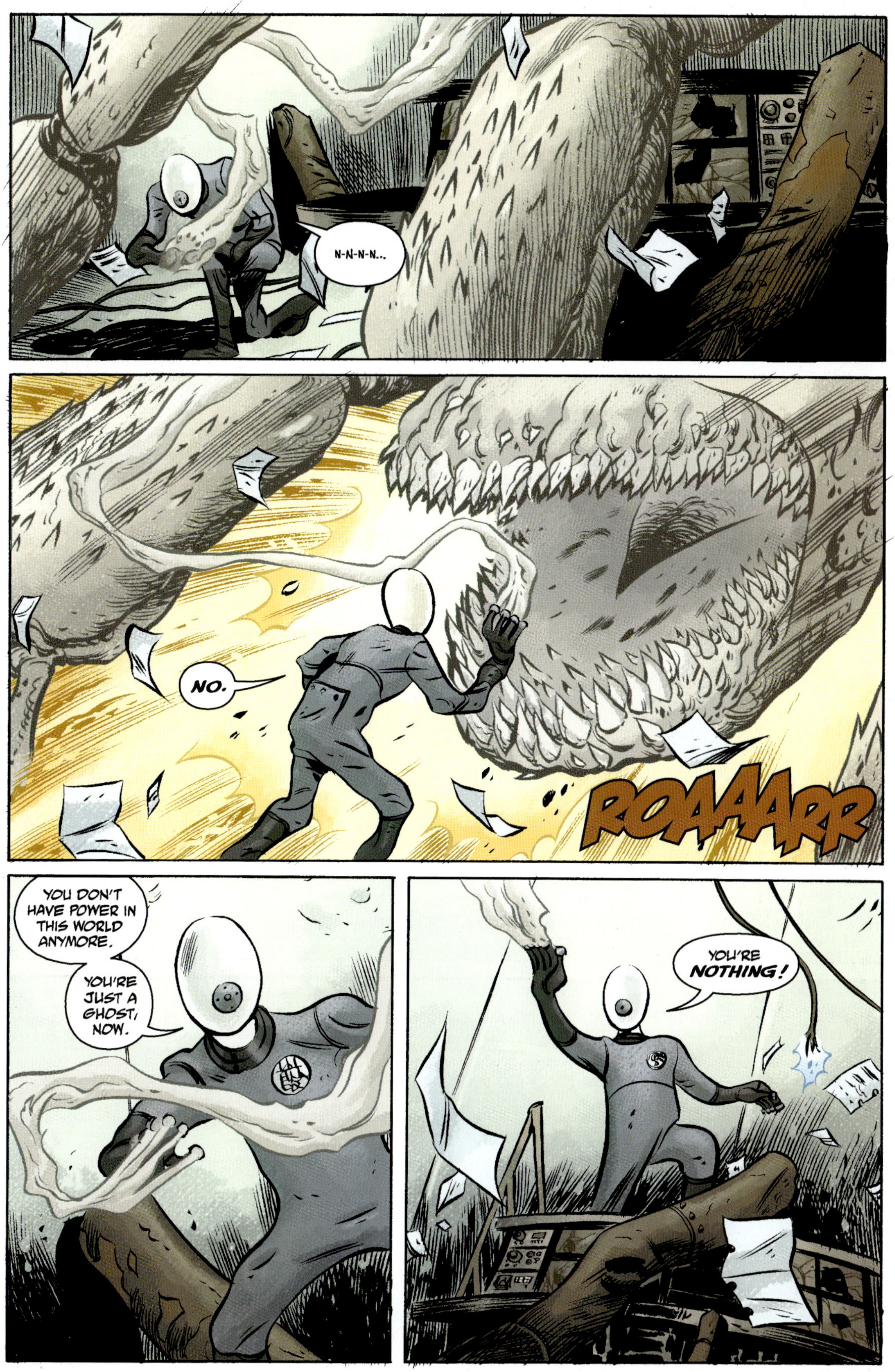
N-N-N-N...
NO.
ROAAAARR
YOU DON'T HAVE POWER IN THIS WORLD ANYMORE.
YOU'RE JUST A GHOST, NOW.
YOU'RE NOTHING!

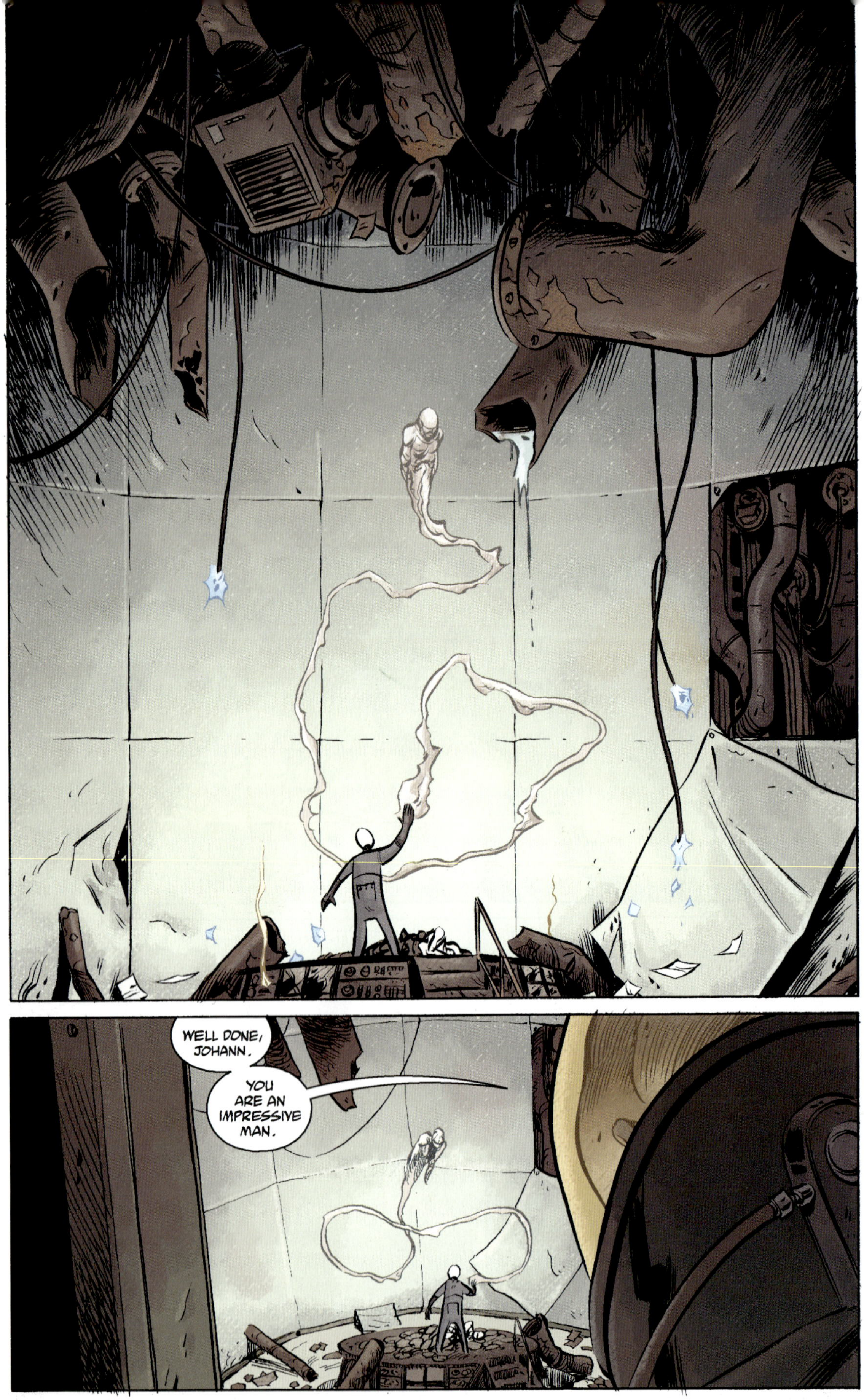
WELL DONE, JOHANN.
YOU ARE AN IMPRESSIVE MAN.

⟨WHAT WAS ALL THAT?⟩
⟨I HEARD IT FROM THE SECOND FLOOR!⟩
⟨HAS IT STOPPED?⟩
⟨WHAT'S ALL THIS ABOUT? WHAT HAPPENED TO THAT DOOR?!⟩
⟨WE DON'T KNOW, DIRECTOR. SOMETHING INSIDE...⟩
⟨THEN FOR GOD'S SAKE, LET'S SEE WHAT'S IN THERE!⟩
SHRAK
⟨LORD CHRIST!⟩
HERR KRAUS! ARE YOU ALL RIGHT?!
I AM QUITE WELL, IOSIF.
AND I HAVE YOUR ANSWERS.

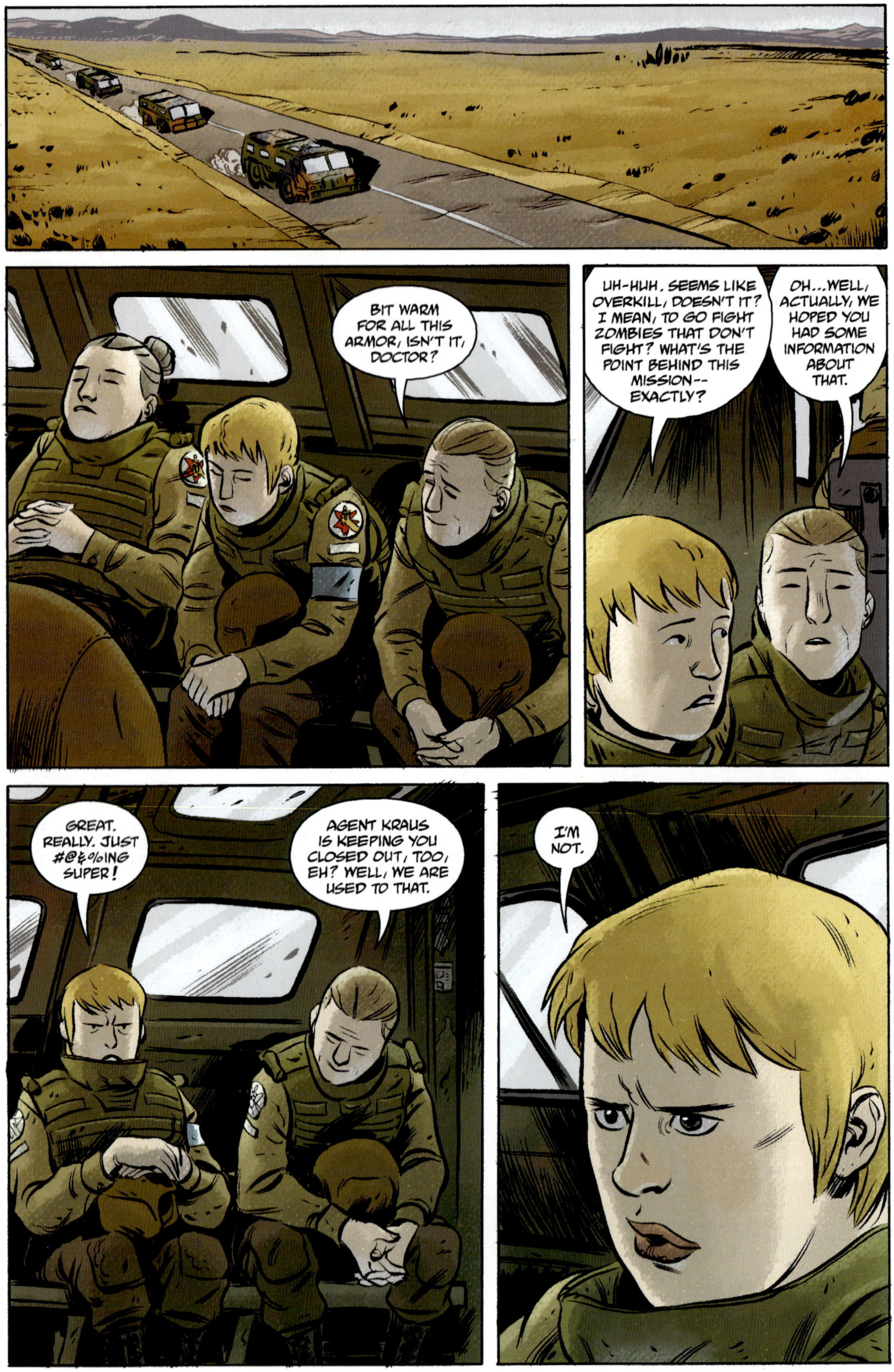
BIT WARM FOR ALL THIS ARMOR, ISN'T IT, DOCTOR?
UH-HUH. SEEMS LIKE OVERKILL, DOESN'T IT? I MEAN, TO GO FIGHT ZOMBIES THAT DON'T FIGHT? WHAT'S THE POINT BEHIND THIS MISSION--EXACTLY?
OH...WELL, ACTUALLY, WE HOPED YOU HAD SOME INFORMATION ABOUT THAT.
GREAT. REALLY. JUST #@&%ING SUPER!
AGENT KRAUS IS KEEPING YOU CLOSED OUT, TOO, EH? WELL, WE ARE USED TO THAT.
I'M NOT.

DOCTOR, THOSE WIKILEAKS FILES TOLD US A LOT, BUT THEY DON'T REALLY--THEY DON'T "CONNECT THE DOTS" FOR US, AS YOU MIGHT SAY.
YOU MENTIONED SOMETHING ABOUT INCUBATORS?
RIGHT, BUT IT GOES BACK A LOT FARTHER THAN THAT.
"BACK TO THE FIRST APPEARANCE OF THE FROGS IN 1994.
"WE THOUGHT WE WIPED THEM ALL OUT THEN, BUT IT WASN'T THAT EASY. A KIND OF FROG PLAGUE WAS SPREADING TO HUMANS THROUGH A FUNGUS IN A SMALL MICHIGAN TOWN."
FILES SAY BUREAU CAPTURED SOME OF CREATURES.
THEY DIED. QUICKLY. PUT 'EM IN A CAGE, THEY'RE LIKE ORCHIDS.
PLENTY MORE WERE STILL OUT THERE, THOUGH.

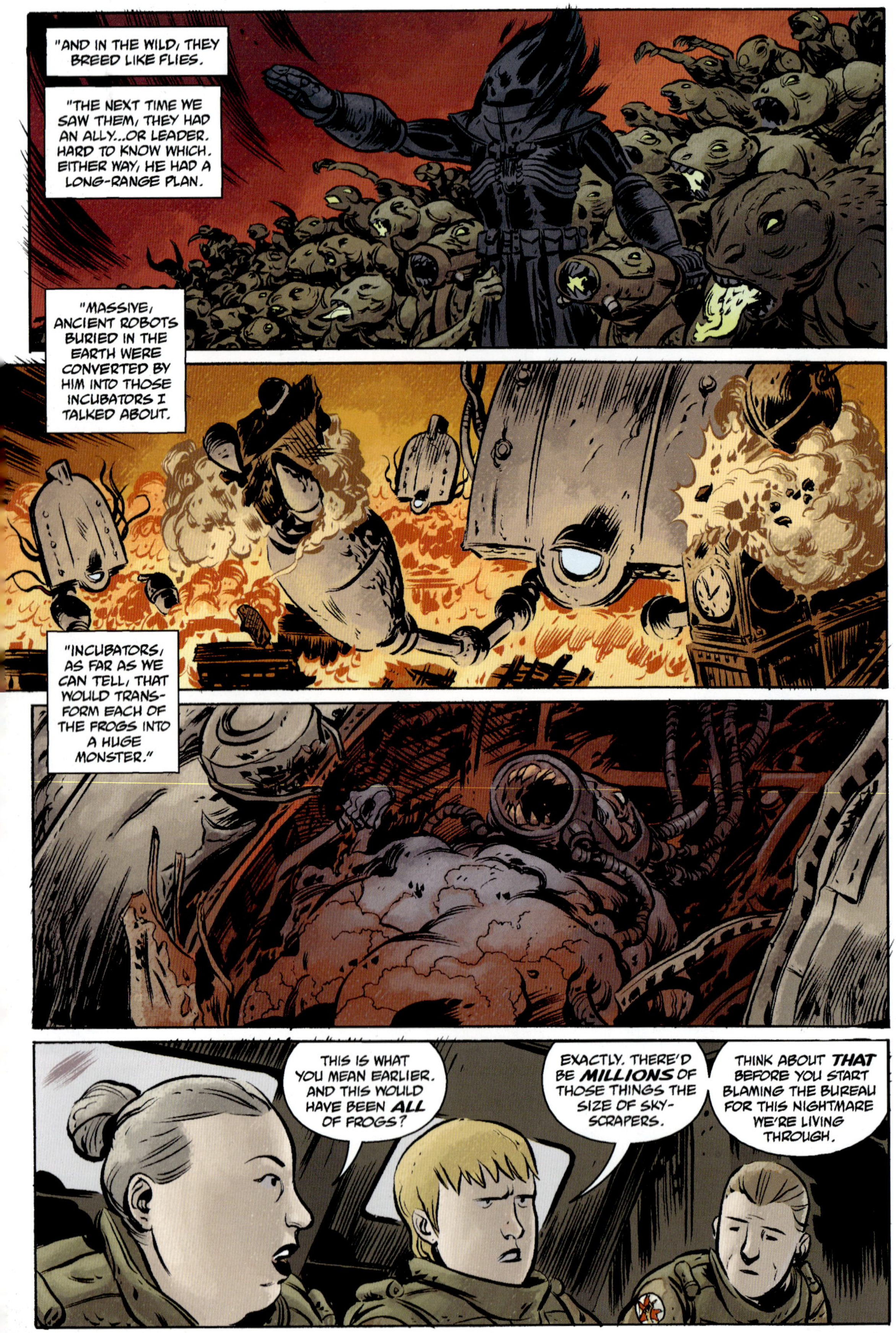
"AND IN THE WILD, THEY BREED LIKE FLIES.
"THE NEXT TIME WE SAW THEM, THEY HAD AN ALLY...OR LEADER. HARD TO KNOW WHICH. EITHER WAY, HE HAD A LONG-RANGE PLAN.
"MASSIVE, ANCIENT ROBOTS BURIED IN THE EARTH WERE CONVERTED BY HIM INTO THOSE INCUBATORS I TALKED ABOUT.
"INCUBATORS, AS FAR AS WE CAN TELL, THAT WOULD TRANS-FORM EACH OF THE FROGS INTO A HUGE MONSTER."
THIS IS WHAT YOU MEAN EARLIER. AND THIS WOULD HAVE BEEN ALL OF FROGS?
EXACTLY. THERE'D BE MILLIONS OF THOSE THINGS THE SIZE OF SKY-SCRAPERS.
THINK ABOUT THAT BEFORE YOU START BLAMING THE BUREAU FOR THIS NIGHTMARE WE'RE LIVING THROUGH.

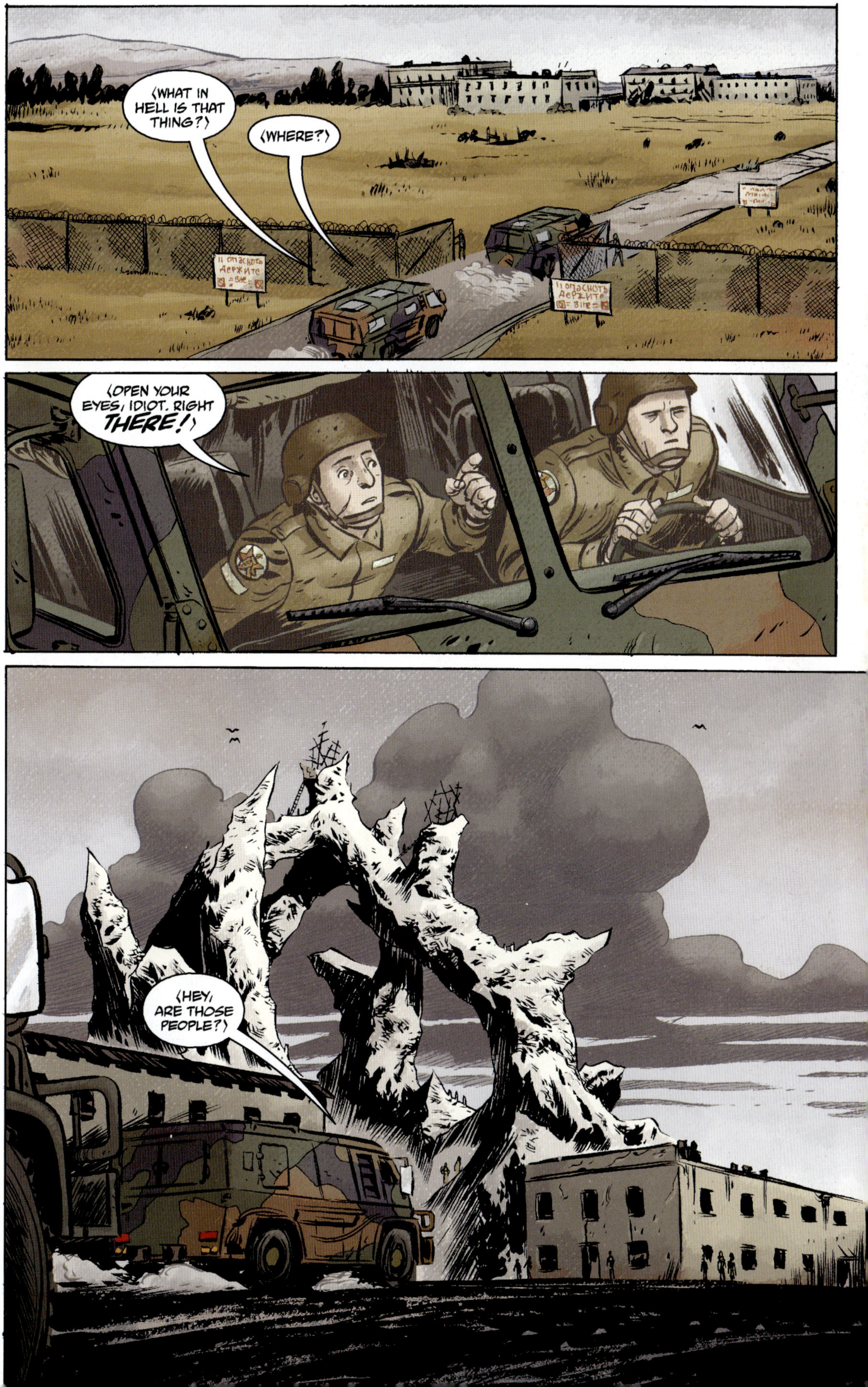
⟨WHAT IN HELL IS THAT THING?⟩
⟨WHERE?⟩
⟨OPEN YOUR EYES, IDIOT. RIGHT *THERE!*⟩
⟨HEY, ARE THOSE PEOPLE?⟩

⟨NOT EXACTLY.⟩
⟨JESUS! SO THEY ARE REAL. WE SHOULD JUST RUN THEM ALL DOWN.⟩
⟨THEN YOU WASH THE TRUCK AFTER-WARD.⟩
THINGS ARE BECOMING CLEARER. THIS IS THE COAL MINE WE TOLD YOU ABOUT. I THINK WE WERE LIED TO. I THINK THIS IS THE OBJECTIVE.
WHAT ARE YOU...? ANOTHER DESCENT? NO WAY. NO WAY.
ASK YOUR FRIEND IF HE AGREES.

JOHANN, WAIT!
WHAT'S GOING ON?
DON'T WORRY, KATE. I WILL SEE YOU SOON.
OR I WON'T.
?
I'M SORRY YOU WEREN'T BETTER INFORMED, DOCTOR.
THAT WASN'T MY IDEA. IT WAS JOHANN'S.

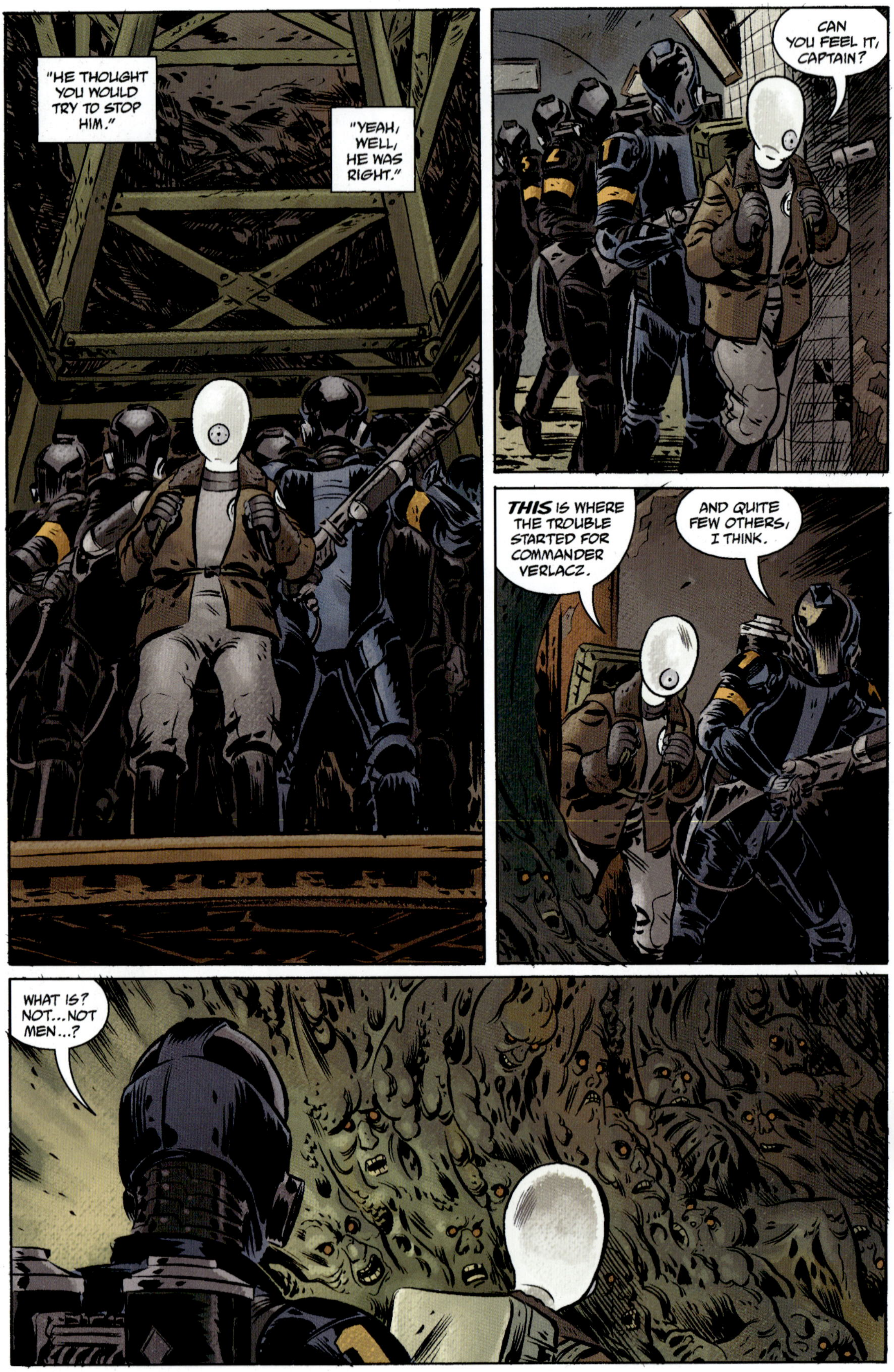

"HE THOUGHT YOU WOULD TRY TO STOP HIM."
"YEAH, WELL, HE WAS RIGHT."
CAN YOU FEEL IT, CAPTAIN?
THIS IS WHERE THE TROUBLE STARTED FOR COMMANDER VERLACZ.
AND QUITE FEW OTHERS, I THINK.
WHAT IS? NOT... NOT MEN...?

THEY *WERE.*
LONG DEAD. EVEN THEIR SPIRITS ARE GONE. VERLACZ WAS RIGHT ABOUT THAT.
CLACK
HUH?

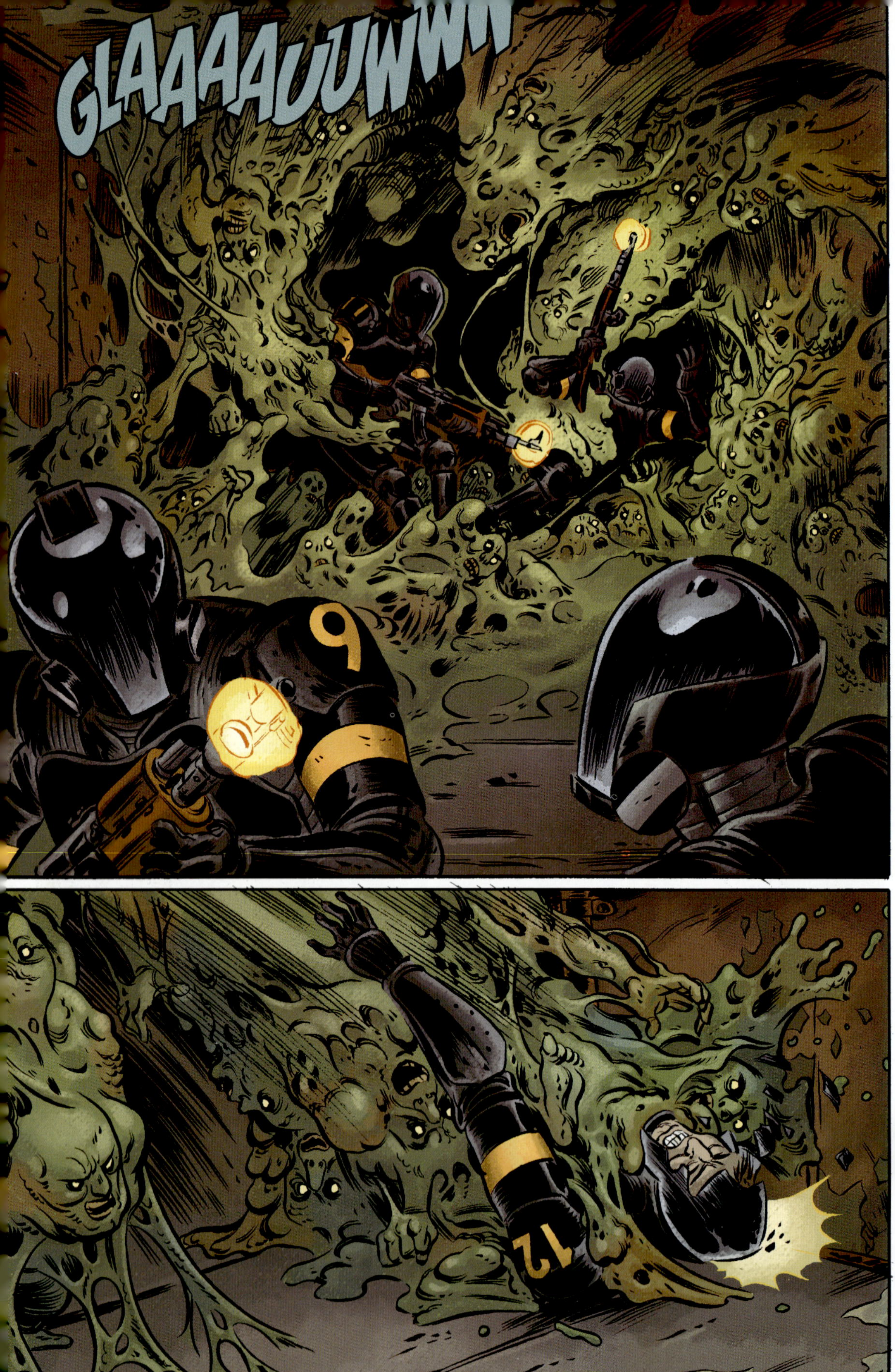
GLAAAAUUWWW

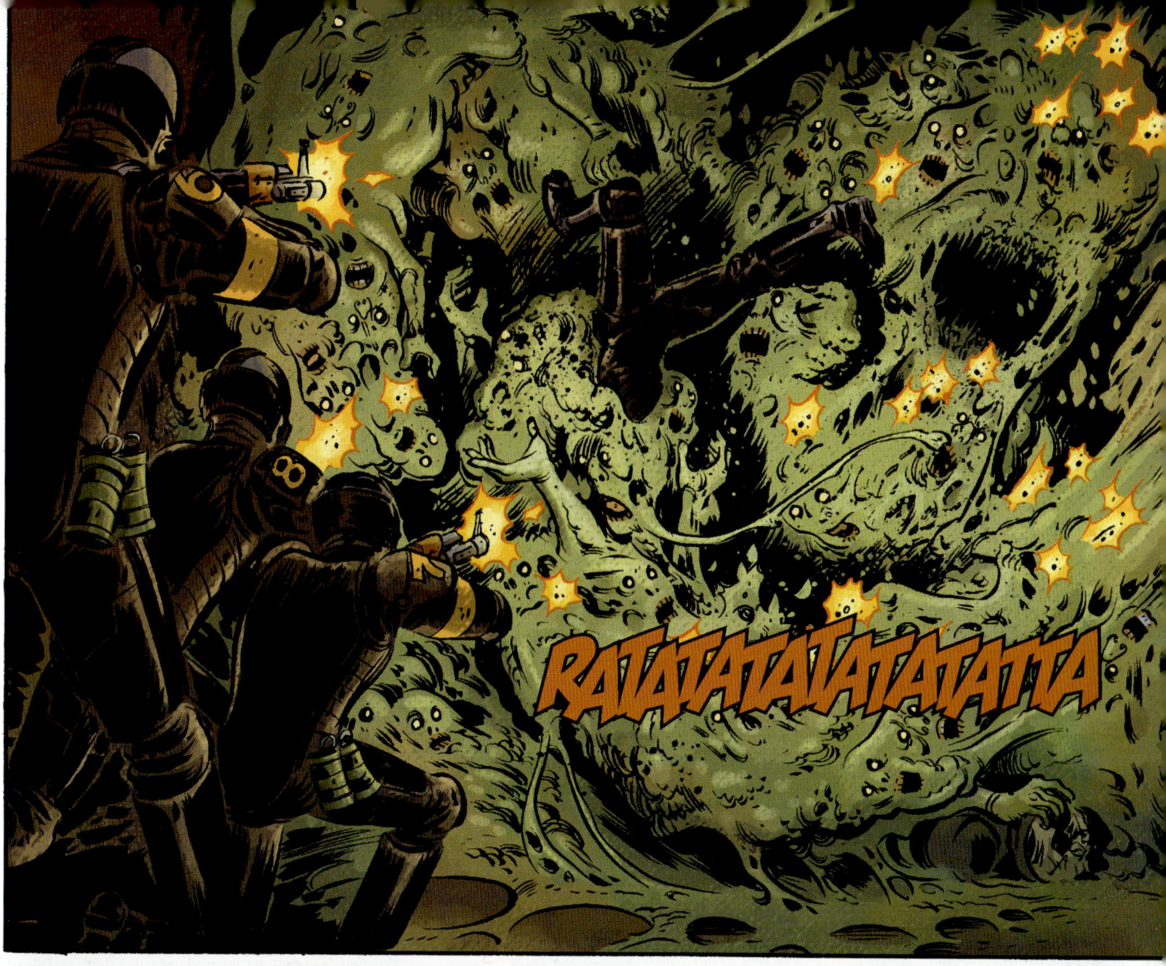
RATATATATATATATTA

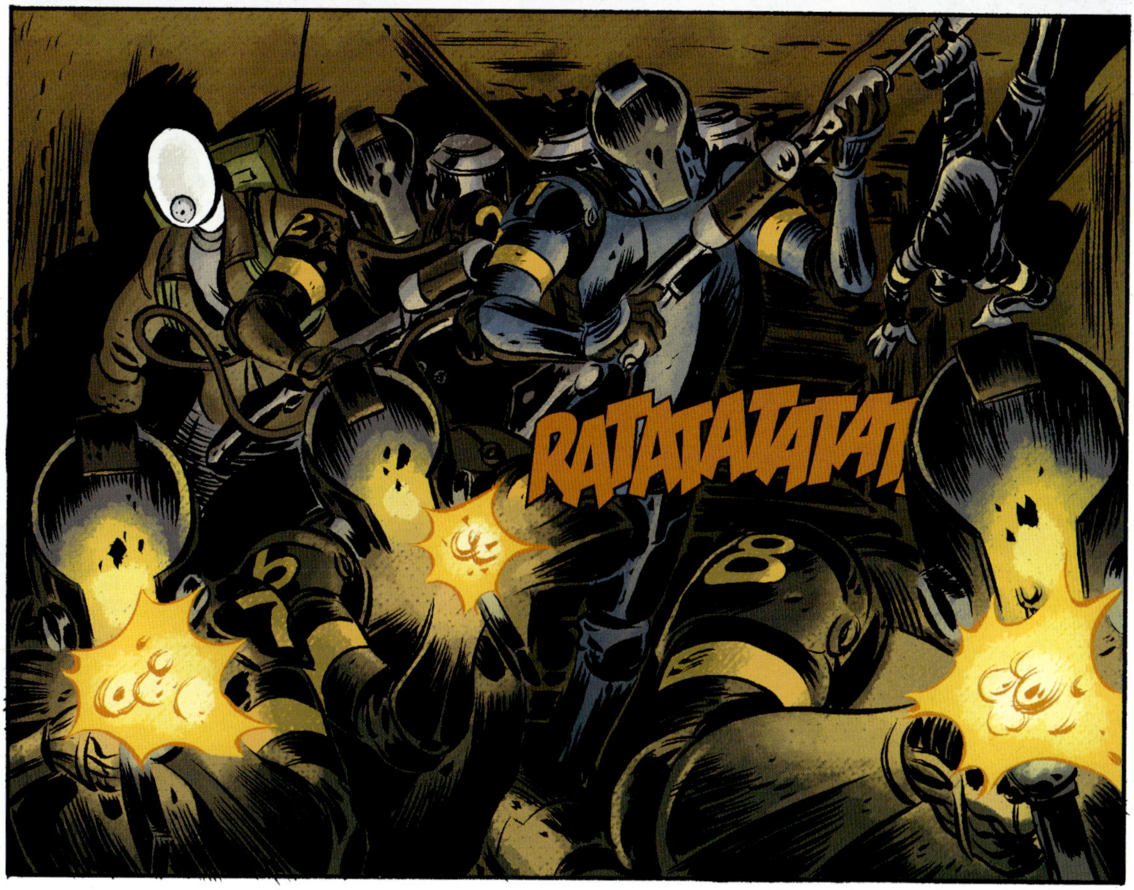
RATATATATAT

HEEEEEEEEEEEE
RATATATATATA
EEEEEEEEEEEEE
HYDROFLUORIC ACID?
IS WORKING, NO? YOU SAID FIRE IS FASTEST, I KNOW, BUT IN COAL MINE IS NOT GOOD IDEA.

AND KIRIL? IS HE...?
⟨COME. THERE'S MORE KILLING AND MORE DYING TO BE DONE.⟩
LOOK AT HIM! **WEEPING!** GRIEVING, SHOULDERS SHAKING.
THIS MAN, I ALWAYS KNOW HE IS TOO WEAK FOR SPETSNAZ.
NO. YOU'RE WRONG.
HE ISN'T CRYING.

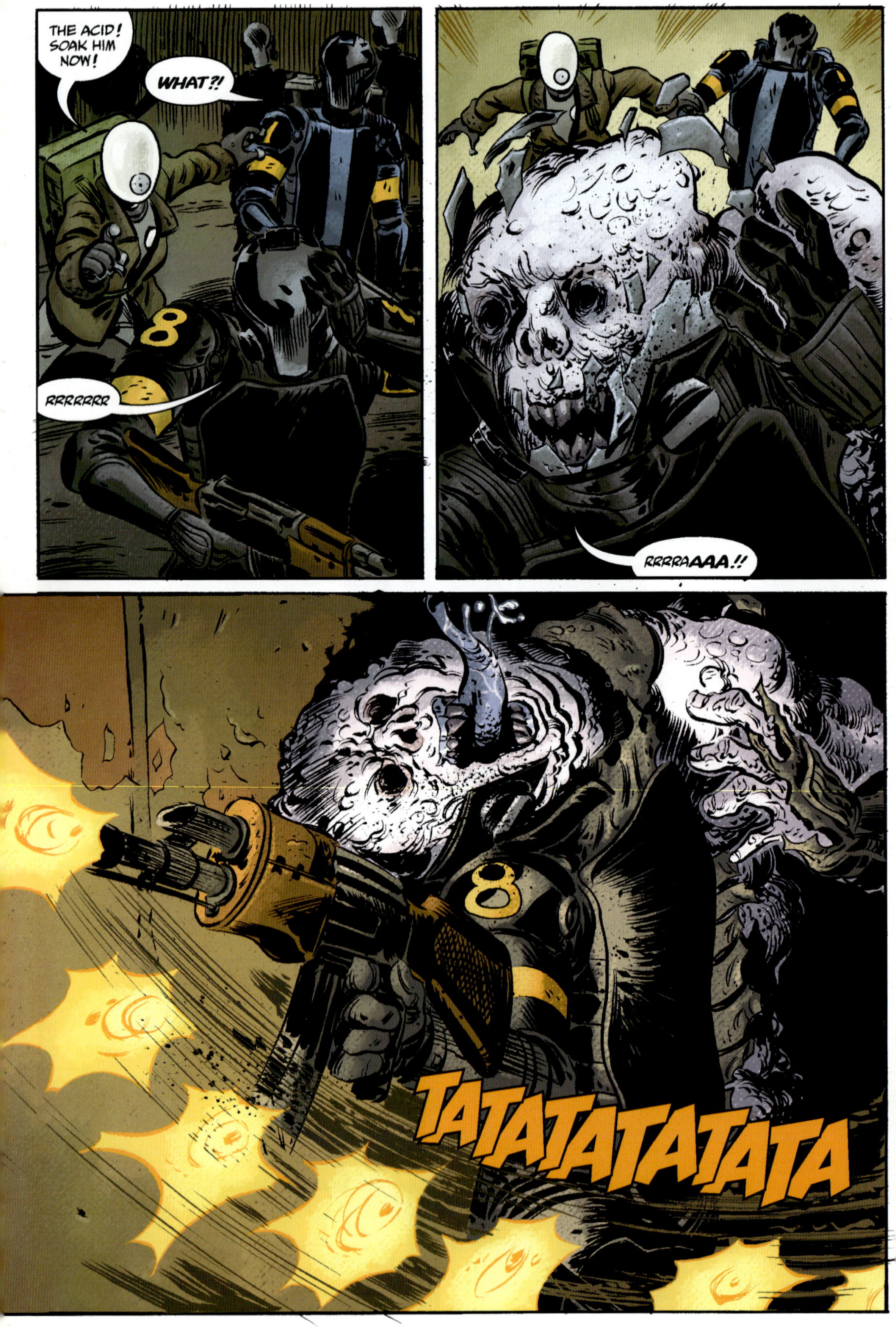
THE ACID! SOAK HIM NOW!
WHAT?!
RRRRRRR
RRRRAAAA!!
TATATATATATA

ILLUSTRATION BY DAVE JOHNSON

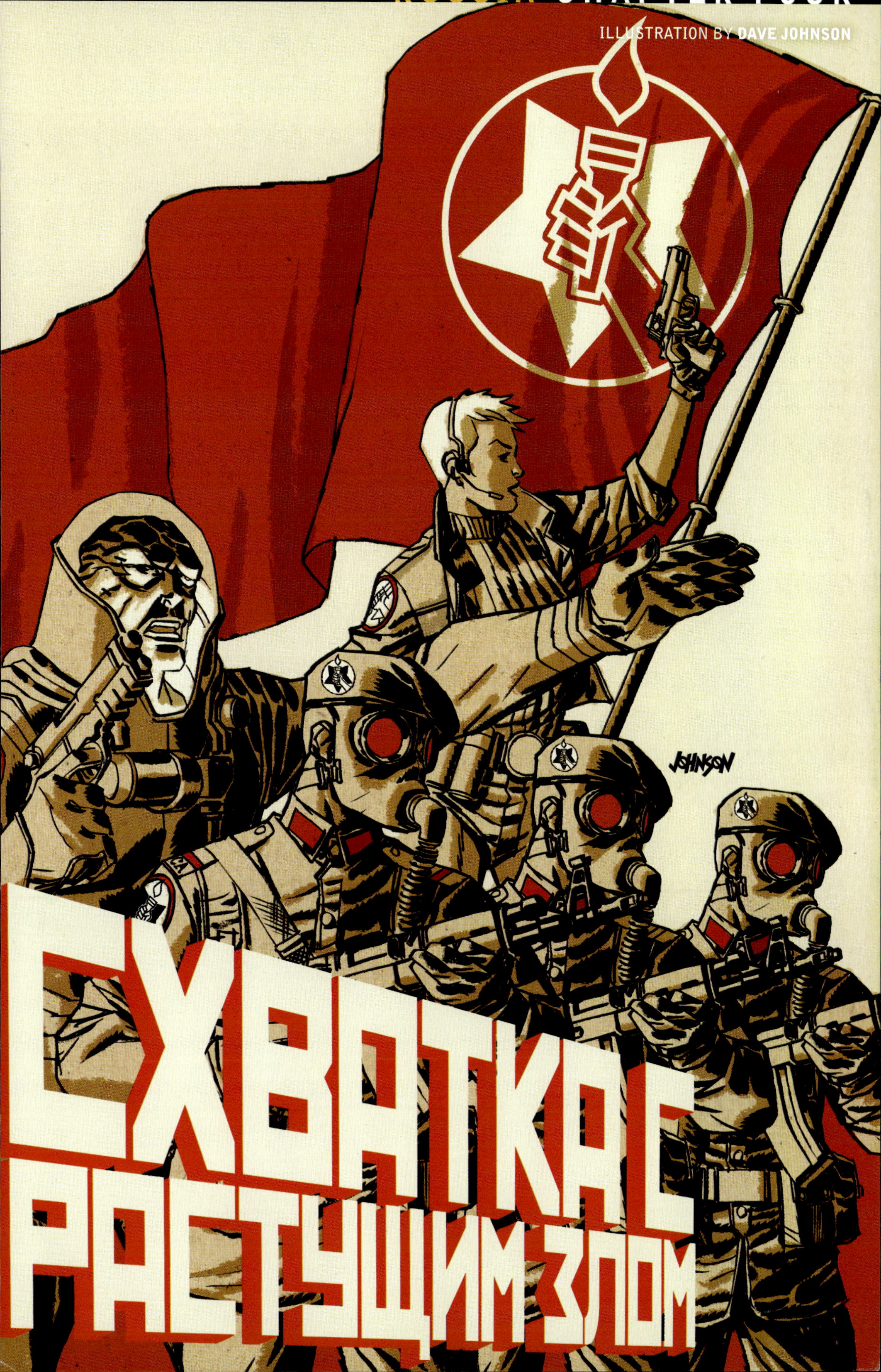
JOHNSON
СХВАТКА С
РАСТУЩИМ ЗЛОМ

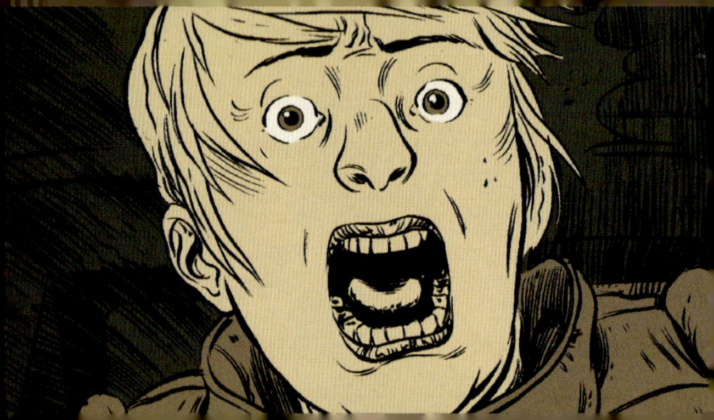

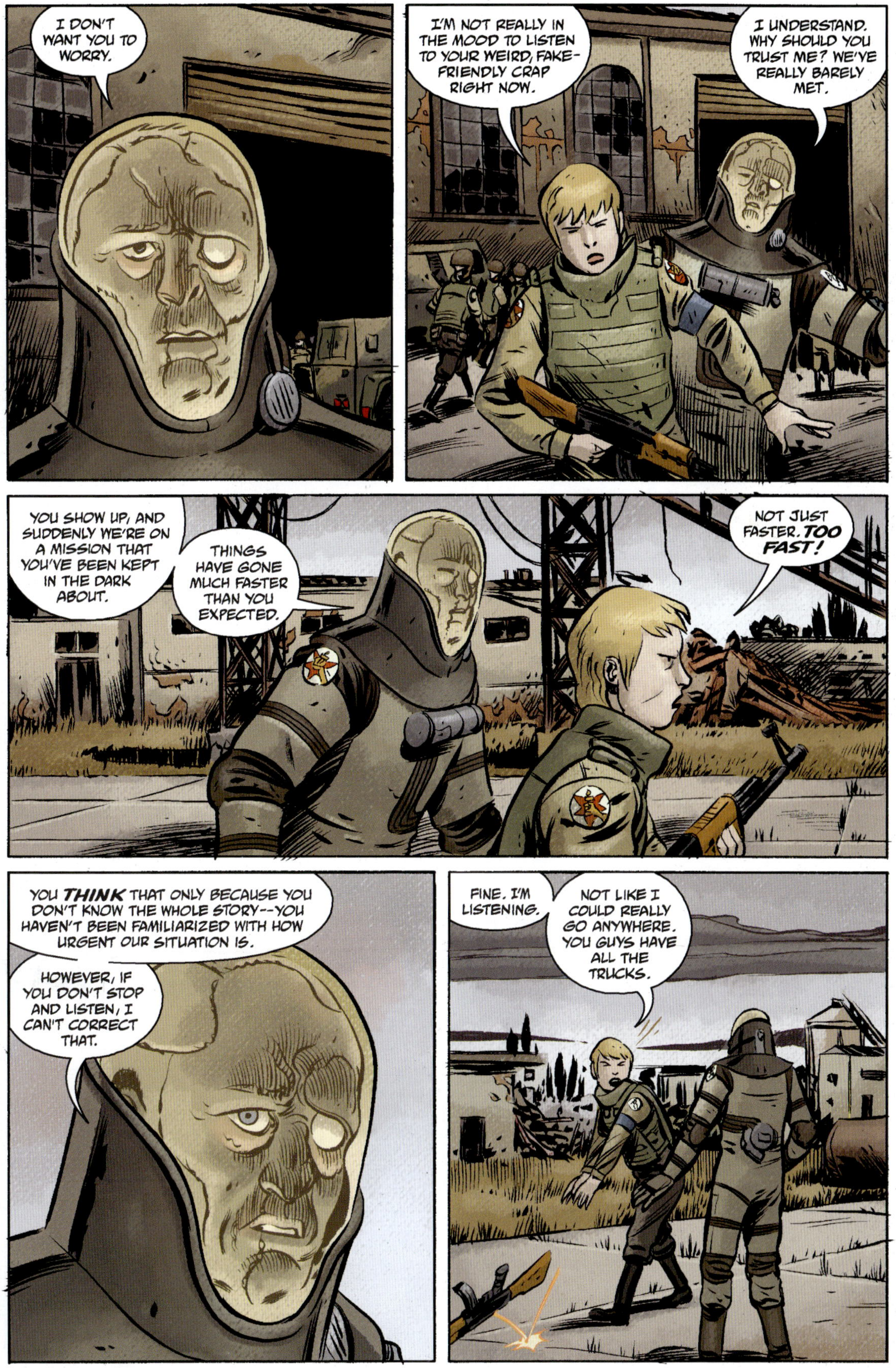
I DON'T WANT YOU TO WORRY.
I'M NOT REALLY IN THE MOOD TO LISTEN TO YOUR WEIRD, FAKE-FRIENDLY CRAP RIGHT NOW.
I UNDERSTAND. WHY SHOULD YOU TRUST ME? WE'VE REALLY BARELY MET.
YOU SHOW UP, AND SUDDENLY WE'RE ON A MISSION THAT YOU'VE BEEN KEPT IN THE DARK ABOUT.
THINGS HAVE GONE MUCH FASTER THAN YOU EXPECTED.
NOT JUST FASTER. TOO FAST!
YOU THINK THAT ONLY BECAUSE YOU DON'T KNOW THE WHOLE STORY--YOU HAVEN'T BEEN FAMILIARIZED WITH HOW URGENT OUR SITUATION IS.
HOWEVER, IF YOU DON'T STOP AND LISTEN, I CAN'T CORRECT THAT.
FINE. I'M LISTENING.
NOT LIKE I COULD REALLY GO ANYWHERE. YOU GUYS HAVE ALL THE TRUCKS.

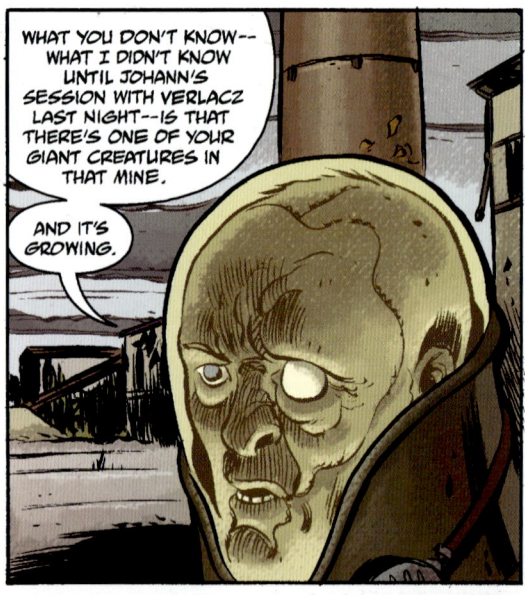

YOU'VE ALREADY HEARD THAT COMMANDER VERLACZ WAS SENT BELOW INTO THE MINE, AND HOW HE CAME BACK POSSESSED.

RIGHT.

WHAT YOU DON'T KNOW-- WHAT I DIDN'T KNOW UNTIL JOHANN'S SESSION WITH VERLACZ LAST NIGHT--IS THAT THERE'S ONE OF YOUR GIANT CREATURES IN THAT MINE.

AND IT'S GROWING.

"JOHANN'S SESSION"--? VERLACZ IS DEAD?

HE DIED WEEKS AGO, IF WE'RE BEING HONEST WITH OURSELVES. THE ONLY SPIRIT LEFT IN HIS BODY WAS A SMALL PIECE OF THIS GIANT BEAST'S WILL.

JOHANN LEARNED THAT WHEN IT'S GROWN LARGE ENOUGH TO EMERGE, IT WILL NEST IN *THAT* STRUCTURE THAT THE LIVING DEAD ARE BUILDING.

IF WE HAVE ANY HOPE TO KILL IT, *NOW'S* THE TIME.

KILL IT HOW?

THAT, SPECIFICALLY, IS WHAT JOHANN DIDN'T WANT YOU TO KNOW.

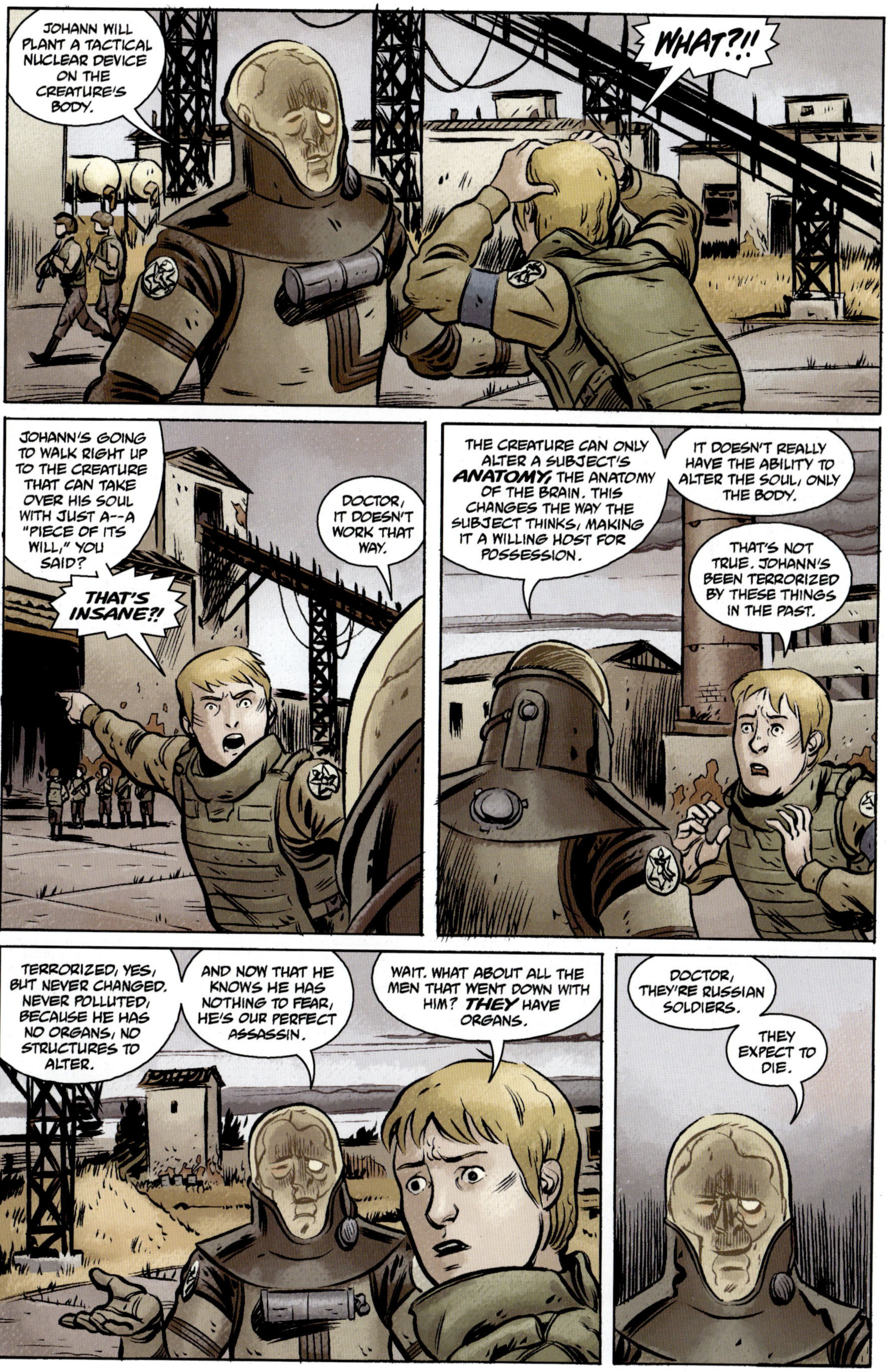
JOHANN WILL PLANT A TACTICAL NUCLEAR DEVICE ON THE CREATURE'S BODY.
WHAT?!!
JOHANN'S GOING TO WALK RIGHT UP TO THE CREATURE THAT CAN TAKE OVER HIS SOUL WITH JUST A--A "PIECE OF ITS WILL," YOU SAID?
THAT'S INSANE?!
DOCTOR, IT DOESN'T WORK THAT WAY.
THE CREATURE CAN ONLY ALTER A SUBJECT'S ANATOMY, THE ANATOMY OF THE BRAIN. THIS CHANGES THE WAY THE SUBJECT THINKS, MAKING IT A WILLING HOST FOR POSSESSION.
IT DOESN'T REALLY HAVE THE ABILITY TO ALTER THE SOUL, ONLY THE BODY.
THAT'S NOT TRUE. JOHANN'S BEEN TERRORIZED BY THESE THINGS IN THE PAST.
TERRORIZED, YES, BUT NEVER CHANGED. NEVER POLLUTED, BECAUSE HE HAS NO ORGANS, NO STRUCTURES TO ALTER.
AND NOW THAT HE KNOWS HE HAS NOTHING TO FEAR, HE'S OUR PERFECT ASSASSIN.
WAIT. WHAT ABOUT ALL THE MEN THAT WENT DOWN WITH HIM? THEY HAVE ORGANS.
DOCTOR, THEY'RE RUSSIAN SOLDIERS.
THEY EXPECT TO DIE.

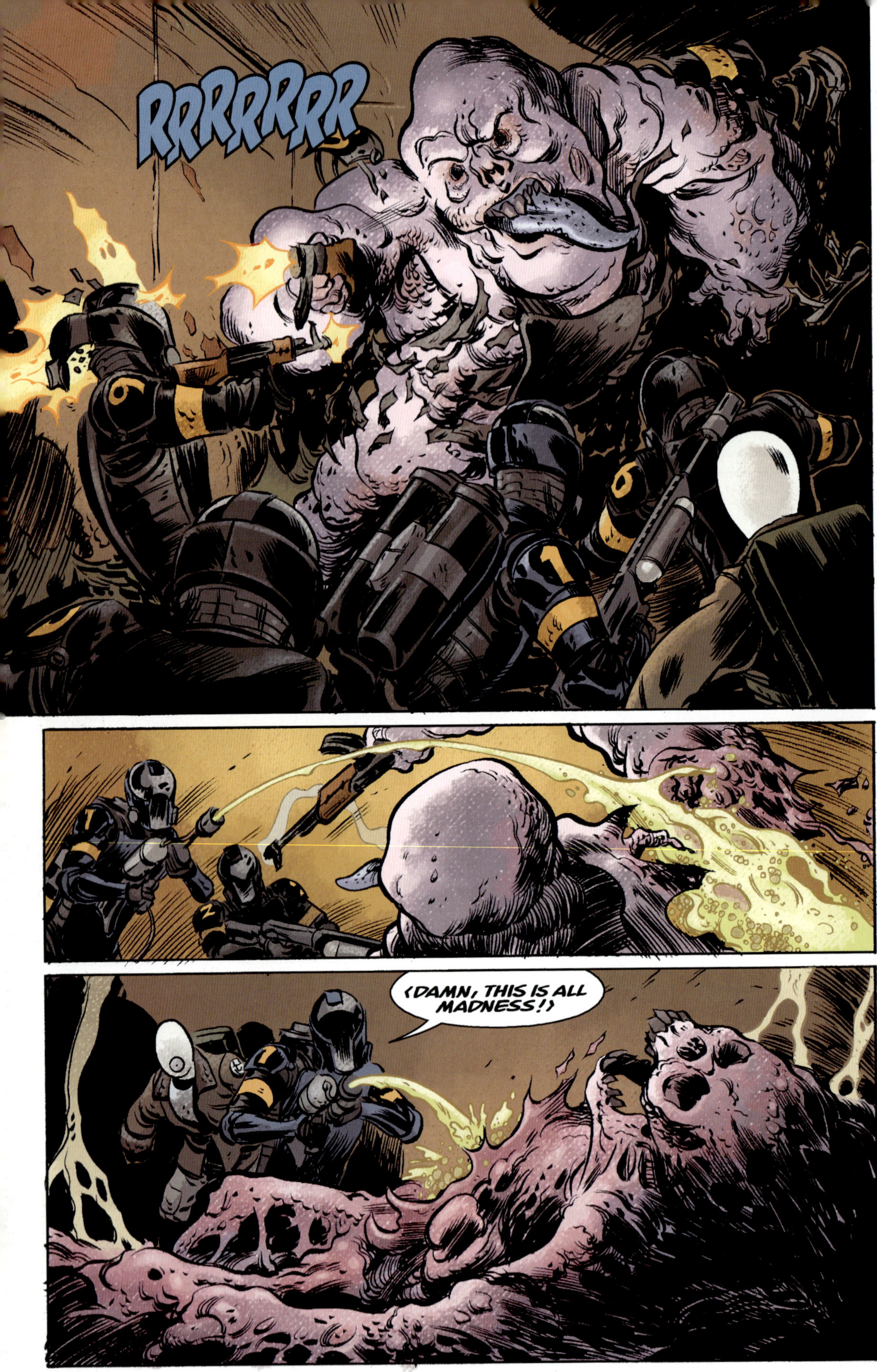
RRRRRRR
‹DAMN, THIS IS ALL MADNESS!›

POK
POK
POK
AAAIIII!
TATATATA
CAPTAIN! CAPTAIN, ARE YOU--?
AAAAHH, GOD DAMMIT! YOU KILL THAT THING, KRAUS. YOU KILL IT!!!!

POK
TATATA
HUUU!
‹SAINT SERGIUS, I'M NOT STRONG ENOUGH FOR THIS!›
GLF!
ARGH!

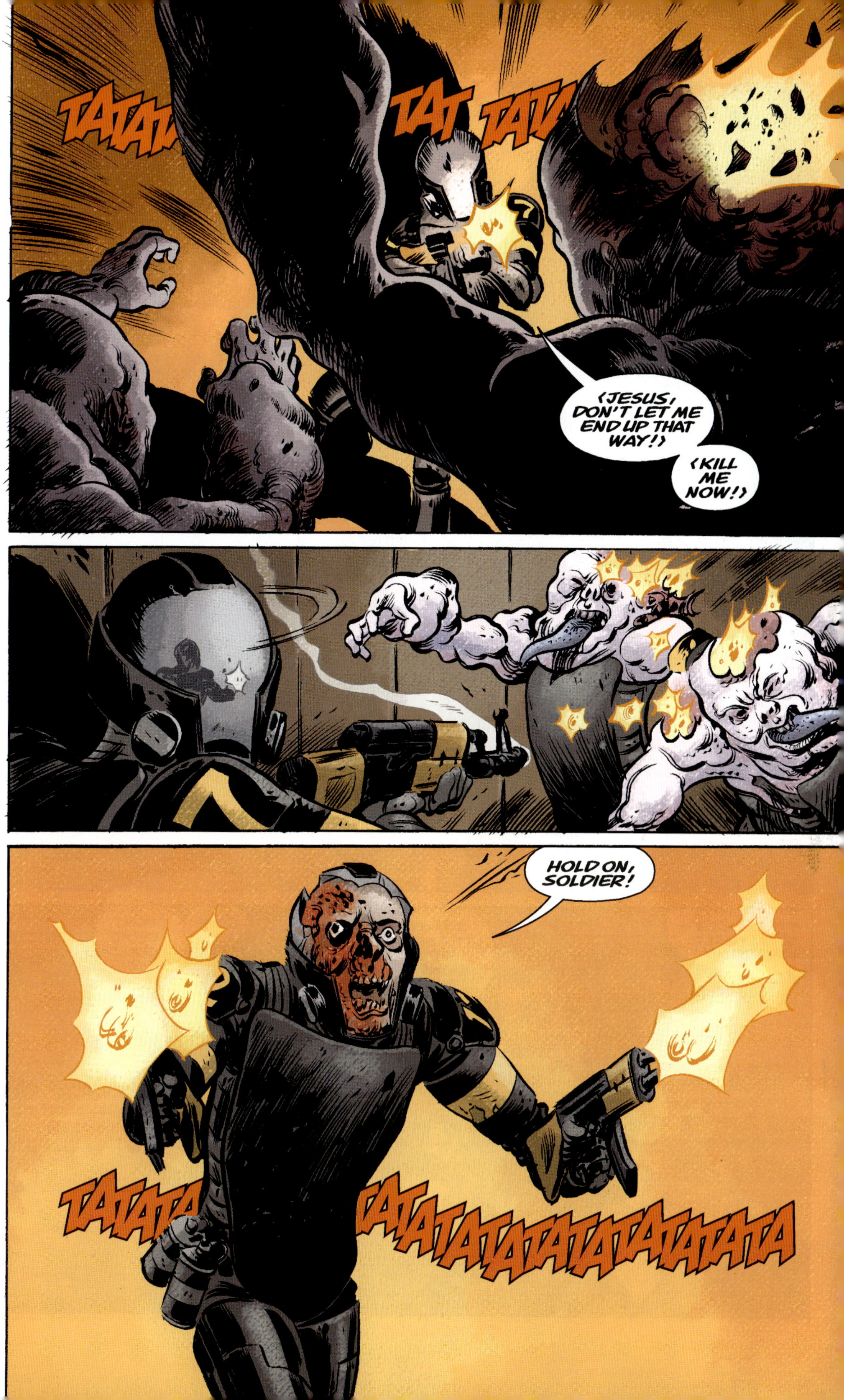
TATATA
TAT TATA
‹JESUS, DON'T LET ME END UP THAT WAY!›
‹KILL ME NOW!›
HOLD ON, SOLDIER!
TATATA
TATATATATATATATATATATATA

TATATATATATATATATATATATATATATATATATA
‹KIRIL? KIRIL, YOU ARE DEAD. THAT MUST MEAN THAT...THAT YOU ARE ONE OF THOSE--›
‹FOR GOD'S SAKE, PAVEL!›
‹IT'S KRAUS, THE GERMAN GHOST WHO WAS IN THAT FLIGHT SUIT.›
‹DON'T YOU REMEMBER THE DEBRIEFING?›
IT IS SO? YOU ARE GERMAN INSIDE KIRIL'S BODY?
IT TAKES A LITTLE GETTING USED TO, I IMAGINE, BUT YES. I'M JOHANN.
COME.
I DON'T THINK WE HAVE MUCH TIME.

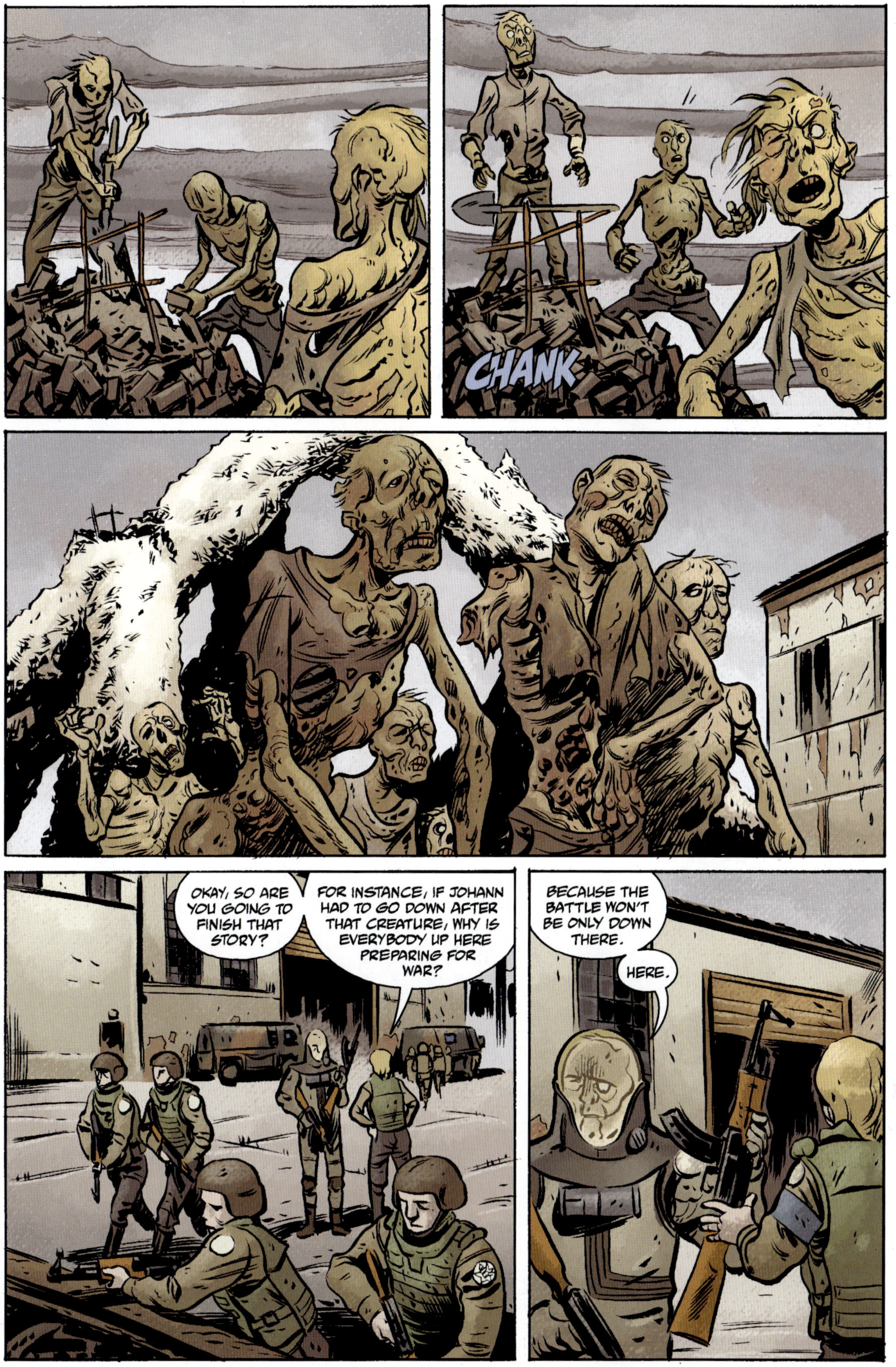
CHANK
OKAY, SO ARE YOU GOING TO FINISH THAT STORY?
FOR INSTANCE, IF JOHANN HAD TO GO DOWN AFTER THAT CREATURE, WHY IS EVERYBODY UP HERE PREPARING FOR WAR?
BECAUSE THE BATTLE WON'T BE ONLY DOWN THERE.
HERE.

JOHANN DOESN'T BELIEVE THAT CREATURE WILL SIT STILL FOR THE ATTACK.
IF JOHANN CAN GET THROUGH THE FIRST LINE OF DEFENSE, IT WILL HAVE TO CALL IN REINFORCEMENTS-- AND WE'RE HERE TO CUT THEM OFF.
WHAT'S THAT NOISE?
THAT, I BELIEVE, IS YOUR WAR.
EEEEEEEEEEEEEEEEEEE

WHY THE OTHERS TURN INTO MONSTERS? WHY NOT ME?
THE THING THAT DID THAT IS, I THINK, DISTRACTED RIGHT NOW.
WHAT IS LIKE? INSIDE KIRIL? IS ALL YOU, OR PART HIM?
HE'S GONE, IF THAT'S WHAT YOU'RE ASKING. I'M THE ONLY ONE IN HERE NOW.
YOU CAN'T DIE, NO? HOW CAN YOU? JUST GO INTO NEW BODY.
NOT "NEW," PAVEL. THEY'RE ALWAYS BROKEN--USELESS TO ANYBODY ELSE. YOUR BODY IS YOUR OWN. AND IT ACTUALLY WORKS.
DA, BUT YOU CAN LIVE FOREVER.
WALKING AROUND INSIDE OTHER PEOPLE'S CORPSES IS NOTHING LIKE LIFE.
PAVEL? ARE YOU ALL RIGHT?
TIRED. HOT DOWN HERE. NO AIR.

MY BODY IS NOT WORK SO GOOD NOW.
YOU STAY BEHIND, THEN. REST.
IT PROBABLY WILL BE SAFER BACK HERE FOR YOU ANY-WAY.
12
SOME SORT OF NIDIFORMIS FUNGI. BEAUTIFUL.
BUT WHY...I SHOULDN'T BE LOOKING AT...WHAT'S WRONG WITH ME?

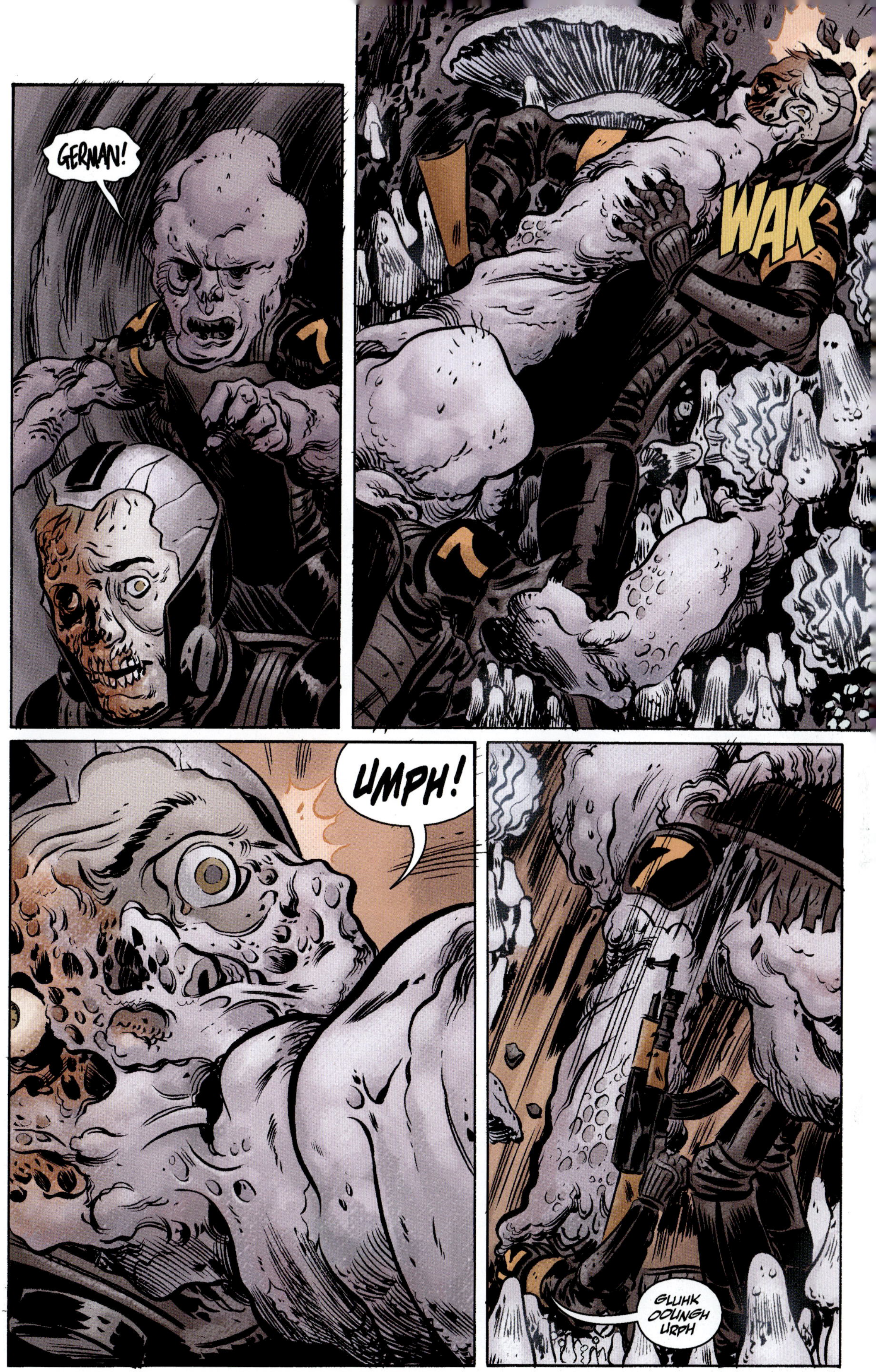
GERNAN!
WAK
UMPH!
GLUHK OOUNGH URPH

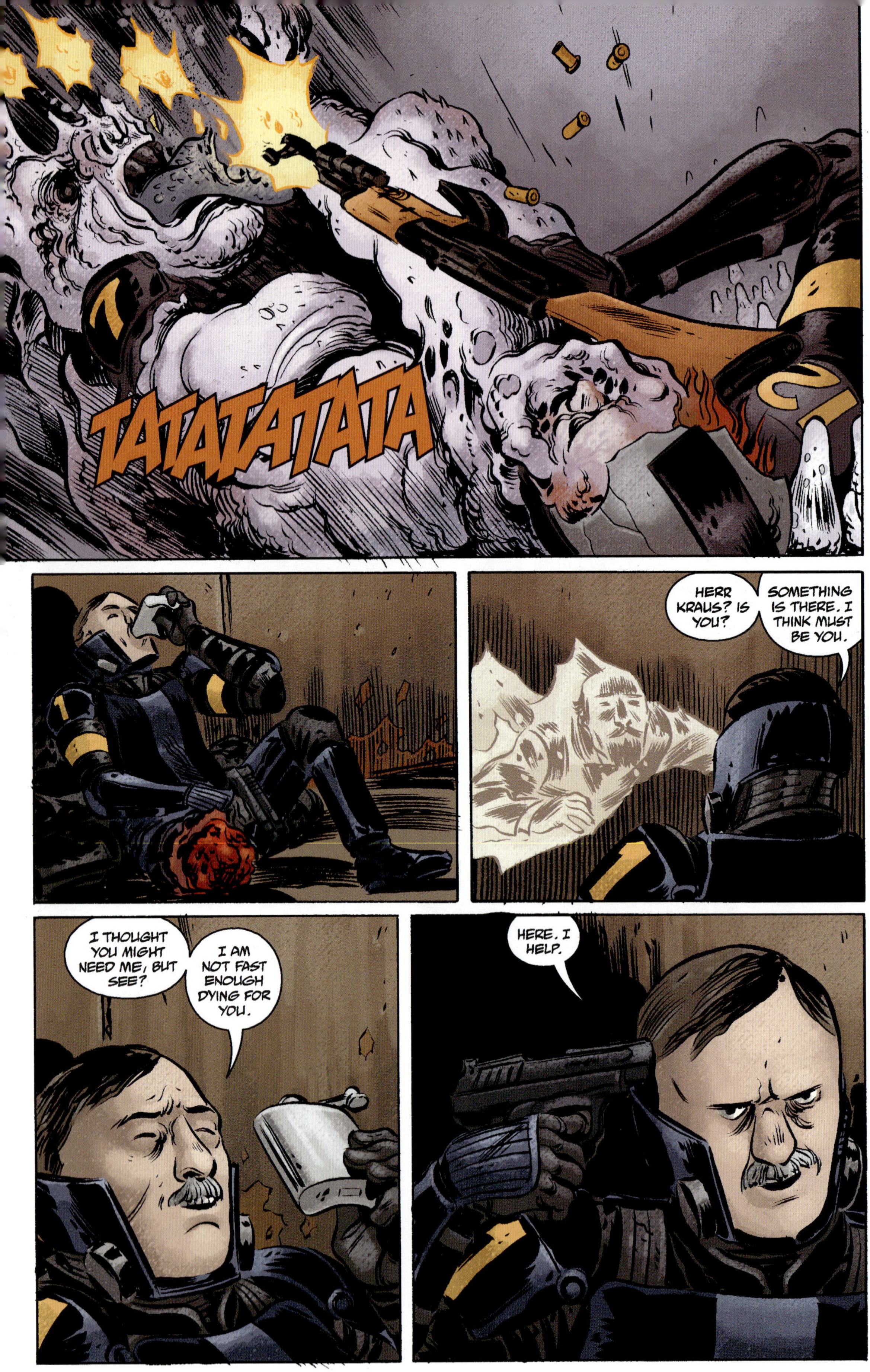
TATATATATA
HERR KRAUS? IS YOU?
SOMETHING IS THERE. I THINK MUST BE YOU.
I THOUGHT YOU MIGHT NEED ME, BUT SEE?
I AM NOT FAST ENOUGH DYING FOR YOU.
HERE. I HELP.

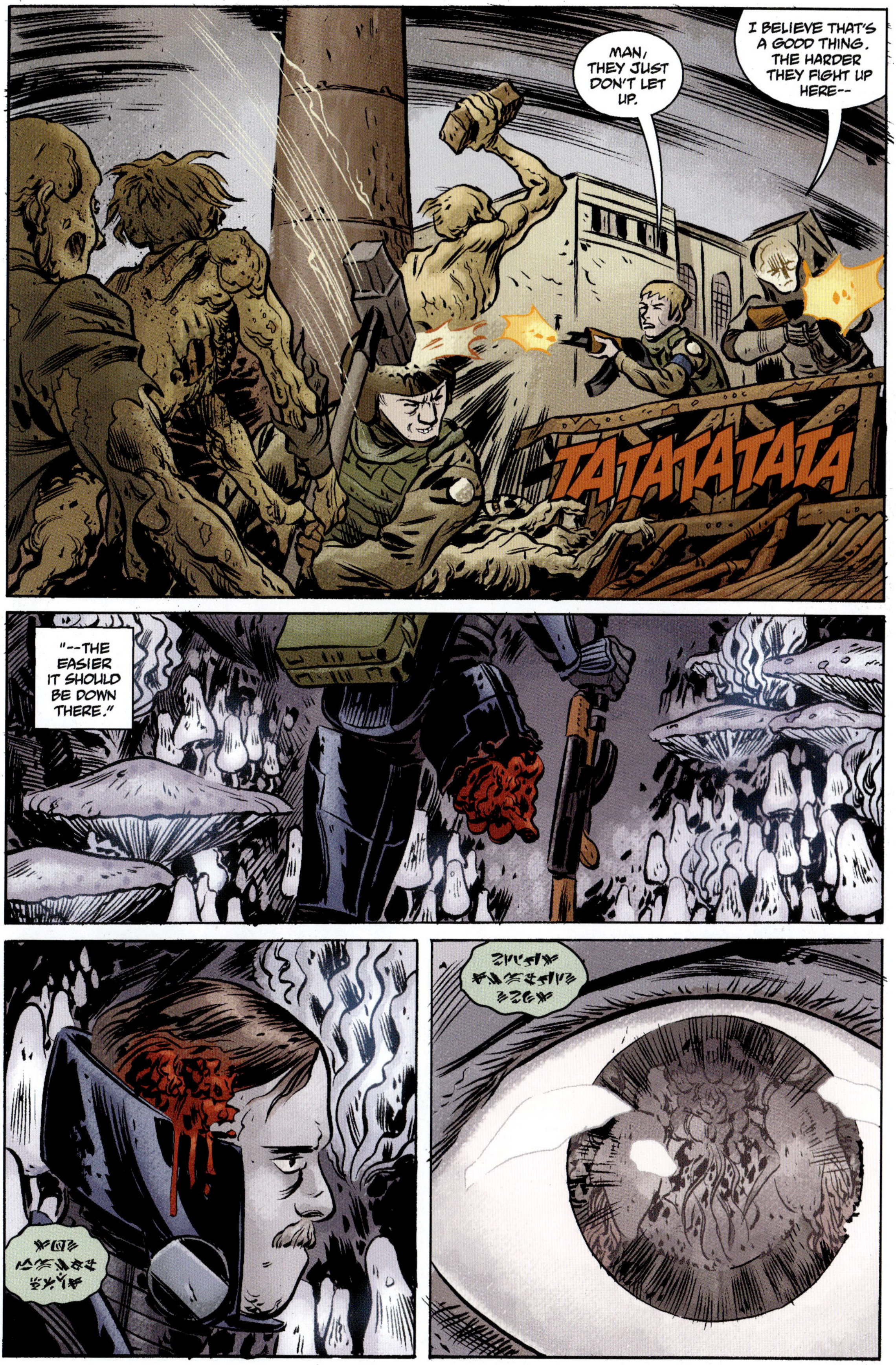
MAN, THEY JUST DON'T LET UP.
I BELIEVE THAT'S A GOOD THING. THE HARDER THEY FIGHT UP HERE--
TATATATATA
"--THE EASIER IT SHOULD BE DOWN THERE."

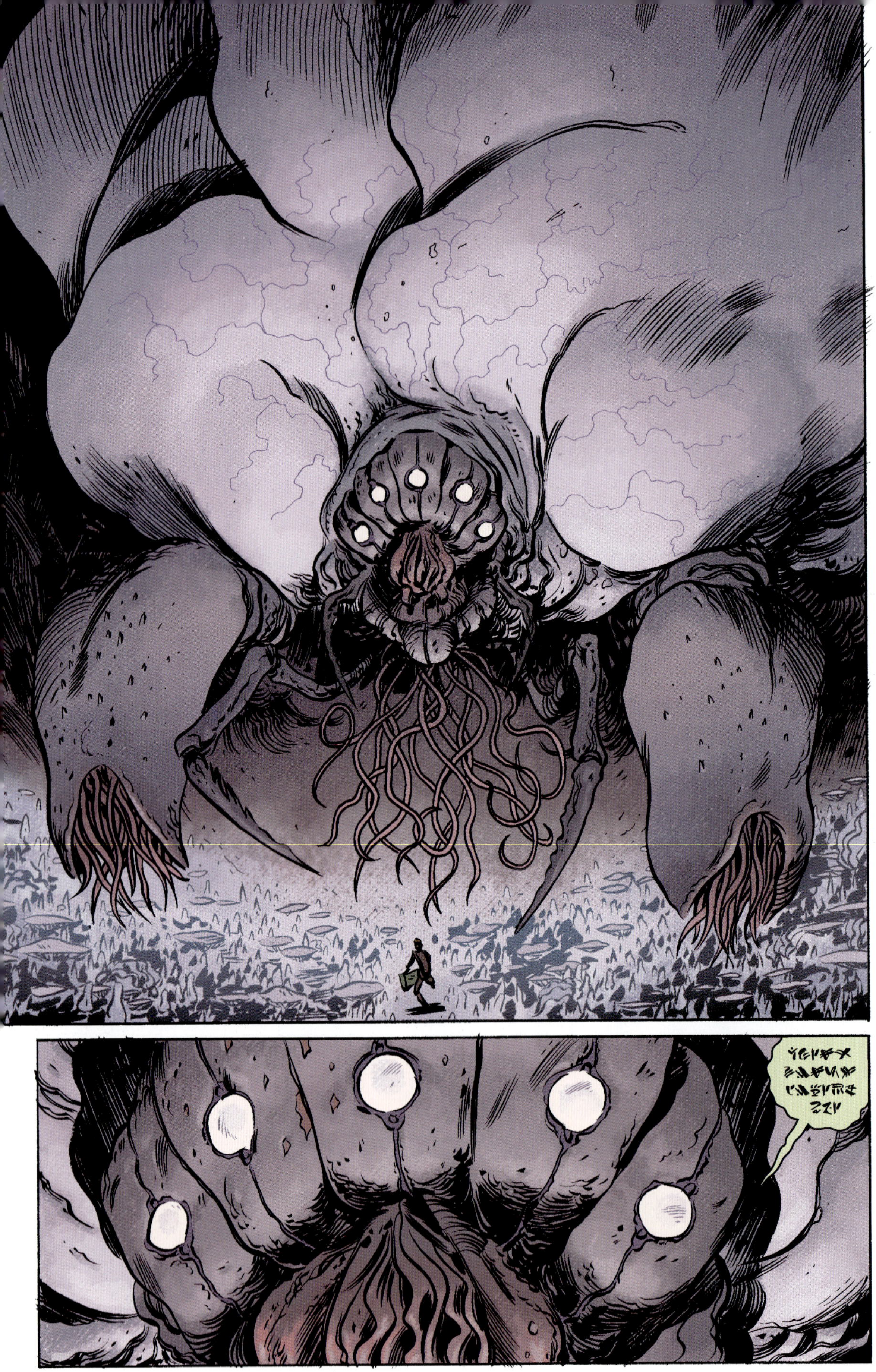

NUHPH DAONN ENGREN
YOU CAN'T REACH ME ANY-MORE.
WITHOUT ANY BRAIN TISSUE TO MANIPULATE, YOU CAN'T EVEN SLOW ME DOWN.
UUUUUUUU
?!

WAS IST...?
YOU'RE GOING TO FIX ME UP A BODY.
AND I WON'T HURT YOU BECAUSE... BECAUSE THAT'S WHAT I...
HEH HEH. YES, POOR LITTLE JOHANN.

THAT'S WHY PAVEL SEEMED OKAY FOR SO LONG--ASKING ME QUESTIONS.
LEARNING ABOUT ME.
BUT THAT MEANS YOU KNOW...
I'M GOING TO LIVE FOREVER.
NOOOOOOO!

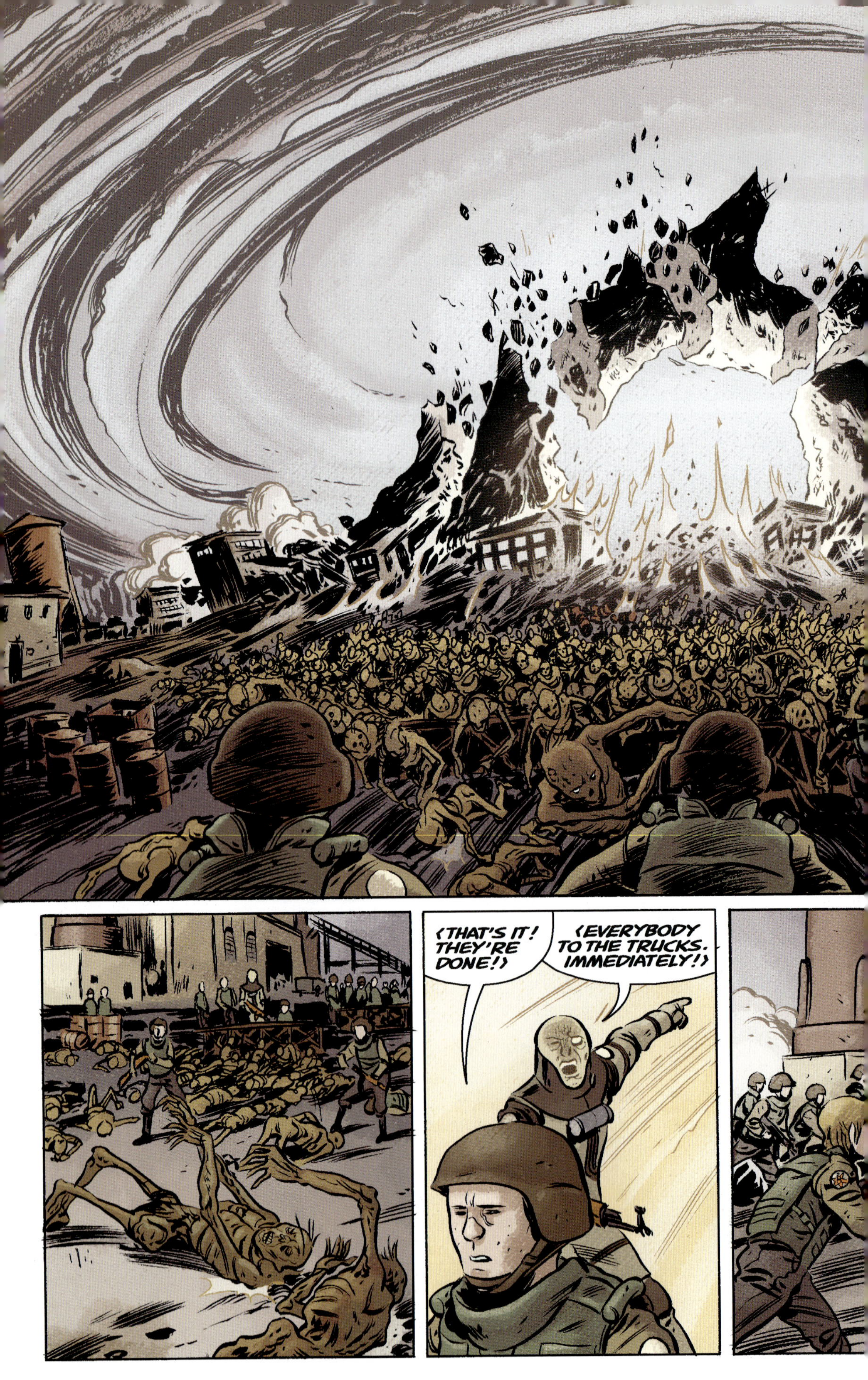
‹THAT'S IT! THEY'RE DONE!›
‹EVERYBODY TO THE TRUCKS. IMMEDIATELY!›

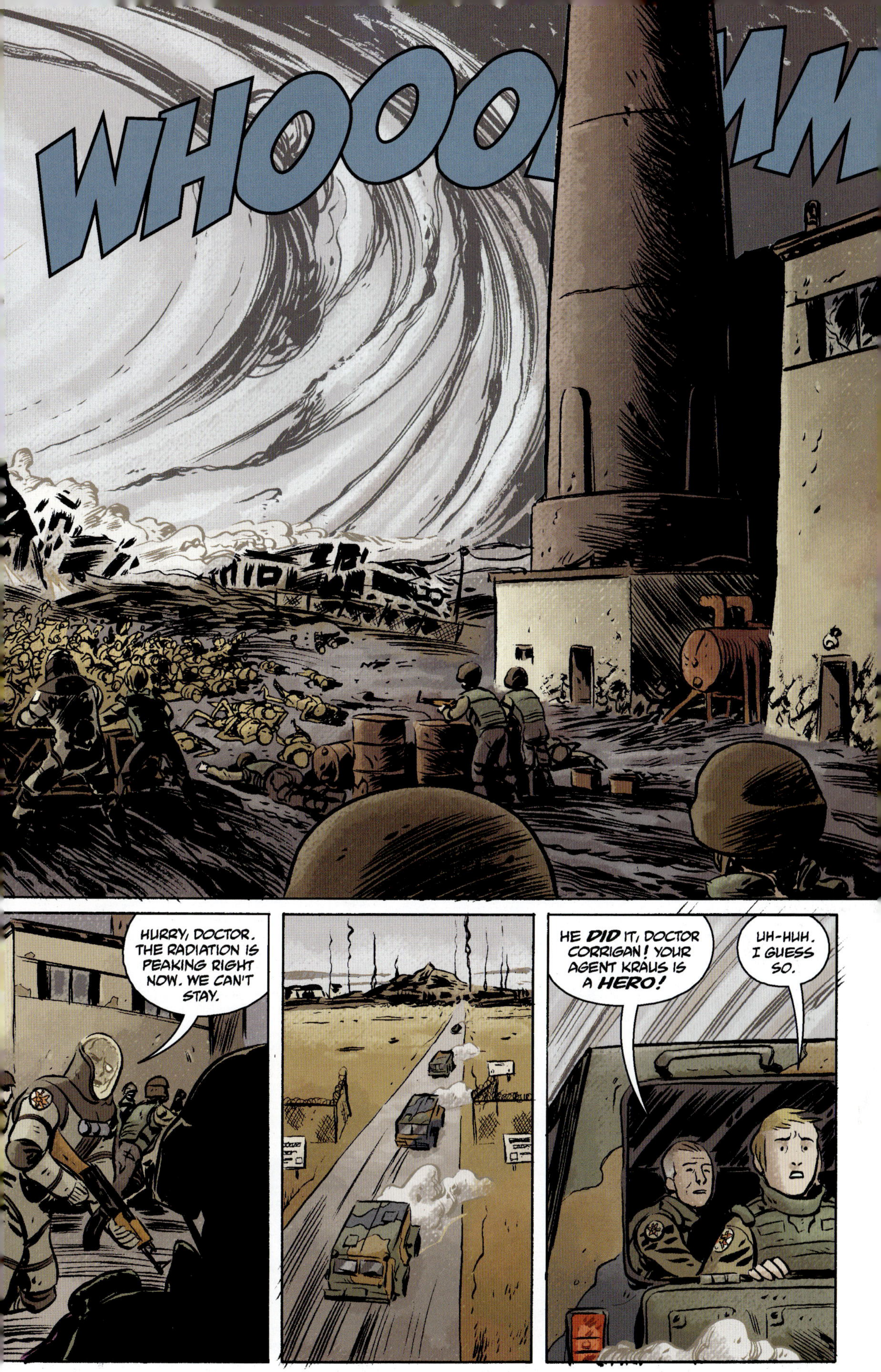
WHOOO MM
HURRY, DOCTOR. THE RADIATION IS PEAKING RIGHT NOW. WE CAN'T STAY.
HE *DID* IT, DOCTOR CORRIGAN! YOUR AGENT KRAUS IS A *HERO!*
UH-HUH. I GUESS SO.

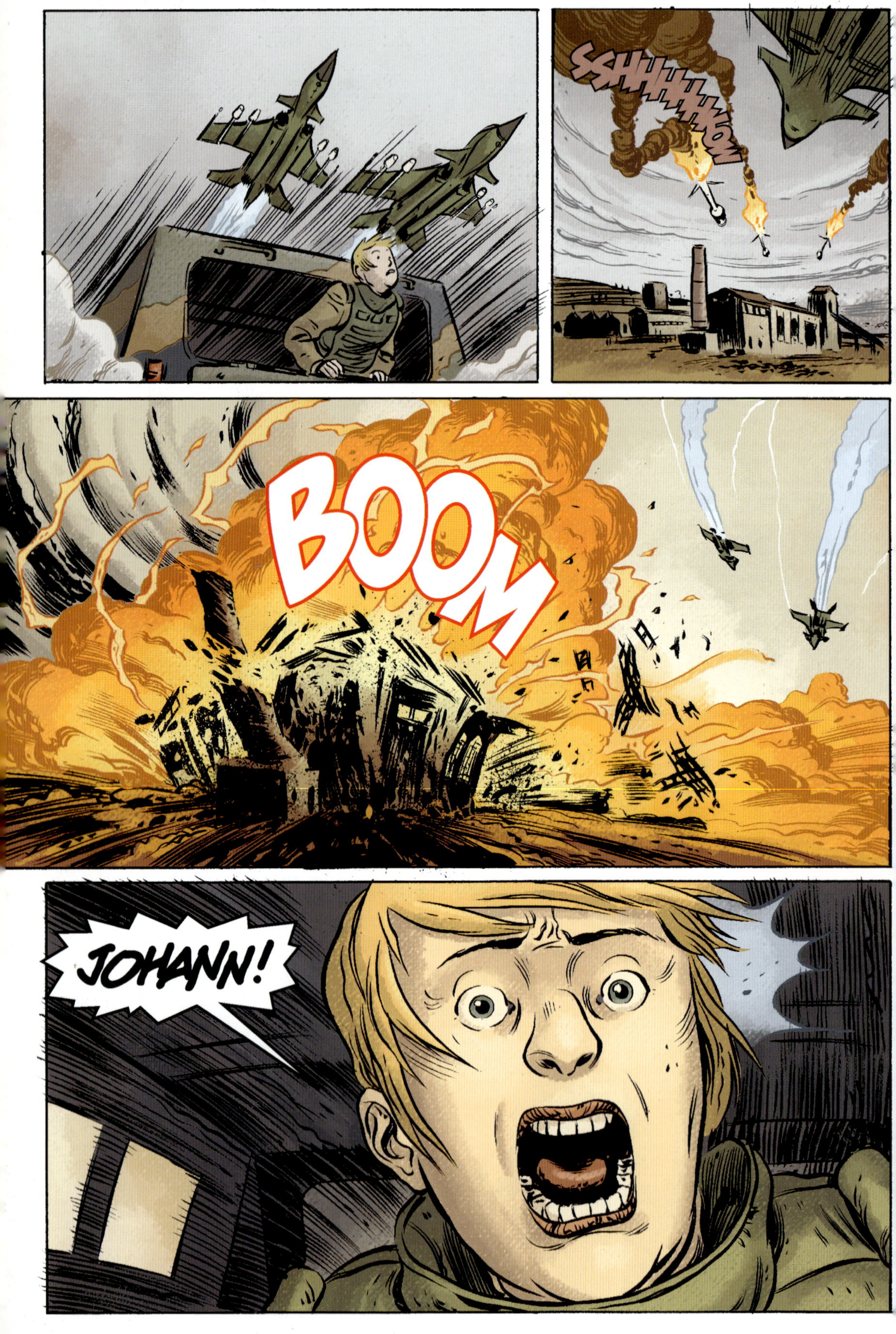
SSHHHHHOW
BOOM
JOHANN!

ILLUSTRATION BY **DAVE JOHNSON**

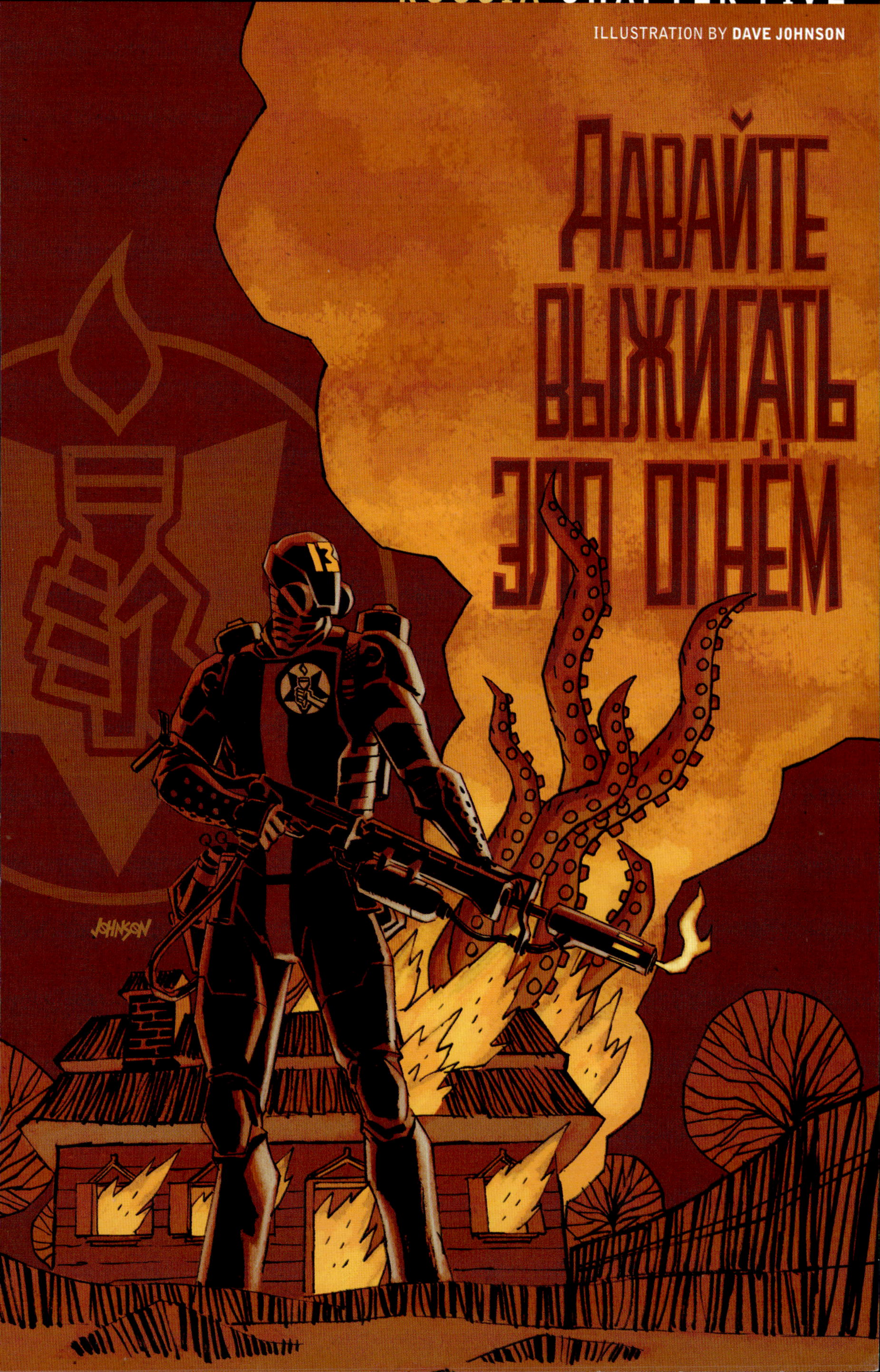
ДАВАЙТЕ ВЫЖИГАТЬ ЗЛО ОГНЁМ
13
JOHNSON

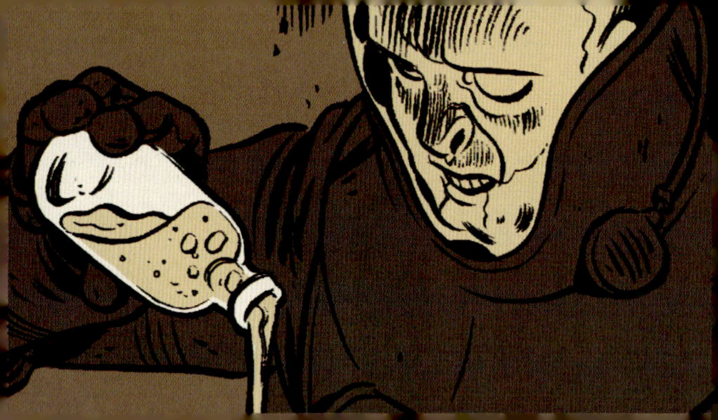

WHAT THE HELL ARE THEY DOING?!! JOHANN'S STILL DOWN THERE!
DR. CORRIGAN, AGENT KRAUS CAN'T BE PHYSICALLY HARMED.
HIS CONTAINMENT SUIT! DON'T YOU UNDERSTAND? HE NEEDS IT TO HOLD HIMSELF TOGETHER.
DOCTOR, THE SUIT MIGHT HAVE BEEN DAMAGED IN THE MISSION ANYWAY.
RIGHT, BUT I DIDN'T REQUEST TO BRING THE SPARE BECAUSE--THAT GOD DAMNED IOSIF! HE KEPT THIS WHOLE THING QUIET.
HE DIDN'T TELL ME THAT JOHANN WAS GOING TO BE A COMBATANT.
DIRECTOR NICHAYKO WAS SAYING IT IS KRAUS WHO KEEP SECRET.
WHY WOULD I BELIEVE WHAT HE SAYS?
WEREN'T YOU ALL TELLING ME HE LEAVES YOU OUT OF THE LOOP ALL THE TIME?
MORE REASON TO BELIEVE THAT DIRECTOR NICHAYKO MADE A CONTINGENCY PLAN.

AND AGENT KRAUS CAN TEMPORARILY INHABIT ANY DEAD CREATURE, ISN'T THAT SO?
"THERE IS NO SHORTAGE OF HOSTS FOR HIM TO BORROW. AT LEAST UNTIL WE CAN MAKE OTHER ARRANGEMENTS."

THOSE BODIES ARE HIGHLY RADIOACTIVE. WE COULDN'T GET NEAR HIM.
OR IS HE SUPPOSED TO WAIT OUT HERE FOR THE BUREAU TO SHIP IN ANOTHER SUIT?
HEY, ARE WE STOPPING?
MAYBE. WE SHOULD BE A GOOD FIFTEEN MILES AWAY BY NOW.
GREAT! NOW I CAN TALK TO YOUR ESTEEMED DIRECTOR!
DR. CORRIGAN, IT'S NOT WISE TO APPROACH HIM ANGRY.
FOR CHRIST'S SAKE, VASILY. GROW A PAIR!
AH, THERE YOU ARE!
WHO THE HELL DO YOU THINK YOU ARE?! MAYBE YOUR TROOPS EXPECT TO DIE, BUT YOU CAN'T TREAT JOHANN LIKE TOILET PAPER! I SWEAR, I'M GOING TO--
KATE, PLEASE.

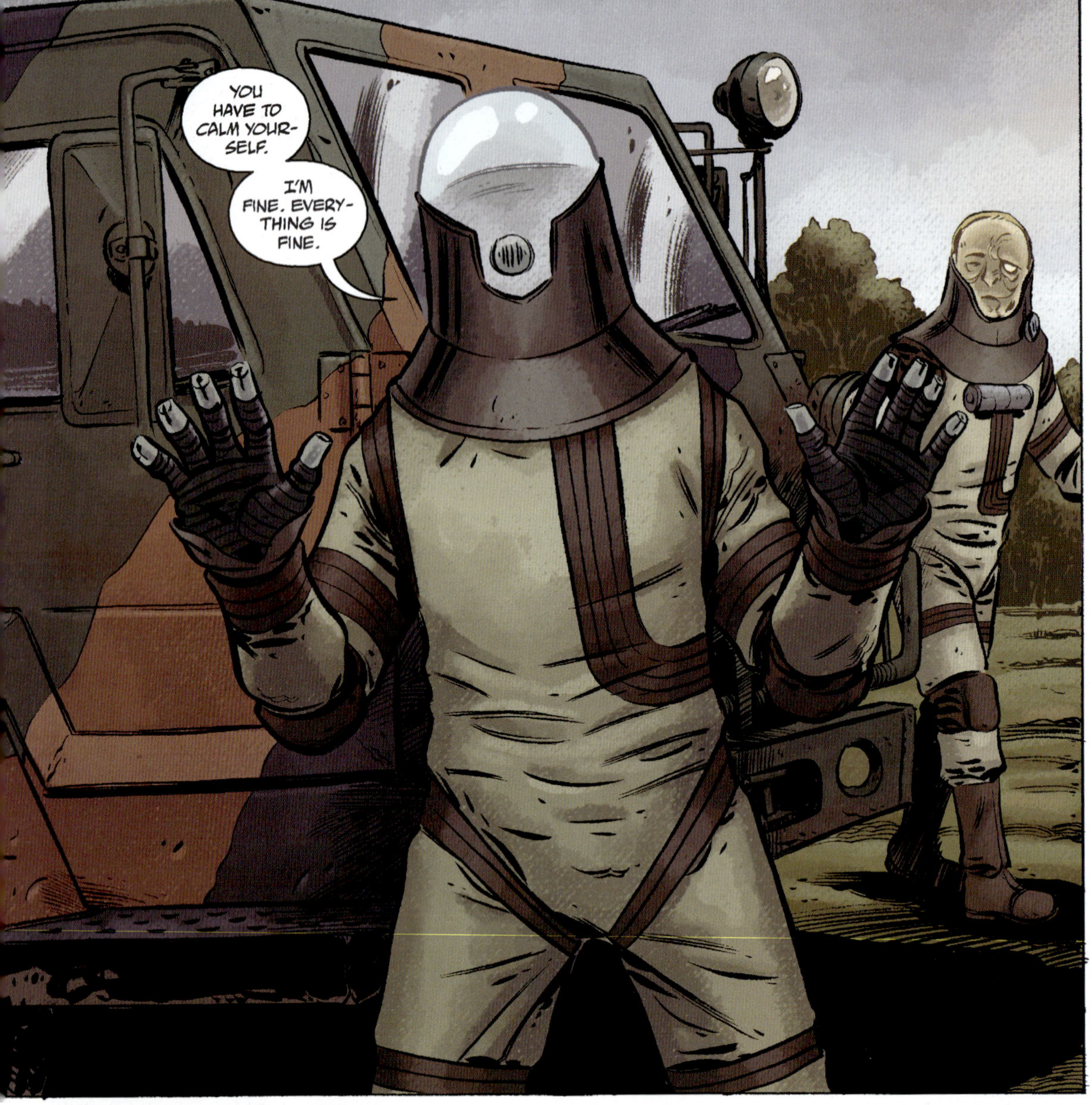
YOU HAVE TO CALM YOUR-SELF.
I'M FINE. EVERY-THING IS FINE.

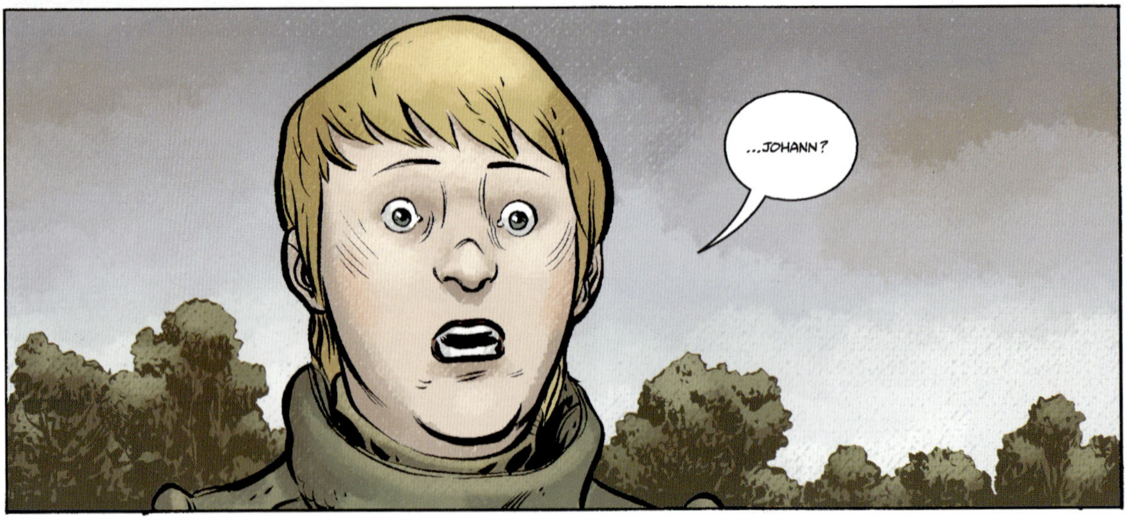
...JOHANN?

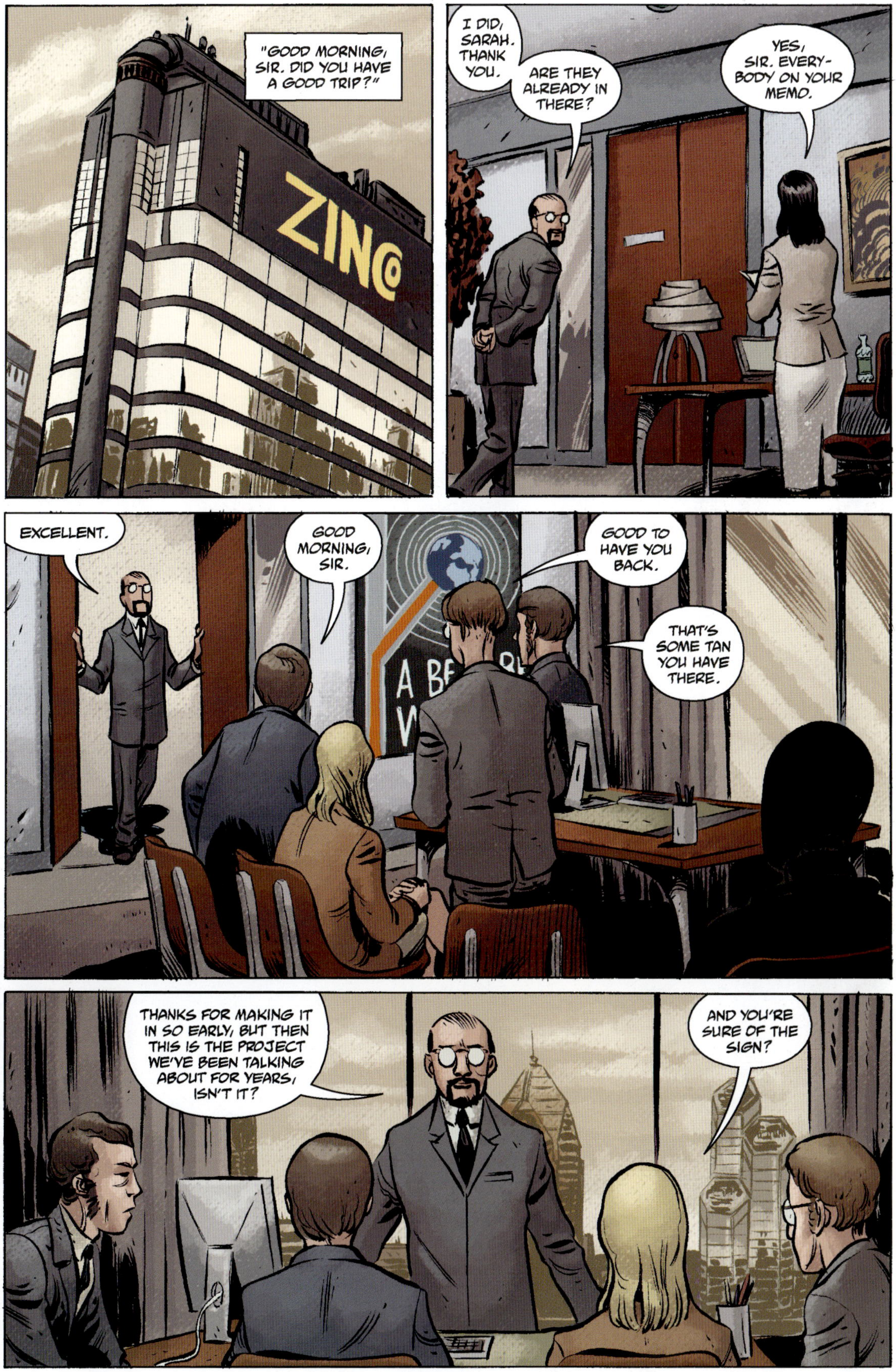
"GOOD MORNING, SIR. DID YOU HAVE A GOOD TRIP?"
ZINCO
I DID, SARAH. THANK YOU.
ARE THEY ALREADY IN THERE?
YES, SIR. EVERY-BODY ON YOUR MEMO.
EXCELLENT.
GOOD MORNING, SIR.
GOOD TO HAVE YOU BACK.
THAT'S SOME TAN YOU HAVE THERE.
THANKS FOR MAKING IT IN SO EARLY, BUT THEN THIS IS THE PROJECT WE'VE BEEN TALKING ABOUT FOR YEARS, ISN'T IT?
AND YOU'RE SURE OF THE SIGN?

IF YOU'RE ASKING ME IF THE PHOTOGRAPHS I SENT YOU WERE "SHOPPED," THEY WERE NOT.
IF YOU'RE QUESTIONING MY INTERPRETATION, TRUST ME, HAD YOU BEEN THERE WITH ME, YOU'D HAVE NO DOUBTS.
MR. MARSTEN, WHY SHOULD WE NOT TRUST YOU?
IT ONLY MAKES PERFECT SENSE.
ZINC
A BETTER
WOR
THIS IS THE TIME OF BLOOD, RIOT, AND FIRE, ISN'T IT?
IT WOULD BE SURPRISING IF WE HAD NOT SEEN A SIGN BY THIS POINT.
IF NOT NOW, WHEN?
ZINC

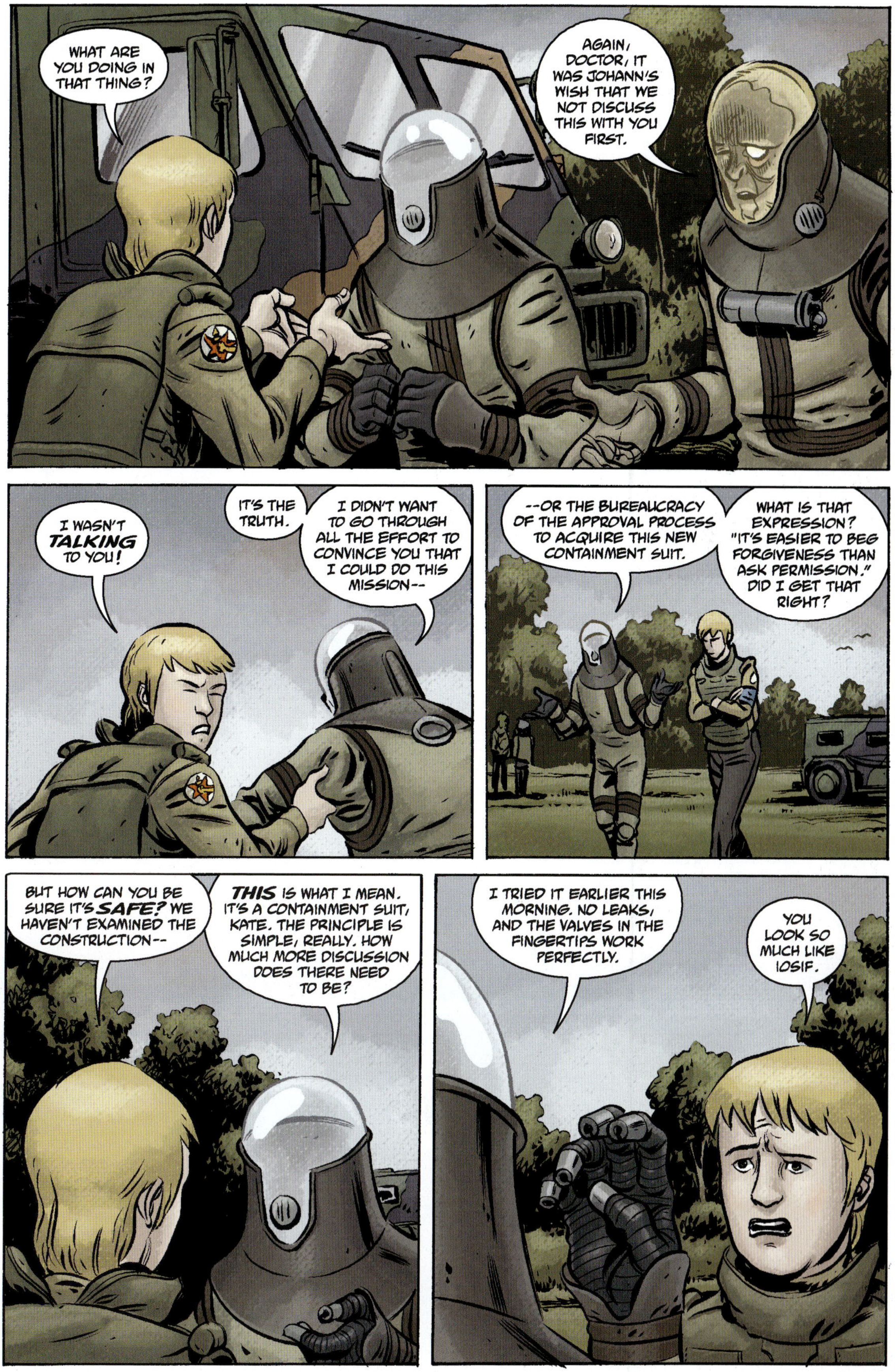
WHAT ARE YOU DOING IN THAT THING?
AGAIN, DOCTOR, IT WAS JOHANN'S WISH THAT WE NOT DISCUSS THIS WITH YOU FIRST.
I WASN'T TALKING TO YOU!
IT'S THE TRUTH.
I DIDN'T WANT TO GO THROUGH ALL THE EFFORT TO CONVINCE YOU THAT I COULD DO THIS MISSION--
--OR THE BUREAUCRACY OF THE APPROVAL PROCESS TO ACQUIRE THIS NEW CONTAINMENT SUIT.
WHAT IS THAT EXPRESSION? "IT'S EASIER TO BEG FORGIVENESS THAN ASK PERMISSION." DID I GET THAT RIGHT?
BUT HOW CAN YOU BE SURE IT'S SAFE? WE HAVEN'T EXAMINED THE CONSTRUCTION--
THIS IS WHAT I MEAN. IT'S A CONTAINMENT SUIT, KATE. THE PRINCIPLE IS SIMPLE, REALLY. HOW MUCH MORE DISCUSSION DOES THERE NEED TO BE?
I TRIED IT EARLIER THIS MORNING. NO LEAKS, AND THE VALVES IN THE FINGERTIPS WORK PERFECTLY.
YOU LOOK SO MUCH LIKE IOSIF.

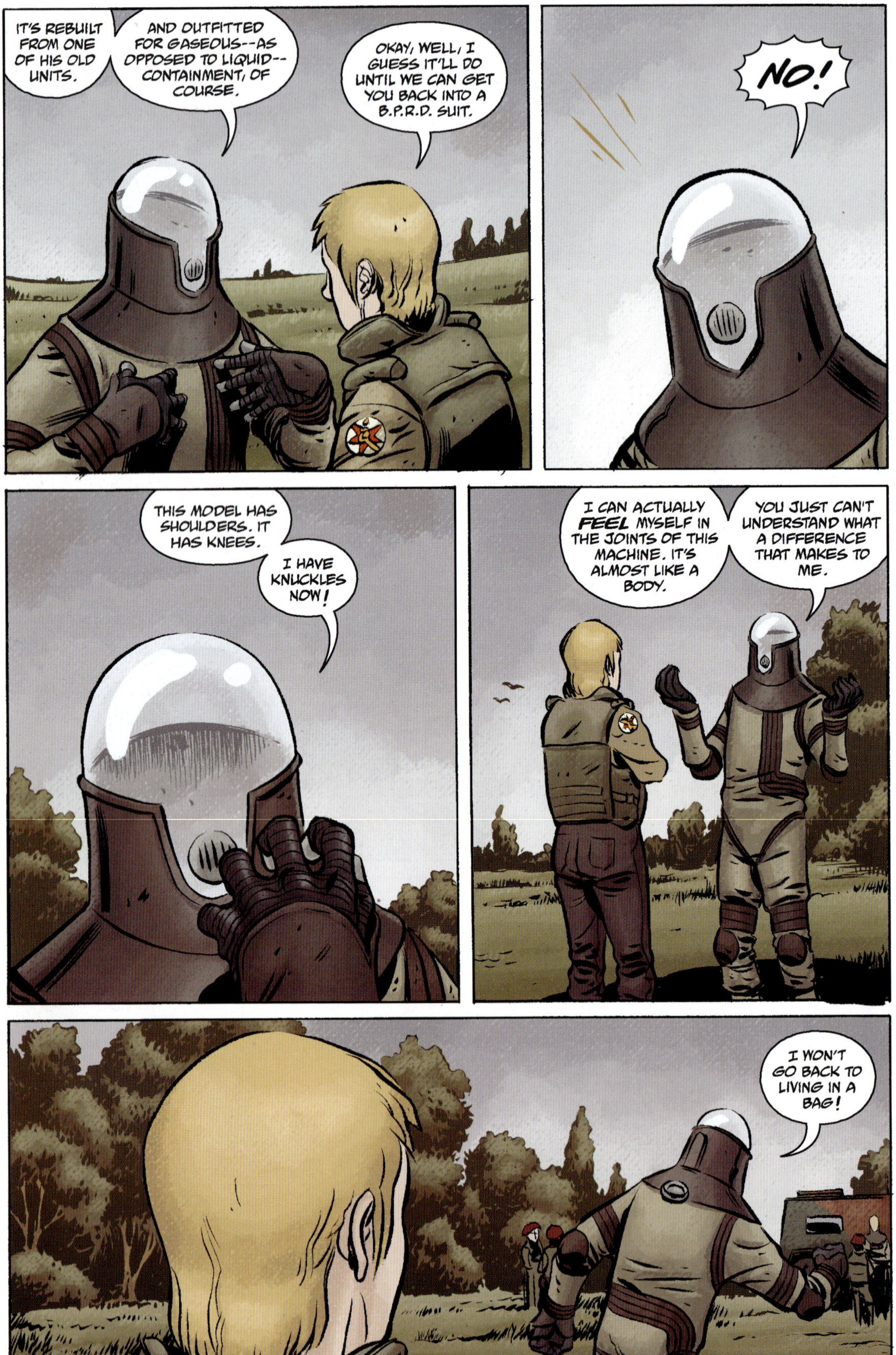
IT'S REBUILT FROM ONE OF HIS OLD UNITS.
AND OUTFITTED FOR GASEOUS--AS OPPOSED TO LIQUID--CONTAINMENT, OF COURSE.
OKAY, WELL, I GUESS IT'LL DO UNTIL WE CAN GET YOU BACK INTO A B.P.R.D. SUIT.
NO!
THIS MODEL HAS SHOULDERS. IT HAS KNEES.
I HAVE KNUCKLES NOW!
I CAN ACTUALLY FEEL MYSELF IN THE JOINTS OF THIS MACHINE. IT'S ALMOST LIKE A BODY.
YOU JUST CAN'T UNDERSTAND WHAT A DIFFERENCE THAT MAKES TO ME.
I WON'T GO BACK TO LIVING IN A BAG!

NORTHERN NEW MEXICO.
I CAN'T BELIEVE YOU GUYS. NAB ME, THEN LEMME GO, THEN GO RIGHT ON AND TRACK ME DOWN, MAKE ME YOUR RAT.
AIN'T RIGHT, JERKIN' ME LIKE THAT.
MM HMM.
THERE, ALL RIGHT? RIGHT **THERE.**
I AIN'T GETTING NO CLOSER. AND THIS IS ***IT,*** Y'FEEL ME? YOU LOSE HER AGAIN, THAT'S ON **YOU.** NOT ME.
AIN'T GONNA FIND ***ME*** AGAIN!
HEY, LOOK AT THIS LOAD.

OKAY, YOU DONE YOUR SLUMMIN'. NOW BACK THE #&*% OFF, TIGER WOODS!
I PROMISE, I'M NOT HERE TO HURT ANY-BODY.
NO $#&%! WE'RE THE ONES 'BOUT TO HURT YOU!
SHUT UP, TANK.
CHANGE YOUR MIND, MR. NAVY SEAL? WANNA TALK TO ME AFTER ALL?
I'M NOT NAVY.
I KNOW WHAT YOU ARE. I DON'T KNOW WHY YOU BOTHERED HUNTING ME.
I WAS COMING FOR YOU.

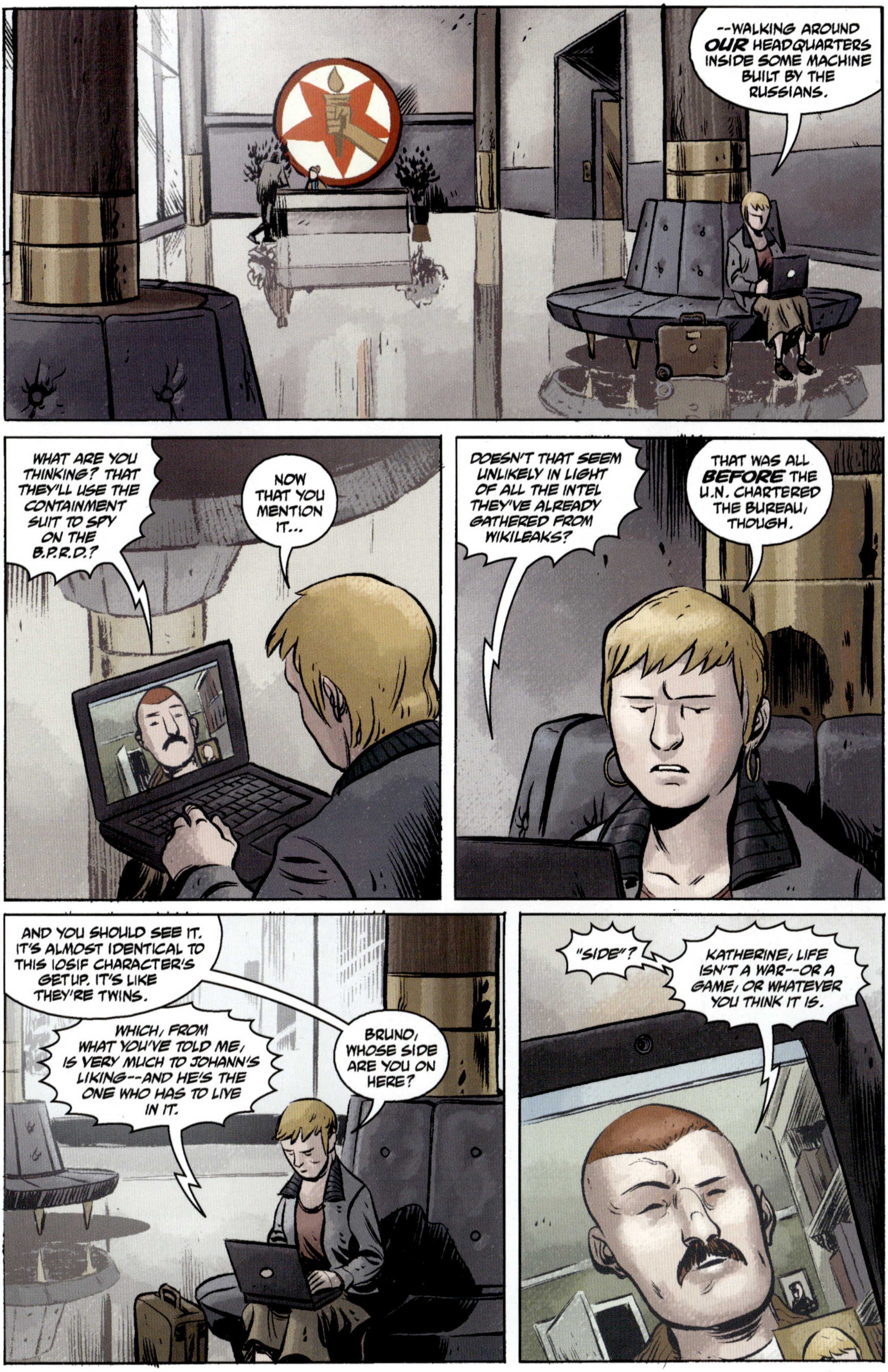
--WALKING AROUND OUR HEADQUARTERS INSIDE SOME MACHINE BUILT BY THE RUSSIANS.
WHAT ARE YOU THINKING? THAT THEY'LL USE THE CONTAINMENT SUIT TO SPY ON THE B.P.R.D.?
NOW THAT YOU MENTION IT...
DOESN'T THAT SEEM UNLIKELY IN LIGHT OF ALL THE INTEL THEY'VE ALREADY GATHERED FROM WIKILEAKS?
THAT WAS ALL BEFORE THE U.N. CHARTERED THE BUREAU, THOUGH.
AND YOU SHOULD SEE IT. IT'S ALMOST IDENTICAL TO THIS IOSIF CHARACTER'S GETUP. IT'S LIKE THEY'RE TWINS.
WHICH, FROM WHAT YOU'VE TOLD ME, IS VERY MUCH TO JOHANN'S LIKING--AND HE'S THE ONE WHO HAS TO LIVE IN IT.
BRUNO, WHOSE SIDE ARE YOU ON HERE?
"SIDE"?
KATHERINE, LIFE ISN'T A WAR--OR A GAME, OR WHATEVER YOU THINK IT IS.

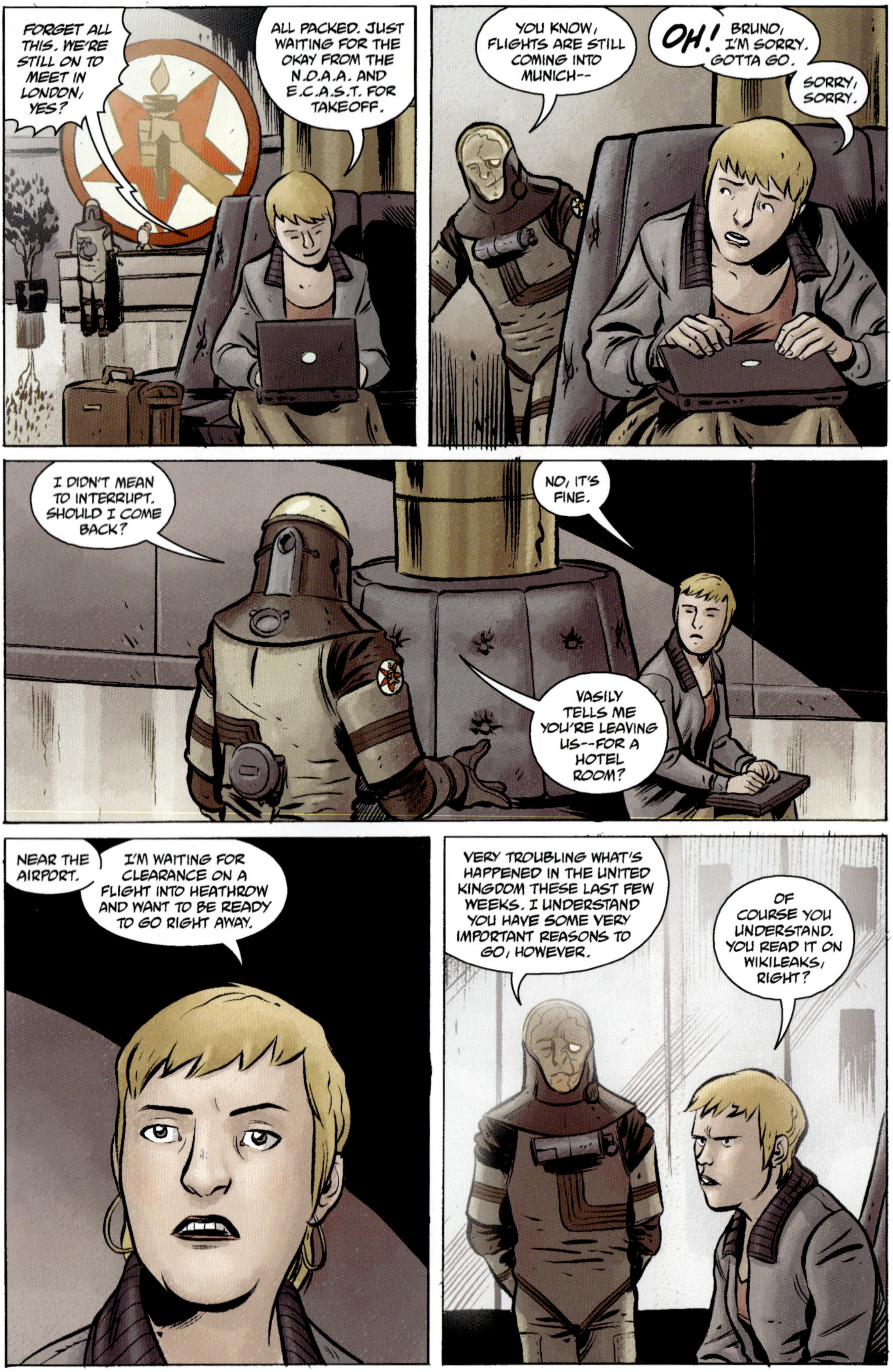
FORGET ALL THIS. WE'RE STILL ON TO MEET IN LONDON, YES?
ALL PACKED. JUST WAITING FOR THE OKAY FROM THE N.O.A.A. AND E.C.A.S.T. FOR TAKEOFF.
YOU KNOW, FLIGHTS ARE STILL COMING INTO MUNICH--
OH!
BRUNO, I'M SORRY. GOTTA GO.
SORRY, SORRY.
I DIDN'T MEAN TO INTERRUPT. SHOULD I COME BACK?
NO, IT'S FINE.
VASILY TELLS ME YOU'RE LEAVING US--FOR A HOTEL ROOM?
NEAR THE AIRPORT.
I'M WAITING FOR CLEARANCE ON A FLIGHT INTO HEATHROW AND WANT TO BE READY TO GO RIGHT AWAY.
VERY TROUBLING WHAT'S HAPPENED IN THE UNITED KINGDOM THESE LAST FEW WEEKS. I UNDERSTAND YOU HAVE SOME VERY IMPORTANT REASONS TO GO, HOWEVER.
OF COURSE YOU UNDERSTAND. YOU READ IT ON WIKILEAKS, RIGHT?

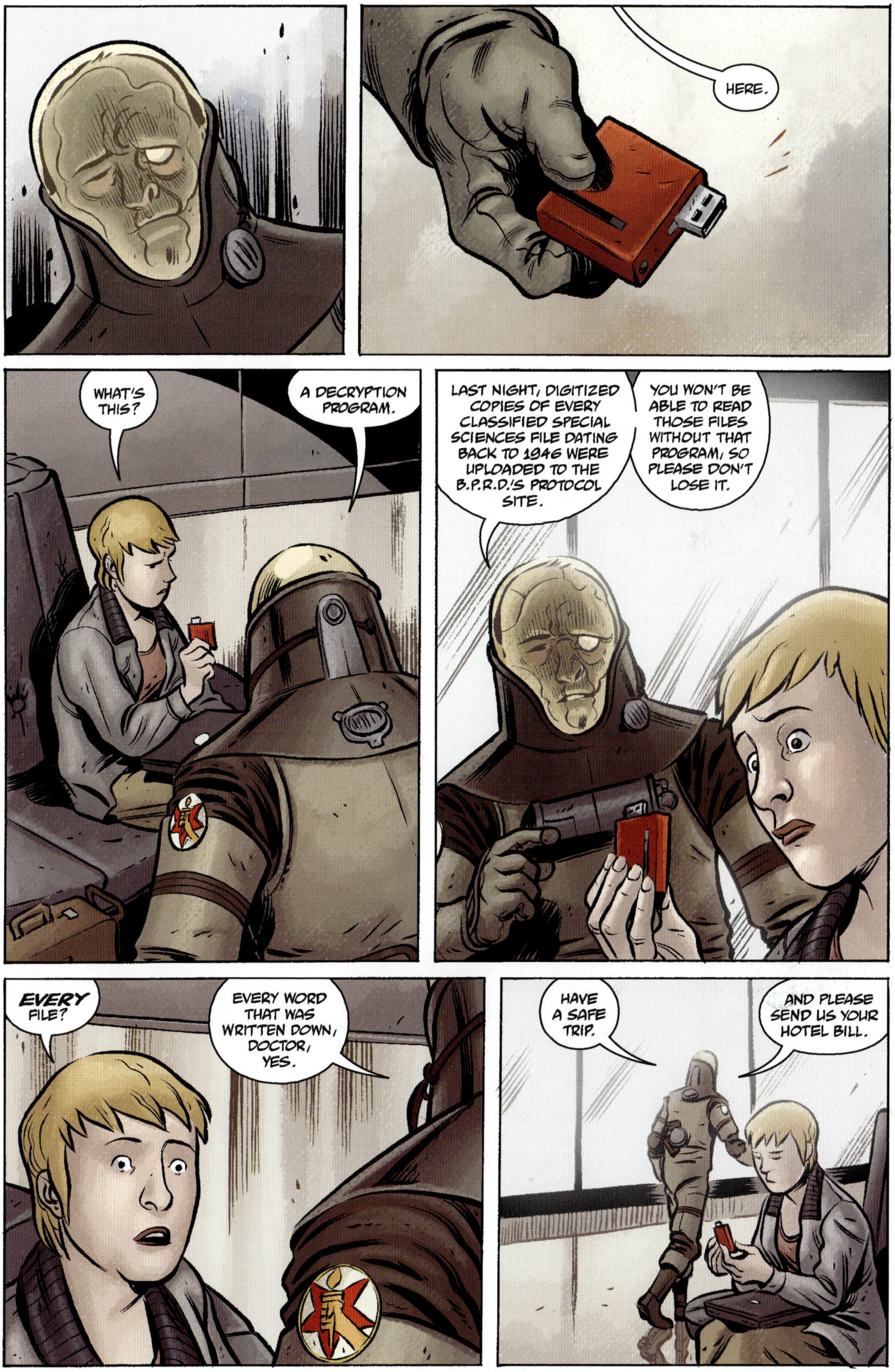
HERE.
WHAT'S THIS?
A DECRYPTION PROGRAM.
LAST NIGHT, DIGITIZED COPIES OF EVERY CLASSIFIED SPECIAL SCIENCES FILE DATING BACK TO 1946 WERE UPLOADED TO THE B.P.R.D.'S PROTOCOL SITE.
YOU WON'T BE ABLE TO READ THOSE FILES WITHOUT THAT PROGRAM, SO PLEASE DON'T LOSE IT.
EVERY FILE?
EVERY WORD THAT WAS WRITTEN DOWN, DOCTOR, YES.
HAVE A SAFE TRIP.
AND PLEASE SEND US YOUR HOTEL BILL.

BZZZZZZ
HELLO.
HELLO, DOCTOR. I WAS TOLD YOU'RE ON YOUR WAY BACK, BUT THIS COULDN'T WAIT.
IT'S AGENT SAPIEN.
HIS HEART'S BEATING ON ITS OWN, AND BRAINWAVE ACTIVITY HAS RESUMED. OUR DOCTORS ARE ALL BAFFLED.
HE'S ALIVE? YOU'RE SAYING ABE'S ALIVE?!!
YES, DOCTOR.
OH MY GOD! THAT'S AMAZING! THAT'S GREAT!
YES, DOCTOR.
THERE'S JUST ONE THING...

--HEY, WON'T YOU PLAY ANOTHER--SOME-BODY-- ♪
⟨TROUBLE?⟩
⟨FUEL PUMP, I THINK. CAN I GET A LIFT?⟩
⟨YOU ARE LUCKY. NOBODY EVER TAKES THIS ROAD BUT A FEW FARMERS. ARE YOU LOST?⟩
⟨NO. JUST VISITING A FRIEND.⟩

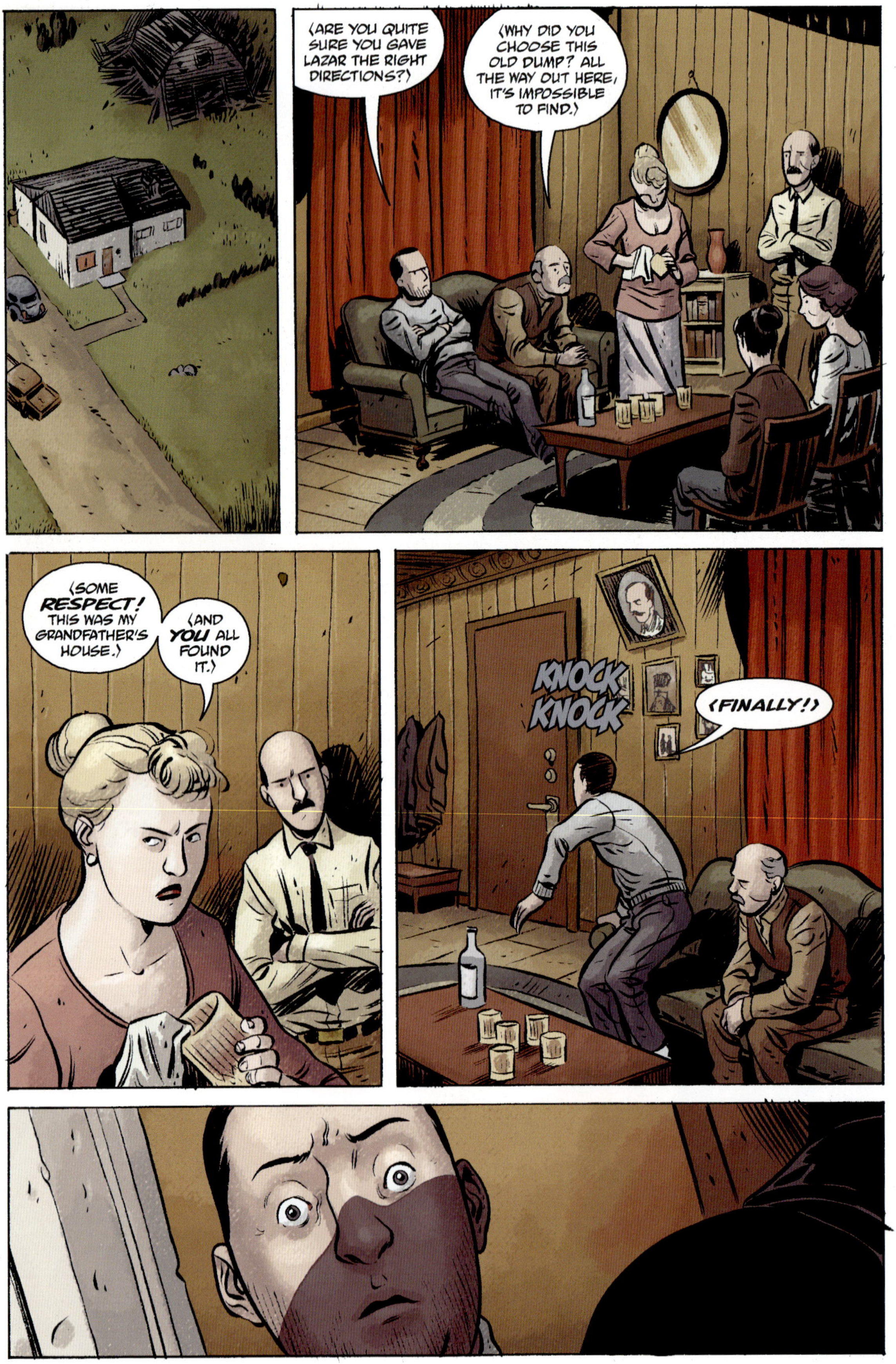
(ARE YOU QUITE SURE YOU GAVE LAZAR THE RIGHT DIRECTIONS?)
(WHY DID YOU CHOOSE THIS OLD DUMP? ALL THE WAY OUT HERE, IT'S IMPOSSIBLE TO FIND.)
(SOME RESPECT! THIS WAS MY GRANDFATHER'S HOUSE.)
(AND YOU ALL FOUND IT.)
KNOCK KNOCK
(FINALLY!)

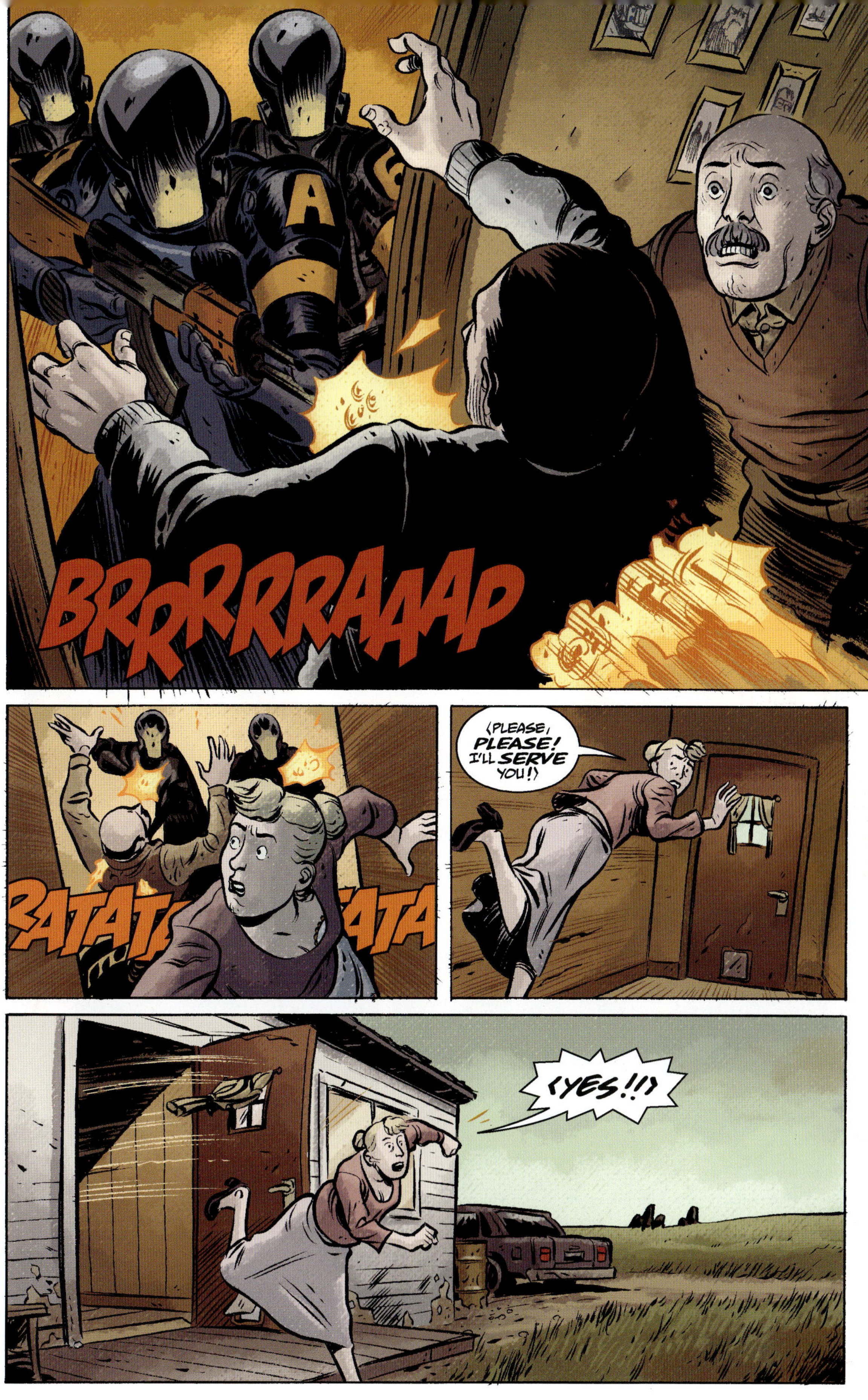
BRRRRRAAAP
RATAT
ATA
‹PLEASE, PLEASE! I'LL SERVE YOU!›
‹YES!!›

BLAM BLAM BLAM
BLAM BLAN
⟨SO, AVEL. MORE SECRET MEETINGS?⟩
⟨SECRETS... SECRETS ARE NOT GOOD.⟩
⟨I'M S-S-S-SORRY, DIRECTOR. FORGIVE ME.⟩

⟨I WISH YOUR FRIENDS HAD ADVISED YOU BETTER. I WISH THEY'D BEEN A POSITIVE INFLUENCE.⟩
⟨I'M BEGGING YOU.⟩
⟨LIKE MY FRIEND.⟩
⟨SEE THIS?⟩
⟨HE GAVE IT TO ME. SOMETHING LIKE HOLY WATER. MORE SCIENTIFIC, THOUGH.⟩
AAIII!
⟨INFECTED, BUT STILL NASCENT.⟩
⟨ALL RIGHT, YOU KNOW WHAT TO DO.⟩
IIUHHLECCH

⟨LOOK AT THAT. NOT ONE CLOUD.⟩
⟨WHEN I FIRST CAME TO THE SERVICE, I WAS RESTRICTED TO THE SUB-BASEMENT LEVEL.⟩
⟨SIX YEARS AND SEVEN MONTHS BEFORE THEY EVEN LET ME UP TO THE FIRST FLOOR. DID YOU KNOW THAT?⟩
⟨MY GOD, WHAT A DAY THIS IS!⟩

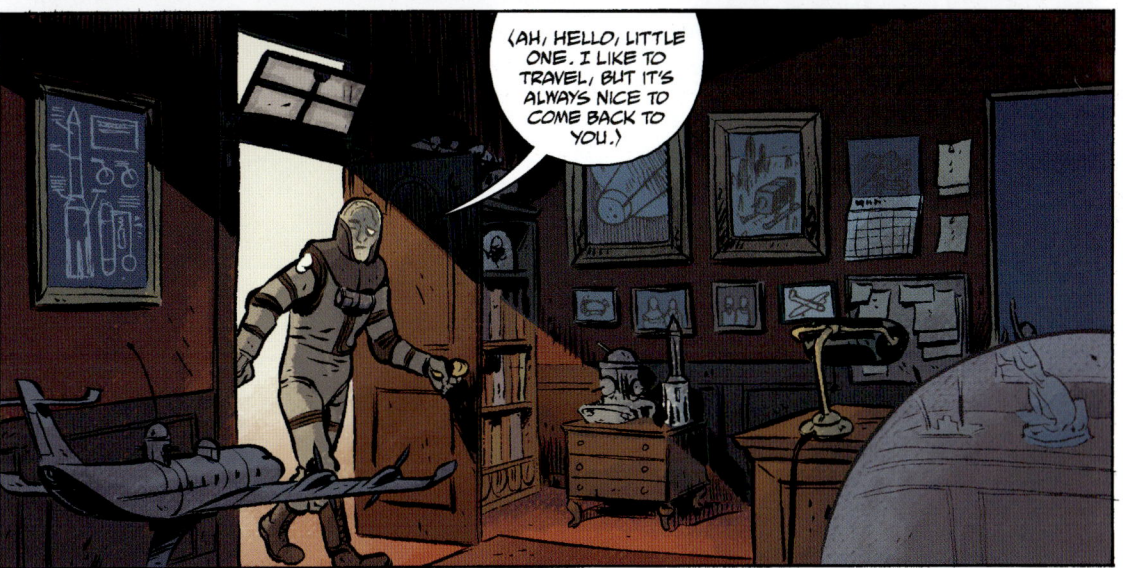

⟨AH, HELLO, LITTLE ONE. I LIKE TO TRAVEL, BUT IT'S ALWAYS NICE TO COME BACK TO YOU.⟩

⟨I'M AFRAID I HAVE SOME UPSETTING NEWS, THOUGH.⟩

⟨AND I DON'T WANT YOU TO BE ANGRY.⟩

⟨DOCTORS KHANIN, TARASOV, FEDOSEEV, CHUZHOI, AND PROFESSORS ABEZGAUZ AND PANUSHKIS--⟩

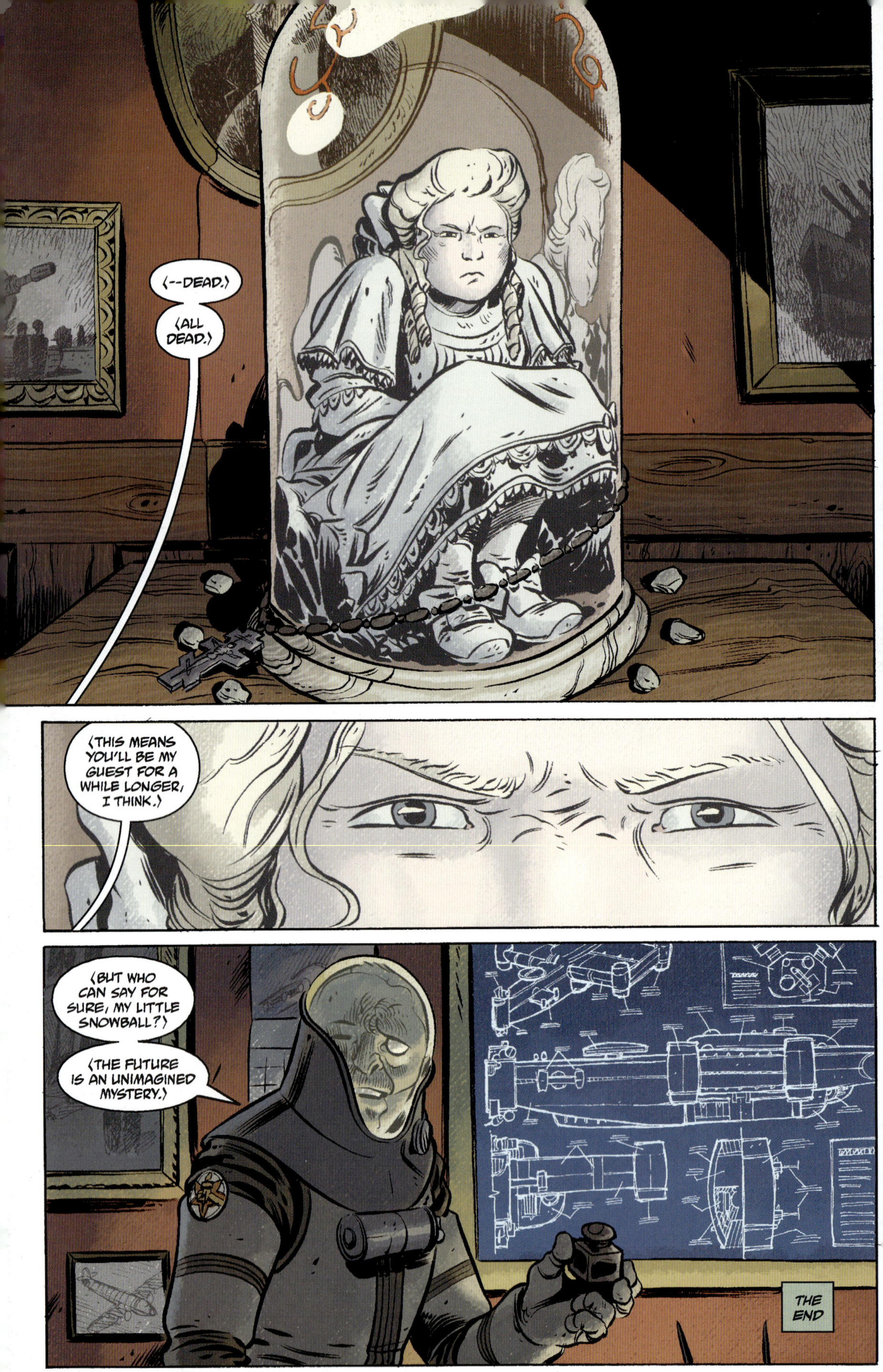
‹--DEAD.›
‹ALL DEAD.›
‹THIS MEANS YOU'LL BE MY GUEST FOR A WHILE LONGER, I THINK.›
‹BUT WHO CAN SAY FOR SURE, MY LITTLE SNOWBALL?›
‹THE FUTURE IS AN UNIMAGINED MYSTERY.›
THE END

AN UNMARKED GRAVE

ILLUSTRATION BY **DUNCAN FEGREDO**

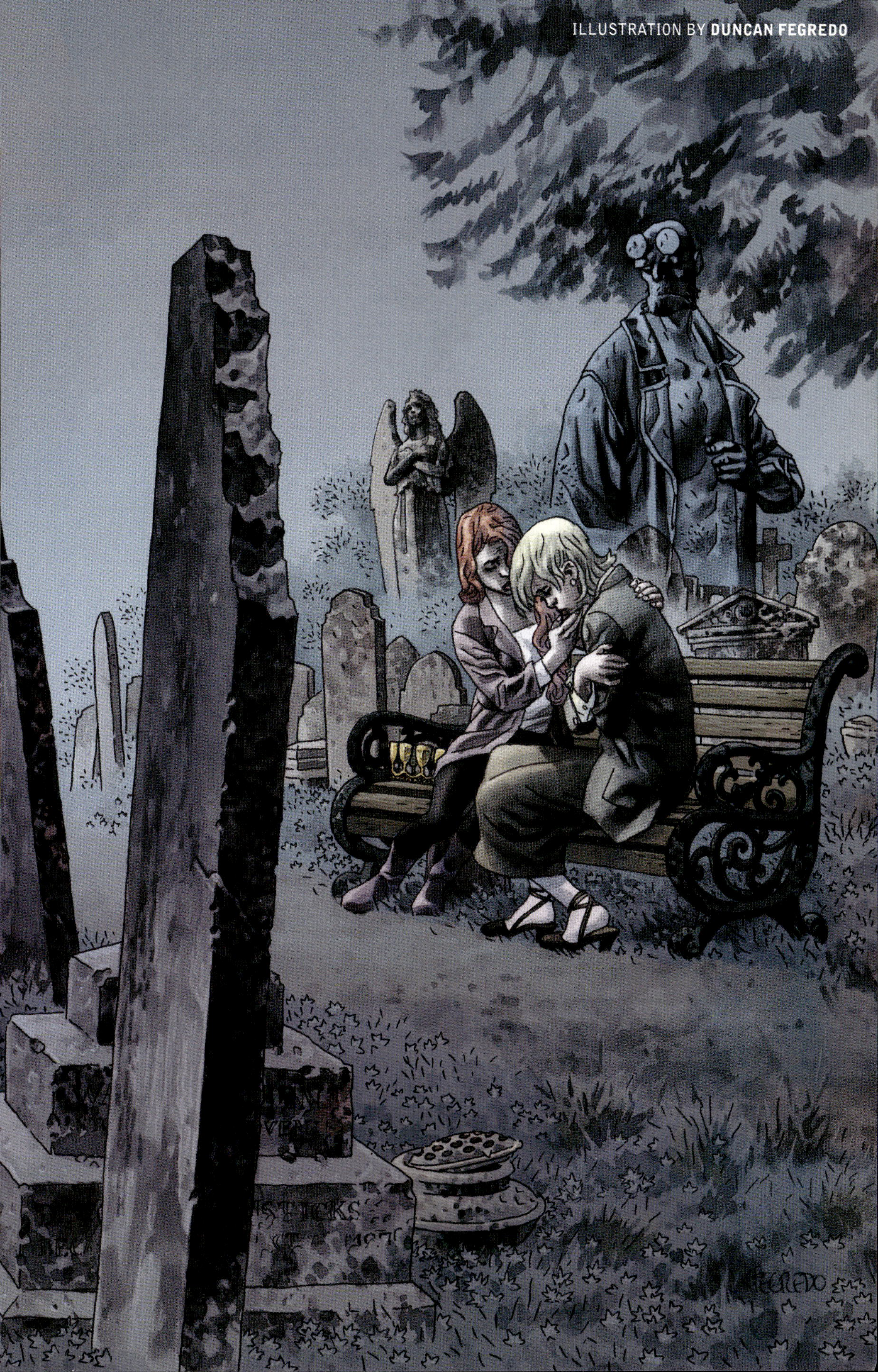

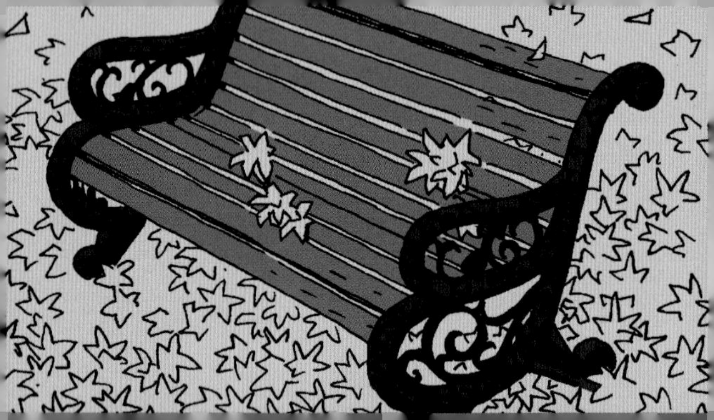

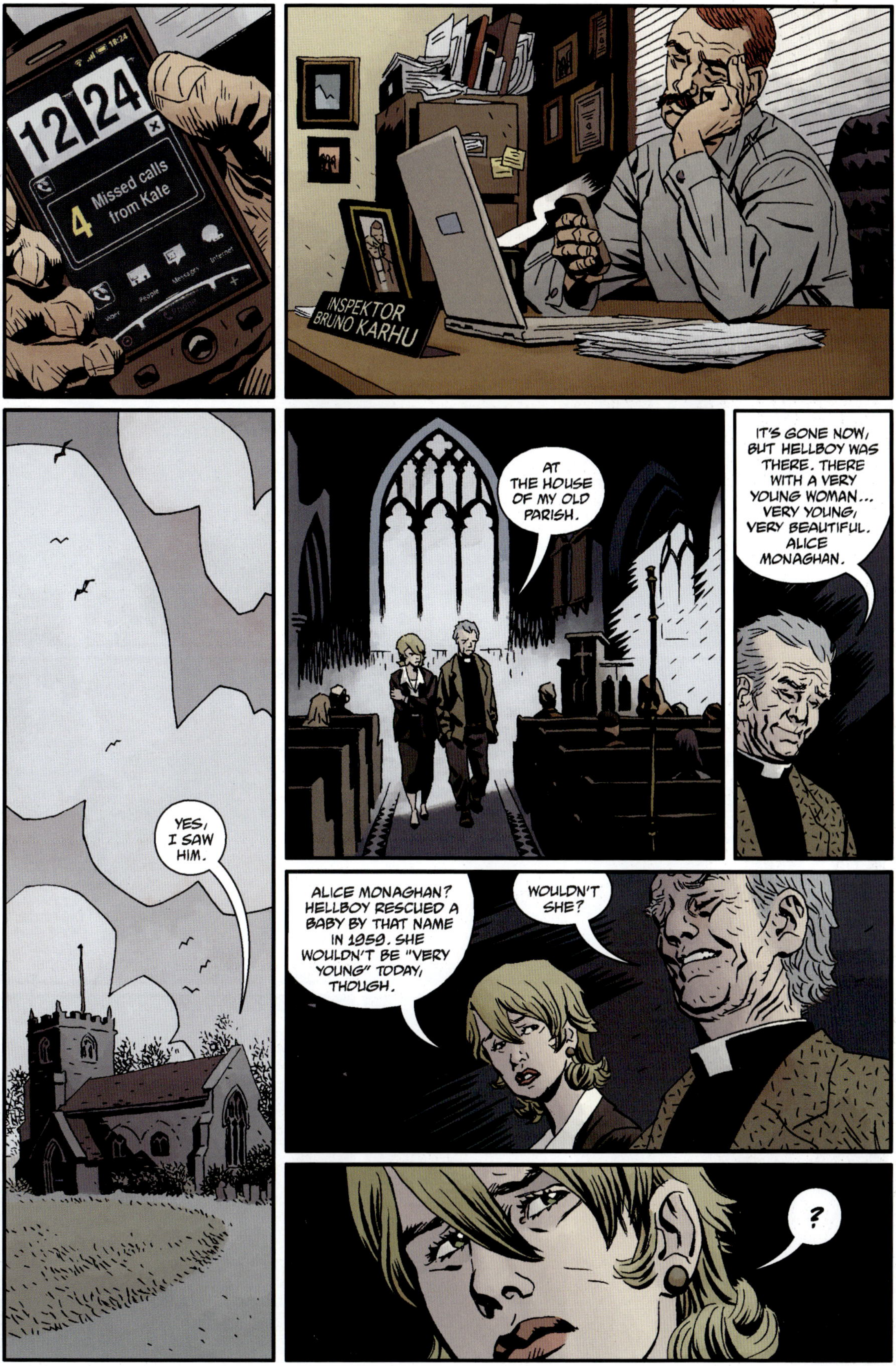

12 24
4 Missed calls from Kate
INSPEKTOR BRUNO KARHU
YES, I SAW HIM.
AT THE HOUSE OF MY OLD PARISH.
IT'S GONE NOW, BUT HELLBOY WAS THERE. THERE WITH A VERY YOUNG WOMAN... VERY YOUNG, VERY BEAUTIFUL. ALICE MONAGHAN.
ALICE MONAGHAN? HELLBOY RESCUED A BABY BY THAT NAME IN 1959. SHE WOULDN'T BE "VERY YOUNG" TODAY, THOUGH.
WOULDN'T SHE?
?

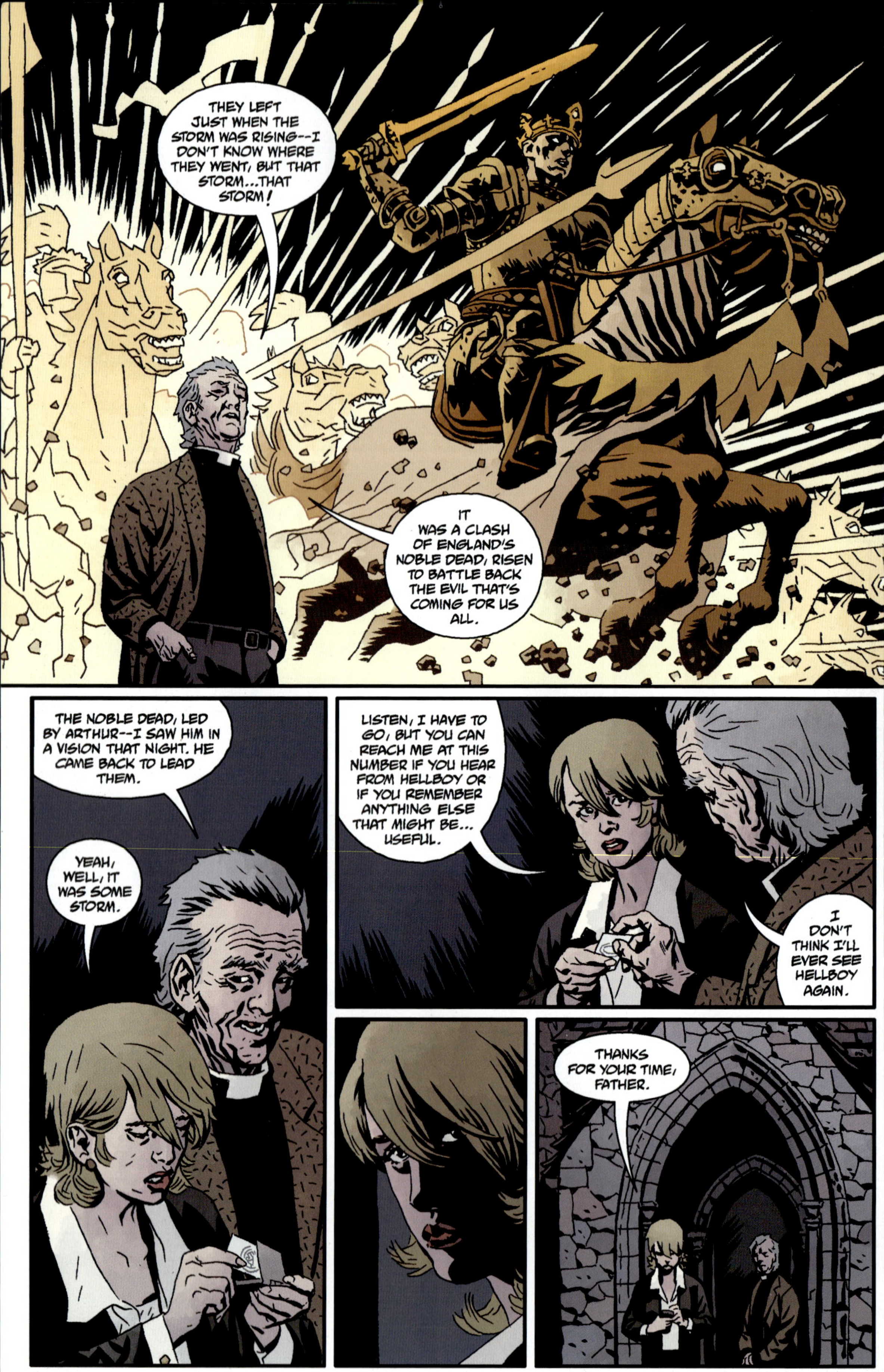
THEY LEFT JUST WHEN THE STORM WAS RISING--I DON'T KNOW WHERE THEY WENT, BUT THAT STORM...THAT STORM!
IT WAS A CLASH OF ENGLAND'S NOBLE DEAD, RISEN TO BATTLE BACK THE EVIL THAT'S COMING FOR US ALL.
THE NOBLE DEAD, LED BY ARTHUR--I SAW HIM IN A VISION THAT NIGHT. HE CAME BACK TO LEAD THEM.
YEAH, WELL, IT WAS SOME STORM.
LISTEN, I HAVE TO GO, BUT YOU CAN REACH ME AT THIS NUMBER IF YOU HEAR FROM HELLBOY OR IF YOU REMEMBER ANYTHING ELSE THAT MIGHT BE... USEFUL.
I DON'T THINK I'LL EVER SEE HELLBOY AGAIN.
THANKS FOR YOUR TIME, FATHER.

Calling
Bruno
IT'S NOT THE SAME.
I'M SORRY?
THIS CHAPEL, IT'S NOT SO GRAND AS FATHER BILL'S OLD CHURCH.
YEAH, FATHER BILL. TOOK ME A WHILE TO HUNT HIM DOWN, BUT I'M LOOKING FOR A FRIEND--
HE WAS RIGHT ABOUT THE ARMY, YOU KNOW? I SAW THEM, THE NOBLE DEAD OF ENGLAND.
AND HELLBOY MIGHT HAVE LED THEM. HE WAS ENTITLED.
HE DISCOVERED THAT HE WAS A DESCENDENT OF ARTHUR AND HE DREW THE SWORD OUT OF THE STONE.
HE WAS KING--OR COULD HAVE BEEN. HE COULD HAVE BEEN.
BUT IN THE END HE CHOSE TO FACE THE ENEMY ALONE. HE SLEW HER...AND SHE SLEW HIM.

...WHAT?
IT'S TRUE. IT IS.
I SAW THAT, TOO.
I...I DON'T EVEN KNOW HOW YOU...
YOU'RE SURE? YOU'RE REALLY SURE HE'S--
HE DIED SO ENGLAND WOULD SURVIVE.
"SURVIVE"? I DON'T KNOW. IT LOOKS WORSE THAN MOST PLACES TO ME.
I CAME THROUGH LONDON. THAT'S GONE. ALL OVER ENGLAND MILLIONS OF PEOPLE ARE DEAD. EVERYBODY ELSE--THEY'RE LEAVING.

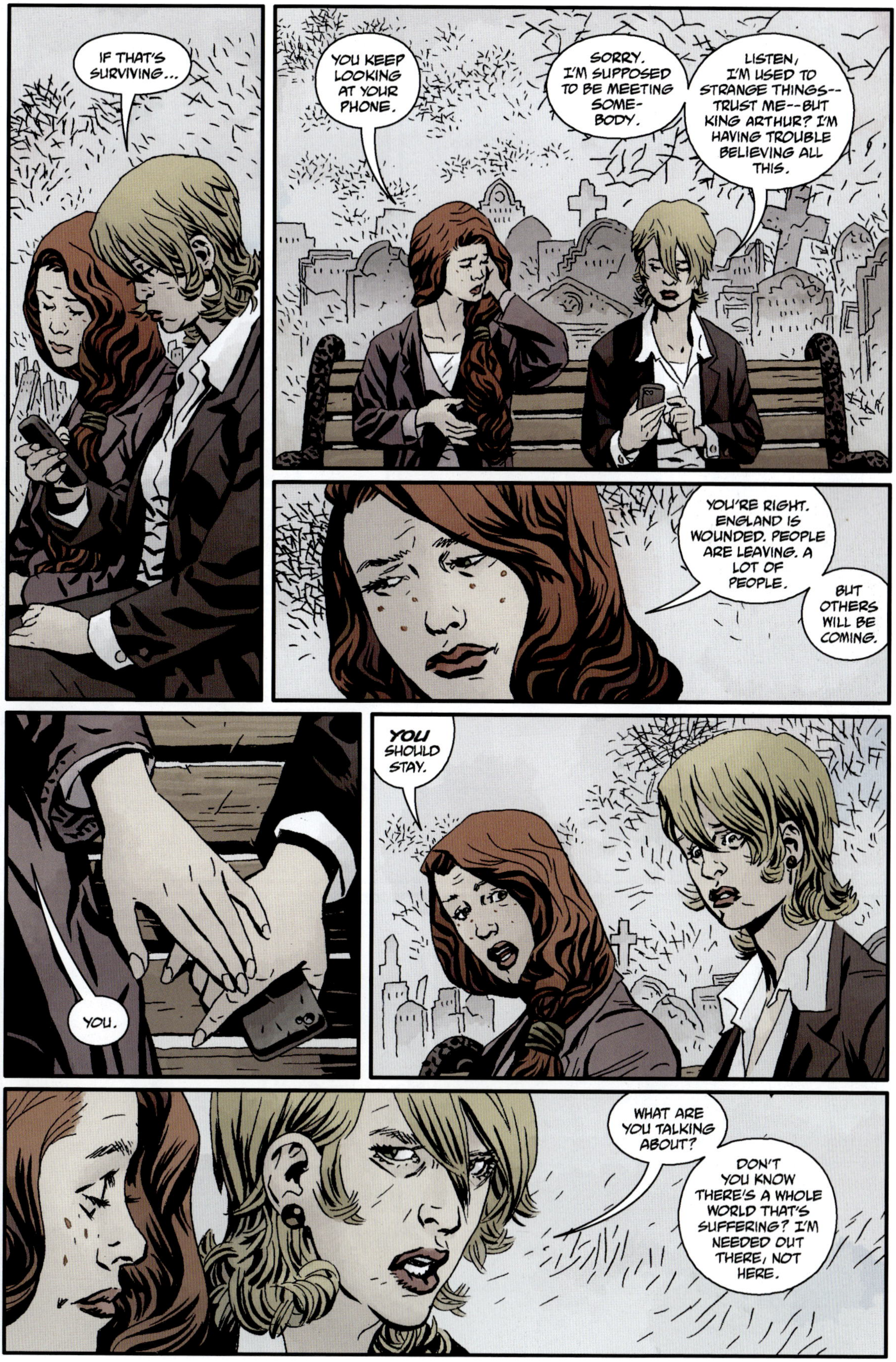
IF THAT'S SURVIVING...
YOU KEEP LOOKING AT YOUR PHONE.
SORRY. I'M SUPPOSED TO BE MEETING SOME-BODY.
LISTEN, I'M USED TO STRANGE THINGS--TRUST ME--BUT KING ARTHUR? I'M HAVING TROUBLE BELIEVING ALL THIS.
YOU'RE RIGHT. ENGLAND IS WOUNDED. PEOPLE ARE LEAVING. A LOT OF PEOPLE.
BUT OTHERS WILL BE COMING.
YOU.
YOU SHOULD STAY.
WHAT ARE YOU TALKING ABOUT?
DON'T YOU KNOW THERE'S A WHOLE WORLD THAT'S SUFFERING? I'M NEEDED OUT THERE, NOT HERE.

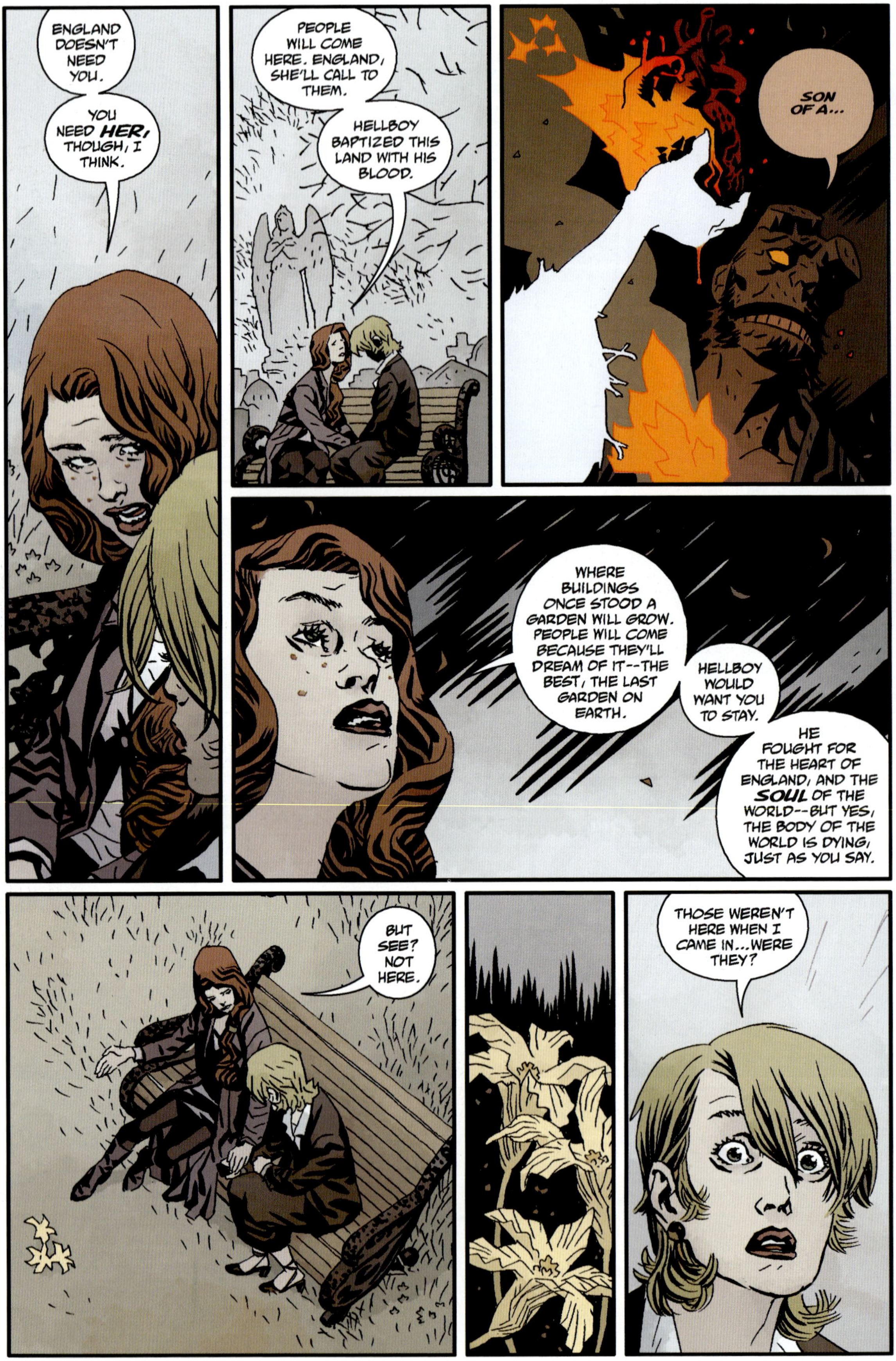
ENGLAND DOESN'T NEED YOU.
YOU NEED **HER**, THOUGH, I THINK.
PEOPLE WILL COME HERE. ENGLAND, SHE'LL CALL TO THEM.
HELLBOY BAPTIZED THIS LAND WITH HIS BLOOD.
SON OF A...
WHERE BUILDINGS ONCE STOOD A GARDEN WILL GROW. PEOPLE WILL COME BECAUSE THEY'LL DREAM OF IT--THE BEST, THE LAST GARDEN ON EARTH.
HELLBOY WOULD WANT YOU TO STAY.
HE FOUGHT FOR THE HEART OF ENGLAND, AND THE **SOUL** OF THE WORLD--BUT YES, THE BODY OF THE WORLD IS DYING, JUST AS YOU SAY.
BUT SEE? NOT HERE.
THOSE WEREN'T HERE WHEN I CAME IN...WERE THEY?

LIFE IS A CYCLE, KATE. THINGS HAVE TO DIE SO OTHERS CAN LIVE. I'M NOT TELLING YOU ANYTHING YOU DON'T KNOW--
BUT IT'S TERRIBLE SOME-TIMES. VIOLENT, AND TERRIBLE--AND IF YOU GO NOW, MAYBE YOU WON'T BE ABLE TO COME BACK.
ALICE... IT IS "ALICE," ISN'T IT?
HE'S GONE? HE'S REALLY GONE?
YES.
I CAN'T BELIEVE IT'S HOPELESS. HOW CAN I TURN MY BACK ON EVERY-BODY, EVERYTHING ELSE?
I CAN'T JUST STAY HERE AND GIVE UP.
I CAN'T! AND I DON'T THINK HELLBOY WOULD WANT ME--
RRRING
Bruno Calling
App Store
Contacts
iTunes
iPod

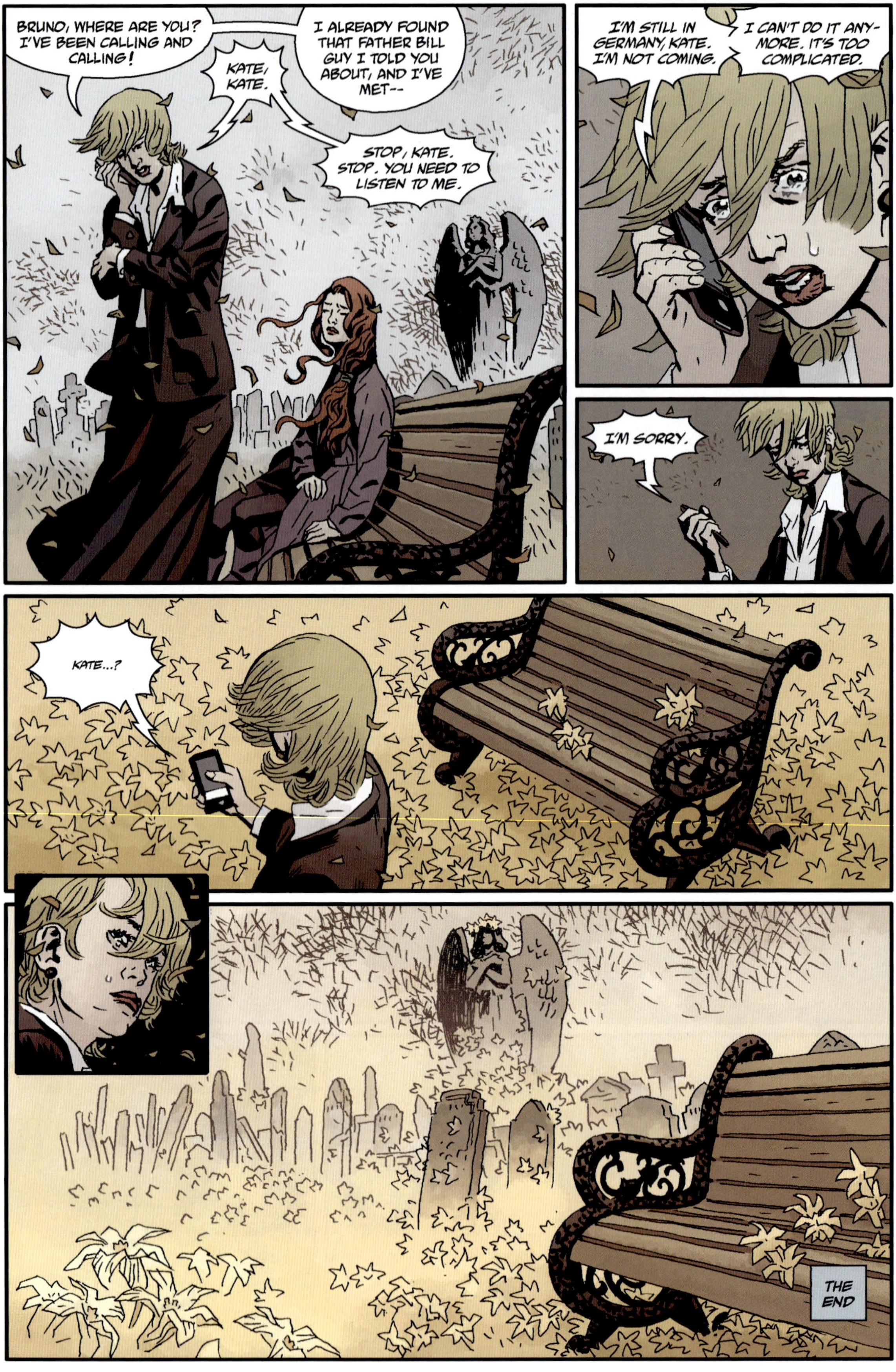
BRUNO, WHERE ARE YOU? I'VE BEEN CALLING AND CALLING!
KATE, KATE.
I ALREADY FOUND THAT FATHER BILL GUY I TOLD YOU ABOUT, AND I'VE MET--
STOP, KATE. STOP. YOU NEED TO LISTEN TO ME.
I'M STILL IN GERMANY, KATE. I'M NOT COMING.
I CAN'T DO IT ANY-MORE. IT'S TOO COMPLICATED.
I'M SORRY.
KATE...?
THE END

B.P.R.D.
SKETCHBOOK
NEW WORLD
Notes by Guy Davis

BULLDOG LIKE

THICK ARM CLAWS

HARD SHELL HEAD

NO EYES

With the *Plague of Frogs* menace wrapped up, it was time to focus on new dangers ahead for the B.P.R.D. team, and of course that meant a bunch of new monsters to take the place of the frog creatures! It started with just doing a few random creature sketches to see if I was going in the right direction, but my first pass at a sort of "bulldog" monster didn't have the right feel for the story.

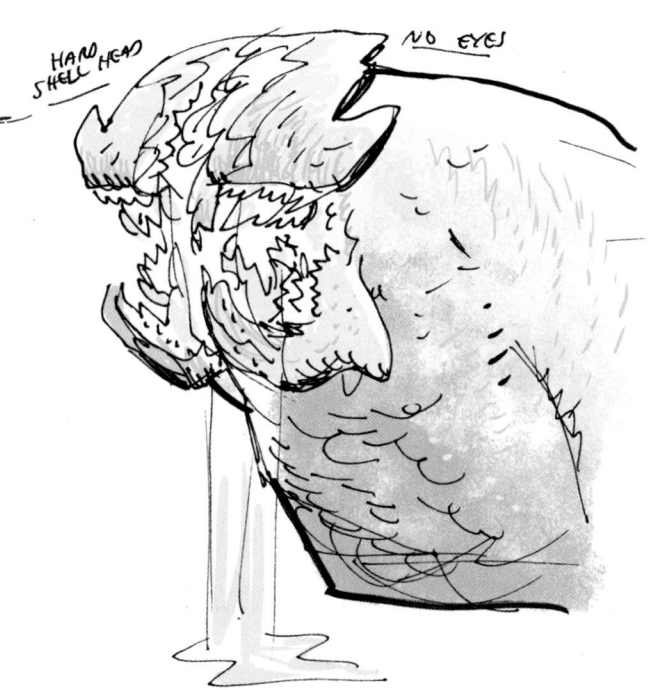

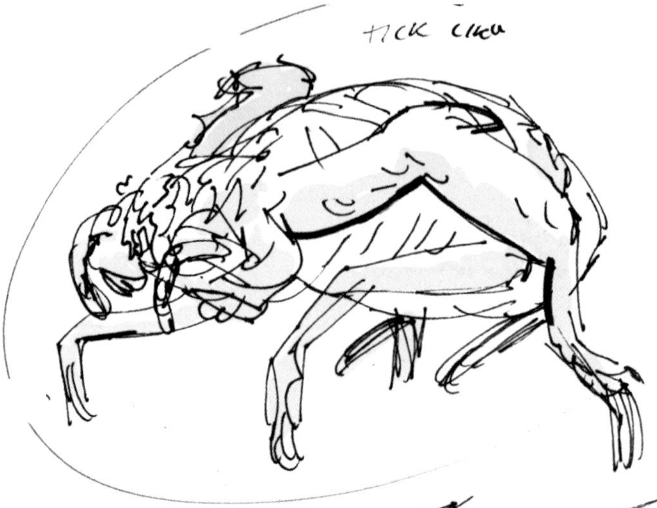

Next was a sort of tick-like creature that I thought would look fun wandering around the Canadian wilderness, but Mike thought this was still too similar to the other Ogdru Hem creatures we've seen through the series.

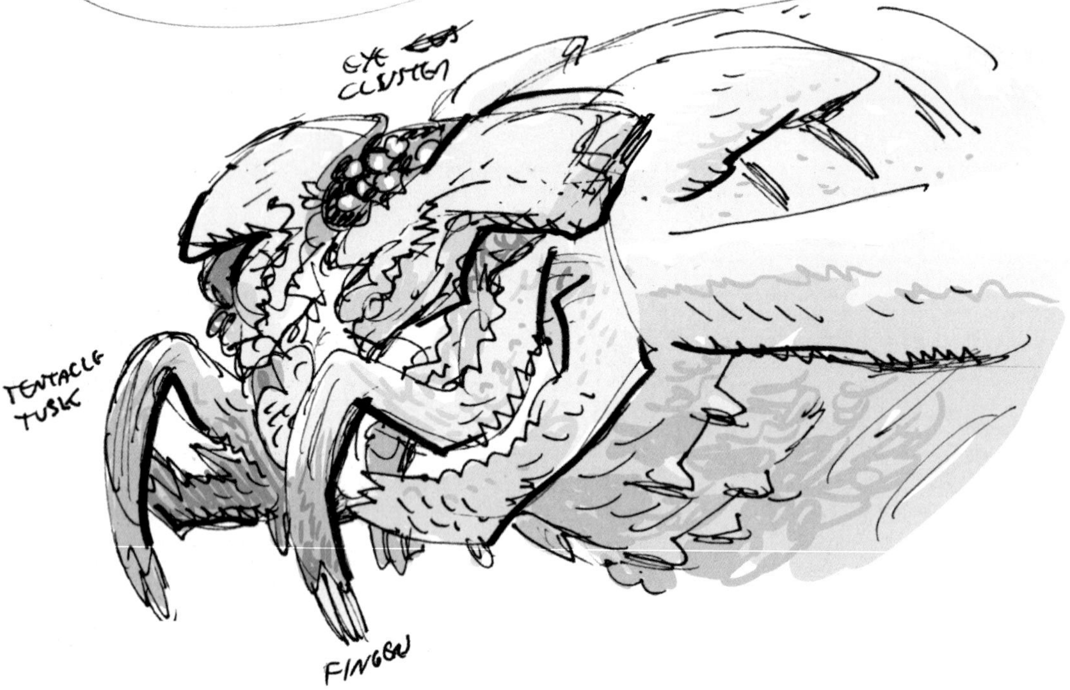
EYE CLUSTER
TENTACLE TUSK

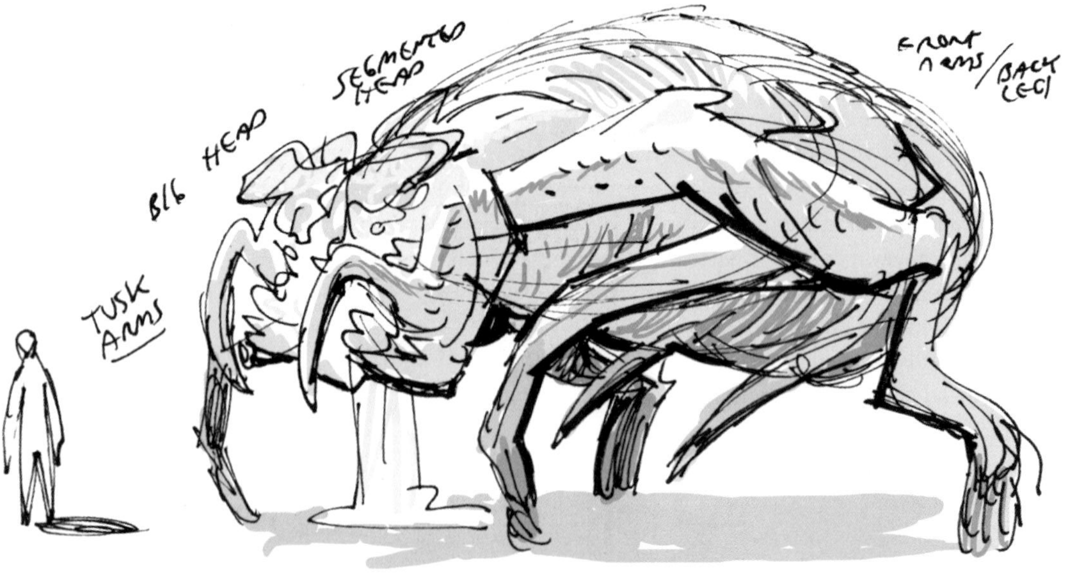
SEGMENTED HEAD
BIG HEAD
TUSK ARMS

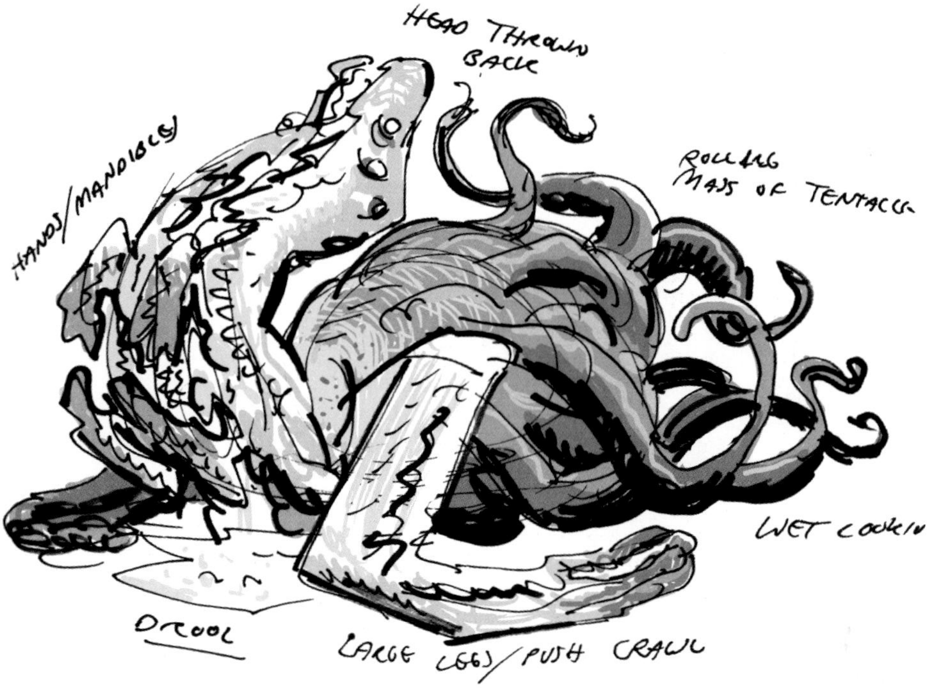
HEAD THROWN BACK
HANDS/MANDIBLES
ROLLING MASS OF TENTACLES
WET LOOKING
DROOL
LARGE LEGS/PUSH CRAWL

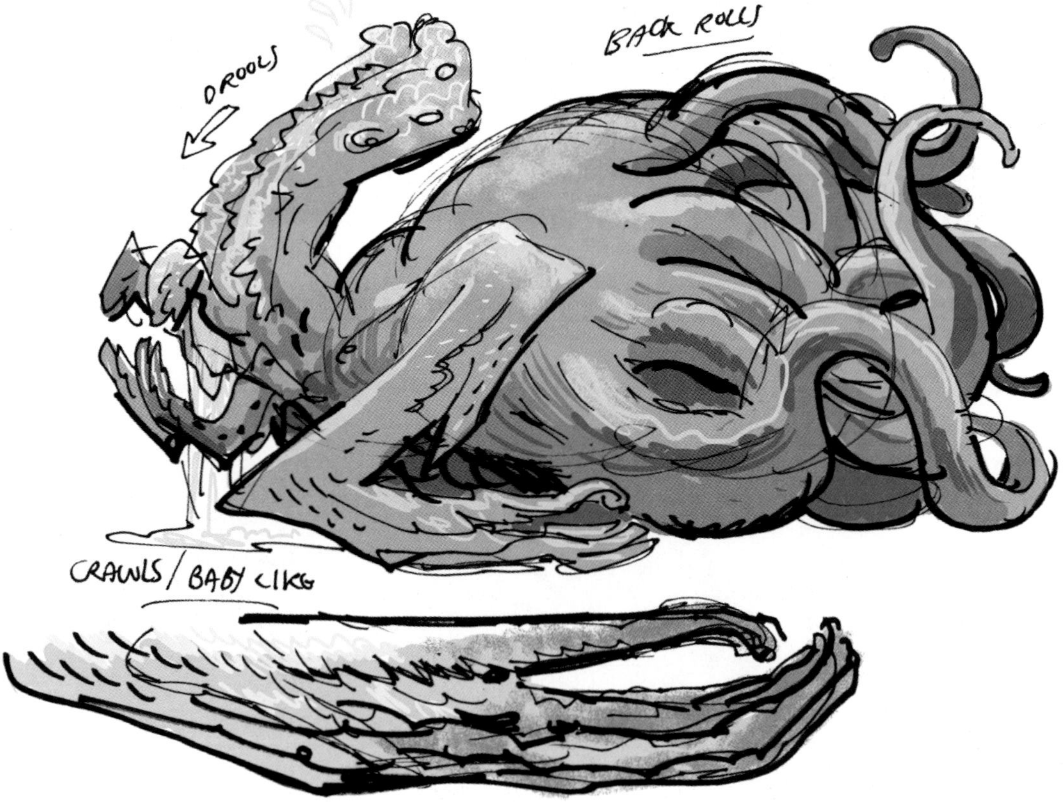
BACK ROLLS
DROOLS
CRAWLS/BABY LIKE

Time to add some tentacles! Mike and I liked the idea of it crawling along through the woods like some sort of infant (which it was) or larva. Almost there but not right yet . . .

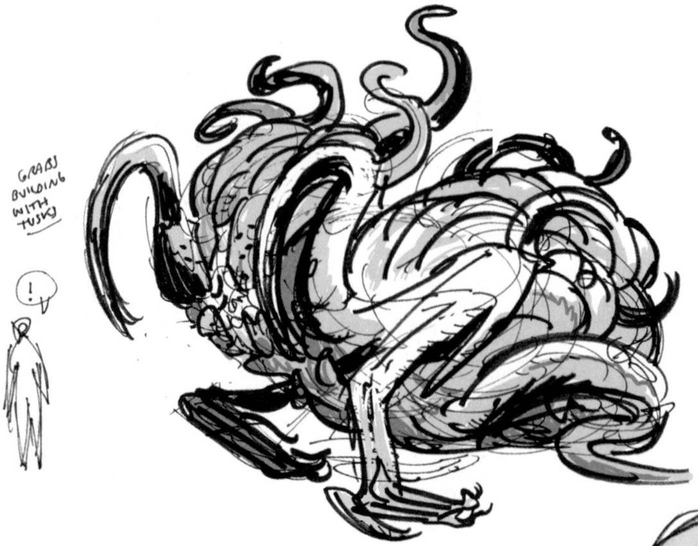
GRABS BUILDING WITH TUSKS
!

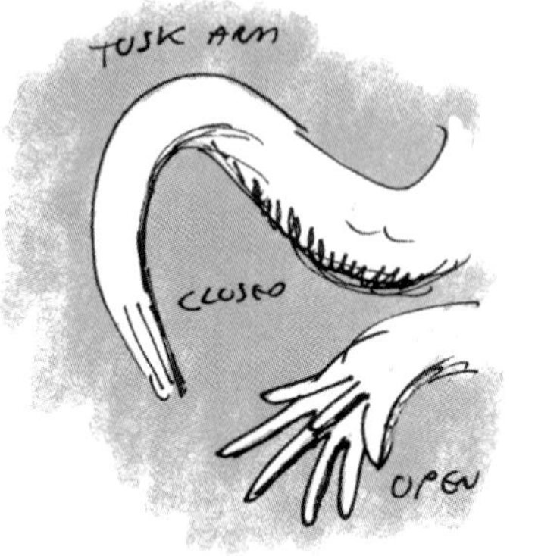
TUSK ARM
CLOSED
OPEN

With the final pass I kept the crawling arm and mass of tentacles but worked that up to the head design, too, so the tentacles were used as smaller arms and "holding" tusks around a hidden mouth of teeth. Mike liked this direction, and it made for a nice, spooky image as this mass rolled, whipped, and crawled through the woods!

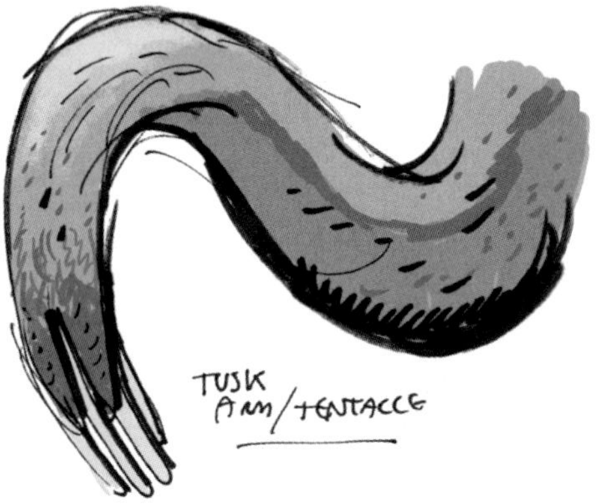
TUSK ARM/TENTACLE

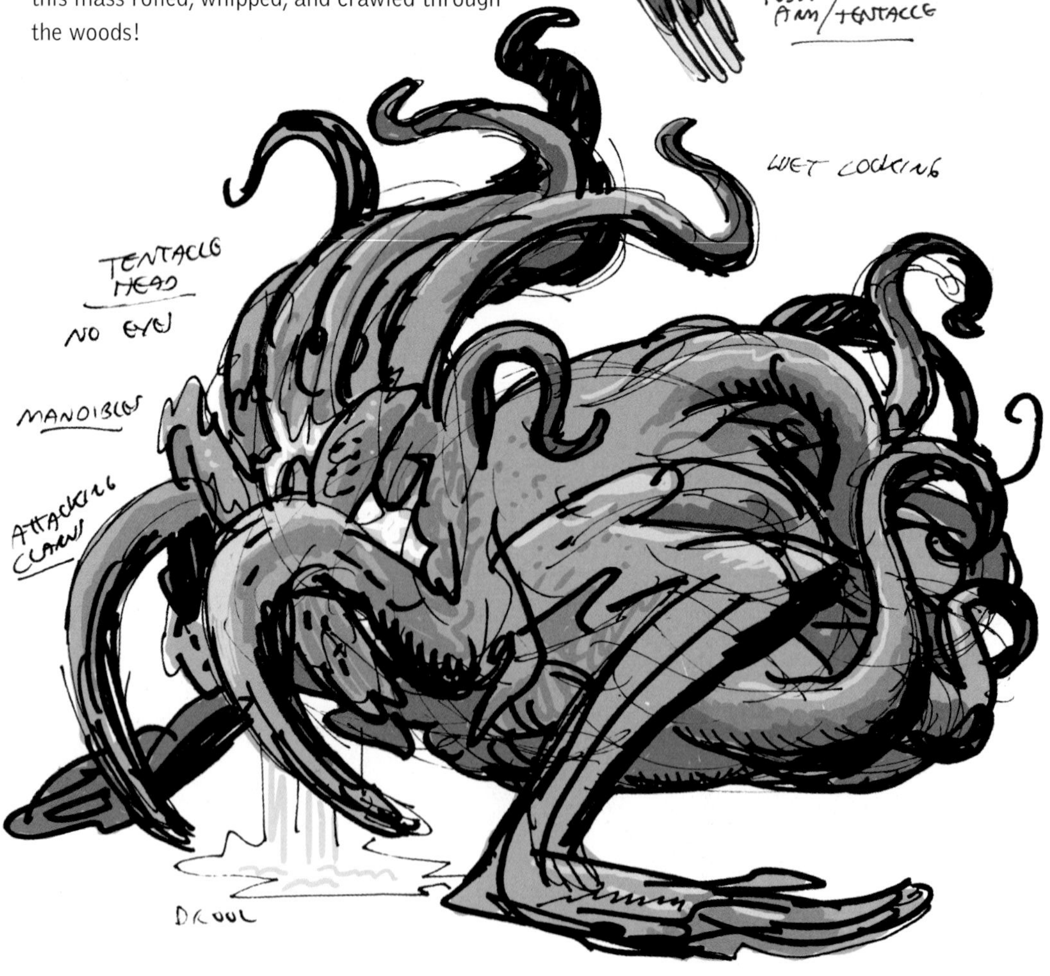
WET LOOKING
TENTACLE HEAD
NO EYES
MANDIBLES
ATTACKING CLAWS
DROOL

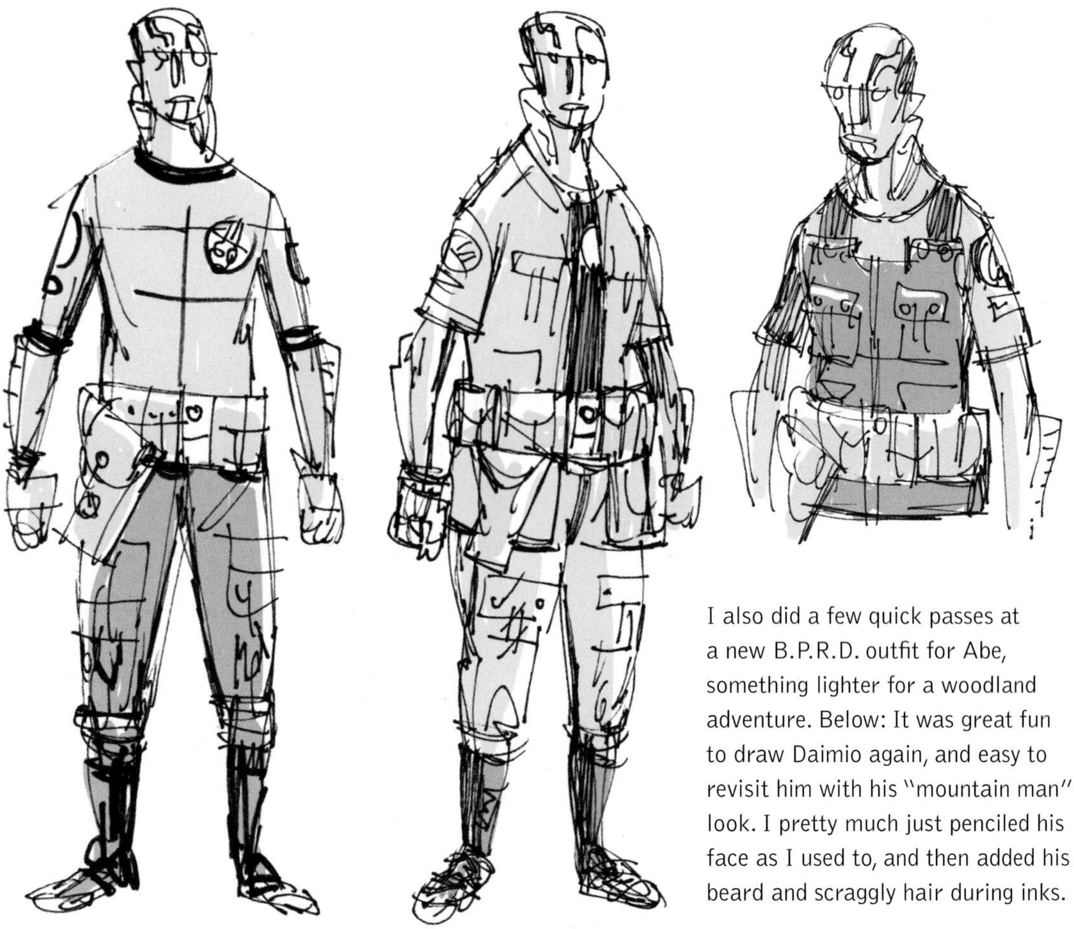

I also did a few quick passes at a new B.P.R.D. outfit for Abe, something lighter for a woodland adventure. Below: It was great fun to draw Daimio again, and easy to revisit him with his "mountain man" look. I pretty much just penciled his face as I used to, and then added his beard and scraggly hair during inks.

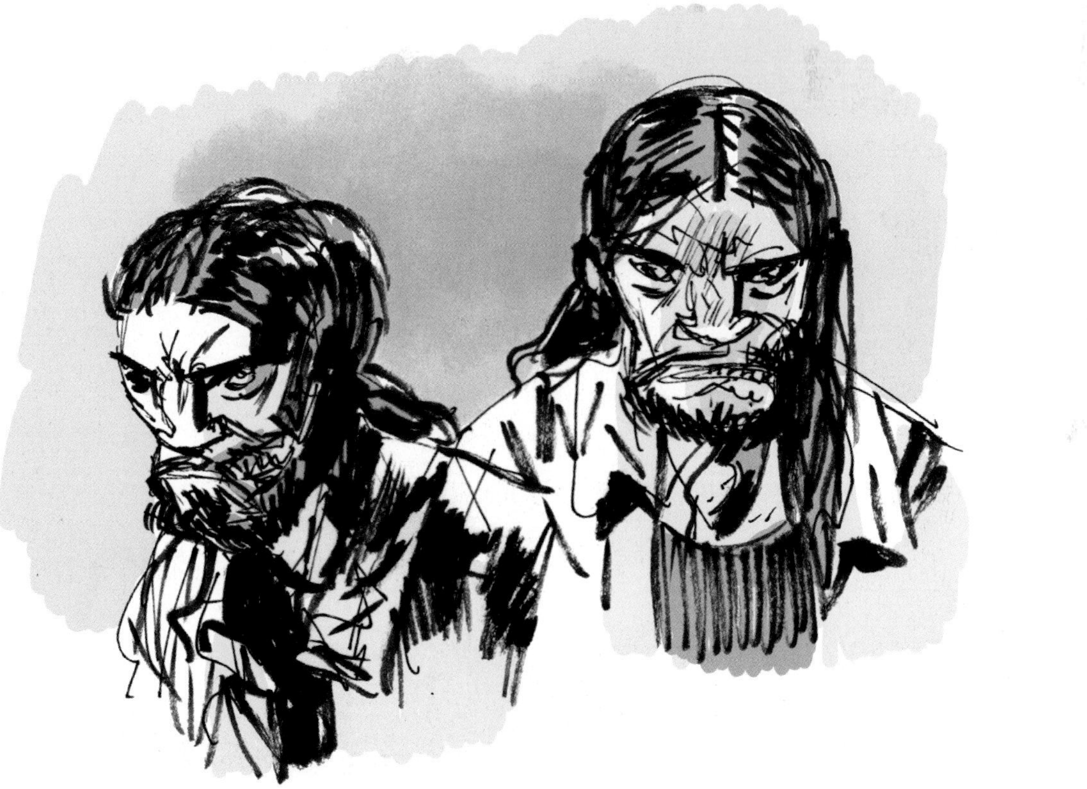

Along with Daimio, it was great to return to Daryl the wendigo for a bit. I wanted him to seem more feral and detached from his human side when we saw him again and tried to get that haunted feel in his stare.

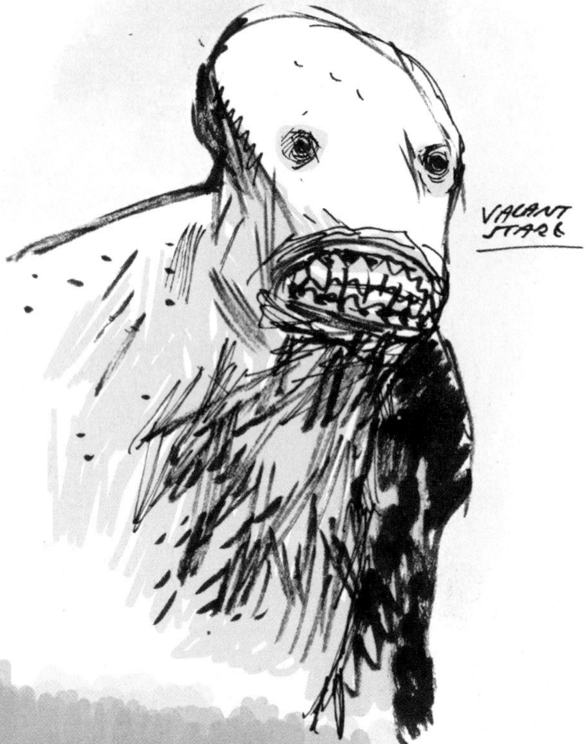
VACANT STARE

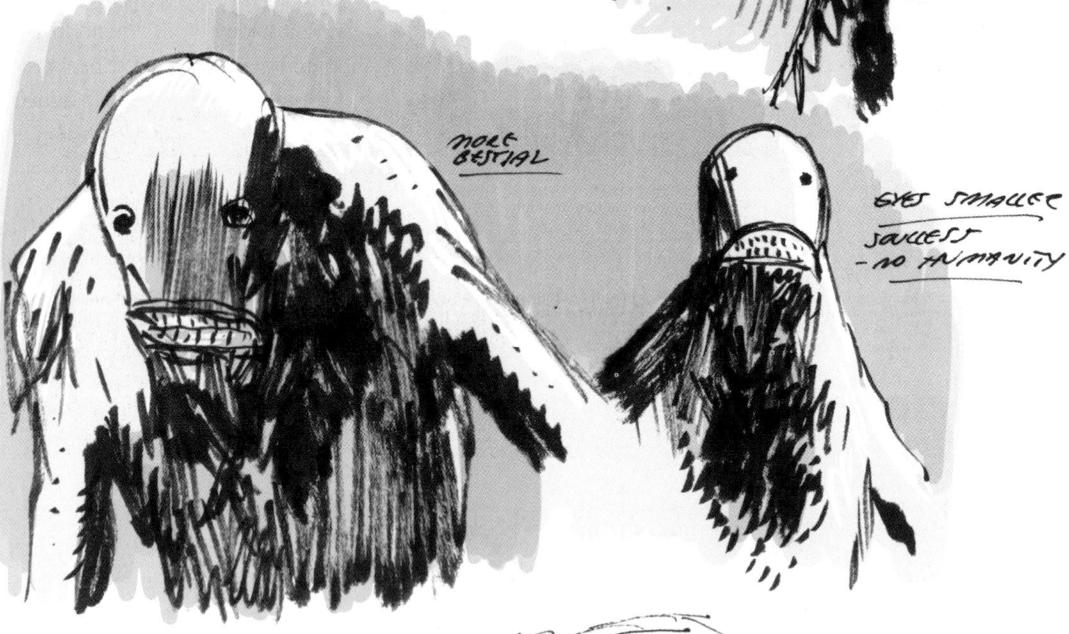
MORE BESTIAL
EYES SMALLER
SOULLESS
-NO HUMANITY

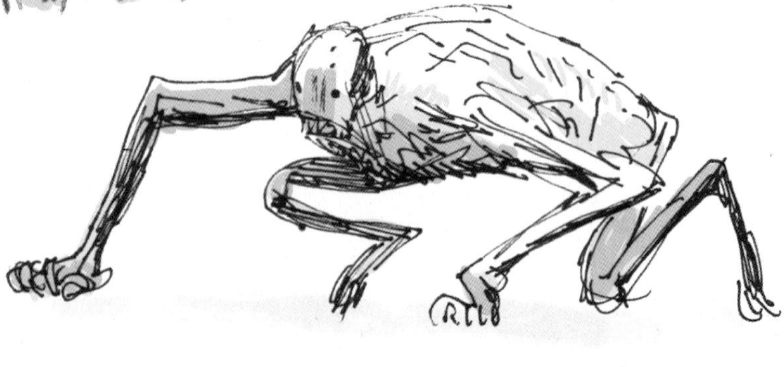

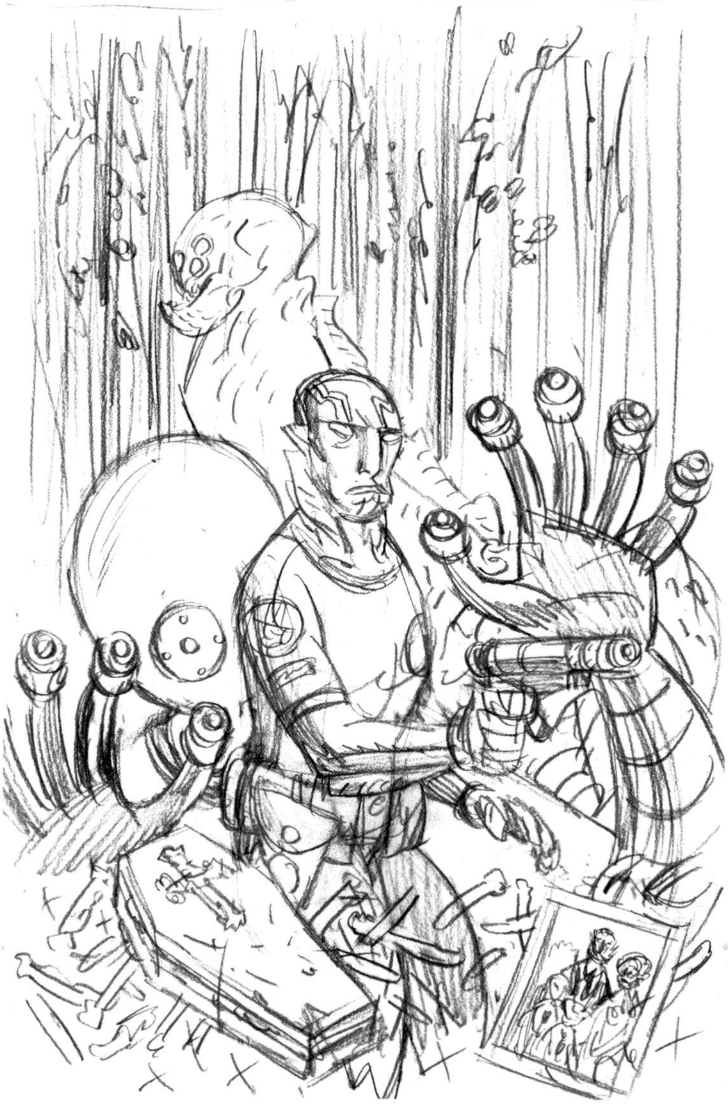

Left: The pencils to the first issue's cover, including the Salton Sea monster and the "gothic" coffin shape that didn't work and was changed for the final cover. Below: Some rough sketches for covers to *New World* #4 and #5 (we knew Daryl would have to get a cover spot for one of those!)

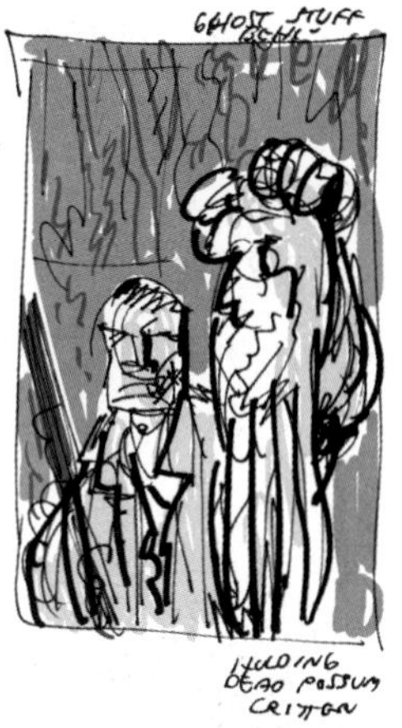
GHOST STUFF
HOLDING DEAD POSSUM CRITTER

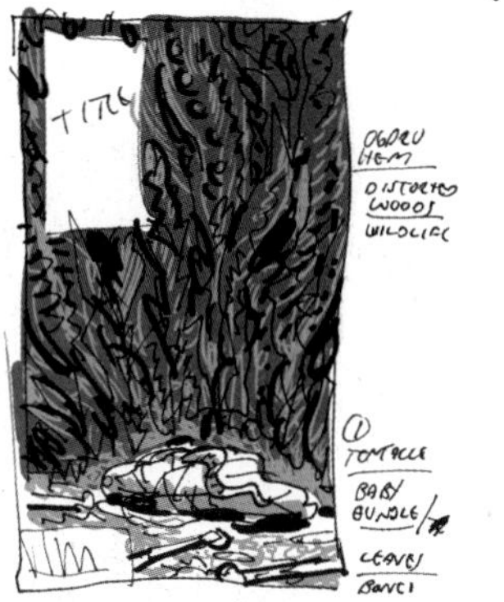
TITLE
DISTORTED WOODS
WILDLIFE
TENTACLE
BABY BUNDLE
LEAVES
BONES

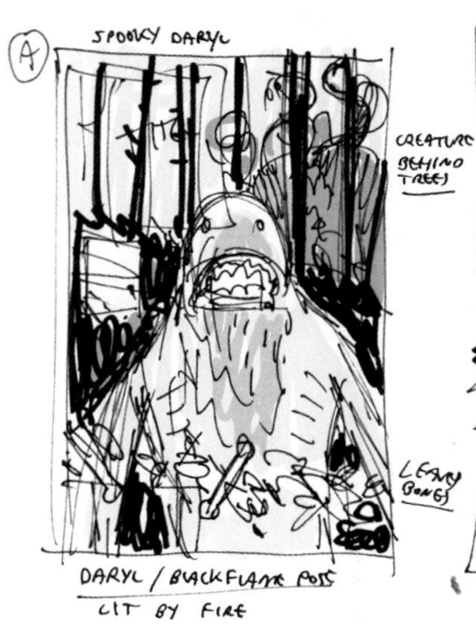
A
SPOOKY DARYL
CREATURE BEHIND TREES
LEAVES BONES
DARYL / BLACKFLAME POSS
LIT BY FIRE

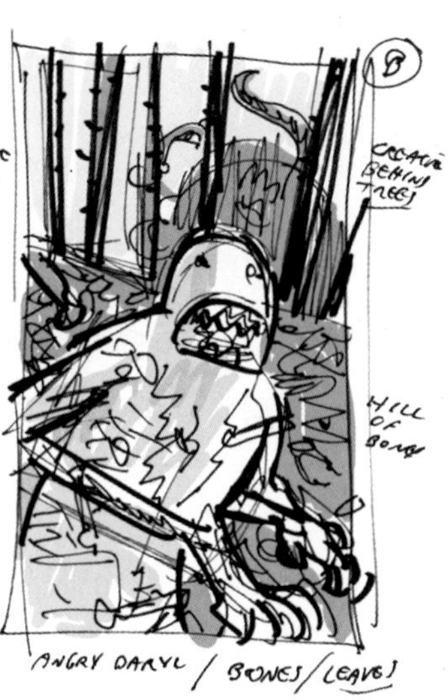
B
CREATURE BEHIND TREES
HILL OF BONES
ANGRY DARYL / BONES / LEAVES

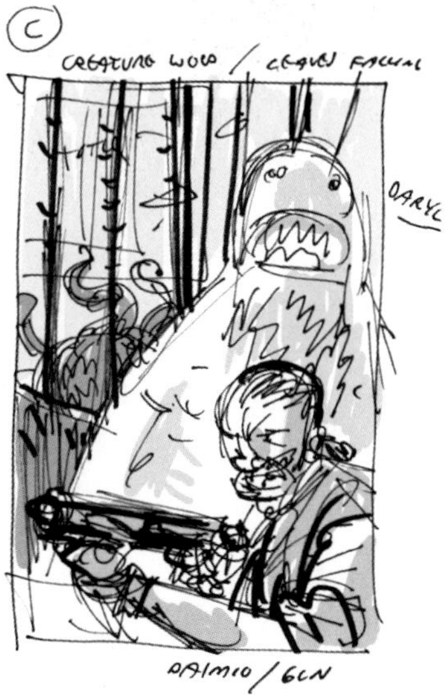
C
DARYL
DAIMIO / GUN

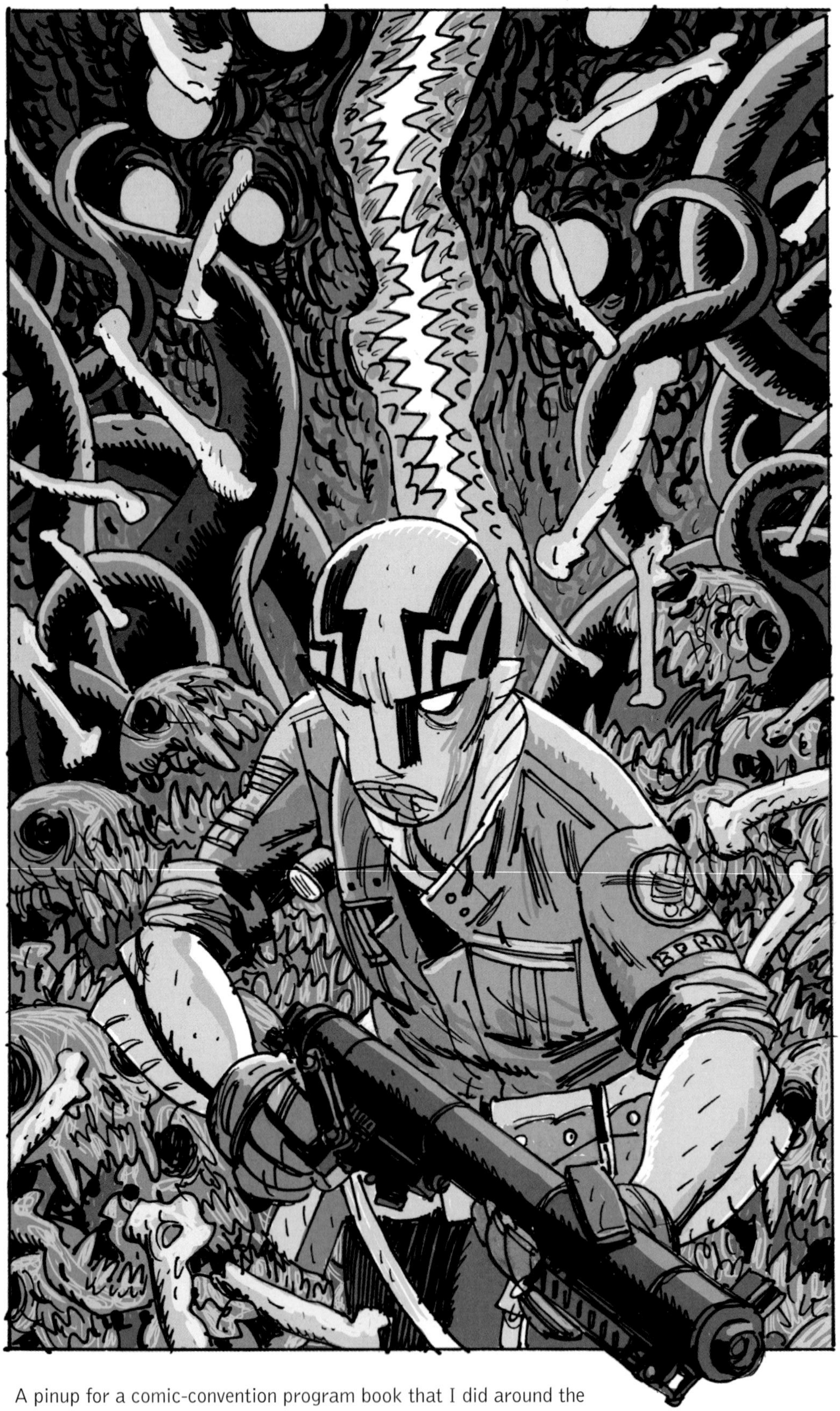
BPRD

A pinup for a comic-convention program book that I did around the time of the first issue with Abe in his woodland garb and an early look at the infant creature in the background before I settled on the final design.

GODS *and* MONSTERS

Notes by Katii O'Brien

Character sketches for Fenix.

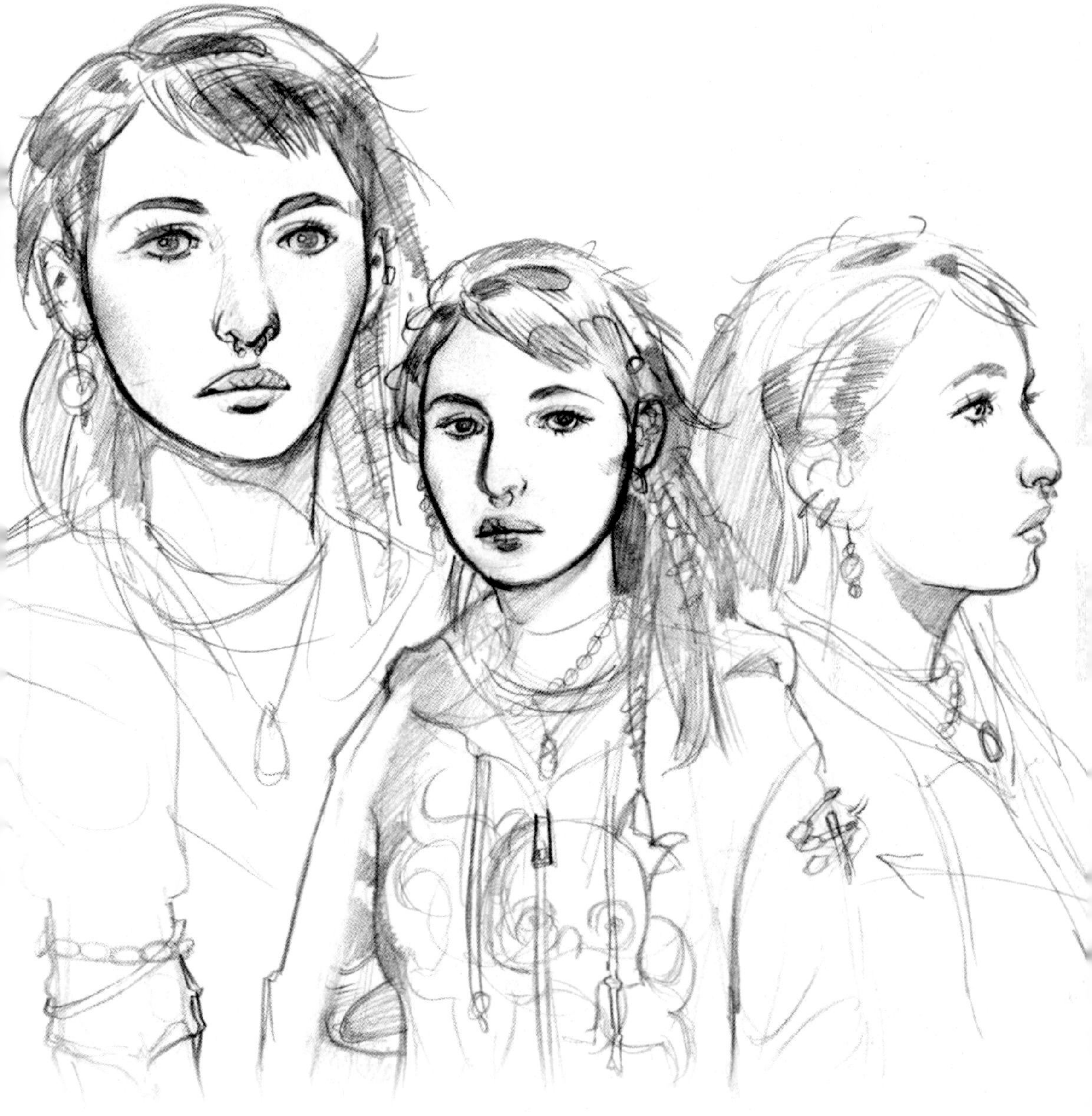

Symbol For Hyperborean Priest

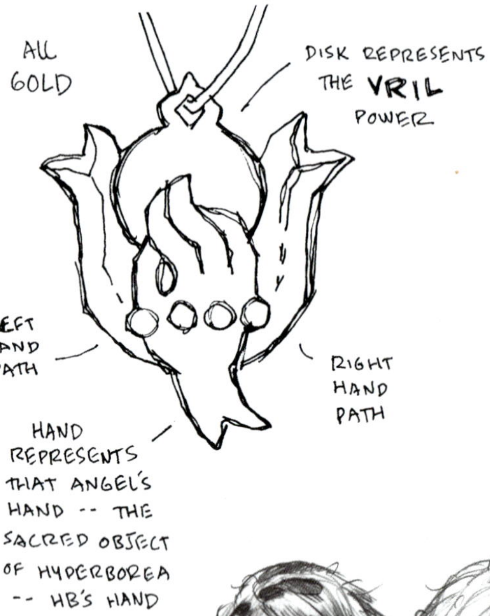
ALL GOLD
DISK REPRESENTS THE VRIL POWER
LEFT HAND PATH
RIGHT HAND PATH
HAND REPRESENTS THAT ANGEL'S HAND -- THE SACRED OBJECT OF HYPERBOREA -- HB'S HAND

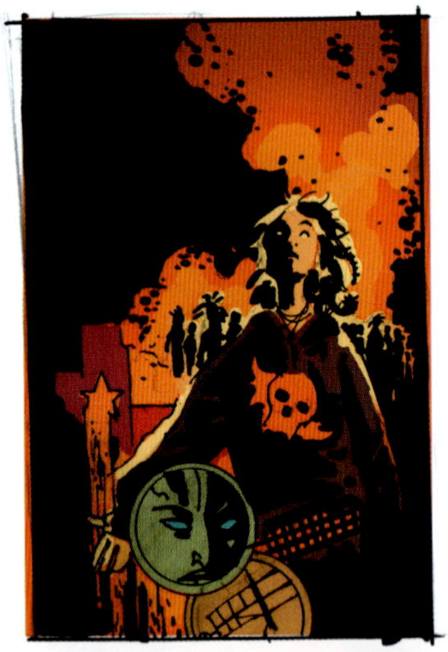

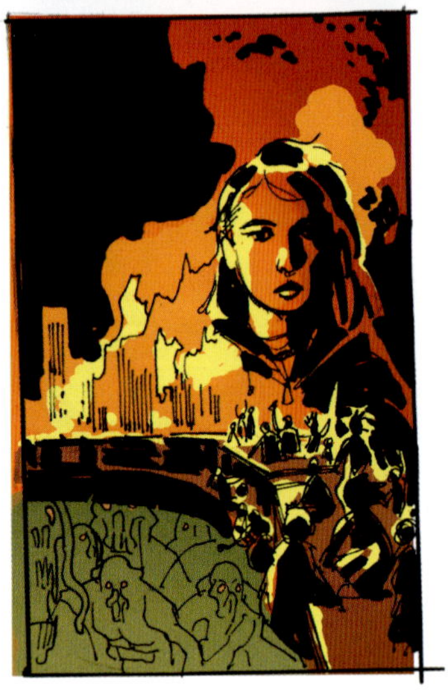

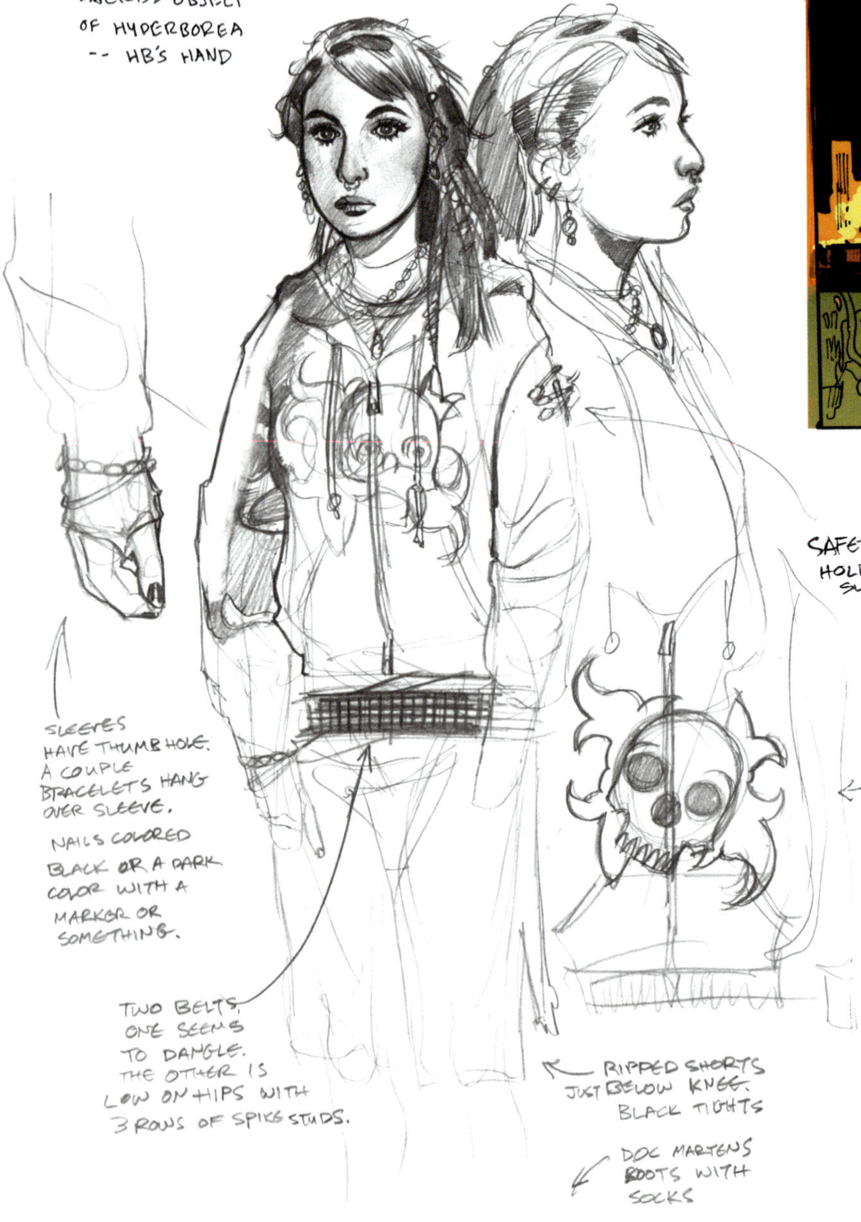
SAFETY PINS HOLD SWEATSHIRT SLEEVE TOGETHER.
SLEEVES HAVE THUMB HOLE. A COUPLE BRACELETS HANG OVER SLEEVE.
NAILS COLORED BLACK OR A DARK COLOR WITH A MARKER OR SOMETHING.
SWEAT SHIRT EMBLEM SOMETHING LIKE THIS. SKULL IS SPLIT BY ZIPPER.
TWO BELTS, ONE SEEMS TO DANGLE. THE OTHER IS LOW ON HIPS WITH 3 ROWS OF SPIKE STUDS.
RIPPED SHORTS JUST BELOW KNEE. BLACK TIGHTS
DOC MARTENS BOOTS WITH SOCKS

Facing, upper left: Mike's designs for the amulet.
Facing, top right: Ryan's sketches for the *Gods* #1 cover.

Facing, bottom and this page: Fenix studies.

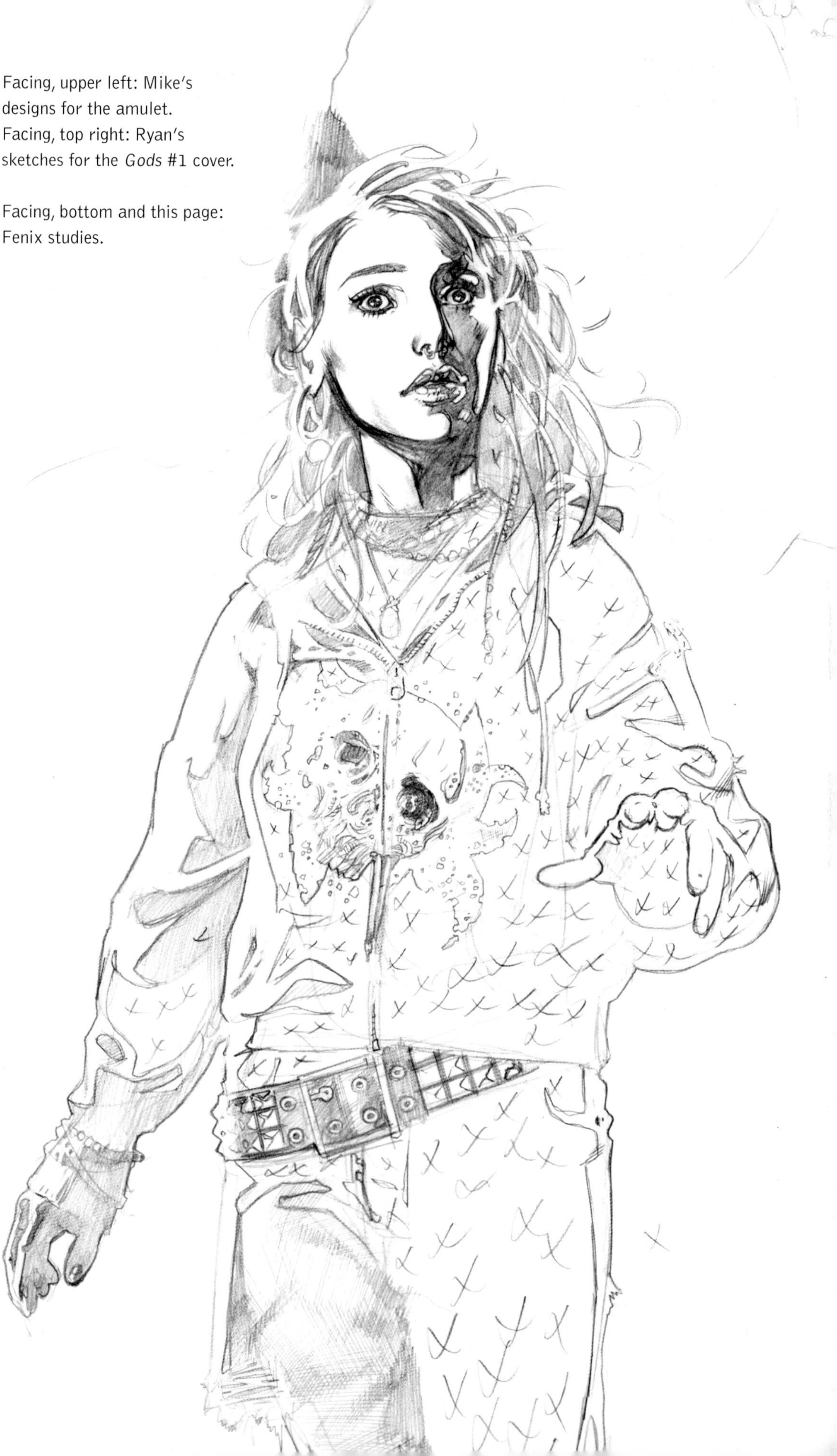

Process work for the *Gods* #1 variant cover. Line art by Guy, color by Dave, lettering by Clem.

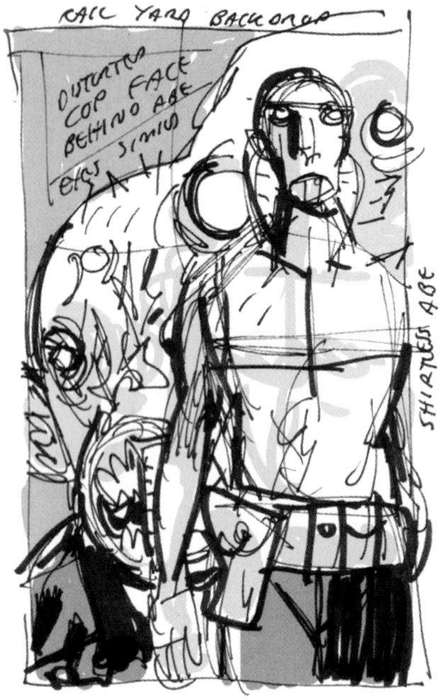
RAIL YARD BACKDROP
COP FACE
BEHIND ABE
SHIRTLESS ABE

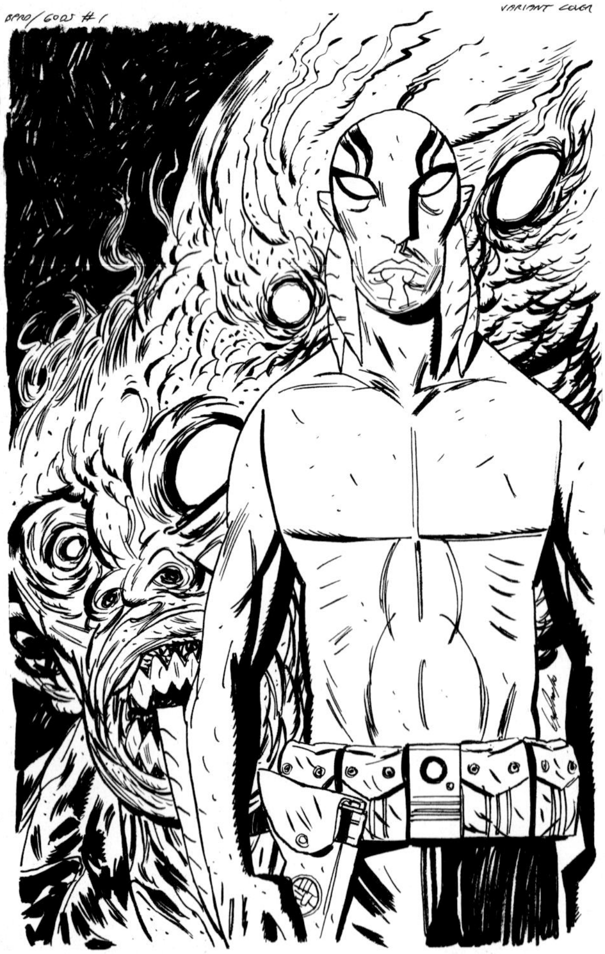
BPRD/GODS #1
VARIANT COVER

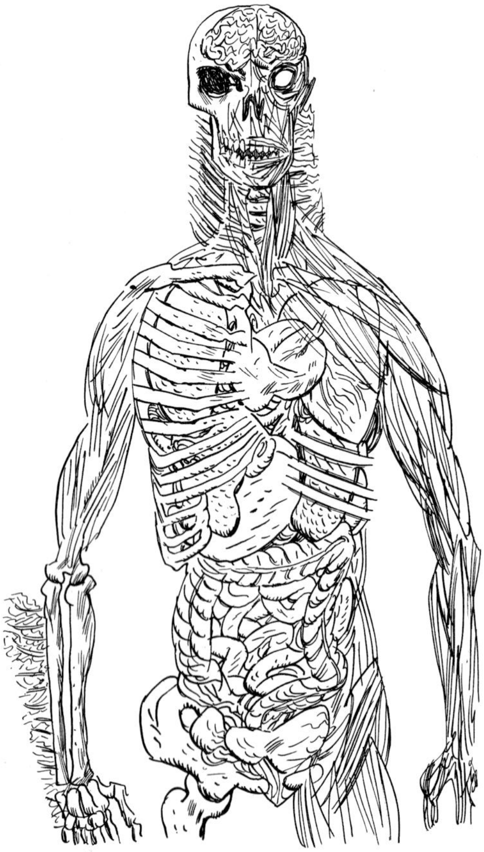

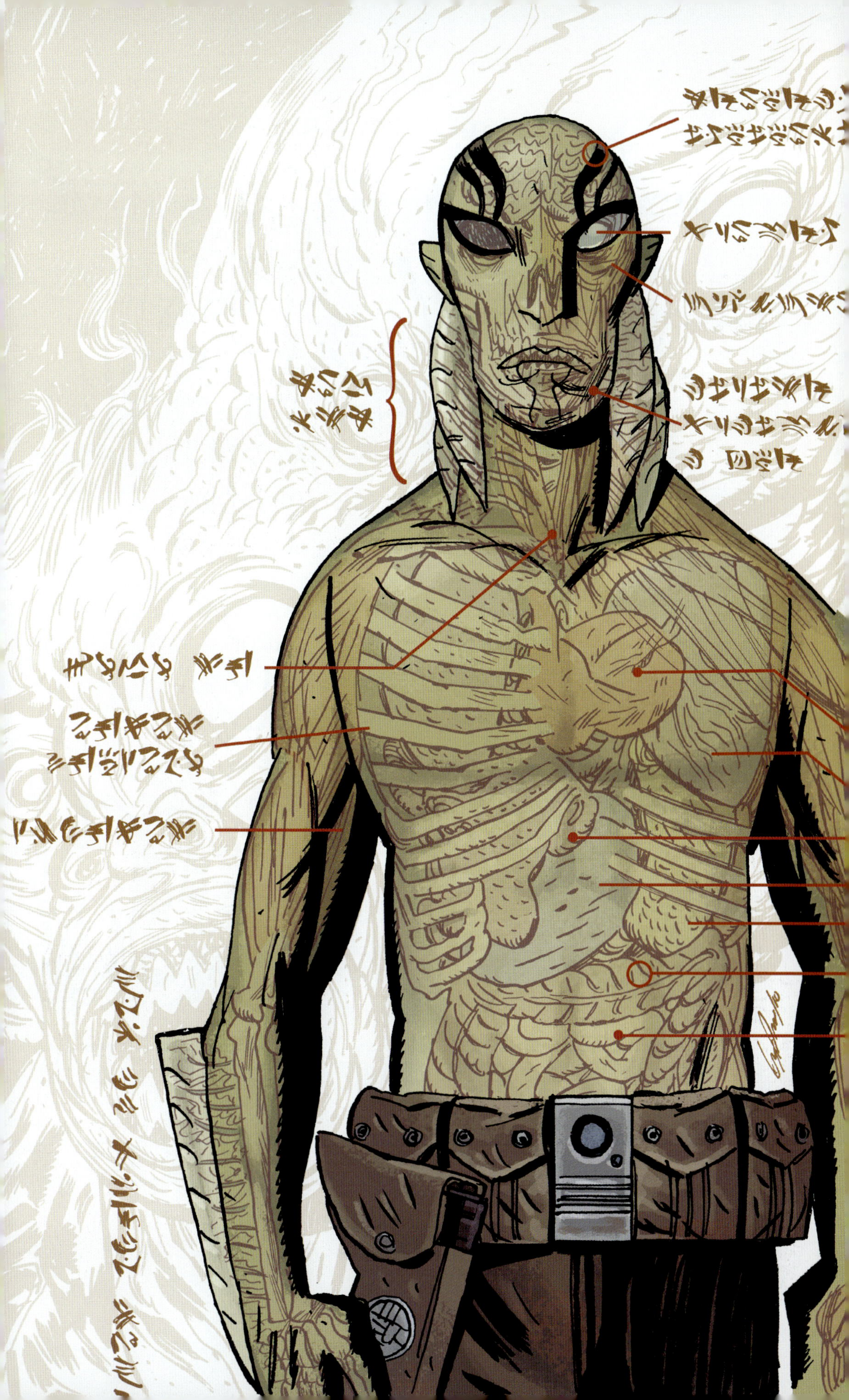

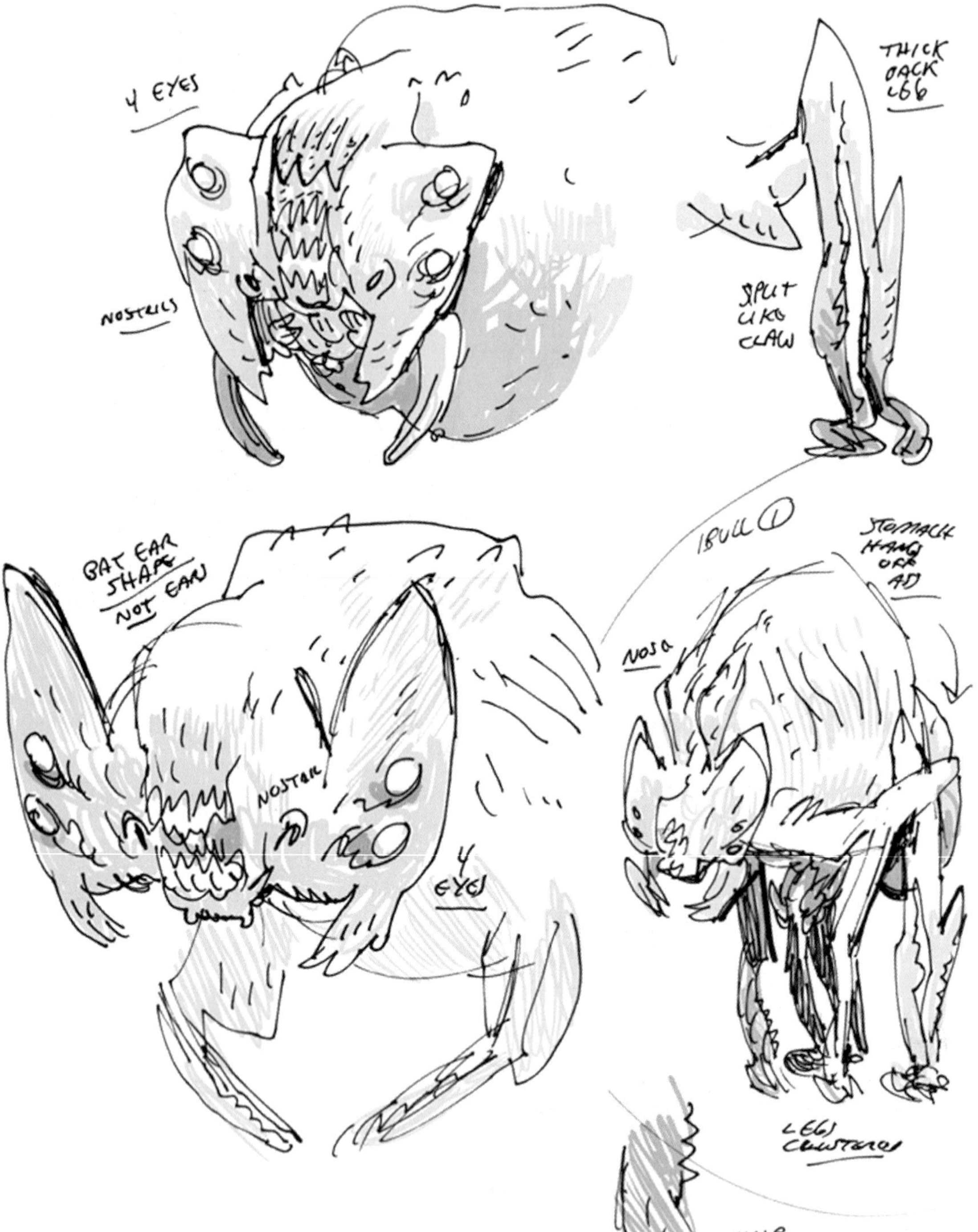
4 EYES
NOSTRILS
THICK BACK LEG
SPLIT LIKE CLAW
BAT EAR SHAPE NOT EAR
NOSTRIL
4 EYES
NOSE
LEGS CLUSTERED

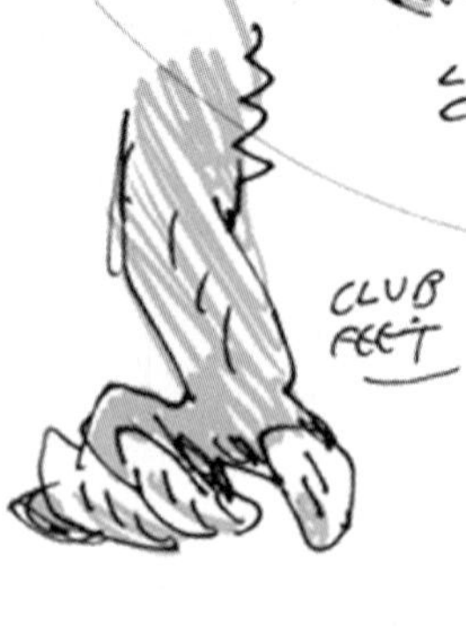
CLUB FEET

Some of Guy's monster designs.

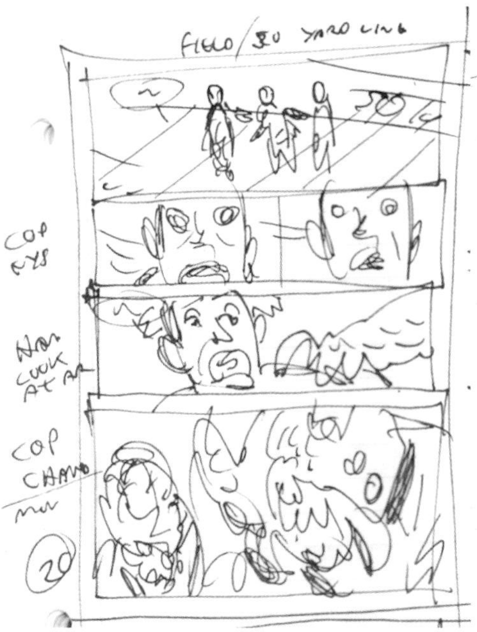

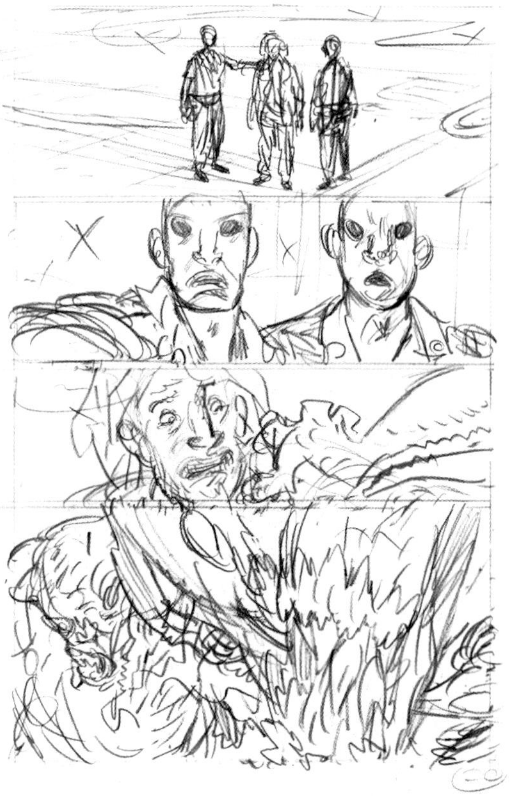

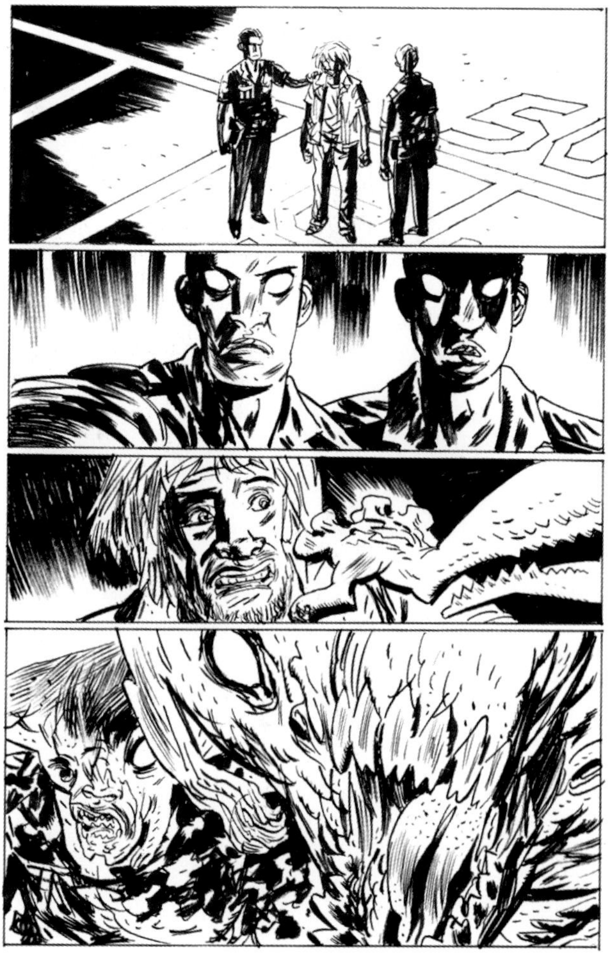

Guy's layouts, pencils, and inks for a page of *Gods* #1.

Ryan's process work for the *Monsters* #1 cover.

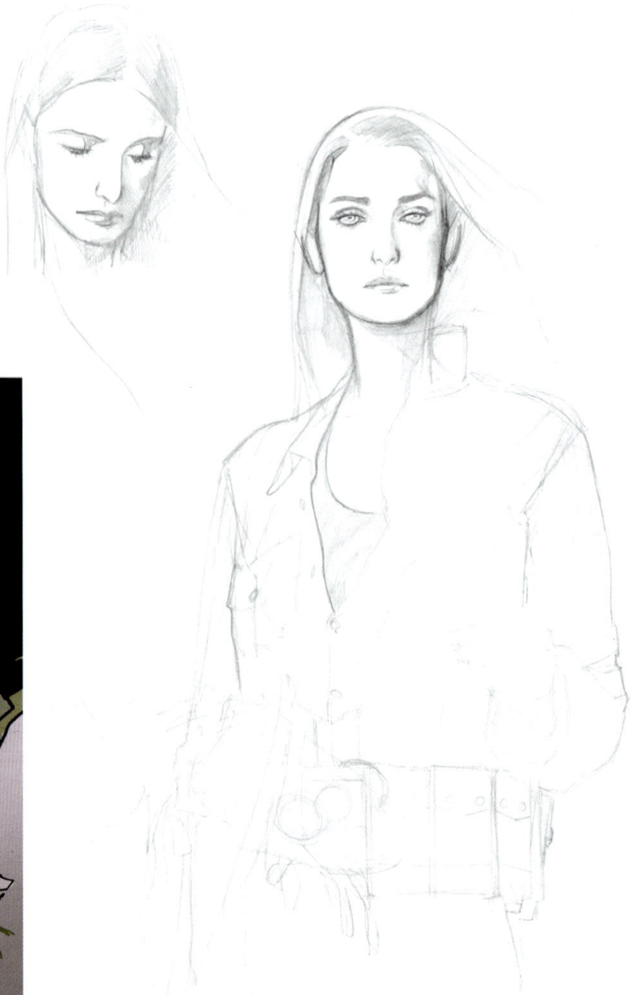

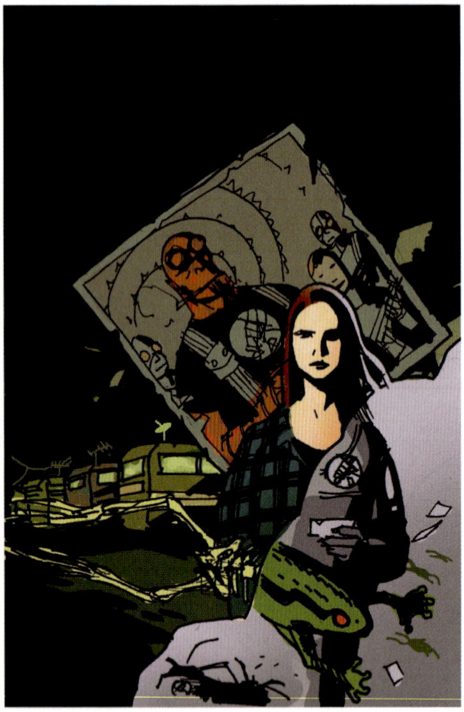

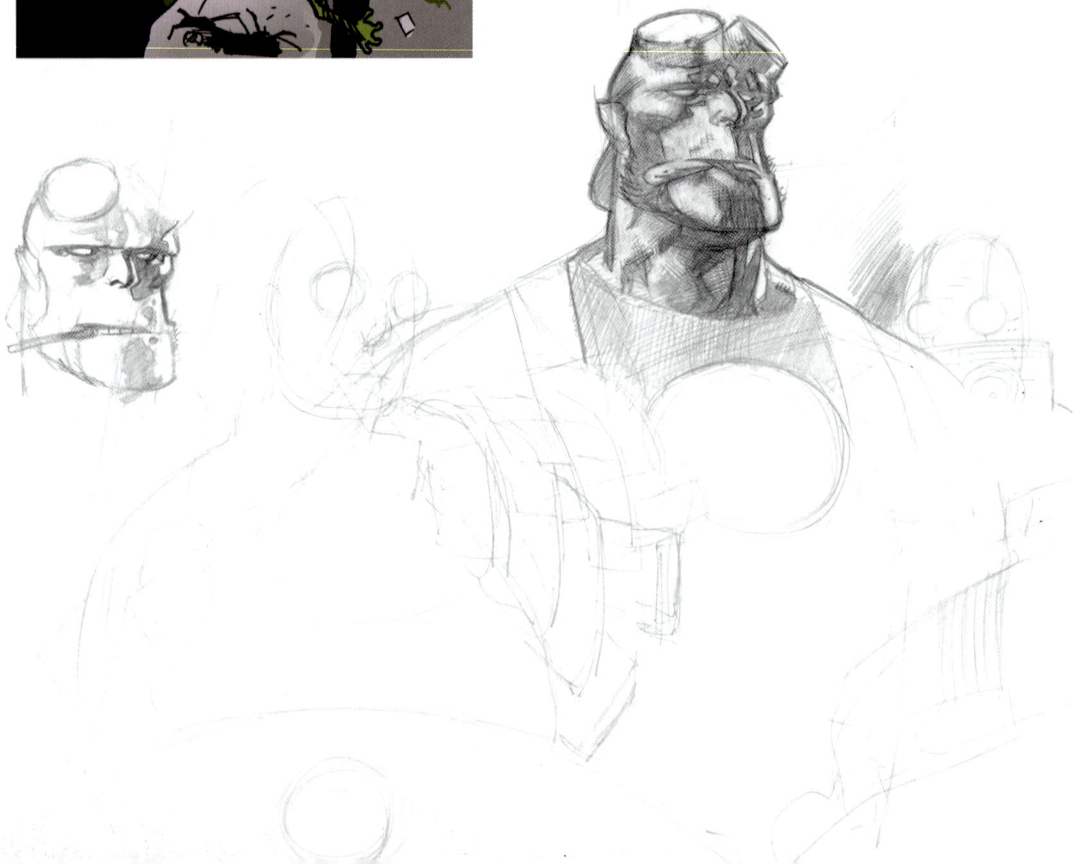

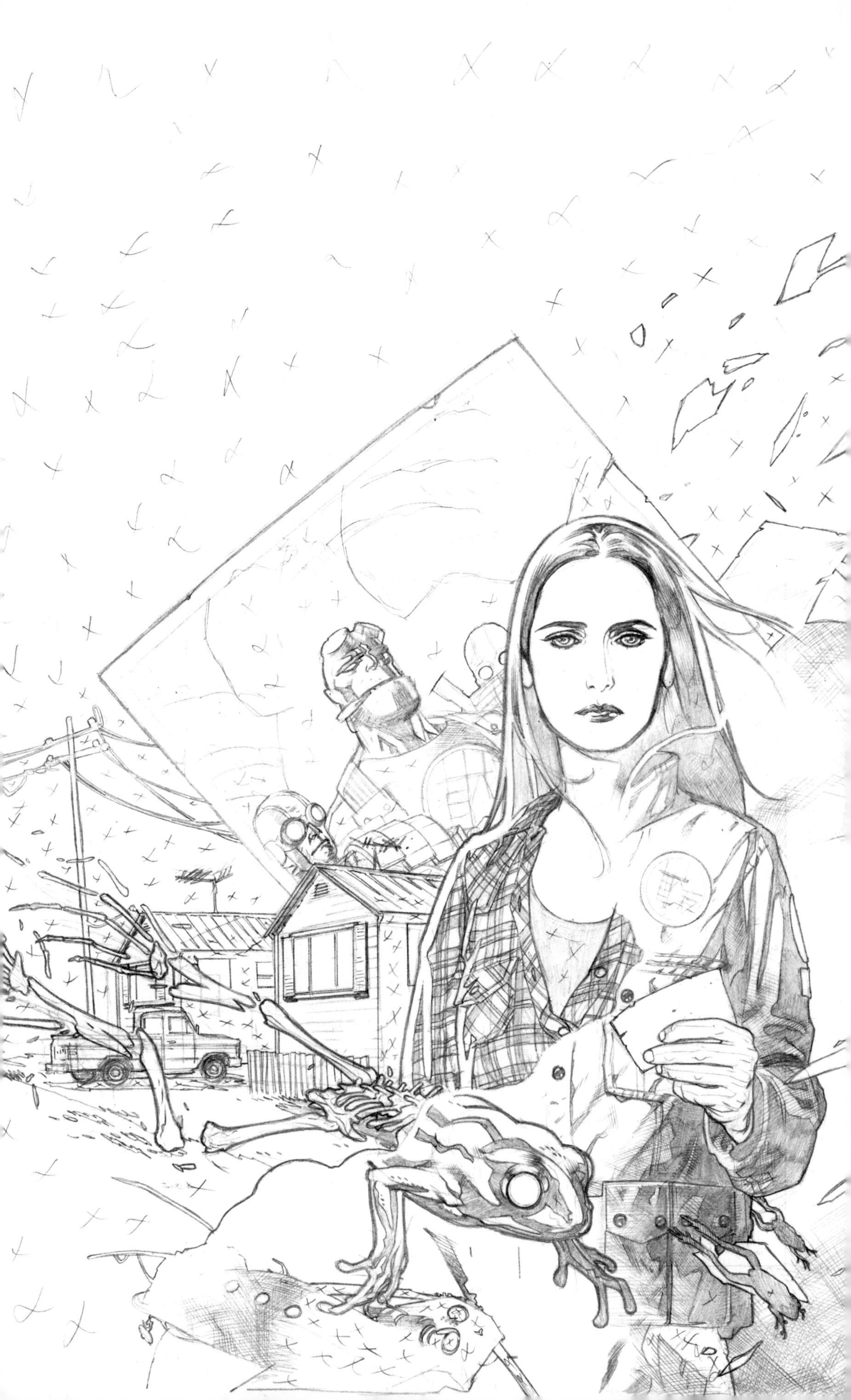

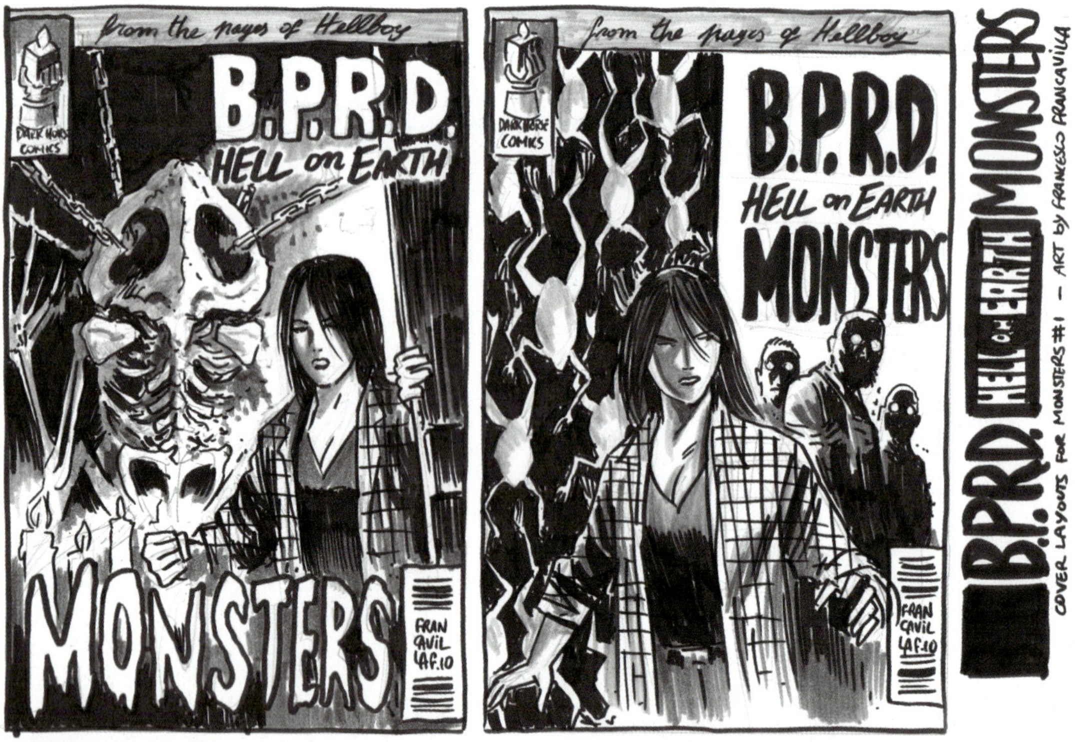

from the pages of Hellboy
DARK HORSE COMICS
B.P.R.D.
HELL on EARTH
MONSTERS
FRAN CAVIL LA F.10
from the pages of Hellboy
DARK HORSE COMICS
B.P.R.D.
HELL on EARTH
MONSTERS
FRAN CAVIL LA F.10
B.P.R.D. HELL ON EARTH MONSTERS
COVER LAYOUTS FOR MONSTERS #1 — ART by FRANCESCO FRANCAVILLA

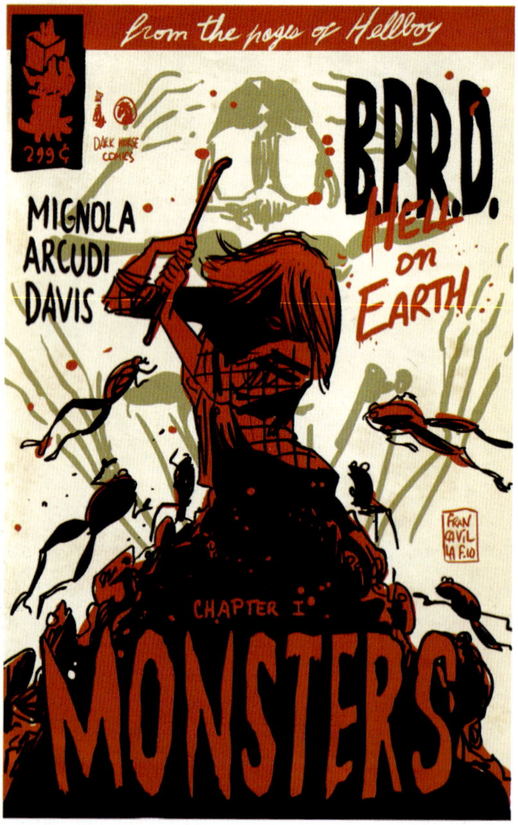

from the pages of Hellboy
2.99 ¢
DARK HORSE COMICS
B.P.R.D.
HELL on EARTH
MIGNOLA
ARCUDI
DAVIS
FRAN CAVIL LA F.10
CHAPTER I
MONSTERS

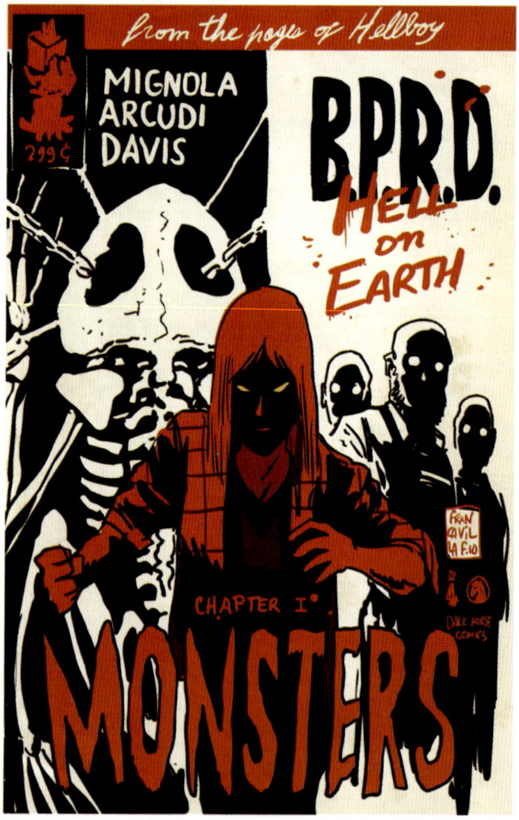

from the pages of Hellboy
2.99 ¢
MIGNOLA
ARCUDI
DAVIS
B.P.R.D.
HELL on EARTH
FRAN CAVIL LA F.10
DARK HORSE COMICS
CHAPTER I
MONSTERS

Francesco Francavilla's process work for his variant to *Monsters* #1 (above) and the final cover (facing).

from the pages of Hellboy
MIGNOLA
ARCUDI
CROOK
350¢
FRAN
CAVIL
LAF.10
B.P.R.D.
HELL on EARTH
A DARK HORSE COMICS
PRODUCTION
MONSTERS
1 OF 2

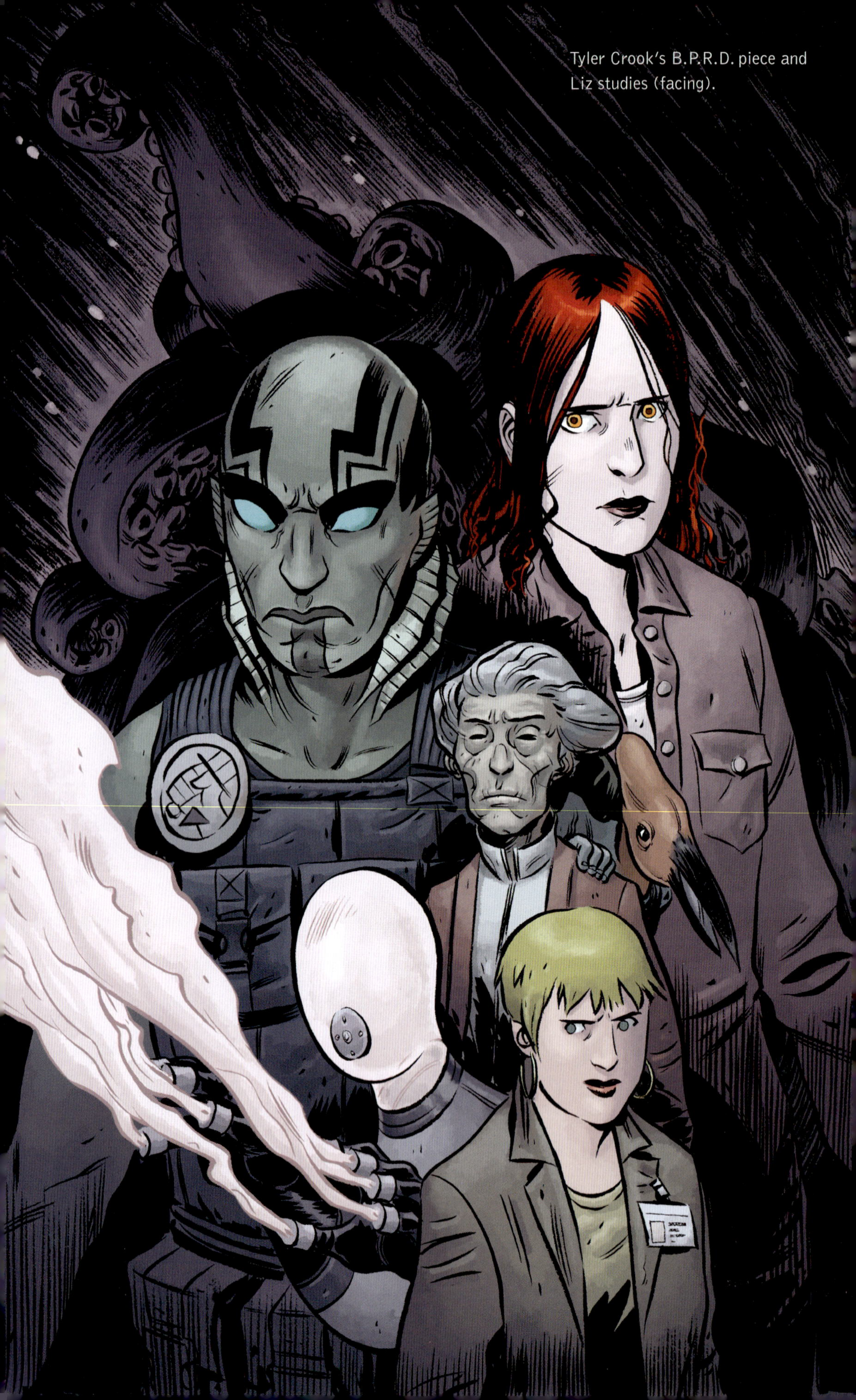

Tyler Crook's B.P.R.D. piece and Liz studies (facing).

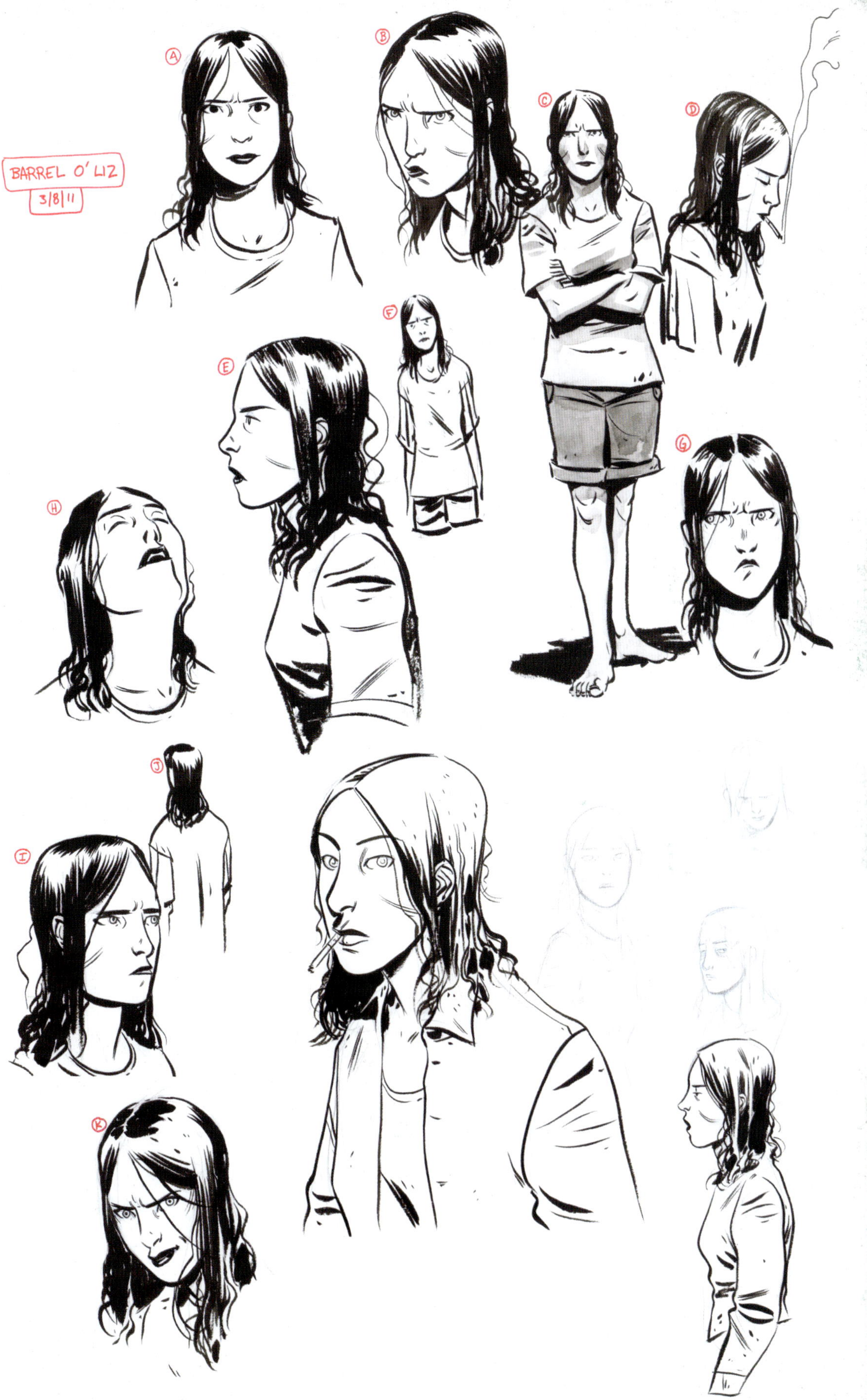
BARREL O' LIZ
3/8/11
A
B
C
D
E
F
G
H
I
J
K

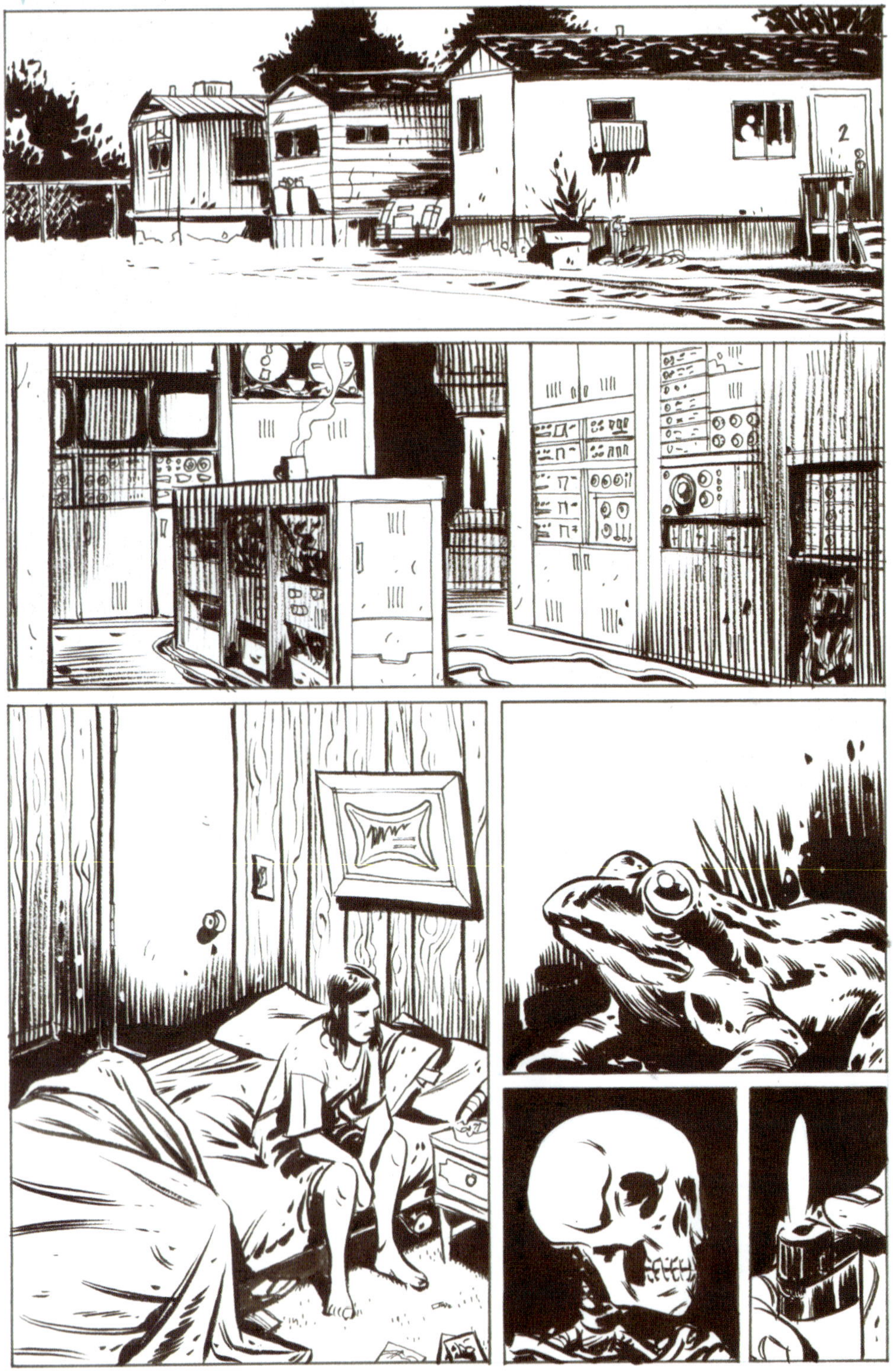
2

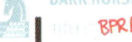

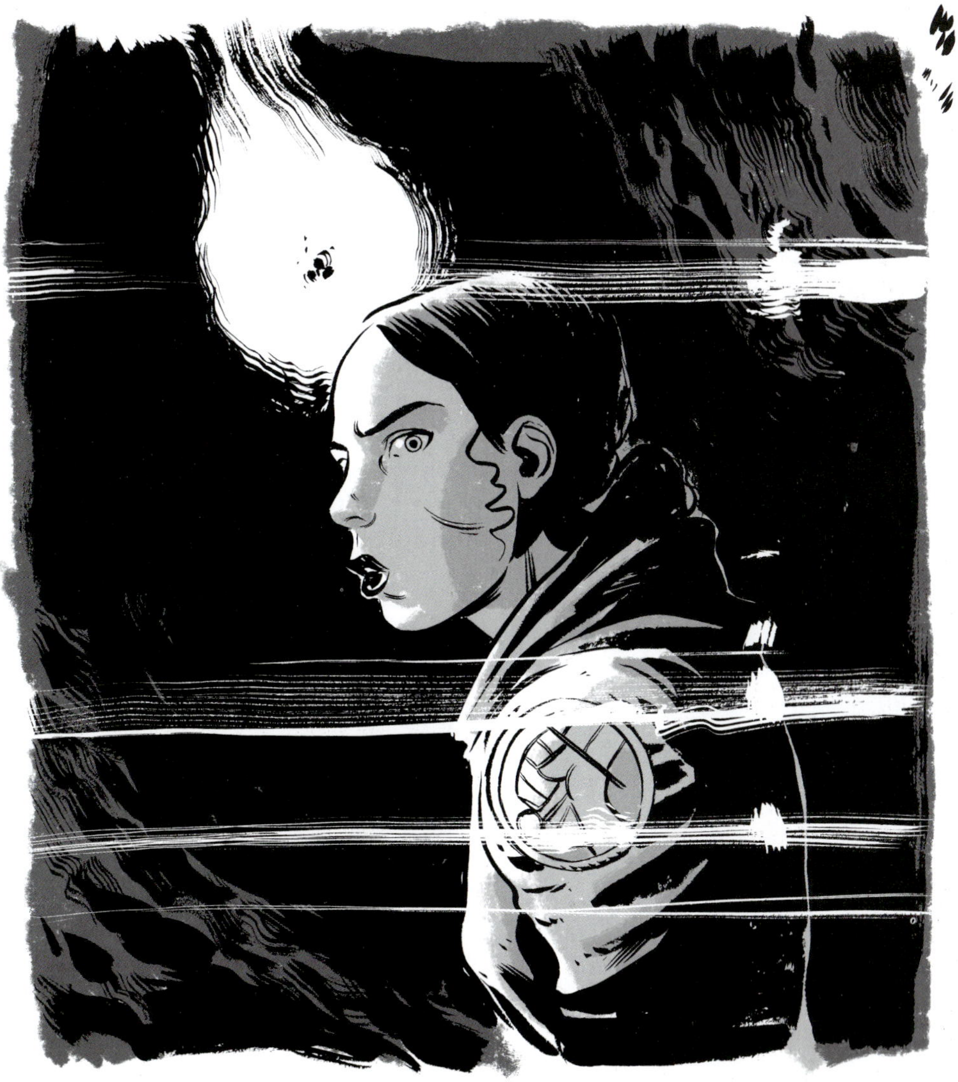

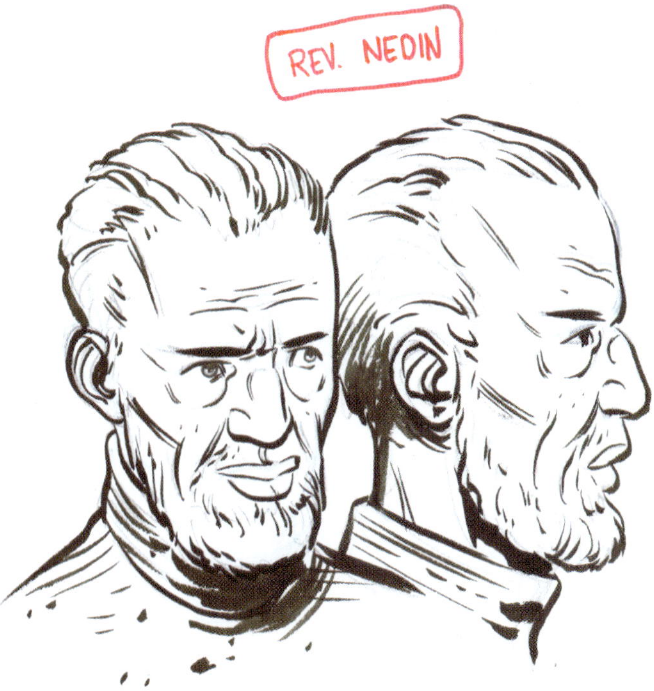
REV. NEDIN

Above: Tyler's art for the inside front covers of the *Monsters* issues.

Facing: A warmup piece.

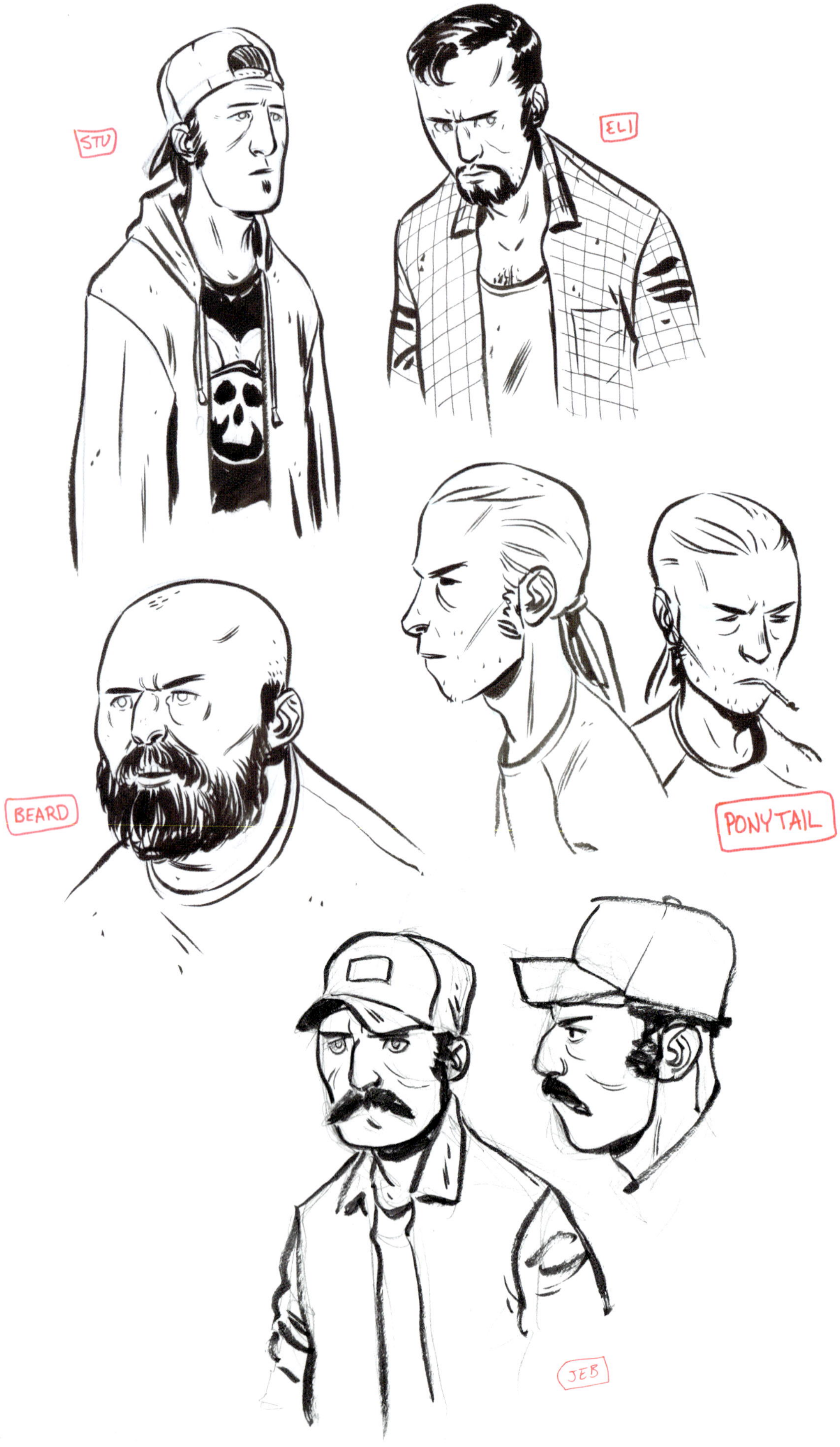
STU
ELI
BEARD
PONYTAIL
JEB

TALL GUY
V. 1
4/12/11
NASCAR
MEETS
METALLICA
HOODIE WITH
ADDED SKIRT
FROG
WRITING
I DON'T
KNOW IF
THE CIRCLE
PART IS
IMPORTANT
EMBLEM
IF YOU ROTATE THIS
90° CLOCK-WISE IT IS
A RUNE THAT MEANS
"CLEANSING FIRE"
I ADDED THE DOTS
FOR FUN

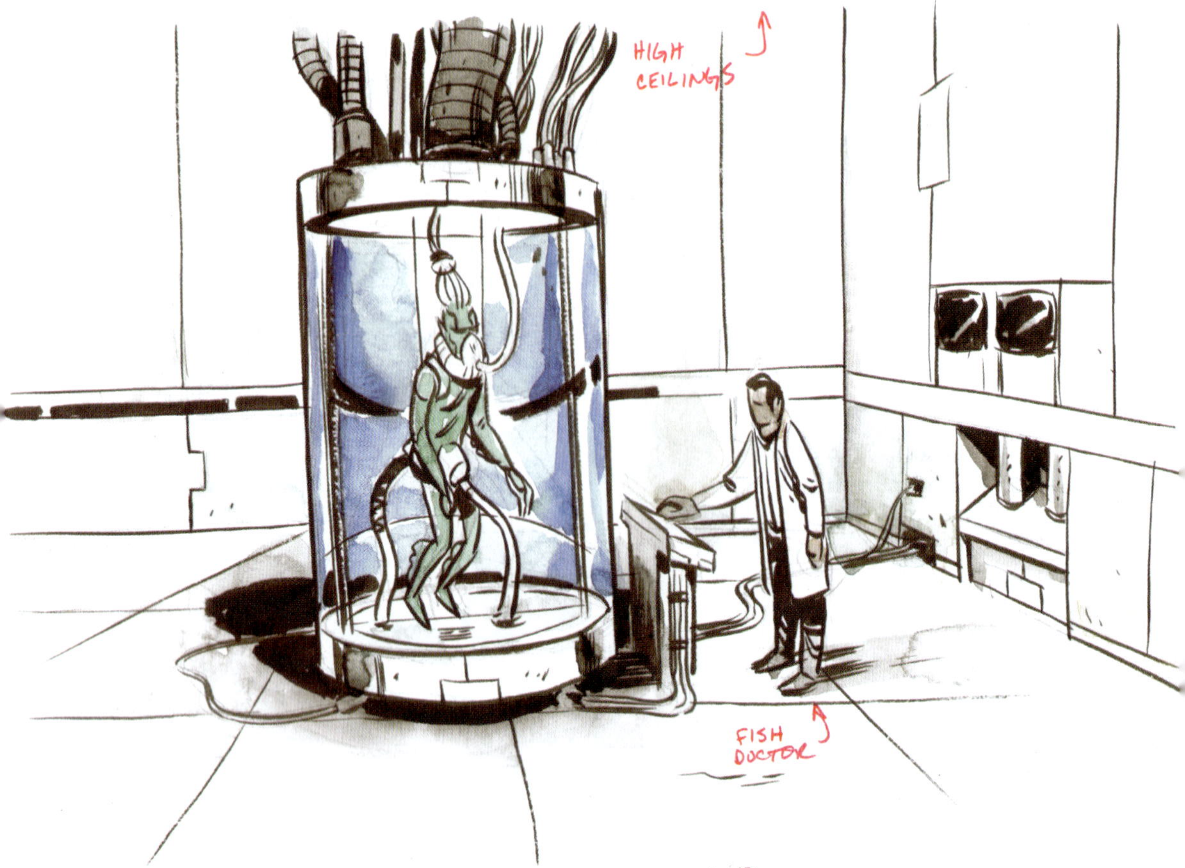
HIGH CEILINGS
FISH DOCTOR

POOR ABE V. 1 4/12/11

A lot of work went into designing Abe's tank, making sure Tyler's tech synced up with how Guy designed Bureau settings, and also making sure it all would work with scenes planned for upcoming issues.

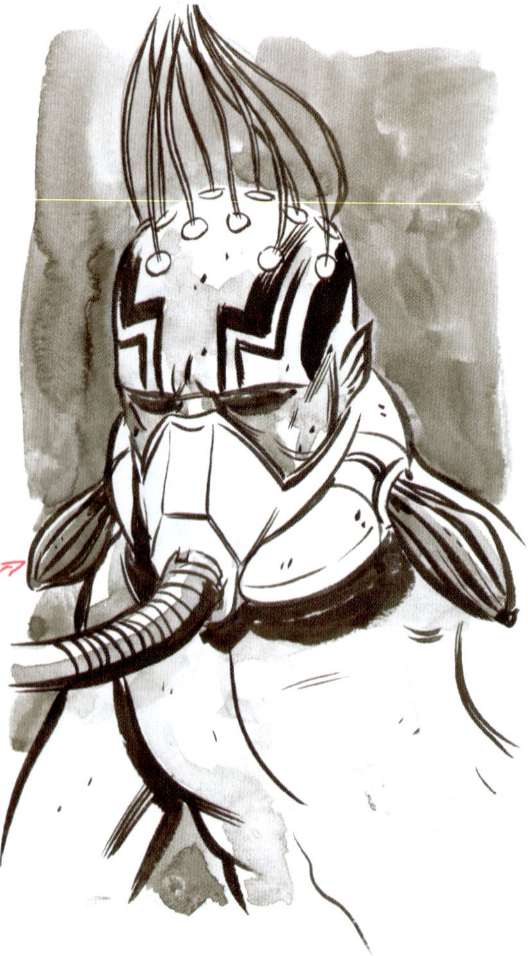
THESE LITTLE BAGS WOULD INFLATE IF HE WAS BREATHING.

ABE'S BREATHING THING V.2
OUTSIDE TANK
AREA AROUND BANDAGE SHOULD BE BRUISED
PEE + POO

47/12

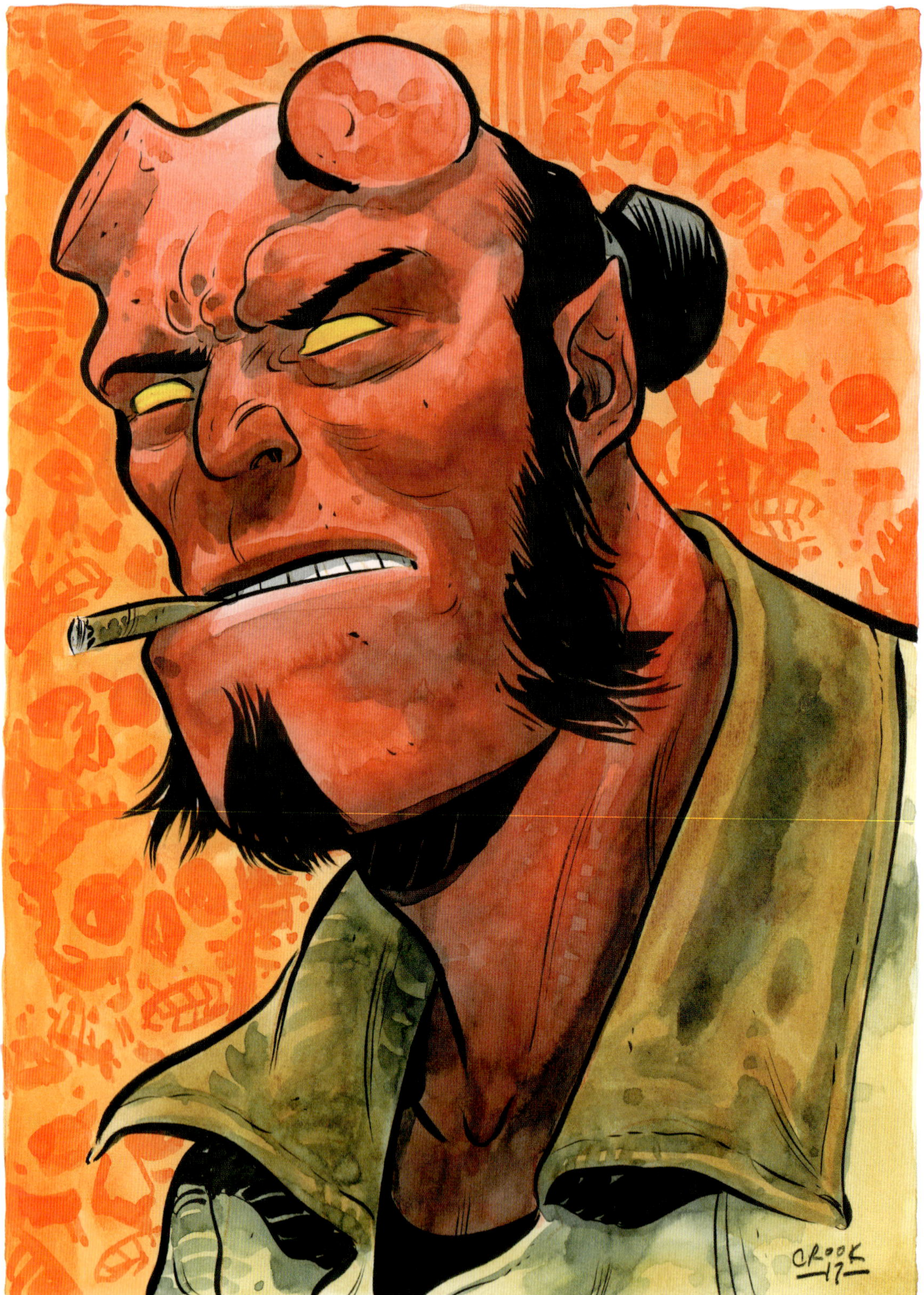
CROOK
17

Commissions Tyler did after leaving *B.P.R.D.*

-1859-

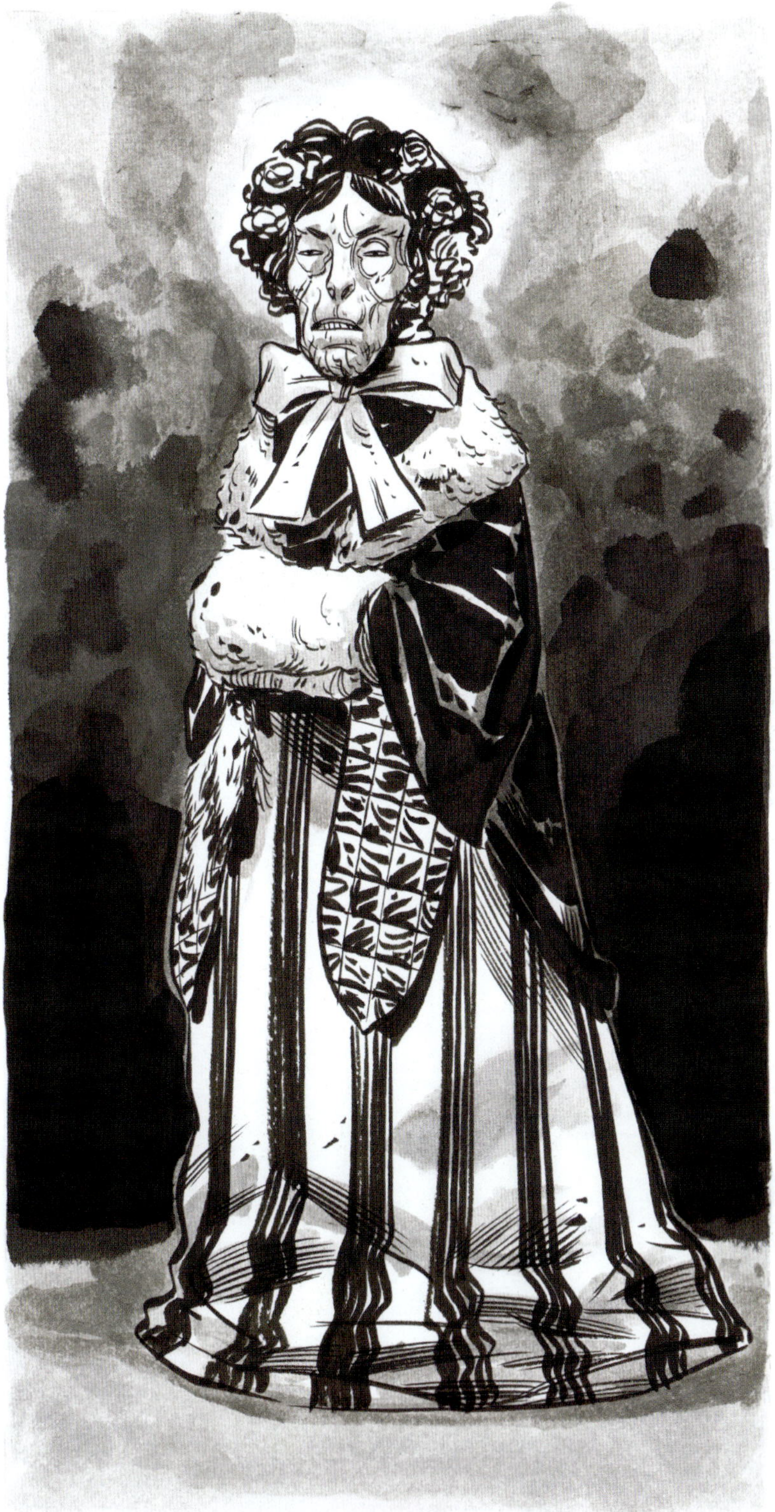

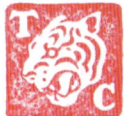

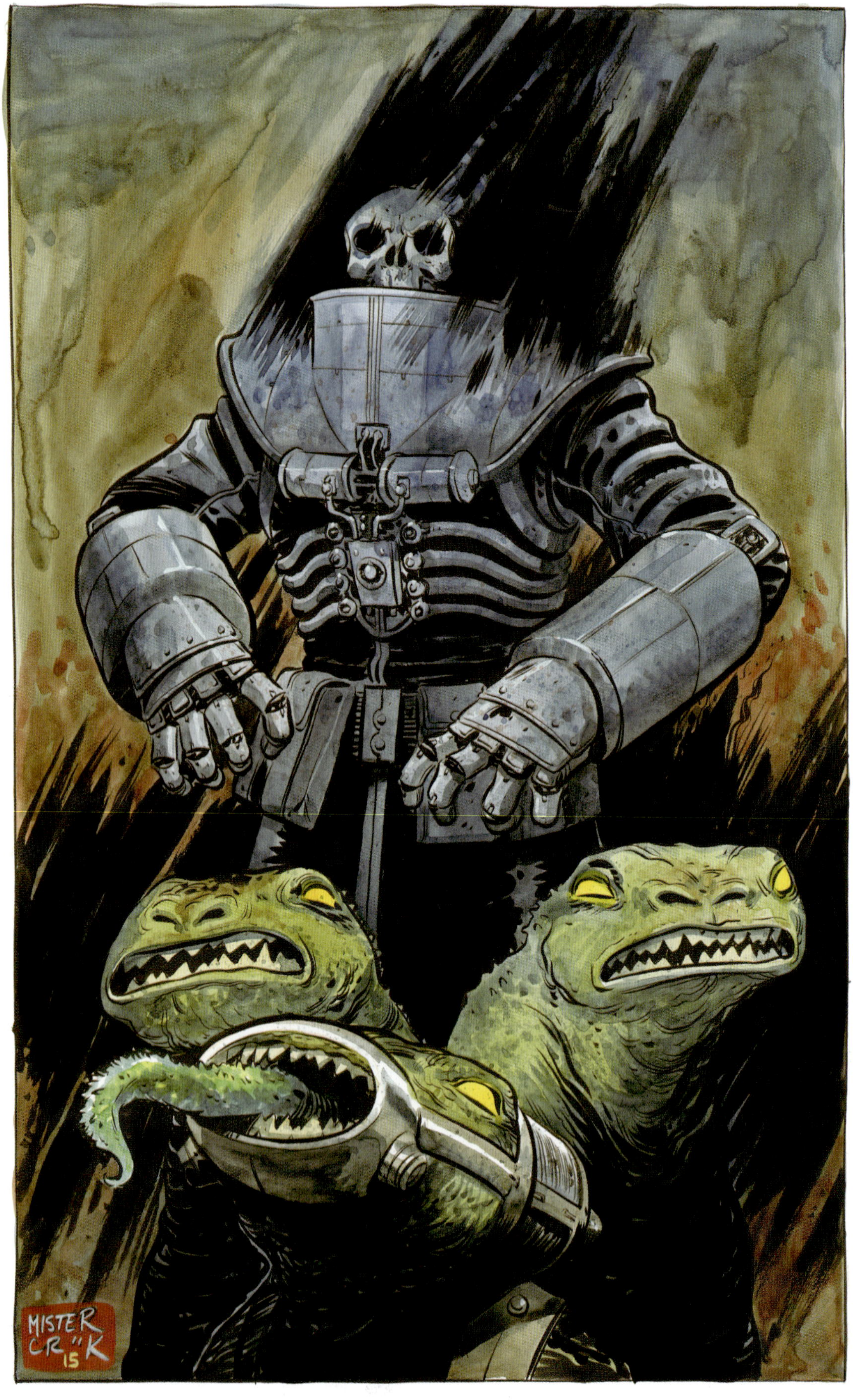
MISTER
CR"K
15

RUSSIA

Notes by Tyler Crook

Guy Davis started designing Iosif and Johann's new suit long before I started on the project. For Iosif's final design, we used the head from this page . . .

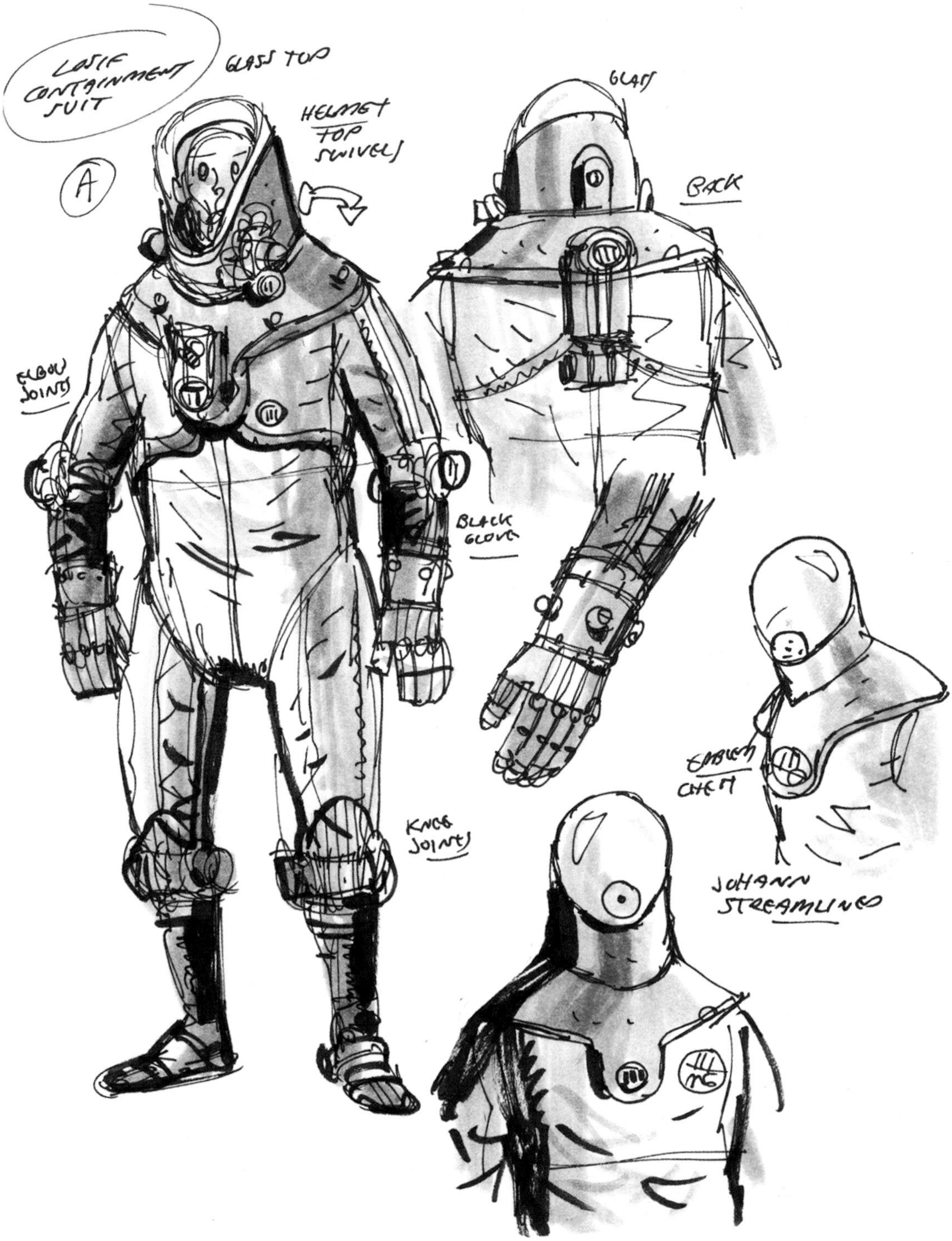

GLASS TOP
HELMET TOP SWIVELS
A
GLASS
BACK
BLACK GLOVE
KNEE JOINTS
JOHANN STREAMLINED

. . . And the body from this page.

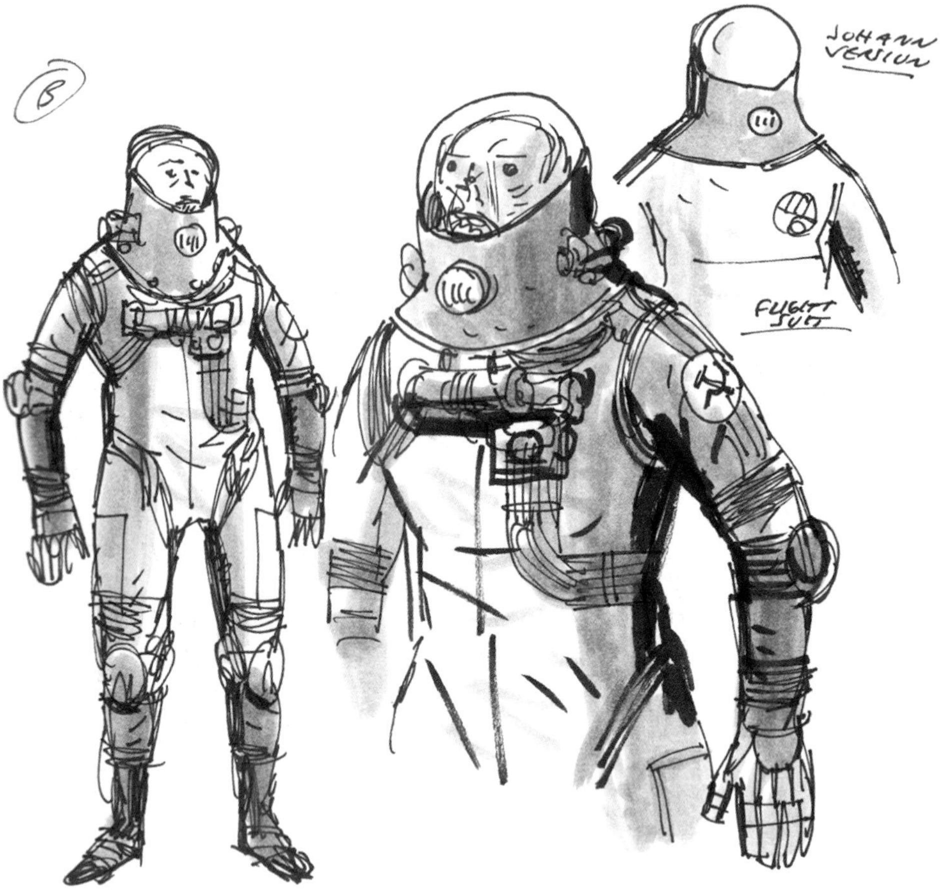
B
JOHANN VERSION
FLIGHT SUIT

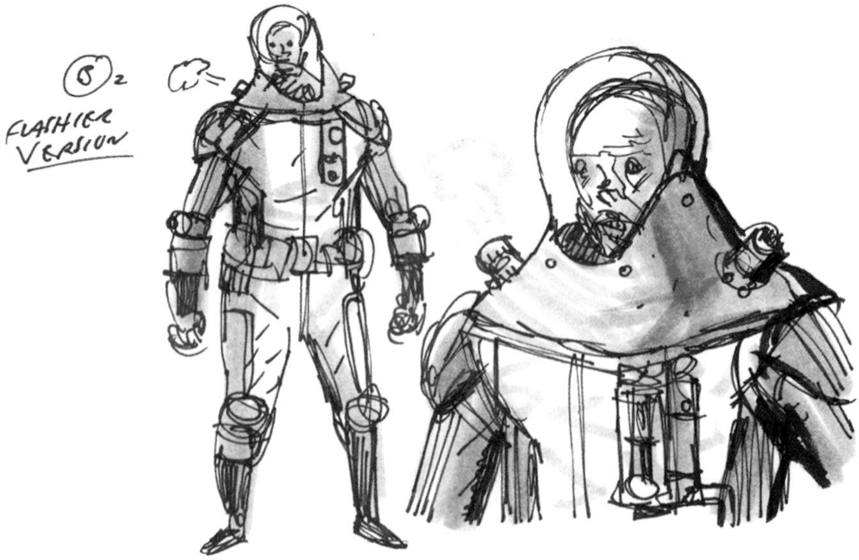
B2
FLASHIER VERSION

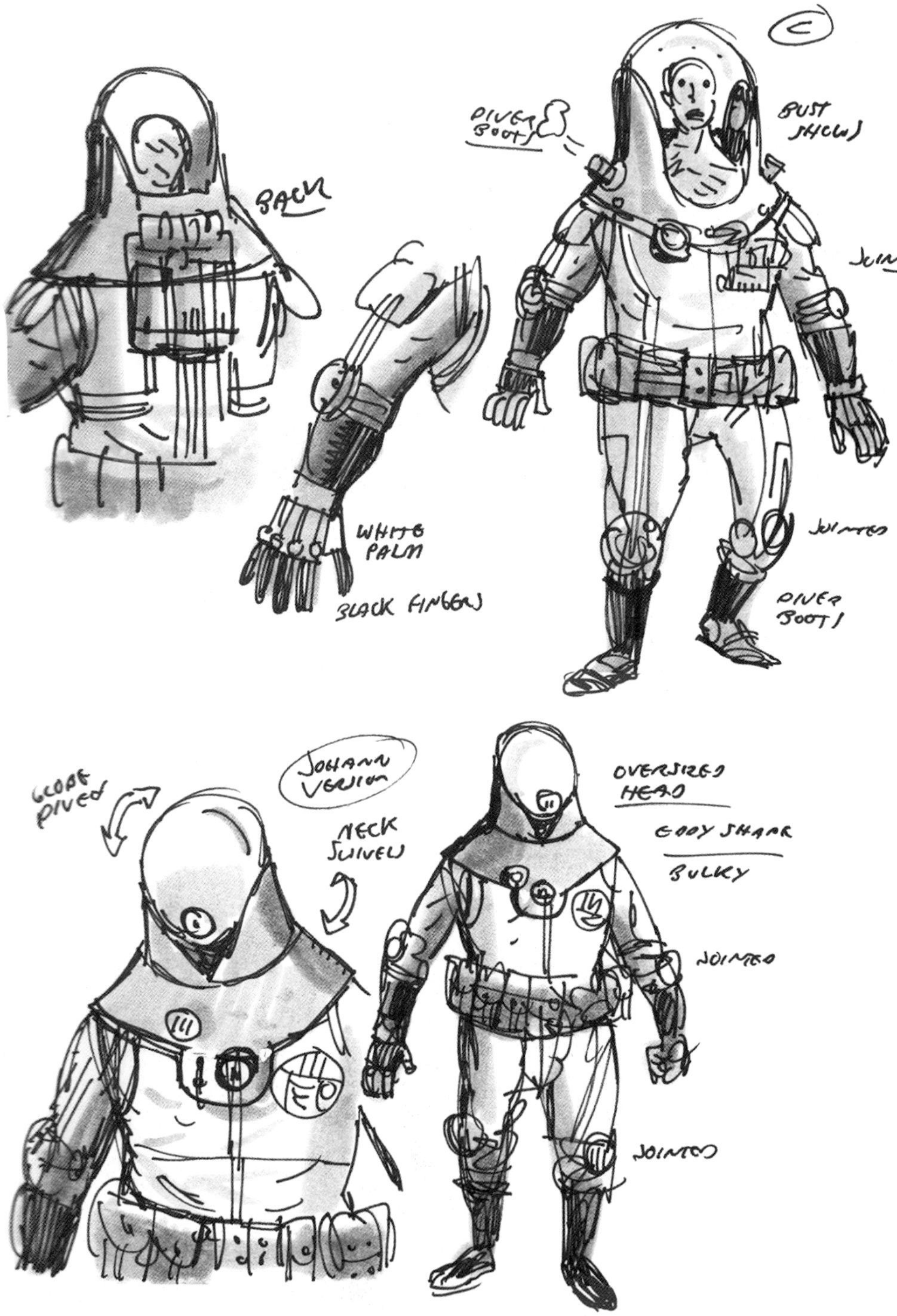

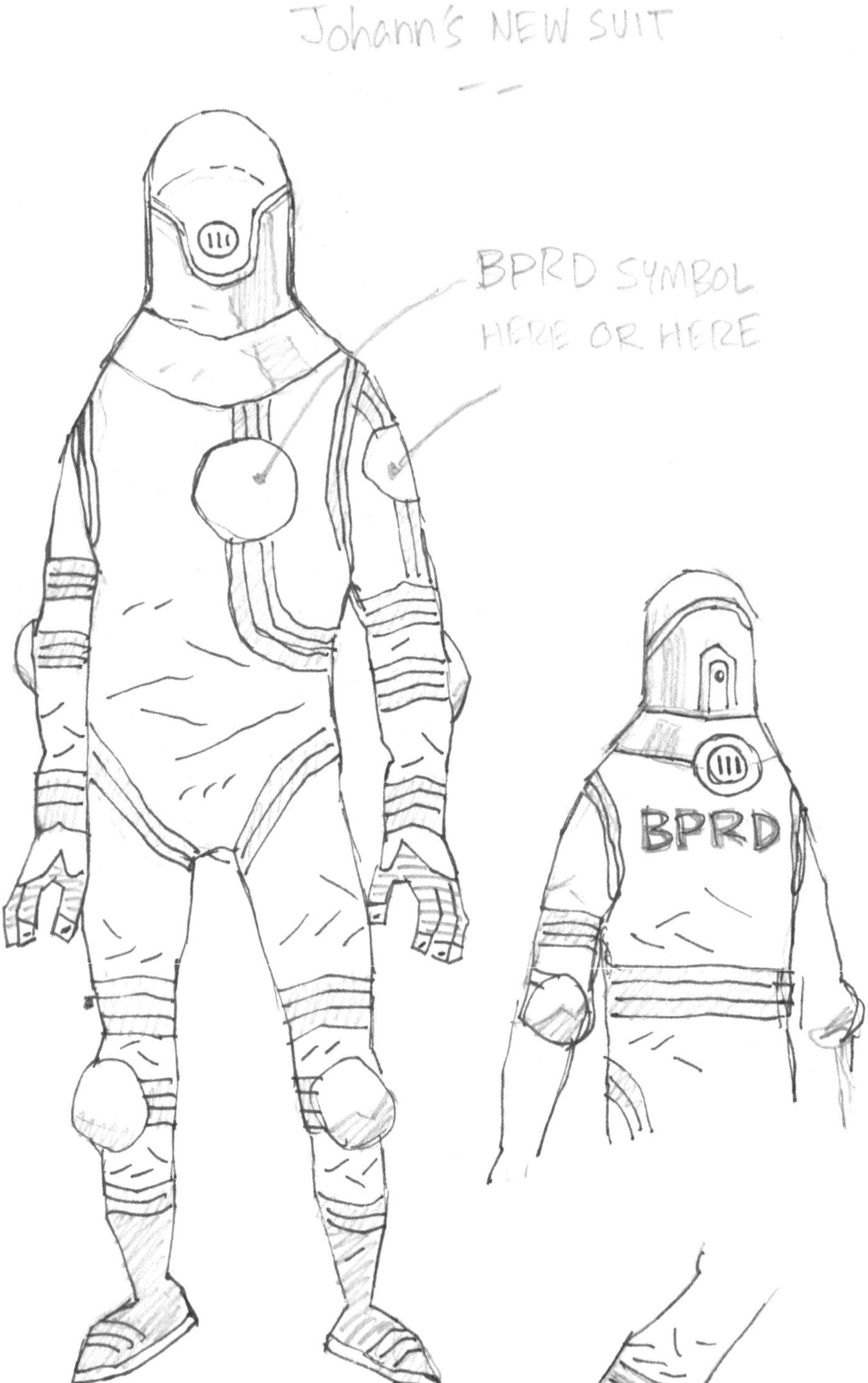
Johann's NEW SUIT
BPRD SYMBOL HERE OR HERE
BPRD

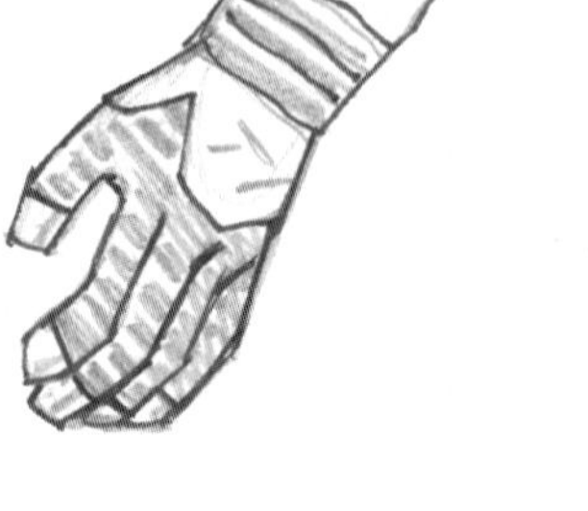

Working off Guy's designs, Mike tweaked Johann a little bit, and voilà! You got yourself a new containment suit.

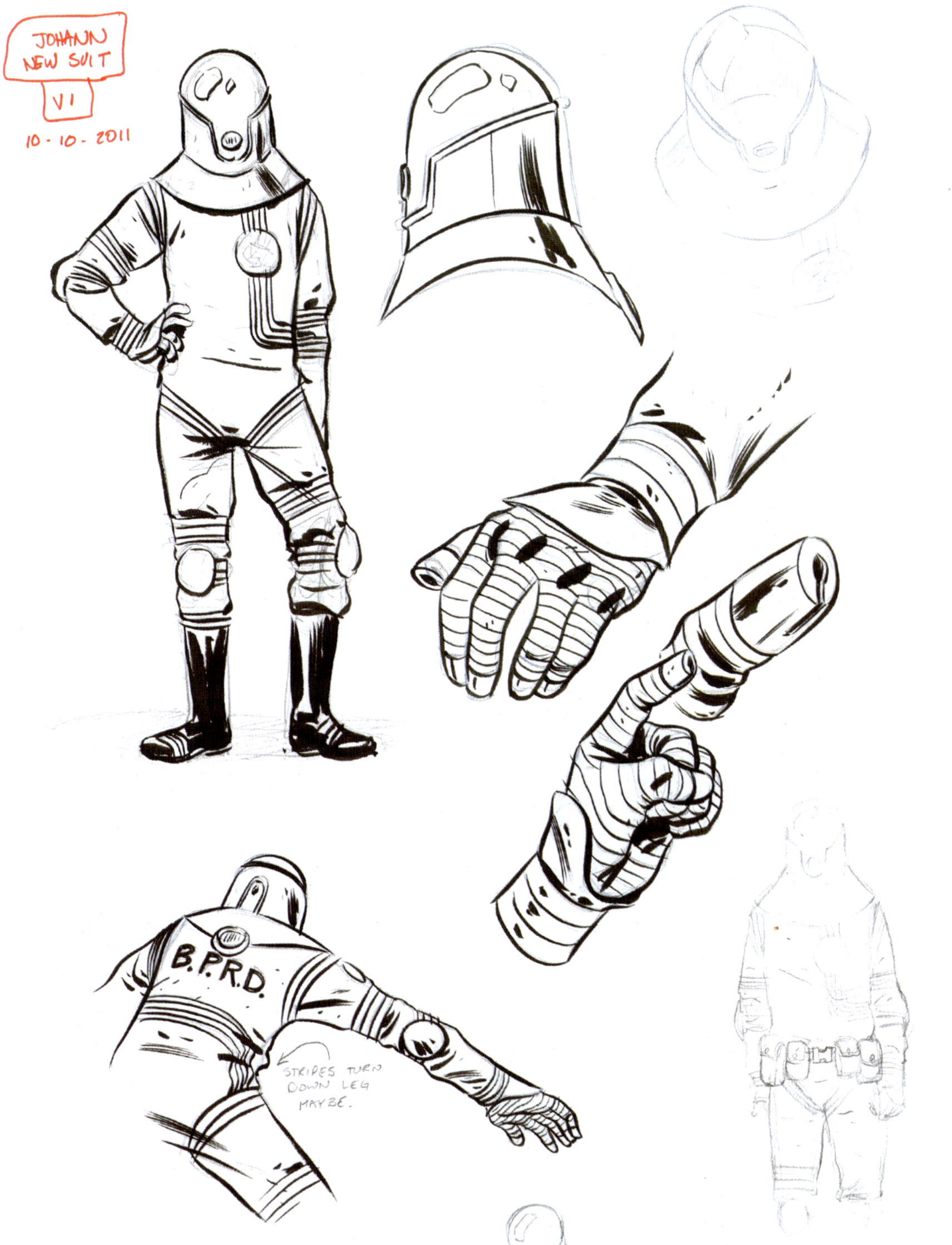
JOHANN
NEW SUIT
V1
10-10-2011
B.P.R.D.
STRIPES TURN
DOWN LEG
MAYBE.

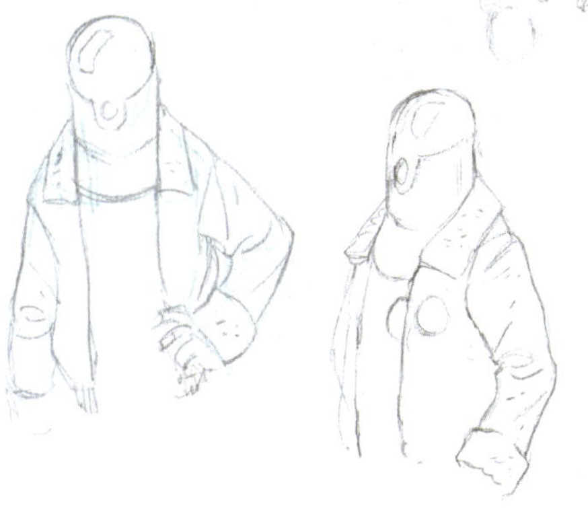

Of course, I instantly started posing Johann like his suit came straight out of a J. C. Penney catalog.

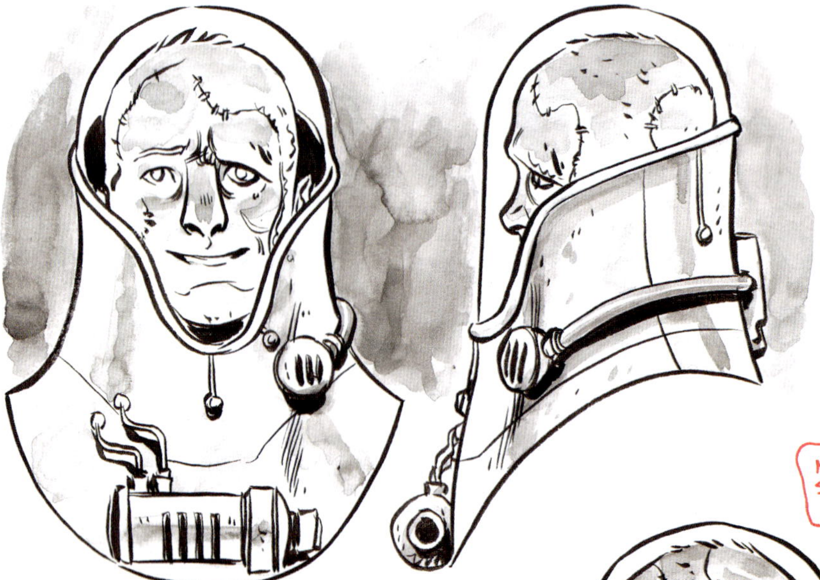
IOSIF HEAD
6/13/2011

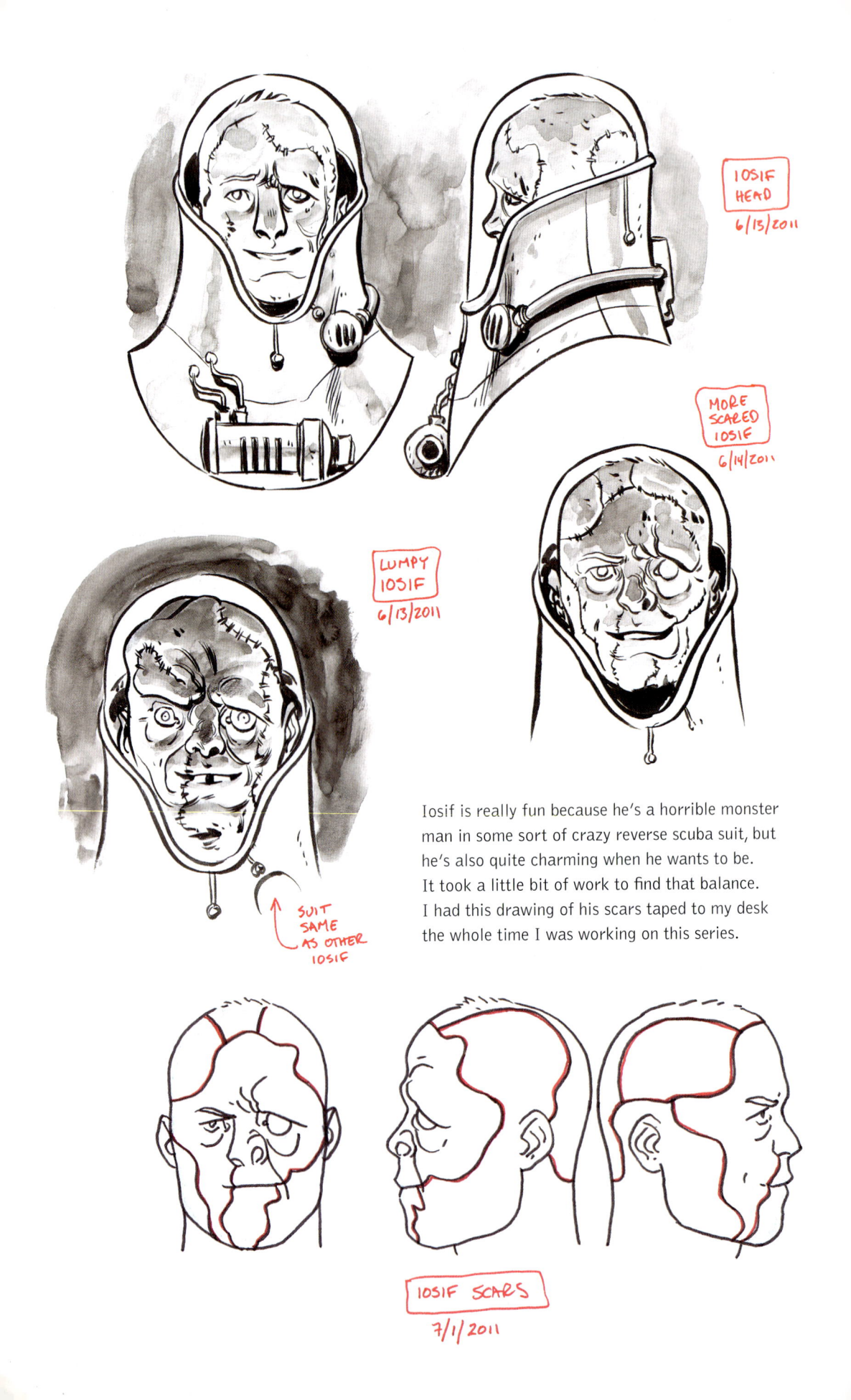

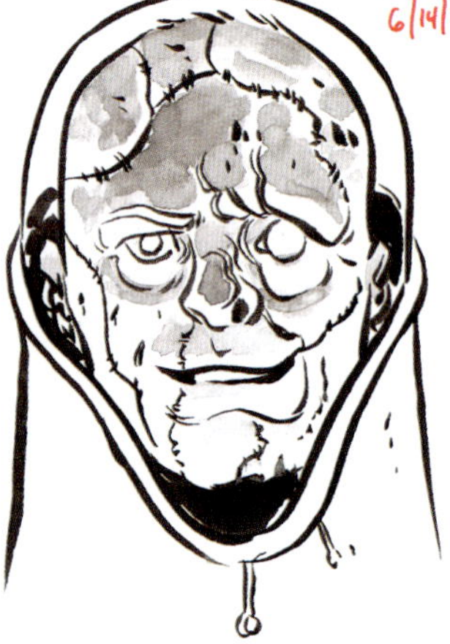
MORE SCARED IOSIF
6/14/2011

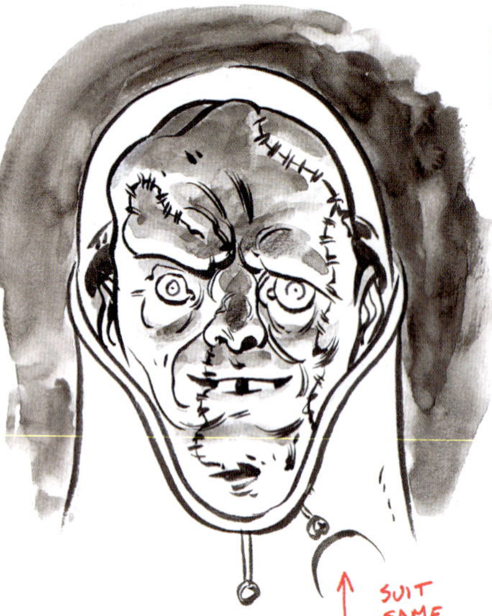
LUMPY IOSIF
6/13/2011
SUIT SAME AS OTHER IOSIF

Iosif is really fun because he's a horrible monster man in some sort of crazy reverse scuba suit, but he's also quite charming when he wants to be. It took a little bit of work to find that balance. I had this drawing of his scars taped to my desk the whole time I was working on this series.

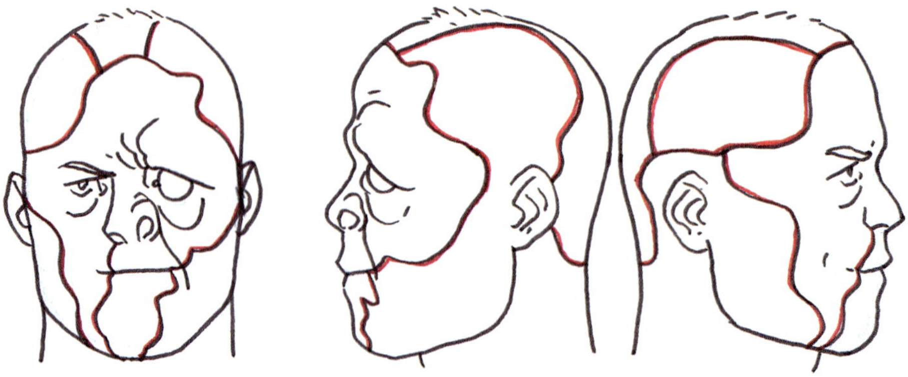
IOSIF SCARS
7/1/2011

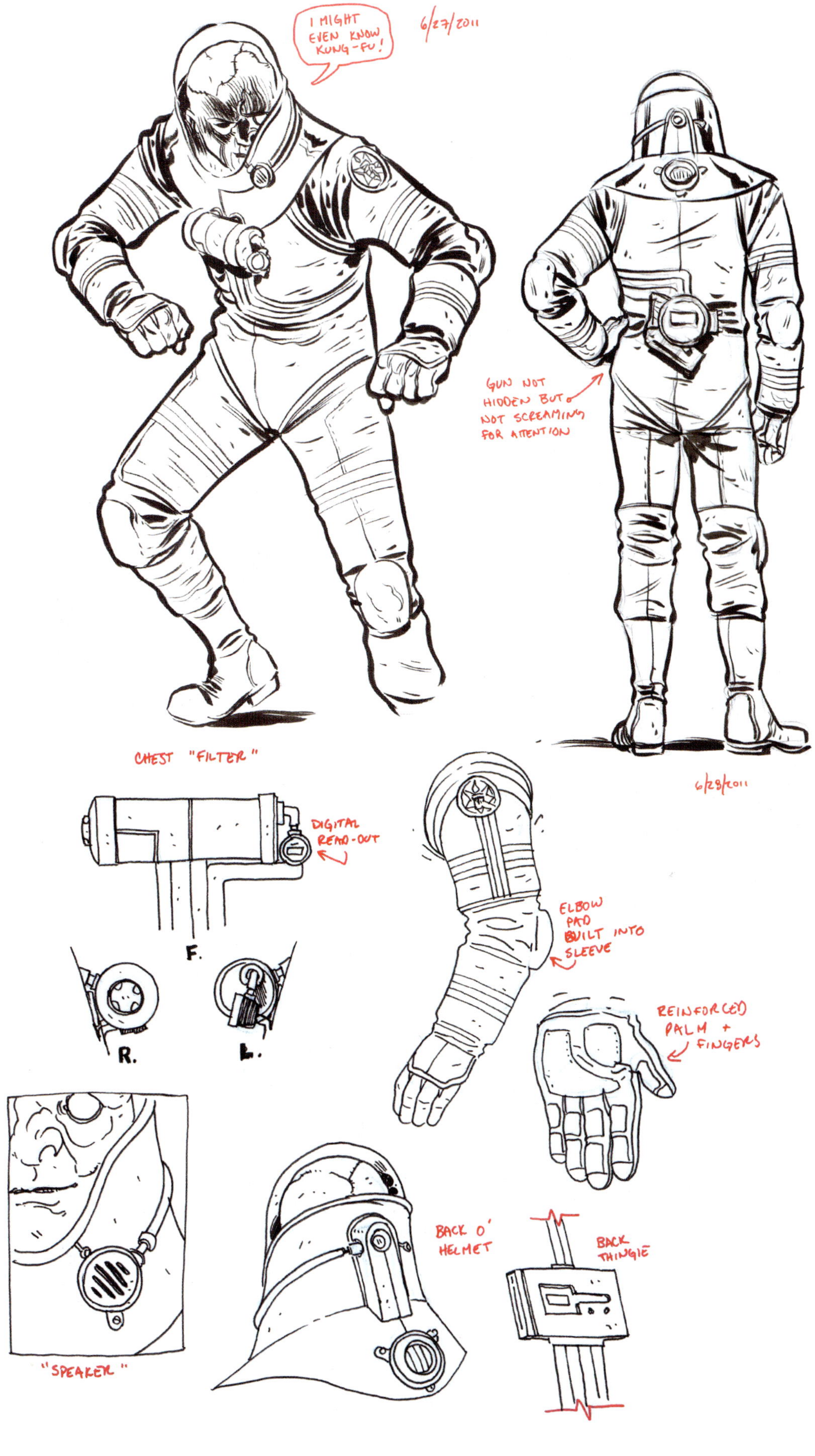
I MIGHT EVEN KNOW KUNG-FU!
6/27/2011
GUN NOT HIDDEN BUT NOT SCREAMING FOR ATTENTION
CHEST "FILTER"
6/28/2011
DIGITAL READ-OUT
F.
R.
L.
ELBOW PAD BUILT INTO SLEEVE
REINFORCED PALM + FINGERS
BACK O' HELMET
BACK THINGIE
"SPEAKER"

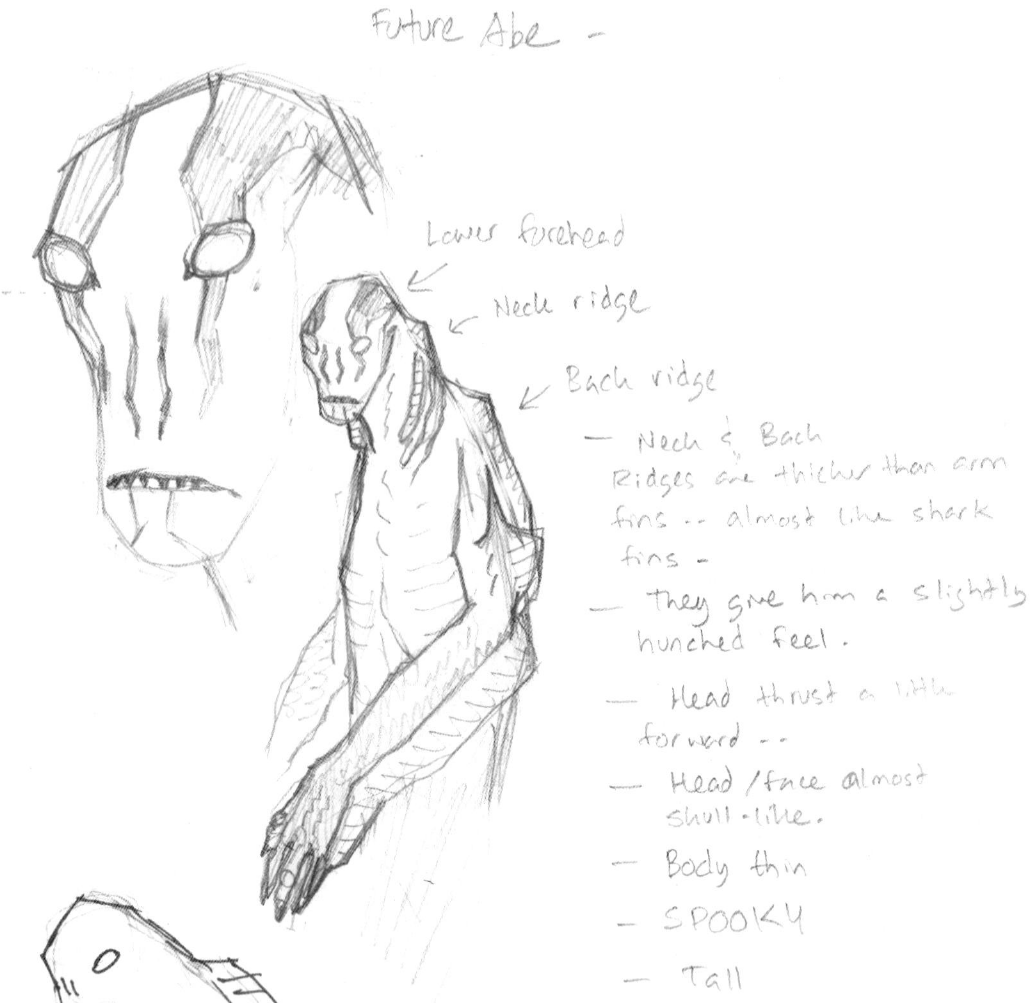
Future Abe -
Lower forehead
Neck ridge
Back ridge
— Neck & Back
Ridges are thicker than arm
fins -- almost like shark
fins -
— they give him a slightly
hunched feel.
— Head thrust a little
forward --
— Head / face almost
skull-like.
— Body thin
— SPOOKY
— Tall

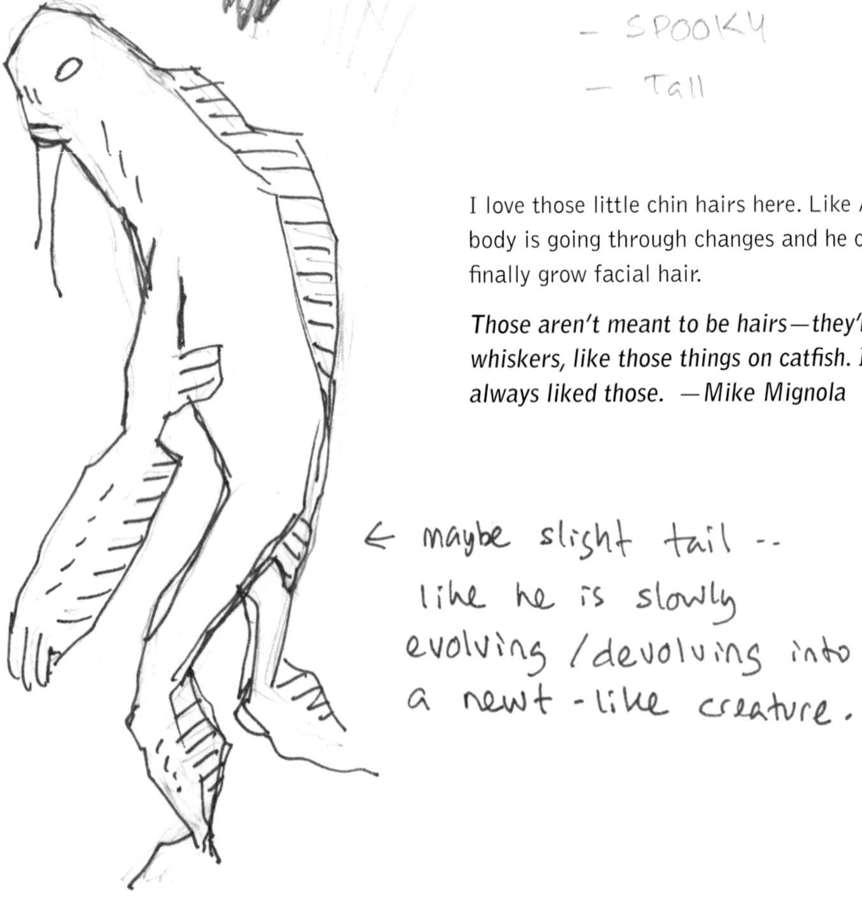
← maybe slight tail --
like he is slowly
evolving / devolving into
a newt-like creature.

I love those little chin hairs here. Like Abe's body is going through changes and he can finally grow facial hair.

Those aren't meant to be hairs—they're fish whiskers, like those things on catfish. I've always liked those. —Mike Mignola

Guy Davis was so good at drawing Abe that I felt a little relieved that he was going to be mutating, hopefully into something that would be easier for me to get right.

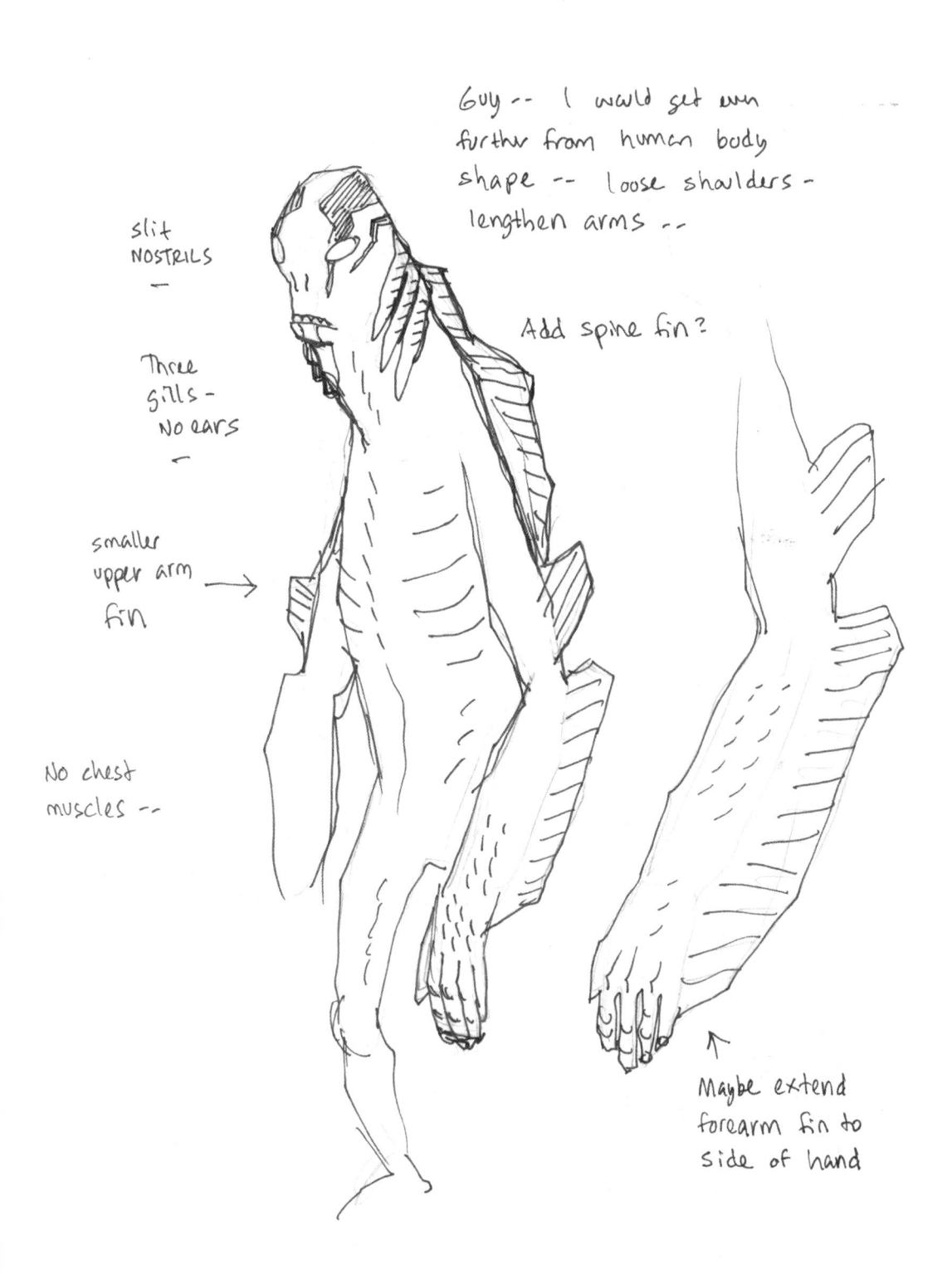

Guy -- I would get even further from human body shape -- loose shoulders - lengthen arms --

slit NOSTRILS

Add spine fin?

Three gills - No ears

smaller upper arm fin

No chest muscles --

Maybe extend forearm fin to side of hand

It turns out that even mutated
Abe is hard to get right.

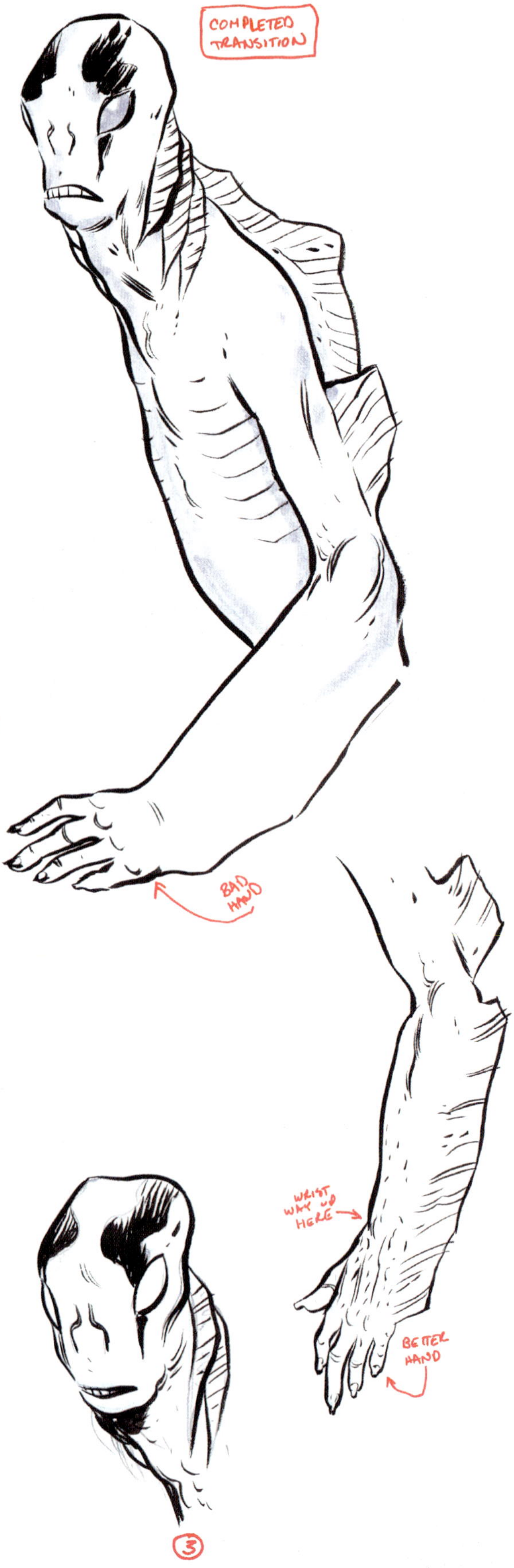
COMPLETED TRANSITION
BAD HAND

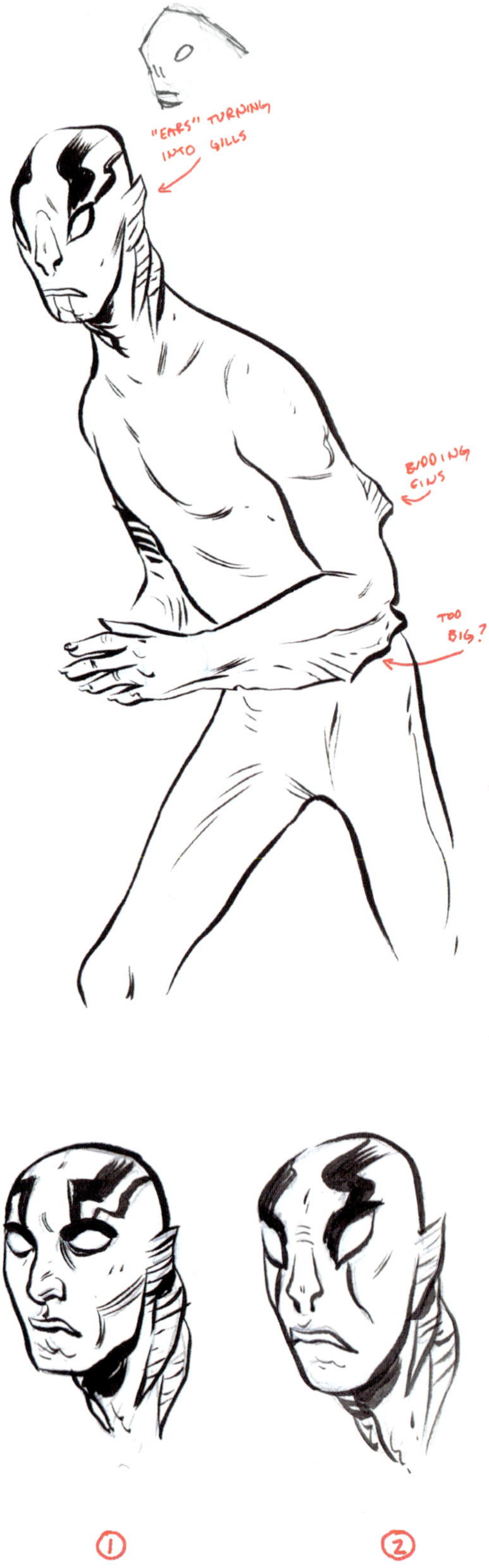
"EARS" TURNING INTO GILLS
BUDDING FINS
TOO BIG?
WRIST WAY UP HERE
BETTER HAND
1
2
3

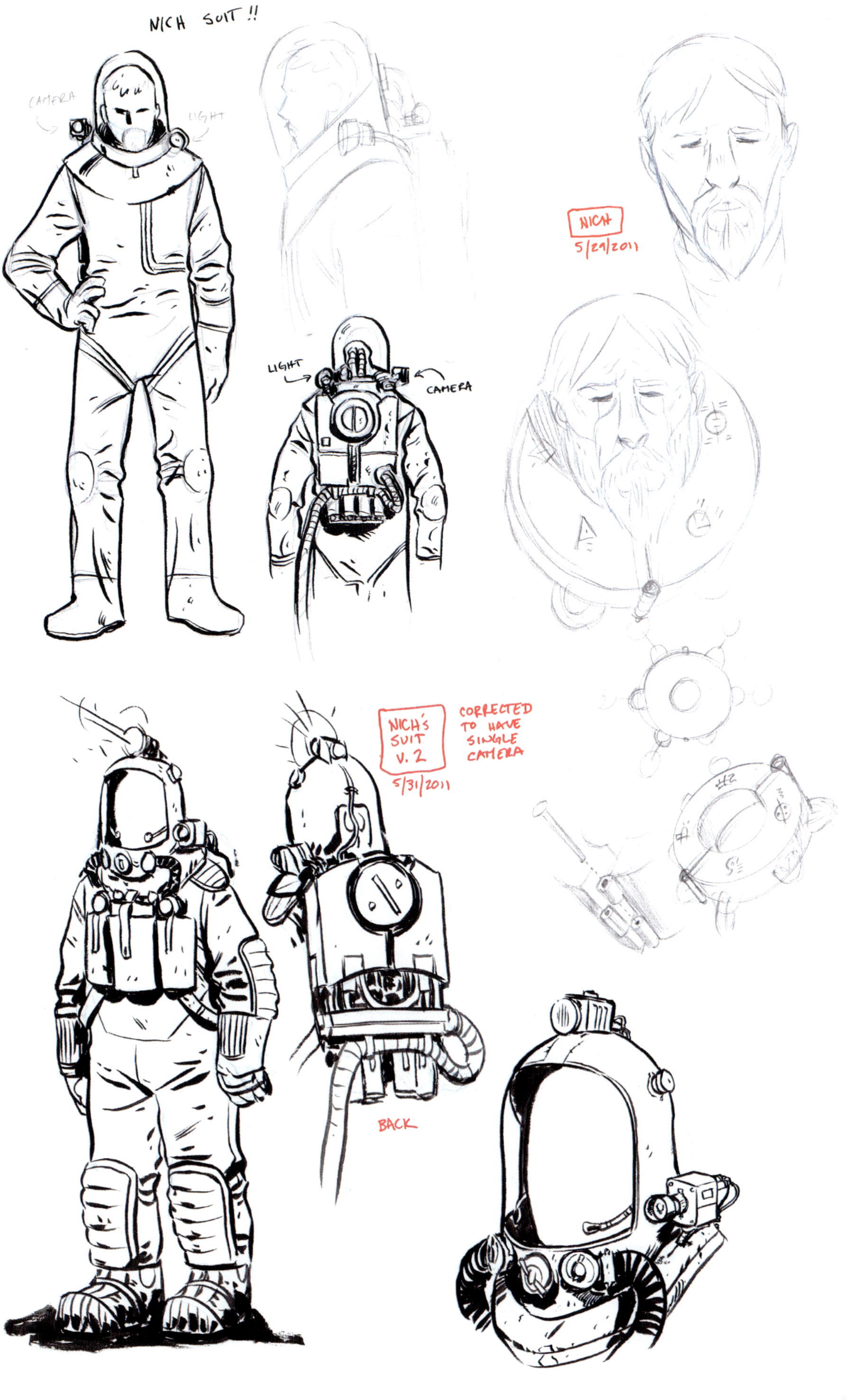

NICH SUIT !!
CAMERA
LIGHT
LIGHT
CAMERA
NICH
5/29/2011
NICH'S SUIT V. 2
5/31/2011
CORRECTED TO HAVE SINGLE CAMERA
BACK

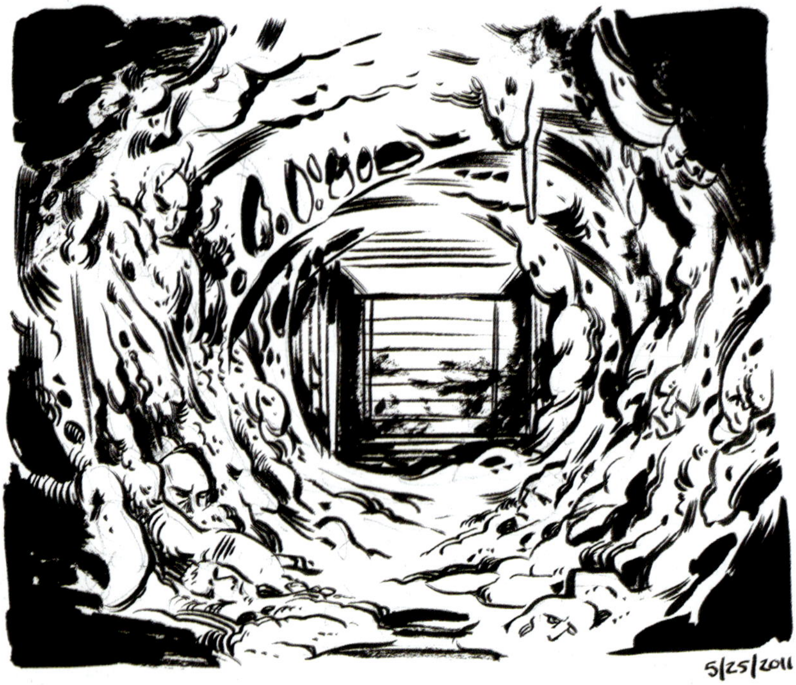
5/25/2011

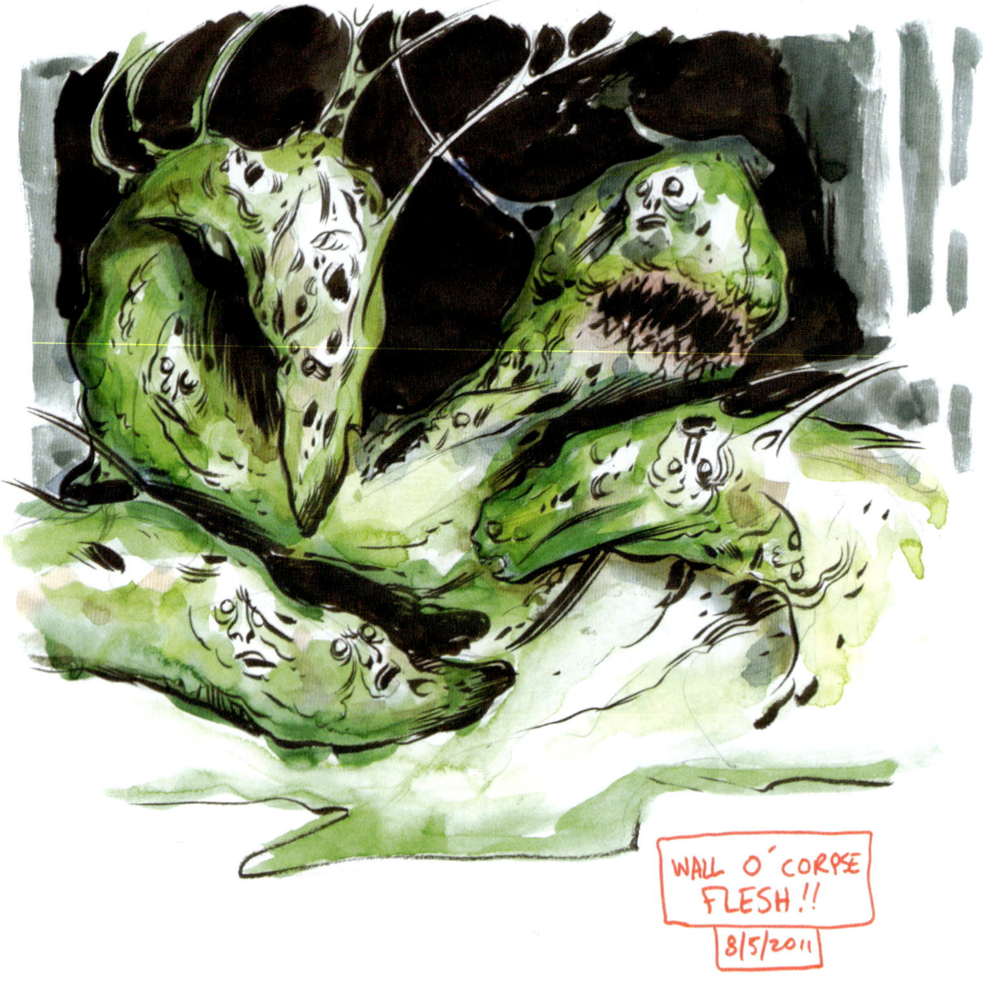
WALL O' CORPSE
FLESH!!
8/5/2011

"Wall of corpse flesh" is one of those things that is pretty easy to write but a lot harder to draw. In drawing this I learned that you can always add more corpses. Always.

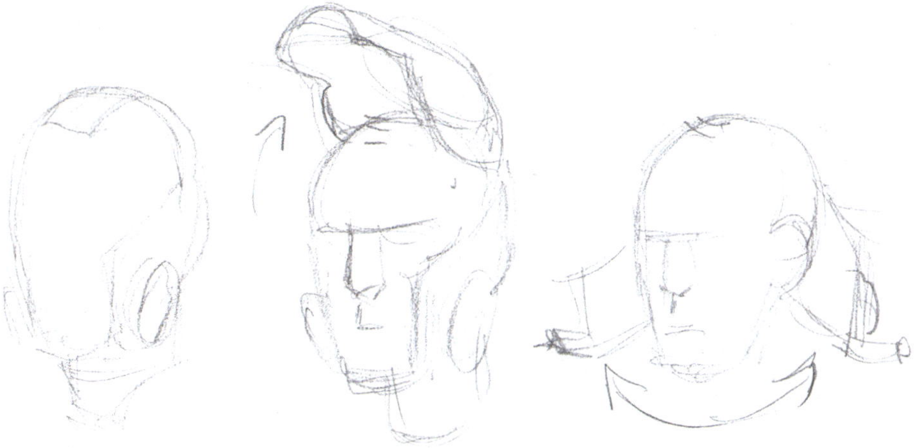

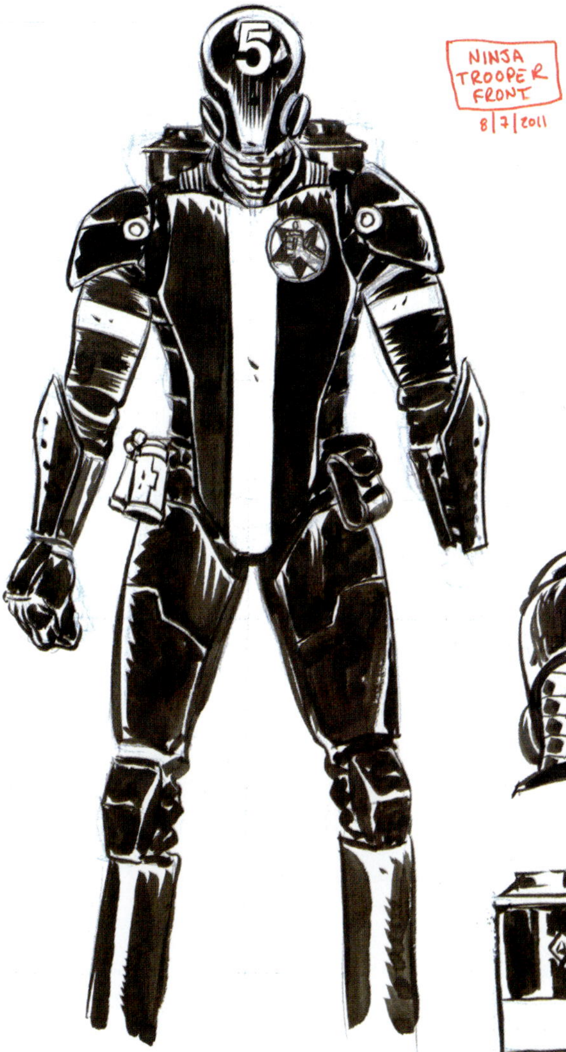

NINJA TROOPER FRONT
8|7|2011

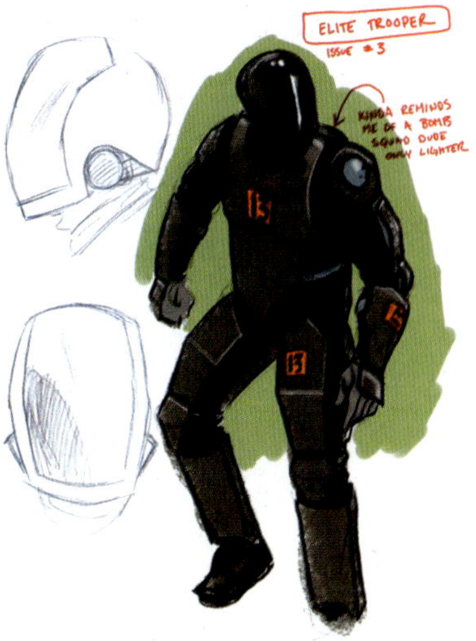

ELITE TROOPER
ISSUE #3
KINDA REMINDS ME OF A BOMB SQUAD DUDE ONLY LIGHTER

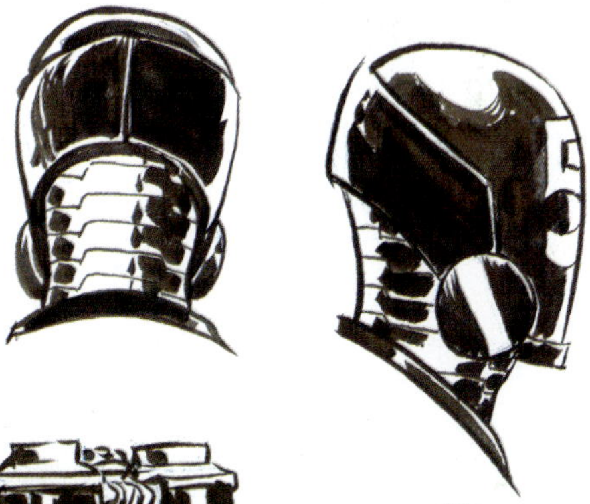

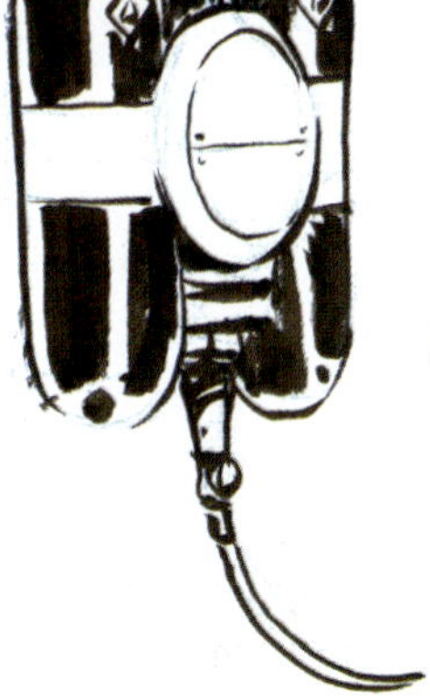

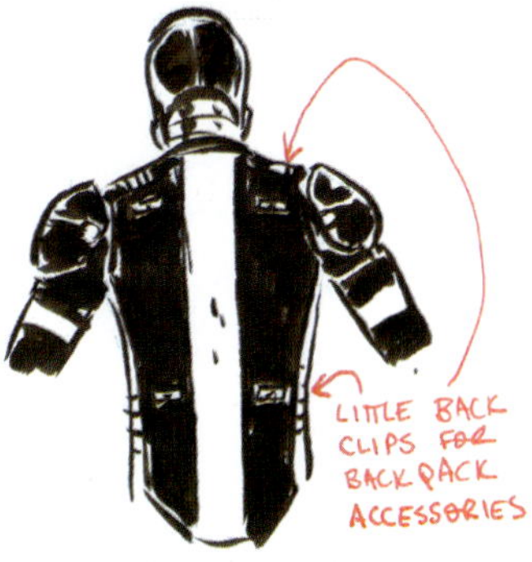

LITTLE BACK CLIPS FOR BACKPACK ACCESSORIES

The numbers on the troopers' faces were a bit distracting, so we moved them to their shoulder pads. I eventually had to make a chart so I could keep track of which numbers get killed on which page.

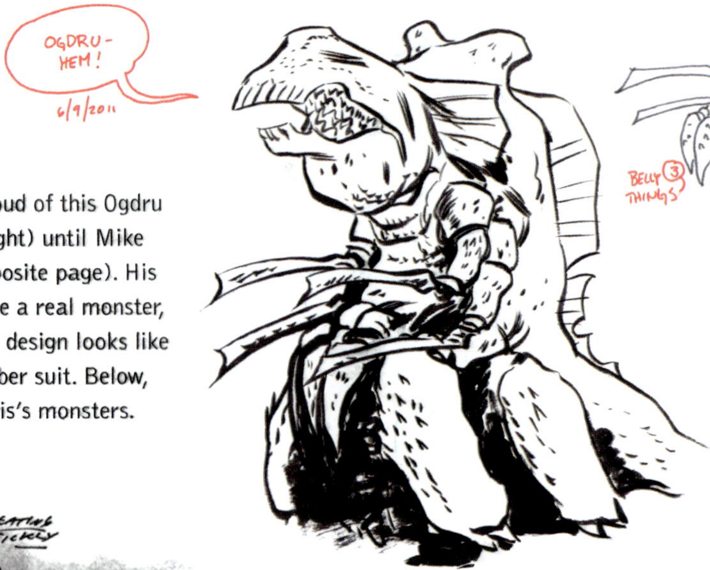
OGDRU-HEM!
6/9/2011

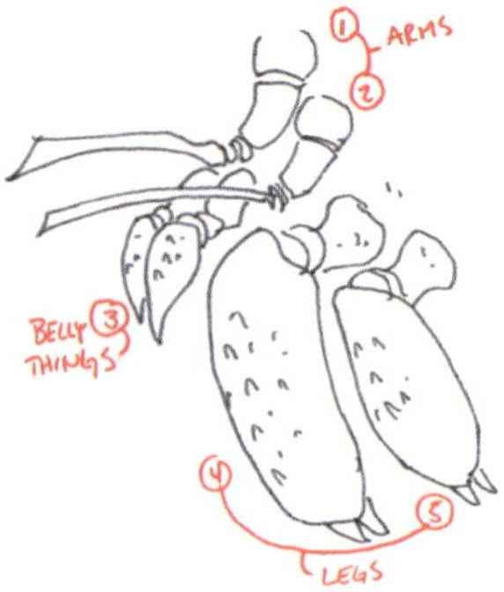
1
ARMS
2
BELLY THINGS 3
4
5
LEGS

I was really proud of this Ogdru Hem design (right) until Mike tweaked it (opposite page). His sketch looks like a real monster, while my initial design looks like a dude in a rubber suit. Below, one of Guy Davis's monsters.

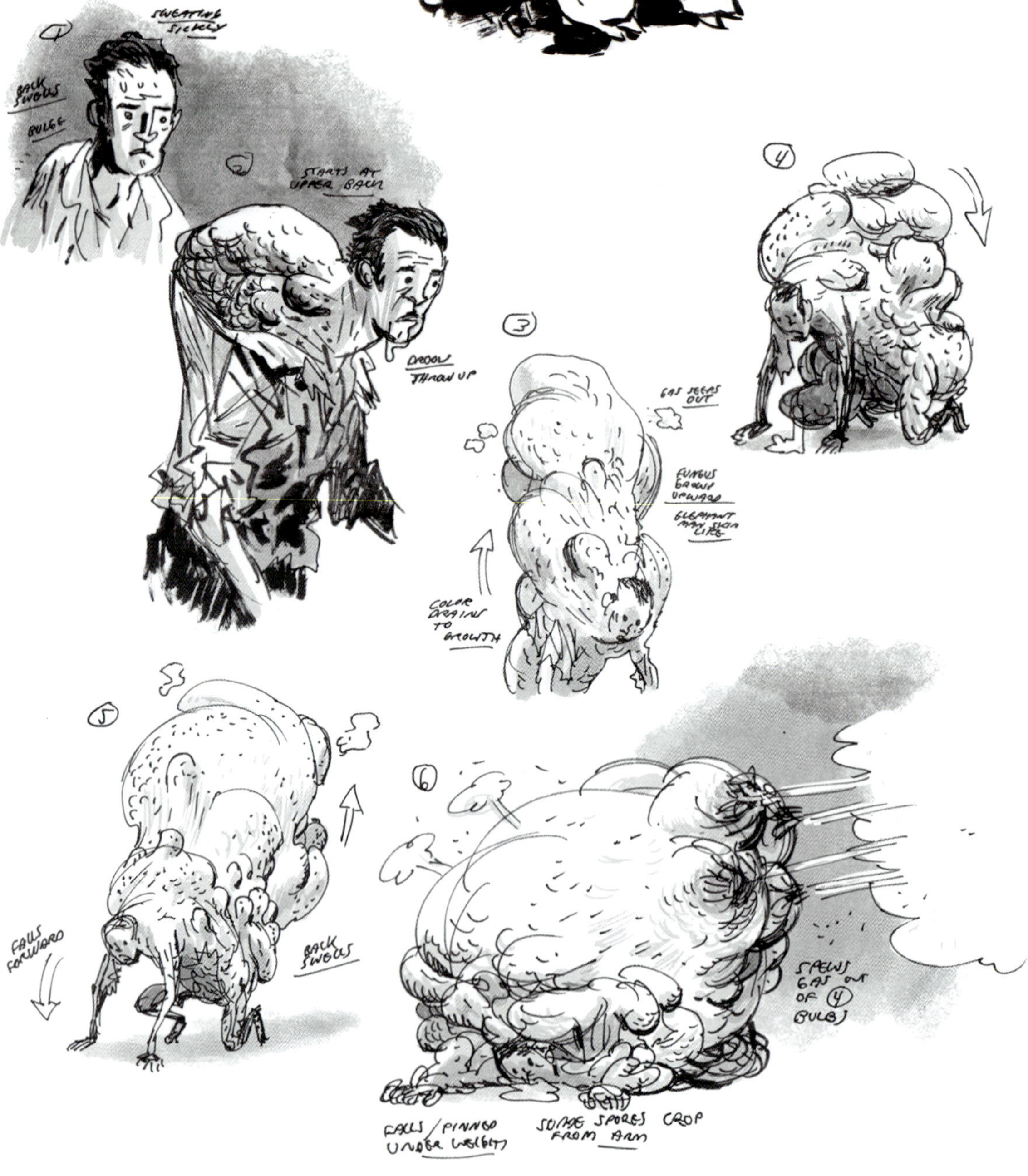
1
SWEATING SICKLY
BACK SWELLS
BULGE
2
STARTS AT UPPER BACK
DROOL
THROW UP
3
GAS SEEPS OUT
FUNGUS GROWS UPWARD
ELEPHANT MAN SKIN LIKE
COLOR DRAINS TO GROWTH
4
5
FALLS FORWARD
BACK SWELLS
6
SPEWS GAS OUT OF 4 BULBS
FALLS/PINNED UNDER WEIGHT
SOME SPORES CROP FROM ARM

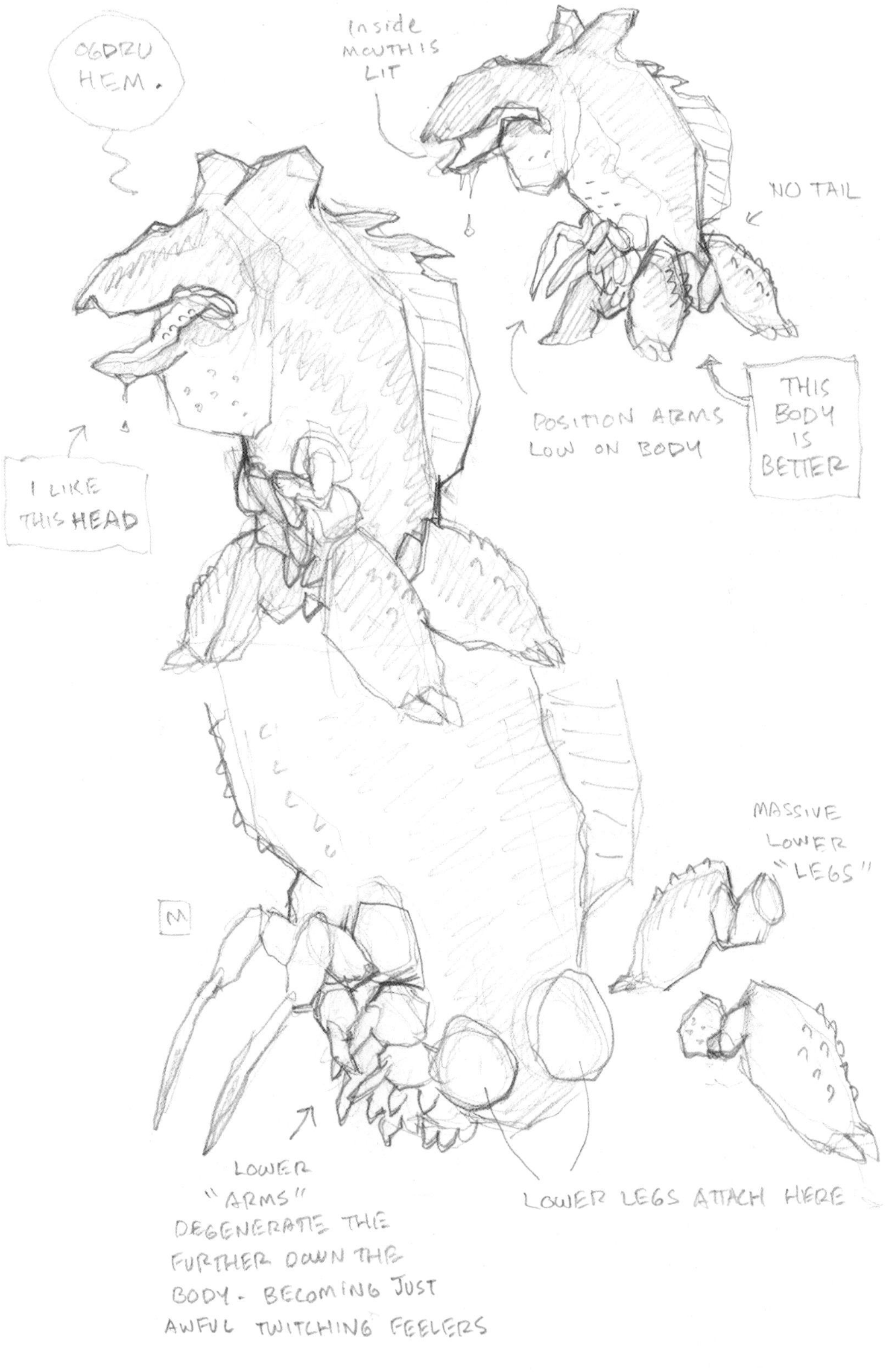
OGDRU HEM.
inside mouth is lit
NO TAIL
POSITION ARMS LOW ON BODY
THIS BODY IS BETTER
I LIKE THIS HEAD
M
MASSIVE LOWER "LEGS"
LOWER "ARMS" DEGENERATE THE FURTHER DOWN THE BODY - BECOMING JUST AWFUL TWITCHING FEELERS
LOWER LEGS ATTACH HERE

On this one I think Mike told me to either have eyes or a mouth but not both. We went with a mouth for obvious reasons.

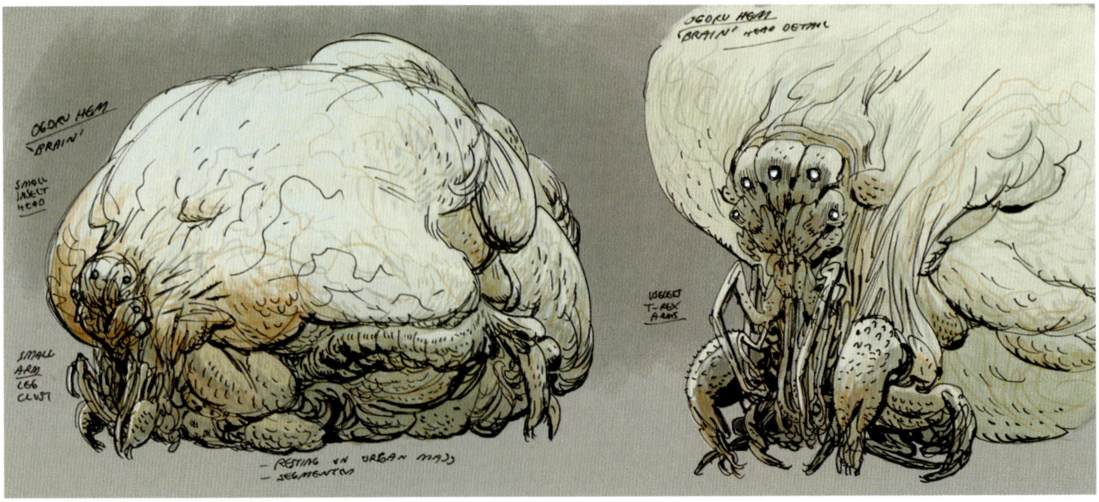
'BRAIN'
SMALL INSECT HEAD
SMALL ARM
– RESTING ON ORGAN MASS
– SEGMENTED
'BRAIN' HEAD DETAIL
T-REX ARMS

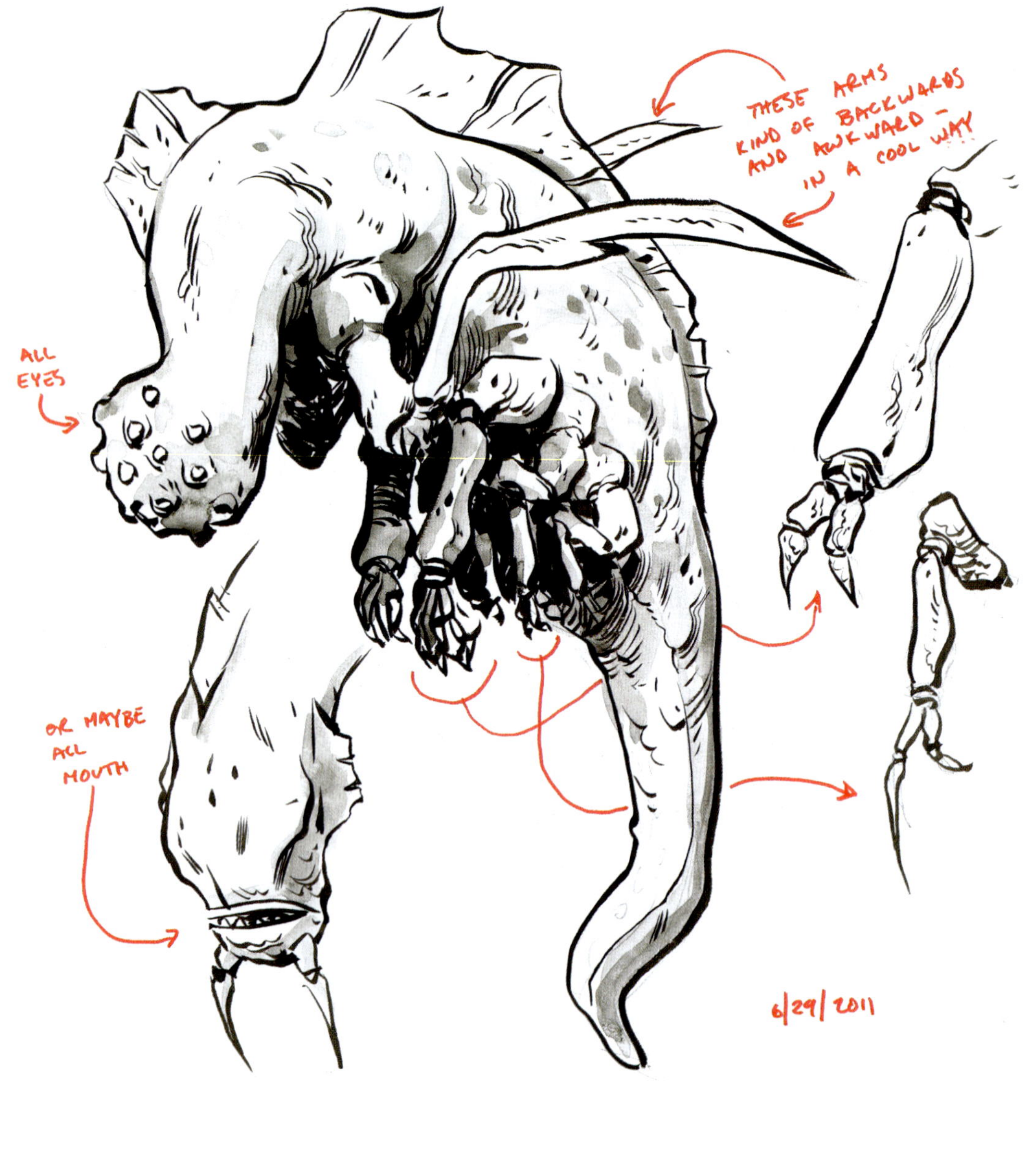
THESE ARMS KIND OF BACKWARDS AND AWKWARD – IN A COOL WAY
ALL EYES
OR MAYBE ALL MOUTH
6/29/2011

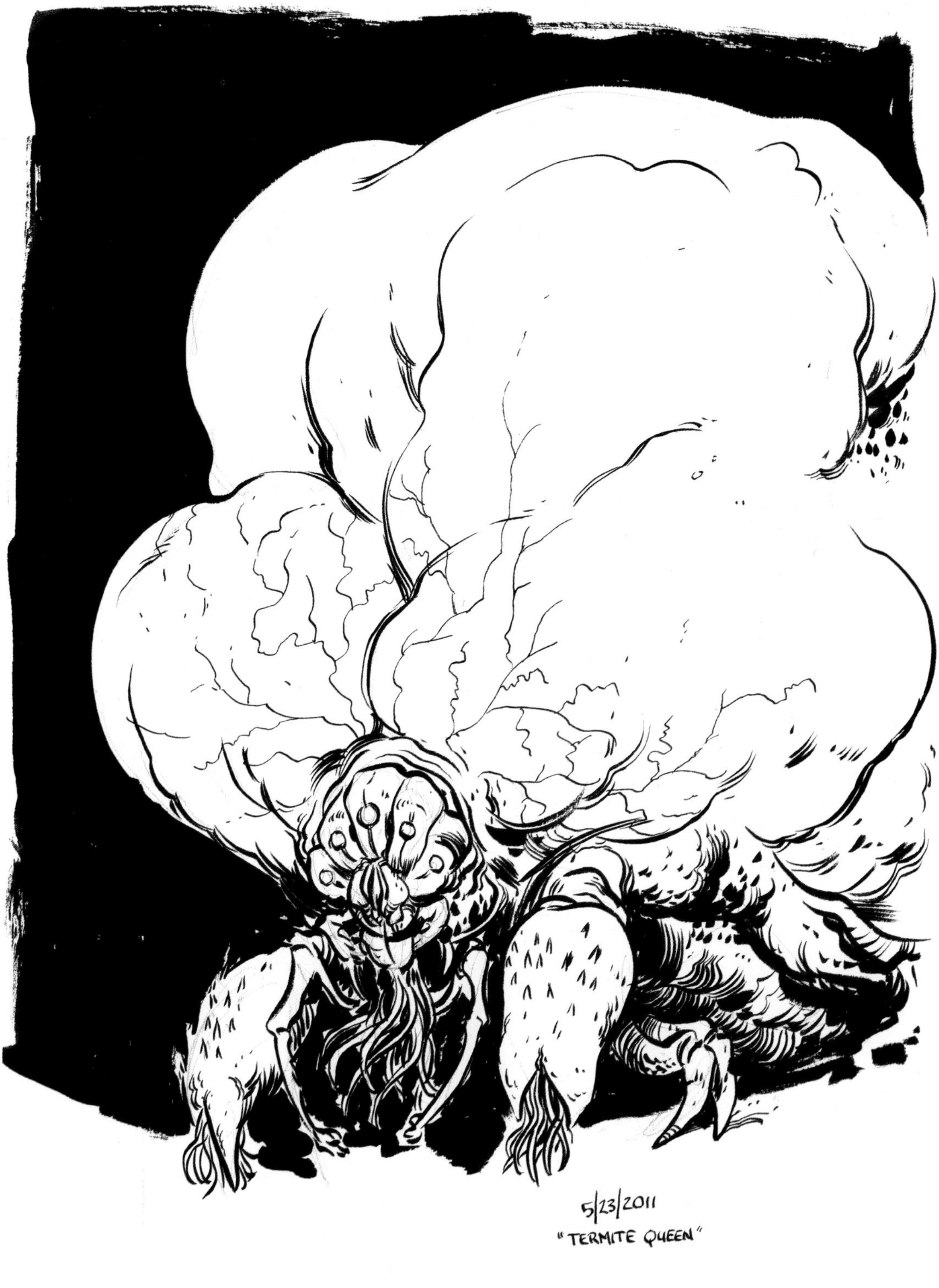
5/23/2011
"TERMITE QUEEN"

This was my first attempt at getting a handle on Guy's design (opposite page, top). It turned out okay, I guess, but looking at it right next to Guy's design still makes me cringe a little.

I had done a few sketches of different kinds of monster bug thrones, but they all looked like they had hired architects and contractors to build them. Mike nailed it with his zombie-built design.

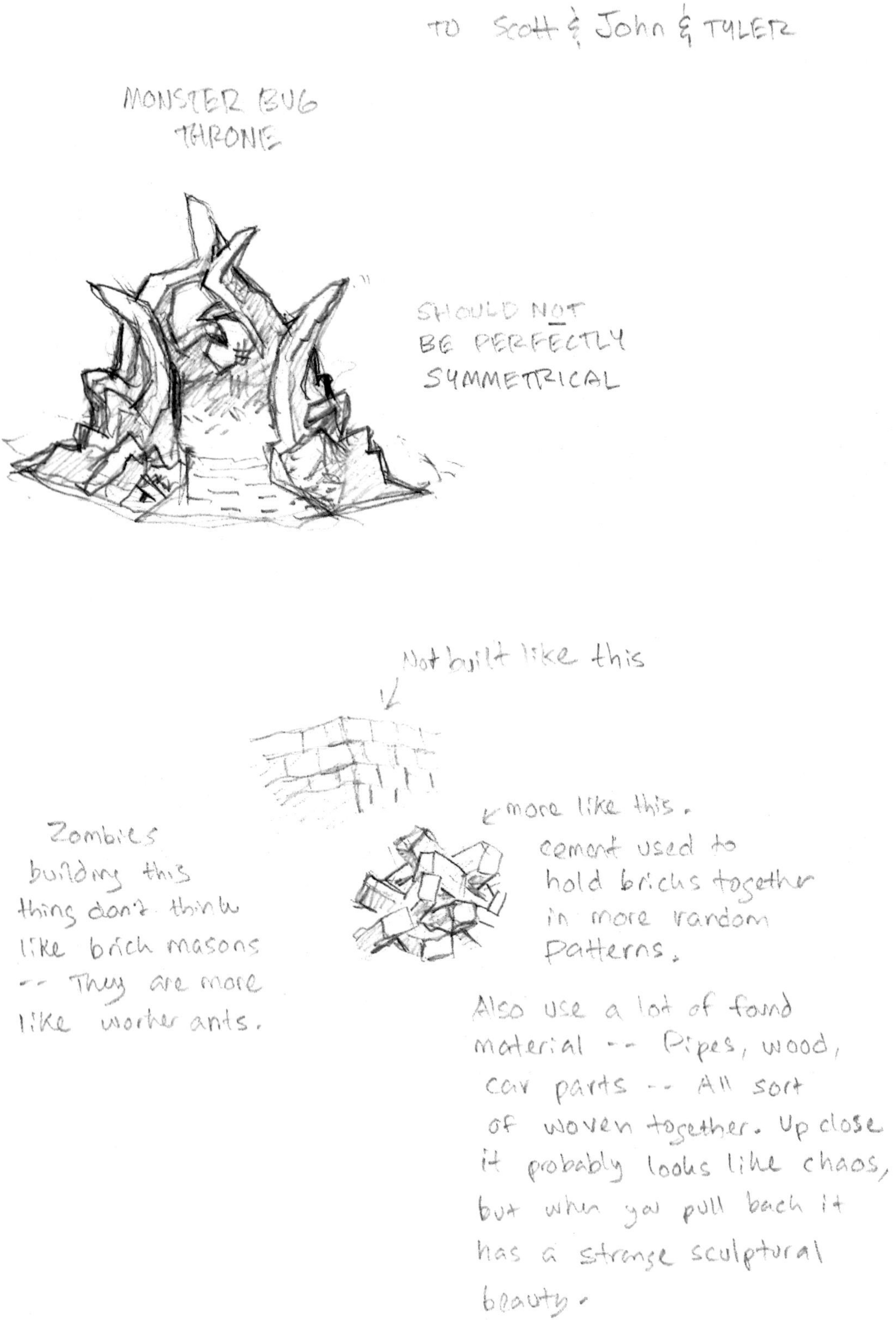
TO Scott & John & TYLER
MONSTER BUG THRONE
SHOULD NOT BE PERFECTLY SYMMETRICAL
Not built like this
more like this.
cement used to hold bricks together in more random patterns.
Zombies building this thing don't think like brick masons -- They are more like worker ants.
Also use a lot of found material -- Pipes, wood, car parts -- All sort of woven together. Up close it probably looks like chaos, but when you pull back it has a strange sculptural beauty.

At one point I got the chance to go hang out with Mike for the afternoon and we kind of worked out the design for this room and the design for Nich's chains. That was a fun day.

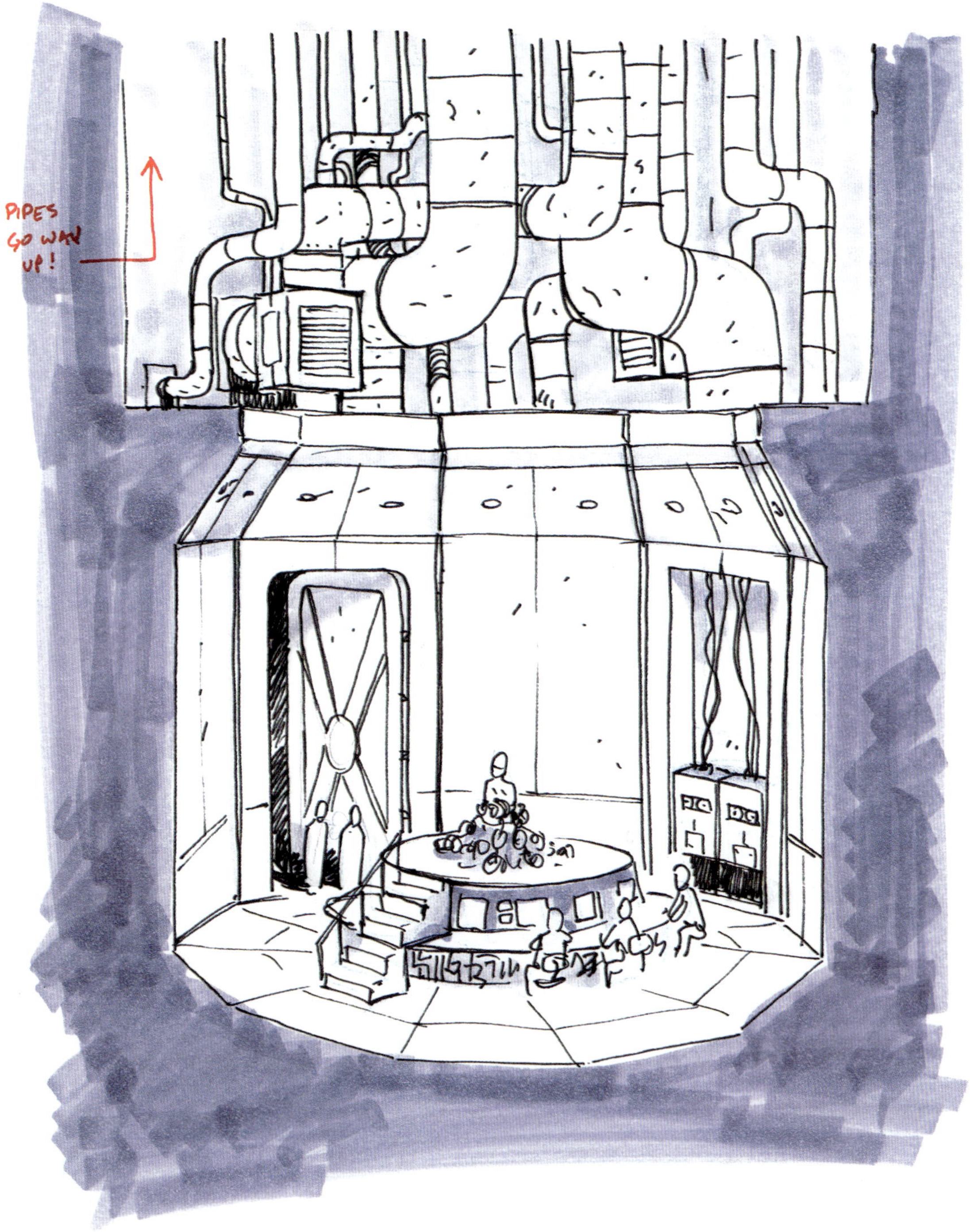
PIPES GO WAY UP!

After I finished the layouts for an early draft of this scene, Mike and John decided it needed a rewrite. When they were done the scene had a much more epic feel. I worked right off Mike's thumbnails (see pages 307, 315, 316, 317, and 318).

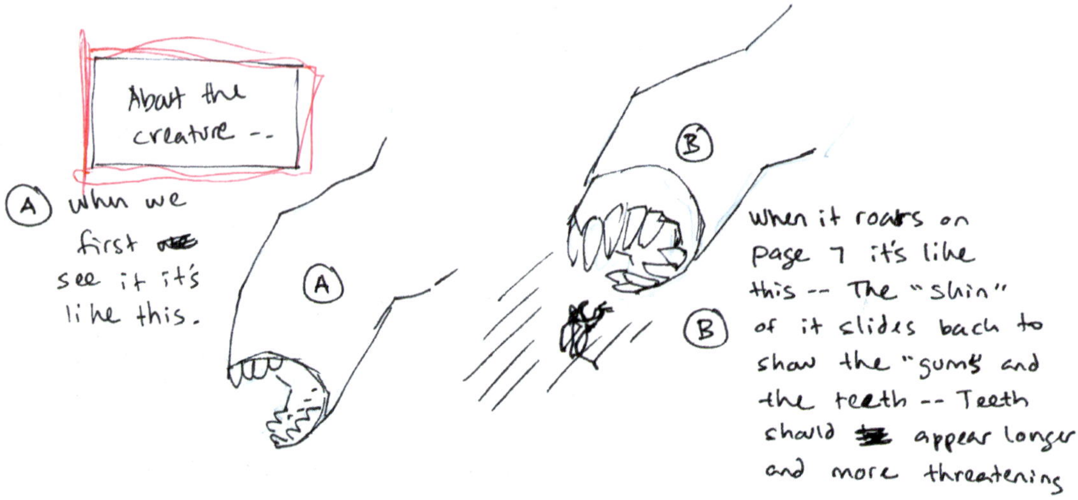
About the creature --
(A) when we first see it it's like this.
A
B
(B) when it roars on page 7 it's like this -- The "skin" of it slides back to show the "gums" and the teeth -- Teeth should appear longer and more threatening

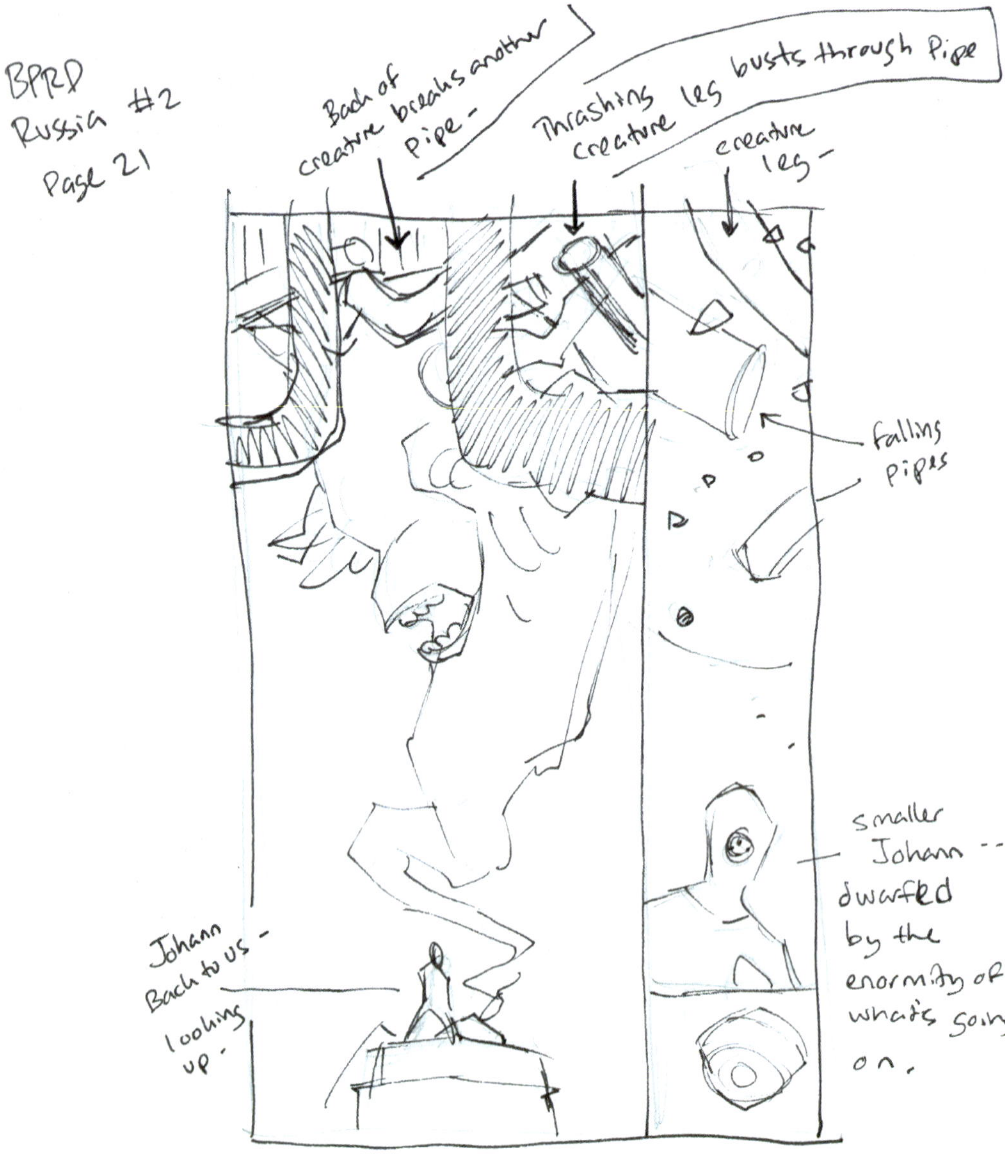
BPRD Russia #2 Page 21
Back of creature breaks another pipe -
Thrashing creature leg busts through pipe
creature leg -
falling pipes
smaller Johann -- dwarfed by the enormity of what's going on.
Johann Back to us - looking up -

BOTTOM OF ⑤

We see papers and scraps of metal blowing around -- like there is a windstorm blowing in that lab.

---

① CREATURE'S ROARING AND/OR THE WIND THROWS JOHANN BACKWARD OFF THE PLATFORM --

② JOHANN IS WEAK -- Ectoplasm is being sucked out of him to grow the creature. We are close on Johann here but we should see that he's starting to crumple as his bag-body empties --

MORE STUFF blows around in the air around him.

FURIOUS WIND STORM INSIDE LAB --

CREATURE HAS INCREASED IN SIZE -- SWELLING to FILL UPPER PART OF LAB - CAUSING MORE DAMAGE to THOSE PIPES -- ⑥

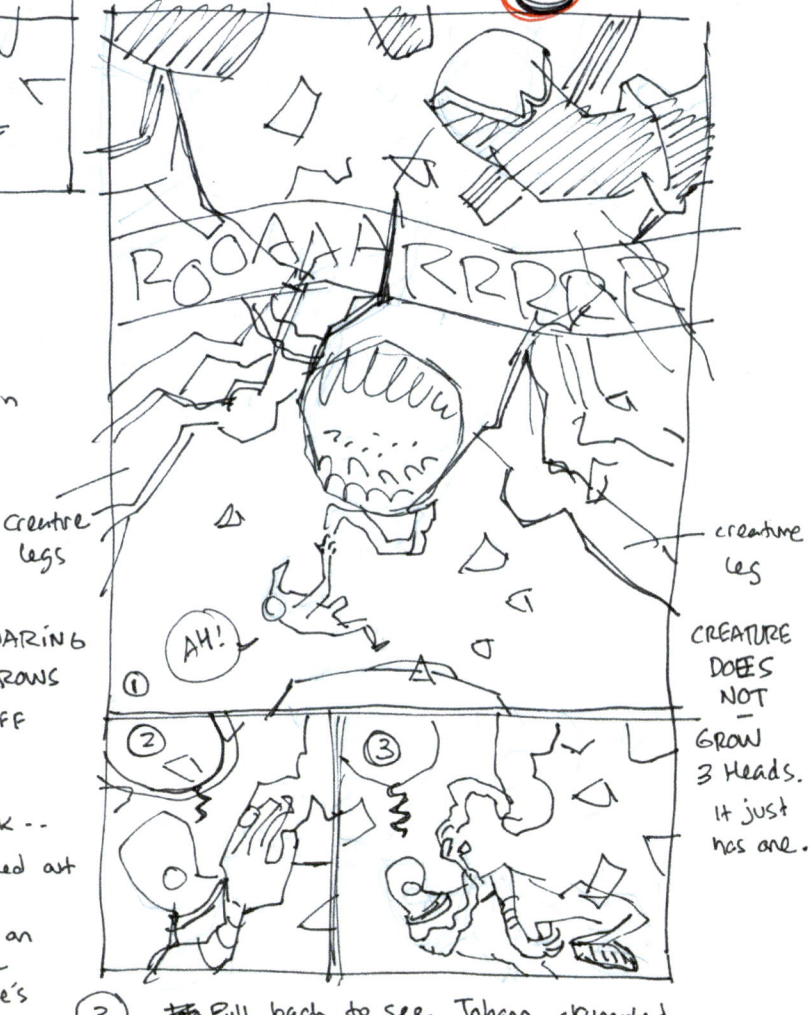

ROOAAARRRRR

creature legs

creature legs

CREATURE DOES NOT GROW 3 HEADS. It just has one.

AH!

③ Pull back to see Johann crumpled on the floor - shoved up against a wall. We clearly see that his suit is nearly empty -- Like a discarded, mostly unstuffed, scarecrow. -- Wind storm is still blowing stuff around like crazy -- He continues to speak but is weak -- shaky tail on balloon and small letters.

The wind storm rages in the lab on this whole page.

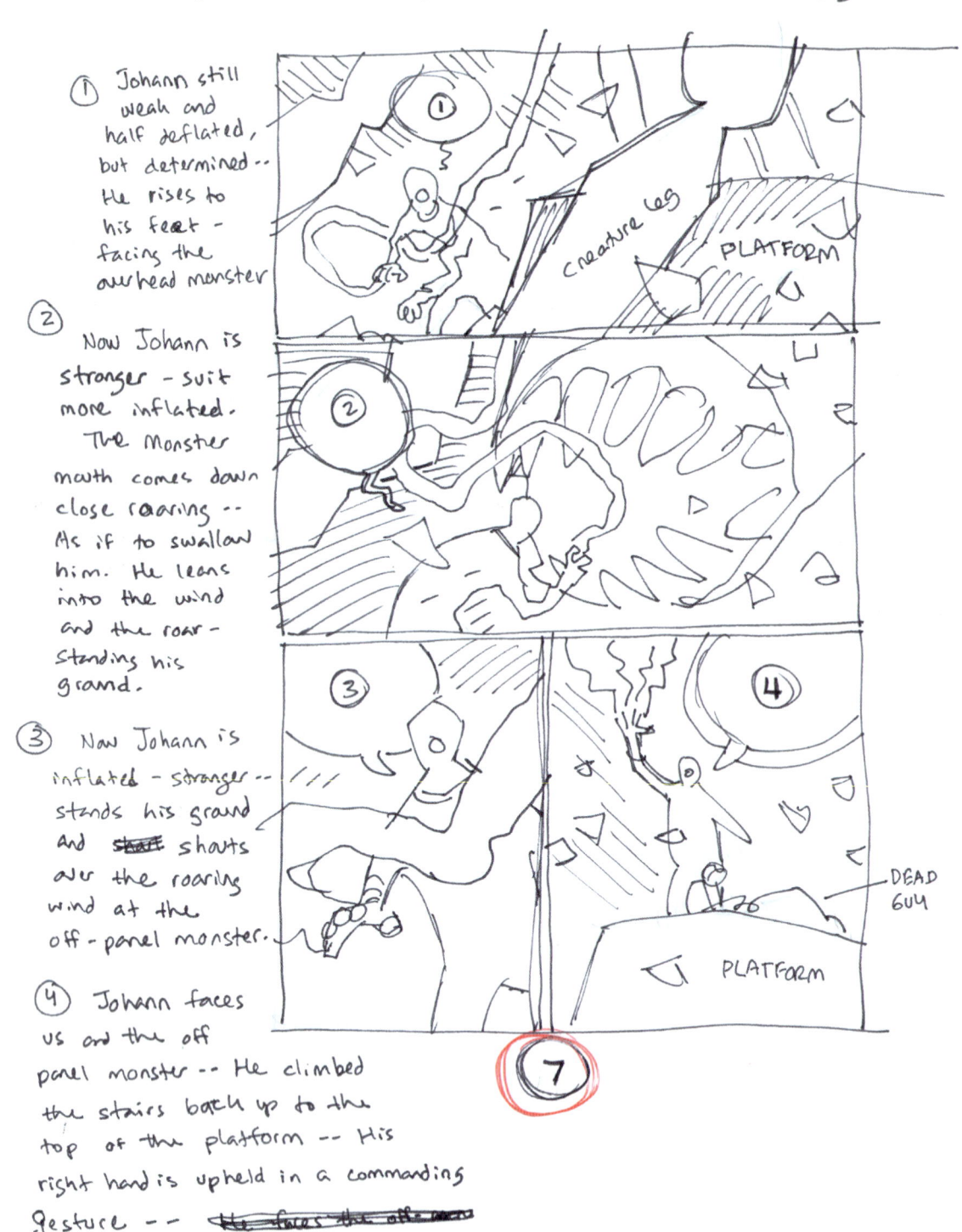

① Johann still weak and half deflated, but determined -- He rises to his feet - facing the overhead monster

② Now Johann is stronger - suit more inflated. The monster mouth comes down close roaring -- As if to swallow him. He leans into the wind and the roar - standing his ground.

③ Now Johann is inflated - stronger -- stands his ground and ~~staff~~ shouts over the roaring wind at the off-panel monster.

④ Johann faces us and the off panel monster -- He climbed the stairs back up to the top of the platform -- His right hand is upheld in a commanding gesture -- ~~He faces the off man~~

This is where he tames that off-panel monster but we don't see how much he's tamed it till the next page.

(labels in panels: creature leg, PLATFORM, DEAD GUY, PLATFORM)

7

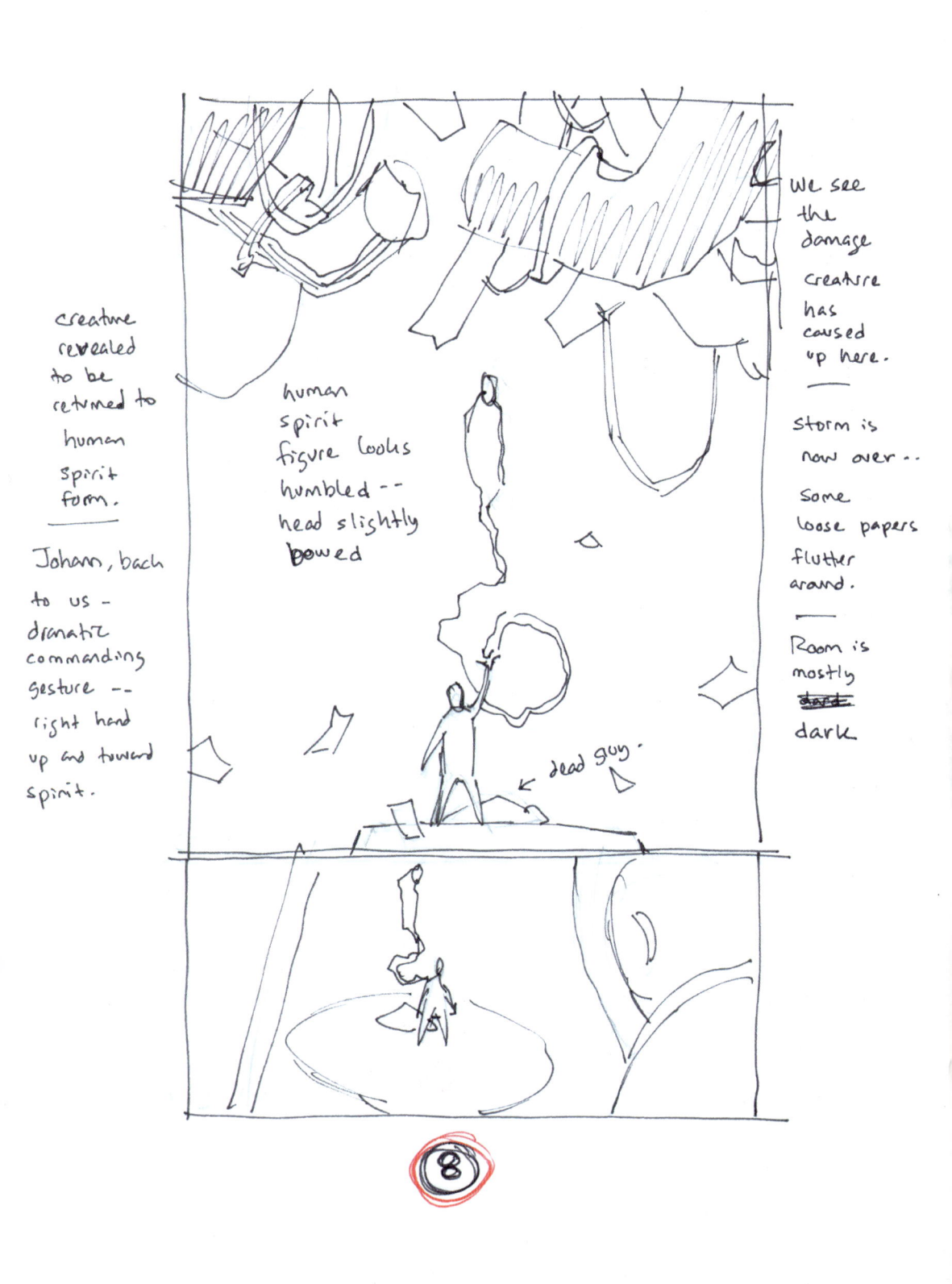

creature revealed to be returned to human spirit form.

Johann, back to us - dramatic commanding gesture -- right hand up and toward spirit.

human spirit figure looks humbled -- head slightly bowed

We see the damage creature has caused up here.

Storm is now over --

Some loose papers flutter around.

Room is mostly dark

← dead guy.

8

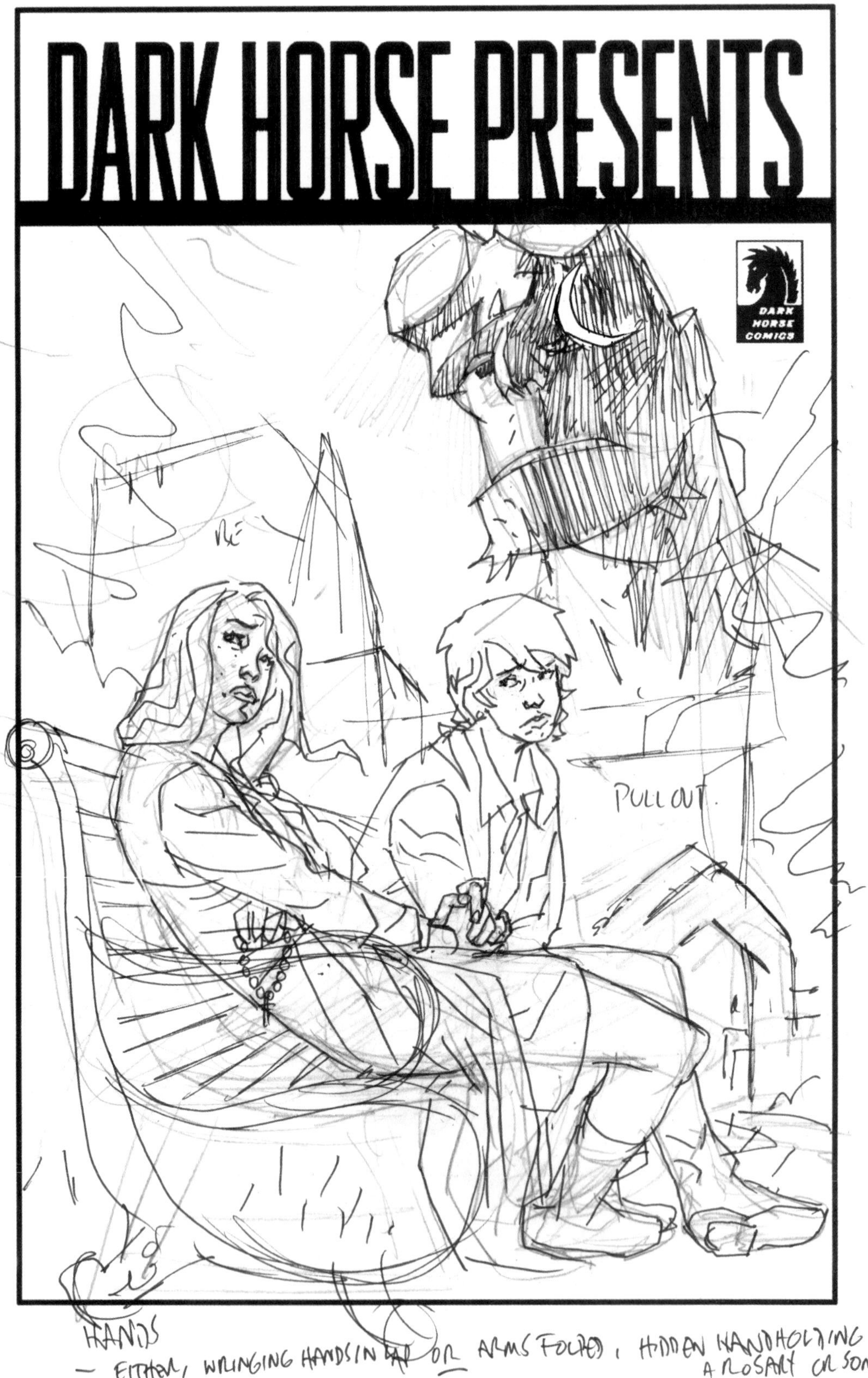
DARK HORSE PRESENTS
DARK HORSE COMICS
PULL OUT

HANDS
– EITHER, WRINGING HANDS IN LAP OR ARMS FOLDED, HIDDEN HAND HOLDING A ROSARY OR SOMETHING

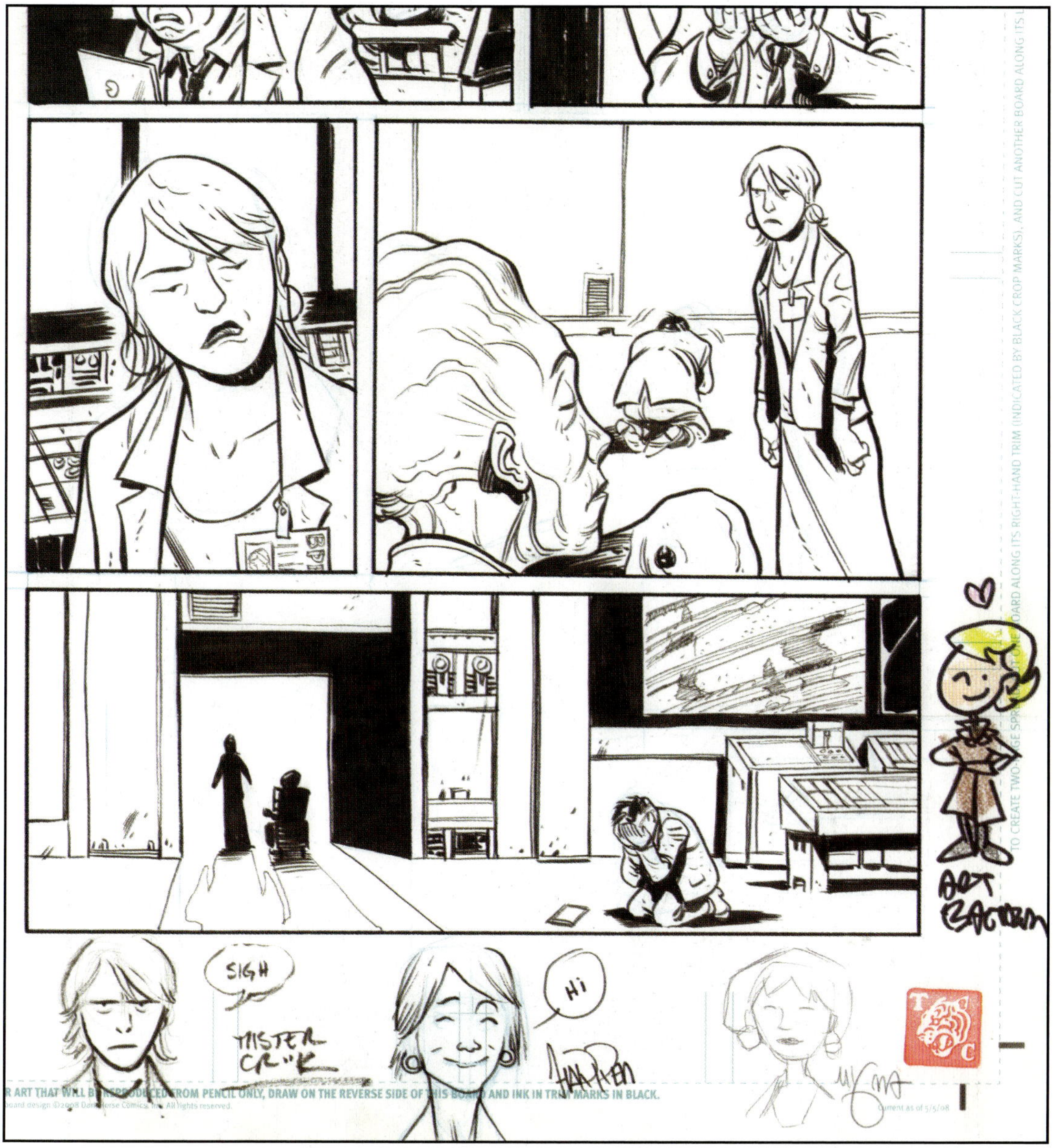
SIGH
HI

A page of *Hell on Earth* purchased by Liz Kozik, who got Mike, Tyler, James Harren (who debuts next volume), and Art Baltazar (*Itty Bitty Hellboy*) to draw Kate.

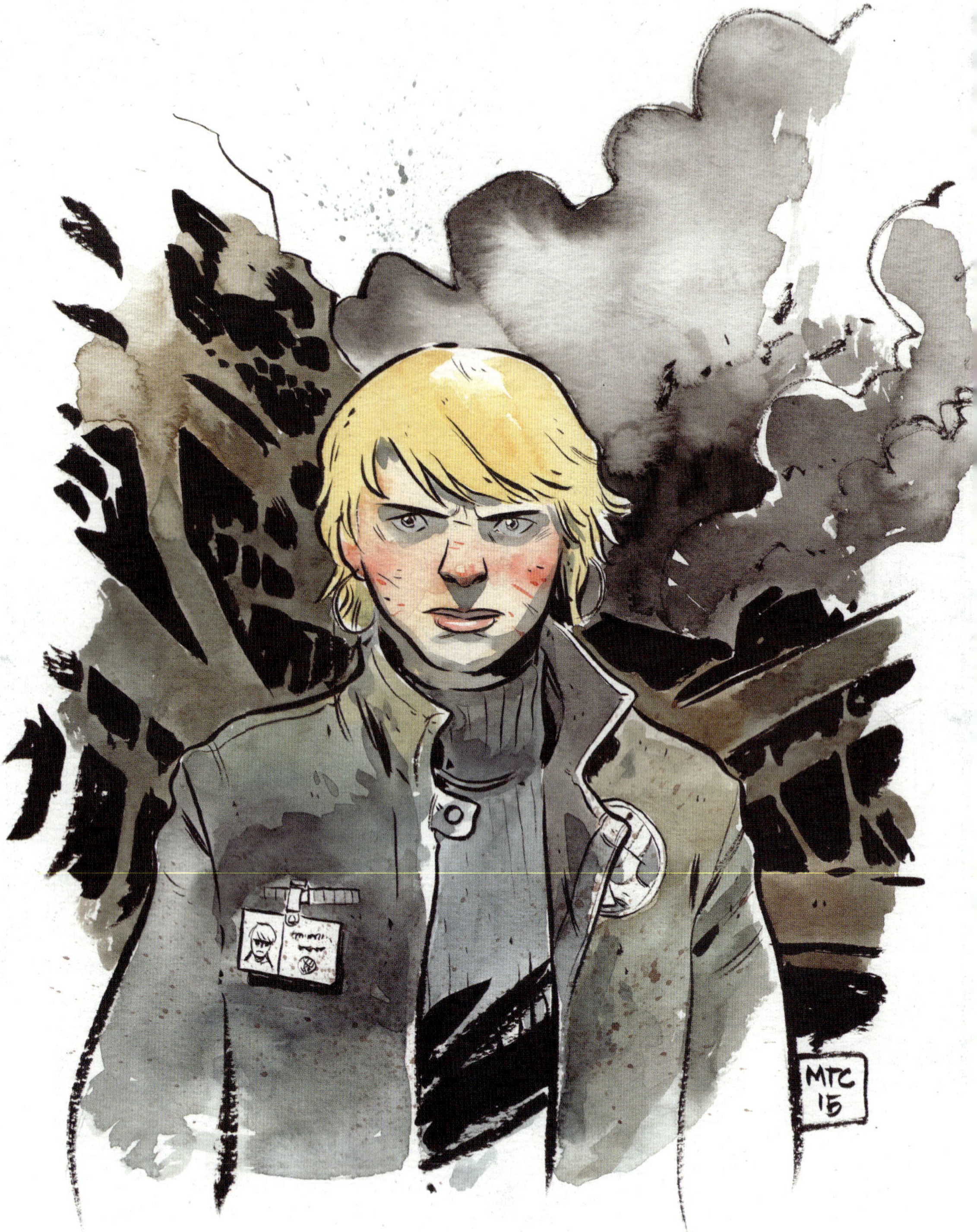
MTC
15

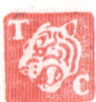